THE CONTROL SERIES BOXSET

ANNA EDWARDS

Megan,
Surrender to Control!
Anna
Edwards
x

Cover Design by www.CharityHendry.com

Logo Design by Charity Hendry

Editing by Tracy Roelle

Proofreading by Sheena Taylor

Formatting by Charity Hendry & Anna Edwards

To Charity.... I can never repay your kindness.

PART ONE
SURRENDERED CONTROL

ONE

Amy

Amy emerged from the water to the sight of the full moon glistening over the endless volcanic sand. The bright illumination shone on her honey-blonde hair, and she brushed her fingers through it to separate the wet strands. The day of travelling had left her tired, and the warm water eased her aching muscles that had been cramped by the budget flight. This was her first holiday in many years because aspiring writers didn't tend to have the money to travel. Nor dancers in a gentlemen's club, forced to work just to make ends meet. But it wasn't as bad a job as it sounded because she was well protected. Her uncle ran it and made sure she was sheltered from the seedier side of the profession. She enjoyed the dancing side, it was her second passion after writing. Her uncle, Stephen, paid for this holiday to Lanzarote as a twenty-first birthday present. Ever since her parents died in a car crash two years ago, he'd looked out for her. He was the only family she had left, and she respected him and trusted him implicitly.

She took a towel and wrapped it around her body, the aroma of the freshly caught fish being cooked in town was everywhere and made her mouth water in anticipation. She decided on a small tavern which was filled with more locals than tourists. She wasn't big on the mass-market tourism of the island and preferred places of culture and history, but as the holiday was a gift, she couldn't refuse it. She ordered the grilled catch of the day with salad and a glass of the local *La Geria* wine. As she watched the sun slowly set over the shimmering waves, the tension in her shoulders began to dissipate.

When she had finished her delicious meal, Amy ordered another glass of wine and pulled out a little notebook from her bag to begin writing down some of the details of the island so far. She liked to bring her personal experiences into her writing. She wanted to get everything noted down, in case she should need it for future stories.

She'd just finished a passage on the chaotic wait for her luggage at the airport when an uneasy tingling warmed her skin, as though she were being watched. Looking up, she met the alluring sky blue eyes of a man sitting across the room. Had he just arrived? Or how had she not noticed him previously? He too was sitting alone with a glass of wine for company. Upon making eye-contact, she couldn't help but blush. He was exquisitely handsome. He'd a rugged, yet, smart look; a defined jawline; and short dark hair, which he ran his fingers through as he watched her. The top few buttons of his blue linen shirt were undone and revealed a muscular upper body, which oozed a primal masculinity. His stare was intense, and she felt herself being drawn into it even more. When his lip twitched at her blatantly checking him out, she pushed the other chair at her table out with her gladiator-sandalled foot and looked up. She smiled at him with a cheeky grin, masking her excitement. For a moment, she thought he wasn't going to move, but then, he got to his feet. Even the way he walked was sexy. She was glad she was sitting down as her legs felt like jelly at his presence. He took a seat and held his hand up to the waiter, who promptly took his order for a more expensive bottle of wine. Neither of them spoke at first. They continued to take each other in.

"James." His voice was deep and inviting, and she was pleased to note he was speaking English.

"Amy." Her voice was smooth and possibly a little bit too sexy when she spoke.

Silence.

"Well, if this isn't awkward." He ruffled his hands through his hair again. The bottle of wine arrived, and the waiter poured them each a glass.

"Shall we start again? I'm Amy. I'm twenty-one. I come from London, and this is my first holiday in a while. I've come away to finish writing my first novel."

"I'm James. I'm twenty-eight. I also come from London, well Kent initially. I haven't had a holiday myself for a while. I tend to be a workaholic."

"What do you do?"

"I work in property. It's all very boring, I'm sure you don't want to hear about it. So, a novel? Is it all hush-hush, or can you tell me something about it?" He sat back in the chair, his left leg resting over his right, the wine glass tantalising-ly resting at his full lips. Lips that she couldn't tear her eyes away from. She wondered what they'd taste of, if she kissed him? He seemed happier to be asking questions than answering them, so she decided to respond to him to continue that line of conversation.

She chuckled and took a mouthful of her wine. "It's a classic boy meets girl, boy loses the girl, boy wins the girl back forever."

"Interesting. So this boy? What's he like?"

"Tall, dark, and handsome."

James nodded with genuine interest.

"And the girl?"

"Pretty, slim."

"Blonde?"

"Blonde."

"I like this story already."

"Told you it was a classic."

"Certainly is." He raised his eyebrow as he spoke. "So, is the man proficient in the bedroom?"

"That's a little presumptuous isn't it?"

"Why?" He chuckled, as he refilled the glasses that they both seemed to have drunk rather quickly.

"They've only just met."

He shrugged, "Why should they waste time, if there's an attraction between them?" James reached forward and took her hand. Their eyes met in an intense stare, as sparks of electricity flowed through them both. She wasn't drunk, so it wasn't that. "Are you staying nearby?"

The question hung thickly in the air between them.

She'd had only one previous partner, and that was a boyfriend of four years. Strange as it seemed, she felt that she already knew James, even though they'd only set eyes on each other not fifteen minutes before. "Yes, the Rivera apartments."

"Do you want me to walk you home?"

She didn't doubt from the look on his face that this would turn to sex if he did. But something about him, something about the mystery of his tone prevented her from saying no. He had a presence about him that drew her under his spell.

"Yes."

James pulled out his wallet and put forty euros on the table. The walk back was short, and they talked a little more. Just general facts, where they grew up, favourite foods, drinks, and a particularly funny story about an encounter that he'd had with a flock of seagulls in Brighton. She didn't tell him she worked in a Gentleman's Club.

When they entered her apartment, she was suddenly nervous. James took a seat on the cream sofa, and she went to look in the kitchen for a drink. She found two glasses and a semi-chilled bottle of wine and returned to the lounge. His big body was so commanding in the small lounge.

"Sorry, it isn't more. I only arrived today."

"It's fine. I still haven't bought any wine for my apartment, so you're a step ahead of me."

"How long have you been here?"

"A week now. I've just a few days left. How long are you here?"

"Only a week."

"Not long to finish that novel then."

"No. Not really. I'll have to forgo sunbathing and do lots of writing."

She put the bottle down on the table, because she needed a corkscrew to open it. "I won't be a minute. Just have to figure out which drawer the corkscrew is in." She turned back to walk into the kitchen but stopped as James called out 'wait'. It was the way he said it—it sent shivers of anticipation down her spine. Slowly, she turned and looked at him, her eyes wide. He'd risen from the sofa and was walking towards her.

"Take your dress off."

"I...."

"Take your dress off."

She had no answer. Her mind was telling her this was crazy, but her body was doing as he asked, completely disobeying the part that was telling her to tell him to fuck off. She reached down to the hem of her dress and pulled it over her head. She wasn't big breasted, so underneath the summer dress, she hadn't worn a bra. She stood in front of him in a pair of white lace panties. He walked around her, studying her, taking in every inch of her prickling flesh. She could feel the heat of his gaze marking her. She was never *naked* in front of the clients at the club, although she did wear revealing clothing, but that could not prepare her for what she was feeling right now. He leaned over her and took a deep breath, he was smelling her.

"You're beautiful." His tone was calm but had a stern undercurrent to it.

"I was supposed to be getting you wine."

He laughed. "I'm going to kiss you now. Are you sure you want to do this?"

"I don't think I'd be standing in front of you in my panties if I didn't. Now, are you going to remove some of your clothing?"

"Eager. I like it. But we will do this my way." James pulled his shirt over his head, and she noted that she was indeed correct about his superbly toned chest. She couldn't see his back, but she saw on his left arm he had a tattoo. It looked like the tips of wings.

"What's your tattoo?"

His face went momentarily blank. He didn't answer but pressed his body closer to hers. He leaned in and kissed her. Tender at first, and then with intense passion. She could feel her knees weakening as she was pushed back against the wall. "Place your hands above your head and don't move them." Again with that authoritative tone.

"Why?"

"Will you do as I asked? Or should I leave now? I told you, we will do this my way. You'll enjoy it. Don't worry." A hot kiss was again pressed to her lips and without thinking anymore, she moved her hands above her head. "Good girl. You'll be rewarded for that later."

Rewarded? James moved his mouth from her lips down to the peaking tips of her nipples. His tongue swirled around the sensitive buds, and she let out a yearning moan. He looked up at her, a mischievous look in his eyes, and began to lower his body to trail his tongue down the flat line of her stomach until he knelt on the floor in front of her. He placed his hands on either side of her panties, and in one fluid motion, ripped them from her body. She was breathing fast now. This whole experience was so damn intense it almost seemed like a dream. Her body was on fire, and she longed for him to touch her.

James put his hands between her legs and parted them to reveal her neatly trimmed sex. He groaned. "I haven't even touched you, yet, and you're ready for me. Have you been like this all night? I can even smell your arousal."

She sure as hell wasn't going to let him know that he was turning her on more than she ever had been before. "You know how to kiss a lady and get her excited. It's a good start but it all depends on what skills you have now."

He gave her a little tap on the top of her thigh which brought a scream from her, and then ran a finger over her displayed folds before moving it slowly into her inner channel.

"If you doubt my skills again, I'll put you over my knee." Her body writhed against his hand, and she found herself being excited about having her bottom spanked.

Holy hell. Where had that come from?

His thumb found the hidden bundle of nerves between her thighs and teased it. She could feel the heat within her starting to build. "If you don't stop doing that,

I'm going to come all over your hand." James abruptly withdrew his finger and got to his feet with a tutting sound.

"No. Not yet. You'll come when I tell you that you can." He looked her in the eyes, and it was almost like he was controlling her body with his words.

"You're not in charge of me, you know that right?"

He didn't answer, only sniggered. He reached into the pocket of his trousers, brought out his wallet, and retrieved a condom from it. The wallet was then tossed aside. She watched him lower his trousers and pants to reveal a substantially thick cock which he then covered with the condom. It was jutting up towards his stomach and was a work of art. It should have been framed and hung in an art gallery. It was that perfect. She was panting now. Although she was terrified that the length and girth of his manhood was going to hurt, at the same time, she needed him buried deeply inside her. *Now!* She wanted to know what he felt like. She pulled her hands down and reached out to touch the muscular sinews of James's shoulders.

"No. You don't touch me, unless I give you permission." He slammed her hands back against the wall and held them there with one hand. With the other, he lifted her leg from the floor and in one slow thrust pushed inside her.

"Oh God," she groaned. This was nothing like she'd felt before. Her ex-boyfriend wasn't small, but sex between them had always been something that they seemed to do just because they were boyfriend and girlfriend. This was different. It was raw, and it was dangerous. James began to move slowly. Their eyes locked together as with each long movement he stroked against the sweet spot deep within her.

Their lips joined in a tango of passion. His hand still held her in place, and she was glad for it, because she was barely able to support her weight. She felt the build-up of her climax again. She tried to suppress the feeling. James had told her that she couldn't come until he gave her permission, and she wanted to please him.

Jesus, what was this man doing to her? This was her body. Why was it responding to his control like this?

He seemed to know she was close and trying to control herself; she could tell by the little curl of his lip. She wanted to hit him. She wished he'd let her release. He finally let her out of her misery when he leaned forward and collected her lip between his teeth. He nodded consent, and she exploded around him. Wave after wave of earth-shattering pleasure rolled over her shaking body. She called out, and he joined her over the precipice as he released himself into her.

They were both covered in sweat. They were breathing rapidly, and their legs were quivering. James lowered her leg to the floor and withdrew from her, checking the filled condom as he did so.

"Are you alright? I didn't hurt you, did I?" She shook her head. She couldn't find her voice just yet. "Good." He pressed another kiss to her now-bruised lips and looked into her eyes. At that moment, something within him changed. She saw it. Gone was the dominantly splendid lover he'd been; he withdrew into himself. He pulled up his trousers, quickly found his shirt and put it on. "I'm sorry. I shouldn't have done that." And with that, he left her: confused, standing naked, covered with the scent of the best sex she'd ever had, and her hands still above her head.

TWO

James

James could still smell her scent, no matter how many times he showered. She'd got under his skin. Why had he walked out? He cursed himself for being such a fucking idiot. He could've been with her again and again, and he grew hard at the thought. He could never be normal. He could feel the tattoo burning on his back, the permanent reminder of what he was. Why did he continually torture himself?

He'd been sitting in his office overlooking the sights of London and remembering for an hour now. He angrily swiped his paperwork to the floor. He walked to his safe, opened it, and took out a file. It hadn't taken Matthew, his bodyguard, long to find Amy's details. He was ex-MI5, after all.

He read the words on the cover sheet again:

STRICTLY CONFIDENTIAL,
"Amy Jones, D.O.B. 25th January 1996. Brentwood, Essex.
Only child of Gavin and Judy Jones: both deceased 14th October 2012.
Resident in Kennington, London, SE11. Purchased April 2013.

He returned the file to the safe and locked it. This had to stop. He already regretted having Amy's details, plus he had a meeting shortly and needed to concentrate on that. It was a holiday fling. If she saw him again, after the way he'd left her, she'd probably slap him in the face. He gathered his papers and headed to the boardroom. His secretary flicked her hair as he passed. She clearly had a thing for him, and he was starting to find it irritating.

"Marie, can you ask Simon to have the figures on the Argentinian project on my desk in the next half hour. Could you also tell him to stop flirting with the girls in Accounts if he wants to keep his job?"

"Of course, Sir. I'll see to it at once," she called after him, but he barely heard her. He was lost in the memories of Amy.

Amy

Amy pulled the collar of her thick coat up around her ears when she emerged from Kennington tube station. It was difficult to keep warm, since her return home. She had acquired a beautiful tan but was unable to show it off in the miserable February weather.

The final few days in Lanzarote had been occupied with a flurry of writing. She managed to nearly finish her novel, but she couldn't help but feel disappointed with it.

When she'd returned home from the holiday, she put her computer in a drawer and vowed not to look at it for at least a couple of weeks. Until then, she'd immerse herself in her dancing. She could, perhaps, seek some overtime and try to forget about both her writing and her brief encounter with James. That was going to be hard, however, given how often she'd been replaying the events of that evening over in her mind. Why had he been able to control her that way? How had he done those things to her body? And why did he disappear? What did she do wrong?'

When she entered the club, in which she worked, her uncle greeted her with a warm embrace. "Hello, little kitten. You have fun in the sun?" He kissed both her cheeks and then stood back, looking proudly at her.

'Kitten' had been her nickname since she was four years old. She'd been given a cuddly toy cat from her parents as a birthday present, she carried it everywhere as a young child, and to this day she still owned it. It now sat on top of the wardrobe in her bedroom, albeit in a slightly worse for wear condition, with one eye and half a tail.

She hesitated, blushed, and then responded. "It was lovely Uncle Stephen. Thank you so much. It was ever so generous of you."

"I'm pleased," he said. But then his familiarity changed to a business-like demeanour. "Sara called in sick," he moaned. "I'll need you to dance on both stages tonight, and you'll only get a fifteen-minute break between." He chuckled and gestured to her tummy. "But I'm sure you ate and drank far too much in Lanzarote, so it will do you good."

She hadn't actually put on any weight whilst away. She'd been very careful with what she'd eaten. She didn't mention anything, however, but giggled. Her uncle always liked to have the last word. "Of course, Uncle Stephen, Not a problem. I'll go get ready now."

He was already walking away from her towards his office when he called back, "Good girl. I knew I could rely on you."

She shrugged off her heavy coat and headed towards her changing room, which she shared with Sara. They'd been friends ever since she started working at the club. Sara was a few years older than her and had been there for almost a decade. She had an Amazonian look, with jet black hair and big sultry eyes. She was stunningly beautiful and was much sought-after by the punters in the club; a fact she often used to her advantage in generating additional income. For not only did the club provide public dancing, it also offered private lap dancing in the backrooms. Not that Amy would consent to doing any of these despite how much her uncle complained about it.

She couldn't recall a time that Sara had taken a day off sick and was worried that something could be wrong. She quickly took her mobile from her bag, texted her to check how she was, and offered to drop round at the end of her shift.

She sat down at her dressing table to apply her makeup. She could see the freckles on her face and shoulders which always appeared when she spent any time in the sun. Although she was supposed to wear thick makeup, she decided that tonight she was going to opt for a more natural look. She applied a little dab of blue eye shadow, a fine amount of black eyeliner, and a touch of long-lash mascara. She had a gentle wave to her strawberry-blonde hair, so she decided to leave it down, giving her a bohemian appearance. She selected a studded bodice with a short, jagged-edged silk skirt from the wardrobe, and after putting it on, she slipped on her favourite pair of small, silver heels. There was a sense of anticipation and excitement in her belly to be returning to the dance stage. She loved to dance. It was a shame she didn't have any training and could actually do something like theatre work with it. All she had was dancing for drunken men. There had to be something more to her life than this.

James

When he arrived home later that evening, James went straight for a workout and then a shower. He stood in his large shower, resting his head against the wall of his ensuite bathroom. He'd managed to put Amy out of his mind for the last few hours. The scorching water ran over his powerful shoulders and down his defined masculine chest and lean waist. Grabbing a towel from the rail, he dried his body, put on a pair of black jeans and a blue linen shirt, and headed to the kitchen.

His mother lived with him, although she had her own floor in his large Kensington house. She helped with the housekeeping and looked after the place while he was away. He kissed her on the cheek when she handed him a chilled bottle of beer from the fridge.

"Did you have a good day at work?" she asked him with a devoted smile.

He nodded. "Did you speak to Sophie?" he asked.

"Yes, she's finally chosen the navy gowns."

His sister was getting married and was being a bit of a bridezilla. At twenty-three, she was five years younger than him, and he adored and protected her as he did his mother.

He approved of her fiancé, even though the pair of them were rather wayward and likely to float through life on a soft breeze and see where it took them. He had insisted on paying for most of the wedding. Sophie didn't need to accept his offer, as her fiancé was a millionaire in his own right. However, she knew how much it meant to him to be able to provide this for his sister, given their father was totally out of their lives. He had left under an extremely black cloud a few years previously. His mother placed a plate of food in front of him and wandered off to her room, leaving him alone with his thoughts.

He was finishing his dinner when his bodyguard entered with a pensive look on his face.

"Evening. Is everything alright?"

"Um, yep. Oh, your secretary said that the Enquirer has been on the phone again asking about the interview for their magazine," Matthew replied.

"They don't take no for an answer, do they? Perhaps I should agree to it. At least it would get them off my back." While he accepted the media's focus on his business affairs, he liked to keep his private life just that.

"I'll have to protect you from even more female attention if you agree to it. I'm not sure how I'll cope." Matthew chuckled and sat down with his own food.

After a short silence James asked, "So, did you follow her?"

Matthew nodded.

"Is it safe?" he asked.

This time, he shook his head and frowned.

"It's a gentlemen's club. Run by her uncle, a Mister Stephen Jones."

Matthew put his cutlery down.

"What does she do there? Waitressing? Bar-work?"

"No Boss, She's a dancer. An erotic pole dancer. But from what I could establish, that's all she does." The bodyguard took a deep breath and continued. "Her uncle, though...." Matthew reached into the pocket of his suit jacket and handed James his phone with a video on it. He pressed play and clenched his jaw.

"Is she there now?" he asked.

"Yes, Boss."

"Give me ten minutes." How could she be so stupid? Or was he the stupid one? Did she know who he was? Was she playing him? "Matthew, we're going in hard. Make preparations."

THREE

Amy

When it was Amy's time to dance, Mrs Barton, the stage manager, called at her door.

"There's a full crowd out there tonight. Make sure you dance well. Could get a few decent tips." The middle-aged woman peered behind the curtain. "If you'd remove a bit more clothing, you'd earn a fortune."

"My act is more about the illusion of sexuality, Mrs Barton. It works better with my clothes on."

"Well suit your bloody self. More money for the other girls, then."

"As long as I have enough at the end of the week to cover my living costs, I'm happy."

The first half of her set went well, although during it she felt strange. Like all the hairs on her body were standing on end, and a heat flooded through her body. She put the feeling to the back of her mind, tucked her tips into the bra part of her corset, and headed to the bar to get some water and take her short break.

The club was heaving. It was a Friday night and the city traders were celebrating the end of the week. One of them, looking totally inebriated, staggered into her slurring as he spoke. "Care to give me a private dance, darling?"

"I never kiss on a first meeting," she said. "Now, how about you go find your friends."

He groaned and staggered backward, struggling to stand up properly, as a security guard approached and escorted him unceremoniously away. She looked over to where she knew her uncle would be sitting. She smiled cheekily at him, as if to say she had matters completely under control, and he winked back.

When she finally made it to the bar, the barman presented her with a glass of water containing ice and a squeeze of lemon. He knew what she liked.

"Thank you, Pierre," she said, blowing him a playful kiss, and he dramatically bowed.

"You're welcome, Miss Amy. How was the holiday?"

"Hot, wet, and relaxing."

"Sounds like a typical day in here without the relaxing bit." The barman chuckled, and Amy joined in.

"You ever wanted something more than this, Pierre?"

"What, like waiting in a high class joint?"

"No, a different job. Do you have a dream?"

"Nobody can make as good a Manhattan as me."

"You're right there. Save me one for later."

"You aren't paid to talk and flirt, Pierre. I believe you've people waiting for drinks." Pierre instantly turned and served another patron.

She turned towards the voice. "Hello, Leon."

"Aren't you supposed to be working as well?"

"I'm on my break."

Leon was one of her uncle's 'henchmen'. He was also a total slimeball.

"I think your break is about to finish. Unless you want to come and share some of it with me. I know a room that's free. You can show me how much you missed me."

"Well, that won't take long. I didn't think of you once while I was away."

"One day, you'll beg me to stick my cock in your tight little cunt."

She stepped off her stool and headed back to the stage. "In your dreams, Leon."

James

As they entered the club, James and Matthew showed their I.D. The bouncers and girls on the door were experienced in recognising wealthy clients, and they were both quickly offered a private booth. Shortly after they were seated, a bottle of Dom Perignon was brought to the table by a scantily-clad brunette. She was followed by a smartly-dressed man who introduced himself as a senior member of the management team and requested that they ask for any services they may require.

He looked around trying to locate Amy. It took him a few moments and a double take before he realised that the girl dancing on the back stage was her.

God she looked sexy. The seductive, swaying movements of her curves were intensely erotic. If he'd touched himself, he would have exploded in an instant.

"You better drink this, Boss," Matthew said, handing him his glass from the table.

He drained it.

He was impressed when he saw Amy deal with a drunk, closely observing as a bouncer escorted him away. He followed Amy's gaze as she smiled at a man who was clearly her uncle, the owner of the establishment. She seemed to think her uncle had sent the bouncer over. In reality, he was paying no attention to the fact that she could have been molested in the middle of the club.

"Have them bring the uncle over," he ordered Matthew.

Amy's uncle didn't take long to arrive at the table. He was greying at the temples, had a slightly portly figure, and his features were harsh. James saw nothing of Amy's warmth or kindness in his eyes. To be polite, he got to his feet and reluctantly held out his hand.

"Mr North. It's a great pleasure to welcome you to my club. Please, anything we can do to make your visit more pleasant, don't hesitate to ask. "

"Thank you, Mr Jones. The blonde with the wavy hair who was dancing earlier." He pointed to the second stage. "I'd like to meet her, privately." He reached for a neatly bound collection of fifty pound notes and placed them on the table. "And I'm willing to pay ten grand for the privilege."

Amy

Amy went to the other stage to check everything was in order for her second act. A fifteen-minute gap gave her no time to relax. She'd be exhausted when she got home.

At the curtain, waiting to commence her second set, Mrs Barton reappeared.

"Change of plan. Your uncle wants you."

"What is it?"

"He wouldn't tell me. He says he'll tell you himself."

She sighed and rushed over to her uncle.

"Mrs Barton said you wanted me?"

"With Sara off tonight, I need a favour from you. We've an important guest asking for a private dance, and all the other girls are busy."

"But what about the stage? There will be no one on it?"

"Mrs Barton is going to shift some of the curtains around, and Jenny will dance for both crowds."

"So why can't I dance for both crowds and Jenny do the private dance? Uncle, please. You know that I don't like the private dances. Don't make me do it."

"Don't argue about this," her uncle replied sternly. "Just do as you're asked. The club is full tonight, and I've a lot to do."

She looked down forlornly, reached out, and tenderly touched his hand. She was so ungrateful, sometimes. He was trying his hardest to look after her, and she was fighting him. What would one dance hurt?

"I'm sorry, Uncle Stephen. Of course, I'll do it. Which room do I need to go to?"

"Number One," he replied, looking slightly calmer.

She quickly went back to her dressing room and freshened up a little. A quick squirt of some perfume always seemed to heighten their senses and made the inevitable 'coming in their pants' happen quicker.

The next thing she knew she was standing outside the private room with the client waiting inside. She took a deep breath, checked her clothing was in place, and opened the door. The room was darker than normal, almost pitch black. With a little unease, she stepped forward and closed the door behind her. She couldn't hear anything. From the centre of the room came a deep breath, followed by a long, drawn-out sigh that sent shivers down her spine. As a single soft light turned on, she heard a voice she never thought she'd hear again. "Hello, Amy."

"James," she gasped.

FOUR

Amy

Amy trembled as James slowly stood, he had the same intensity as before, but this time she sensed anger in him.

"How did you find me?"

He snapped back with a curl of his lip, "Chance. This wasn't the sort of place I expected to find you in. I thought you were innocent. Shows what I know."

"I didn't think I'd see you again after you walked out," she replied, sarcastically. "Did you have to get back to your wife?" Who did he think he was? The man who'd given her the best orgasm of her life was in her place of work and insinuating she was a whore. He'd obviously paid to get her alone in this room. What a bastard. She was furious that he thought he could show up here, after walking out on her the way he did with no explanation, and expect her to submit to him the way she had then. She switched on her business manner. He was not going to control her this time.

"If you'd return to your seat, Sir, I'll begin the dance. First, though, I'd like to remind you that you're not to remove your hands from the side cushions during the dance, and you're certainly not to touch me at any point."

He didn't stop advancing on her.

"Sir, sit down."

"No." She wasn't scared—there were cameras in the room, and her uncle would be having them watched. If he didn't stop, she'd only have to make a signal and a bouncer would be in to protect her. She composed herself with a deep breath.

"Take a seat please, Sir, or I'll call security to have you removed from the premises."

"Answer me one thing, what do you do here?"

"I dance. Why?" She placed a hand on her hip.

"Just dance?"

"Yes."

"And this?" He pointed to the chair where she'd give him the lap dance.

"If I can avoid it, I do. My friend is sick tonight." He winced at the mention of her friend. Why?

"Are there cameras in here?"

"Yes?" She motioned towards one. "What's going on?"

"My name is James North. I'm a billionaire, and I can buy whatever I want. I paid ten thousand pounds for my time with you."

"Time with me?" Her world was collapsing in on her. "Do you mean...?"

"I won't touch you," he interrupted. "But I have to tell you something. Please sit. I need you to listen to me."

Her damn body betrayed her mind again, and she instantly sat down on the chair. James came and perched on his haunches before her.

"Your friend, who is off sick. What have you been told?"

"Nothing, my uncle mentioned she was ill."

"She isn't sick. She's...injured."

"Injured?" she questioned.

"She was violently assaulted by your uncle and several of his men."

"What?" She laughed, was he insane? Her uncle wouldn't do something like that. "I don't believe you," she replied resolutely.

"Please, you have to listen to me."

"No, I don't. I don't even know you. You fucked me and left me. Why should I trust you?"

"You shouldn't, but I need you to. We have to leave here, now."

"You're mad." She pushed him away, ran to the door, pulled it open and was faced with her uncle.

"Mike, Dave, take her back in the room, and hold her down if necessary so Mr North can conclude his business. It's about time she faced the reality of what actually happens in this club. I'm no longer willing to support this spoilt and naive little bitch."

She stood there in shock. What was she hearing? This man was her flesh and blood. He was the only family that she had, and he was condoning and even assisting in rape. Her rape. His niece!

The two bouncers grabbed her arms tightly and dragged her into the corner of the room with James and her uncle watching. Another man she didn't know appeared at her uncle's side.

She lay helpless on the floor, looking up at the four men.

Then, in what seemed like an instant, James threw the back of his elbow into one of the bouncer's faces knocking him to the ground, as the other man, who she hadn't seen before, delivered a flooring punch to another bouncer. What in God's name was going on?

James knelt beside her, removing his jacket and trying to place it around her shoulders. She scrambled to her feet and backed away from him, still looking petrified.

He stood back up and turned to her uncle. "Miss Jones will be resigning with immediate effect. You'll see to it that a good severance pay is prepared for her, which, my bodyguard here, will collect from you tomorrow. You try and contact Amy again, and I'll kill you."

Her furious uncle decided to take a swing at James but was held back by the bodyguard.

James turned to her, offering his hand, but again she shuddered and stepped back.

"Amy," he pleaded, looking tenderly at her. "Please, listen to me. This was all horrible but necessary to reveal the exact nature of your uncle and what goes on in this club. I'm sorry, but he's not the man you thought he was. He has so many secrets." He pulled his phone from his pocket and pressed the play button.

Sara appeared on the screen. She looked terrified, backed up against a wall. Her voice echoed out of the phone, pleading for mercy, but all Amy could do was watch as Leon and several other men rained down punches on her body. When they stepped back, Sara lay unmoving on the floor. All that she knew then shattered when her uncle walked over and kicked her friend in the stomach. She let out a cry when the video stopped. Tears started to stream down her cheeks. He was the man who she thought protected her. The man who'd looked after her since her parents had died. Standing up, she swallowed hard, formed a fist, and sent it flying into the face of her uncle. She followed it up with another and another. She was screaming and crying.

Strong arms circled her waist to pull her away. She swung around and landed a punch on James.

She had to get out. She ran. Behind her, she could hear James calling for her to stop, and her uncle calling for additional security.

The cold night air was like a slap in the face. She stood in the alleyway next to the club, wearing virtually nothing, crying and shaking. What was she doing? Where could she go? Should she go to the police? She stumbled towards the main road. Everything was a blur, but she could tell that people were staring at her. She could hear their exclamations and disgust at her appearance. Nobody tried to help her. Why would they? For all they knew, she was a drugged up prostitute.

She heard footsteps running up behind her and turned to lash out again, but she stopped when she looked into James's sorrow-filled eyes. Here was the lover who'd brought her to blissful levels. The man who she knew she could trust, even after one brief encounter. She sank to the cold pavement, exhausted and freezing. He put his coat over her shoulders and held her in his arms. He took her bloodied hand and gently kissed it. Part of her wanted to pull away from him again. Her head was spinning, trying to take everything in.

"I'm sorry. There's so much I need to tell you. But not now. We need to get you somewhere safe and warm." A car pulled up beside them. "This is my car, and my bodyguard, Matthew Carter, is driving it. You're safe. Please get in the car. I promise I won't hurt you. I'm going to take you back to my home. My mother is there." He held out his phone. "If you want to speak to her the entire time we're driving, you may."

She looked blankly at him.

"I don't know." She shook her head. She looked at the car, the concerned look on the driver's face, and back to James.

"You have my word no harm will come to you while you are under my protection." He waved his phone at her. "Here take this." He unlocked it, and she took it. "Google my name. James North. You'll see that, in the club, I gave you the correct details about myself." She pulled the phone close to her and did as he suggested. It brought up pictures of him and details of the company he owned. She flicked through it while he watched her. "You know exactly who I am now. If I hurt you in any way, you can go straight to the police."

She stood up, and he helped her into the car. She turned to him. "I'm trusting you. Please don't let me down."

FIVE

James

James could feel himself shaking as he slid into the black leather car seat beside Amy. He reached over her to fasten her seat belt, and she flinched again. He wanted to hold her, but even if she never allowed him near her again, at least she'd be away from her uncle.

She turned and looked at him as though he were a monster. Maybe he was. Her eyes were as wide as saucers.

"How?" Her voice wavered as she spoke.

"How what?" he said calmly.

"How did you know where I was? It wasn't chance, was it?"

He shook his head and turned away from her. "The day after I got back from Lanzarote, I asked Matthew..." —he shifted his look in the direction of the driver— "...to find out as much about you as possible."

"Why?"

"I don't know. We had a one-night stand. It was marvellous. Well, it was for me. I wanted to know more about you. Maybe meet you again."

"So you could destroy the only life I know?"

The comment felt like a stab to his heart, and he had no reply for it. They sat in silence for the rest of the short journey to his home.

He helped her out of the car and to the front door. He could see the astonishment on Amy's face. She turned to him,

"You own this?"

He nodded, and she faltered again at the top step.

"You won't force me?"

He stuttered over his answer; her heart-rending pleas were breaking him.

"I promise you."

He opened the door, and his mother came rushing down the stairs towards them. Matthew had obviously warned her.

"You poor thing. You must be half frozen. Let's get you inside. I have the fire on and have made a nice cup of tea for you. How do you like it? Milk? Sugar? You're safe now. Come on."

He watched his mother direct Amy towards the blazing open fire. She sat her down on the cream leather sofa and placed a hot tea on the small table beside it. Tea was his mother's solution for everything.

"James, find Amy something warmer to wear. Your sister must have clothes here that will fit her. Make sure they are nice and comfortable, mind you. Try and find some pyjamas." He nodded. Before he disappeared down the corridor, he turned and gave a final look towards Amy. She was watching him. Even after everything he'd done, he could see she trusted him.

It didn't take him long to find clothes for her to wear. When he went back into the lounge, he saw that Matthew had joined them and was sitting in his favourite chair with a fine cognac.

"I hope you poured one of them for me too."

He could feel Amy fix her eyes on him when he spoke. "I know Mum says that tea cures everything, but I think we all need something a little stronger."

Matthew got to his feet and, with a sarcastic bow, went to pour two more glasses.

"I've put the clothes in the guest bedroom next to mine. Mum, would you mind showing Amy to the room?"

His mother nodded and helped Amy to her feet. Amy continued to watch him until the very last moment, he didn't need to look at her to know this because he could feel the deep scrutiny of her gaze.

He sat down in his large brown, antique leather chair with sudden exhaustion. Matthew returned with the cognac and handed it to him. He drank it down in one long mouthful. It burnt his throat with its rawness, but it was what he needed.

"You alright, Boss?"

He looked up at Matthew and smiled. "Just about. Thank you for everything tonight. You know, I'd be lost without your help."

"Now a good time to ask for a pay-raise?"

He raised an eyebrow.

"Worth a shot." Matthew sat down again, and both of them sat in silent contemplation for a moment. "What happens with Miss Jones now?"

He shrugged his shoulders and slouched down into his seat, "I guess that will depend. But I can tell you she isn't going back to that club, under any circumstance. She'll be staying here for the week at least. I want to check out where she lives, first thing tomorrow, to make sure it's safe. I suspect she left belongings at the club as well. I want you to get them when you collect her severance package tomorrow."

"Do you think her uncle will give up on her that easily?"

"I want her tailed every second of the day. Hire whoever you need. I don't want her out of their sight unless she's safe with me or here in this building."

"You going to tell her that you're having her followed?"

"No."

"Boss, if you're hoping to have a relationship with her, then surely you need to be honest."

"Not yet. I need to get to know her first. I need to know she'll accept me the way I am, especially if I turn..." He abruptly paused when Amy walked back into the room. She looked even sexier in the low-slung pyjama bottoms and tight-fitting top. He could see her erect nipples pushing through the fabric. The look in her eyes told him everything; they had renewed sparkle. She took the seat on the sofa again and tucked her legs up underneath her. He passed her the cognac that Matthew had placed on the table.

"It will help you sleep." He looked at the clock. It was one in the morning, but he was far from tired. His mum yawned. "Go to bed, Mum. You're tired. I'll show Amy your room if she needs you."

His mum looked to Amy, and after a quick look to him for reassurance, Amy responded, "Please, Mrs North, you go to bed. You've been so kind to me. I'll drink this and probably go myself."

"If you are sure?"

"I am." His mother got to her feet and held her hand out for him to kiss before she walked down the corridor to her part of the house. James indicated to Amy where his mother's bedroom was situated.

"I've a couple of errands to run before bed, so I'll bid you goodnight," Matthew said, smiling at Amy, "It's lovely to have met you, Miss Jones. If there's anything you want during your stay here, just ask."

Amy looked a little puzzled, "My stay? I'll go home, tomorrow, first thing. I need to find a new job."

"You've had a big shock. Why don't you consider staying here as my guest for a few days? We've a pool, and a gym in the basement you can use."

"Am I a prisoner here?" she asked.

"Of course not. You'd be free to come and go as you please." He got up from his chair and sat next to her on the sofa. She didn't flinch but defensively crossed her arms. "I'm sorry. I promise I'll explain everything. But not tonight. You need to sleep. What you've been through today will have left you shaken and greatly confused. If you wish to return to your apartment tomorrow, then I'll take you myself. But please consider my offer. I know I've no right, but I'd like to get to know you better."

She stared at him. He could see she was weighing up everything in her head, going through all that had happened. She then slowly nodded her head.

"I'll stay until the end of the weekend. Three nights. But I need to return home tomorrow to collect some clothes. It isn't right, me wearing your sister's." She sighed heavily. "And I'll need to go to the club. My bag, phone, and keys are there."

"I'll send Matthew first thing in the morning to retrieve them. I'm sorry, but you can't go back there"

"You don't control me. I'll do what I want."

"It's for your safety. Please trust me," he entreated.

"Tomorrow, I want you to tell me exactly that's going on. I want you tell me everything you know about my uncle"

"I promise you. I'll tell you everything."

She got to her feet. "Goodnight."

"Goodnight."

He watched her leave, then switched the TV on low and began to flick through the channels. Amy was in the bedroom next to his, and she was hurting. He was going to have to explain to her why he walked out on her in Lanzarote. He wanted to bury himself inside her to make it all right, but that was where all his problems had started.

His hand reached down and undid his trousers. He pulled his cock out and began to stroke it. He shut his eyes and thought of Amy in the costume she'd been wearing in the club. He remembered the scent of her as they'd had sex in Lanzarote. The little cry she'd made as she came. He was gripping really hard now and roughly tugging at his throbbing shaft. He was going to come. He needed to come, but at the last minute he pulled his hand away. That was his punishment.

He'd never be worthy of her.

SIX

Amy

A shaft of light shone through a small crack in the curtains. Amy slowly opened her bleary eyes and looked around the unfamiliar room. Expensive-looking tapestries decorated the pristine white walls. A large mirror sat on top of an ornately-carved wooden dressing table, and a matching wardrobe was on the other side of the room. She reached for her phone on the bedside table to check the time, but it wasn't there. When she rolled over, her body ached, and she remembered the night before. She pulled the bedcovers over her head and screamed loudly into them.

She was alone.

She slowly got out of the bed and pulled on a dressing gown that had been left on the back of the door. A hairbrush was on the dressing table, and she pulled it through her hair. She looked at her reflection in the mirror and saw dark circles under her eyes. She still didn't know what the time was, and so she quietly opened the bedroom door and peered out. The house was silent. She remembered her way to the lounge and went to see the time. It was eleven in the morning. She'd slept for much longer than she had thought.

A voice made her jump, but when she turned and realised it was James's mother, she relaxed.

"Good morning, Mrs North."

"Please, will you call me Miranda? Come, I have some breakfast in the kitchen. You must be famished."

She was, so she followed Miranda into the kitchen, where laid out before her was an assortment of pastries, fresh fruit, and on the stove were sausages and bacon. The smell of freshly ground coffee permeated the room.

She looked around the room for signs that James had woken and had already eaten his breakfast.

"He left early. Urgent business meeting, apparently. He said he'll be back as soon as possible and for you to relax, take a bath, swim, watch TV, do whatever you want, and he'll take you to get your belongings later."

She sat at a large family table, and Miranda poured her coffee.

"He seems a very busy man. Is that how he became so successful?"

Miranda busied herself at the massive stove while she answered,

"He works more hours than I care for him to do. The holiday he took recently was his first in about five years, and I'm sure he was constantly on his phone and laptop while there."

"He seemed relaxed and happy. He certainly didn't have a laptop when I was with him." She blushed when she realised the implication of what she had said. "I mean when we had dinner."

Miranda served her cooked breakfast and sat beside her, "It's alright dear, I'm not daft. It was obvious to me that something had happened between you both."

Amy cut a piece of the toast and egg and popped it in her mouth. It was delicious, and she swallowed it down hungrily before going back for more.

"He scared me last night, and I still don't fully understand why he acted the way he did. But I can see he's a good man. I see the way he treats you. I would like to get to know him." The words came out of her mouth before she could think about what she had said. She was still angry with him, but she wanted to understand him. She was intrigued by his intensity and wanted to peel back his layers to discover what was beneath.

"I'm glad of that." Miranda smiled as she topped up her coffee.

Amy surveyed Miranda when she took her empty plate. She was slim, smartly dressed, and held herself well. Her hair and nails were clearly attended to professionally, and on a regular basis. She looked like she was in her mid- to late-forties, but, with a twenty-eight-year-old son, she suspected she may be a little older.

"I'm going to see what clothes Sophie has, that you can wear." Miranda went to the door.

She called after her, "Is Sophie his sister?"

Miranda called back, "Yes. Help yourself to another pastry. Nobody leaves my kitchen hungry."

She chose a ripe apple from the fruit bowl instead. A phone vibrated on the counter, she looked and saw the message was from James to his mother. She knew she shouldn't, but she read the brief notification header.

It's all trashed. Keep Amy there.

She read the message again before it disappeared. Trashed? What was trashed? She grabbed the phone and sped through the house, calling for Miranda who appeared quickly from another bedroom with clothes in her hand.

She held her phone up to her. "Where's James?"

The elder lady snatched it from her. "What did you see?"

"Where's James?" she shouted.

"Amy calm down, please. Sit down." She didn't sit, in fact she remained standing in defiance. "He went with Matthew to get your belongings from the club. Your uncle wasn't there. James was told he was at your apartment." She looked down at her phone and pressed her finger against it to unlock it. Amy didn't need to hear the rest.

"He's destroyed it, hasn't he? I need to go."

"James said you need to stay here. It isn't safe--" ·

"Isn't safe? It's my apartment." She grabbed the clothes and stormed along the corridor to her room. "I'm going with or without your help. I'll walk the entire way, if I need to."

The traffic was light so it only took Miranda half an hour to drive them to her apartment in Kennington. She got out of the car and sped up the six flights of stairs to her door. The door was slightly ajar, and she nervously pushed it open. A vintage mirror—a Christmas gift to herself—was shattered in front of her. Further down the hallway, an array of ripped furnishings and smashed ornaments were scattered over the floor. This was her first home; these were her possessions, and they were completely ruined. She heard a noise from the lounge, and when she entered, she saw James and Matthew carefully trying to pick up pieces of furniture. Her stereo system and TV had been smashed. The sofa had been cut and its filling pulled out. Her eyes focused on an empty picture frame on the floor. It was the one that contained the last ever photo taken of her with her parents. It was now torn into tiny pieces scattered beside the frame. It could never be replaced.

She let out a loud sob, and James turned. "Amy. What are you doing here?"

James let go of his half of the coffee table, much to Matthew's anguish when he was left to balance it himself, and wrapped his arms around her. She didn't shy away. She needed the comfort. "You were supposed to stay with my mum." Miranda breathlessly appeared at the door.

"Amy." He cupped her cheek, his piercing blue eyes trying to calm her obvious distress. "Let my mum take you back to my place. Matthew and I will sort everything here."

She leaned further back into his warmth. "Is every room the same?"

"Yes. I'm sorry."

"Why did he do this? I don't understand."

"I don't know. But he'll pay for it."

"You've called the police?"

"No. The police will do nothing. He had your keys. They'll view it as a domestic." She knew what James meant by 'he'll pay'. For now, she was too raw with anger to argue.

"I had my mum's jewellery in my bedroom." James let go of her waist, took her hand, and led her to the bedroom. Matthew and Miranda stayed in the lounge and continued cleaning. She went straight to her jewellery box which was on the floor. Relieved to find her mum's wedding and engagement rings there, she placed them on her fingers.

"I need to get the police involved. Without a crime reference, I won't be able to get my insurance to fix and replace everything." She pulled her hand through her hair in desperation and looked back at James. The look of concern was gone from his face. He had the look of determination and control again. The one from that night.

"You won't need money. I'll sort everything."

She interrupted, "I'm not going to let you repair everything at your expense."

"I won't be repairing anything at my expense."

"My uncle won't be repairing this either. I want him gone from my life. After what he did? I want to forget him."

"I'll deal with your uncle my way, but you won't be returning here."

She wanted to defy him, to scream at him, and tell him no, but she couldn't. She didn't want to stay here. He was overruling her common sense again, but she had fallen completely under his spell. She looked at the pile of her clothes, her intimate undergarments strewn all over the floor.

"I agree. On some conditions."

"You've a thing for conditions. We'll need to work on that."

She turned back to him and accepted a kiss from his lips that shocked them both.

"I'll pay my way. You won't keep me."

He raised an eyebrow, "We can negotiate that." She laughed. "The other conditions?"

"Just one."

"I'm all ears." He put his arm around her waist again.

"Whatever this is between us, it won't last if we don't get to know each other properly. No lies. No secrets. You messed up last night. You should have come to me and told me everything, not made a public display of it. This..."—she waved her hands at the chaos of the room—"is partly your fault."

"And I'll never stop apologising for it. It's why I want to help you correct it. It's why I'm here cleaning it myself."

"I was a little surprised at that. I thought you'd hire someone. But, if you accept my conditions, I'll stay with you and take your help. If not, leave now, please." She brought her finger to her lip and nervously chewed on the tip while she waited for his answer.

He placed both his hands around her waist.

"I agree."

SEVEN

James

It didn't take them long to finish packing what remained of Amy's belongings. A locksmith arrived and changed the locks while they were there. He went to hand Amy the key to lock up, but she shook her head and told him to keep it.

She didn't seem to really have much fight left in her. The past twenty-four hours had been too much for her, and he felt overwhelming guilt for his part in it. He had allowed his controlling nature to overrule his common sense, again, and she was suffering as a result.

On return to his home, James helped her out of his mother's Audi and carried one of her suitcases into the house. She carried the lighter of the two, although neither one was heavy. She didn't have many belongings that were salvageable.

Amy went straight to her room. He thought she needed a moment alone and went to make them some drinks. When he returned, she was hanging up her final dress. She looked up at him, pleading, "I want you to tell me everything."

He took both of her hands and pulled her close. She kissed him gently on the lips. She tasted so good. Why couldn't he take her away somewhere and make her forget everything that was happening, instead? He really didn't want to see her crying.

"I trust that you did it for the right reasons. I'm still so confused by my uncle. He's not the man I grew up believing him to be. I need to know everything to get it all straight in my head."

He took her hand and, in silence, led her to his study on the top floor of the house. Most of the Georgian house was in keeping with the period, but it had modern twists. This room was no exception. He had a massive, curved oak desk in the middle of it. To the right, on the wall, he'd three large screens which could be concealed under pictures that descended from the ceiling.

He showed Amy into the room and sat her on a velvety chaise longue. He went to a safe, which was again hidden behind a picture, and pulled out a folder. He handed it to her.

"This is everything I found out about you."

He felt ashamed of the file when she took it from him. That folder contained so much personal information about her. If she put the folder down and walked out on him now, he wouldn't blame her. It made him look like a stalker. However, she just flicked through all the information and stopped at the details he had on her uncle's business.

He knew that her uncle used the premises as a front for drugs and prostitution. He imported girls from Eastern Europe with the promise of a brighter future only to have them carry out sex acts in a property he owned nearby. Amy wiped a tear from her eye.

"I thought Sara got some of her extra money from…selling her body. I didn't know he had another property that did all that. Those poor girls."

"Matthew and I will be working to shut that part of the business down."

"Let me know when you have," she mused, still concentrating on the folder.

She turned over another page and looked up at him in shock.

"Sara?"

He nodded. "Sara isn't her real name. She's Gabriella Martinez. She's from Latin America. Did you know she was your uncle's lover?"

"She can't have been. We used to complain about him together. I never thought she liked him only that she tolerated him, because she earned good money."

"The video I showed you was from a week ago, when you were in Lanzarote. It's security footage from the club. Matthew had someone hack into the systems. She was pregnant with your uncle's child. He didn't want it, though. The only reason your uncle paid for your holiday was so that he could get you out of the way while he got rid of the baby." He handed her back the papers but turned to a page which had photos of Sara's body after her uncle had enacted his cruel termination on her. Amy's hand flew to her face, and she paled.

"Yesterday, Matthew found Sara in her apartment. She had taken an overdose of painkillers. I'm so sorry, she didn't survive." Amy let out a loud cry that almost tore his heart apart. He wanted to lash out. He wanted to punish her uncle for the pain he was inflicting on Amy.

For now, though, he needed to concentrate on the girl he was cradling in his arms. She sat up, and he wiped away the tears from her eyes. "That's why I came for you straight away. I wasn't thinking straight, when I heard about her death. I had to get you away and protect you."

"She has no family?"

"Matthew found her family. We're arranging to get her home to Brazil. Sara was duped by your uncle. There were letters and a diary in her flat that showed she thought he'd marry her. She was a good girl and took her life as a last resort because she felt so much shame."

"Thank you for returning her home." Amy's voice broke. "How can he have done that to her? To make someone think that death is preferable to life? I should have been here to help her."

"Your uncle is a sick man. He's perverted and dangerous, and there's nothing that you could've done. Please let me protect you from him?"

She pushed him away and stood up.

"You must be crazy, getting involved with me. I should go. It isn't fair to you."
He frowned but didn't move.

"You're going nowhere. As you said earlier, we've a connection, and we owe it to ourselves to explore it. Come here."

She instantly obeyed him.

"You're safe, and we can learn about each other now. Trust me. If I didn't want to do something, I wouldn't. Sara made a mistake and paid with her life."

He didn't finish what he was saying because she crushed a passionate kiss to his lips. He reciprocated at first and then pushed her away.

" I need to feel something other than the pain. I need to be back in Lanzarote."

He froze. He wanted nothing more than to tear her clothes from her and bury his aching cock deep within her. But she was vulnerable at the moment.

"Lie back." His tone was stern, and she immediately did as instructed. He pulled the trousers, she was wearing, down her legs and ripped her thin panties from her body. "Open your legs."

She did so, revealing her already-glistening pussy to him. He leaned forward to trail his tongue over the length of her folds, parting them and savouring her juices. He was throbbing with his own need. He flicked his tongue over and over her clit, and every time, she groaned in pleasure. Slowly, he inserted a finger inside her then two, and she thrust herself against his hand. His finger hooked, and he teased her g-spot. She was close. He stopped, and she moaned.

"Not until I say, remember? That's my rule."

She cried out, "And you complain about me with rules and stipulations."

With his free hand, he gave her two quick, sharp smacks to her peachy rear.

"Answering back gets you into trouble."

"James, please," she begged.

"Please what?" he teased.

Breathlessly, she clutched at her perfectly formed breasts and gyrated against his hand. "Please, let me come."

He chuckled. "Come."

James flicked her nub with his tongue, and she exploded. She gushed over his tongue and gripped his fingers in pulsating waves of ecstasy. He longed to bury himself inside her, but as she came, her tears flowed. She sobbed. He moved to cradle her and held her close until she calmed and fell asleep.

EIGHT

Amy

A month had passed since Amy moved into James's home. She was enjoying learning more about him and had made wonderful friends in both Matthew and Miranda. Two days after her laptop had been smashed, James presented her with a brand new MacBook Pro. A variety of writing software had been installed on it, and all her work, she had thought lost, had been neatly stored in what he called a 'cloud'. He gave her a new iPhone as well. She was told that it was linked to his account, so she could download anything that she wanted on it. Her contacts were all on it, minus her uncle. She didn't complain but made a mental note to pay him back one day. In the mean-time she would enjoy the modern technology, even if it baffled her a little bit. He also had pictures of her with her parents, recovered from her old laptop, printed out and put in frames in her room. She bawled like a baby when she saw them. They spent a lot of time together just having what James termed 'dates'. Today was one of those dates, and he was taking her shopping. Matthew pulled the car into Sloane Street, and all she could see were top designer brands.

"I can't afford to shop here. In case you forgot, I don't have a job," she scolded.

"I can buy you a present."

"No. Please, can we go somewhere cheaper? I don't want you having to buy me expensive clothes. You seem to think that it's one outfit that I need. Most of my clothes were destroyed. I pretty much need everything."

"Then I'll buy it for you."

She groaned and placed her head in her hands.

"You aren't listening to me. I'm not going to let you buy me everything."

"I have the money. I can spend it how I want, and I want to spend it in these shops." He had a defiant look on his face that told her, he wasn't going to listen.

"Fine." She leaned forward and spoke to Matthew. "James is getting out here to spend his money how he wants. Can you take me to Oxford Street, please, so I can spend mine?"

"What. No, that isn't what I meant," James spluttered next to her. "Matthew, you stay here."

"If he stays here then I'm not getting out of the car. You can, but I won't move a single muscle from this seat."

Matthew coughed "Er, Boss? Sorry, but I need a decision as to what I'm doing. A traffic officer is heading this way."

She folded her arms over her chest in defiance and sat back in her seat.

"Fine. Take us to Oxford Street. But I'll be buying your entire wardrobe."

"You'll buy me one outfit, and you won't argue. I'm adamant, and you won't change my mind. I'm not here for your money. I'm here for you."

"I think we need to have a long discussion about defiance and soon." James shrunk over to his side of the car, and she was confident that he was sulking. He had the whole stuck out bottom lip thing. She was secretly cheered by her little victory even though she knew it would mean punishment later. James was very skilled with his fingers and tongue, and if she denied him something, then he denied her. He always relented in the end, normally when she begged. He'd kept to his word and had not pressured her into anything more, even though she could see he was very evidently hard every time he touched her. The rest of the date passed with very little event.

When she returned home, she found a Mulberry Bayswater handbag waiting for her. She didn't protest, even after she had Googled the cost. She liked it and thought he'd made an excellent choice. He had promised her a Chanel one next, and she told him that there was no way he was to buy her one. She'd take it straight back to the store.

"Have you decided what you're doing with your flat?" James asked, as he poured her a glass of Prosecco.

"Well, as you won't let me pay you back for all the repairs, I thought that I'd rent it out."

"Not sell it?"

"I don't have a mortgage on it, so renting it out will give me some money of my own until I find another job."

"You don't need a job."

"Don't start, I'm finding a job!" She rolled her eyes.

"Why? I'm a billionaire. And when we open the hotel in Bangalore, I'll make more money than I know what to do with. Let me spoil you?"

She wasn't going to get anywhere with James in this mood. He wanted to treat her like a princess and protect her, but she could never live her life that way. It was how she had been treated by her parents and her uncle, and where had that got her? No, she needed to stand on her own two feet.

"Tell me how you made your business so successful. Where did you grow up?"

"Changing the subject won't help you win the argument, you know." He looked at her with a raised eyebrow. "But I'll indulge you this once. My parents came from Kent. They'd some money so I went to grammar school and passed all my GCSE's and A-levels with top grades, but I didn't go to university despite being offered a place at Cambridge."

"Why?" she interrupted.

"I didn't want to. I had other plans. I had a trust fund, and when I received it, I bought a plot of land at auction. With a few trusted builders and a trainee architect, I developed three houses on the land and sold them at a triple profit. We went onwards and upwards from there."

"Do you still use the architect?"

"He's a shareholder and chief architect of the company. The head builder is head of my operations team."

"Their loyalty to you paid off and vice versa."

"Certainly did. I wanted my sister to work with us, but after dad left us, she wanted to forge her own way in life. I may have greased the wheels a little bit for her to do that, but please, don't ever tell her so."

"You really adore Sophie, don't you?" she enquired.

"I do. I still can't believe she's getting married. Did you like speaking to her the other day?" They'd had a Skype call with her.

"I did. She teased me something rotten about you, though." She snuggled further into James's arms; shut her eyes and listened to his heartbeat.

"What did she say? I'll have words with her."

"She was laughing at you for, finally, at your ripe old age of twenty-eight, finding a girlfriend."

"That's it. She can pay for her own wedding."

"You wouldn't dare." She patted his chest.

"Try me."

"She did say something that worried me a little bit. She mentioned that when the press finds out about us, they'll want to do interviews."

"They probably will, but we will deal with that when it happens. Maybe I'll give them the topless photo shoot they keep asking for, and they'll leave you alone."

"I'm not sure I like that."

"Getting protective over my body, Miss Jones?"

"Maybe a little. I love your tattoo. I caught a glimpse of it when you were changing the other day. Why a male angel? It's so intricate."

She was sure that she felt his heart skip several beats and start rapidly thumping when she asked the question.

"I saw the design and liked it. Do you want another drink?"

"No, I still have some of this one." Alright, so he wasn't going to talk about his tattoo. Every time she tried to get him to open up about something that wasn't his business or his family, he shut down. She wasn't going to allow it to happen this time.

"Am I your first proper girlfriend? Is that why the press will be so interested in us?"

He groaned. "Shall we watch a film?"

"Stop avoiding the question."

"Stop *asking* the question, and I'll stop having to avoid it."

She sat up. "Please. Why do you always avoid this question? You know everything about my past love life."

"Yes, I do, and I wish I could erase the thought of another man touching you."

"Is that why you won't talk to me about your sex life? Because you think I won't like the thought of you with another woman?"

"Amy."

"No. If we're to have a relationship, we need to be open with each other. You can't keep secrets from me." She raised an eyebrow at him and sat up.

"You aren't going to stop are you?"

She shook her head.

"Alright, I give in. I've had a proper girlfriend. I met her when I was sixteen. We were together for five years. Yes, we had sex, before you ask. No, it wasn't as good as my one encounter with you." He smirked. "Now, shall we watch a film, or do you want to question me more?"

"Why did you break up?"

He got up from the chair and ran his hand through his hair. "We wanted different things from the relationship."

"She wanted marriage?"

"No."

"You wanted marriage?"

"No."

"Then what?"

"We were sexually incompatible."

He downed his glass of Prosecco and turned his back to her.

"Incompatible?"

"I've certain needs. I'm controlling, you know that already, but I also like certain things sexually."

"Oh. So…you're into whips and chains? She wasn't submissive, but you think I will be."

"You already are, whether you know it or not. Whips and chains aren't all what BDSM is about. It's about trust. As your lover, I'll expect you to submit to me sexually. I don't mean like a slave, but I do want to look after you. I'll reward you for this submission. That's important to me." He turned back round to face her, and she could see this was hurting him. "Do you want to leave?"

"Do you think I should?"

"*She* did."

"We've been thrown together by a very intense experience. We still have so much to learn about each other. What you've said, I won't lie, scares me a little. Mainly because I don't know much about it. But right now, I'm not going anywhere." She tentatively reached out and placed her hand over the front of his trousers, his cock instantly sprung to life. "You've given to me a lot recently. Will you let me give to you? I want to have you in my mouth."

"You don't have to?" he almost whispered.

"I want to."

He nodded his consent, and she started to undo his belt buckle, then the zip of his jeans. She turned her attention to his cock, which was right in front of her face. It was perfect. He was broad and long. She would barely be able to fit more than half of him in her mouth. Slowly, she licked up his length towards the tip and flicked her tongue over it. He let out a gravelly moan.

On the next pass she swirled her tongue all the way around his cock. She drew him into her mouth, shallowly at first, but as she moved up and down, she took him deeper and deeper. He was stretching her mouth. She already knew what he felt like in her pussy. She cupped his balls, ran a finger over the tight skin underneath, and he grabbed hold of the bookcase next to them.

"Fuck."

She pulled back and took hold of her glass of Prosecco. She drank some of the cooling bubbles into her mouth and then quickly placed as much of his cock into her mouth as she could. He shuddered and hissed. She swallowed the wine.

"You're far too much of an expert at this. You sure you're a good girl?"

She gave a throaty laugh. Her pace quickened, and she was sucking him hard now, taking him deeper and deeper. She then withdrew to his tip leaving him bereft of the warmth of her mouth. She was tantalising the proud purple crown with little licks. This was all new to her, but somehow, she knew how to please him.

"You'll get the biggest reward ever for this, sweetheart."

She knew he was getting close when she looked at how he gripped the book-case. The whites of his knuckles were showing.

"Harder. Deeper."

She obeyed, and he hit the back of her throat. She gagged a little but swallowed him down.

"I'm going to come. You don't have to take me, but I'll need to pull out if you don't."

She allowed the word 'no' to reverberate around his cock and took him deep again. He came with ferocity. She could taste every pulsating wave of his essence. He withdrew from her mouth, and she swallowed every last drop of him. He bent to kiss her. He had the withdrawn expression of guilt on his face.

"Please tell me I didn't hurt you. That it wasn't too much. I'm sorry. I got carried away."

She ran her hand over his cheek.

"No. It was perfect for me." She kissed him and nestled against his chest. His heartbeat was so fast. She couldn't tell whether it was because he'd orgasmed or because he was terrified. "We will learn this together. Never shy away from telling me anything, please."

He kissed the top of her head.

"I will try."

NINE

James

"We need to be certain on these figures. This deal has always been problematic, and I'm not going to let it run away with us. Simon, what are your percentage errors allowance?" James stood at the head of the large boardroom table, around him were his heads of departments, and they were discussing a contract for building properties in the South American market. He looked towards his head of accounting. He was young for the position and an awful flirt, but he was reliable and had been consistently accurate in his calculations.

"I've allowed two percent fluctuation; this should be no more than one million pounds either way. I know it sounds a lot, but the market is borderline, and the specifications are tightly controlled. We've already greased the wheels, so we shouldn't have to deal with as much bureaucracy in the long term either. I would say the leeway is minus point-five to plus two-point-five percent. A lot of the work has been done upfront. To not sign now would give us a significant loss."

"And the plans?" He turned to his head of architecture.

"Agreed in principal, subject to your signature on the contract."

"Any repercussions likely over the tensions in the Falklands?" This time, it was his commercial director to whom he turned.

"Good publicity for improving them. Especially with your donations to the orphanage and women's refuge."

"So, let's put it to a vote." Ultimately, any decision on the signing of contracts was his responsibility, but he allowed his close team to convey their opinions to him. "A show of hands for yes?"

All of the team put their hands up.

"Motion carried. I'll sign the documents tomorrow."

At that moment, Matthew appeared. He made a sign that he needed to speak to him and, from the look on his face, it was something to do with Amy.

"Thank you, everyone," James said.

Matthew walked in the door while the members of his board left.

"What is it?"

"Miss Jones, Sir, she's boarded a train out to Essex."

"What?" He looked at him in astonishment.

"You didn't know."

"No, I didn't fucking know. Did she tell you? Why didn't you say anything before now? What the hell is she playing at?"

"She didn't tell me, Sir. I had a phone call from your mother, and she told me. She assumed we knew and that Amy was with me."

"Does she have anyone with her?"

"Miss Anderson is tailing her, as requested. She won't interact unless vital for Miss Jones's protection." Miss Anderson was Amy's personal bodyguard, not that Amy knew anything about her.

He pulled his phone out of his pocket and flicked onto a tracking app.

"What train is she on?"

"According to Miss Anderson, it's a fast train to Shenfield, in Essex."

He rubbed at his temple as he left the room and returned to his office. Marie stood to give him his messages, as he passed, but he waved her away. He went straight to his safe and pulled out the file. "Damn it. It's her mum's birthday today. Get the car. She must be going to her grave. She won't be thinking straight, and she won't be looking out for danger. Why didn't she tell me? I could've taken her."

"Do you think that's wise?" Matthew didn't move. "Maybe she needs time alone for this? If Amy had wanted you there, she'd have told you. She's safe. Miss Anderson is watching her, and she's good."

Matthew didn't often question his orders. That was one of the reasons they got on so well.

"I'll be there for her afterwards. I won't impact on her mourning, but I'm not risking anything happening to her. We still don't know what her uncle is up to. He was looking for something in that flat. We don't know if he found it or not. I have to protect her. I won't lose her."

"She isn't Colette. She's completely different. You have to trust her."

He turned away and clenched his fists. "Don't ever mention her name near me. Go get the car." The last words were spoken with cold demand. Matthew had pressed the wrong button. He was doing all he could to maintain his control when he was around Amy. He wanted to do so much to her, but it was wrong, all wrong. He needed to protect her and keep her safe. He needed to prove that he could put that part of his life aside and be the perfect boyfriend.

"As you wish, Boss."

When they pulled up outside the park, where the app indicated Amy was, Matthew turned to him again,

"Please let her have this moment alone. She lost both her parents so tragically. It will still be raw, especially after recent events."

"I will. Thank you. I'm sorry for my attitude earlier."

"I'm used to it, Boss."

He got out of the car and wandered through the trees, past numerous statues of creatures he recognised from the story of the Gruffalo. He eventually saw Amy, sitting on a bench, talking to herself. She had tears in her eyes. A bunch of lilies lay by her feet. The steam of her breath flowed from her mouth as she spoke. James made no attempt to move forward. He could just about hear her voice, and she was sobbing as she spoke. He wanted nothing more than to pull her into his arms and hold her, but he knew she needed space.

"I trusted him, Mum. I thought he was all that I had left in the world, and he betrayed me in the worst way. Did you protect me from his real nature? You should have told me. Why didn't you say anything? You always treated me like a princess and hid the nastiness of the world from me. How am I supposed to protect myself now, when I know nothing about real life?" He felt guilty, he was the one who'd shown her what her uncle was.

Amy's one-sided conversation changed to a discussion on him. "I really like him, Mum. He makes me feel so special. I know he's hiding so much from me. I want to trust him, but I'm scared. What if he's hiding something dangerous? He's very intense, and everything feels so strange at the moment. I barely know what normal is anymore. Why did you have to die? I need you so much. I need to talk to you. Why did you leave me?" Her voice broke on the last words, and she bowed her in to her hands. He knew, at that moment, what it would do to him if he lost his mother. He saw it in Amy's breaking heart. He went to step forward to comfort her, but something stopped him. He couldn't give her that support now, there was still so much that he hadn't told her. He took a step back and returned to the car. Matthew opened the door for him, when he came alongside the vehicle.

"Take me to the nearest train station. I'll get a train back to London. I want you to return here and bring Amy home."

"You sure, Boss?"

"Yes. She needs this time to herself. I don't say it often, but you were right."

"You're doing the right thing."

"I can't let it happen again. I need to control this."

"No, you need to forget everything they did to you."

He looked up at his bodyguard as he sat.

"That will never happen."

"Why not?"

"Just drive."

"Answer me this? What does she honestly know about you except that you have money?"

"Nothing."

"Then if you want to keep her, talk to her."

He looked out the window as Matthew turned the car around. Could he really take the risk and open up to her?

Amy

"Need a lift, Miss Jones?"

Matthew pulled the Aston Martin Rapide S up next to her.

"What are you doing here? How did you find me?"

"Tracked your phone." She should have known. "If you'd told me where you were going, I'd have brought you here as well. That's what I'm here for. It's my job."

"I thought James may need you, and I didn't want to disturb you," she replied.

"I spend most of my time sitting around his office reading the newspaper."

"Sorry. I thought he kept you busy."

She wiped away the tears to try to disguise the fact that she'd been crying, but when he offered her a tissue, she knew that she'd failed. They didn't really speak on the journey back to London. She was emotionally tired. She shut her eyes and must have fallen asleep for an hour, when she next opened them they were pulling up outside James's house. She sat up and rubbed her sleepy eyes.

"Thank you. I'm sorry to have made you drive all that distance."

"Not a problem Miss, I like to get out of the city sometimes. Anytime you want to go to the country just ask. We'll take a picnic next time." He winked.

She laughed but secretly vowed that she'd take him up on the offer. "Will you tell James what I did?" He was paranoid about her security, and in the few weeks that she'd been with him, he'd always ensured that either Matthew or himself accompanied her when she went out. She found it a little stifling after being able to travel wherever she wanted for the last few years, but she also found a degree of comfort in it.

"If he asks, I'll say I took you both ways."

"Thank you. I know he's worried about my uncle, but this was something I needed to do on my own."

"I know." He got out and came round to open the door for her before she could question him further. "Go on up. I better get going to pick up Mr North. Don't want him getting grumpy 'cause he has to travel with the regular people." Matthew's cheeky laugh made her chuckle as well. And a laugh was what she needed. "Miss Jones, can I say something?"

"Of course."

"Don't give up on asking him about himself. He'll open up eventually." The bodyguard jumped back into the car and sped off before she could answer him.

Miranda handed her a cup of tea when she entered the front door. "How was your day out?"

She pondered her answer. Miranda's question was so genuine and kindly put. The woman had been so helpful. She decided on the truth, even if it did get back to James. Matthew said he'd cover for her on the aspects of her safety.

"I went back to Essex, where I grew up. There's a park there I often visited with my mother. It was her birthday today, and I wanted to sit and remember her for awhile."

Miranda came up to her, put her arms around her, and brought her close, which took her a little by surprise.

"That sounds a wonderfully comforting thing to do. Places full of memories always give us what we need in times of anguish. Come and sit down, you must be tired."

"I slept in the car on the way home."

"Have you told James that it was your mother's birthday?"

She shook her head, "I thought he'd know. He has that file on me, so I figured he'd know everything already. He didn't say anything this morning, though."

"Oh Amy, dear. He's a man. He may have a file on you, but he's no idea how to use it. You'll still have to remind him when your birthday is." The elder lady smiled.

Amy felt deflated and collapsed onto the sofa. She really was naive in so many aspects. She knew nothing and was falling for a man of the world. He'd probably tire of her soon and throw her back out on the street. Nobody could fall in love with someone who could barely tie their own shoe laces without some sort of advice.

"I'll tell him later. Matthew has gone to collect him from work."

"I'll leave you two alone tonight. You need some time together. Why don't you get a takeaway of your choice and relax?"

"I'd actually like to go out for dinner with him. It isn't something we've done yet."

"Then tell him that. I know my son can be a little full on at times, I've no idea why, but his heart is kind. If you aren't happy with something he wants to do, don't let him dictate to you."

"Do you stand up to him?" She bit her lip, she hadn't meant to ask such an impertinent question, but it seemed to roll off her tongue. Things often did. She really needed to learn to control that.

"It's alright, I know that I'm speaking of something that I don't often do myself. My son changed a few years ago. He wasn't always this closed off. He was attacked. I don't know the full details, but I think it scared him. I'm sure he'll tell you about it, but he hasn't exactly been forthcoming with me. For now, though, you must keep to your strengths. That's what attracted him to you in the first place. You've a strong sense of your own worth. If you want to go out to dinner, tell him. And make sure you choose the restaurant as well. I know that he seems to do everything for appearance, but actually, he loves the simple things in life." Miranda squeezed her hand.

An idea suddenly hit Amy. She knew what she was going to do and where she was going to take James for dinner. It was traditionally British, but with an elegant flair. She got up from her seat and gave Miranda an immense hug. "I know exactly where I'm going to take him. Matthew should be bringing him home soon. Tell him I want him dressed in jeans and a t-shirt and ready to go by six-thirty." She set off back to her room as she spoke. "Oh and Miranda, he's to leave his wallet at home."

"I can't promise that last one, but I'll tell him."

TEN

Amy

At just gone seven, Matthew pulled the car up outside a vintage fish and chip restaurant by Liverpool Street Station. Amy was so excited she was almost bouncing in the car as they drove. James had a scowl on his face. She'd heard him grumble at his mother when she told him that he was to leave his wallet at home. As soon as she appeared in her long jumper and leggings, with knee high boots, James quietened and reluctantly agreed. Miranda had given her a wink of good luck.

"What's this place?"

"It's a compromise."

"Compromise?"

"My treat for dinner. I would have taken you down to the coast for fish and chips, but that would be a long drive."

"We could've gone to the coast for dinner. That's what I've got Matthew for, to drive us wherever we want to go." The bodyguard groaned from the front of the car. James got out of the car and held his hand out to help her from her seat.

"Matthew has already driven out that way today." She was going to tell him when they'd got to the table, but considering the mood he was in, maybe outside in the open was easier.

"Why?" He didn't let go of her hand but led her towards the restaurant.

"I went back to where I grew up." She stopped outside the entrance. "It would have been my mother's birthday today. We often went to a park together, and I wanted to go there to remember her." She bowed her head. This was crazy. She was feeling guilty for lying, "I...um...I got a train there." His hand clenched tighter on hers.

"Alone?"

She nodded.

"I know."

She looked up and straight at him. His eyes were soft and full of affection for her. "You know? Matthew told you?"

"No, I saw you there."

"What?"

She let go of his hand and stepped back. He was there? He'd been watching her? "I don't understand."

"Matthew brought me down when I saw where you'd gone. I thought you might need me when I realised that it would have been your mum's birthday."

"But when Matthew found me, you weren't with him?"

"I got a train back to London."

"Why didn't you come to me?" she questioned.

"Because you needed that time to yourself. It was your personal time to grieve and reflect on the last few weeks."

"It was."

He pulled her closer to him and brushed his hand through her hair.

"I know this is all new, and we're still getting to know each other, but you can talk to me about things like this. If you'd mentioned it, I'd have come with you but given you the time you needed to be alone." She kissed him lightly on the cheek. "So are we eating? I haven't had proper fish and chips for a long time now. I must have been a kid on Hasting's seafront the last time." He led her into the restaurant and allowed her to order for them. She had a glass of white wine. He had a beer, and they both had beer-battered fish with chips and mushy peas.

"Do you look like your mother?" he asked, while sampling the peas.

"I do."

"Sophie is the spitting image of my mum. I think I've too much of my father in me."

"When was the last time you saw your dad?"

"I'd rather not talk about him. He hurt my mother badly, and I need him out of my life forever."

"Alright. How about a favourite subject at school then?" she asked.

"What?"

"Come on, allow me some questions. You've a whole file of information on me, but I've to find out about you the old-fashioned way." She popped a chip in her mouth.

"History."

"History? I wouldn't have guessed that." She almost spat the chip across the room in shock.

"Why?"

"I would have thought craft, design and technology."

"I like learning about people's pasts. How they lived." He shrugged.

"You're somewhat of an enigma. Shock me again?"

"With what?"

"Something else that I wouldn't expect from you?"

"There isn't really a lot to tell. What you see is what you get."

"I don't believe that for one minute. Come on? There must be something," she pestered.

"Really, there isn't."

"Ok, first kiss?"

"Colette, unfortunately. We were together when we were sixteen. Your kisses are so much better, though."

"You lost your virginity to her?"

"No." She could see that he was getting reluctant to answer these questions, but she needed to know.

"Who then?"

"Can we just enjoy this meal, please? Why don't you tell me your favourite subject at school instead?"

"English. Now answer my question."

"A prostitute."

"What?" she screeched her answer a little too loud.

People turned to stare at them.

"I'm not proud of it. It was the done thing amongst my mates and I."

"Do you and your friends still use prostitutes?" she asked.

"They're no longer my buddies."

The look in James's eyes changed to one of shame, and she knew that she wouldn't get another answer from him on this subject.

"So you like history. Have you visited any of the old houses in the country?"

He looked straight into her eyes. The shame disappeared and was replaced by affection.

"Lots. I really want to take you to my place in Yorkshire. It's the stuff of Pride and Prejudice."

"I'd like that very much."

She hesitated on her next question.

"So, you said you were into this BDSM thing."

"Was. I'm not any longer."

"Alright, but I read Fifty Shades of Grey. They seemed to enjoy it, well in parts. I don't think that woman. I forget her name...was interested in the contract part. Is that why Colette didn't want to do that?"

"We're having a nice meal. I really don't want to talk about my ex-girlfriend. She's out of my life, end of story." Somehow she didn't believe that one bit. Someone who was relaxed about ex relationships didn't change the subject every time they spoke about them.

"We aren't talking about your ex-girlfriend. We're talking about BDSM. I want to know more about it."

"I don't do it anymore." James shoved a piece of fish in his mouth and frowned at her.

"Humour me, alright?" Jesus, he could be so tetchy sometimes. She wished he'd tell her whatever it was that was buried so deep inside.

"You don't have to have contracts. It can be mutually agreed between two parties what you do. The Dom's job is to protect the sub, and in return, she gives him her submission. Sometimes this is just sexually, but in some couples it extends to him choosing what she eats, wears, and more," he reluctantly replied.

"So like the Dom would lay her clothes out for her in the morning?" She continued her questioning.

"Yes, but he'd reward her for that by washing her all over before she dresses."

"Would she have to wash him and get him dressed?"

"Depends on the nature of the agreement between them."

"Did you want this?"

"Partly."

"Partly?"

"I want to take care of any woman who is mine, and I'm in a position to do so. I'd want to buy her the best clothes to make her look and feel beautiful."

"That explains your insistence on our shopping trip."

"I wanted you to feel beautiful."

"I don't have body issues. I've 'being beholden to someone' issues. My entire life has been governed. I want to be able to look after myself a bit."

"Even if it gets you into trouble?"

"You mean my uncle?"

"It was only a matter of time before he had an offer like the one I gave him, from someone who didn't have your best interests at heart."

"I know." She looked down and shuffled a bit of fish across her plate into the ketchup. "So, BDSM basically means the woman putting her day to day control into the hands of a man?"

"Only if both parties agree."

"Hmm. And what about the sex stuff? Is that why you won't let me come until you say I can? Or is that you being Bossy?"

"You're impatient. Too much playing with yourself, if you ask me."

"Hey. I don't. Well I do...but we aren't talking about that." She couldn't believe *that* had come up in the conversation.

"Of course. Was the orgasm I gave you good?"

"Yes."

"Better than when you do it yourself?"

"Yes." She thought about it for a second and then added, "but I thought you weren't a Dom anymore?"

"Part of it will never leave me. But the scenes and stuff, I'll never do again. It's wrong."

"Scenes?"

"Yes. There are certain clubs that you can go to and perform more exotic acts with women. You can also perform these in a private bedroom as well."

"You mean like my uncle's clubs." She rolled her eyes.

"No, clubs where both are willing participants, and they consensually agree to engage in acts without money changing hands."

"Oh. You use these clubs often?"

"Not anymore."

"You've spanked me a couple of times when we've been playing. Is that part of it? Because I don't remember my ex-boyfriend doing that."

"Don't mention your ex-boyfriend. I don't wish to know he existed."

"And the spanking?" She was on a roll and wasn't going to let up on her questioning.

"I shouldn't do that. I'll stop."

"Why?"

"I shouldn't do it."

"What if I liked it?"

"You don't."

"How do you know?"

"I just do."

He was shutting down again. She was going to get nowhere with that question. Even if she did like the spanking.

"Is your fish good?"

"Yes. I'll probably need to do double my gym session tomorrow, but I'm enjoying it."

"Good." She was trying her hardest to think of more questions to get him to open up again. She knew she'd probably have to do most of her research on the internet. "How long have you had the tattoo? I want a tattoo. I don't know what yet, though."

"A few years now. If you decide you want one, I'll take you to my artist. He's the best. You don't go anywhere else."

"I don't go anywhere else?" She raised an eyebrow.

"Yes."

"Is that a Dom thing?" she teased.

"No it's an *I have the best artist* thing."

"Why the angel?"

"I liked the design."

"Did it hurt?"

"A lot."

"How long did it take?"

"Three sittings. How is your book coming? Have you had any more time to write it?"

And that was the end of that. He shut her down again. Still, she got more out of him than previously. She was determined. She wasn't going to stop.

They finished the rest of the meal. When it came to the bill, Amy snatched it before he could pay and went straight to the cashier. She felt smug until, the next morning, she found the money had been transferred to her bank account. He may deny he was into BDSM, but she had a feeling that he was more into it than he realised.

ELEVEN

James

James could not believe that Amy hadn't walked out on him.

When he told Colette what he wanted sexually, she laughed at him and ended their relationship. She insulted him, and he had to buy her off to prevent her from selling stories about him. He forked out a good million. It nearly broke him. Thankfully, they'd signed contracts, and she couldn't come at him for any more money when his business didn't falter but prospered.

He longed to try new things with Amy. She was under his skin and in his head. She tested his control but obeyed him entirely when he demanded it.

He shook his head. He was at his desk in the middle of his London office, and he was fantasising about her. He hadn't invited Amy to his office. He wanted to protect her from any scrutiny at the hands of prying employees—well mainly his secretary—but it was time for that to change, he could still protect her when she was at his side. He picked up the phone and pressed the quick dial for home.

"Hi, James. You alright?" Amy's sexy voice answered.

"Are you dressed?"

"I've a towel around me. I can dress in a few minutes. Why?"

"Just a towel? You want to send me a picture...without the towel?"

"Mr North, I hope your work calls aren't monitored."

"Miss Jones, I'm the chairman of the company. I'll have them erased."

She giggled playfully. His cock jumped.

"Hush and listen." She instantly complied. "I want you to bring my lunch to the office. Bring some for yourself. I don't have many meetings today. I want to show you around." She was silent, had he said something wrong? "Amy?"

"What should I wear?"

"What you usually wear." He chuckled as he answered. "Jeans, jumper, boots."

"You sure? I've a smart skirt and jacket I can wear."

"Come as you are."

"I'm wearing only a towel? Are you sure?"

"Maybe put some jeans and a t-shirt on. Don't forget my favourite pickle."

"That stuff makes your breath stink."

"You planning on kissing me in public?"

"Not if you eat the pickle."

"Amy!" he scolded.

"I'll be there in half an hour."

She put the phone down. He pulled up his instant messenger and quickly typed.

Actually, wear the skirt...no knickers.
    J

She replied instantly with a picture of her middle finger. He laughed.

Amy arrived pretty much on the half hour. Matthew escorted her up, and when his secretary tried to stop them, Matthew scowled at her and said that Amy was Mr North's girlfriend. His secretary's face was a picture. He suppressed a chuckle and stood to greet them.

"Marie, it's fine. I asked Matthew to bring Amy here. Amy this is my secretary Marie. Marie, my girlfriend, Amy." Marie gave the best-nonplussed greeting she could muster, and Amy reciprocated with all her sweetness. He nodded to Matthew. "Thank you. I'll call you when Miss Jones is ready to leave." His body-guard left. "This way?" He placed his hand on the small of her back and guided her into his office, shut the door behind them, and flicked a switch to turn the glass opaque.

"She fancies you."

"I hadn't guessed." He chuckled.

"That was mean. You should have told her I was coming before I appeared."

"She'll live. She's read far too many romantic books where the millionaire boss falls for his secretary. She wants a fantasy; the reality is very different." She raised her eyebrow at him, and he motioned for her to lay out his lunch.

"You shouldn't lead her on."

"Are you jealous?" He patted her on the backside.

"No."

"She's excellent at her job, and part of that's probably because she wants to please me. What's the harm in that?"

"Just watch that she doesn't send you to all the wrong meetings tomorrow."

Amy stuck her tongue out at him.

"Did you follow my instructions?"

Amy opened her bag and laid out sandwiches and a salad on the table.

"What?"

"You're wearing a skirt, but what's underneath?"

She sighed heavily and slid her hands down the silky fabric of her skirt. She gripped the hem and pulled slowly up to reveal her slender, toned thigh. Amy lifted it up even further, watching him the entire time, awaiting his reaction, but he gave nothing away. Finally, she pulled the skirt all the way up and revealed to him that, indeed, she was not wearing any underwear. He ran his tongue over the back of his teeth, as he savoured her neatly trimmed pussy.

"Satisfied?" she asked.

"Not yet. Touch yourself."

"Not here." She looked around nervously.

He switched on the authority in his tone.

"Touch yourself."

Her hand went between her thighs. James watched as she slid a perfectly manicured finger over the folds of her sex.

"What would you like me to do now?"

"I want you to make yourself come."

"Do you have security cameras in your office?"

"Of course I do."

"Monitored?" She moved her hand away from herself.

He reached out and pressed a button on the phone. It rang twice before it was answered.

"Mr North? How can I help?"

"I want all the cameras switched off in my office immediately."

"Sir?"

"Please, Harry."

"At once, Sir." There was a small background noise. "All done, Sir."

'Thank you. Turn them all back on in an hour." He hung up. "Happy?" He smiled at her.

"Has anyone ever said no to you?"

"Doesn't happen often."

"I'll have to remember that."

"Enough talking."

"Bossy."

He slid his hands down to his hardened cock. He undid the zip, pulled himself out, and began stroking himself. Amy put her hand down and circled her clit. She held herself so that he could see everything. She was breathing heavily, and her perfect breasts swelled within her t-shirt. He wanted to touch her, but he wanted to watch her satisfy herself, first. He gripped himself harder, his control wavering. Amy was getting close. He knew the soft whimpering noise she made already. She was breathing harder and harder, and her head fell back against the edge of the chair.

"Don't come yet. "

"Fuck you."

When her eyes flashed open, she met his gaze with intense ferocity. He lost his control, rushed forward, grabbed her hands, and held them above her head. His weight pressed against her, his cock close to the entrance of her sex. All he needed to do was push inside her.

His face was inches from hers, and her eyes glistened with devilment. She was testing him.

"I should deny you for that."

"You won't," she replied confidently.

"Do you really want to test me?"

He took both of her hands in one of his, and the other went to his cock. He thrust hard into his hand and came instantly upon her thigh. He groaned out loud as his soul poured out of him and marked her delicate flesh as his. He could scarcely believe this was happening. She looked beautiful with his cum on her. She was definitely his now, not that she hadn't been from the first moment that he'd seen her. He looked up, and she was watching everything. He let go of her hands and put himself back in his trousers.

"Keep your hands above your head." She did as he demanded. He went to his sink and got a cloth, which he brought back and used to clean her thigh. "Right, I need to show you the office. Up you get."

"James?" Her eyes were full of questioning.

"Punishment, Amy. You wanted to test my limits."

She sat up and pulled her skirt down.

"Really?"

"Really." He smirked.

She huffed, but she stood and took his hand.

The tour of the office seemed to take a long time.

Everyone had heard that the Boss had a girlfriend from Marie, and they all wanted to meet her and talk with her. Amy was polite and took her time to speak to everyone, but she had a healthy glow to her cheeks. She was seething at him for this punishment. If he hadn't just come, he'd be hard again with the excitement of watching her. After about an hour and a half, they finally finished, and he saw her into the lift that would take her back down to the car park. He got in with her, and as the lift started descending, he pulled her to him. She'd waited long enough. Before she could argue, he had his hand under her skirt and was massaging her clit.

"Are you going to be a good girl this time?" He removed his pressure.

"James, please." He could tell she no longer cared they were in a lift, which could stop at any time, and someone else could get in. All she wanted was to orgasm at his touch. It was all he wanted now as well. He gave her what she needed again, harder, circling the little nub in tantalising pleasure.

"Come, Amy. Come, now."

She did, shuddering and pulsating against him, her groans of euphoria causing him to hiss into her neck in need. He was rock hard again and longed to sink balls deep into her, but he'd made a promise. He'd keep it, even if it killed him. He held her tightly, as he felt her legs caving. The lift stopped.

He righted her skirt and almost carried her to the car. He knew she couldn't speak, so quietly, he placed her in the Aston Martin to a questioning look from Matthew.

"I think it was all a bit much. Miss Jones is fatigued."

Matthew nodded.

"I'll see her home safely, Sir."

"Thank you."

He watched the car pull away and brought his hand to his nose. The smell of Amy's orgasm was on it. The guilt suddenly washed over him. What had he done?

TWELVE

Amy

Amy could feel the throb of the orgasm between her thighs for days. She was floating. He had denied her. She'd struggled not to touch herself for almost two hours, and then, he touched her, and she had exploded. It had been in a lift. Damn. What if there had been CCTV? She was sure that James would get rid of any evidence. She wondered if he could get the tape for them to watch together? Amy shook the thought from her head.

Where was Matthew? He was late.

She hadn't told James, but she'd made a decision. They were testing each other's limits. James had been close to pushing inside her, and he'd have come the second he did.

It was too risky.

She'd booked an appointment to get checked and make sure she was clean. After she'd learned about James and his ex-girlfriend and the prostitute, he'd left a file for her detailing that he had regular annual health checks. The last one having been shortly after Lanzarote. She was his girlfriend now, and as such, she needed to take precautions to prevent any unwanted accidents.

Matthew finally buzzed up, and she grabbed her Mulberry handbag and raced down to the car.

"I need to go to Kennington Lane please."

"Of course, Miss." He started to drive and she checked her watch. She had twenty minutes until her appointment. Hopefully, the traffic was going to be light. She looked out the window at the sights of London speeding past. When they rounded Green Park, they headed north.

"This isn't the way."

"It is, Miss."

Her phone rang before she could answer him. The caller ID said it was James.

"Is it urgent? Matthew has taken the wrong direction."

"No, he hasn't. He's taking you to my private physician at Harley Street. I'm sorry. If I'd known earlier what you were planning, we could've discussed it together, and I could've come with you. This is something we're both in together."

"What?" She couldn't believe what he was saying. "How did you know?"

"I told you I know everything about you."

She didn't know whether to be flattered that he cared so much or annoyed that he was telling her what to do, again, and was paying for it. "There's nothing wrong with my doctor. Matthew will be there the entire time. Well not in the examining room but...oh, you know what I mean. I'll be safe."

"I mean no offence to your doctor, but mine is the best money can buy. He'll offer you the best advice and give you the right contraception for our needs."

He had smooth-talked her around. "Ask me before you change my plans next time. That's all I ask."

"You can punish me later." She could hear him chuckling.

"Go do some work, Mr North, I have to go spread my legs for your doctor."

It was her turn to laugh this time.

"Do whatever he suggests. Don't think of the cost. Phone me when you're done."

"I will. Later."

"Goodbye."

She hung up.

"Is everything alright with the change of plans, Miss Jones?" Matthew looked at her through the mirror. He looked guilty.

"Do you tell James wherever I ask you to take me?"

"It's what he pays me to do, Miss."

"He's as bossy with you, then."

"Always." He laughed.

"One thing he can't make you do, though, is call me Miss Jones. I give you permission to call me Amy. Please do so."

"As you wish Miss....Amy." He stopped the car, "We're here." He got out of the car and came to open the door for her, "Just up those steps."

She had never been to Harley Street. There were so many doctors' practices. She chuckled and thought maybe she should enquire about getting her breasts enlarged while she was here. See if that got back to James. He'd have a fit. She went to reception, told them her name, was escorted into a private room, and offered a drink from a vast menu of branded beverages. She decided on water but even then had to choose a particular make, she had expected it to just come from the tap. The doctor appeared almost immediately after her drink had been brought. She was suddenly very nervous. This all felt really serious, but she didn't need to worry, Doctor Baudin was very friendly. The doctor examined her and gave her a clean bill of health. A blood test was taken, and he promised the results would be available later that day and couriered straight to her. They discussed various forms of contraception, many she didn't even know existed. She was given the injection but was told to be careful for seven days as she wouldn't be covered until then.

James was going to India in two days. She wouldn't see him for at least a week. She thanked the doctor and was told the bill had been sorted by Mr North. She didn't argue. She probably couldn't afford the prices in there anyway.

It was the start of April and exceptionally warm. She'd been cooped up in the house for a long time, so she asked Matthew to drop her at the North side of Kensington Gardens on the way back, and she'd walk home from there. He grumbled his reluctance, but she insisted, and he had no choice but to comply. The gardens were full of spring colour. Tulips and daffodils lined the walkways. She looked to the sky, shut her eyes, and inhaled deeply. She was in the middle of a very busy city, but it was so peaceful here. She must get James to walk here with her. Maybe she could ask him to take the day off before he went to India. Spend the whole day, just the two of them together.

She rounded the corner of the Serpentine, by the Princess Diana Memorial, and her peace was shattered when she was suddenly set upon by a man with a camera and a woman holding an iPhone to her mouth.

"Miss Jones, tell me what's it like to be dating one of the most eligible billionaires in the UK? Where did you meet him? Is he as good in bed as the rumours say? Can we get a picture of you posing by the fountain?"

The camera flashed in her eyes and she blinked. "Who are you?"

"Sally Bridgewater, London Daily Magazine. Come on Miss Jones, no need to be so shy. Mr North is quite the catch. You're a very lucky girl."

The camera flashed again, and people stopped to stare. She felt very exposed.

"I don't wish to talk about my relationship. If you'd excuse me." She went to push past the buzzing paparazzi, but Sally Bridgewater was persistent.

"Come on, one quote for our readers. Is he as sexy under those suits as we all imagine?"

She was suddenly hoisted backwards. A lady she'd never seen before stepped in front of her.

"Miss Jones has no comment. If you have any questions, you'll address them to Mr North's press secretary, as is the correct procedure. Miss Jones, this way, please. Matthew is waiting in the car to escort you home."

The lady grabbed her arm and pulled her away from the now-sullen Miss Bridgewater. Amy tugged her arm free.

"Who are you?"

"Sonia, Miss Jones, I'm your personal security."

"My what?" she spat out.

"Miss Jones, the car, please. We need to get you away."

"No." She turned and began to walk off in the other direction from where she was being led. Her phone rang, and she didn't need to look at it to know who was ringing. "When were you going to tell me you were having me followed everywhere?"

"Please go with Sonia." James's commanding voice ordered.

"No."

"Amy!"

"Fuck you."

She hung up. The phone rang again, but she didn't answer. She muted it and put it back in her bag. She hurried out of the park, though she didn't really know where she was going. Sonia was probably following her.

He was supposed to not keep secrets from her, yet he had someone following her around. Why hadn't he introduced her to Sonia? She understood the need for protection. Without thinking, she slammed her fist into a nearby wall. People around her began to stare.

"What are you looking at?" she shouted at the onlookers.

Matthew pulled up in the car beside her. "Amy, please get in."

She folded her arms across her chest and refused to budge.

"Please. If I don't get you back to the house safely, it will be more than my life is worth. I know him. He'll have left the office and be heading home now. He's scared you'll get hurt. That's the only reason he did this."

She rolled her eyes and sighed with defeat. She opened the door and got in the car. Sonia jumped in the front seat next to Matthew. The short journey to the house was made in silence. When they arrived, she didn't wait to have the door opened for her but stormed into her new home without so much as a thank you. She was so angry; she was fuming. Her knuckle hurt and was bleeding, but most of all, she realised that the freedom she'd had in the past was gone. Did she want this?

She felt suffocated, claustrophobic.

She went to the kitchen sink, took a cloth, and washed her knuckles. She heard the front door open, and James called out her name. He was angry.

"In the kitchen," she shouted but kept her back to the door and washed her hand. James thundered into the room and threw his briefcase on the counter.

"What did you think you were doing? You never not answer the phone to me. Look at me." His voice was full of fury but had undercurrents of deep concern. She turned. Tears had started to tumble down her pale cheeks. The cloth she held at her hand was covered in watery blood. "Jesus." He halted in shock. "What happened? Did they do this? I'll sue every last penny out of them." He rushed forward, grabbed her hand and checked it. He brought it to his lips to kiss it, but she pulled her hand away.

"I did it. You lied to me. I asked you not to, and you did it again. In fact, you did it all morning. You cancelled my appointment and rearranged it with your doctor. I know you've a need to control but...." She stopped and turned away again.

He stumbled backwards and took hold of the counter. "You want to leave me?"

She couldn't turn to face him yet. She needed to figure this out without looking at him. "I know you need to control, and I accept that. In many ways, I like it. You look after me and ensure I'm safe when I can't do it myself, but you need to tell me what you're doing." She took a deep breath and turned back to face him. He looked so scared. Neither had spoken of the feelings that were developing between them, but they were starting to run deep on both sides. "If you'd told me about Sonia, I might have complained for a few hours, but I understand the reasons you're doing it. I know that in your business, you make decisions and people follow without questioning, but our relationship isn't a business. We're in it together. No more secrets from me. Please."

"'You aren't leaving me." He took a tentative step towards her.

"If you promise me, here and now, that important matters such as personal protection or things which cost large sums of money, will be discussed between us as adults, then I'll stay."

She expected him to come and cradle her in his arms, but he didn't. He reached for his briefcase. "I should tell you about this then?"

She was instantly worried. What now?

"Our relationship has hit the gossip columns, and I've arranged an interview tomorrow for us both to officially come out as a couple."

"Alright. It isn't with that foul woman from the park?"

"No, someone much nicer."

"Good, anything else?"

"Will you accompany me to India. I want you to be at my side throughout the entire opening. I want everyone to know that you're my girlfriend. Please. I've sorted a visa for you and everything."

"India?"

"Yes. I may want to surprise you and keep that a secret, but you have my word. Big decisions, I'll talk to you about. What do you say, Amy? Will you come with me? Be my partner for all the world to see?"

She smiled. "You better take me shopping for summer clothes."

THIRTEEN

James

James rolled over in the bed, and his arm felt Amy's smooth, naked frame next to him. It wasn't a dream. They hadn't slept together before, but last night, it seemed the right thing to do. They hadn't been intimate in any way. It was not the time for that. They had lain on the bed in each other's arms until they fell asleep. He totally lost it yesterday, when he got the phone call from Matthew saying that she was being hounded by Sally Bridgewater. His lawyers were now working on an injunction against her. When she'd then defied him and refused to answer the phone, he'd almost combusted. But mostly, he was scared. He was afraid that he'd pushed her too far and that she'd walk away from him. He had never felt this way about anyone before. She was driving him crazy. He wrapped his arms around her, she stirred, her bright blue eyes opened and greeted him.

"Morning, beautiful." He kissed her lips.

"Morning, handsome. You sleep well?"

"Best sleep I've ever had."

She nuzzled closer into him.

"What time are the magazine people coming?"

"Around ten. They'll bring someone to do your hair and makeup. They'll have someone find the perfect clothes for you as well. I have a phone call with India at nine, but I'm not going to the office today."

"That's good, as long as they dress me in clothes I like." She looked at the clock. "So we have half an hour more in bed."

"Well, I was going to make you a cup of tea and breakfast in bed."

"Oh. That gives me a big dilemma. I'd like breakfast in bed, but I also want to lie in your arms a bit longer."

"Decisions, decisions." He ran a hand down her flat stomach.

"Breakfast, please."

He groaned. "Really?"

"Go."

He slid from the bed and pulled on a pair of jogging bottoms. He felt Amy's heated gaze scan over his body as he did.

"My wish is your command, Miss Jones. But just so you know, in future, I've an intercom into the kitchen and could've asked Mum to bring it and leave it outside the door instead." Before she could say anything, he pulled his T-shirt over his head and left her moaning.

His mother was in the kitchen preparing breakfast as normal. He kissed her cheek.

"How is Amy this morning?"

"Nervous."

"You sure about this? You aren't pushing her too quickly are you? You've only been together for just over a month."

"If I could hide her away and protect her from all of this, I would, Mum. I'm terrified of losing her."

"You need to tell her everything."

"I know. I'm going to book a week off after the opening in India. Maybe go to the Seychelles or Maldives. I'll tell her everything then." He shrugged. "But for now, I need to get her breakfast."

His mum handed him a tray full of pastries and coffee.

"One step ahead of you."

"Thanks, Mum."

"I'll make myself scarce today."

"You don't have to."

"Oh I do. I've a date."

His mouth dropped in shock.

"You've a what?"

"Take Amy her food, or she'll get hungry."

"Mum…"

"Go. I'll be careful."

He shuddered. "Mum, I don't need to know that."

"I meant I'll follow all your security advice."

"Phew." He picked up the tray and wandered back into the bedroom. Amy had got out of bed and had wrapped a dressing gown around her naked body. He felt deflated, he'd hoped to have some fun with her. A quick glance at the clock showed him there wouldn't be time anyway. If he were late for his call, there would be trouble.

"Here, beautiful. Breakfast." She turned, took the tray from him, and gave him a peck on the cheek.

"I'll take it back to your mum and eat there. You get ready for your call." She kissed him again and smiled, "We can breakfast in bed tomorrow." And with a cheeky wink, she meandered off back down the hallway. He ran a hand through his hair and sighed. God, he hoped she was ready to have sex soon. His balls were tight and turning blue, and he felt like he was permanently stiff when she was around. It was time for a shower. A freezing cold one. Again!

He could barely concentrate on his phone call. They'd important final details to confirm, but all he could think about was Amy and this damn interview. Why couldn't they leave her alone? So what if he had a girlfriend? He wasn't a famous rock star, actor, or royalty. Why couldn't they go and pester one of them instead? He'd never realised that being a, supposedly, good looking billionaire meant you had no private life. He guessed it was his own fault because he was regularly seen out with different girls, at different celebrity functions. He'd a reputation as a playboy. What the press saw couldn't have been further from the truth. He'd have been quite happy to have not attended them, but he didn't have a choice. It was what was required to keep the business in the spotlight.

When they finished, he went to find Amy. The stylists and the reporter were already there, and she was in the centre of a hive of activity. She'd someone curling her hair in soft waves which accentuated the perfect features of her face. They were using a scary looking piece of equipment, though, and he hoped it wouldn't leave any permanent damage. She smiled at him and held her hand out. He took it and pressed a kiss to the soft skin. A camera flashed, and he turned and glared.

"Mr North." The reporter stood and held his hand out to him. he shook it. The journalist was a little too enthusiastic and made him feel a little uneasy, especially when he looked down at James's crotch with a lick of his lips. "It's so good to meet you, finally. I'm sorry. Ellie couldn't make it, so she sent me instead. I'm Sean. Your girlfriend is so lovely. A perfect little doll." He turned to her and winked. "We're making her look very natural." The reporter turned back and looked him up and down again. "I think you need to complement her. I'd say a nice pair of tight jeans and a plain T-shirt. That will be perfect."

"I wear what I want to," he replied in an outraged voice.

"Oh no, James. You have to wear what you're told. Besides, I like the idea of tight jeans," Amy responded. He raised a questioning eyebrow at her. Sean enthusiastically bounced next to him.

"Let's go and check out your wardrobe, Mr North. I'm sure you've something suitable." Before he had a chance to protest, he was swept up by the reporter and led to his room. He could hear Amy laugh as he went. She'd suffer for that later. Only he knew she wouldn't. He didn't do that anymore. He couldn't.

The interview started off well, general questions on how they met, how long they'd been dating, that sort of thing. Amy held her own with the questions. She even admitted to being a dancer when questioned on what her job was. He was proud of her. However, when the sexual questions started, he was on the verge of kicking the reporter out of his house

"So Miss Jones, we've all seen pictures of Mr North after he's been exercising and has his shirt off. He's very toned. I know a lot of our female readers would like to lick his abs and see where else he's particularly toned." Sean paused and looked him over again. Why did they have to send him the gay interviewer who had spent most of the interview trying to come onto him? Did they think that would make him want to do more work with their magazine? Amy squeezed his hand in reassurance. "Are you able to give our readers an insight into what lies beneath all those fabulous designer suits and how talented he is with it?"

He went to hold his hand up to stop the interview, but Amy took hold of it and smiled.

"Well, I'm not sure if that's something we can talk about in public, because it's a very private thing between us. But I know you have loyal readers, so all I'll say is…"

He held his breath. What was she going to say? And how much would he have to pay his lawyers to get it taken out of the interview?

"He is even better in the flesh than the pictures, and as for his talent? I can completely assure all your readers, here and now, I'm not with him for his money." She giggled and licked her lips. It sent shivers down his spine. He wanted to pin her to the sofa and fuck her while still doing the interview.

"Hmm. I can see. You're a very lucky lady indeed." Sean licked his lips.

James jumped to his feet. He realised that gave a better view to Sean of his now even more snugly fitting jeans, and quickly jumped behind a chair.

"The interview is done. I've work I must do. I trust you got everything you need?"

"I certainly did." Sean got to his feet. He held out his hand, "It's been a pleasure, Mr North. A great pleasure indeed."

He reluctantly shook his hand again and quickly headed for the door.

"Amy, can you see them out, please? I need to make a phone call."

She nodded, and he returned to his office as quickly as possible. He pulled up his laptop and checked his emails. Nothing of any importance. He'd still answer a few, though, just so he could stay in his office.

As he finished, Amy entered the room.

"It's safe to come out now."

"Don't." He looked up at her and glared.

"Oh come on, it wasn't that bad. I was terrified, but he put me at ease."

"Well, he didn't do that to me."

She came over to him and put her arms around his shoulders.

"My poor baby. Did the nasty man mentally undress you?"

"Amy."

She laughed again.

He should think of a reason to leave the house until he could calm down.

"I'm sorry." She leaned forward and kissed his cheek. The heat of her lips pulsated through his body straight to his cock. Fuck, he really had to get out of there.

"I have to go to the office. Some forms need signing before I go to India." He stood up and went to the window to put distance between them both. He was shaking, his fists clenched to try to maintain control.

"Can't you have Matthew bring them over here? I thought we could have some lunch together and then maybe go for a walk."

"Matthew isn't here to courier papers around for me. He's here for protection. If I were to have a walk with you, he'd need to be with us," he snapped at her.

"I'm sorry." He could hear the pain in her voice. This was killing him. "I'll go change. I'll see you tonight."

"Amy." She paused, her head was down. "I'm sorry. That guy threw me off. I wanted to enjoy the interview. I wanted it to be the first of many we do together. You did well. I'm proud of you."

She turned back to face him.

"Now you know how I feel when you look at me that way."

He came up to her and dared to put his arms around her waist, but he waited to be thumped and pushed away.

"You don't like the way I look at you?"

"I didn't say that."

"I'm sorry I shouted at you."

"I know. I'm sorry I teased you."

He was relaxing again. He was bringing himself back under control. Just her closeness tamed the wild beast within him. He kissed her tenderly on the lips.

"Do you really have to go to the office?"

He shook his head. "No."

"We can have lunch together?"

"Yes."

"Can we have lunch in bed?"

"Of course."

She took his hand and led him from the study. Instead of heading to the kitchen, she went straight to the bedroom.

"We need to get the food first."

She looked at him from under her long fluttering lashes,

"I was thinking of a different type of lunch."

He stopped dead. Did she mean what he thought she meant?

"James, I want you. In every way a boyfriend and girlfriend should be together."

"Are you sure?"

"I trust you. In fact, I think I may be falling in love with you."

He couldn't speak. He'd known from the moment he first saw her in Lanzarote that he was in love with her. Could he do this? Should he do this?

She didn't know the truth of his past.

No, that was just what it was. It was his past.

Amy was his future, and she was standing here in front of him offering everything that he wanted. He growled,

"Get in the bedroom, because I'm not going to let you change your mind. I'm going to make love to you until you can no longer walk."

FOURTEEN

Amy & James

Amy took James's hand and held it tightly. He pulled her towards him, and a passionate kiss engulfed them both. She parted her lips slightly, and he delved his tongue inside her mouth to taste her sweetness. She could feel the urgency of the heat building inside her already. She'd never wanted a man as much as she wanted James right now. She needed him, tasting her body. She needed him inside her. She ached for it.

They were still in the hallway, though. She had enjoyed their first time up against a wall together, but she wanted more time to explore. She pulled her mouth away, breathless.

"I want to take this slowly. I want to learn your body. Can we go to the bedroom, please?"

He sighed, scooped her into his strong arms, kicked his bedroom door open, placed her tenderly on the bed, and went back to shut the door.

"My hero." She laughed and pulled her top over her head to reveal her breasts in a lacy cream bra. She pushed them together a little and smirked.

James quickly flipped her over and brought her back against his taut body. She could feel the strain of his cock within his trousers.

She turned in his arms. He was standing at the end of the bed, and she was on her knees in front of him. The air was thick with the sexual anticipation between them, she slowly started to unbutton his shirt. Neither said anything, they just watched as her delicate fingers lingered over each of the buttons in a tantalising reveal of his broad chest. She gasped as she lowered his shirt over his shoulders. He had the most beautiful body she'd ever seen. It was hers to learn to pleasure in ways he liked. And learn everything she would. She reached her hand out to trail a path over one of his pecs and up his shoulder to where the feathers of his tattoo started. It was intricately designed. She placed her finger at the start, he hissed and abruptly grabbed her hand.

"No."

She looked at him hesitantly. Why would he not want her to touch it? She leaned forward and kissed his lips again.

"It's an amazing design. Let me look at it, please?"

He again shook his head, his eyes still carnally focused, but she saw the sadness buried deep within them. What did this tattoo mean? He was not telling her something again. Why did he have to do this? She wanted to know everything about him. She'd accept this little secret for now because he was mellowing around her.

James reached around her body to unfasten her bra. He slowly and softly circled a finger around her left breast to where its peak stood proudly erect. He leaned forward, taking it between his teeth and holding it while his tongue moistened the bud. She let her head fall back and groaned. This man did wonders with his tongue. She could think of so many more things she wanted him to explore with it. Tentatively, she reached for the waistband of his trousers. She needed to see him fully naked. His cock was beautiful. She knew what it felt like to have it within her, and she wanted that again. However, James had other ideas, and he pushed her back against the bed. He trailed a path down her body, taking in every element of her taste and storing it for exploration further at a later date. He reached the waist band of her jeans and undid the zip. She was wet, and her very core was throbbing. This teasing between them was killing her. She wanted him to touch her where she needed him the most. He looked up, grinned, and then helped her to shimmy off the jeans over her slender legs.

"Please."

"Patience. I'm going to make this special for you, for both of us."

She thrust her hips into the path of his hands. He slapped at her thigh.

"I'm seriously going to have to punish you one day."

She giggled but stopped as soon as she saw a flash of pain flicker behind his eyes again. She reached up and brought his lips down to hers. They kissed again, their eyes open, captured by the overwhelming emotions bonding them together. He broke the moment by tearing her pants from her body. He was beginning to make a habit of that. At least she now had what seemed like an endless supply of them after she'd returned home one day to find her wardrobe looked like a lingerie shop.

She was naked before him. With her ex-boyfriend, she had always felt a little self-conscious in this position, but with James, she knew how much he adored her body and craved every part of her. She lowered her eyes to see the straining need, which he still insisted on being kept encased within his trousers.

He left a path of kisses over her body as he lowered himself between her thighs, kissing either side of where she needed to be touched. She thrust her hips forward again, and he lightly bit the skin of her left thigh, sending shivers through her body. Her core ignited, and she felt she may come just from that one touch. God this man played her like no other. He knew how to control her so that her body responded to everything that he did.

In the back of his throat, he gave a gravelly groan. It reverberated around her as he finally parted her wet folds and traversed his tongue between them.

"You taste perfect " he said, looking into her eyes, "I've never experienced anything like it before. You're what I've always dreamed off."

He bent again and dipped his tongue within her sweet haven. She cried out when he rubbed a finger over her straining clit. She was ready to explode. She needed to come but stopped herself. She wanted James's consent. He delved his tongue deeper and kept up the pressure on her engorged bud, she writhed on the bed like a sexual goddess.

"Please. I need to come. Oh. Please."

He removed his tongue, mid thrust, and she moaned at the loss.

"Come. Come."

His tongue thrust straight back into her, with a finger, and she exploded. He held her tightly until she stopped shuddering and then stood up beside her and freed himself from his jeans.

"I could watch you come all day. It's the most amazing sight. You ready for some more?"

"More?" She was breathless and could barely feel her legs as it was. "More."

He chuckled, "Oh yes. Much more."

James reached in a drawer and pulled out a condom packet. She watched him tear it with his teeth and then roll the barrier over his throbbing length. His magnificent cock was going to rip her apart. He seemed bigger than in Lanzarote. If that were possible. He was thick and long.

Their mouths met again when James slid up her body, skin on skin, her legs parted wide, and he positioned himself at her entrance. She looked down; he was about to slide into her. She tensed a little as his cock breached her and slowly slid in, inch by inch. He paused when he was about halfway, allowing her to adjust to the feel of him. She was stretched wide, but the twinge of pain brought her pleasure.

"Are you alright?"

She lifted her gaze from where she and James were joined and met the concerned hues of her lover's eyes. She exhaled a long breath that she didn't even realise had been held.

"I can feel you gripping tight onto me. Is it hurting?"

She gave him a reassuring smile and kissed him.

"I'm fine. I'm watching us." Her eyes glanced down again to where his cock was half in her. James's eyes followed hers.

"Fuck." He hissed and pressed another inch in.

"You're so big, but my body already doesn't want you to leave."

He gently thrust the last few inches in and filled her. Stopping for a moment again, he kissed her forehead and then ran kisses down her jawline to her neck. She shut her eyes and relaxed her head back against the pillow. She felt complete. He, fully inside her, was everything she had ever dreamed of.

He bit down hard on her nipple, and she screamed out as white-heat pulsated through her body to the core. She was going to come again. James withdrew from her until only his tip remained inside. She groaned ruefully at the emptiness, the ecstasy she was feeling subdued but remained beneath her skin ready to enflame again.

"I want you back in me." He rocked his hips, teasing her.

"James." She shut her eyes and rotated her hips nearer. She needed friction down there.

"There's a word?" His tone had changed, he was masterfully rasping at her and in control. His words alone were sending quivers shuddering through her body.

"Please. Please?"

She opened her eyes and met the dark carnal circles of his. He was like a man possessed. He was captivated by her. He slammed back into her, she gasped with pain and absolute delight. He flicked his hips around and withdrew from her again. His pace quickened as he filled her then left her empty. She caressed his hair, tugging on the ends every time he hit the sensitive spot inside her. Sweat was glistening on both of their bodies. She ran her hands down the back of James's head and neck and then began to claw her nails into his back in her need to get him even closer. He stopped thrusting, adjusted his position so that his weight was supported on one rippling triceps, grabbed her hands, and held them tightly above her head. James never liked her touching him intimately when naked. She needed to know why, but before she could think anymore, he began to thrust again, and the pressure within her body built to a final crescendo.

" I'm coming again."

"Come!" he demanded.

She did. She flew high into the sky as the most intense orgasm she'd ever felt pulsated over every inch of her body. Before she could come down again, the feeling hit her again.

James groaned out, and she knew the tight walls of her pussy were milking his climax from him. They seemed to exist in this state forever, both high and shuddering together. Eventually, he collapsed on her, reached between them to hold the base of his cock, and withdrew from her body. She felt empty.

That's when the panic hit her.

The last time this happened, he had walked out on her. She desperately searched his eyes for signs that he was about to do the same again. She saw none, though, he either wore a very clever mask or he was as thoroughly sated and happy as she was. He rolled from her and pulled her into his arms. He was shaking. She entangled her arms within his.

"James?" She was worried.

"Did I hurt you?"

She shook her head vehemently.

"No. It was unbelievable. I've never, ever, felt that way before. How did you manage to know my body that well? I can't even get a multi-orgasm from a vibrator."

He didn't answer her straight away. "You never found the vibrator that was a perfect fit."

She slapped at his chest. He stopped shaking and kissed her.

"I know. I'm never going to get rid of this one." The words came out of her mouth before she even realised what she was saying, "I mean...if..." She blushed, as he interrupted to spare her embarrassment.

"Well, this one never wants to get rid of its new owner either."

It wasn't a conventional declaration of love.

The front door slammed, and Miranda called out that she was home. The spell between them was broken.

"Mothers have the worst timing."

She laughed as he slid from the bed, and she got a last look at his perfect body while he retrieved his jeans from the floor and disappeared into the bathroom. She didn't want to leave the wanton carnality of the sweat-soaked bed. She was happy, for the first time since the death of her parents. She felt settled, like she was finally getting her life back.

James was her future.

～

James pulled the condom from his deflating cock, checked it, wrapped it in tissue and tossed it in the bin. He went to the sink and splashed water on his face. He was shaking again. Fuck. What was she doing to him?

He hadn't hurt her. He hadn't hurt her. She'd told him that, and she seemed so happy. That's what he needed to remember. He loved her so much it was killing him, because he'd destroy it. He was vermin. That's why they did to him what they did. He splashed more water on himself. If he could just keep his control, everything would be alright.

FIFTEEN

James

James held Amy's hand tightly as he assisted her to manoeuvre gracefully out of the car in the short skirt she'd chosen to wear. He tried not to look at the lissom length of her legs. The press would be waiting, and he didn't need to be photographed with a telling bulge in his jeans. A camera picked up everything, and the press jumped on it. Matthew and Sonia appeared at their side. Sonia took Amy's bag, and they strode purposefully towards the airport with the flashes of cameras going off around them. Why people were interested in his love life, he would never understand. He was nothing remarkable, ultimately, he was a builder. If you have money, your life becomes public interest, although he'd been told on numerous occasions that his good looks helped.

They breezed through first class check-in and were escorted through the security check with ease, even when Amy set off all the alarms and panicked. He stood back and laughed while she was searched by the butch security lady. She frowned at him and cuddled a little tighter into him when, instead of going to the first class lounge, they went straight to the plane to board. He had developed the fine art of minimising the waiting times at the airport to the least possible inconvenient length. As much as the lounges were comfortable and well stocked, he wanted to get on the plane and get travelling. The stewardess greeted them, and they were fast-tracked straight onto the plane and into their luxury seats.

To ensure their privacy, his company had booked every seat in first class. Matthew and Sonia travelled in business class. Usually, he'd go with Matthew and not bother with such extravagance, but he wanted Amy to himself. He didn't want to make polite conversation with anyone else. He wanted to hold her in his arms while they watched a movie, slept and ate. A stewardess appeared, introduced herself to them and handed them both a glass of champagne and a luxurious gift bag filled with toiletries, an eye mask, socks, and a toothbrush and toothpaste. He looked over to Amy, her eyes were wide with excitement. She'd told him before they'd left for the airport that she'd only flown a few times and never in business class, let alone first class; it had always been on cheap package flights. She was enjoying the experience. He sat back, closed his eyes, and let her converse with the stewardess. It was almost a ten-hour flight to Bangalore, and he had a busy day ahead after they landed.

They'd been working on developing the hotel for years now. It was a different direction for his firm, a new output. The expansion of business in India meant Bangalore was becoming a vibrant and wealthy city. Many Europeans and Americans were travelling there for business meetings, and he, himself, had done so on numerous occasions for business with his office development branch. He'd found the hotels lacking. They had top brands emerging, but they were all generic. None of them captured the magic of the country blended with the modern facilities that a business traveller was expecting. There were one or two authentic, high-class hotels, but their location was not optimal. He'd managed to secure a prime piece of land and paid attention to the right people to get his planning permission approved easily. As with virtually all government departments, he knew a little cash donation sweetened the path to getting what he wanted. They worked together with a traditional Indian architect, and the hotel was designed as a palace. It was colourful, like the country itself, but not overly so, and the furnishings were luxurious and classy. It had two swimming pools, spa facilities, tennis courts, a fully equipped gymnasium, several different types of restaurants, and a whole first-floor wing devoted to branded shops and smaller jewellery shops. The suites all had twenty-four-hour butler service. All staff members had received top class training and would be rewarded for keeping very high standards.

He was looking forward to this trip. The hotel was going to open, and months of hard work would come to fruition. But mostly because Amy was going to be at his side all the time to enjoy it with him. He couldn't be prouder to show her what he had achieved.

The plane sped down the runway and into the air, Amy gripped his hand tightly. She told him earlier that she was nervous of flying. Once in the air, she was okay, but the going up and down terrified her. He held her close to his chest and hummed softly to calm her. They must have both fallen asleep for a few moments, because the air stewardess suddenly appeared at their side with menus, and he noticed the seatbelt signs were off. Amy studied the menu intently, while he, pretty much knowing what was going to be on it, scanned quickly and gave his order. He requested more champagne and flicked through the movie listings. He'd seen most of them, so when Amy finally made her order, he pushed the screen away and brought her back into his arms.

"You feeling better?"

"Much. I don't think I've ever fallen asleep on a plane. I was listening to your heartbeat, and it soothed me."

"Glad I could be of assistance. Anything else I can do to make your flight more comfortable, Miss Jones?"

Amy looked around the cabin. "You can pass me that blanket. My legs are getting cold."

"Well, if you didn't wear a ridiculously short skirt..."

"You don't like it?"

"I didn't say that."

The stewardess brought them their dinner, and they chatted a little bit more about the hotel and what they'd be doing in India. He could see that Amy was a little bit worried about the full schedule, but when he told her that, after the opening, he'd booked for them to go to the Maldives for a week, she was stunned into silence.

"You didn't have to do that."

"I wanted another holiday."

"The holiday to Lanzarote was the first one you'd taken in years. And now another one in a few short months. People will think you've gone crazy and are having an early mid-life crisis."

"Maybe I am." He raised a playful eyebrow at her and slid his hand further up her leg. When they were in the Maldives, she was going to spend the entire time naked if he had his way. She leaned into him and whispered into his ear.

"So, the bathroom in this cabin, is it ours alone?"

"Yes. Why?"

"I think I need to visit it. Do you want to join me?" She winked. Was she suggesting what he thought she was suggesting? His jeans suddenly felt decidedly snug. No. He needed to keep their sexual liaisons to a bed. Since the other night, they'd been together several times but always in bed. He was better able to control himself that way. He wouldn't hurt her that way.

"I'm not sure that's a good idea."

Her face fell, "You don't want to? Would we get into trouble? I thought that's why we have first class to ourselves."

Damn. He shot himself in the foot there. One time wouldn't hurt. He held his hand out to her and stood to follow. The stewardess poked her head around the curtain, saw Amy kiss him, and quickly shut it again. They'd be the talk of the crew by the time they emerged from the toilet, but he didn't care. Amy was all that he ever wanted, and any opportunity he got to be inside her, he was going to take it.

He closed the door after them and locked it. She was already removing her tiny pants.

"I only have one spare in my hand luggage, so I don't want you ripping these ones." She laughed and put them by the sink. He pulled her close, and they kissed, mouths tangling in an unspoken urgent need. They'd had sex before coming to the airport, but they both still wanted more. He ran a hand down her body and under her skirt to prepare her for him to enter her but was surprised when he found her pussy dripping already.

"How long have you been like that?"

"Since we left the apartment."

She blushed.

"But we'd only just..."

"I know. But I've never seen you in such tight jeans before." She ran her hands around to his backside and gave it a little squeeze. "I like the way your arse looks in them."

"You're a bad, bad girl."

"Punish me then?"

He pulled back and opened his jeans, pushing them half way down his legs. His magnificently erect cock proudly leapt towards Amy's erotic scent.

"Shit. I don't have a condom. They're in my wallet." He went to pull his jeans back up, hoping that he'd be able to get his dick back in them.

"No worries." He looked at her, confused, and she pulled a condom from her skirt pocket. "I'm always prepared."

"How many more days do we have to be careful?"

"Five."

"Stock up."

She laughed, and he took the condom from her and put it on.

She braced herself against the sink, with one foot on the toilet, and displayed herself to him. The bathroom was a tight squeeze, but he got himself close and thrust, without warning, into her. She gasped and clamped down on his cock. Fuck she was so tight. He felt every undulation of her muscles, and when they massaged him, he struggled to keep his control. This wasn't going to be a sensual lovemaking. It was going to be raw and animalistic. He pulled out and rapidly thrust back in again, repeating this until he found his rhythm. She placed her hand on his neck, she looked at him to check that this was alright. He was conscious that whenever they made love he refused to have her touch him when he was naked. He still had his shirt on, and she wouldn't be able to get at his flesh. He gave her a small nod, and she let her head fall back. Her eyes fluttered shut, and she became lost in what he was doing to her.

All around him came the noises of the stewardesses in business class looking after their guests. He wondered if they could hear him every time he slammed into Amy and knocked her further back against the sink. He wondered if they could hear every cry of lust she made when he swirled his hips before he pulled back out again. His legs began to quiver. This was too good. He was struggling to maintain his control. The fact that he was pleasuring the woman he loved in a place where anybody could hear them and realise what they were doing was sending him over the edge. His balls drew up tightly. He was ready to unload within Amy, but he needed to hear her come first.

"Touch yourself. Make yourself come for me."

Her head snapped up, her eyes opened, and her hand instantly went between her legs and sought out her sensitive clit.

Fuck, when they were in a place with more room, he needed to get her to do all kind of things to herself. She obeyed him so freely. He needed to be able to watch her pleasure herself, see her slip her fingers into her wet pussy, coat them with her juices, then he'd make her suck them afterwards. Knowing what she tasted like, he shut his eyes tightly. It was already starting—he was imagining things.

Amy screamed out when she came. He clapped a hand over her mouth to silence her as he released in the condom deep inside her. Their movements stilled, and he withdrew and brought her into his arms. They were both breathless. He'd need a shower as soon as they got to the hotel. Maybe Amy would join him. He quickly shook that thought from his head. He didn't need to get excited again. In bed. You can only do it with her in a bed. You can't risk losing her now.

"We better get back to our seats. I'm sure the crew is talking already."

"You think so? Will they be angry?"

"Matthew will have given them a tip to keep quiet."

"Seriously? Have you done it for all the girls you have flown with? Or did you plan this before we boarded?"

"Neither." He pulled up his jeans and disposed of the evidence. He pulled the freshly laid out wash cloth and wet it before running it over Amy's pussy to clean it. She didn't push him away, but he got the feeling she was angry at him now. "You aren't the only one that got inducted into the mile-high club. I promise you, Matthew just does these things. It's why I pay him so well. I didn't plan this. If you remember rightly, you were the one who suggested it. And to clarify, I've never had sex with someone on a plane, until now."

She pulled her skirt back down and smoothed it before putting her knickers back on.

"Sorry." She put her arms around him, "I got jealous."

"I like it, shows how much what we did means to you."

A knock came to the door.

"Yes," he answered sternly.

"Um, Sir. Sorry. The Captain says we're about to hit a patch of turbulence and that he'll need to switch on the seatbelt sign. You'll need to return to your seats at once."

Amy tried to suppress a giggle at the unease in the stewardess's voice.

"She probably thinks you'll take the tip back because she interrupted us."

He laughed and opened the door to the flushed face of the stewardess.

"It's alright. We will return. I think my girlfriend is feeling much better now. She's a terribly nervous flyer."

The seat belt sign flashed on. He helped Amy back to her seat, did her belt up, and then lowered her chair to a fully reclined bed. He got into the seat next to her and did the same with his. They both lay on their sides staring at each other in silence as the first bumps came. The lights in the cabin switched off. The next thing he knew, they were being woken for breakfast, and it was forty-five minutes until landing.

SIXTEEN

Amy

They were met at the airport by an Indian man, who was introduced to Amy as Naresh, their driver for the duration of the stay. She queried why Matthew wasn't driving as normal and was told that driving in India was completely different to the UK and that it was better left to those who knew the rules of the road. She quickly learnt what this meant on the hour-long trip from the airport to the hotel. Despite the fact that it was six in the morning and the roads were what she deemed to be country roads marked with potholes, it was busy. People walked wherever they wanted, and bikes laden with whole families, at times, zoomed around the car. Green and yellow tuk-tuks (Indian rickshaws), full to busting with people and goods, turned with a moment's notice, and they even had to stop for five minutes while a cow crossed the road and was worshipped by locals. She stared wide eyed out of the window all the time. She was taking in everything that this strange city had to offer. James held her hand and laid back and closed his eyes again. He'd seen it all before and nothing felt alien to him. The driver was giving her a bit of a running commentary on points of interest, as they entered the district of Whitefield. The city landscape changed into what she'd expected: high-rise office buildings, and malls devoted to tempting the Western visitors into spending their abundance of money. All the companies' buildings had their names on them, and she recognised quite a few. They pulled into the driveway of a hotel, which she saw was called The Malu Palace, and the car stopped. Security guards appeared and placed a mirror under the front and rear of the car. They then opened all the doors so that a security dog could sniff within the car. She looked at James in concern.

"It's standard procedure everywhere. You'll get used it. It makes you feel safer in the end."

The security guard didn't speak to her but smiled and shut the door.

It was seven in the morning Indian time, one-thirty am Greenwich Mean Time, when they pulled up outside the hotel and the doors were opened by traditionally dressed porters. All she wanted was to have a shower and sleep for another couple of hours, but she needed to support James. Sonia took her bag and pointed to a scanner. She nodded. Security was tight in this country. But James was right, it did make her feel safe. Or maybe it was the fact that he had barely let go of her hand since they had left London. She could feel people looking at her, and she didn't know whether it was because she was James's girlfriend; or the fact that she'd a next-to-nothing skirt on, when everyone else was covered; or the fact that she was blonde and most people here were dark.

They entered the lobby of the hotel, and the manager greeted James. He let go of her hand to reciprocate. Two young girls came over and bowed before her and wished her *Namaste*, something she'd been told meant hello. She responded in kind, and they placed a flower garland over her head and then blessed her with a red-painted bindi (dot) to her forehead. James was having the same done to him, as were Matthew and Sonia, the former not looking that impressed with the garland. Another girl brought them a cloth to wipe their hands on, and a fourth presented them with a drink in a coconut shell.

"What is it?" she whispered to Sonia.

"Coconut water."

"Is it nice?"

"I like it, some don't."

She took a little sip. It tasted quite sour, but she liked it. It was refreshing, and despite being only seven it was hot outside already.

"Thank you," she said to the girls, and they scurried away. James called her to his side,

"Raji, this is my girlfriend, Amy Jones. She'll be accompanying me to all the opening ceremony events. We will need to get her a Sari made for the grand opening on Friday."

Raji shook his head like he was saying no then held his hand out to her, and she shook it,

"Nice to meet you, Miss Jones. I'm Raji, the hotel manager. Anything you need, please don't hesitate to ask. Mr North, I'll have my wife personally escort Miss Jones to the city, today, to source a Sari. I know just the shop."

She looked at him confused. "But didn't you shake your head to say no?"

James laughed out loud. She turned and glared at him.

"In India, when a person shakes their head like that, it means yes."

"Really."

James shook his head in demonstration, and Raji laughed this time.

"Except we don't look as silly as Mr North doing so."

"He looks like a nodding dog," she exclaimed with a giggle.

James frowned at her.

"No more encouraging Amy to tease me, Raji. She's perfectly capable on her own." He chuckled.

"I think I like your girlfriend, Mr North. Come, let me show you to your suite. I've put Mr Kumar and his entourage in the presidential suite. I hope that's alright. You've the second best rooms in the hotel."

"Makes sense to me." James motioned for him to lead the way.

She caught up with James and held his hand again.

"Who is Mr Kumar?"

"He is one of the most famous Bollywood stars. He's officially opening the hotel for us."

"That's nice."

"He is being paid well to do it."

"Oh."

"It's all good publicity."

"Maybe he can get someone to teach me Bollywood dancing. It's always looked fun."

James didn't answer that statement because Raji began talking to him again.

The lobby of the hotel was vast, it had ornate carvings all over it and displays of exotic flowers on plinths. Staff bustled around cleaning everything. Amy didn't know why because the place looked spotless to her. The lift was decked in beautiful pale marble, which matched the floors of the hotel. Raji opened the door to their suite, and James ushered her in. She stood there amazed. The walls were adorned with exquisite carvings and artwork, and the fabrics were the finest hand printed silks. This was the entrance hall to their suite, and doors led off into a huge lounge area with a separate working space to the right. To the far end were two further rooms which she guessed must be for Matthew and Sonia. Their ensuite was the size of her flat back in Kennington. She was scared to even open the door to the bedroom she'd share with James, but she eventually found the courage. It took her breath away. The marble flooring ending halfway to the bed and was replaced with hand-made carpets. The bed itself was the size of two double beds pushed together, but it was only one, because it was four posted and bedecked in the most fabulous silk fabrics. The tables, wardrobes and television units were hand carved from wood. She had tears in her eyes, because she was somewhere so beautiful and all due to a vision that James had and saw through to fruition.

He appeared behind her and wrapped his hands around her waist.

"Do you like it? Do you think it's too much?"

"It's so beautiful. I feel like I'm in paradise."

"All of the furnishings and fabrics have been sourced from within India, and the contracts have gone to families where it will make a complete difference to their lives."

Tears started to tumble down her cheeks.

"I love you."

He turned her around in his arms.

"What?"

"I love you."

"I love you as well."

All she wanted to do was take him into that big bed and spend the rest of the day with him there, but he had business meetings, and she didn't want to be a distraction to him. She wiped her tears of happiness away.

"You go shower, and I'll unpack. You need to get all your work done so we can have a dinner in the roof top restaurant tonight."

"I'll look forward to that all day, Miss Jones."

"Go."

James disappeared into the bathroom, and she began to unpack the suitcases, which had appeared in the room as if by magic. She took his toiletry bag to him as he stepped into the shower. She wanted to join him, but she had to be sensible and not distract him. He was here for work and not romance. There would be time for that when they went to the Maldives. Oh, my god, she was going to the Maldives. She tried not to let out a little whoop of joy.

She left the bathroom with a final quick look at James's sculpted body and went back to the bedroom. She still felt so tired, despite the fact they'd slept for a few hours. She took her clothes off and tossed them into the linen bin provided. Part of the duties of the butler was to ensure that all their clothes were washed, ironed, and returned. This was truly unlike any hotel she'd ever stayed in before. She slipped a tiny nightdress over her head and got between the sheets. She should shower, but she wanted to rest her eyes until James finished in the bathroom.

The next thing she knew the phone next to the bed was ringing.

"Hello?" She picked it up and sleepily spoke.

"Miss Jones? *Namaste*, I'm Ratu, Raji's wife. He's asked me to escort you to choose a Sari. Is now convenient?"

She sat bolt upright in the bed.

"What time is it?"

"It's midday, Miss."

"Midday. Oh. I'm sorry. I've been sleeping." She looked over to the pillow and saw James had placed a little note on his pillow and a lotus flower. "Could you give me half an hour?"

"Of course Miss, I'll meet you in reception."

"Thank you so much."

She picked up the note and read the declaration of love from James and his promises for the evening. She placed it in her bag. Next, she got out of the bed, stripped the nightdress from her body, and jumped into the shower. In half an hour, on the dot, she was in reception. She'd dressed in a long maxi dress and had a shawl draped around her shoulders. She'd been told that, in the city, it was best not to draw attention to your flesh. Ratu greeted her with a firm handshake and a nod of the head. Ratu was dressed in Indian attire; she was wearing an outfit that, Amy learned, was called a *salwar kameez*. Gold bracelets were all the way up her wrists, she had numerous piercings in her ears, and a jewelled bindi in the middle of her forehead. Amy was informed that they were going to the city to a place called Commercial Street. It was one of the main shopping streets in Bangalore and was something that she needed to experience. Sonia appeared at her side, as they got into the car, and presented her with a bottle of water.

"You'll need this, Miss Jones. It will be hot out there."

Sonia was right, as they got out of the air-conditioned car, the heat hit Amy. It was early afternoon in the middle of the country's summer. The temperature must have been hitting thirty-five degrees Celsius or more in the shade. She was instantly sweating when they walked up the steps to the store. Ratu had another bag with her, and this was taken away and placed into a security locker. Their handbags were searched. Again, she was reassured that this was all normal.

They entered the store, it was like she'd walked into a rainbow, a sparkly one, everything seemed to be embedded with beads and gems. People milled every-where. Ratu explained that most of them were staff, and that, on a busy weekend, the store could almost be impossible to move in. She didn't know how anyone could actually shop in somewhere like this. A friendly gentleman greeted them in perfect English, and when Ratu explained what they needed, she was ushered to one side of the room and provided with a seat. A drink was brought to her—coconut water again—and two ladies began to question her on her favourite colours.

She was a bit overwhelmed by it all.

They turned to the walls, which were covered from top to bottom with fabrics, and pulled out several blues.

"Light or dark, Madame?"

"I like the darker ones."

"Good choice, Madame."

"This one?" The other lady spoke and held up an aquamarine length of fabric with embellishments, which she thought looked like millions of sequins.

"A bit darker?"

The other lady held up a sapphire-coloured one this time. This had beads sewn onto it in patterns.

"This is hand sewn, Madame."

"Matches your skin and hair perfectly."

She looked to Ratu for help.

"Why don't you try it on, Miss?" one of the ladies offered.

"I don't know how to wear one."

"Stand up please, Madame." The other was on her feet.

She did as instructed. One of the girls took her shawl away. It was neatly folded and placed beside her. The other showed her how to stand, and in what seemed like a fluid movement, the Sari was wrapped around her with ease. A mirror was brought in and she stood before it looking at her reflection. She loved it. It suited her colour perfectly. James would like it.

"How much?"

Ratu interjected. "Mr North has taken care of it, Miss."

"Of course." She couldn't be angry at him; she'd expected it. "But I'd still like to know the cost."

Ratu looked at the girls, and they said something between them in the regional dialect. "It's around two hundred pounds in your money, Miss."

She gasped.

"It's hand sewn in the finest silks."

"Oh."

"Mr North will love you in it. He stated that cost was not an issue."

"He would." she smirked. She was going to let him get away with it this time, though, as she absolutely loved the Sari. "We will take it."

The sale was rung up before she could change her mind. She thanked the staff, and they returned to the car. She was told that usually they'd take the Sari to a shop nearby to choose fabric for the underskirt and lining. It would then be taken to a seamstress to complete the work, but Ratu would arrange all of that without the need to impose on her time even more.

She was hungry and hadn't eaten since they'd had breakfast on the plane. Ratu gave instructions to the driver, and they pulled up next to a well-known fast food restaurant. She sighed. She really didn't fancy a burger.

"Is there not something different?"

Ratu looked out the window. "Oh no Miss, we aren't going there. The restaurant is on the other side."

She turned her head and looked at a restaurant, which said 'Veg Only'. It didn't look anything special. In fact, it looked like a cheap diner. They were shown to a table, and she ordered a lemonade and allowed Ratu to order the food as most of the menu wasn't in English.

"I haven't ordered you much. Mr North has a big dinner planned tonight, so you don't want to be full up."

The food arrived quickly, and the lemonade she ordered turned out to be genuine, freshly squeezed lemonade. Ratu told her that in India if you wanted lemonade like in the UK, you needed to order the brand. She stored that bit of information for the future but still enjoyed the real lemonade. The meal consisted of vegetables only.

"Many of the people in India are vegetarian." Ratu told her.

"I don't mind. You'll have to tell me what some of the food is."

"These are *chapatti*, Indian bread; and this is *gobi Manchurian*, it's spicy cauliflower; and this is *paneer masala*, which is Indian cheese in a butter gravy; and this final one is a *dahl*, which is lentils infused with spices."

She sampled all the dishes, thoroughly enjoyed them, and even ordered some *gobi Manchurian* to take back to James.

By the time they got back to the hotel, it was getting late and she found James asleep. She stood there for a few moments watching him as he slept. He was sprawled out naked on the bed with only a thin sheet covering him. He really was the most handsome man she'd ever known. He must have been exhausted. His clothes where strewn upon the floor. His back faced her. She'd never had a chance to have a proper look at the tattoo on his back. It was very intricate in its detail. The wings of the angel circled his shoulder blades, and in the middle sat the figure of a man. She'd never noticed before the sad expression on the angel's face. Tentatively, she reached out to touch it lightly. She wanted to wipe away the tears she imagined it was crying. The skin underneath felt different. She leaned in for a closer look and saw that his back was marred with ugly scarring. The tattoo was hiding it all.

James stirred in the bed. She stood back, and he turned to face her.

"Hello beautiful. When did you get back?"

"Just now." She smiled.

"What's the time?"

"Just after six."

"Good." He pulled her towards him, "Just time to christen this big bed."

She wanted to ask him about the scars but now wasn't the time. Instead, she pulled her dress over her head and climbed into the bed next to him.

SEVENTEEN

James

"Make sure that you check all the rooms, and *personally*. I'm not leaving anything to chance. They all need to have one of the gift bags in them." James ran his hand through his hair. "And the press packs. Make sure they're all laid out in preparation as well. I'm trusting you Raji." Amy appeared at his side and handed him a glass of water with ice and a slice of lemon. Raji nodded and hurried away.

"You need to come and have an hour's rest. I'll help Raji check the rooms."

"I don't have time for a rest," he snapped at her. "The hotel's opening is in four hours, and there's still so much left to do." He was distracted by two waiters laying a table out incorrectly and started towards them, his fists clenched. Amy jumped in front of him.

"Bedroom now." She stood with her hands on her hips and lips pursed together in defiance. "You'll do as you're told. I'll sort the tables and check the rooms. You've barely sat down or slept in three days. If you don't rest now, you'll collapse during the opening. And *that* will be the headline news and not the hotel." He tried to walk around her, not having time for this, but she continued to block his path. "James, please. Listen to me."

He could see the worry in her eyes when she looked up at him. He drew her to him and cuddled her.

"I'm sorry. You're right. Let me sort the table. Raji will sort the rooms, and then, you can come and keep me company while I rest?"

"Alright. But if I join you in the bedroom, no sex. Deal?"

"Deal." He couldn't be bothered to argue. He sorted the table layout and then virtually dragged Amy to their suite. Matthew was there cleaning his shoes for the evening. Sonia was watching television and grumbling at the poor choice of channels. He instantly vowed to rectify that. He didn't want anyone to find any faults. Amy led him into the bedroom and shut the door. She took his jacket and shirt off, helped him onto the bed, and removed his shoes and socks. He lay on the pillow and instantly relaxed. He tapped the bed for her to come and lay next to him. She shook her head.

"No. Shut your eyes and sleep."

"At least lay down with me."

"No."

"Seriously?"

"You can't always have your own way."

"Why not?"

"Because I said so. Shut your eyes and go to sleep."

"Yeah. That's going to be a little difficult." He looked down at the rapidly expanding tent in his trousers.

"You're insatiable."

"You're incredibly sexy." She'd forced him to stop running around but he wasn't going to allow her to win. He needed to take back the control. "Remove all your clothes."

"No." She folded her arms at him in a challenge. His cock jumped, and he gripped the bed to maintain his dwindling restraint. God, she loved to test him. He slid slowly from the bed and lowered his trousers, so his erect cock jutted out straight towards her.

"Are you really going to leave me like this?" He prayed the answer that she gave wouldn't be no.

"I'm not going touch you. I told you that." She turned away from him, and his mouth dropped open. He'd never had a woman defy him like this. He looked down at his hands. They were shaking.

" Come here and suck me, or I'll put you over this bed and spank your arse until it's red." The words left his mouth before he had a chance to think. What was she doing to him? He was losing it.

She turned back around, and he noticed she'd undone the buttons at the front of her knee length dress. She slipped the dress to the floor. He met her eyes, which were still full of defiance. What was she doing?

"I won't be sucking you. I won't be touching you. If you want to come, you'll have to do it yourself."

"What?" His answer came out in a strangled moan of longing. Her bra followed the dress to the floor. He reached out to touch her breasts, but she smacked his hand away.

"You don't touch me, either."

"Come on, enough is enough. Stop fooling around."

"I'm not." She walked over to the chair in the corner of the room and sat on it. She parted her legs and brought one foot up onto the seat. His blackening eyes followed the path of her hand as she trailed it over her breasts and down to the cleft between her legs. She pulled the flimsy material of her pants across and displayed herself to him—she was glistening with dewy moisture. He hissed, and his hand grabbed hold of his cock and began to stroke it. What in the hell was she doing to him? He watched her use one hand to hold her delicate folds apart and with the other ran a finger down in between them and circled her clit, massaging and teasing it. He tugged harder on his cock, groaning with each stroke around the head. His eyes flicked to Amy's. She was mesmerised by the way he played with himself.

She lowered her middle finger and stuck it within herself. He wiped away the bead of pre-cum that appeared on his cock. She was writhing against her finger. She put another one in and then let go of her folds and began to massage her clit again.

He had dreamt of this moment. He couldn't believe it was happening. It shouldn't happen. This was wrong, wasn't it?

He had no control. It was all Amy. It wasn't in bed. It was erotic, and he was more turned on than he knew. Fuck, he was losing his mind. He was a pervert. That's what they'd called him. He had the scars.

Amy moaned.

" I'm going to come. Are you close? I want us to come together."

"Yes." Was all he managed before he violently came into his hand. His legs began to quiver as Amy cried out with her own release. He tried to focus on her, but his head was swirling, and his cock was still pumping what seemed like an endless swathe of essence into his hand. He couldn't move. He could barely catch a breath.

What had actually just happened? He caught, out of the corner of his eye, Amy lowering her legs and getting up from the chair. She fetched tissues from the box on the dressing table, and he watched her wipe his hand. No. No. She shouldn't be doing this. His mind was endlessly twisting, his heart beating so rapidly he thought it would explode.

He was heading down that dark path again. He was going to lose her. He was forcing her to do his dirty stuff. She sat beside him on the bed. She kissed his now sweating forehead. He needed air.

"I'm sorry." He pulled up his trousers and, without looking back, ran from the room. He was shirtless and barefoot, but he needed to put distance between them. He heard Amy call after him, but he couldn't stop. The roof was the nearest place. He needed to breathe. He was struggling. He couldn't find any air. He hurtled up the fire escape exit and burst out onto the roof. Gulping, he tried to get as much air into his lungs as possible. He didn't hear the footsteps behind him until the last minute.

"You can't hide the truth from her any longer."

He spun around. Matthew stood before him his strong arms folded across his chest.

"Leave me alone."

"No. Whatever that bitch did to you, Amy is different. She loves you, and I think, even though you're trying to deny it, she's exactly the same as you."

"She'll hate me. I can't see that happen. I love her."

"She'll hate you if you keep walking out on her like this." Matthew reached out and grabbed his arm. "Go talk to her."

"Fuck you. You don't know anything." He took a swing at his friend to try and shake him off, but his bodyguard ducked. James turned again and caught Matthew hard on the side of the face. The bodyguard reciprocated and pushed him hard against the wall. His back stung as it hit the rigid surface. The scars beneath his tattoo instantly burned. He tried to push Matthew off him, but the bodyguard was too well trained and too strong.

"I took you to the hospital that night. I stayed with you until your mother could get there and remained in the waiting room for hours after. Don't tell me I don't know anything. I couldn't get to you in time to save you, but I'm not going to let you make the biggest mistake of your life here and now. Because if you continue down this path then that's what it will be."

"She'll hate me." He sent a pounding blow into his bodyguard's stomach, but his own hand came off worse against the steely abs he found there.

"Did she hate you during whatever you just did that triggered this off?" He froze. "She's in your room crying right now. Wondering what she's done to upset you."

"She didn't leave?"

"No, you're a complete idiot." He relaxed into Matthew's grip, and the body-guard let go. "Sonia is in there consoling her."

"Fuck," he screamed at the top of his voice and a flock of pigeons, which had been quietly nesting nearby, cascaded into the sky below the rooftop. "I need to solve this, don't I?"

"Yes. You let her go, and you're on your own. I'll quit."

A cough came from behind them. It was Sonia.

"I'm sorry, Sir, Mr Raji is looking for you, urgently. The press is showing up already and several of the guests as well."

He slouched against the wall.

"Amy?"

"Mrs Ratu is with her helping her dress and put on her makeup."

"Stay with her, but tell her as soon as this opening is all over, I'll explain every-thing to her. And Sonia, tell her I love her." He turned back to Matthew. "Go get me my suit. I'll change in your room."

Matthew nodded and disappeared with Sonia back down the stairs.

He stood on the rooftop breathing in what he could of the city's 'fresh air'. He thought his past had been just that, the past. He thought he could suppress it and hide it, but, if he was to save his relationship with Amy, there was the one big demon he needed to face. He'd get through this evening, and tomorrow he'd tell her everything. Then she'd be able to make her own decisions about him and whether she wanted to stay with him or not.

He prayed that she did.

EIGHTEEN

Amy

The door opened, and all the guests filed into the elegant ballroom. Amy stood at James's side ready to greet them. Raji and his wife were with them, along with several executives, including James's Indian and UK-based architects. She followed Ratu's lead and presented a little curtsey to everyone, rather than a handshake. She didn't need to speak to them; women were merely a decoration for their men, in Indian culture. She didn't mind tonight. Her head was all over the place. A smile was about all she could manage.

She felt like a princess in her Sari. She had her long blonde hair pulled up into a fancy hair style which was decorated with delicate jewelled pins. Her makeup had been done for her, and the hotel had loaned her gold bracelets so numerous that they covered her wrists and forearms. She even had a bindi on her forehead. It was a beautiful sapphire colour to match that of her Sari. James was dressed in a jodh-puri suit. His jacket was a special Indian design, similar to the hotel's logo, blue and gold in colour. Raji was dressed the same, and she knew that the suits had been specially made for them because they fitted each man like a second skin. After the final few guests shuffled through the welcoming committee, James took her hand and led her to their table for the Indian banquet. She could tell he was nervous; his palms were sweaty. She whispered quietly to him, while they walked,

"You're doing well. Everybody looks happy."

He smiled down at her, "I love you. I'm sorry. I wish I didn't have to do this now. I owe you an explanation."

"I love you too. Please, forget that for now. I'm here to support you. You've worked so hard for this." He pulled her seat out as they reached their table. "Tomorrow we can talk. Tonight we celebrate." She stretched up and kissed him.

"Thank you." All the gentlemen stood as the ladies took their seats, and then they sat. She sat next to James and the Bollywood star, Mr Kumar, and next to him was the most beautiful woman she had ever seen. Her jet black hair was as elaborately decorated as hers, and her hands were covered in Mehendi designs. They were beautiful and intricate. The starter was brought, a mixture of *pakoras*. These were pieces of vegetables deep fried in garam flour. The sauce served with it was incredible. Champagne was flowing, and while James chatted to one of his big investors on his left, she engaged in conversation with Mr Kumar and his wife, Meena, the woman with the jet black hair. They had met on the set of a film where she played his love interest and married after a whirlwind romance. They had three children, though the woman didn't look as if she'd ever been pregnant.

When she told them that she used to dance in England, she didn't divulge where, they promised to show her how to do some of the Bollywood dancing later. She was so excited.

The main course was brought. For most people this consisted of a vegetable biryani, but if you wanted, you had the option to have chicken instead. She opted for chicken and found it really alien that she had to opt for meat. James told her that unlike England, meat was the opt-in here. Animals were sacred and worshipped. She'd never actually find beef to eat due to the cow being the most sacred animal in Indian culture. She wondered about fish, cheese and eggs. James laughed and told her not to mention eggs. A lot of people didn't eat them because of where they came from. It had been a nightmare for his chefs to decide on a dessert. The Indians weren't overly bothered by desserts, but he was keen to offer one, because it would be what his travelling guests preferred. But they struggled with simple things, such as flour. It was made differently in India, so they'd had to import a load. She squeezed his leg under the table to show him she adored what he'd done. Dinner was cleared away and the speeches started. James and Mr Kumar took centre stage, and she proudly clapped, when they officially declared the hotel open and cut a ribbon. She could visibly see James relax as the ribbon was cut and everyone cheered. He'd done it.

The live band started, and Meena begged Amy to join her as some lively Indian music struck up. She stood beside the dance floor and removed her high heeled shoes at Meena's direction. Meena demonstrated a couple of basic steps. As soon as Meena realised that Amy could pick up the dance as they did it, she launched fully into a proper Bollywood dance. Amy followed her, and the crowd cleared a part of the dance floor for them. They were clapping as Meena performed the dance, and Amy followed her movements a few seconds later. She was smiling so much her cheeks were hurting. She wasn't quite sure how she was keeping the Sari on as she danced, but it seemed to be staying in place. Mr Kumar joined them and performed the moves with them. Everybody stopped what they were doing and watched them. A big finale came to the dance, it saw first Meena and then her twirled in the air by Mr. Kumar. The band stopped playing and everyone cheered. She was sure she must have looked a sweaty mess, but she didn't care. Through the haze of faces, she saw James watching her. He had the biggest smile on his face, and he was clapping so hard she thought he must be hurting his hands. She curtsied to the group, left the dance floor, and went straight to his arms. He embraced her and pressed a kiss to the top of her head.

"I didn't know you could dance like that."

"I've been dancing since I was four. I have always picked it up really easily. I miss it in some ways. I'll have to dance more for you." She giggled and then realised what she had said. "I'm sorry."

"No, don't be. I want you to dance for me. You can teach me as well. I've two left feet." He laughed. "Maybe something a bit less energetic for a start, though. I always fancied learning the tango."

"I think I could oblige you there."

They stayed at each other's side for the rest of the evening. Stalls were laid out, selling different products from the country, and one even did Mehendi, which she dragged James to. He refused to get any done, saying it was for girls despite the fact that Raji had it all over his hands. However, he helped her pick out a winding pattern that snaked down her forearm, over her hand, and down her middle finger. It reminded her of his tattoo. She loved it and actually told him she was going to consider getting it done permanently. James whispered into her ear. "You do that, and I won't be responsible for how hard you make me." She reached out with her painted hand and stroked it down his face.

It was two in the morning by the time the final few guests made their way to their bedrooms. She was almost dead on her feet. The staff busied themselves, changing around settings, so that the banquet room would be ready for a buffet breakfast the next morning. The evening had been about Indian food, but the breakfast would be a traditional European affair.

She couldn't remember where, but she lost her shoes somewhere around midnight. She was tiny, now, when she stood next to James, though he still used her as a leaning post to say goodnight to the final guest.

"Come on you. Time for bed."

She could barely keep her eyes open when they headed for the lift. He scooped her into his arms and carried her from the lift to their suite. Matthew opened the door and bid them good night. He placed her on their bed, and as she sat there dozily aware of what was happening, he removed the pins from her hair and brushed it out. He next helped her to remove her Sari and guided her, naked, into the bathroom. He waited outside while she did her business, and by the time she emerged, he'd undressed. He reached behind his back, produced her nightgown and put it over her head. He then led her to the bed, laid her down, and covered her up with the sheet. She waited for him to kiss her, but he didn't. He went to the bathroom without a word. What was he doing? She was baffled. When he came out, he climbed into the bed beside her and brought her into his arms. He kissed her on the forehead and whispered, "Goodnight."

She responded in kind, and he turned out the lights. She lay there in the dark, suddenly wide awake. She was in bed with a man who she knew held a secret from her. One that made him terrified of her when they made love in any way that wasn't vanilla sex. He'd run out on her twice now. He was going to tell her, but she didn't think she could sleep before he did. James groaned. Was he asleep or, like her, thinking. She turned in his arms and sat up to reach a bottle of water beside her bed. She'd had a few drinks that night but not many. She certainly wasn't drunk, and she knew James wasn't either. She took a sip, and when she turned back to lay down, he had rolled over, so his back was facing her. The wings of the angel were caught in a flicker of moonlight, which streaked through the drapes.

She reached out, the tip of her finger millimetres from the tattoo and the scars she'd seen hidden underneath. He turned in the bed and looked up at her with his sorrow-filled eyes.

"What you have to tell me. Does it have anything to do with your tattoos and the scars they hide?"

NINETEEN

James

James's world fell apart at Amy's words. She knew. She'd seen them. He'd always been so careful to make sure they were covered in full light. You had to get so close to study them and see the scars. She couldn't have seen them in this light. "How?" Had Matthew told her?

"The first night we got here when I returned from shopping. It was still daylight and you were sleeping in the bed. You've never let me look at the tattoos properly. I wanted to see them."

"Are you horrified?"

He sat up next to her and she brought her hand to his stubbled face. "No. I want to know how you got hurt. Is it related to why you ran from me?"

"I don't want to lose you."

" I know we were going to do this tomorrow, but I think you need to talk to me now. I need to know what happened to you."

He nodded, reached over, and took a sip of his water. He was shaking; he was so scared. She was going to walk out on him, here and now, and he'd never see her again. He owed her an explanation, though.

"Please hear the whole story, before you say anything. Before you make your mind up about me. Please, will you promise me that?"

"Of course." She moved her hand down to his and squeezed it with reassurance.

"I told you I had a girlfriend, and we broke up about five years ago. Our split was not amicable. In fact, it was completely the opposite. By the end, she despised me. We'd been together since we were sixteen. Our relationship didn't become physical until we'd been together for four years. She was very religious and wanted to save herself until she was sure I was the right one. I wasn't ready for marriage, though. I wanted to build my company first. Eventually, and I didn't pressure her, she decided that I was the one, and we consummated our relationship." He saw Amy wince at talk of him being intimate with another woman. "Her view of sex, though, differed from mine. She believed anything that wasn't the missionary position was wrong. Eventually, I began to find it hard to get off during sex with her. I loved her, or well, I thought I did. So I suggested different positions, and she'd punish me and deny me sex for weeks. We'd argue about it a lot. I was masturbating more than being with her. I used to enjoy going away on trips because it meant I could stick on a porn video and wank to it. One night, I decided that I needed to do something or our relationship was going to fall apart. I brought her a blindfold."

"What did she say?"

"She agreed to try it. I tied it around her eyes, and we started to...you know." Amy winced again.

"I know."

"Except I got carried away. I flipped her over and went to enter her from behind. I smacked her arse. I was so erect, I thought I was going to come then and there. It felt so good. So freeing. I wanted more. I pushed into her, and she screamed. She scrambled away, ripped the blindfold from her face, and called me the devil. She quickly dressed and left the house. I tried to see her the next day, but she refused. Her brothers told me I was unholy and a freak. I was never to go near their sister again. They wanted compensation for her suffering. She felt like a whore. She'd need counselling for life, and the odds of her being able to form another relationship were slim to none. I had to give them money. I was already a millionaire, but it nearly bankrupted the company. If I hadn't paid them, they'd have gone to the press and sold stories about me." He stopped and drew breath. He'd spoken so fast he wanted to make sure Amy had taken everything in. "Do you understand everything?" She looked at him blankly or in shock. He really couldn't decide. "Amy?"

"They made you pay compensation to your girlfriend of five years because you tried to have sex with her doggy style?"

"Yes."

Her tiny fists were tightly clenched. She was angry. No, she was seething. She thought he was sick as well.

"That doesn't explain the scars." She spoke through clenched teeth.

"You sure you want to hear that bit?"

"I want to hear everything."

"I didn't want another girlfriend after that. I thought I'd throw myself into the business. I watched porn and BDSM videos to satisfy my needs. One night, I was passing a club, and I went in and found a sub for the evening, and she did things. Things the way I wanted them. The way I'd seen them on the videos. After that, I visited her on other occasions."

Amy interrupted.

"What sort of things?"

"I tied her up. I whipped her. We used toys." He paused and looked away. "We masturbated in front of each other." She inhaled sharply. He really was a disgusting freak. She'd hate him.

"Is that how you got the scars? Did she go too far?"

"No. One night, I was leaving the club. I sent Matthew to get the car. I'd had a little too much to drink and wandered into a nearby park. My ex-girlfriend's brothers were walking home and saw me. They knew what the club did. They saw a way to make money; except the first time I drew up a watertight contract. I refused. A fight started. Two against one, and the one wasn't entirely sober. I was outnumbered. They got me on the floor. They took my belt from my jeans and hit me with it."

Amy gasped. He couldn't look at her. He couldn't bear to see the judgment in her eyes that told him that he'd got what he deserved. "The entire time they called me so many names. I was sick, perverted, a freak, and the devil. I didn't deserve to live or love. I'd ruin everything. What I wanted wasn't sex. It was bestiality and degrading to woman, and I deserved to rot in hell. I eventually blacked out. Matthew told me he found me and took me to the hospital. My skin was so badly marred that I was told I'd be scarred for life. I vowed from that day I would take control. I'd never put myself in that situation again. That's what I have done. I covered my back with the angel to remind myself of that vow. Then, I met someone." He went silent. All he could hear in the room was Amy's small sobs. He still couldn't look at her.

"You...you...mean me?" She struggled to get her words out.

"Yes—and I lost control again." He finally looked up at her, and she had tears streaming down her face. "I don't want to lose you, please. I'll try to be good. I'll get counselling. I'll do anything that it takes so that I don't make you hate me. I'm sorry. I made you do things I shouldn't have. Please, please don't hate me. I don't want to be that person. I want to be the boyfriend that you need."

She turned away and let out an anguished cry. He'd lost her. He knew it. She walked over to the table and picked up a scarf she'd placed on it earlier. She came back to the bed.

"Stand up." Her words were barely distinguishable.

"What are you going to do?"

"You say you love me? Do you trust me?"

"Amy?"

"Do you?"

"Yes."

She shut her eyes, and he watched as she took a deep breath.

"I'm going to blindfold you."

"What?" Blindfold? She was going to teach him a lesson. She was going to show him what a disgusting monster he was.

"Trust me." She came close to his face and whispered. He moved the sheet from over him and stood. He was still naked and extremely vulnerable before her. She tied the scarf around his face, so he couldn't see. Maybe she was going to leave him like this and walk out on him. He may have just seen her for the last time.

She came close to his ear, again, and rested a hand on his chest. His heart was thumping so rapidly.

"You're not a freak. You aren't the devil. You're none of those things. What you wanted is natural. Between two consenting adults, it's perfect, and I enjoy everything that you do to me. Your ex-girlfriend wanted something different. What her brothers did to you was assault, and it was wrong." She put a finger over his mouth when he went to correct her. "No. You've spoken, and now I will. You're blindfolded before me. I'm going to touch you wherever I want. You won't stop me.

However, if at any point you really wish me to cease, you'll say Lanzarote. Do you understand?"

He nodded.

"I need you to say yes."

"Yes. I understand." He couldn't quite take in what she was saying to him just yet. It was confusing. It was not what he expected to hear from her. She should be angry; she should hate it. Yet here she was telling him that what he wanted was natural.

"These scars…" She was behind him now. "to you, show you to be nothing but vile and dirty. I'm going to give them new meaning. I'm going to show you that you're everything to me, that I love you, and we will try new things together that aren't sinful. They're right. They're right, because we're in love, and we consent." She kissed the centre of his back where he knew the heaviest of his scars were. The angel's sad face covered them. He groaned. She kissed him again. He felt his cock beginning to rise. His back was burning. Every time she pressed her lips against a part of it, it sent shivers throughout his body. She repeated the process again. Her delicate fingers traced the outline of the scars hidden beneath the fanciful artwork. His thick cock was jutting rigidly out by the time she finished. He was ready to explode.

"Amy."

"No talking. We're a partnership. No secrets, no lies. We're equals. If we don't agree or like something, we use the word Lanzarote."

She stopped talking, and he couldn't hear her moving. He was trying to listen out for where she was when her lips wrapped around his cock.

He moaned long and loudly. She was sucking him hard, her tongue twisting around his shaft as she savoured every inch of him. He wouldn't last long. He was listening to her. They were both consenting to this. He wasn't hurting her or pushing her away. She wanted the crazy stuff as much as he did. She was enjoying it. That's why he lost his control with her. That's why she frustrated him, in equal parts to him loving her. He groaned again when he felt her swallow him deep. He was hitting the back of her throat. He wanted to rip the blindfold off, so he could watch her, but he needed to come like this. The scars on his back were no longer stinging painfully. They were vibrating. They were pulsating waves of pleasure into his balls, and he felt the fires surging through his body. He called out her name as he came into her mouth. His legs threatened to give way, so she helped him to sit back on the bed. She removed the blindfold and was kneeling before him. Her hands rested on his toned thighs as his exhausted cock settled.

"I love you. I'm not your ex-girlfriend. I don't want just vanilla sex with you. You want to blindfold me, whip me, use toys, fuck me in any position you want, I consent. I consent because it isn't wrong. It's something we're agreeing on together. I may not say yes to everything, and equally, there may be things I want to do to you that you don't. But we make this decision together, we discuss it, and we have a relationship of equals." He drew her up into his arms.

"You really don't hate me?"

"No. I can't live without you. I'll be at your side forever."

He moved a strand of hair that had flipped over eyes and then wiped away the tears.

"I thought I was wrong for so many years. I never let anyone have control. God I must have annoyed Matthew and my mother."

Amy laughed.

"I don't expect you to change overnight. I think I'd miss it actually. Shows you care."

"Equals."

"Equals."

Amy looked at the clock.

"You do realise we have to be up in three hours for the buffet breakfast."

He pulled her back into bed with him.

"I'd rather have you for breakfast. If I'm not a freak, I've a lot of things I want to try with you. I think I may have to send Matthew out to buy a copy of the Kama Sutra tomorrow."

TWENTY

Amy

Amy ran the brush through her hair and scooped it up into a ponytail. There wasn't any time to shower nor to wash the hairspray, from the previous night, out of her hair. She took her foundation and tried to disguise the bags that had appeared under her eyes. James was frantically running around trying to get his clothes on.

"Are you ready?" His voice was tense.

She gave herself a spray of her favourite Marc Jacobs perfume.

"Yes."

"Come on, then."

They opened their bedroom door. Matthew and Sonia stood there immaculately prepared as if they'd had the regulation eight hours sleep. She wanted to go back to bed. She looked and felt a mess.

"I know. We're late." James held his hands up apologetically. "We had a lot to talk about."

Matthew scowled at James.

"Raji has been calling every five minutes. I told him to start without you."

"Thank you. Let's go."

James took her hand, and they almost ran to the lift.

"Everything alright, Boss?" She heard Matthew try to whisper to James.

"It's perfect. I've a few things I want you to fetch for me later, if you can find them."

She tried not to gulp too loudly; she knew he was referring to the newfound sexual freedom that she'd given James and his urgency to explore it.

The breakfast buffet was already in full swing when they arrived. She took her seat, but James was immediately dragged off to engage in conversation with those who he hadn't managed to speak to the previous evening. Most people were helping themselves to the breakfast. It was a mixture of cereals, cheeses, hams, fruits, yoghurts, and of course, all the traditional British fry up ingredients. She wasn't really hungry so she asked Sonia if she would fetch her some fruit and a poached egg on toast. Her bodyguard had a look of worry on her face. She knew Sonia could see that she wasn't physically exhausted, but she was mentally.

"Are you alright? If you want to talk, you know I'm a good listener."

"Thank you." She hadn't wanted Sonia as her bodyguard. She felt she'd impact on her freedom. She'd often been harsh and not even spoken to her. However, during the trip they had spent a lot of time together, and she eventually told her to call her Amy, as Matthew did. She actually counted Sonia as a friend. "Do you know everything?"

"Matthew asked permission from James to inform me of all the details." She noticed Sonia clench her fist in anger. "What they did to him was wrong. He didn't deserve that."

"No. Not at all."

"I'm glad he told you and that you stayed with him."

"He never did anything to make me want to leave him. What he wants is natural to me. I have to help him realise it as well." She blushed, "I'm sorry. You probably don't really need to hear of my sexual preferences. It won't assist you in guarding me."

Sonia took her cup, "The more I know about you, the better I can protect you. Please don't ever fear telling me anything." Sonia smiled and went off to find her breakfast.

Amy looked around the room for James, he was animatedly chatting with an elderly American couple. She couldn't believe how relaxed he looked. Last night, his shoulders had been hunched up, and his face was full of tension, but despite only about two hours sleep, he looked free from all the cares in the world. She was still struggling to get her head around how someone could've made him feel so dirty for a natural urge to want to explore his girlfriend's body. She wanted to explore his, to find out what he liked and what he didn't. She wondered if the ex-girlfriend had been as controlling in their lives outside of the bedroom as she had been in it. Would he have been allowed to kiss her apart from a peck on the lips? What about holding hands in public? She could see why James was so controlling with her. After what happened, he closed down. He hadn't allowed himself to think about anything that he didn't prescribe.

The breakfast passed peacefully, and when she saw that James wasn't actually going to be allowed to sit down and eat, she had a coffee sent to him and a load of pastries taken to their bedroom. She returned to the bedroom without him, despite assurances he wouldn't be more than a few moments behind her, and took a shower. The warm water cascaded off her aching muscles, and she shut her eyes to allow herself to really dream of a future with James. They hadn't known each other long, but to her, it felt as though he was a part of her now. To not be in his arms would kill her. It must have been another hour before he appeared. He was chatting animatedly with Matthew as she and Sonia sat in chairs watching a Bollywood film.

"They wanted to leave around one. How long is the flight?"

"A little under an hour, I think."

"Alright. I want you to book us into one of the cabins for the night. Raji can see to the guests tonight. I'm not the manager, merely the owner. And if I don't get some sleep this evening, I'm liable to collapse."

"You want me to have Miss Amy flown back here so you can sleep."

James glared and then thumped Matthew on the back.

"Miss Amy will do as she's told. Especially after I've exhausted her."

"You want to bet on that, James?" She butted into their conversation, and Sonia laughed. "Where are we going now?"

"A few of the guests want to take advantage of a package we can put together for them. It flies them down to Kabini Nature Reserve for a visit. Sorry beautiful, but we have to join them."

"I wondered why the hotel had the helipad. What do I need to wear?"

"Shorts and a t-shirt will be good. It will be hot down there."

She looked at the clock. It was already close to midday. "I will pack us an overnight bag. You go shower and shave. Make sure you eat something as well."

"I will do," he replied. Matthew nudged him, "Oh, yes. I need you to sign this as well. It's some papers for the landing cards at the Maldives."

She picked up a pen, signed, and handed them back to James. She couldn't be bothered to read them. She trusted him. "I'm sorry. I'd hoped we could spend some time together."

"This means the world to you. I'm fine. Relax and go with it. Stop worrying. Besides, a nature safari sounds fun."

"You won't say that when you see the tour vehicles."

James was right. As she boarded the bus, which didn't have any glass in the windows and looked like it might not make the tour, she suddenly felt a little nervous.

"What animals are we likely to see?"

"It will be mainly elephants, antelope, and monkeys, but there have been tigers, crocodiles, and leopards before."

"You sure it's safe?" She looked at the opening that was a window.

"Hold me tight, so you don't bounce out?"

"What?" He laughed, and she punched him in the chest. "Don't tease me like that."

The tour was breath-taking. To see the animals in their natural habitats, especially the elephants, was just fantastic. They were happy and relaxed. She noticed lots of little tree stumps on the plains. She asked the guide about them and was told that during monsoon weather the plains flooded, due to the amount of rain, and thus the trees didn't grow. She couldn't imagine the amount of rain it would take to flood such a vast area, and she lived in England where it never seemed to stop raining. There was suddenly a lot of commotion between the driver and the guide. The bus halted abruptly. She looked to her right, and there, striding out of the bushes not more than about ten metres from them, was a leopard. It was magnificent. It seemed to be posing for them. Its sleek, spotty coat was beautiful in design. The way its paws padded along the ground showed off its powerful feline abilities. James got out his phone and began to snap pictures as he spoke. "This is unique. I've never seen a leopard before."

The whole bus hushed and watched the big cat, as it walked past the bus and then ran into the bushes on the other side. She reached up to him and kissed him.

"Thank you for bringing me here."

"Thank you for coming here with me."

They returned to the helicopter and waved their guests off before they got into a nearby Jeep. Matthew and Sonia stayed with them, of course. She wondered if they ever got bored following them around; mind you, the job did have some perks.

The vehicle bounced its way along the unmade roads towards the holiday cabins on the outskirts of the reserve. The farmers were in the fields tending to the crops. They still used cows to pull equipment like ploughs. She didn't see a single tractor. Out here, unlike the city, it was as if time had stood still and everyone continued to live life like it had been in the olden days. Except for the satellite television dishes on all the houses, of course. The cabins they were staying in were old-fashioned wooden ones, except with modern conveniences. She knew what James liked by now, and so she wasn't surprised. It was dusk by the time they arrived, and, as they walked into their cabin, they saw a romantic dinner for two had been laid out on the veranda, next to a hot tub.

A waiter appeared and began placing dishes on hot plates. James tipped him, and he left them alone.

"Dinner, Miss Jones?"

"Why thank you, Mr North."

He pulled her chair out for her, and she took a seat. The meal was a traditional Indian affair, but she didn't mind because she'd got used to it and was really enjoying the variety. What she particularly liked, though, were the sweets placed out for dessert. They were made of marzipan and covered in gold and silver leaf. She could've eaten far too many of them, but she also fancied some time in the hot tub.

"I'm going for a soak in the hot tub. Ease the aching muscles from the dancing last night and the bouncing around in the tour bus."

"Did you bring your bikini? Do you want me to fetch it?" James asked.

"Damn it." She sighed and rolled her head. "You didn't tell me I needed it, so I didn't bring one." She pulled her t-shirt over her head and dropped it to the floor with her shorts. "I could go in, in my bra and knickers, what do you think?"

James sat back in his chair and brought his leg up over the arm and pretended to be deep in thought. "Well you could, but personally, I've heard stories of the chlorine in these things ruining clothes. I think you need to take them off completely."

"Oh, yes. I wouldn't want to damage such beautiful underwear." She stepped into the candlelight so that she knew James could see her and teasingly lowered the straps of her bra. She kept her eyes on him the entire time. She unhooked the bra and freed her breasts. She went to lower her knickers, but James was upon her. He took hold of the fabric and tore them from her body. "So much for not getting them damaged."

"I'll buy you new ones." His voice rumbled with its gravelly tones of lust. He dropped his shorts and pants, and then pulled his t-shirt over his head.

"James." She reached out and touched his hand. "This is normal. I want to do it."

"I know. If you didn't then you'd say Lanzarote to me. And we'd discuss it."

She nodded at him. She felt so happy, as he guided her into the tub and pulled her onto his lap. She slid down on his already hard cock, and he reached over and turned the jets on. At first, they didn't move. They enjoyed being rocked by the current of the waves. She stared into his eyes, her forehead resting on his. This was intimate and intense.

" I'm past the seven days that we needed to be careful. If you want, you can come inside me without a condom on."

'Do you want that?"

"Yes."

"Then I want it too."

He placed his hands on her hips and began to guide her movements up and down his shaft. She let him take control. He needed this. She became lost in the feeling of his thick cock, free from any barriers, thrusting within her. He felt closer and deeper. She felt more connected to him than she ever had. James increased the pace, and she bobbed up and down in the water. Her breasts were just resting on the surface when she went down. He pushed her up, his teeth sank into her breast, and she cried out. Shivers ran through her body. She could feel her orgasm building, but she wanted their first time skin on skin to be special. They needed to come together. She wanted him to feel every muscle of her private havens milking his cock for everything that he could give her. She wanted to drink it all inside her. Too much tension had existed between them, and this moment was about freeing it all.

"Can we come together?" Her heart was beating rapidly, and she was beginning to feel the pressure in her thighs as she now helped James with their movement.

"That's the only way I ever want to come again. Whenever you're ready. I'll be there right with you, beautiful." He looked down between them to where their movements were becoming so frantic that the water was fountaining over the sides of the tub.

She leaned forward and kissed his lips. What started as tender lovemaking was now inflamed passion. The kiss was bruising in its urgency, and their bodies were driving together. She flung her head back. When the orgasm came upon her vigorously explosive, she cried out and shuddered as she felt his cum flow within her. Their essences combined, as she returned to his lips and, neither of them moving now, just stayed there. All around them came the sounds of nature, the calls of the elephants over in the reserve, and the crickets as they sang their evening songs.

TWENTY-ONE

James

"Come on. Stop being a wimp." James rolled his eyes.

"But what if something bites my toes? Do they have teeth?" Amy whined.

"Nothing will eat your toes. They may suck on them, but they won't eat them."

"That doesn't sound much better. Argh. I can see fish swimming."

"That's usually what fish do, beautiful."

"But they'll touch me. They'll be slimy." She stuck her tongue out in revulsion.

"They won't come anywhere near you. They're more scared of you than you are of them."

"I don't want to touch the bottom. You have to hold me the entire time so that I don't have to put my feet down. There may be crabs, and they'll bite my toes."

"I'll hold you every single minute. Trust, remember?"

"Why did I agree to this?"

"Because you're the best girlfriend in the world."

"No, because you had me tied to the bed, blindfolded, and were sucking my clit so hard I was screaming."

"Exactly, the best girlfriend in the world."

"James North, I'm never letting you between my thighs again."

"Yeah right. I give you a day on that. Now get in the water."

He steadied himself so that Amy could finally dive into the water and cling to him like a limpet.

"Something touched my backside."

"That's me."

"Don't you even think of trying to get me horny."

"It was the furthest thing from my mind."

They'd been in the Maldives for almost a week now, and this was the first time they'd actually ventured out of the bedroom. Amy had failed in a task the previous night, and this was her punishment. He found out that she'd never been snorkelling before, as she was terrified of swimming with fish. He wasn't going to let her miss out on such a fantastic experience, so when she'd come, twice, without his permission, he had Matthew book the excursion at once.

"Please. They're going to touch me."

"Relax. They're fish. Why don't you put your head under the water and have a look?" She shook her head rapidly. "I'm going to pull your mask down and put the breathing part in your mouth. Relax. I'm protecting you." He pulled the mask over her eyes, and before he could put the breathing tube in her mouth, she spoke, "If so much as one little fish touches me, you're having no sex for a month."

"Alright. If one fish touches you, then I'll satisfy myself for a month."

"That's not what I meant."

"I know." He shoved the breathing part of the snorkel into her mouth before she could answer him. All he could hear was mumbled words. He was sure they involved numerous swear words. "Right, put your head under the water. See what you can see. Remember to breathe normally but through your mouth." He could see that she was absolutely terrified, but she did as he instructed. Her head must have been under for at least two or three minutes before she came up gasping for breath. She spat the piece from her mouth,

"I saw an angelfish. It swam so near to me. It was so colourful. I want to go under again. But don't let me go."

"I won't."

Amy disappeared back under the water and eventually relaxed. He held her the entire time, and whenever a fish came too close, she jumped up into his arms a little further. He couldn't believe that he was here, in the middle of the Indian Ocean, with such an astounding woman. He'd been such an idiot to believe the things that his ex-girlfriend and her family had called him. What they had done together was natural. He could only put it down to the foolishness of youth that he'd been sucked into believing them. He hadn't relinquished all of his controlling nature yet, though. He still expected high standards, and where Amy was concerned, she was to be treated like a Princess at all times. She was his, and he'd make sure of that. He had the money so why not.

He had a surprise for her tonight. He was nervous about it, as she didn't want him to keep secrets that concerned them as a couple, but this had to be kept a secret. She'd understand. Wouldn't she? God, he hoped so.

When they arrived back at shore, Sonia fell ill, and Amy became very upset that her friend was so ill. Matthew stayed with Sonia while she slept, and he took Amy back out into the sunshine to try and distract her from worrying. He connected his laptop and answered a couple of emails while she picked up a romance novel and began reading. He wondered if the romance was on a par with theirs. Amy laughed and told him theirs was better, and maybe she should write about it. That would shock the press. He turned back to his emails happily picturing the expression on the faces of the likes of Miss Sally Bridgewater. The afternoon passed far too quickly.

He sent Amy up to the villa to dress for dinner, whilst he made the final few arrangements with Matthew and checked on Sonia, who was feeling much better. He wanted everything to be perfect. When he entered the villa, he was delighted to find Amy naked and freshly showered. Dinner plans went out of the window for a few moments while he gave her a little reward for her bravery in the water. He left her basking in the afterglow of her orgasm while he showered and changed into a pair of casual linen trousers and a shirt. When ready, he checked on her and found she was dressed in the white skater dress that she'd worn the first time they met in Lanzarote. He thought that most of her clothes hadn't survived her uncle's destruction of the flat, but he was certainly glad that this one did.

"You ready?"

"Yes. Are we going far?"

"No, not far at all." He picked up the blindfold from the table and handed it to her. "I want you to put this on, please."

"Oh no. The last time I wore that, I ended up swimming with fishes."

"No punishment, this time." He swallowed. "I've a surprise for you?"

"A surprise?" He could sense the nervousness in her voice.

"Are you upset?"

She came up to him. She pulled his shirt from his trousers, then moved round behind him and ran her hand over his tattoos. He moaned as sparks of pleasure coursed through his body. His tattoos no longer represented pain but portrayed happiness. She came back around to face him, took the blindfold, and put it over her eyes.

"I'm ready."

He held her hand and led her down to the beach. He was certain that he had butterflies in his stomach. Nothing had ever meant so much to him. When they got to the shore, he kept her a little distance away while Matthew and Sonia lit the candles that they had placed out on the beach. A massive picnic hamper stood next to the blanket and cushions that had been laid out on the beach. Eventually, Matthew and Sonia left, and he lifted the blindfold from Amy's eyes. The sun was setting and the moment was perfect. He took a seat on the blanket, and she nestled into his arms so they could watch the sunset together. He wasn't normally soppy, but it was probably the most romantic moment of his life. He opened the hamper, gave her some strawberries, and he popped the cork on a bottle of the finest champagne. He handed her a glass, and they chinked to happiness and love. He was about to speak when Amy started up a conversation.

" I've decided something while I've been here. I want to sell my flat and use the money to rent a dance studio and teach dance. I have experience, though no real teaching qualifications. I'm sure I can find a qualified teacher to help me out. What do you think?"

"What about your writing?"

"I'll still be able to do that. It won't be full time. I write novels. It isn't journalism or anything like that. As long as I manage a daily quota, I'll be alright."

"You know that you don't need to work right? I can provide for you, and I want to."

"I know. And that's why I want to set the dance studio up. It doesn't have to be for money. It can be for fun and for teaching others to do something that I love. It would be nice if it made some money, but I'm not business-minded at all. I'll leave that to you."

"You want me to help you?"

"Not with money, but maybe with things such as finding the studio."

"It would make more financial sense to keep the apartment in Kennington and use the rent and the money you have saved, so far, for a deposit and any other payments. Maybe I could invest a little to make up for any shortfall you may have. I'd expect a return on my investment, though." He grinned at her. She didn't reply to him, but he could see she was working a response out in her head. "I'd be a silent partner. I can draw up an official loan contract for the money. I would expect regular returns, when you can afford it, and even payment for my business' services to you."

"At a commercial rate?"

"At a rate that we sit down, discuss together, and agree on."

"I don't know. Wouldn't it be easier to get rid of the flat?"

"I'd prefer you to keep it for a safety net."

"In case we break up?"

"No, because that won't be happening. In case you need it in an emergency for any reason."

She smiled.

"Alright, we will work out a deal when we're back in England. No wonder you're so successful, Mr North. You drive a hard bargain."

"It's what I'm known for."

"Can we toast it with a little more of this champagne?"

"I hope that you aren't going to get drunk on me. This isn't the only romantic surprise I have for you tonight."

"Oh yes? What else?"

"You'll have to wait a bit."

"Tease."

"I think after this week, you've learnt that if I want to tease you, I can. And I'll make you scream my name while doing it."

"I love it when you talk all masterful."

"I love it when you submit. Food?"

"Only if you eat it from my stomach."

"Amy!"

"Spoilsport."

He handed her a plate of food, and they sat watching the rest of the sunset while eating. When the sun finally disappeared beneath the ocean, it was time. He got to his feet and tried to disguise the fact he was shaking.

"Amy?"

"Hmm," she sleepily replied and laid back against the cushions.

" Look at me."

She instantly snapped awake and scrambled up onto her knees in front of him. He loved the way she reacted to him. He didn't even need to try to be masterful with her; she just natural in her response to him.

"Sorry, is it time for another romantic surprise?"

"It is." His palms were sweating. He'd never been so nervous. He could stand up in front of a room full of people and speak, but this one simple thing, and he was a quivering mess. He'd a whole speech prepared, but his mind was like jelly. He couldn't remember a thing, even his name it seemed.

"What is it? What's wrong?"

She tried to get up, but he got down on one knee in front of her. He pulled a little box from out of his pocket. The sea lapped around them onto the white gold sand. The candles flickered in the moonlight, and a thousand stars shone down on them, expectantly.

"I know that in the grand scheme of things we haven't known each other very long, but I'm confident about this. I'm more certain than I've ever been about anything in my life. I love you, and I want to share the rest of my life with you." He cleared his throat. "Will you marry me?" He opened the little box he he held in front of him. Inside was a platinum ring with a princess cut diamond. He'd had the ring flown in from Dubai, and it had been made to his specifications. He held his breath as he waited for her to answer.

He knew what was in his heart. He never wanted to even look at another woman. From the moment he'd met her in Lanzarote, he'd been enthralled with her. She'd got under his skin and helped him recover from his past. Yes, he was still demanding, but she understood him and could temper that with her playfulness. Had he made a big mistake? Had he ruined everything?

"James." Here was the put-down. He could hear it in her voice.

"It's ok. I'm sorry. I shouldn't have asked. It's too soon, right? I should have told you. I shouldn't have got the ring. I'm taking control again and not telling you things. I'll put it away and send it back." He got to his feet and shut the box.

"James North, will you stop over-analysing things and let me answer. Open that box up and come and put that ring on my finger." She held her hand out.

"What?"

"I love you. Even if you're an idiot sometimes. Yes, I'll marry you. I don't ever want to be apart from you. I can't take a breath when I am." She was crying now. His eyes were watering; he must have sand in them. He took her left hand and slid the ring on. He could've spent more money on a ring for her, but she had delicate hands, and anything ostentatious would have looked wrong. He had judged it right.

"Perfect."

"It is." She held her hand up and looked at the ring. "Oh my God. I'll be your wife."

"That's generally what happens when two people get married."

"Can we celebrate our engagement?"

"What do you have in mind?" She reached down to his trousers. He stopped her. "Alas beautiful, not really the best thing to be doing in the open in this country. However, let's go back to the bedroom. I've one more surprise for you."

TWENTY-TWO

Amy

James led Amy into the bedroom. They left everything on the beach, but she knew Matthew would dutifully arrange for it to be cleared up. She wondered what they'd ever do if Matthew left them. They'd probably never get anything done and get arrested for doing something wrong. He was only a couple of years older than James, but he was almost like a big brother.

She looked down at her hand and the glistening gem on her ring finger. She'd had no idea that he was going to propose to her, let alone present her with the most beautiful ring she'd ever seen. It caught her completely by surprise. She had to take a few minutes to repeat his words in her head until she fully understood what he was saying. When she realised, she had no hesitation in saying yes. She loved James; she wanted to be his wife more than anything in the world.

When her parents died she thought her life was over. She relied on them for so much love and support, and all of a sudden, she was alone. Yes, she had had her uncle, but now that she looked back, she always seemed an inconvenience to him. She was glad he was out of her life and hoped that she never had to see him again. She had a new life; she'd be Mrs North. She'd look after the man to whom she was devoted, but she'd still have time to herself to pursue her dancing interests and to write. In Matthew and Sonia, she had friends and close ones at that. They'd all eaten together one night on the trip as a thank you from James for all their hard work and support. The evening had been so joyous and full of laughter that she had been certain, by the end, that they would all ache the next morning from collapsing in fits of giggles. She was sure something was going on between Matthew and Sonia as well. The atmosphere between them had changed. She mentioned it to James, who laughed and said he thought Matthew was celibate. He'd never even so much as looked at a girl since he'd been with him.

And, finally, she had Miranda, who'd become like a surrogate mother to her.

She was so caring and reminded her of how much she missed her own mother. She hoped Miranda would be pleased to hear of the engagement. She was a little nervous about telling her.

"Did your mother know you were planning to propose?"

When they entered the room, James went to the drawer where she knew he kept some of the 'provisions' that Matthew had purchased for him in India. He turned around and looked at her.

"Way to ruin the thoughts in my head. I really don't need to be thinking about my mother at the moment."

"Sorry. I just wondered. Would she be worried that we haven't been together long?"

"She adores you as much as I do. Yes, I did tell her that I was going to propose. I told her what happened after I told you everything about me. She's over the moon for us and said that if I do anything to chase you away, she'll disown me."

"I like your mother. She's a sensible lady."

"I like her, too. But right now, I'd rather you remove all of your clothes, and we banish any more thoughts of my mother from our minds. It isn't conducive to what I've planned." He looked down at his groin.

Amy lowered her dress to the floor, the sides of her mouth curled up in amusement. Something about getting naked before James and seeing the way he looked at her body had her quivering with anticipation.

"What do you plan on doing to me tonight?" She sauntered up to him. As in Lanzarote, she hadn't worn a bra with the dress. She didn't need to, so all that she had on was her knickers. He pulled some lubricating gel out of the drawer and placed it on the counter top. He then pulled out a vibrator as thick as he was. It pulsated at such a rapid speed that one touch against her clit the other night almost had her screaming out in orgasm.

"Normally, I'd ask that you don't question me on what I'm going to do to you. I want you to feel the heightened sense of knowing that I'll get you off hard but not how I'll do it." He tore her knickers from her body and ran his hand over her sensitive mound. She was wet for him already. She didn't know why he needed the gel. She was always dripping for him with one look. "But this is a big thing for us both. I own here; this is my pussy. It responds to any commands that I give it, even when here,"—he pressed a kiss to her forehead—"is being stubborn."

James removed his hand from where he'd been massaging her, and she pouted at the loss of friction. He gave a quick tap to her clit, which elicited a moan of shock and pleasure from her. He then traced his hand over her hip and around her back and down the crack of her backside. He stopped at the small puckered hole. "I want to explore here."

She heard him inhale a breath when he spoke and waited for her response. "I've never done that before. Have you?"

"Yes. Once with the lady I told you about."

He was honest with her. That meant a lot.

"She'd have been used to it, I suspect."

"I suspect as well. I've been preparing you all week to take me, though. You may not have realised, but every time I used a butt plug with you, I used a bigger one. If you don't want to, please say. I'll do something different. We've a lifetime together to explore these things, when and if you feel ready."

"It isn't that I don't…I like it when you play there. It heightens my orgasms. I'm scared though. I worry it will hurt. You aren't exactly small."

"We will take it slowly. See how you feel. You ask me to stop, and I will."

"Alright. Let's try." She knew she could trust him.

James dropped his clothes to the floor and led her to the bed. He laid her down affectionately and climbed on beside her. She put her left hand on his face. The ring sparkled in the dim light of the room. A gift from her fiancé. The man who held her heart. They kissed, and the kiss turned more passionate, as yet again, they sought to feel every part of each other's bodies. She no longer worried about her hands caressing James's back. He allowed her to touch him freely. He even called out in pleasure when she ran a path over his scars. They no longer meant pain and suffering to him, they were love. Her love, a love she gave freely and with no constraints. Their bodies moved together as one when he entered her pussy and re-claimed it as his own. His thrusts became animalistic and hard as she writhed underneath him. Then, he slowed again. She trembled on the precipice of orgasm. She cursed him as she always did, but she knew that there was more and better to come. He pulled out of her and flipped her over and in one fluid movement plunged his rock solid cock deep into her pussy. She screamed out. She wanted him to move, because in this position he'd rub against her g-spot every time that he did. He didn't move. He reached over, took the lubricant and squeezed some of it on to his hands, while she tried desperately to get some friction where she needed him moving the most. He slapped her bottom, and she called out in desperation again.

"Please."

"Wait." His tone was masterful. He was at his dominating best at that very moment. She'd do anything he wanted, because she and her body were completely under his control. He was the only one who could give her the feelings that she craved. She hissed. She felt his finger test the pucker of her anus. Fuck. She wanted him there as well. She wanted him everywhere. He was already in her brain, her heart, her pussy. He teased his finger in slowly, and started to move his cock within her. It felt painful for a mere second, but after the pop, which sucked him in, it felt so good. He his finger deeper and then gently pushed another in. She felt full. She felt complete.

"God I can feel my cock inside you. I can feel every time I move. Is it hurting?"

"No." She struggled to reply as she suppressed the orgasm bearing down on her like a stampede of wild horses.

"Come for me like this?"

She didn't need asking twice. She exploded around his cock. Shuddering and pulsating in an orgasm so fierce she could barely keep a sense of what was going on. When she stilled, James removed his fingers from within her but kept his cock inside her pussy. He didn't move. He leaned forward and held her until she got her breath back.

"Are you alright?"

"Yes. That was intense."

"Do you feel sore?"

"No."

He withdrew himself from her pussy, covered himself with a condom, and moved his cock to her arse.

"Can I try this, Amy?"

"Yes." She didn't care if it hurt at first. She wanted him inside her. Anywhere. She needed to be joined with him. It was the only way she felt satisfied. James leaned back on the bed and got the vibrator. He slid it inside her pussy, turned it on, and the fire ignited within her belly again. He took some of the lube and massaged it into her before pressing the head of his cock against her puckered hole. He was so big it burnt when he pushed in. He paused, to allow her sphincter to relax, then moved again and paused again. She shut her eyes and tried to concentrate on the vibrator pulsating within her pussy and the pleasure that she got every time that it rubbed against her sweet spot, but still the burn came through. She didn't think she could do this. It was too much. But then the sense of delight hit. James was completely in her arse, and he was grinding against the vibrator. She knew he was completely lost in the feeling. She could hear it in his breathing.

He withdrew from her. She instantly felt empty. He thrust back in, and she squealed.

"Again." The word left her mouth before she was even able to fully register the feelings that were flooding her body. He pulled out and thrust into her again until he found a steady rhythm.

Their bodies were covered in sweat. This coupling between them was raw and untamed. It was new, and they were learning. It was setting them both free from fear. Every time he thrust into her, she felt herself on the verge of soaring. She was ready to fly. She'd never felt so in love. She'd never felt so free and so much pleasure. She was close. She could tell James was as well. The thrusting was getting quicker. He moved his hand to her clit, and that was all she needed. She came in a furious explosion, and then, she felt him coming inside her. Their bodies shuddered together. James withdrew, and she collapsed down on the bed. He pulled her into his arms, holding her tightly and stroking her damp locks from her forehead.

"Are you alright?"

"Yes, how do you know my body so well?"

"Because it was made for me. Just as I was for you."

He got up from the bed, disposed of the condom, fetched a cloth, and gently wiped her down. He then climbed into the bed beside her, and she snuggled into his arms.

"I need to sleep. I think you've pushed me to the limit that my body can handle," she moaned.

"Oh no, you can handle a lot more, but for now I think I could do with some sleep." He chuckled,

"I don't think I want to go home tomorrow."

"I don't either, but we have to."

"Damn."

"Goodnight, Mrs North to be."

"Goodnight, Mr Jones to be."

TWENTY-THREE

James

James swept Amy into arms and carried her across the threshold of his mansion in Knightsbridge.

"You do realise that we aren't married yet, don't you?" She squirmed in his arms and tried to get him to put her down. He shrugged in reply.

"I know, getting in practice for when we are. Besides, I know it's quicker for me to get you to the bedroom if I don't let you walk."

"How did you work that one out?"

"You're a woman. You'll want to show my mum the ring and then talk about the holiday and India. It will be at least five hours by the time I get you naked again."

"You had me naked, and in the mile-high club again, not more than two hours ago."

"Yeah but that was two hours ago."

She bashed his chest with her tiny fist, and he reluctantly put her down with a lamenting grumble. He wrapped his arms around her waist and affectionately kissed the top of her head.

"How you are going to survive a whole day at work is beyond me."

"You'll be bringing me my lunch every day, Miss Jones. That's how."

"Oh, yes? I thought that was what you had Matthew for?"

"I don't find him nearly as sexy as you. He likes to try and take the lead. He isn't a very good submissive."

The bodyguard grunted from behind him as he carried a heavy bag and dumped it on the floor.

"At least that's one duty I can stop performing for him then. I don't get paid enough to listen to that sort of moaning."

Amy laughed, and he frowned at Matthew.

"You wish." He looked around. He had expected his mother to greet them. "Mum?" he called out.

"I bet she's gone out to get the ingredients for your favourite meal. She told me when I texted her earlier that she was going to cook it in celebration." Amy took her hand luggage from him while she spoke. "I'll put this in the bedroom and then make us a cup of tea. I don't know about you lot, but I don't think I've had a decent cup of tea for two weeks now. You need to look at that for your hotel." He smacked her bottom for her teasing.

"I'll have you know I've had the finest English teas imported. And this is in a country that's famous for making the stuff."

Amy glided along to the bedroom, he watched the seductive sashay of her hips. She was his woman. They'd be married soon and able to spend the rest of their lives happily together. He couldn't believe it. He needed to find a wedding planner for Amy straight away. He didn't want to wait for her to become Mrs North. He wondered if she'd consent to going to Gretna Green at the weekend and marrying there? His mother would kill him if he did. And so would his sister. She'd been planning her wedding for ages, and she had to be the first. He wanted to make sure Amy would never escape from him, though. Not that he thought she actually would want to go anywhere despite how annoying he could be at times. He placed his hand luggage down on the floor and began heading for the kitchen to put the kettle on for Amy, when he heard her scream. It was a bloodcurdling scream, one of sheer terror and panic. He turned quickly, and he and Matthew stormed for the bedroom. He almost skidded into Amy who was running from the bedroom.

"The bed" She was sobbing. "He has her."

All the covers had been torn from their bed. Blood covered them, and a massive knife was embedded in the centre of the mattress. He nodded to Matthew, and he went forward to look at it. James edged closer, next to the knife was a fingernail that had been pulled off someone. That's where the blood came from. He swallowed back the feelings of compounding unease. The knife was stabbed through a picture of his mother, gagged and bound to a chair. There was a note beside it. He looked to Matthew as the bodyguard picked it up. Amy was still sobbing in his arms.

"What does it say?" he asked.

"If you want her back, and not a piece at a time, you'll meet me and give me what I want. Come alone. My whore of a niece will tell you where."

He fought back the bile that was threatening to launch from his mouth with the thought that Amy's uncle had his mother and was hurting her. Why now? How did they get in here? This place was impenetrable. After Amy came to live here, he made sure of that with a thorough review of his security.

"We need to call the police?"

Amy lifted her head from his chest and spoke but still clung tightly to him.

"No." His tone was unwavering. "No police." He nodded to Matthew, "Go fetch everything we need. I'll meet you in the car in a few moments. Get Sonia in here now."

"You, you have to call the police. You can't go to him." Amy's big eyes stared up at him in panic. She thought he was crazy.

He picked the picture up, his hand was shaking with fury. "Where is she?"

"James."

"Where's my mother?" he shouted, his blood had reached boiling point. She backed timidly away from him.

"Call the police, and I'll tell them where she is. I'm not telling you, while you're in this frame of mind."

She turned away from him and refused to look at the picture anymore. He really didn't need her being stubborn right now. He needed to get to his mother and rip her fucking uncle's head off. He swung her back to face him. Probably a little too forcefully but all he could feel was the worry for his mother. His fingers dug into the delicate flesh of her arms.

"Stop messing around with me. I don't have the time for this. He said you could tell me where he has my mother. Now tell me." He positioned his face mere inches from Amy's.

"I don't want you going to him. He'll hurt you. Please. Please, call the police." Amy dared to reach up and touch his heaving chest. He could see that she was absolutely terrified, but he couldn't back down. His need to control had taken over him, and he needed to be pointed in the right direction to go kill.

"Your uncle had no qualms in killing his girlfriend, Sara. Remember her? He's a fucking psychopath. He was going to allow me to rape you. His own flesh and blood. Please, that man has my mother. I'll be okay. You have to trust me, alright? Please, Amy, tell me where he is, tell me where he has her."

He held the picture up to her face. Defeat washed over her, and she bowed her head. "It's a room in the club, furthest from the stage, to the right. It's called the 'night' room. It's where he has the girls who do the darkest stuff. Please, if you're going then I'm coming with you. He wants me. For whatever reason, he wants me."

He cupped her chin. She was shaking, tears streamed from her eyes. He needed to calm her down and reassure her before he left her alone. "He asked for me, not you. I made him lose face by taking you away the way I did. He thought he'd get ten thousand pounds. He got nothing. He'll want money. I'll give it to him, and this will all be over. You stay here and make that cup of tea. Mum will need it when I get her back."

"Is that what Matthew has gone to get? Money?"

"Yes. Matthew is getting him money. More than I promised him before."

Sonia coughed at the door. He kept his eyes focused on Amy, still trying to calm her down.

"Matthew is ready in the car, Sir."

"You stay here, Amy. I'll be okay. Sonia will be with you the entire time. I'll phone you as soon as I have my mother."

He saw her look to the door behind him, and her eyes widened with shock. She saw the gun that Sonia held for him. Shit! Sonia quickly tried to hide it, but it was too late.

"You're taking a gun." She whacked him in the chest and pushed him away.

"Calm down. It's for protection."

"You aren't going to give him money, are you? You're going to kill him." She ran her fingers through her hair and pulled on the ends.

"If he doesn't see sense, yes."

She pushed past him and headed for the telephone on the bedside table. He didn't have time to think. He ripped it from the wall.

"No police. This is personal, and I'll deal with it my own way."

"You're scaring me." Amy had flattened herself against the wall. Her eyes were bewildered as she tried to take everything in. Mere moments ago, they had returned from a romantic break full of love and excitement for their engagement, but now, now the world was falling apart around them.

"You think I haven't done something like this before? What do you think happened to the brothers? I made sure they wouldn't hurt anyone else with their misguided preaching. Why do you think I have an ex-spy as my personal protection?"

"You killed them?"

"No. I've never killed anyone. But I've had to take people to task before. Matthew trained me to be strong and protect myself. I have to go. We will talk more later. My family is my responsibility, and I won't let anyone hurt them and get away with it." He stroked her cheek, and she leaned into his caress despite being angry at him.

"You aren't going anywhere without me."

"I'm sorry." Her face registered too late what he was about to do, and he pushed her into the bedroom, slamming the door shut behind him. Sonia handed him a key, and he locked the door. "I'm so sorry."

His head rested against the door as her tiny fist pounded it from inside. He shut his eyes, composed himself, and turned to Sonia. "Stay with her. Don't let her out for any reason until I get back. If you do, you'll never work again in this country, even if you're fucking Matthew. Do you understand me?"

Sonia nodded. He took the gun from her, placed it into his jeans, and headed down to the garage to find Matthew. He was certain he could still hear Amy's screams when he reached the basement. He hoped she'd forgive him for this.

TWENTY-FOUR

Amy

Amy's hand hurt from thumping the heavy oak door. She fell to the floor, wiped the tears from her eyes, and sat there in disbelief. James had lost it and locked her in their bedroom. He was racing off to do god knows what and maybe even get himself killed. She had to stop him. He didn't know her uncle. Yes, in the past she had thought butter wouldn't melt in his mouth, but she had also seen the dark side of him. She had seen the damage that his hired thugs could do, like the time when a punter got out of hand at the club and left with broken limbs. She had to get to James.

"Sonia, you have to let me out. Please." She got to her feet and calmed her voice to speak through the door.

"I'm sorry. You know I can't do that." Sonia's voice was tempered with concern. Her bodyguard was also reeling from the rather unexpected welcome home.

" James is in trouble. He doesn't know what he's headed into. Please. Matthew will be in danger too. I've seen the way you look at him. I know that look. I wear it on my face all the time. Please, I love James so much if anything happened to him I wouldn't survive. Do you feel that way about Matthew?"

"Matthew will be level-headed the whole time. He'll know what he's doing. I want to let you out, but I can't. Take a seat and wait. It won't be long and we'll hear something. I'm sure of that."

"Wait for the police to come and tell me that my fiancé is dead? Not going to happen. I'll get myself out, even if I have to tie sheets together and climb out of the bedroom window."

She yelled out in frustration and smashed her fist into the door again. She saw her bag on the floor. Her mobile was in it. She could phone the police. She scrambled across the room and began to frantically pull all her belongings out. Where was it? Damn it. Why did she have so much rubbish in her handbag? When she finally found it, she hugged it to her chest and almost let out a squeal of jubilation. Until she turned the screen over to face her.

"No, No, No."

It was out of battery.

"What are you doing in there?"

Sonia's voice came through the door.

"Trying to sort this mess out since you won't help me."

"Whatever you're doing, stop it. Please? Just wait."

"Open the door and stop me then."

She got to her feet and went to James's side of the bed. He kept a spare iPhone charger plugged into the wall there. She quickly plugged the phone in and waited, not very patiently, for it to charge.

"Come on you damn thing. Work."

How long had James been gone? Ten? Fifteen minutes? He'd be there soon. She didn't have much time.

Hurry up, hurry up.

" Please, just be patient." Sonia's voice was desperate now.

"Patient? Like fuck. Do you know what my uncle is capable of? He's the reason you're employed to protect me."

" Lock yourself in the bathroom" Sonia screamed her name and advice this time. A thud came from the other side of the door.

"Sonia?" She stepped towards the door. No sound came from the other side.

"Sonia?" she shouted louder and ran to the door. The key turned, and it opened.

Sonia lay on the floor. Dead? Unconscious? She didn't know. She looked up and into the dead eyes of two of her uncle's thugs. She had to think quickly. She couldn't get out of the bedroom, and hiding in the bathroom wasn't an option.

The knife. Matthew left it on the bed. She made a dash for it and grabbed it, just as one of the men caught her around the waist. She turned and slashed at his face. He screamed out in pain and let her go. Blood spurted from a gash which tore down his stubbled cheek.

"Stay away from me," she yelled.

"Fucking bitch." A stocky man with a rather pissed off look responded.

"You touch me, and I won't hesitate to use this knife."

"Don't be so stupid. Your uncle just wants a little chat." The other man spoke and strode confidently into the room. His hands were held high in supplication.

"Where's James's mother? If you've hurt her…" She looked towards the finger-nail on the bed.

"We only took one."

The man who didn't have blood pouring from his face lunged for her, but she slashed at his arm and managed to dash for the door. She wanted to check on Sonia, but she didn't have time. She had to get to the club. She sped through the hallway and noticed the keys for the Audi on the side table. She grabbed them and headed down the stairs to the garage. Her heart was beating so fast she could hear it in her head. Footsteps echoed on the floor above. She stumbled on the stairs but managed to grab hold of the banister to keep herself upright. She tore into the garage and clicked the keys for the Audi. It opened, and she jumped in and started the engine. She had never driven this thing. It had so many different buttons. She wanted the button that allowed her to go. She found drive, pressed it, and floored the accelerator as the two thugs hurtled down into the garage. She clipped one of them as she sped past. His body flew off the bonnet and landed with a sickening crunch on the floor. She didn't have time to worry if she'd killed him. The garage door was, thankfully, still open and she emerged onto the street above.

A car pulled in front of her. She slammed on the brakes and whacked her head on the steering wheel. She tried to reverse but couldn't. She was trapped. The feeling of failure began to constrict in her stomach. The door was flung open and her uncle's head guard, Leon, appeared. He pulled her from the vehicle like a rag doll.

Leon was the only guard with half a brain. He was strong, devious, and liked to get his own way. There'd been many a time in the club that she had seen him hit some of the girls if they'd done something wrong. He was also well known for taking pleasure from the girls, whether they wanted to or not.

"Miss Jones, can we stop with the feeble escape attempts now? If you want to see your lover alive again, I'd come quietly."

She kicked him in the shin, but she couldn't get herself free. She was screaming, hoping that someone would hear something and call the police if she could stall them for long enough.

She stilled immediately, however, when a gun was pointed at her head.

"Come on Leon, let me shoot the bitch."

"Boss wants her alive. We won't get our payoff if she's dead. I'll let you play with her afterwards though. She always did think she was better than the rest of us," he sneered.

"I heard the rumours that your dick was so small it wasn't worth worrying about," she retorted.

He whacked his calloused hand hard across her face. She tasted blood in her mouth. He then pulled her face towards him and held her tight.

"I'll show you how much satisfaction I can give. Maybe a little display in front of your lover?" She spat in his face. Leon threw her at the other thug, whose face she'd slashed. "Get her in the car. Somebody may have already called the police. We need to get out of here."

"What about Jase? She hit him with the car."

"Is he alive?"

"No idea."

"Let's hope he isn't. Now get her in the car."

She was thrown forward and into the car that she had crashed into. She needed to relax, keep her calm, and use her brain. She knew her uncle better than anyone. He must have a weakness. What was it?

TWENTY-FIVE

James

"Are you sure about this, Boss?" Matthew pulled the car up outside the club. "He isn't like anyone you've faced before."

"He has my mother." That was the only answer that James could give.

"He's also your fiancée's uncle."

He gripped the dashboard tightly; his knuckles were white with fury. Matthew would do as he was asked, even if he felt James was going about it the wrong way.

He checked the gun, handed it to Matthew, and got out of the car. "Wait here. I'll sound the alarm, when I need you. Get my mother out first. I'll get myself out."

"As you wish, Sir."

Matthew turned the engine off and waited, eagle-eyed, as instructed. James hated this bit His palms were sweating. They'd only done this a couple of times together. He really hadn't lied to Amy when he said that he hadn't killed anyone. He hadn't, but Matthew had. On his say so.

On leaving the hospital, after the beating, he'd had Matthew follow the brothers. One night, they discovered them about to attack a gentleman outside a gay club. They prevented the attack and dispensed their own justice on the brothers. Matthew killed the older of the two. The other brother they forced to leave the country for good, and he wouldn't walk properly again.

So this was nothing new to them, but it felt so much more personal. His mum was everything to him. She'd supported him through so much. He wasn't about to let anything happen to her. Amy was his future, and the thought that the man doing this was related to her made matters even worse. He knew that no matter what happened, Amy was going to end up hurt—better emotionally, though, than physically.

He entered the club and was immediately frisked by a bodyguard, his phone was taken away, and he was led down the corridor to the back. The club was empty. He was shown into a dark room. Knives, whips, and chains were on the wall. His mum was in the centre of it. He ran to her and checked her. She was crying, and her hand was covered in blood. Somebody would pay for this. She pulled away from him. She was blindfolded and had headphones over her ears. She didn't know it was him. He went to remove them, but a voice behind him spoke. "I wouldn't do that Mr North. She tends to scream a lot when you remove the blindfold. I wish I'd taken her tongue instead of a nail. Mind you, it wasn't as bad when I was fucking her, pretending to be her loving boyfriend."

He slowly stood up, his fists clenched, and he exhaled sharply to keep his composure. He spun to face Amy's uncle and three guards.

"So that's how you got in my house. Clever. Name your price. I'll pay. Then I can get home to my fiancée, and we can forget you ever existed. My driver is in my car, and I can send him to get it."

"Oh no, Mr North, this has gone so much further than that. You see, I found something out. Those papers I sent to you in India for Amy to sign? Well, they're worthless."

He swallowed hard. Something he thought was over and forgotten was coming back to haunt him.

"Worthless? They handed the club over to you, which is what you wanted. And Amy doesn't know that she even owned it in the first place."

"Yes, she can't sell the club. A stipulation of her father's will, not until she's twenty-five. And I'm sure you can appreciate that I'm not willing to wait that long." Amy's uncle rolled his eyes.

"I'll get my lawyers to look into it at once. She doesn't have to know about that. She thinks you're out of her life. She doesn't want you back."

"No. That isn't enough anymore. I've waited long enough, and as it seems that things are very serious between you and my niece, why shouldn't I profit from it? I want ten million."

"I don't have that money lying around." James raised an eyebrow in derision.

"I've researched your finances, and I know you can access your money at any time. I could however, take a down payment until you can get the rest to me. I'll post one piece of your mother back to you each day until I get what I want. I'm thinking a finger next. What do you say?"

"I won't be able to get that sort of money from here. Let me send my bodyguard in to stay with my mother, and I'll go get the money."

Amy's uncle rubbed his head. "Micky. Remove Mrs North's finger. It seems Mr North is determined to play with us."

Micky moved towards his mother with a knife in his hand. James moved his hands together, as if to plead, and pressed a button on his watch signalling Matthew to come in and put an end to all this. He just needed to buy a little more time.

"No. Please. If I take that much money out of my accounts, the system's designed to trigger alarms. I need to do it in person. I'm not messing with you. I wouldn't risk my mother. Please." He kept his voice deliberately calm.

He moved forward to try and distract the guard who had the gun pointed at him. The guard put the gun down and went to grab him. He allowed himself to be restrained. Matthew appeared and, with one quick shot, fired a bullet through Mickey's head. Matthew turned the gun on the guard beside Amy's uncle and shot him in the leg before he could get a clear aim at either him or his mother. James flipped the guard, who was holding him in place, over his shoulder and rammed him head first into the wall. The guard slumped to the ground. James grabbed the gun from the table, while Matthew knocked the other guard out. Both he and Matthew then turned their guns on Amy's uncle, ready to shoot. But something was wrong.

He didn't look scared. In fact, he still wore a confident smile on his face.

"Matthew, untie my mother and get her out of here."

Matthew nodded and removed the blindfold.

"Do you even know how to use that gun?" Stephen Jones was taunting him, but he responded by cocking the pistol and pointed it squarely at Amy's uncle's forehead.

"I may be a simple businessman, but unfortunately, I've seen enough fuckers like you in my life to need to know how to protect myself."

"You ever killed any of them, though? Isn't that what he's for?" He raised his eyebrows towards Matthew.

"We shall see very shortly won't we?"

"We will. Because you won't be killing me here, today. You'll be giving me what I asked for."

"Are you an idiot?"

"No but it would seem you are. And a predictable one at that."

"What's that supposed to mean?"

Matthew appeared at his side with his mother.

"Let's go, Boss."

"Oh, I wouldn't." Amy's uncle laughed with a cackle. "Our party is just beginning. I'd suggest you drop the guns." His eyes flicked towards the back of the room. Matthew turned his head, whilst he kept his eyes boring into the evil before him. Matthew sighed and bent to put his gun on the ground and kicked it away.

"Boss, drop the weapon."

He spun around.

Amy stood before him, her hands cuffed behind her back, a bump on her head, and blood staining her mouth. Next to her stood a man who held her tightly, whispering in her ear so that Amy's face screwed up in revulsion. He didn't need to lip read to know what was being said, especially when the man licked Amy's face. Tears tumbled down her face. To the other side of her stood a man with a gun at her head. He pointed his own gun down and bent to lay it on the floor. It had all been a trap. His mother was a ruse to allow them to take the real prize. The woman he loved more than anything. He'd vowed to protect her, but he'd failed. He needed to get his head straight, but he couldn't. His need to control would destroy everything. It already had.

TWENTY-SIX

Amy

Amy recoiled when Leon licked her face. He'd been touching her and insinuating all sorts of lewd things on the way to the club. She wanted nothing more than to smack him in his tiny balls.

James put the gun down and stood with his hands up. The guard with the weapon at her head gave his gun to Leon and stepped forward to collect the ones Matthew and James had placed on the ground. Her uncle's guards were rapidly dwindling, two lay unconscious on the floor, one lay dead from a bullet to his forehead, and the one she had injured disappeared for medical attention the second they dropped her there. He probably went back to collect his mate, who she'd run over. She tried to remember how many other guards were around. She thought this was it. The guard with the guns placed them on a table. At her uncle's command, he then strapped Matthew into a set of chains on the wall. They knew he was the one to watch. Miranda kept close to his side.

She looked at James, and she could see that he was lost again. She'd seen that fear before. He was suffering. He'd seen that Amy was hurt and shut himself down because he blamed himself for causing her pain. She needed to bring him back, and the only way she could do that was by being the strong one as she'd been in the past. This was how their relationship worked. When one needed the other, they were always there for them.

She was shoved roughly down into a chair. The handcuffs at her back rubbed against her wrists; they were tearing the skin and causing bleeding. She made a note that if she ever tried handcuffs with James they'd be fur-lined.

Her uncle barked out another order, which made her jump. Leon came back around to her side and pointed the gun at her temple again.

"Now, I have your full attention, Mr North? After your wilful attempts at escape, I now have funeral costs and medical bills to cover. I think I'll have to increase the amount that I require from you. And I'd suggest you waste no more time in trying to delay the inevitable. I want twenty million in my account in the next half hour. Or..." He pointed toward Leon, "I'll let you watch as my associate here takes whatever he wants from my niece. And believe me, he's some very peculiar tastes that tend to leave his ladies a little broken." Leon cracked his knuckles in her ear, and she felt sick.

"Get me my phone. I'll show you how to transfer the money to whatever account you want. It'll be done in moments." She knew the tone in James's voice. He was waiting for what he now saw as the inevitable. His death or hers. Her uncle sent the only other guard in the room, who was conscious, to get James's phone. While they waited, her uncle strode up to her and patted her cheek.

"So naive, so pretty. Such a waste. You were too much like him." She turned her head away. She didn't want to be touched by this man. She wanted him to rot in hell. He pulled it back and gripped her tightly by the chin. "You know; you're just like your whore of a mother. She was always playing hard to get, but the reality was she loved it rough."

The moment of clarity that she needed hit. Her uncle had fancied her mother, but she'd chosen her father. She had her advantage, and she was damn well going to use it.

"I'm surprised you wanted me around if you felt that badly towards my mother. After all, everyone always said I was the spitting image of her when she was my age. Were you trying to make me into the whore you thought she was?"

He laughed out loud and pulled her towards him and away from Leon. Leon stepped to the side and pointed his gun at James's head. James still stood silent and in his own world.

"Your mother *was* a whore. How do you think we met her? She was one of the girls at the club. Entrapped your fucking father with her feminine ways. Got him to marry her, the money-grabbing bitch. She went for the brother with the bigger share of the fortune."

"You know that isn't true. She wanted nothing to do with this place. It's why we moved out to Essex."

"No, you moved because nobody would accept she was the Boss. And she sweet talked your father into giving up his business and his blood family."

"You don't mean that."

"Yes, I do."

She screamed at him, "You agreed to their marriage. You gave your blessing. You were my dad's best man."

"You think I had a choice? Your dad had all the control. I did what he wanted, or I was out. Your mum had him wound around her little finger so tightly that he didn't know the truth from reality anymore."

"That's complete bullshit."

"For fuck's sake. Wake up. You know it's the truth."

She was struggling. She did know the truth, not the twisted version that her uncle had painted in his mind. She shut her eyes. She needed to calm this down. The fighting was making them both angrier, and it wasn't shaking James from his sorrows. She quietened her voice and forced the tears out of her eyes.

"We had a conversation about you one day. Mum and dad had a big argument.

He stormed out. She said she wondered what her life would have been like if she'd married someone else. I asked her who, and she told me you."

"She'd have been treated like a princess. She'd have been the centre of my world."

"I thought she was to my father. I guess I saw nothing that went on behind their closed bedroom door. It was all hidden from me."

The guard returned to the room with James's phone and handed it to her uncle.

"You know how your parents died don't you?"

"A car accident." They'd skidded over the central reservation and into the path of a lorry coming the other way.

"The police report stated that it seemed as though they'd been arguing. The cameras caught a heated discussion between them on the lead up to the point of the accident. The camera at the point of the crash showed your mother's hands, as well as your father's, on the wheel. It looked as though she'd grabbed it. She caused the accident. She was responsible for the death of my brother."

She turned her head away again and began to cry. This time, though, her pain was for real. James lifted his head. Was he coming back to her?

"No. No." She screamed the last no in the desperate hope that it penetrated James's befuddled mind.

"I'm sorry. It's the truth. I'll show you the police reports if you want." Police reports, police report... James had researched her, had he seen these reports? Had he kept the truth from her? Her heart was ripping apart. She could feel it tearing in two. Out of the corner of her eye, she saw Matthew move his hand. He'd freed himself from the chains. She needed to get her hands free as well. She was no use as she was.

"Uncle Stephen, will you unchain me, please? It doesn't have to be this way." She looked down at the phone. "I'll ask James to help you out. He'll do it for me. You've suffered as much as I have. My mother is at fault here. She killed my father and has destroyed us both." Her uncle hesitated. "Please. At least Dad left you the club. You can make it great without her interference. James could invest in it. We could do something great with it together. Please. It doesn't have to be this way. I want you in my life. You're the only family that I have."

The solemn expression on her uncle's face changed. The corners of his mouth curled upwards, and he began to laugh out loud. A cackle that made her jump. He grabbed her and shoved her to the floor.

"I want twenty million pounds. And your fiancé, over there, is going to give it to me."

"What do you need money for? You own this club."

"I don't own this fucking club. You do. Your father left the whole thing to you in his will. And you're lying, deceiving boyfriend, well he tried to sell it to me, without your knowledge. So you see, you're just the same as your mother. A deluded little whore."

She opened her mouth to speak to James, but she noticed the expression on his face had changed. Gone was the defeat, and back was the murderous intent. This was something she could work with...but at what cost to their relationship?

TWENTY-SEVEN

James

The sound of Amy's anguished cry permeated the hazy fog that had become James's brain. She was suffering, and he had to stop it. That was his duty to her. He looked up and saw that she was bent over a table, and a man was on top of her. He lunged forward, but a gun was pointed at his head. He stilled.

He looked to see where Matthew was and got the sign from him that he was free and ready.

Amy had tears tumbling down her face. What was that man doing to her?

She looked at him. "Is that right?"

Her uncle turned.

James nodded. He needed to be honest. He couldn't lie now. He had promised her he'd never do that again.

Her uncle laughed, and he wanted to rip his stinking head from his body and feed it to the lions in London Zoo.

"Just as I thought. You didn't even know that you owned the club. He never told you. God. I figured I was good at keeping you in the dark. But your own lover? Is that how he made his millions? Stealing off his dumb blonde girlfriends?"

"I never lied to her."

"You never told me the truth, either," Amy spat. He stumbled backwards. Her eyes were full of daggers.

"You didn't need to know. You were away from the club. Matthew was keeping an eye on everything to ensure that he didn't do any damage to your name. I was protecting you."

"Protecting or controlling?" Amy turned her head and pushed against Leon. "Will you let me up, creep? I'm not here for you to rub your sad little erection all over." Amy's uncle nodded, and Leon reluctantly pulled her up. He didn't move too far from her, though. "So did I get any income out of this club I'm supposed to own, or have you both pocketed that for yourselves?"

"You got money. You really think a dancer earned what you got paid for, pretty much, doing nothing? You want to make money in this club, you have to give the clients a bit more special attention."

"Or you'd sell them to the highest bidder," she sneered.

"You know I don't need any money you earn. I was letting your uncle keep everything. I wanted your name away from the club. I wanted that man away from you."

"Isn't that something that I had a right to decide for myself, James?" She turned to her uncle, "And as for you, if this truly is my club, then I guess you can knock the value off the money you want from James."

"You can't sell it."

"What? Why? I don't want it."

"It can't be sold until you're twenty-five, apparently. But I'll get my solicitors to work on it, if that's what you want."

"Oh great. I'm stuck with the local brothel. That's perfect. I can see the headline news now. 'Billionaire's girlfriend is local Madame'. Sally Bridgewater will love that one." She turned her head to look at the guy behind her. "Will you stand back? I know you get your kicks from rubbing your tiny dick against women, but I'd rather you keep it to yourself."

He watched the man's face redden, and then he grabbed her around the throat. He rushed forward, but Amy's uncle lunged straight for him and smacked him down on the table. Amy was thrust down next to him. They were millimetres from each other.

"Enough." Her uncle's voice came in a tone of finality. "I'm getting rather bored. I want my money, now." He brought James's phone close to his face. "And then, this ends here. Mr North, transfer the money."

"One thing, first." Amy struggled to get her words out.

"No, enough. The money."

"You're going to kill us the second you get the money, so let me die knowing this one final thing."

"What." Amy's uncle spat his answer at her.

"What was the date that I signed the papers?"

No, she didn't need to know that. "Please."

"No, I want to know."

"How are you two supposed to be in love? You have done nothing but fight since you entered the room. Alright. I don't know the exact date, but it was when you were in India."

"India?" Amy looked into James's eyes, and he could see her heart breaking. He knew what was coming next. "Was it before or after we talked?"

"Please, if this is to be our final moments, let's not do this."

"Before or after?" She was shaking and her demanding eyes bore into him.

"After."

He watched as she shut her eyes. She was breaking down before him, and he couldn't hold her. He wasn't sure she'd let him anyway. "I love you. I only ever wanted you to be safe."

Amy kept her eyes shut and didn't answer him.

"Hey Boss, while he transfers the money, can I show her what a real man can do to her?" He looked up and saw a malicious grin on, the soon-to-be dead, Leon's face. If only he could figure a way out of this.

"Go for it. It will provide some entertainment, and I bet it makes Mr North transfer the money a bit quicker. I wonder if she'll scream as much as Sara did when we all took turns with her?"

He tried to struggle as he watched the man pull up Amy's skirt. He was too heavily pinned down. Was he really going to have to see her so utterly destroyed? Amy's uncle pulled him up and handed him the phone.

"Transfer the money, now, or I let him have a go. I might even throw your mother in as well." He motioned towards the guard by Matthew and his mother.

Amy kicked back out at the man about to rape her and smacked him hard in the balls. Leon stumbled backwards and groaned loudly. Amy slid to the floor. Leon grabbed his gun and pointed it at her.

"Fucking bitch. You're dead."

A gunshot rang out, and a bright red dot of blood appeared on Leon's forehead. He gurgled and fell to the floor. James turned his head towards the direction of the shot and saw Sonia stumble into the room. She had a cut above her eye, where she'd obviously been attacked. She was swaying, so he guessed she'd been knocked unconscious. From behind him came another groan of agony, as Matthew, who'd freed himself, sideswiped the guard that was standing beside him and ran him into the wall.

James was standing next to Amy's uncle, so he lashed out with his elbow and sent the old man flying to the floor. He launched himself around the table and grabbed Amy. He needed to check she was alright. He pulled back the hair that was over her face. She had dried blood on her mouth.

"Amy. Look at me."

"Is it over?"

"Yes, beautiful. You won't be hurt now."

"James." The panicked call from Matthew came from behind him. He saw the gun on the table, grabbed it and spun around. Amy's uncle had gotten to his feet and pointed a gun at them.

"What were you saying about this being over?"

He followed the trajectory of the gun's aim straight to Amy. He pulled back the trigger of his gun. Falling sideways as he shot, he pushed Amy out of the way. His shot hit her uncle and ripped through his chest. The old man stumbled forward, dropping his gun. Matthew tackled him to the ground. Blood frothed at Amy's uncle's mouth. He suddenly registered a searing agony from his side. He clutched at it, as he landed on the floor and rolled onto his back. A crack came from the other side of the table as Matthew broke Amy's uncle's neck. He could barely register it, though. His head was spinning, and everything was turning cloudy. The pain in his side was travelling and burning. He pulled his hand away from his side and held it up. It was covered in blood. He could hear Amy hysterically screaming and screaming. Matthew appeared at his side and placed his hand hard onto where it was hurting him. His head started spinning more, as he heard calls for an ambulance. All the time everything was growing darker. Amy came to his ear and was pleading, pleading for him to hold on, to live. He tried to answer her, but nothing came out. The pain was so intense he couldn't take it anymore. Darkness engulfed him, and everything went silent.

TWENTY-EIGHT

Amy

The ambulance seemed to take an age to weave through the London traffic. Amy wanted to scream at everyone to get out of their way, but instead, she stayed silent and watched the paramedic work on James. He was pale, because he'd lost a lot of blood. Her hands were stained with it. His top had been ripped away, and all these things stuck to his chest. Machines beeped around him, but James lay there silently. He hadn't regained consciousness. As they pulled into the A&E emergency bay, the ambulance doors were flung open, and the trolley that James was on was wheeled out. Doctors crowded around him and began to discuss his vital signs. She felt so helpless. She wanted to make him better, but she had to let the doctors do their jobs. All she could do was pray.

James was wheeled straight into the resuscitation room. She was stopped from following, so she stood there as the doors closed on her. She was still crying. Her mouth and her head were both hurting, and she was shaking. What did she do now? How long before she could see him again? What were they doing in there? Why couldn't she be in there with him? Did he know she wasn't there? Was he upset?

A nurse came over to her and put a hand on her shoulder. She jumped.

"Miss Jones, is it? Please, I won't hurt you."

She sobbed in response.

"Please, come this way. I've a room you can wait in." She suddenly became aware of the faces of those waiting to be seen all watching her. The nurse, again, placed a hand on Amy to guide her. "I'll get you a nice cup of tea. You look like you need one. I think some ice for that lip as well. We should get a doctor to check that bump on your head."

She allowed herself to be directed to a room. She was numb. "What are they doing to him?"

"They're trying to stabilise him. His blood pressure fell in the ambulance, and his heartbeat is erratic. They're worried about the damage the bullet did."

"Will he be alright?"

"Honey, I'm going to be honest with you. I don't know. We need to let the doctors do their thing."

She let out a shuddering breath, as she nodded her acceptance of what the nurse was saying. The nurse helped her to sit. The room smelt of cleaning fluid. The whole place did. The fact she was in a hospital was beginning to sink in. Everything still seemed so scattered in her brain. The gunshots were still ringing in her head.

"Thank you."

"I'll get you that tea, and I'll get a doctor to come and look at you here as well. You may need a CT scan on that bump, but we will see what he says."

She turned away and looked at the door. Her right hand rubbed over the diamond of her engagement ring on her left. She felt like she was in a nightmare. It was hard to even process everything that had happened.

She felt like it had been days since she'd slept. It probably was, actually. They'd left the Maldives early in the morning, and the flight had been a long one.

A doctor returned with the nurse and her cup of tea. He examined her and asked her loads of questions. She may have answered them correctly; she may not have. She really didn't know, but he seemed satisfied and said that, as she hadn't blacked out, she could be observed while they waited for news of Mr North. The door was suddenly flung open, and Matthew, Miranda, and Sonia entered the room. The doctor immediately went to Sonia. She was virtually being carried by Matthew and still appeared to be dizzy. The doctor demanded that she be admitted straight away and sent for a scan. The nurse and the doctor then hurried away with her. Matthew tried to go with the female bodyguard, but Sonia demanded that he stayed with Amy. Matthew did as he was told. Another nurse then came and took Miranda for examination. This left her and Matthew alone in the waiting room.

"Have they said anything?"

"They're stabilising him. We're to wait."

"I hate these places."

She turned her head to look at him. Her eyelids were heavy.

"I suppose, in your line of work, it's one place you never want to see."

"Yeah. Means we have failed in our duty."

"You didn't fail. It was an intense situation."

"He'll be alright. It's probably the blood loss causing the trouble."

"Are you always this casual afterwards?"

"After what?"

"Killing someone?"

"Your uncle?" he asked.

She swallowed and met Matthew's eyes for the first time. They were red-rimmed, and he looked tired. She saw in that instant that nothing he'd done was easy for him. "I'm sorry. He deserved it."

"Nobody deserves death. I don't make the decision to take someone's life lightly. I ended your uncle's life, because he was already dying. James's shot may have hit the mark, but it wasn't going to be a quick death. Snapping his neck ended it with less pain and fear."

"You should have let him suffer. He wouldn't have done the same for you."

"You don't mean that."

"Don't I?"

"No, you have an amazingly kind heart, and you saved James. He was on a path to total destruction, but your love and perseverance with him have made him an entirely different man."

"You really think that?"

"I do."

"So why did he lie to me?"

"Because he loves you and wanted to protect you from what you were too naive to understand."

"Naive." She got to her feet and walked to the small window. She leaned against the frame. It was cold to touch and made her shiver slightly. "So you think I'm a child as well."

"No. I don't. I believe you're wiser than you give yourself credit for. I do, however, think you choose not to see things. You worked in a brothel for a year. You must have known what went on? What about signing stuff for the club? Did you never have to sign anything for your uncle?"

She turned back to face him.

"You're right. I knew what went on. I chose to believe the best of my uncle. I wasn't forced to do it, so I ignored it. And there were times I signed things. I never read them. I always believed what he told me. I trusted him. Just the same as I trusted James."

"This was never malicious on James's part. I promise you. He wanted to protect you from being hurt. He hated seeing you in pain. The night in the club when he had to show you that video. It killed him. I saw him punishing himself that day and every day afterwards until you forgave him. You're his world."

"You know, if he had told me I would've told him to sell the club. I don't want that sort of place."

"I know. I think he knows that as well." She looked down at her engagement ring again. So much had happened in such a short space of time, and she didn't just mean the events of that day. She'd only known James for a few months. She felt like she was drowning in it all. "What are you going to do?" Matthew got up from his chair and came over to her. He touched the engagement ring.

"I don't know." She loved James so much. But it was as if everything was too intense. One thing after another kept coming at her. She needed to slow it down. She needed to find her own pace, and even her own breath again.

Matthew brought her into his arms and comforted her. It was the first time since her father died that she felt like she was being watched over with a familial warmth. She mumbled into Matthew's jacket.

"Can I ask you something?" She brought her head up so she could see his reaction. "What my uncle said about the way my parents died. Do you know if it was true?"

He sighed.

"I've seen the police reports. There was no indication they were fighting. I spoke to an associate of mine about the accident." He paused. "All indications pointed to the fact that your uncle had them murdered. But it couldn't be proven. Your mum was never supposed to be in that car. The meeting they were heading to was supposed to be between your uncle and your father. It was meant to be about your father selling his half of the club to your uncle. She didn't want him to go through that alone, it would seem, and so she went with him. They died together, very much in love."

She went silent; she couldn't speak. Her brain was unable to process any more information.

The door opened, and a doctor came in.

"Miss Jones?"

"How is he?" She jumped to her feet.

"He is stable and awake. We've moved him to a private room. He's asking for you."

"Oh, thank god." Amy brought her still-bloody hands to her face to stifle the relieved sobs.

"I'll take you to him now if you wish?"

"Yes, please." She turned back to Matthew. "Thank you. You should go find Miranda and tell her. Go be with Sonia afterwards. She needs you."

"I will."

She nodded at him and then followed the doctor to where James was.

The room was sterile and cold. Machines surrounded James and beeped in time with his heart beat. He had a drip in his arm and another one feeding blood into him. He still looked pale. He had his eyes shut, but as soon as she closed the door, he opened them and looked at her.

"Amy." His voice was croaky and weak.

"I'm here." She came beside the bed and took his hand.

"I love you."

"I love you, too." Her voice broke.

"What happened?"

"We're all safe. My uncle...he is dead." James groaned and shut his eyes again. "Your mum will be here soon. A nurse took her to assess her injuries."

"I'm sorry."

"You need to rest. Now isn't the time to talk. Get some sleep. I'll go home and change then come back and sit with you."

"Don't leave me."

Please. I'm covered in blood. I need a shower."

"I shouldn't have got you to sign that paper."

"Not now." Her voice was breaking.

"I need to know you forgive me. Please."

She pulled her hand away from his and turned away. She couldn't do this now. Everything was still so confusing.

"I'm going to go and change."

"Don't walk out on me." His tone was pleading but also had the air of control in it.

"Please."

"Look at me."

Her body betrayed her, and she turned around. "I can't, I can't do this now."

"Tell me that you forgive me for what I did. I won't do it again. You have my word. I'll change. I love you so much."

She brought her hands up to her face and covered her eyes as she started shaking her head. "Oh god, I'm so confused." She was shaking.

"You need to sleep. Everything will be better tomorrow. I'll come home. We can go to my country estate for a while and rest. I think I'll need some time to recover from this."

"No."

"We need time. Everything has been a big shock. You have been through so much today."

"No. It isn't that." She looked down at her engagement ring and took it off her finger. She placed it on his chest, tears now streaming down her face.

"Stop it. Don't be silly. Come here and put your ring back on. You aren't going to do this." The machine next to him started beeping as his heart rate accelerated.

She leaned over the bed and kissed his lips. He tried to move his arms to pull her back to him, but he was sluggish from all the drugs, and she evaded him.

"Lanzarote, James. Lanzarote."

To Be Continued......

PART TWO
DIVIDED CONTROL

ONE

Amy

Six months later.

"You need to point your toes when you spin to the left. It makes the movement seem more fluid as if you're water flowing over the floor. Roll your arms more from the wrists."

"Like this, Miss?"

"A little bit more. Feel the music; become lost in it. Shut your eyes. Let it flow through you, and your body will respond."

The sixteen-year-old performed the move again, this time perfectly.

"Yes, yes, just like that."

She jumped for joy, and Amy stepped back proudly. She'd been working with her for a couple of months in preparation for her audition at a dance academy. It was fantastic to see the way her pupil was developing, and she was sure Emily would easily pass the test.

"Well done. We're done for the day. Go home and get some rest. Feet up. Lots of carbohydrates. You'll need it for tomorrow. You'll do brilliantly, though. I can feel it. Break a leg." They both giggled.

"Thank you, Miss Amy. You've been so wonderful. I'll text you tomorrow to let you know how it went."

"Please do. I'll be anxious until I hear."

It had been two months since she opened the dance school. It took about four months to convert the club into a suitable venue for a school. She had to redecorate and disinfect so many of the rooms, although the dark room at the back remained sealed up. She never went in there. Some of the smaller rooms were rented out to music teachers and after-school clubs. She kept the stage area as it was, to rent out to local groups who wanted it for their own performances. She would also plan an end-of-term display for all her students.

She had worked night and day on this project. It was all she had left. It hadn't been easy. People knew what the club had once been. They knew about the deaths that occurred there, and it took a lot of word of mouth and advertising just to get people in the door.

She was sleeping in one of the back rooms, so that she was still able to rent out her flat and use the income to put into the school. Her uncle's patrons hadn't taken kindly to the change, either, and she'd had to pay out a lot to the previous employees to ensure that they didn't cause trouble.

It hadn't been easy.

At first, she'd thrown herself into the work just to stop crying. She was utterly destroyed by the events on the day James was shot. She tried not to think of him, but he always seemed to come into her mind when she least expected it, and she would break down.

Elena, her qualified teacher, tried to get her to go to clubs with her, or even just down to the pub for a drink, but she wasn't ready. She said she'd lost all her confidence, but the reality was she was still very much in love with James. She saw him on the news and in newspapers. He was busy working on his hotels. A few weeks ago, he was photographed out clubbing with two girls. The heading stated he was 'back on the market' and was certainly enjoying himself. She didn't even get out of bed that day.

"How'd Emily do?" Elena interrupted her thoughts.

"She did well. I think she's finally ready. She'll ace the audition."

"Brilliant. You should really start your teaching exams. You're a natural dancer. You don't need me apart from the qualifications bit."

"You want to leave me already?"

"Well no, just saying." Elena came and gave her a big cuddle. "Right. I'm not going to take no for an answer today. I'm going out tonight dancing, and you're coming with me."

"Lena, no."

"No arguments. You're twenty-one, and you need to live more. Come on, let's get you some clothes to wear."

Elena dragged her through the club to the room that was used for a bedroom. The teacher opened the small wardrobe she had and sighed.

"Is that it? You've like three outfits."

She had walked out of James's life with her bank card and the clothes she had on. Clothes that were covered in blood and had to be thrown away.

"Sorry. I'll just put my PJ's on and relax in front of the TV instead."

"No, you won't. You can come to my apartment. We're a similar size, so you can wear something of mine."

"El...," she began but didn't get to finish before she was dragged from the room and towards the doors of the club. Part of her wanted to run back and lock herself in her bedroom, but she had to begin living again.

Four hours later, in the night club and on their second drinks, she was actually enjoying herself. She felt a bit overdone—her hair had been pulled and twisted into an elaborate style; she had more makeup on than she usually wore, and the skirt Elena had chosen for her ... well ... she wouldn't be bending over in it anytime soon. Not unless she was prepared for the whole club to see everything that it barely covered.

Elena downed a Jägerbomb. "Come on, let's show these people how you actually dance to this."

She looked at Elena's friends. "Is she always this excitable in a club?"

They all nodded in unison. A brunette, Samantha, shouted over the music, "She downs the drinks and then dances them off. Never gets a hangover."

"Unlike you, Sammy," Elena teased.

"True, but then, I look like a grandma when I dance."

They all laughed again.

"Come on, please."

"Alright, I'm coming. But if I break my ankle in your sky-high shoes then you'll have to take all my classes for a month."

"You won't." Elena started to groove with the music as they both headed to the dance floor and began to perform a bit of a routine to the song. People around them started clapping. The tune finished, and Elena drifted off into her own world when the next one came on. Amy did the same.

For the first time in months, she was happy and relaxed. She was glad she allowed Elena to bring her here. From behind her, a pair of masculine hands slid around her hips. She turned to look at the guy. He was cute. She smiled and slowed the rhythmic movement of her hips in time with his. She was single even if she didn't feel like it. She might as well enjoy herself.

His hands gripped tighter. She gyrated against him. One song flowed into another, and she became lost in the freedom of the beat.

Then a voice sent shivers down her spine. "Get your fucking hands off her."

She swung around to see James grab the guy that she was dancing with and pull him off her. The guy pushed James back.

"Get lost, loser."

She jumped between them and pressed her hand against James's broad chest. Her betraying body sparked with energy from his closeness.

"Wait your turn. I'm going to fuck her first." The man she'd been dancing with ordered.

She turned back to the now not-so-cute guy. "What did you say?"

"Come on, babe. You're begging for it."

"You think I'm going to sleep with you?"

"Nobody dances like that unless they are asking for my rock-hard cock inside them."

People around them began to give them some space.

"Please, can I, Amy?" James spoke from behind her.

"You're asking my permission?" she questioned.

"I know, and I've only had one beer."

"Only one. You must be getting old. Be my guest."

And with that, she turned on her heel and left the dance floor. Elena stopped her,

"Is that *the* James?"

"Yes, it is. I've had a good night, but I'm going to grab a taxi home. I'll catch you tomorrow."

"I'll come with you."

"No, you stay and enjoy yourself. I'll text you when I'm home."

"If you're sure."

"Yes, I am."

She hugged her friend as the sounds of a fight broke out behind them. Matthew appeared in front of her.

"I left him for one minute." He spoke through clenched teeth.

"Sorry," she offered.

"No worries, Miss Jones, it's my job."

Matthew sped past her and into the fight. She headed out into the fresh air. So much for a new start.

TWO

James

The first punch reverberated down James's knuckles, but that didn't stop him landing another one in quick succession. The crowd around them cleared and chants of 'fight' arose. The fight wasn't going to look good for his business, but he didn't care.

He hadn't even wanted to be at the club. They'd had a couple of colleagues over from Europe who'd wanted to sample some nightlife. He knew she was in the club before he even saw her. When he saw her dancing alone on the floor, she looked so lonely but free. She was lost in the sensations of her movement. That was how she always got when she danced. He was mesmerised by her and had watched her intently for ages. Matthew had told him to stay away. But the second that creep touched her, that was never going to happen.

Matthew grabbed him by the shoulders and pulled him off the now-bleeding and dazed idiot.

"We have to go."

"Yeah, run on home to your skank girlfriend before she opens her legs for someone else."

He lunged, but Matthew held him tight. "Go after Amy. This is your chance. Don't waste it with this loser."

Matthew's words hit home. He nodded, and the bodyguard let him go.

"Just teach him a lesson."

"Okay I will. Take the car. I'll get a cab."

Matthew threw the keys to him, and he walked off the dance floor. Outside, he found Amy at the taxi rank; she was shivering and waiting for a cab. She was even more alluring than he remembered, and his body ached for her. She looked strange with so much makeup on.

"Can I give you a lift home?"

She looked up at him.

"I don't think that's a good idea, do you?" She looked down at his hand. It had blood from the guy's nose on it, and he tried to cover it with his jacket. "You taught him a lesson then?"

"I left Matthew to administer the harsh lesson."

"James…" She looked worried.

"He was disrespecting you. He needs to be taught how to treat a woman."

"He won't…kill him?"

"Matthew doesn't kill everyone to teach them a lesson."

"I still have nightmares."

She shivered again.

"Here, put this on." He took off his jacket and handed it to her. She took it and placed it around her shoulders. He had a breakthrough! This was a start.

"I would've preferred to be at home, in front of the television, in my PJs."

"You haven't changed much. I remember many a movie night."

"Have you changed?" She looked up at him. The streetlights reflected in her eyes.

"Only you can tell me that."

"I don't want to do this now. Please."

"All I'm asking is that you let me take you home. Nothing more."

"You promise?"

"I promise."

"Where's the car?"

"Over here." He led her to a brand-new Audi.

"To replace the one I crashed?"

"Yeah. You sort of totally wrote it off."

"I'm sorry. I'd pay you back, but I could barely afford to get you a push-bike."

He opened the door for her, and she got in. She did her seatbelt up while he went around to the driver's side, climbed in, and did the same.

"Maybe I should have bought a push-bike to replace the Harley."

"Oh god. Did I write that off as well?"

"It was nothing a good mechanic couldn't fix. I should take you out on it some-time." He paused. "Your choice. No pressure."

She nodded and looked out of the window. He switched the engine on and waited.

"Are we not going?" She looked back at him.

"I need to know where I'm taking you."

"You don't know?"

"You told me to stay away. I did as I was asked."

"You didn't even ask Matthew to find out?"

"You used our safe word. It killed me, but I gave you what you wanted."

She went quiet for a long while. "The club."

"The club?" He swallowed hard and gripped a little tighter to the wheel. He pulled out of the parking space and onto the street.

"I turned it into a dance school, but I can't afford to live somewhere separate, so I use one of the rooms as my bedroom."

"Alone?" His tone was shocked.

"Yes, alone."

"I didn't mean it that way. I meant…after everything that happened there?"

"I don't go in that room, and it doesn't look like the club anymore. I've worked hard on getting it all changed." She held her hands up. "Broke nearly every nail."

He laughed.

"I'll have you know I'm pretty good with a paint brush. We opened a couple of months ago, and the client books are already filling up."

"I'm really happy for you. I know it's what you wanted to do."

"It is. I have Elena, the girl I was with at the club. She's a qualified dance teacher, and she works with me."

"The one with the appalling taste in nightclub wear."

"The exact one." She laughed. It was music to his ears.

He stopped at a traffic light and turned to face her. She had lost weight, and she looked tired. It must be all the dancing. He just wanted to scoop her into his arms and hold her close. A horn beeped behind them. He looked up to the light, and it had turned green.

She giggled again. "Eyes on the road, Mr North. I expect better from my chauffeur."

"Surely, if I'm your chauffeur, you should be sitting in the back."

"Pull over and I will."

"It's ok, I'll let you stay in the front. I forgot my peak cap so I'm off duty tonight."

A few minutes later they pulled into the club's car park. The club had changed. It couldn't have been easy to get a business off the ground in a place tainted with the kind of reputation that it had. She had done well, but he wasn't at all happy with her staying here alone.

"Thank you for the lift." She leant over as if she were going to kiss him and then turned to open the door instead.

"Amy." She turned back.

"Yes?"

He tentatively leant forward and pressed a little kiss to her lips. He pulled back looking for signs of anger on her face.

Instantly, she was on him, her hands in his hair as they feverishly kissed again. She slid herself over to his seat so that she was on top of him. He pushed his chair as far back as it would go. He could smell her arousal; he could see it in the flush on her cheeks. If he touched her, she'd be wet and ready for him. He just knew it. He couldn't though. If he touched her, he wouldn't be able to stop. This time, she needed to take control.

"I need you."

"I want you. But are you sure?"

She began to undo his jeans to free his hardening shaft. With this proof of her consent, he tore her knickers from her body, and she rose above him. He grabbed hold of her hips and held her in place.

"I need to put a condom on."

She froze. "Have you been with someone?"

"No. You?" He didn't want to ask, but he had to know.

"I have barely left this building. Tonight was the first time I've been to a club."

"We still need protection. I wouldn't want you to fall pregnant."

"I had the injections. I managed to get my doctor to give them to me."

Would he be able to be inside her skin on skin and walk away if she asked him to? He should slow this down and think, but his brain was sending all the blood to his cock. He pulled her down hard onto it. His whole body shook, and her tight pussy captured him.

This was even better than he remembered. He was home. He moved her slowly up his length and then back down.

"God I love you."

She stopped. Whimpered.

Then she scrambled from his lap and out of the car. What the fuck?

He shoved himself back into his trousers and followed her to the door. She fumbled with the keys.

"What's going on?"

"I shouldn't have done that. I'm sorry. Thank you for the lift." She found the right key, opened the door, entered, and went to shut it in his face. He put his leg in the door to prevent it from closing.

"No, you ran away last time. I'm not letting you do it again. Talk to me."

"I can't speak to you."

"Why not?"

"Because I want you."

He pushed the door back and followed her into the main area of the club. A few tables were laid out, and the bar area looked similar, but it was no longer tacky and looked more in keeping with a theatre show.

"Then, fuck me, so we can talk."

"Be serious."

"This is because I said I love you. I'm not going to lie to you; I've always loved you. You know that." He reached inside his shirt and pulled out the chain around his neck. On it, he had hung her engagement ring. "This hasn't left my neck since the day you left me."

She came closer, and his heart beat faster. He needed to slow down. Six months ago he had hurt her atrociously, and since then he had stayed away from her as she had asked. But when she left, he'd wanted to rip the drains out of his arms and die, and he'd been sedated for several days after he tried. He couldn't blow this chance.

She reached out and took the ring in her hands.

"I don't know how to trust you again. I'm scared we'll end up hating each other."

"Listen to your heart. What does it tell you to do?"

She snorted a little laugh,

"I told you what it's telling me to do."

"Then do it. Let me put myself inside you and make you scream with pleasure; you know I can. Afterwards, I'll stay if you want me to. You ask me to leave, and I will. I'm giving you the control."

"You'll never be able to do that."

"I know you don't trust me but try. If I fail, then I'll leave your life forever."

She took his hand and led him to the bar. "I always wanted to have sex on this bar." She spread her legs and leant forward over the counter so that her breasts were pressed against the marble and her bottom was in the air. He nearly shot his load when the non-existent skirt rode up.

"I think I can oblige you there, Miss Jones."

"No pressure." She turned back to face him, and he could see in her eyes that she was turned on but also very scared.

"Only between your beautiful thighs." He ran a finger over her folds. "Always ready for me."

"I've been ready since I first heard your voice in the club."

He dropped his trousers and pants and pulled his cock free. He stroked it a few times. Amy watched over her shoulder. She had always liked to see him touch himself. He positioned himself at her entrance. He entered her slowly, savouring every second as her heated centre welcomed his rigid length. He stilled when he was all the way in, to tease her. She began to rock her hips, and he smacked her oh so beautiful naked bottom.

"Patience."

"I thought I had the control."

"You want the control here as well?"

"If you don't start moving soon then, yes, I do." She ground her hips again. He whacked her bottom harder, and she hissed. He withdrew and slammed back into her several times at a frantic pace. He ran his hands over her back to her shoulders and gripped them. His pace was scorching.

His legs were already feeling weak, and his balls burned every time he thrust into her welcoming warmth. "Part your legs wider. I want to get deeper inside you."

"I don't think you can." She was breathless, gripping the bar with her broken nails. He spread her legs farther apart and rammed himself back inside her again. She screamed with pleasure when he rotated his cock inside her before pulling out again.

"Let me come. Please. I beg you."

He bent over her and bit her shoulder, a silent sign between them of his consent. He thrust forcefully, and she shuddered underneath him as she came against the cold marble of the bar top. He followed her and released deep inside her. All the tension that he'd lived with for the last six months flowed from his body. Basking in the afterglow of their orgasms, they remained entwined together. Neither moved. Neither spoke. He knew he must be crushing her, but she never asked him to move.

He finally withdrew from her and pulled his jeans up. He ran his hand along her tender pussy, and she shuddered with an aftershock. He helped her stand and supported her because she was rather unsteady on her high heels.

"What do you want me to do?"

She mumbled sleepily, "Do?"

He scooped her into his arms and carried her into the hallway.

"Which one is your room?"

She pointed down the hall. He carried her there, nudged the door open, and placed her on her bed. He removed her shoes and skirt and pulled the covers over her. She hadn't told him to stay, and she hadn't told him to go.

"Amy?"

No reply came. She was asleep.

He walked out of the room and closed the door. Back at the bar, he poured himself a brandy and took a seat on one of the soft sofas. He decided that he was going to stay there until she woke. He couldn't risk losing her a second time. It would kill him if he did.

THREE

Amy

Amy rolled over in the bed and let out a long sigh of contentment. That was the best night's sleep she'd had in months. Suddenly, the satisfied ache between her thighs reminded her of what had happened. She sat bolt upright in the bed.

"James."

He wasn't in the bed with her. Had she told him to leave? She tried to think back. But after they'd had sex, she'd been exhausted and had collapsed. She couldn't remember anything. Maybe it had all been a dream.

She got out of bed and removed the remainder of her clothes from the night before. She'd only had two glasses of wine, but the way he'd played her body had completely knocked her out.

She jumped into the shower in her room and washed away her now crazy hair-style and excessive makeup. She made a quick coffee and headed out into the club, towards the bar. When she opened the door, she heard the sound of someone's breathing. She froze and peered around the corner of the door.

On one of the sofas and fast asleep in the most awkward position was James. He hadn't left, but why had he slept here?

She must have fallen asleep before she gave him an answer. He didn't want to leave, but he didn't want to stay in her bed without her permission, either. Her heart leapt.

She placed the coffee down silently and tiptoed up to him. He'd be aching today; the sofa was tiny for someone of his build.

"James?" She tapped him lightly on his arm, and his eyes blearily opened. "Did you sleep here all night?"

He stretched out an arm and sat up. He cracked his neck and then nodded.

"What time is it?"

"A little after nine. Do you want a shower? Might ease the aching bones a bit?"

He took her hand.

"Did I do the right thing? I wasn't sure what to do."

She leant forward and kissed him.

"Yes, you did the right thing. Go shower. I'll bring you a coffee. I don't have any clothes that will fit you, so you can't change."

"That's alright. When Matthew saw I wasn't home last night, he would've dropped some off here earlier."

"He would've presumed that we were...doing what we did and brought you clean clothes." She frowned. Her mind started racing. "But how would he know where you were? You haven't looked me up?" Had he lied to her?

"Relax. You know Matthew does these sorts of things. It's what I employ him for. " He pulled his phone from his crumpled jeans pocket. " GPS. He can track me at all times. The Audi has it. Not to mention, I have some device on my watch that I really don't understand."

"Oh, sorry." She laughed to ease her discomfort at automatically assuming the worst. "I'm just glad he doesn't have video reception on those things."

"I'd draw the line at that. Why don't I shower and change? We can go and get some breakfast? Now you've got the fucking out of the way, do you think we can talk?"

"I'd like that." She smiled, and her stomach let out a loud gurgle. "I want a full English breakfast, though. I seem to have my appetite back."

He laughed as he left the room. She sat on the sofa, picked up his jacket and brought it to her nose. It smelt of him—a heady, spicy essence that was her safe place.

She was still so nervous, but she needed to give him a chance. She hadn't lived the last few months, and that was no way to exist.

Forty minutes later, they wandered into a posh restaurant in Guildhall.

"I wanted a fry-up."

"You'll get one. This place is the best in London."

"There was a cafe a minute's walk from the club."

"Really? Can you see me in a greasy spoon?"

"Essentially you're a builder, aren't you?" She laughed. He grunted.

"Sit down."

She did as she was told. Damn you, body!

The waiter came over and greeted James in a friendly manner. He was obviously a regular. Two full English breakfasts, accompanied by freshly squeezed orange juice and coffee, were quickly brought over, and they began to eat. She wasn't going to admit it to James, but the food was fantastic.

"So, what happens now?"

James wiped his mouth when he finished and sat back to drink his third cup of coffee.

"What do you mean?" She looked at him confused.

"Us? If there is an us?"

"There is." She placed her knife and fork together on her plate. "But it can't be the same way as last time. Not yet. It was too intense. The way we were going, we would've ended up hating each other."

"I'll never hate you." He folded his arms.

"If you're not even going to try to listen and understand then I should just walk out now."

"Alright. I'm listening," he said hastily.

She bent down to her handbag and pulled out the paper and pen that she had packed while James was showering.

"We're going to develop some rules and agree to them."

"Rules?"

She picked her bag up and stood up.

"Alright, sit down. Rules. What's the first one?"

She sat back down and began writing.

"The first one is that if either of us find out anything about the other, we'll tell them straight away. No secrets or lies."

"You've my word on that. Although, I ask to be allowed to keep secrets if I want to surprise you. I love you, and I have the finances to buy you things if I want to."

"Alright, I'll give you some leeway on that. Twice a month and no massive surprises that involve holidays or purchases over one hundred pounds."

"A thousand."

"Two-fifty."

"Five hundred."

"Please. I can't reciprocate those sorts of gifts."

"You give me everything I need when you're in my arms. However, I'll reluctantly agree to two-fifty."

She wrote that down.

"Lastly, I won't be moving back in with you. I want to take this slowly."

"Amy…"

"This is non-negotiable. I don't work Wednesday mornings. I can come to you Tuesday night and stay over. You can come to me on Saturdays since the school is closed on Sundays. Do you agree to that?"

"Two nights. That's all I get to see you?"

"Yes, at first. We need our space. You still have a company to run, and I'm trying so hard to get my business off the ground. I'm also trying to find spare time to write. When I lived with you, I didn't have a job, and I had time to write. I need to be able to do that still. I'm not saying that you can't phone me and talk to me during the days we don't see each other. In fact, I'd like that."

"Can we have phone sex?"

"Yes, we can have phone sex."

"Alright, but I want two rules of my own. I know I promised you I'd give you all the control, but I'm adamant on these just as you are on the taking it slowly."

She swallowed. This had been going so well. "I'll listen to them and consider them."

"Firstly, your room at my house is exactly the same as the day you left it. I want you to feel free to use any of the clothes, underwear, handbags, jewellery, cosmetics, and so on that I bought for you. They're yours." She timidly nodded. She needed clothes, and it made sense to use what she already had even if most of it was designer brands. "I'll have Matthew return your phone and laptop later today."

"I have a new phone already; I don't need another one."

"Is it a contract? Or pay as you go? Does it have GPS? FaceTime?"

"Pay as you go. It's just a basic one."

"Then, I'm not arguing with you on this point. It'll be returned for my peace of mind, if nothing else."

"Is that it?"

"No." James sat forward in his chair and rested his arms on the table. "I don't like you living in the club. I'll worry about your safety. You know me. You'll find Matthew or myself camped outside in the morning if I can't control that worry. To be able to stick to your rules, I'll need to feel you are safe."

"I do understand that, but I can't afford anywhere else. I need the rent from my flat to fund the business. The income from the school isn't enough to cover all my costs yet."

"Then that's the choice you have to make. Either you allow me to assign Matthew or Sonia to protect you on the nights I'm not with you, or I have a property just down the road which you can use. It's nothing fancy, but it is in a safe location and fully furnished."

"Sonia is still with you?" The bodyguard had saved their lives.

"Yes, she is. She's been looking after my mother." He frowned at her.

"What do you say?"

"You know I don't want to live rent-free in a place you own, but equally, I can't expect Sonia and Matthew to give up their comfort to look after me." She looked over the list of rules that they'd already written down. This was a big sacrifice for her pride, but he was also sacrificing for her. He wanted nothing more than to have her by his side twenty-four seven, but she wasn't ready for that. He was going to find this hard. He'd worry about her all the time, and it would severely test his control.

"Alright, I accept. You can take me to see the place later."

He took her hand and brought it to his lips.

"Thank you. I'd worry too much if you stayed at the club alone."

"I know. We just need to learn a bit more about each other. But that has to take place without living in each other's pockets all the time."

He let go of her hand and brought it up to the ring around his neck.

"What do we do about this?" The morning sun caught the diamond and glistened.

"Keep it there, for now. We're boyfriend and girlfriend only. When the time is right, we'll both know, and I'll wear it again."

He looked deflated. She hurt for him. But she needed to find her own feet. For most of her life she'd been under someone else's control: first her parents, then her uncle, and then James. She'd never built anything for herself, and she was taking great pride in what she was achieving with the dance school.

"Shall I get the bill?" He looked back at her.

"Yes. We can go look at the apartment, and if I like it, you can help me move in."

"Can we christen the bedroom? It's a Sunday after all."

She laughed. "I wouldn't let you out of the place without doing so."

FOUR

Amy

"Can I get two skinny caramel lattes and a decaf Americano with a splash of milk please?"

"Eat in or take away?"

"Eat in, please."

"Anything else?"

"El, you want a muffin?" She turned to her friend, who was eyeing up a ginger-bread cake.

"Please."

"Three gingerbread muffins as well, please."

"What is with the three of everything? Something you aren't telling me?"

She paid the barista and pulled out her phone while they waited for the coffees to be made. A few days had passed since she and James had reconciled.

"We've company."

"Who?"

She put her hand up to silence Elena as the call was connected.

"Hey Sonia, your coffee and cake are in here."

"Am I that obvious?"

"No, but James is."

"I'll be there in a minute."

She hung up and placed the phone back in her bag. The coffees were ready, so they took them to the table and sat down just as Sonia walked in and joined them.

"Elena, meet Sonia. She's my bodyguard, and I suspect she probably knows everything about you already."

"Matthew gave me a file this morning. Happy to meet you." The two shook hands.

"And you." Elena looked towards her. "A file? What does that mean?"

"That you're not a mass murderer."

"I'm not?"

"Nope."

"That's good to know. Does he do this sort of thing often?" Elena had such a puzzled expression on her face that she was trying not to laugh.

"It's his quirk."

"Are you angry at him?" Sonia leant forward and took a sip of her drink.

"I thought I would be, but no, I'm not. It's something James needs for his peace of mind. Just don't sit out in the car again. It's too cold."

"I won't. However, don't tell Matthew. I get more attention from him if he thinks I have."

"How are you both?"

"We're good. Magnificent in fact." Sonia blushed.

"Matthew is James's bodyguard, right?" Elena asked.

"Yes, he is."

"And you and he are together?"

"We are."

"Right, Amy. I need a full catch up because I'm totally lost. But first, I want my muffin."

All three of them laughed. The next hour was spent giving Elena a rundown on who was who, and Sonia gave Amy a brief update on what had been going on during her six-month absence. She felt so badly at how poorly James had taken their break up, but she was glad that it had provided him with an opportunity to focus his thoughts.

"You said that reporters are interested in your relationship with James, right?" Elena sat down with another coffee.

"Yes, unfortunately."

"Well, I think the guy over there might be one. When I was buying the coffees, he was staring over at you the entire time."

She turned her head to where a middle-aged man was pretending to read a newspaper. He had rugged features framed by salt-and-pepper hair. He seemed familiar to her, but she couldn't place him.

Sonia stood and grabbed her hand.

"We need to leave, now."

"What is it?"

"No time for questions. Come on."

She grabbed her bag, and Elena did the same.

The man was out of his seat and walking towards them. "Miss Jones, I mean you no harm."

"Amy, move." Sonia was tugging her now, pulling her out of the shop. "Out of the way, sir. She has nothing to say to you."

"I disagree, Miss Anderson," the man replied. Everyone in the coffee shop was now looking at them. Elena had a puzzled look on her face, and Amy was confident she wore the same. They reached the door, however, as they were about to exit the man spoke again, "She's my son's girlfriend, after all."

She ground to a halt and turned. "Mr North?"

"Yes."

"We have to go. James doesn't want anything to do with his father," Sonia urged.

"No, he doesn't, but I haven't got a clue why." She shrugged Sonia off and stepped forward with her hand outstretched. "It's a pleasure to meet you. Maybe we should take this conversation back to the dance school. I'm sure it's one we shouldn't have in such a public place."

"I couldn't agree with you more." James's father stepped forward and held the door open for her and the others to walk through. When they reached the street, Sonia pulled her aside.

"You know I have to phone Matthew."

"I wouldn't want to get you into trouble. Do what you have to." Sonia peeled away and pulled out her phone. "Elena, are you coming back?"

"No, I'll go and collect the new t-shirts for the uniforms."

"Thanks."

"Not a problem." Elena left her alone with James's father. She had so many questions going around in her head. All she knew was that he had left Miranda for another woman, and none of the family ever spoke about him. There were no photos in the house, and any Google searches she had performed in the past while looking for information on James, made no mention of his father. If it weren't for Sonia's reaction, she would have questioned the true identity of this man.

"Mr North, the school is a few minutes' walk this way." Amy gestured in the direction of the club.

"I hope that I won't get you into too much trouble." His expression was genuine. "I just wanted to see you. Your friend must have thought me a stalker."

"She thought you were a journalist."

"The rumours in the magazines this morning are true then. You're back together with my son?"

"We're taking things slowly, but yes, we're back together."

"I'm glad. I've seen the way he looks at you in pictures. I don't think I have ever seen him so happy before."

"Mr North. Please. I don't understand why you've searched me out." She stopped.

"I need to tell you some things about my son. I don't want him to hurt you."

"If you mean about the scars on his back? I already know." She started walking again. She went round the corner into the parking lot of the school.

"He told you?" Mr North scrambled to catch up with her.

"Yes, he did. We've no secrets from each other."

"You've changed him."

She opened her Mulberry handbag and searched inside for her key. She retrieved it from amongst all the other contents of her bag and used it to unlock the door. "I haven't changed him. He's just open with me."

"What about his mother?"

"He's more open with her than I would have expected. Look, I don't want to be rude, but James told me you left Miranda for another woman. He doesn't want anything to do with you, and I wish to respect his wishes. If there is nothing that you specifically want to talk to me about then I think you should leave."

"I wondered what his version would be. Controlling as always."

"What?" Controlling. That word that summed her lover up completely.

"He hasn't changed a bit, has he?"

Before she could answer that, Sonia appeared beside her.

"I think we'll have company very soon."

"I'd better put the kettle on. Are you coming in, Mr North?"

FIVE

James

"Er. Boss. I've just had a phone call from Sonia." James looked up from where he was examining a set of architectural drawings spread out over the boardroom table.

"And?"

"You might want to sit down."

"What has Amy done this time?" James turned his attention back to the drawings. "She's probably just testing me. I'm going to give her the benefit of the doubt."

"I don't think it's her testing you."

"What is it then?"

"Your father's with her."

"My father!" He gripped the desk so tightly that his knuckles turned white. "What the fuck is he doing with her?" He strode around the desk and grabbed his jacket off a chair. "Let's go."

Matthew followed him from the room and down to the garage.

"Apparently, they were in a coffee shop, and Mr North was there. He approached Amy, and she invited him back to the school to talk. Sonia tried to warn her against him, but you know Miss Jones."

"Get us there, quickly."

"Yes, boss."

He settled back in the passenger seat while Matthew drove. His fists were still clenched to calm himself. Even though he wanted to go in all guns blazing and beat his sperm donor—he sure as hell wouldn't call him father—to a pulp, he needed to stay as calm as possible in front of Amy. They'd only been back together a few days, and he couldn't risk losing her again because of his temper. Why did his father have to come back into his life now? He thought that he'd never see him again.

The car pulled up to the school, and James jumped out.

"Boss."

"It's alright, Matthew; I know I must stay calm."

"I'll wait outside for you."

He entered the school. "Amy?" he called out.

"In here."

He entered and saw Amy sitting across from his father with cups of tea in front of them.

Sonia stepped forward. "I'm sorry, boss. I did inform her that I didn't think she should speak with him."

"It isn't Sonia's fault. I asked your father to stay," Amy interjected.

He nodded at Sonia. "Matthew's outside." She left to join the other bodyguard. He walked closer to the table and pulled out a seat for himself.

"I thought I made myself clear when you left. You're not a part of this family anymore. You lost that right when you cheated on Mum." He reached out and placed his hand over Amy's. She was watching him suspiciously, probably waiting for him to lash out.

"I'll never stop being a part of this family. I'm your father."

"In biological terms only." He shifted forward in his chair.

"I know how much you care for your mother, but maybe you should listen to what he has to say. That was in the past. A lot has happened since then."

"No."

"Please, just listen to him?"

Why was she doing this? Why would she not leave it be?

"She's a smart girl. Not one of your usual then?"

Okay, that was enough. He was trying to hold it together, but his father was pressing his buttons, deliberately trying to wind him up. "I'll not lay a hand on you, but if you don't get out now then I'll have Matthew throw you out."

"You'll never change, will you? All I wanted was to find out how my family is."

"We're not your family. You lost any right to that when you fucked that whore."

"Whose whore?"

"Get out!" He jumped to his feet. The chair flew back into the wall. Amy stood and pressed her body into his. Her presence calmed his temper.

"Maybe it would be best if you left, Mr North. You said you had something to tell me about James, and so far I don't think I've heard anything that I didn't already know."

"So he told you that he'd paid for that woman as well."

"James has done a lot in the past that he regrets now. It's in the past." She was defending him.

"I had such high hopes for you. You were my first-born son, my glory. I was so proud of you when you started the business and worked so hard to make it the success it was. I was amazed that someone so young could be that intelligent and determined. But you got consumed by the darkness of your own mind."

His father blamed him. He blamed him for everything that had happened. And James was back there; he could hear the argument in his head.

"What the fuck are you doing?"

"James?" His father withdrew from the woman, one of James's ex-escorts, and scrambled from the bed. He turned his head as his father found his trousers and put them on. "It isn't what it looks like. It's a mistake."

"Too fucking right it's a mistake."

"Please don't tell your mother. It won't happen again."

"No, it won't." He strode to a wardrobe, pulled out a suitcase, and began to throw all his father's clothes into the bag. "Because as soon as you're dressed, you're leaving and never coming back."

"You can't do that."

"I can and I will. You will not hurt Mum."

"Like you are with this dominant stuff?" His father took a step back. "Shit, sorry I didn't mean that."

He pulled his hand back and sent it flying into his father's face.

"Get the fuck out, now. I swear, if I ever see you again I won't stop punching 'til you're dead!"

"James, please look at me." Amy's voice permeated the fog of recollections in his brain. "Mr North, please leave. Matthew, Sonia!" She called out for their bodyguards.

"You think I deserved it, don't you? Everything that happened? Everything's always been my fault. That's why you used her. To teach me a lesson."

"Finally, you understand."

"Enough." Amy interrupted just as Matthew appeared at the door. "Matthew, escort Mr North, Senior, out." He could tell she was fuming. She had heard the blame for his beating being laid firmly at his door by his own father. Matthew did as he was instructed, and his father made no effort to fight the inevitable. As the room went quiet around them, she nestled into his chest.

"I'm sorry."

"Why are you sorry?" He didn't understand.

"I allowed him in, and he was obviously trying to insult you."

"You weren't to know. I hadn't told you about that day. I still haven't really."

"No, but you will when you're ready." She went up on her toes and gave him a tender kiss.

SIX

James

He looked at his phone for what was probably the fiftieth time. He had texted Amy in the morning. She had immediately sent him a brief reply saying there was a problem with the club, and she'd message him later. That was three hours ago. He was sure everything was fine. She'd probably just got caught up in her work and would message him again soon.

Jesus.

Surely it should be Amy moping over her phone, waiting for him to call or text.

He put his phone in his pocket. She would be around later, so he'd get some lunch and then look for a present for her. It had been a month since they'd laid down the rules, and they'd both stuck to them. He even found that he was able to relax in the time he was at home alone. He marched out of his office. Marie instantly jumped to her feet, pouting and pushing her breasts together to accentuate her curves. It did nothing for him.

"Mr North, how can I help you?"

"I don't have any meetings this afternoon, so I'm going to take off. I have a call at eleven tomorrow morning. Please, can you move it to one in the afternoon?"

"Of course, Mr North. Aren't you feeling well? Do you need me to get anything for you? I could bring it over to your home."

"No, I don't need anything. I'm going shopping for my girlfriend."

"Oh, her. Yes." He watched her sit back down and pull up her contact list.

"Marie, there is something you can do for me. I want you to arrange to have some flowers sent to Amy. Make sure the bouquet includes lilies and lots of blue to match her eyes. I want the note to read, 'To my beautiful angel, I can't wait to see you tonight. Love James.' Please get them to add a couple of kisses at the end."

His secretary's lips pursed tightly while she wrote the message down.

"I'll do that for you, sir." She was seething, but he didn't feel guilty for one minute. That woman needed a reality check.

A few hours later, he was still wandering the shops looking for something for Amy which was under the budget that had been set. It was proving a challenging task. Perfume, clothes, a watch, handbag, jewellery—he had already bought her all of those. He looked towards Matthew and could tell that he was completely bored.

"Does she really need a present, Boss? Didn't you get her something last week?"

"I was hoping she'd count it as the start of a new month."

"The new month will start from thirty days after the last present."

"Why did I have to pick the stubbornest girl in the world to fall in love with?"

"Because she's the only one who'd put up with you." Matthew chuckled.

"There goes your Christmas bonus."

"You cut my Christmas bonus, and you can lug your own Christmas tree up the stairs."

"I'm sure I wrote that into your contract as a requirement of the job." He groaned. "Christmas. That's going to be fun. I'll probably have to negotiate and agree to more rules. Come on Matthew. You must have an idea. Help me out."

"Do I get my bonus back?"

"If you can find me the perfect gift for Amy, and it doesn't get me into trouble, I'll double your bonus."

"Follow me." Both left the store and headed down the street to a small alleyway. Matthew led him down it and stopped outside what appeared to be an ordinary house.

"What's this?"

"A place I learned about when in the employ of Her Majesty."

"Is it legit?"

"They may not pay their taxes, but yeah, it's cool."

Matthew knocked on the door, and a man opened it. James stood back while Matthew spoke to him in a language that sounded Russian or Eastern European. What the hell were they talking about?

"Come in, sir." The man who opened the door motioned with his left hand for him to enter. "You are most welcome. I'm Sergey; I help you find what you look for."

He smiled and followed Sergey into the building.

"What is this place, Matthew?"

"You'll see, Boss."

The ragged-looking man, dressed in jeans and a Chelsea football shirt, opened a locked door and revealed a large room filled with every sex toy he could imagine. And a lot more besides. He visualised Amy writhing in pleasure, her pussy wrapped around his cock or one of the massive dildos, and the smile on her face when she was completely sated and unable to move.

He walked around, taking in everything. These were gifts for him, as far as he was concerned, so he could buy whatever he wanted. Amy's gift would be free when he used them on her. Half an hour and two rather full carrier bags later, he handed an amount well over the two hundred and fifty-pound limit to the shop owner.

"If you ever need more, my door always open for you and Mr Matthew. All best quality. Guaranteed to make women very happy."

"I hope so. Thank you."

He and Matthew headed back to the car.

"We don't have a normal Boss/employee relationship, do we?" He laughed when Matthew took the shopping from him to put in the boot.

"Would you have it any other way, sir?"

"Not at all."

He pulled out his phone. He had forgotten that he'd put it on silent. He'd six missed calls, all from Amy. He usually returned her calls immediately, so he dialled her back quickly. She answered, after the second ring, in tears, and his heart froze in terror.

"What's wrong?"

"I thought it would be easy, but I've ruined everything…" Her sobbing was so fast he could barely understand her. He leapt into the car. Matthew got in the driver's side.

"Beautiful. Calm down. I can't understand you. Tell me what's wrong. Matthew and I are on our way. Are you at the school?"

"Yes," She let out a distressed howl. "There's water everywhere."

"Water?" He looked over to his bodyguard who was currently swearing under his breath. The lights had turned red against them, and Matthew had taken a turn a bit too fast in an effort to escape the wait.

"There was a leak. I tried to fix it. I don't know how to turn the water off, and I've made it worse. It's flooding the stage, and the ceiling came down. I can't get a plumber to come and help me. They're all too busy."

He let out a long sigh of relief.

"Is that all? I was terrified."

"What do you mean is that all? James, the stage is ruined. It's all such a mess. I'll have to cancel classes. I'm going to be cleaning up for weeks."

"Sorry, I didn't mean it that way." Matthew tried to hide a smirk at his faux pas. "Look. Matthew and I'll be there in a few minutes. Try and find where you turn the water off and get some buckets under the leak."

"Ok." She started sobbing again.

"It'll be alright. Come on. You're strong, remember."

She hung up. He put his phone back in his pocket, placed his head against the headrest, and shut his eyes.

"You alright, Boss?"

"Yeah, you'd better get us there quickly."

"Two minutes."

When they pulled up to the club, Amy ran out to them. She was covered in dust and grime and was thoroughly wet. He was barely out of the car before she had his hand and dragged him to the stage. Water cascaded through the ceiling which had indeed collapsed, and the remnants of it were all over the stage.

"Matthew." He turned to his bodyguard. "Go with Amy and find where you can turn this water off. There should be details in the office. It's a requirement of all the health and safety crap."

"Sure, Boss." He watched them disappear. He took off his jacket and folded it neatly onto a chair then removed the cufflinks from his shirt and pulled it over his head. It was his favourite; no way was he getting it ruined. He took the ladder and the few tools that she'd apparently been using and held them at an angle, away from him, to ensure he'd get the least amount water over him. He climbed and began to screw the bolt back onto the pipe. Amy had actually undone it. He sighed. She would feel like such an idiot, but if he lied to her, she'd be angry at him.

The water stopped gushing. They'd found the stopcock and turned it off. He tightened the bolt. Amy and Matthew returned. Her eyes were red from crying, and her tears made streaks through the dirt on her face.

"Have I severely damaged it? Oh God, is it going to cost much to get fixed? I'm so stupid. I should've just put a bucket under it and called a plumber in the first place. I just knew they'd charge me so much."

He got down and brought her to his chest as she started crying again. Matthew went to the side and began to tidy up.

"The pipes are fine. You turned the bolt the wrong way. That's all."

"What?"

She pushed back from his bare chest.

"The bolt. You undid it, rather than tightened it."

Her anguished wail echoed against him and she buried her head in him again.

"It's an easy mistake to make. You aren't a plumber."

"You didn't make it," she said grumpily into his chest.

"I used to build houses, remember." He carried her to one of the sofas and sat her on his lap.

A lady in dance gear entered the room. She brought her hand to her mouth, saw him comforting Amy, smiled, and went to help Matthew with the tidying. Amy lifted her head. "How much will it all cost to fix?"

"A couple of thousand for the ceiling, same for the floor. Maybe more, depending on whether we can get matching parts or the whole stage has to be replaced. I'd get all the pipes checked, though. There's no guarantee how old they are or what condition they're in after your uncle's time as landlord."

"I don't have that kind of money. We're supposed to be renting it out to a drama club for their Christmas production next weekend. I've let them down, and it's all my own stupid fault."

He pulled her chin up so that he could look into her doleful eyes.

"You're trying to do too much on your own. Repairs to pipes? Come on."

"I just don't want to be a failure all my life. I want something for myself. Something I've achieved myself."

"And you're doing brilliantly. But you're tired and worn out, and you're not thinking straight." He swallowed. "Let me help you, please?"

"Not now."

"You said you wanted honesty. Well, I'm going to give you that. You carry on in this way and you will never get this school off the ground."

She looked at him with her mouth open. He took a step back and braced himself, ready for her to launch herself at him, but her whole body shrank.

"You're right."

"Pardon?"

"You're right. I need help. I need your help."

His mouth dropped open. "You, young lady, never stop surprising me." She gave him a weary smile. "Look, we once discussed the idea of me investing in your dance school, for a return of course." He stressed that bit. "We never got to discuss the finer details, but we can do that later tonight. I'll get my maintenance team to come and fix everything. I'll get them to check the electrics and water, and fix anything else that needs to be repaired. If you've more decorating, or anything else that needs doing, they can do that as well. I'll have it all done and ready for the show next weekend. You won't let the drama club down, but you will need to shut the school so my guys can do everything. We can give Elena paid leave and offer bonus sessions to students, to apologise for the inconvenience. I want you to step back while that's all done, though. I'll take you away to my country home. It'll be peaceful, and you can rest. We need to be there over Christmas, anyway, for my sister's wedding. What do you say?"

"I..I.." She looked around the room at the mess. "I can't leave my business for two to three weeks which it would be if you include the Christmas break."

"You won't. Anytime you want to check on the club, we can fly back and be here within a few hours."

"It's all too much money."

"In my lifetime, I'll never spend all the money I have. Even if one day you give me twenty kids and I have to put them all through university and set them up with cars and houses…my primary concern is you. You've worked yourself to the bone. As for fatigue? Fatigue is an understatement. You're making errors, like that pipe, because you are so very tired."

"It'll be an investment. I'll pay you back every month."

"Of course."

She turned to Elena and Matthew who were watching them and waiting.

"Please. That's what I want to do." Her words were music to his ears. He was certain, while he held Amy to his naked chest, that he could hear Matthew and Elena cheer. She gave him a passionate kiss, transferring dirt from her face to his, before standing to go and help Matthew and Elena. "Oh, and James…We're having two children… maximum."

He gave an elaborately faked sigh. "Does that mean we stop having sex after that?" Amy picked up a sodden cloth and threw it at him as hard as she could.

SEVEN

Amy

The light aircraft touched down, and James removed Amy's seatbelt before his own. Matthew did the same for Sonia.

"I'm starting to feel a bit left out here." Miranda chuckled.

"Sorry, Mum." James leant forward and undid her seatbelt.

It only took a few hours for them all to pack and decamp to the City Airport for the short trip up to the Yorkshire Dales. Amy was drained and fell asleep the instant she sat in her plane seat. All she wanted now was some food and a bath. She hadn't had time to shower, and although she had changed her clothes and rinsed her face, she could still feel the grime all over her body and in her hair.

She had been foolish to think she could do everything alone. She wanted to be independent, but James was right. She was a dancer and a writer. She had no skills in DIY or building repairs, and why should she have? She had never been taught. She needed to be less stubborn and actually let him help her a bit.

Following touch down at Leeds, Bradford, there was a short drive to James's country home. They pulled up to his estate and her mouth dropped in awe. It was dark, but lights lit the path all the way up to a mansion. At the top of one side were turrets, giving the building a look of a castle. She couldn't see properly in the dark, but she just knew the place was genuinely old. She imagined it was somewhere a Queen, or at least an Earl and his family would have lived. Lights also illuminated a formal garden. How much land did this place have?

"This is yours?" she spluttered out.

He nodded and the car stopped. He helped her from the car whilst Miranda was assisted by Matthew. A man in a suit came running out and greeted them.

"Welcome home, sir. Do you wish to clean up first or have dinner?"

James looked to her,

"Any preference?" Her stomach gurgled the answer. "Dinner it is then."

Another member of staff came out and took her bag.

"I'll take this to your room, Miss."

"Thank you." She tugged on James's arm. "How many people work here?"

"The majority of the property is run by Mr Aimes, my steward, and his family. That was his eldest daughter who took your bag. I keep several people from the village on retainer for when I'm up here, and there's the garden staff. It's a local business. They've started to offer weddings, etc. I open the house in the summer to visitors, so I have staff for that. It has some history behind it from the War of the Roses. Edward hid out here for a while."

"How old is it?"

"The oldest part is thirteenth century, but most of the remainder originates from Tudor and then Georgian times. It's gone through a lot of changes. You can see the Tudor in the red brick work to the east, but the west wing was added later. The main entrance is the thirteenth century part."

"I'm not even going to ask how much it cost."

"You know me. I got it for a bargain and did it up."

As they walked through the house, she took in all the traditional architecture and furnishing. The entrance hall had a vaulted ceiling, and it was decorated with portraits which James told her were of previous owners. She was led through to a large banqueting hall where the wooden tresses gave the room a Tudor feel. It was as if she had stepped back in time and should be dressed in corsets and long flowing silk skirts. She most certainly should not be at the house of a man who was not her husband.

They finally reached the dining room where an elaborate table had been laid out with crystal glasses, fine china, and silver cutlery. The dining room was a formal room with a table that could seat at least thirty guests. There was a massive fire in the Inglenook fireplace which was alight and providing warmth, and the walls were covered in silks of a rich burgundy colour. She was beginning to feel like she shouldn't touch anything and nestled closer to James.

"Is it overwhelming?" He looked down at her.

"You own this?"

"It's my home. If you want me to do a 'Mr Darcy' from the lake for you, I'll be happy to oblige."

"You've a lake?" He pulled out a gilded chair for her, and she sat on it with a thud. It creaked; she groaned and checked for breakage.

"I have a maze as well. I plan on getting lost in it with you for several hours tomorrow."

His mother coughed politely. "Not at the dinner table, James."

"Sorry, Mum." He took the seat at his mother's right. Miranda continued to talk.

"I was nervous coming here, at first, but it really is so beautiful and so rare to actually be allowed to live in a place like this. Once you get past the resident ghost of course."

"Ghost?" she shrieked

"Mum. I only just got her here. Please, she'll be walking out the door in a minute." Matthew and Sonia both chuckled. James took her hand. "It's fine. There's no ghost." She let out the long breath that she had been holding. Glasses of wine were poured and their first course arrived.

"Do you always eat like this, here?" She took a mouthful of her delicious spicy pumpkin soup.

"Not always. It depends on what we're all doing, but we do try to have an evening meal or breakfast together," Miranda replied. "It's the one thing I insisted on when James bought the place. Too many people don't do enough things as a family nowadays." She turned to James. "When are Sophie and Grayson arriving? Did you tell her we came up early?"

"I texted her. She said they'll be here at the weekend. She has lots of things she wants to organise before the wedding. I think I'll put her in the West Wing. Amy and I are going to camp out in the East."

"Don't you annoy her. It's her big day. She just wants everything to be perfect."

"Would I annoy my sister? Really? When has that ever happened?"

She sat back. She loved watching them banter. Matthew joined in, and Sonia also added a few words. She just sat with a smile on her face, taking it all in. For the first time in a long time, she felt like part of a family. She was nervous at the thought of meeting Sophie but excited at the same time and prayed that Sophie would like her.

"Come on. You're supposed to stick up for your boyfriend. They're accusing me of all sorts of stuff. Tell them I'm not annoying."

She took his hand and squeezed it. "No, of course you're not. Frustrating, grumpy, and nagging, yes. But you're not annoying." Everyone at the table exploded in laughter. James clicked his tongue in his mouth and scanned her face down to her breasts. Under the table, he slid his hand up her leg. She shut her legs tightly to stop him going too far. He leant over and whispered into her ear. "You will pay for that later."

She licked her lips. "Promise?"

The steward appeared beside her and took her soup bowl. Dinner was brought in: roast chicken with assorted vegetables and potatoes, delicious gravy, and of course a real Yorkshire pudding. Would they really be getting a three-course meal every night? She'd need to go running every day. Wine was served throughout with a different one to accompany each course. Finally, a dessert of a chocolate cake completed the feast. Would she have room for it? It was so decadent, but she managed to force it all down. She did draw the line at licking the plate though. Matthew didn't which earned him a whack from Sonia.

By the time she ended up in the cast iron bath in her en-suite bathroom, she was virtually falling asleep. She laid back and let herself sink into the water to wash her hair clean of all the bits of ceiling dust. When she came back up, James had appeared with a hot chocolate for her and brandy for himself.

"How are you feeling?"

She hummed a contented sigh.

"That good, eh? I'll have to bring you here more often."

"I still can't believe you own this place. I feel as though I've died and returned to Earth as a member of the Royal Family."

"Well, I don't have a peerage yet. But maybe, one day."

"Lady Amy North," she chuckled "I like it."

"North?"

"One day."

James came to kneel beside her, and she reached a hand over the side of the bath and pushed the collar of his shirt apart, so she could see the engagement ring.

"One day."

He leant forward and kissed her.

"Do you want me to wash your hair?"

"Please."

He picked up the bottle of shampoo, squirted a little of the jasmine-scented liquid into his hands, and began to massage it into her hair. She hadn't had it cut for a while, so it was long and probably in terrible condition. She should ask him if he could arrange a hairdresser for her; she already knew the answer would be 'yes'. She shut her eyes while he massaged the soap into her scalp. He used the strength of his fingers to ease the last vestiges of tension from her.

"Amy?"

"Yes."

"This room is not my master bedroom. Mine is reached through a door inter-connecting the two rooms. Just as it would've been in the olden days. The husband and wife didn't sleep together; they only met for the purpose of making babies."

She sat up and turned to face him. "I wanted to give you a choice while you're here. If you prefer to spend a night alone then you can, but equally, if you want to spend a night with me, you can." He pulled out a key and placed it on the sink. "That's the key for the door. I don't have a copy."

She pressed a finger to his lips to quieten him. Her heart was beating so fast. He was giving her a choice and freedom. He was giving her the control over the rela-tionship, still.

"I want you to take the key and open the door. If we want a night apart while we're here, all either of us have to do is just say so. Besides, I'd need a thicker wall to dampen down the noise of your snoring."

"Hey." He flicked water at her.

"Oh yeah? Two can play that game." She splashed a massive shower of soap suds and water over him.

"You are really going to be in trouble later."

She shrugged, a telling, playful smile on her lips. "You keep saying that."

James stood, removed his clothes, and got into the bath behind her. He slid his hand under the water and pushed her thighs apart. His finger circled her sensitive bud with expert pressure. She rocked in the water as she lay against his chest, listening to his heart beating with excitement. The pressure between her thighs built, and the heat from her core began to spread throughout her body. The lapping of the water brought more stimulation to where she wanted it most. Her back arched, and her breasts thrust up into the air.

"Told you that you were in trouble."

"Please."

"No." He had a tone of menace in his voice as he removed his hand and uncere-moniously moved her forward in the bath so that he could get out.

"What the fuck? Get back here."

"No, I think I'll sit here and finish my brandy while you finish washing your hair."

"James." She pouted pleadingly at him. "Please."

He picked up his brandy and held it aloft in a salute.

"Here's to frustrating, moody, and if you don't hurry up, wash your hair, and get in the bedroom with your legs spread, then nagging."

She sunk back under the water, silently cursing and planning revenge on the man with whom she was head over heels in love.

EIGHT

James

James's cock twitched with anticipation as he watched Amy stomp sullenly around the room. He was lying naked on the ornately carved four poster bed in his room. He had wanted to have an antique bed, but they'd been too small, and his feet had hung over the end, so he'd had one made.

Amy pulled a fluffy dressing gown over herself.

He loved to tease her this way; she got so stroppy with him and spent most of the time with the cutest glower on her face.

"Amy?"

"What?" Her answer was short.

"Can you pass me some pants out of the top drawer please?"

"When did your last slave die?"

"She hasn't. She's wiggling her sexy little arse at me at the moment."

"Bite me."

"I will later, thank you."

"You think you will be so lucky?"

"Oh, I will, don't worry."

Amy pulled open the drawer which contained his underwear and chose a pair, slammed the drawer shut, and threw them at his head.

"I'm going to your library to pick a book to read."

"Amy."

"What?" She turned with her hands on her hips and a look on her face that would melt ice. He stood up, next to the bed. "Drop your dressing gown and lay on the bed on your stomach."

"Thought I was in big trouble."

"You are." He turned on the authority in his voice. "Do it now."

She instantly dropped her gown to the floor and scrambled onto the bed to lay with her perfect little backside facing up. He opened the door to a vintage wardrobe and began to pull out a few pieces that he had bought from the shop. He set them aside on a dressing table. He heard Amy shift on the bed, so she could get a better view of what he was doing.

"Keep your head forward and down on the pillow."

She groaned but did as she was told. He loved how responsive she was. She may control him everywhere else, but in the bedroom, she was his to dominate. He took a blindfold out first, went back to the bed, and put it over her head.

"This will make sure you can't cheat."

"James?" There was a little hint of trepidation in her voice.

"Trust me." He pressed a soft kiss to her forehead.

"I do," she whispered the words back to him and put her head back down. He stood for a moment and just looked at his woman. He hoped she meant it, in all aspects of their life, and not just in the bedroom, kitchen, lounge, back seat of a car, or wherever the mood took them. He went back to the wardrobe, pulled a few more items out, and took them all back to the bed. He pressed a hidden switch on the wall, and the lights dimmed. She hadn't moved. He bent down beside her and nudged against her ear with his lips as he spoke.

"I want you to put your hands above your head." She instantly obeyed. "Good girl. You'll be rewarded for your obedience. You have my word." He couldn't quite hear her muffled reply from amongst the pillows, but he was pretty confident it involved a few swear words and vows of abstinence for him if she weren't. He smacked her hard on each of her peachy cheeks, and she wiggled, asking for more. She was insatiable, and that made her just perfect for him. He took two lengths of silk material, tied her hands to the bed posts, and then stood and lit a couple of candles which he had placed around the bedroom.

"Amy?"

"Yes?"

"We need a safe word."

"We do. What do you suggest?"

"Something personal to you?"

"How about rose?"

"Rose?"

"My mum always smelt of it."

"Rose it is." He climbed over her and knelt with his legs either side of her body, being careful not to bear his full weight down on her. He blew a warm breath up the length of her spine until he reached the spot at the bottom of her neck. Then he leant over to the table beside the bed, took a sip of a cold drink he had placed there and repeated the trail with now-cold lips. He was sure he could see the skin on her back prickle. He did the same thing a few more times until she began to gently squirm beneath him. He reached for a bottle of oil, poured a little onto his hands, and began to massage the tension away from her back. She was full of knots, and he made a note to have a proper masseuse—not a masseur— visit her tomorrow.

"Are you ticklish there?"

"Not ticklish, but every time you touch there, I can feel sparks of electricity hit me straight in my clit."

"You're not to come until I say you can." He ran a hand teasingly over her lower spine again, and she clenched her legs together.

"James..."

He stopped and slid his body up her spine until he was able to bite down on her ear lobe. She gasped and turned her head for a kiss. He pressed his finger between her lips, and she wrapped her tongue around it and sucked it hard. He removed it and brought his hand down to his cock and stroked it against her back.

"Feel what you do to me? Feel it."

"Put it inside me, please? Anywhere. I just need to feel you."

He took a long, slow inhalation of breath to prevent himself from doing just that.

"Not yet. Put your head back down." She did as he commanded. "What I'll do next will sting at first. Try to last as long as you can. It'll be worth it. I promise you."

"Ok." Her voice came from within the Egyptian cotton pillows.

He took a lit candle from the table and blew it out. The plume of smoke cascaded into the room.

"Use your safe word if you want me to stop, remember, beautiful?"

She nodded.

He tipped two drops of the wax onto the top of her back. She thrust forward and let out a moan of delighted pain. He pulled an ice cube out of his glass with his other hand and ran it around where he had dropped the wax. She pulled hard on the restraints at her wrists. He poured a few more drops of wax a little lower and followed it with the ice. She was writhing beneath him now. Her little sounds of whimpering pleasure had his cock rock hard, its purple head throbbing for stimulation that it wasn't going to get yet. Fuck, she was beautiful like this. He was the luckiest son of a bitch on the planet.

He dropped a few more pearls of wax onto her newly-discovered erogenous zone. He watched it cool and form jewels upon her silky skin. He put the candle down and ran his hand over her back, removing the wax. Next, he placed the ice cube in his mouth and ran it over the spot where the wax had left a little red mark. Her body undulated under his touch, and she fought the restraints again. She parted her legs and angled her hips to try and get some contact between her slender thighs. He put his hands under her stomach and pulled her up onto her knees. From behind, he trailed the ice cube in his mouth down the crevice between her, oh-so-beautiful, cheeks; over the puckered hole which she ground against his lips; and down to her folds and the hidden bud within them.

She was fucking his face with her movements. She was so desperate to get herself off. He dropped the ice cube and drove his tongue into her. She let out a cry of relief. He pulled out long enough to tell her to come as he moved his hand to circle her clit. She dutifully obliged: in his mouth and all over his face. He lapped it up as her release continued, wave upon wave. It was the best taste he had ever known. It was her taste just for him, and only he could do that to her body. He withdrew his tongue when she stopped quivering and leant forward to remove the ties to her hands. She threw her arms around him and kissed him deeply, but he drew back.

"Slow down, beautiful. I'm not finished with you yet."

"More?"

He removed the blindfold, and she took a few seconds to adjust to the dim light. "Tonight is all about getting you to relax."

"I don't think I can be more relaxed than I am right now."

"Yes, you can." He got off the bed, and she propped herself up on her arms to see what he was doing. "I went shopping today." He opened the door of the wardrobe and showed her the assortment of sex toys that he had bought. They ranged from dildos of different lengths and thicknesses, clitoral stimulators, nipple clamps with delicate bells attached, soft whips, restraints, paddles, love balls, a love swing, and several lengths of rope. He was not a shibari master, but he had practiced under one when he was training. Her mouth was wide open, and she stumbled to her feet to get a better look.

"This is all for me?" She frowned. "How much did this lot cost?"

"Is it too much? Have I scared you? The cost doesn't matter."

"I'm not afraid, but please, how much?"

James stroked his cock as he watched her surveying everything. He couldn't wait to use them on her.

"Over the limit? Remember you brought me earrings last week."

He grinned a superior, smug smile. "This isn't your present. These are presents to myself. So, it's not part of your budget. Your part is free so choose what you want."

She gave a throaty moan which nearly sent James over the edge. She picked up a little vibrator, about the width of his thumb, and a bottle of lubricating gel.

"I want these?"

He frowned. "Out of all of this stuff, you want that."

"Yes." She wiggled her backside at him as she went back to the bed. He caught her meaning straight away and went after her.

"On all fours then."

She shook her head.

"It'll be easier to get it inside you that way."

"It isn't going inside me."

He screwed up his face in confusion. "Where is it going then?"

"Inside you."

"Like fuck."

"But it's your toy. You bought it for yourself?"

"I bought it to use with you, not on me."

She licked her lips. "That is a shame. I have been doing some reading, and apparently there is a spot on a man that makes him come hard. I thought we could find it."

"You are punishing me for spending too much."

"That and not letting me come in the bath. Now, you get on all fours."

She had such a mischievous look on her face. His cock was still rock solid, and he needed to come. Something about this was actually turning him on.

"Hurry up, or I'll get Matthew to buy me a strap-on, and I'll use that instead."

He laughed at that. "You're lucky I love you."

"Give me ten minutes, and you will be saying that the other way around."

He tackled her onto the bed.

"For teasing me, you don't get to come again."

And with that, he pushed his rigid shaft deep inside her.

She dug her nails into his skin and dragged her hands down his body. Then, with one hand she stroked her still-swollen clit while the other massaged his balls. He knew she was close when she began to breathe quickly. She moved her hands away and put them back on his arse. They were wet from her juices. What was she was doing? She then trailed a path of her own lubricant around his puckered hole. Fuck, it was good. He had never allowed anyone near there, but he wasn't stopping her. When she saw he wasn't going to resist, she collected more of her own juices and went back to press her index finger against his hole.

"James?" she breathlessly uttered

He looked at her and nodded consent.

She pushed her finger deep. Her finger moving within him was strange at first and put him off his rhythm, but she soon found what it was she was feeling for, and he got it back. Without any warning, his balls tightened, and he was coming. Would it ever stop? He became vaguely aware that she was coming as well, but he couldn't focus to enjoy it. He had never felt anything like this before. When she finally withdrew her finger, he collapsed down on top of her, gasping for air.

"Fuck...what was that?"

"That was your prostate, and I just massaged it."

"I definitely want you to do that again."

"Next time I get to use the toy that you bought yourself?"

"If you make me feel like that again, you can use whatever you want." He laughed and turned to bring her into his arms. "I'll even ask Matthew to get you a strap-on... myself."

"I'll hold you to that." She nuzzled against his sweat-soaked chest. He should shower, but he didn't think his legs would get him off the bed let alone hold him upright to wash. His eyes shut. "Thank you."

"What for?"

"For showing me you only want what's best for me."

"Always. Now shush, I need sleep after what you did to me."

"Goodnight. I love you."

"I love you always."

NINE

Amy

Over the following few days while staying at his 'palace', for want of a better word, their relationship continued to solidify. James did as he said and spent a good hour chasing her around the maze on the second day. Mind you, she made herself an easy target to catch. Being ensnared by a six foot something giant with bulging arm muscles, wickedly devilish lips, and a lascivious look on his face, wasn't something that she wanted to run away from. Ever. She was just glad that the weather for this time of year was mild, or she was sure she would've caught frostbite. Not that James seemed to have any issue with that, he spent most of the time buried within her warm depths. But again, she couldn't complain with the miracles he worked there.

The next day they went up to the moors. The very tops of the hills were snow covered, and she learnt that Sonia had excellent skills when it came to driving on ice and snow. Sonia mumbled something about Siberian winters, and she and Matthew nodded at each other and went quiet.

They found a pub with a roaring open fire and enjoyed steak and kidney puddings with mushy peas and mint sauce. Several of the pint-swigging, flat-cap-wearing locals greeted James with a strong handshake and a firm look in the eye. They weren't well manicured and polished like the city traders that she was used to. The hands of the locals were indeed rough and calloused from manual labour, and they were more muscular in build from innumerable hours a day working on the farms. She struggled to understand what they were saying sometimes with their broad accents, but they kept their dialogue clipped. What they did have to say was always highly pertinent.

After lunch, they took a long walk along the river banks of the River Wharfe to try to excise some calories. That night, Amy settled in the library to examine all the incredible titles that James had collected. He also showed her some of the daring books the previous generations had collected, and they'd spent a few hours experimenting with gravity-defying positions, often failing and collapsing in laughter.

All the time he had his people call her, and not him, to keep her up to date with what was going on at the school. All decisions were made by herself, without his involvement unless she asked him for his views. Elena kept sending her photos.

She stood in the hallway fiddling nervously with her mother's ring. James took the call ten minutes ago to say that his sister and her fiancé just touched down and would be with them soon. She couldn't remember a time when she had been more anxious. Meeting James's mother had been very much thrust upon her when her brain wasn't exactly functioning properly. She never had a chance to worry, but with Sophie, it was different. She knew how much his sister meant to him even if he did complain endlessly about her being a bridezilla. She just wanted to make the right impression and not cause any problems for James.

He pulled her closer, and she withdrew from her reflections,

"Stop fidgeting."

"I'm trying."

"You've nothing to worry about." He looked down at her and dropped a little peck to her forehead. "She'll love you as much as I do."

"I hope she doesn't like me that much." She pretended to look shocked.

"Well now, she hates smelly feet, and yours really are the worst, so that may be a problem. "

"My feet don't smell." She scowled and pursed her lips.

"It's alright. You can't hide it from me. I saw the mouse nibbling them this morning thinking they were cheese."

"I did not have a mouse biting my toes."

James let out a howl of laughter, and she whacked him hard in the chest.

"Well, it's nice to see that she has the measure of you already big brother." The silky voice came from behind her, and she spun around quickly.

"Sophie." James ran to his sister and drew her into a big bear hug.

"Watch it. I don't want bruises for the wedding." He dropped her instantly and began to smooth down the wrinkles of her designer dress with a flurry of exaggerated brushes. "Are you going to introduce me, or are you going to allow the poor girl to stand there gawping."

James took her slightly perspiring hand and led her forward.

"Sophie, this is Amy. Amy, this is my sister, Sophie, and the biggest pain in the arse ever." James's sister had exactly the same colouring as him, but she was slender and about the same height as her. She had captivating blue eyes which glowed with the warmth of her personality. She definitely had a model's looks if she had chosen to be one.

Sophie rolled her eyes and blew out her cheeks at her brother's description of her. Amy whacked him again.

"It's nice to finally meet you, Sophie." She took his sister's hand and shook it only to be brought into a friendly hug.

"He has told me so much about you. I have never been so excited to meet someone. I can see already that you are perfect for him."

"Where is Gray?" James interrupted them as he looked past his sister.

"He's coming in a little while. He can't stay here with me until our wedding night. Mum arranged for him to take residence at the lodge in the grounds instead."

"I somehow think you're not going to be a virginal bride, Sophie."

"Tradition, dear brother, tradition."

He snorted. "I give it one night."

"Sophie!" Miranda's cry of joy came from behind her, and Mother and Daughter embraced with warmth and happiness. She just stood back and enjoyed watching them all. Her family had always been very formal. James came to her side and put his arm around her waist.

"You alright?"

She nodded "She's lovely."

"Have you asked her?" Sophie enquired.

"No, I thought it would be best coming from you," James responded.

They were talking about her. She swallowed. "Ask me what?"

"Men. They never do anything you ask. Have you learnt that about him yet?"

"I discovered that during our first date." She chuckled. "Still here, for some strange reason."

"I'm a stud, babe. You just can't resist my animal magnetism."

Both she and Sophie held up a sceptical eyebrow. Miranda went to James's side as his bottom lip began to playfully quiver.

"My poor baby. Mummy will always adore you." She gave him a great big kiss on the cheek.

"Mum. Not in front of my girlfriend. I'm trying to look good."

"The one thing you have to know about James is he's a mummy's boy. And you've passed her test, so you will be okay. Anyway. I wanted to ask you...will you be one of my bridesmaids?"

She looked to Sophie in shock and then to James who was smiling proudly.

"Are you sure? You're getting married in two days, we can't get a dress by then."

"Darling. A dress is not an issue, believe me." Sophie winked at James and she looked at him with suspicion. Had he put her up to this? "Besides, it's my wedding, and I want who I want. You're the woman who my brother loves, and that makes you a part of my family. You will accompany Mum up the aisle. Please say yes. I want to bring you into my special day so much."

"Put like that, how can I refuse? Of course I will."

Sophie screamed her delight, and James took Amy's hand and squeezed it.

"Everything is going to be perfect. It's going to be such a beautiful day. If you get me my snow."

"Working on it." He shrank back behind her to hide.

"You'd better. Mum, can you help me unpack? I want to put all the dresses in the dressing rooms and make sure they're all alright."

"Of course." Mother and Daughter giddily ascended the magnificent spiral staircase and disappeared in a fit of laughter and banter. She turned to James; she needed answers as to the looks that had passed between him and his sister. He stepped back with his hands held up.

"Before you ask. I did not know until last week. I had nothing to do with it, and that is why I didn't tell you."

"What about the look with the dresses?"

"She has the dress that she bought for you, before." He looked at the ground squirming with his head bowed. "Before we broke up."

"Before we broke up? She was going to ask me to be a bridesmaid then?"

"She knew how much I loved you. Everything she said about you being a part of her special day because you are family to her, is true."

"Oh. Does the fact I'm a bridesmaid mean that I don't have to wait to dance with you until all the other bridesmaids have?"

"Well technically, it's the best man who has to dance with all the bridesmaids. I'm the acting Father of the Bride. I think that means I get to dance with my mum all night."

"Really. Oh. You're not even allowed to have a little flirtation with a bridesmaid?"

"Wouldn't want to cause a scene."

"And there was me thinking I might be one of the bridesmaids who gets to score under the table when everyone else is drunk."

"Don't worry, beautiful. You will score. And not just the once."

A throat clearing cough came from the doorway.

"Matthew, I'm really starting to wonder about your timing."

"Sorry, Boss."

She flushed.

"What is it?"

"I have briefed Mr Moore's security. Sonia is with your sister's bodyguard ensuring that she's up to speed. "

"Does he have a large retinue?"

"The usual. Manager, stylist, personal trainer, dietician, and several body-guards. His best man flies in tomorrow, apparently."

She tugged on James's arm.

"Just who is Sophie's fiancé?"

"I'll leave you to explain that one, Boss. I'm going to check that they're adhering to British rules. Don't want any paparazzi shot on my watch."

James nodded. "This is going to be a nightmare." He ran his hand through his hair. "Grayson Moore, a well-known, hell-raiser actor marrying my sister."

"Grayson Moore? You mean Sophie is marrying the actor behind the Aban-doned Renegade films? Oh, my god. He's so cute." She flushed with excitement. She and Elena had gone to watch the latest film only a few weeks ago. It was the usual beat them up, solve the crime story, with fast cars and even faster women. But this one had heart. The leading man captured the female audience with his portrayal of pain and suffering. She was confident that he had suffered from something that he touched upon to make his acting so real. She had loved the film so much that she had downloaded the previous ones and had watched them over the next few nights. She hadn't read anything about his hell-raising past, though.

"Do I need to be worried here, Miss Jones? Are you crushing on my sister's fiancé?"

"Er. No."

"Liar." He chuckled. "I never had you down for enjoying that kind of film."

"Elena's bad influence, I guess."

"Remind me to keep an eye on her."

"She's harmless. She thinks you're better looking than Grayson, anyway." She slapped her hand over her face and mumbled, "Don't tell her I said that."

James suddenly had the look of the devil on his face. "Leverage. I like it."

She placed her hands on her hips and snarled at him.

"Bedroom. I have a very sudden need that only that stern look can satisfy."

He scooped her into his arms and took the stairs two at a time. He placed her down at the top, and their mouths met. Clothes came flying off in all directions. They managed to reach their bedroom, and as the door shut them away from the world, James pushed her against the bed post, lifted one of her legs, and thrust inside her. She came immediately, calling his name and grinding out her orgasm against his cock. He spurted his climax within her and bit down on her shoulder as he shuddered a final time.

"Fuck."

"I think I need to buy a chastity belt for the wedding."

"What?" Both of them were breathing heavy.

"I'm not sure I'll be able to get through the entire day without that. We barely made it into the bedroom. I mean, what if your mother and sister find the pile of strewn clothes?"

James pulled her down onto the bed and brought her into his arms.

"They won't. They'll be tidied before that happens. But as for the chastity belt. I have something much better for you to wear on the day of the wedding."

"What?" She sat up.

"You will have to wait and see."

TEN

James

James's gaze shifted from his breakfast of egg on toast to his alluring girlfriend as she padded sleepily into the kitchen in just her fluffy dressing gown. Mrs Aimes handed her a fresh cup of tea made with water boiled over the fire. Amy's hair was still tousled. Her lips were plump from kissing, and she looked well and truly like she had been fucked senseless. She came over to him and placed her tea on the table before wrapping her arms around his broad shoulders.

"The bed felt cold."

"I'm sorry. I always go for a run Christmas morning. We tend to eat so much."

"You should have woken me. I would've come with you."

"You needed your sleep."

"I can't argue with that."

"Merry Christmas." He kissed her.

"Merry Christmas."

His sister and Grayson almost fell through the kitchen door. Grayson had his hands over Sophie's backside, squeezing tight. They'd very little clothing on.

"I thought you were abstaining until your wedding night, Sis?"

They both jumped and separated. Sophie instantly tried to right her clothing while Grayson sought to hide something in his pants that James really did not want to think about, let alone see, though Amy cast an appreciative look.

"I didn't think anyone would be up yet." Sophie blushed a deep crimson.

Mrs Aimes brought them both cups of coffee, and they joined him and Amy at the table.

"I'm excited and waiting for Father Christmas." He laughed and eased the embarrassment in the room.

"Where is Mum?" He shrugged before Amy replied,

"She's checking all the presents under the tree."

Matthew entered the room. "Mrs North wants you all in the lounge, sir."

"It's Christmas day, Matthew. It's your one day of holiday a year. There is absolutely no need to stand on ceremony. Please, call me by my name." Amy removed her arms from around him. He took her hand to lead her to the lounge, and Matthew followed at their side. "You taking Sonia somewhere nice today?"

"I thought of taking her away for the night, but with the wedding tomorrow, we decided to stay here."

"Christmas day with us again?"

"If that is alright."

"You know it is. Your part of the family."

He thumped Matthew on the back, and they all filed into the lounge to the start of 'Do they know it's Christmas' on the music system. His mother popped the cork on a bottle of champagne and passed round glasses. He kept Amy close. He still couldn't believe she was here with him. They clinked their glasses together in a toast. The others began to sort all the presents out under the tree, but he pulled Amy to the side.

"Most of your presents are in the bedroom for later."

"I have your main one there too." She looked up at him adoringly.

"My main one is right here next to me."

"James." Sophie shouted at him and threw him a neatly wrapped present.

He lifted the label and read. "From Mum and Amy?"

"I hope you like it? You have to wear it."

He scratched his ear. His mother and girlfriend colluding. He was suddenly apprehensive.

"Open it." Sophie bounded up next to them clapping her hands. "Mum told me what it is. I think it's a brilliant idea."

He pulled apart the red and green wrapping paper and revealed a black jumper.

"A jumper?"

Sophie giggled.

"Hold it up to you." Amy bit her lip with nervous energy.

He unravelled the jumper. It was a cheesy Christmas one. A great big Rudolph, complete with bright red nose on it. He groaned.

"Put it on!" Sophie screamed in delight.

Amy reached out to touch the nose, and it played a song. "Do you like it?"

"Do you want me to answer that honestly?"

"My family always had a tradition of wearing something silly on Christmas Day. I asked Miranda if we could continue it. We bought jumpers for everyone."

"Even Grayson?"

"Even Grayson," Sophie replied, and Grayson looked up in shock from where he was reading the back of a book on household husbandry that he had received from Miranda. James pulled the jumper over his head.

"How do I look?"

"Incredibly sexy." Amy smiled at him.

"Well I know that, but how do I look in the jumper?"

A phone snapped a picture; all eyes turned to Grayson.

"I'll ask my followers on Instagram. I'm sure they'll love it."

"Don't you dare." He would be ridiculed.

"Too late." Grayson chuckled.

"You know I can still deny you permission to marry my sister."

"You wouldn't dare." Sophie bashed him in the chest.

"No, you're right there. His punishment is having to marry you and deal with your tantrums." He pulled Amy closer and kissed the top of her nose. "So, what jumpers have you all got?"

Amy went and pulled a bag out from behind the sofa and began handing jumpers out. His mother had a laughing Father Christmas, and Sophie had a dancing snowman. Grayson had a naughty elf— James instantly posted a picture of that on his own Instagram—and Amy had a red jumper with a Christmas tree on it.

"What about Matthew and Sonia?"

"We've ours upstairs. We have Christmas decorations on them." Matthew laughed.

Mr Aimes appeared at the door.

"Sir, my wife says the first course will be on the table in half an hour. Shall I top up the champagne now?"

"Yes, please. Let's get this Christmas party going. Can you get the entire household in here? We will all celebrate together."

By seven o'clock, he was ready for bed. They'd been drinking and eating all day. His stomach hurt from laughing, and he was sure he'd be bruised from the game of Twister. It was the best Christmas he'd ever had.

Amy came to sit on his lap.

"Shall we go upstairs for some time alone?" He had shared her all day, and he just wanted to hold her for an hour and talk. She nodded and stood, and he looked over to his mother. "We'll be back later for cake."

"Of course."

He led Amy up the stairs. Her slender hand was dwarfed by his, but it warmed his whole palm. She was humming 'We wish you a Merry Christmas', and by the time they got to their room, they were both singing it. He removed his jumper and shoes and collapsed on the bed with his arms behind his head. Amy removed her shoes and straddled him.

"Not on the stomach. I think I may have eaten too much."

"We've all eaten far too much. I'm not sure I even have room for your mother's famous cake."

"I can help you work up an appetite again, if you want?" He thrust his groin up, and she collapsed down beside him on the bed.

"I don't think I have the energy for that."

"Miss Jones, have I finally found the key to stopping your insatiable sexual appetite?"

Amy groaned, put her hand on her belly, and laughed. "Fill me full of food. Besides, I think I want my present first."

"I don't know. Have you been a good enough girl for Father Christmas?"

"That is really cheesy. If you're not careful, I'll make you wear your jumper next time we make love, and you will be playing that tune all night."

"I know it was cheesy, but not the jumper, please not the jumper." He leant over and pulled an envelope and a little box from out of his bedside table. "I want no arguments over this Amy. It is Christmas, and you're my girlfriend. I can afford to treat you, and I want to. I have compromised and tried to minimise costs, but ... er ...well, anyway. I hope you like it."

"What have you done?" He watched as she opened the envelope. It contained tickets to Las Vegas for New Year. They'd fly first class, but he hadn't booked the whole cabin out. He had booked The Wynn hotel, but not the best room, just the second best. Finally, he had booked a day trip excursion to the Grand Canyon with one of the local tour groups. He had written it all down on a piece of paper in the envelope. He swallowed as he anticipated her reaction. She read the sheet of paper, looked up at him, and he couldn't read anything on her face. He felt sick. She put the paper down and opened the small box. A clip to go on her clitoris which was remote controlled, and he had the control stored safely away.

"Is this what I think it is?"

"Depends on what you think it is."

"I put it...down there?"

"Down where?"

"James!"

"You have to elaborate."

She went bright red. She always did. For all her love of sex, there was still a naivety about her.

"On my clit?" She looked away, but he brought her eyes back up to meet his.

"Yes. I wanted to buy you something pretty to wear for the wedding, but I didn't want you to outshine my sister and everything I liked would've done that. This is hidden, just between us. You will wear it all day tomorrow."

"What?" Her mouth fell open in his hand. "I can't do that."

"You can. I have the remote control. I'll keep it with me, and I won't let you come until we're alone, but I'll keep you on the edge all day." Amy rubbed her thighs together.

"You won't let me come?"

"No. I want you begging for it by the time I get you back to the room tomorrow night."

She gulped. "Alright."

"Enjoy your present. I'm sure I will." He looked at the piece of paper. "What about that?"

"I think you'd better teach me to play blackjack before we go."

"Does that mean you're alright with it?"

"I can see that you've tried to compromise. I can't wait to go. Just me and you."

"And Sonia and Matthew."

"Of course."

"So do I get a present?"

"My present feels so very lame now."

"I'm sure it isn't."

"It is. I know you can buy whatever you want, so I wanted to get something personal for you. I have been wracking my brain trying to think, and all I could think of was this. It shows you how you make me feel." Amy got off the bed and opened the bag of her laptop. He never went near that. From inside, she pulled out a piece of paper and handed it to him. "I wrote it. I hope you like it." He took the paper and began to read.

Our pressing need pulls us close
With lips entwined in sweet taste,
Masculine fingers trace a path beneath my skirts
Exploring silken flesh at a craving pace.

Anticipation grows of a pleasured state
sonnets of sexuality from breathless lips,
Head thrown back in wanton longing,
I need you, I want you, take me now.

Pleas fallen upon tantalised ears,
As you yearn to take me to a higher state,
Clothes strewn across the floor,
And upon the bed, I get my poise,

A bead of moisture on a fevered brow
Lithe legs part allowing heaven's unveiling,
Golden tresses cascade on pillows soft,
While emotional peaks ripen to solid rocks.

Tumultuous tongues entwine in tango,
A slight hand tears at buttons of metal,
The leather casing of so proud a member
Torn apart with lustful haste.

Scarlet talons mark a trail down muscular flesh,
Your dark head buried in an aching breast,
Small growls of concupiscence resound
Signalling a wavering of all control.

Only you know when I'm at the point of no return,
Will I receive your gift of hardened steel?
Sweet enchantment plundered with one long thrust,
Deep within the welcoming heavens.

Urgency is the need, to quench our thirst divine,
We move in perfect union, rocking, bodies braced,
Our naked forms bonded for passionate elation
As my climatic explosion burns a fiery path

Tumbling over the precipice, finally flying free
Climactic convulsions shudder, jubilation given,
Your name screamed out in breathless waves,
My body clenching and tightening, milking all you give.

Head thrown back in rapture,
Lissom legs of jelly quiver, adoring love repeated,
Fiery passion willing your dramatic release

Give me all your love, burn it within me deep.

Fiery heat surged deep in a convulsing tide,
The flooding zenith of our lust released
As we settle together, gazes rigidly held,
I love you, now, forever and always.'

He could barely catch his breath. He went through it one more time in silence. Every word described why she loved him.

"You wrote this?"

"Yes. It's what I feel for you. I'm sorry it isn't something better. I don't often write poetry, and I really couldn't think of a present."

He put his finger to her lips, "I'm going to get this printed on canvas and hung in my bedroom. I want to get a photograph of us together as the background. And when I say together, I mean naked and my cock buried in you."

"I... You like it that much?"

"This is the best gift I have ever been given. You thought it would be lame compared to my gifts to you, but it's amazing. Mine, money could buy, and I have plenty of that. Compared to yours, it's mine that are lame. You've shared your heart with me and no amount of money could ever get anywhere close to buying that. I'd say I'm speechless, but I realise I have been prattling on and on ..."

He pulled her into his solid body, and their lips met.

"So do you think you're feeling ready for my fiery heat to surge into your parted heavens now?"

"Only if I get to fly free before you do."

"Always."

ELEVEN

Amy

"Where is it? I can't find it. Mum! Help me. James, get your lazy backside in here and get searching." Sophie's voice got louder and shriller as she frantically searched for the garter belt which was both her something new and her something blue. Clothes flew in every direction as Miranda tried to calm her daughter down. Amy ducked when a shoe came flying towards her head.

"Sophie." James appeared and handed her a glass of champagne. "Sit down; drink this. Amy and I will look for the garter. It'll be here somewhere."

"What if it isn't? I can't get married without it. Everything is going wrong. This marriage is going to be a complete failure." Amy began searching again while Sophie started hyperventilating. "What if Grayson has changed his mind? Did Matthew say he was still there this morning? Oh god. What if he stands me up?"

She had heard enough. She knelt in front of Sophie as James turned away and raised his hands in frustration.

"Grayson will be at the altar. Nothing is going wrong. James and I will find the garter, and if we can't, I'll help him bang on every door in the local villages until we can find one. Breathe and relax. You're nervous. That is all. Trust all of us to help make your day perfect."

Sophie burst into tears. Not quite the reaction that she was hoping for.

"I'm sorry," she sobbed through heaving racks of her body while Amy squeezed her hand reassuringly. "I'm such a bridezilla. Gray said we should have just eloped, but I wanted the big white wedding thing. I know I have been driving everyone crazy. I'm so sorry." Sophie collapsed into her mother's arms. James groaned which earned a frown from her. Miranda brought Sophie to her chest and cradled her, telling her that nobody was upset with her. They'd find the garter, and in a few hours she'd be married. Amy got to her feet and tidied the mess of clothes. The garter wasn't amongst them. She was on her hands and knees searching under a futon when she finally found it.

"Got it."

"Yes. Oh, Amy!" Sophie leapt from her mum's lap and almost flattened her as she rushed to embrace her. James mouthed his relieved gratitude to her.

"Thank you, thank you, thank you. James, you never let this one go; you hear me?" She silenced suddenly. He must have told her about their split and all that it had entailed. It didn't surprise her. She loved the fact he was so close and honest with his family. She needed to lighten the mood before it descended into a chaos of tears again

"It's alright. He hasn't annoyed me enough, yet, to warrant me leaving him. Although if he keeps leaving the toilet seat up…"

"Hey. My house; maybe you should be leaving it up for me."

She looked at Sophie and giggled, "And there are his gentlemanly manners. I really need to have a talk with him about them. "

He appeared behind her and pecked her on the cheek. "I think you know only too well that I always use my gentlemanly manners to guarantee your satisfaction first."

Sophie wrinkled her nose up in disgust. "Too much information. We need to change this conversation, right now."

Amy just laughed. "Do you have everything you need now? It is almost eight. The ladies for hair and makeup will be here soon."

"Yes, I think I do." She could see Sophie looking over everything and mentally checking it off as all present and correct.

"Yes, I have everything."

"You sure about that, my little dove? Aren't you missing the father of the bride?" The voice came from behind her back, and she spun around as quickly as James.

"Dad," Sophie whispered in complete shock.

Amy looked at James, and his eyes had gone dead. She shivered. James leapt forward and smashed his fist into his father's face.

"Get the fuck out of here. You're not welcome anywhere near this house." He followed up with another punch. Blood dripped from his father's nose. Matthew appeared at the door.

"Get James out of here." She wasn't totally sure what she was saying, but if Matthew didn't get James away from his father, he wouldn't stop until he killed him. The last time they'd seen this man, he'd said that James had deserved his brutal beating, and that he was ashamed to call him his son. Part of her wanted to punch him as well.

Matthew leapt to action and pulled James, shouting and swearing, from the room. She stepped forward to help James's father into a chair and handed him a towel to stem the bleeding. She may hate him, but she couldn't just walk away.

"Miranda. Would you ring for some ice please?" Miranda didn't move. She was still rocking. "Miranda." She spoke with more authority, and James's mother jumped out of her reveries and called Mrs Aimes.

"I guess my son doesn't want me here then."

"He has good reason to be angry, Mr North."

"Does he?"

"I think you know he does." She needed to be civil to this man for Sophie's sake.

This was her day. But come tomorrow she would offer him no kind words for the pain he was causing James. The selfish way he showed up on his daughter's wedding day. He probably wanted the limelight of the showbiz wedding.

"You don't have to call me Mr North. I'm Peter, Pete normally, though."

"Mr North, I need to check on my boyfriend, if you'd excuse me." She turned to Sophie. "Sophie, this is your day and your decision. I'll go and calm James down. He'll be sorry. I'll send Matthew back down. If you wish your father to stay then let him know, and I'll inform James. If you don't then have Matthew throw him out. The decision is yours and yours alone. This is your day." Sophie whimpered her understanding, and she left them alone to talk. As she went out into the hallway, she could hear James still swearing. Her heart was breaking for him. She approached them and could see that it was descending into a fight between him and Matthew. Sonia was trying her hardest to help Matthew keep his control over James. James's eyes were wild, his hair tangled with the rage he was feeling, and his t-shirt was ripped from where they were trying to just keep a hold of him. His nostrils were flaring, and his teeth were bared. He was like a feral animal, seeking out retribution for his pride.

"Put him in a freezing cold shower."

"Miss?" Sonia stopped, turned and looked at her. That earned Matthew a punch to the jaw, and James a few metres closer to the target that he wanted to rain down blows upon.

"Now," she shouted. The two bodyguard's used their strength and skills to pull James even farther away. She followed timidly behind them; she was scared. The crazy eyes of the man being bundled around were not the man she loved. She stopped by the bedroom door while they pulled him into the bathroom and into the shower. The taps were turned on, and after a few minutes, James cries of rage began to cease. Sonia appeared at the bathroom door to await their next instructions. She was trying to maintain her determination. She set her chin up high and held eye contact with Sonia.

"You and Matthew are to go back to Sophie and obey her instructions with regards to their father."

"We shouldn't leave you alone with him."

"He won't hurt me." Her hands trembled.

"I don't think he knows his own mind at the moment."

"It'll be alright."

Matthew had apparently heard her instructions and also appeared at the door. "Are you sure?"

"Yes." He nodded at her, touched her arm in a caring gesture, and left with Sonia. She took a few moments to compose herself. She was scared of what she would face in the bathroom. Would it be the man she loved or the monster he was capable of becoming?

"James." She took a deep breath and pushed the door of the shower open. He had slid down the wall and was shivering from the cold water. His hair was totally disheveled, but it was the tears coming from his eyes that had her instantly collapsed beside him and bringing him to her breast. "Talk to me?"

"I have made so many errors in my life."

"Errors?"

"My father."

"Your father made the errors on his own. He walked out on you and your family." He pulled away from her. His eyes looked calm but full of sorrow and fear, and he blinked repeatedly. His lip quivered with the effort of trying to keep a check on his emotions.

Tears welled in her eyes. He shook his head before resting his forehead against hers. "I can't help you if you don't talk to me. Trust, remember?"

"I can't. I can't tell you about this. Not now. I need to get back to my sister."

"I love you. Whatever is happening, I want to help you. Please, please talk to me because until you do, I won't let you back in the same room as your sister."

"My dad didn't walk out on my mum. I threw him out."

"But you said?"

"I lied. I lied to everyone. Mum was away on a spa weekend with one of her friends. I thought he might be lonely so I went around to their house to take him out for a beer. At first, I figured he wasn't in. Then I heard noises from the bedroom. The sound of sex. I went to the bedroom, and I saw him having sex with a woman, who was not my mother. Someone you pay fifty quid a night for."

She shuffled closer to him to keep him from going crazy again. She needed to be skin on skin with him. She placed her hand on his toned stomach, under his t-shirt.

"How did you know that she was that type of woman?"

"I paid her to escort me to a function a few weeks before. I knew exactly who and what she was."

She still hated to think of James's use of escorts for publicity events, but he'd had reasons for it. "What happened next?"

"I went mad. I told him to leave. I told him to just go. I gave him money just to get him to never contact us again. He took it and ran off with the whore. I told Mum and Sophie he left with a younger woman. I wanted to protect them from the pain. I took the decision out of their hands. I chucked him out and didn't even give them a chance to know what he was really doing." He closed his eyes to hide from the truth.

She wrapped around him. "You did what you thought was right at the time, but now you must let your mother and sister decide what they want to do. You need to tell them what happened. If you don't want your father in your life that is fair enough, but Miranda and Sophie need to make that decision for themselves."

"I'm never going to change am I?"

"You mean your need to control?"

"I do it to everyone." He looked down to the engagement ring at his neck, "I did it to you and nearly lost you."

She pulled his face towards her's, so she could keep all his attention focused on her, "But you didn't. You're confusing the control; that's all. You see blind rage and react to it because of your past and what you've tried to bury. You don't need to change; we just need to work together. Talk decisions through, not make them on the spur of the moment. You didn't have me then, but you do now, and I'm never leaving you again. You hear that?"

"You should."

She resolutely shook her head.

"You have an overwhelming urge to control? Take me into the bedroom. We will work it out in there and then discuss how to proceed."

"You might never leave the bedroom."

"So be it."

"They'll be so angry at me."

"They'll love you."

A cough came from behind them. It was Matthew.

"Sorry, sir, may I have a word with Miss Amy?"

"It's alright Matthew. You can speak to us both."

"Miss Sophie has requested that Mr North be allowed to stay for the wedding. Your mother has agreed."

"Is he going to give Sophie away?"

"No. Miss Sophie wishes you to do that."

She reached out to take her lover's hand. It was shaking.

"We'll be down shortly. Could you ensure that only Miranda and Sophie are in the room, please? He needs to speak with them alone."

"Of course, Miss Amy."

Matthew left, and she wrapped her arms around James's shoulders.

"If you need to vent your stress at him being here then you find me. Tell your mother and Sophie everything and let them make the decision. I'll be beside you the entire time." He had a wrong to correct, and she'd be there holding his hand the entire time.

TWELVE

James

"Mum, there's no easy way to say this." James stood in front of his mother and struggled to find the words he needed to say. Amy was a reassuring presence behind him. "I found Dad in your bed with another woman. I told him to leave. He didn't leave of his own accord. I'm sorry I lied to you." His heart was in his mouth as the words tumbled from his lips. All the colour drained from his mother's face.

"You took an enormous burden on yourself. Your father should never have put you in that position." She put her arms around him to ease his pain.

Sophie joined in the embrace, and the heat of Amy's body slid farther away, allowing them just to be a family for a moment. They needed it. He loved Amy even more for the way she'd been with him today. He was her safety net, and she was his. Whenever one of them fell, they were caught by the other.

As he led Sophie down the aisle and handed her over to Grayson, he couldn't have been any prouder. He adored his little sister and was so glad to see her happily settled and in love. Sophie hadn't always been the confident woman that she was today. She had hidden away from herself for most of her youth.

Grayson would treat her well. With his half Native American looks and her quintessential English rose features, any children they had were sure to be stunning. He took a place next to Amy for the rest of the ceremony and couldn't help but wonder what any children they'd have would look like. It was an entirely alien feeling. He'd never even thought seriously about children before.

He reached into his pocket and found the remote control of Amy's clitoris clip. This would be fun; he pressed the button. Amy grabbed hold of his hand, and her manicured nails pressed into the flesh of his palm. He stopped and then pressed again. She let out a little hushed moan of longing. His mother turned to face them, and he let go of the button.

"I think someone is a little caught up in her emotions." He put his arm around

Amy and tried not to flinch when she elbowed him in the ribs, as hard as she could.

The rest of the ceremony passed without any issues, and despite being the middle of winter, the sun shone brightly for the photos.

"Can I get the bride's immediate family please?" The photographer called out, and James stepped forward. Amy let go of his hand when he did and shuffled backwards.

"Amy?"

"Immediate family. Just you and your mum, for her."

James nodded and turned back to his sister who was standing next to his father. Hell no!

"I thought it was immediate family." He couldn't keep that to himself.

"Please. I want Dad to be in it too." From behind him, Amy took his hand and gave it a reassuring squeeze.

"Sophie's day."

"What about Amy?" If he was going to have to stand alongside his father for posed pictures, he needed Amy by his side to ground him.

"Of course, she's a part of our family now."

"It'll be wonderful to get a picture of all the family together again. It has been a long time," his father said as they took their places. He set off the clip vibrating again to release his tension. Amy drew blood with her nails gripping into his palm, this time.

The speeches were the funniest part of the day. He recorded the whole thing for posterity and for blackmail purposes later, of course. He was sure Grayson would love to keep the story of his first horse ride and the pile of manure out of the press. He was going to enjoy having a brother-in-law. They'd had an immediate rapport with each other and a degree of one-upmanship which certainly entertained their millions of followers on social media accounts. It was one of the only times that he allowed himself to be scrutinised by people he didn't know. Everything else was kept very private, and only information that he chose himself was leaked. But the bantering with Grayson was different.

He stood at the bar drinking a whisky while the dance floor was prepared. Amy and the other girls had all gone to change into different outfits for the evening part of the celebration. He was so completely lost in his thoughts that it wasn't until his father chinked his glass in a toast that he even noticed he was there.

"She seems like a really nice girl. How'd you meet her?"

He turned his head. His father was shorter than he remembered, and he'd gone grey. He looked old, not like the strong man that he always remembered from childhood. He didn't want to do this, but this was Sophie's wedding day, and he needed to be polite.

"She's more than just nice. She's perfect. And I met her in..." He couldn't say their previous safe word. "The Canary Islands."

"You got building work out there?"

"I took a holiday."

"Really?"

"It happens occasionally."

"How long you been together?"

"Why don't you just say what it is you really want to say, Dad? Do you really want to know everything about Amy, or are you just looking to find out if she's another whore you can fuck?"

"She has the measure of you. That is why I wanted to know more about her. She seems to be the only one who won't take shit from you. But as we seem to be talking about it, I'm not going to walk away from my family this time. No matter how much money you try to give me or what arguments we have."

"That is their decision, not mine or yours. But know this, if you hurt Mum, I won't be responsible for my actions." His eyes narrowed in threat.

"You will kill me? Is that it?" His father didn't seem bothered by his threat.

"I can do worse things than kill you."

"And you do them every day to yourself. Quit judging me by what they made you feel. I made a mistake. Your mother and I were going through a rough patch, and I used a prostitute. I'm not proud of it. I have regretted it every day since. You may never forgive me for what you saw but don't ever think that I'd intentionally hurt your mother. I love her, and I'll do everything that I can to make it up to her."

"Why didn't you come and talk to me, rather than go to that woman."

"Why do you think? You'd shut down." His father placed his drink down on the counter, looked back at his son, let out a heavy sigh, and walked away. James still had his whisky in his hand. He just looked down at it. He didn't know for how long, but the spell was broken when Amy slid her hand over his.

"Penny for them?"

"What?"

"Your thoughts?"

"I doubt they're worth that."

"No, your thoughts probably make billions." She giggled. It was a joyous sound. "Are you ever going to dance with me?"

"What with my two left feet?"

"You can't be that bad. Come on." Amy led him to the dance floor, but after she'd had her feet crushed by his massive size ten's a few times, they both agreed that maybe they should leave the dancing until she had given him some lessons.

"Shall we get out of here for a bit?"

"Our room?"

"No. I thought a walk by the lake. You'll need a coat."

They grabbed winter jackets and stepped outside. As they did, flakes of snow began to fall all around them.

"Snow?" Amy caught one in her hand.

"Fake, I'm afraid. I don't control the weather...yet."

"Well, you're just about useless." The snow was settling all around them. She bent down, picked up a snowball, and threw it at him. It hit him square in the chest.

"You know, two can play at that game."

"You'll have to catch me first." She made a sudden dart for the lake.

"I don't need to catch you," he shouted after her and pulled the remote control from his pocket. "I can stop you with a press of a button."

She ground to a halt and let out an aroused moan. Her eyes were already dark and full of lust. He had kept her at the brink of an orgasm all day, and she was ready to tumble over her zenith. He pressed and released the button with his finger, on and off repeatedly, while he strode purposefully through the snow to reach her. By the time he got to her, she could barely stand. He took her into his arms and carried her to a nearby orangery. It would give them the privacy they needed. He looked over his shoulder and saw Matthew and Sonia standing guard, at a discreet distance, of course. He needed to give them a few days to themselves when they were in Vegas. They'd certainly earned it.

"Please, I can't hold on much longer. I need you. I need to come, or I think I may burst."

He laid her down on a marble table in the centre of the room. He stepped back and pressed the button again. She ripped her coat from her body and arched her back as she lay down. Her hands traced the outline of her breasts in the sapphire silk dress. Her hair was loose and she looked absolutely stunning, writhing under the moonlight which flooded through the carved holes of the building's wooden frame. Her hands slid lower and pulled her dress up and over her thighs until it was bunched around her waist, giving him the perfect view of the glistening, skimpy lace panties that she wore. He leant forward, ripped them from her body, and stood between her open thighs. He could see her laid bare to him as if she was a sacrifice to his needs. His cock was straining against the fabric of his suit trousers, begging to be buried deep. But he was going to savour every drop of her delicious essence first. He pulled her close to him and drove his tongue deep into her flooding vessel. She was going to come soon. He could already feel the onset of the waves that would pulsate through her body, at any moment. He wanted to see her get off so hard, so he took some of the moisture and slid it around to the puckered hole of her anus.

"I'm going to let you come straight away, but I need you to hold yourself open to me." She moved her hands to her cheeks and pulled them apart. He tenderly pressed his finger into her tight tunnel. With his free hand, he pressed the button on the remote control, and Amy screamed. She was loud and uninhibited; she was shuddering in ecstasy against his finger. He kept going, and she came again. She collapsed back against the cold of the marble, her eyes almost rolling back into her head. She struggled to come back down to Earth.

"I... god...huh."

"You liked that."

"Uh-huh"

He laughed.

"You didn't come." She looked down at his straining need.

"Later. I have kept you high most of the day. You needed that."

"I wouldn't have lasted much longer. I was about to go to the bathroom and sort out the need myself."

"You could've told me that sooner. I would've got to punish you then."

He went to a cupboard and pulled out a sealed bottle of water and a towel.

"You bring all the ladies up here?"

"Only the special ones." She laughed, reached out, and hit him as he cleaned her up. "Actually, I typically sit up here to cool down after a run. Matthew always keeps the cupboard stocked up."

"I think I love him."

"I hope not."

She whacked him again, this time with a little more pressure. She went to pull her hand away but stopped at his chest and placed her hand over his heart.

"Marry me?"

"What?" They were the words he wanted to hear but not now. Not like this. He had to do it on his terms. Didn't he?

"Marry me?"

"Alright, you've drunk a few too many glasses of champagne, and you're still high. We can talk about this tomorrow. We better get back to the party." He picked up her torn knickers and gave them back to her before turning away.

"James North. Turn around." He froze. "Turn around." Her tone was stern and sent shivers cascading down his spine. "You doubt I know my own mind. After *everything!*" He watched as she slid from the marble table and came towards him. He was still wearing his tie from the service, but in seconds she had that on the floor and the top buttons of his shirt undone. She took the engagement ring in her hand and held it up between them. "This is mine, and I want it back." She blushed. Her domineering side always came with a fluttering of bashfulness "Please."

He didn't have to control this moment. They managed it together. He pulled the chain from around his neck, undid it, and he removed the ring. She held her left hand out, and he slid the ring onto her finger.

"Yes. I'll marry you. And this time, it doesn't come off."

THIRTEEN

Amy

"I want to go and check on the school before we go to Las Vegas." Amy stood with her hands on her hips and a painfully defiant look on her face. There was going to be no arguing with her. James held his hands up.

"I'll make the arrangements. We fly back to London in an hour, so I'm sure Matthew can make a detour."

"You aren't going to tell me no?"

"Should I?"

"No."

"We will go this afternoon; it's not a problem." James shut his laptop down and looked across the study to where she was still standing. It had been a couple of days since the wedding. All the guests had gone, and Miranda had flown back to London the day after the wedding with James's father. They were going to talk, and they didn't want James around. James himself needed to come to terms with his father being back on the scene.

"You're worrying me."

"Why?"

"You're being too accommodating."

"I told you that if you wanted to see the school at any point then I'd take you."

"You did, but I didn't believe you."

"Come here." He pushed his chair back and patted his lap. She was confused but went over and sat down. He brought her left hand up to his lips and kissed it. He then ran his fingers over the diamond of her engagement ring.

"Divided control. That is what we have."

"I guess I'm still finding that a little difficult to get used to, sometimes."

"I could always take you to the bedroom and exert my control if you wish."

"As much as I'd like that, I think I have only just recovered the use of all my functions after last night, and twice again this morning."

James pressed a button on his phone. Matthew's voice came over the speaker. "Boss?"

"We will be ready to leave in five minutes. I need you to arrange a detour to the school on the way back. Can you have the chief architect there to give her an update on how the renovations are going?"

"He's in the South Downs with his family, sir."

"Damn it. Yes, that is correct. Can you call him and arrange for him to be available to conference telephone should we have any questions? Tell him I'll ensure he is suitably recompensed for the inconvenience."

She put her hand over James's.

"There is no need for that, Matthew. I just want to see how the works are going. I can always speak to him another day when he is back at work. He needs to spend time with his family."

Matthew went silent on the other end of the phone. He was waiting for James to confirm her request. James just smiled at her before speaking.

"Do as the Boss says, Matthew."

"Sure thing. Will there be anything else, or shall I go and start loading the luggage?"

"No, that is everything, for now. Thank you." He hung up. "I thought I was being kind offering a conference call. Normally I would've had a car sent to pick him up and bring him back to London."

"I was surprised you didn't say that."

"I can ask him to send an email update as soon as possible if you wish."

"No, let him have his family time." She reached over and unplugged his laptop from the charger. He physically flinched. She carefully placed it in his bag. "It's the Christmas holidays. Most people are with their family and ignoring anything to do with work. You've spent the last three hours answering emails and making calls. That is enough for the day. In fact, that is enough work until we get back from Las Vegas. I'll give this to Matthew later and have him put an out of office on it and hide it until we get back."

He frowned.

"I have a business to run. I need to keep track of things. People expect answers."

"You have your emails on your iPhone. You can check that and respond to anything *exceptionally* urgent."

"Alright, I agree. But..."

"There is always a 'but'."

He swatted her butt, a playful grin appearing on his face. "I'm upgrading the hotel room in Las Vegas to the best one."

"Fine. But I think that is bigger than my side of the bargain, so I have to add one more."

"What is that?"

"We need to talk with your mother and father."

"No."

"Yes. I spoke to your mother this morning. She and your father are going to take things slowly, but they're back together. I doubt he has told her that he thinks you deserved the beating. She needs to know."

"No, she must never know that." He turned his head to stare out of the window. "Is he at my house?"

"No. He has taken a hotel room for a few days in London. He's going to look for something more permanent with Miranda."

"You mean Mum is going to ask me to pay for her to have a house somewhere with him."

"I don't think they will. He can get a transfer with his job, so a mortgage won't be a problem. The money that you gave him when he left? He never spent any of it. He placed it in a savings account. They'll use that for the deposit unless you want it back."

James shook his head.

"I won't have them having a mortgage and my Mum having to work. I'll arrange for the house for them. They can use any of their money to furnish it."

"This is their decision. They don't want to be dictated to. This is why we need to meet and discuss it with them."

"Was this what you actually came in here to discuss?"

"Yes. I have been pacing up and down our bedroom floor for the last hour, trying to figure out how to tell you."

"Mum phoned you rather than tell me."

"She was terrified how you'd react. She never stopped loving your father. Yes, what he did was wrong, and I'm not too enamoured of the way he spoke to you when I first met him, but she wants to try and forgive him for everything." She could see that he was hurt. His own mother hadn't spoken to him about something so personal to her because she was afraid of his reaction. She wrapped her arms around his neck and pressed the warmth of her body into him in comfort.

"You know I spoke to him at the wedding."

"Your father?" she queried. "What did he say?"

"He said I couldn't see anything in other than black or white, and that I shut down after the attack." He kissed the top of her head. "He likes you. He has you sussed already. He knew that you don't take any shit from me."

"Smart man. And you haven't shut down. You are opening up for me."

"I can't do this right now. I need to get away. I'll talk to them when we return from Las Vegas. Will you tell Mum?"

"I will." She leant forward and kissed him. "Come on, we better go, or Matthew will be stamping his impatient little feet."

They both laughed, and the tension of the last few minutes dispelled.

Two hours later, she was standing open-mouthed in front of the school. Elena had her arms outstretched in a ta-da position, and James fiddled nervously with the belt of his jeans.

"So what do you think? So many people have been commenting on it and asking when we're opening. I have been taking so many bookings and handing out so many leaflets. I think I only stopped to have Christmas dinner and then came back here. Please say you love it? I know you chose the colours and everything, but…Amy say something."

She put her finger to Elena's lips to silence her so she could say something. The whole front of the building had changed. In front of her now was a vibrant coloured space with murals of dance and a whole new glass frontage. What caught her eyes the most, though, was the sign that said Amy's School of Dance. Tears started to stream down her face.

"It is beautiful. I love it. Elena, you've been so wonderful. I should have been here helping you."

James phone rang. "I just need to take this. I'll meet you inside."

Elena grabbed her hand and started to pull her towards the building.

"No, you didn't need to be here helping me. I have loved every minute of it. It's just been the most fun. You've given me a place in life, and I'll never ever forget that."

She was trying to concentrate on what Elena was saying, but her mind was trying to take in all the changes to the school. A new reception area had been built for them to welcome the children, and signposts directed them to specific rooms. The rooms had all been named after a type of dance.

"The names?"

"Oh, I suggested that. I hope you don't mind."

"No, not at all. That's perfect. Just as I would've done."

"See, I told you we read each other's minds."

"I think we do."

"Come, you have to see the stage. It's just amazing."

Elena tugged hard on her left arm and stopped when she saw the engagement ring.

" Oh. My. God!" She was jumping up and down and clapping her hands. "You got engaged! Oh, Amy. I'm so happy for you. Why didn't you text me and tell me? I would've got banners and balloons up to welcome you both back with."

"That's why I didn't tell you." She laughed.

"Am I getting overexcited?" Elena cringed.

"Just a little, but it wouldn't be you if you didn't."

"Right, you can tell me all about the proposal and everything in a minute. First, I must show you the stage area. It isn't properly finished yet, but it's getting there."

Elena opened the door, and Amy almost collapsed on the floor in shock. Gone was the bar where women had been accosted, replaced by a mini theatre. The seats were tiered, so you could see the stage which was set out with all new equipment, and there was a dance floor that the Royal Albert Hall would be proud off.

"Are you imagining all the things we can put on in here? Dance shows, and maybe we can even get a drama teacher and a singing teacher and turn it into a proper drama school." Elena ran up to the stage and began to dance, her heels clicking on the floor. "Listen to those acoustics. How they did it, I'll never know."

"I think I'm lost for words." She just kept looking around. Every time she moved her head, she noticed something different. James came up behind her and wrapped his arms around her waist.

"You like it?"

"This must've gone over budget. I'll never be able to pay you back. The business will never make enough money."

"I have all the financial calculations back at the house. That is what that phone call was about. I knew the second you saw everything you'd want to go through it all. I called in some favours. I promise you; everything is as agreed."

"Amy, get up here and dance," Elena called.

James pulled her jacket from her shoulder.

"Go on. You need to check it out right now. Once they put the finishing touches on, it will be harder to change the floor."

She took her winter boots off, removed her socks and jumper, leaving on just her tight-fitting jeans and a vest top. The opening blast of a favourite song of Elena's and Amy's sounded out from the stereo system. The noise seemed to travel all around her. She looked over to the man she loved, leaning casually and very sexily against a seat. She rolled her shoulders and shut her eyes. She became lost in the music and danced freely. Everything about this place, the atmosphere, the sounds, the floor—it was better than she could've ever imagined. The song finished, and James came up to the stage to join them.

"Is it alright?"

"It's better than alright. It's perfect."

"Good. 'Cause once you get back from Vegas you will be very busy getting this place going."

"Vegas," Elena squealed in the background. "Oh, my God. Are you two getting married there?"

Both of them turned to her and said "No" at the same time.

She was sure she heard Elena say 'yeah right' as she left the stage and melted into James's arms.

"Thank you. I don't know how you did it, but you read my mind."

"I read your mind every day. We read each other's."

"Oh yeah? What am I thinking now?"

"That you really want to spend all evening having me kiss every inch of your body then slide my massive cock into your sweet little pussy and ride you until you can't walk anymore." He began to kiss down her neck. She pushed him away.

"Wrong. It was we better not forget to get steak on the way home."

James groaned. "Wait until I get you home."

"Give me a minute."

He nodded and jumped down. "I'll meet you in the car."

She walked back to the side of the stage and put her boots and jumper back on. She took another look around the room.

"All the demons of this place have finally gone. I know that I'm making you proud, Mum and Dad. I've finally found my place in the world."

FOURTEEN

Amy

"Look, the lights are coming on. That's the Luxor, isn't it? The beam goes right up into the sky. Oh, and look there's the MGM lion. My God, it's massive. Everything is so bright and colourful. New York, New York! We have to go on that roller coaster." Amy bounced up and down in her seat. Las Vegas had always been one of the places on her bucket list, and so far it was living up to her expectations entirely. "Paris." She quickly turned her head in the other direction. "The Bellagio." She looked to Sonia who was excitedly gripping Matthew's hand and staring out the window at the same time.

"Can we go see the fountains one day?" Sonia asked her boyfriend.

"If the Boss says so."

They all looked at James who still wore his Armani sunglasses despite the fact it was dark. He flipped them up. "If I can tear myself away from the gaming tables, I guess we could."

Amy whacked him hard in the chest. "The Venetian! It's massive. We're doing a gondola ride. If these two miserable men don't want to Sonia, we will do it together." She paused "And then spend lots of their money in the shops."

"Why do I have a feeling, Matthew, that we will be spending very little time at the tables?" James grumbled

"Because these women control our balls," Matthew replied with a groan.

The limousine turned right off the strip and then left into the privileged entrance of The Wynn complex.

"Why did you choose this hotel? "she asked James, secretly wishing that they could've stayed in one of the themed hotels.

"I like the service I get here." The car stopped, and the doors were all opened, valets bowed and rushed forward for their bags. He helped her out of the car. It was a long flight, and she wanted to change out of the clothes he'd insisted she wore. Apparently, appearance was everything in Las Vegas, so she had to arrive with Gucci sunglasses and handbag, Stella McCartney skinny jeans and a matching top. She dreaded to think how much the jewellery—a matching necklace, bracelet and earring set—cost.

They had argued over what she needed to pack, and in the end she had told him to just pack the suitcase for her.

He took her hand, and they followed a concierge into the private reception. The walls and floor were covered in white marble and gold leaf. Exotic plants decorated sculptured urns, and everything was opulent. A tall man in a formal grey suit greeted them.

"Mr North, it is a privilege for us to welcome you here again." James shook the man's hand firmly.

"It's nice to be here again. Amy?" James turned and brought her forward. "This is the hotel manager. Anything you need you just ask him, and he'll get it."

She stretched out her dainty right hand in greeting. The manager shook it then clicked his fingers at a nearby employee. "A chair at once for Miss Jones, please. And a glass of champagne and fresh towels for everyone." She was instantly swept into a chair that was more like a throne, and one was brought for Sonia. They cleaned their hands on jasmine scented cloths before the champagne was given to them. James and Matthew followed the manager to a small desk nearby, and instantly two security guards stood beside her and Sonia.

She leant forward and whispered to Sonia. "I suddenly feel a bit out of my depth."

Sonia laughed. "I do, too. I have never been protected before. It feels really odd."

James looked over and gave them a warm smile. She listened to his conversation with the manager.

"The two suites are prepared and fully stocked for your needs. I have left keys in your rooms for the interconnecting door between the chambers. You have the butler and maid you requested. They'll be available to both of you, but obviously, Mr North's requests will take precedence. I have placed the list of items that you both required in the rooms, and your tickets for tomorrow's La Reve show are in this envelope."

"Thank you," James replied.

"Will you be opening a card with us?"

"Of course." James handed over his credit card. "Please put two hundred and fifty thousand dollars on cards for both rooms, I think that will be sufficient for starters." She and Sonia both spat out their champagne at the same time. The two security guards near them took a step back and wiped down their now wet trousers. James handed his credit card to a receptionist who gave him an eyelash-fluttering glance. Amy smiled when James was blind to it and turned to look at her again.

"I hope that you are able to win big, Mr North."

James laughed, "I think you don't, but thank you nevertheless."

The receptionist pointed to something on the screen of her computer and the manager looked. He looked over to her and tried to lower his voice, but she still caught most of the conversation.

"Will you require reservations at the club?"

"No." His reply was very curt, and when the manager looked at Matthew, he shook his head as well although he looked a little more upset. Neither looked over to her, but she could tell by the sudden hunching of James's shoulders that this question had made him very uncomfortable. The manager bowed his head and waved the receptionist away. He handed James and Matthew key cards to the bedrooms.

"You have your usual suite and the one next to it. Your bags will be up there waiting, but I'll send the maid in to unpack them for you shortly. I wish you a pleasant stay, Mr North."

"Thank you." James came back over to her while Matthew pulled out his wallet and handed a handful of hundred dollar notes to the manager. He wasn't telling her something. She took his hand and followed him to the lift. They stood in silence. The lift stopped and the doors opened to reveal the smiling faces of Sophie and Grayson.

"Sophie! I thought that you'd be on your honeymoon. What are you doing here?" she squealed.

"Grayson has some business he needs to attend to. We're heading to the Caribbean in a week."

"Surprise," James whispered in her ear.

"You knew they'd be here?" she looked up at him.

"The reason I chose to come here. I wanted to let you get to know my 'nugget' of a sister better."

"Hey. Watch it, that's my wife you're talking about," Grayson interjected with his American twang.

"I'll never grow tired of you saying that." Sophie smiled as the newlyweds kissed. She felt all warm inside at the display of affection.

"Please. I really don't want to throw up my lunch." James pushed between them and strode towards their suite.

"In now." He held the door open for her.

"He's so bossy sometimes." She rolled her eyes at Sophie.

"Just how I like my men." Sophie giggled, earning her a smack on the backside from Grayson.

The lift rang, and Matthew and Sonia got out. Sophie turned her attention to them and embraced them both. They all filed into the suite that she was sharing with James. Matthew opened a bottle of champagne that was on the table waiting for them and poured a glass for everyone while Sonia handed them out.

She kicked off the three-inch heels that she was wearing and held her glass aloft.

"To a bit of fun in Sin City?"

They all raised their glasses, and Grayson captured Sophie in another kiss and hissed into her mouth, "Very sinful if I have my way.…. especially New Year's Eve."

James glared at him.

She was being kept out of a private joke here. She tried to push the feelings to the back of her mind, but the second that she and James were alone, she was going to have this out with him.

"So what is your business here Grayson? You got a film premiere?"

"No, I own a club, and we've a big night going on." James's face went white. Sophie swallowed hard, and she could see the new Mrs Moore grip her husband's arm tight.

"Amy, why don't we have a shower. It's been a long trip. I'll take you down to the gaming tables afterwards." James stepped forward and attempted to direct her into one of the bedrooms, but she'd had enough. She dug her feet in and shrugged off James's touch with a scowl.

"I don't want a shower. I want to hear more about Grayson's club. Are we all going to the big night? I haven't been out clubbing for a while now. I love dancing."

"Bedroom." James was not asking her this time.

"No." She placed the champagne flute down and folded her arms across her chest. The rest of the room fell silent, and she could see everyone else looking down at their feet in embarrassment.

"We should go back to our room, let you rest." Sophie took Grayson's hand.

"Don't you move a muscle, Sophie. Nobody is leaving this room until you all tell me what is going on. Since I entered this hotel, everyone has tried to keep something from me, and I won't stand here and be made a fool of anymore. James, either you tell me what this club is, or you will spend the rest of the holiday sleeping in Matthew's room."

"Please, can we discuss this in the bedroom?"

"No."

"Alright." He took a step towards her. She took a step back with her eyebrow raised in a stern warning to not even try and touch her. "Grayson owns a club here. It isn't your usual type of place; it's a BDSM club."

"Oh." Her cheeks heated again. "Maybe we should discuss this alone." She turned to the others in the room. "I'm sorry." They all nodded a smile of apology themselves and then fled the room as quickly as they could.

James sat on the white leather sofa and beckoned for her to sit with him. She did so, and he brought her to sit on his lap with her legs stretched out on the seat.

"Are you aware of what a BDSM club is?"

"Sort of. There were a few of the girls into some of that at the club."

"I think what you're referring to is the dominant/submissive side of things. I suspect there was a lot of that in your uncle's club but Grayson's is very different. There are no prostitutes in it. Everyone who goes there does so of their own free will. You don't have to participate in anything. You can simply watch if you want."

"Watch?"

"Yes. There is a big floor area where people meet and pair off, if they wish. Mistress Alexia is the person responsible for the floor staff there. She assists people to find the correct partner which can include her. She acts as an extra to couples, if they require it. There are also private rooms. But everything is consensual, and no payment takes place. To enter, you need to be a member and have had certain checks."

"Are you a member? Sophie? Grayson apparently is as he owns it."

"I am. Sophie is, Matthew and Sonia are. "

"Am I?"

"If you wish to be."

She didn't answer that. She still had more questions. "So are Sophie and Grayson dominant and submissive?"

"Yes, Grayson is my sister's master. I try not to think too much about that side of their relationship. I admit I see her submissive nature to him when we're together, but it's not something we discuss between us."

"So she's a slave to him?"

"No. Sophie has a jewelled collar which she wears to the club of her own free will and Grayson's name tattooed on her wrists, but he does not lead her around like a dog. BDSM isn't about humiliation. It is about worship. As her master, he treats my sister as a goddess. He gets off by seeing how his worshipping can affect her body. In return he expects her to yield certain control to him and trust him to do what is right for her. They're what you call life-stylers. He's dominant not only in the bedroom but also out of it. He dresses her every morning, and he controls what she eats."

"Do you want that from me? Have you participated in activities at the club?"

"I think you know the answer to your first question. My control stays in the bedroom. Out of it, we divide our control. As for the second, yes I have but not for over a year now. I did visit the place when we were apart, but I did not interact with anyone. I simply watched."

"Have people watched you there before?"

"I got Alexia off in the public lounge before, but when it came to satisfying myself, I took her to one of the private rooms. I have never revealed myself on the general floor."

"Did you always go with Alexia?"

"Yes." That was an uncomfortable answer.

"Does she mean something to you?"

"No. Alexia was simply a submissive for my needs at the time. I was one hundred percent certain she was clean." She let out a breath of relief.

"Did you pay her?"

"No, I tried to offer her a present, but she would not accept. Alexia likes sex. We were both single, and we consented to engage in satisfying each other's needs."

"Do you find it strange with Sophie being there? I mean she's your sister."

" We do attend clubs together, but neither of us will engage in any sexual activity in front of the other. That's a hard limit for both of us. I know people may think it strange that we even go to these clubs at the same time, but seeing her kneel at Grayson's feet is as much of her life in BDSM that I see."

"But isn't it disrespectful to women?"

"No, it's very much about championing a woman and using my skills to make sure that she gets off as hard as she possibly can."

"So, um, when you've been there with this Miss Alexia, what have you done with her?"

"Do you really want me to talk about this?" She shifted on his lap and hoped that he couldn't tell that this discussion was turning her on rather than repulsing her.

"Yes. I want to know everything."

"Why?"

She got off his lap and knelt on the sofa with her hand to his face. "Humour me?"

"I have tied her up, blindfolded her, denied her orgasms, licked her out, played with various toys, flogged her, and participated in a threesome with her." She was sure she turned green at him doing all that with another woman. She got off the chair without looking at him, picked up the bottle of champagne, and took a big swig from it. "Talk to me beautiful. Look at me?"

"Give me a minute. I need to process that." He got off the sofa and came and wrapped his arms around her. She was strangely comforted by his affection even when logic said she should push him away. But why? She'd had sex before and so had he. As long as they didn't cheat now that was all that mattered. Even though she was torturing herself she wanted to know more. How could she feel so turned on? "That threesome, was it with another woman?"

"No, it was with Matthew."

"Matthew." She dropped the bottle of champagne on the floor. "I know you have an odd relationship but...did he or you...you know."

"No. God. No. We didn't touch each other. I was in Alexia's mouth while he was fucking her from behind. She had love beads in her arse. Apparently, she likes to get off on being so full."

She pushed him away so she could think. Horny and having him close wasn't a good combination.

"Would you ask me to do that with Matthew?"

"Never. No man touches this..." He reached down between her thighs, cupped her sex, and a grin crossed his face. He had found out that not only were her pants soaked but also her jeans... "It's mine." She let out a carnal groan of need. "All these questions? Do you want to go to the club?"

She shivered when he pressed harder at her mound. "Yes."

He let go of her, and she gasped for air. He pulled his phone out of his pocket and dialled.

"Grayson, get Amy on your books, and get us a private room for the night of the show." He silenced for a moment while Grayson spoke. "Shit, I don't know?" He pulled the phone down to his chest. "Amy? What is an explicit fantasy of yours?"

She opened her mouth to speak, but as several thoughts went through her head, her pussy began to clench. She was suddenly bashful.

"I..err...I don't know."

"Amy." He raised an eyebrow "You want me to satisfy that itch you have in your jeans right now then give me something."

She bit her lip, "You had a threesome? I want to experience that."

"Not happening. No other man touches you."

"Wait. I didn't mean a man, another woman. She mustn't touch you though. Just me for your pleasure."

It was James's turn to stand there stunned. He brought the phone up to his ear, "FFM."

She could hear Grayson's exclamation down the phone.

"I trust Miss Alexia. There are no emotional ties for her or for me. Will you be willing to allow her to be the other woman?"

"Yes." She almost squeaked the answer. She needed to trust him on this. That is what BDSM was about, right, trusting her Dom?

He relayed that instruction to Grayson, hung up, threw his phone on the sofa, and before she knew it, she was flat on her back on the floor. Her jeans were torn from her body, and James sank deep within her, with a primitive roar.

FIFTEEN

James

James wrapped a protective arm around Amy's shoulders, as along with Grayson, Sophie, Matthew and Sonia they strode through the corridor to the high rollers' room. They were flanked on either side by members of Grayson's security team, including the two that he had requested to allow Matthew to be a guest rather than an employee. He didn't expect him to fully switch off, but he hoped that Matthew would at least spend a little time enjoying himself with Sonia. If he didn't, he and Grayson had already agreed with Sonia that they'd chain him up at the club and let her do whatever she wanted to him.

The manager opened a barrier for them and let them all in. James looked at Amy and saw her eyes open wide.

"One thousand minimum!"

"It's expected."

"I'd rather give the money to charity."

"However much I lose, I shall give an equivalent amount to charity for you when we get back to England."

"The same amount as both you and Matthew lose."

"Will I get to put myself in your cute little arse tonight if I do?"

"Maybe."

"Amy."

"Alright." She smiled up at him from under her long lashes.

He guided her to sit with Sonia and Sophie on comfortable chairs which were near to the table that had been set up for the men to play blackjack.

"How much are we cashing in?"

"Shall we start with fifty thousand dollars?" Grayson handed over his card to the dealer. He nodded, and Matthew reluctantly did the same.

"Matthew, you're here as a guest. You've already briefed Grayson's team. Relax. You've earned this break."

"Yes, Boss."

"No more 'Boss' until we're on the plane home, either. It is James."

"Yes, James."

The dealer began to hand the cards out. Amy came over and pressed a kiss to James's cheek when he won the first hand. Approaching midnight, however, he was twenty thousand dollars down. Much to everyone's delight, Matthew was up twenty-five thousand. James threw his cards in.

"You giving up already?" Matthew sniggered, and Grayson joined in the heckling.

"I think my beautiful girl needs my attention." Amy lifted her head up, from where it rested against the side of the sofa in a dozy slumber, and smiled at him.

"Pussy whipped," Grayson replied.

"Like you aren't, Gray." Sophie came up behind her husband and wrapped her arms around his neck. He spun in his seat and gripped her chin. "Baby. You're going to get punished for that remark."

"I look forward to it, Master."

James took his card back from the dealer and stood up.

"Thank you for the game gentlemen." He shook the hand of the dealer and passed him a couple of thousand dollar chips in gratuity. Amy came to his side, he wrapped his arm around her, and she snuggled into his broad chest. His white cotton shirt was soft against her delicate skin.

"Shall we get you to bed?"

"I'm actually a bit hungry. Can we get something to eat first, please?"

"Of course. Night everyone."

Sophie slid into his seat at the table, and they left with two of the bodyguards.

"I can't believe you lost that much money."

"I think your charity of choice will like it, though."

"Did you lose on purpose?"

"Would I do such a thing?"

She smiled up at him, and he directed her through the expansive main floor of the hotel lobby. It was covered in a variety of gambling machines and tables.

"What do you want to eat?"

"A burger."

"Really? At this time of night?"

"Yeah. I really fancy one."

"Well, don't complain to me when you get indigestion and have to spend all tomorrow morning in the gym."

"In the gym. I was planning on hitting a sunbed with a book and staying there all day."

"Only if it is a private cabana that I can join you in."

"Of course." She stopped, grabbed his hand, and tugged him towards a slot machine.

"Please. Can we have a quick go? Do you have any quarters on you?"

"I thought you were hungry?"

"I am, and tired, but I really want to have a go on one of these, please." She gave him doe eyes and a full-on pout. His dick jumped.

"Five minutes." He handed his card to one of the bodyguards. "Can you get me a bowl of quarters? And you better have two burgers delivered to the machine. I'll have a Texan Whisky preferably Balcones, Amy?"

"Amaretto please."

"What the lady requested." He nodded at the guards who scuttled off.

It didn't take long for one of them to return with a bowl of quarters, and James stood protectively behind Amy while she sat at the machine and began to pump it full of quarters. She didn't know what she was doing, but she was laughing. Their burgers and drinks arrived which they ate and drank, despite the fact that they shouldn't eat at the machines. Nobody was going to argue with him. Matthew and Sonia appeared from the high rollers room just as Amy managed to win. It was only about a hundred dollars, but in quarters it looked good, and it made her happy.

"I thought you two were off to bed." Matthew had his hand threaded within Sonia's.

"Women. They can never make their minds up." Sonia let go of Matthew's hand and moved to stand at the machine.

"You want some quarters, Sonia?" Amy held out a handful.

"Yes, please." The bodyguard took them and sat down and began feeding them into the machine.

"We spend all this money in the high roller room to look good for our women, and they'd rather sit at a slot machine. At least the rest of the holiday will be cheap."

"Shush, I'm trying to concentrate." Amy tutted.

"Ok, that is enough." He pulled her from her seat. The bowl of quarters spilt all over the floor.

"Put me down."

He scooped her over his shoulder, so her hair dangled down his back, and her legs were out in front of him. He protectively held her skirt down so nobody could get a view of her underwear. He began to carry her to the lifts. People around them stared.

"Bedtime."

"Put me down this instant! People are looking at us."

"Don't care. Your mine, and I'm taking you to bed."

"James!"

She was squirming in his grip, but he was strong enough to keep a tight hold on her. They got to the lift, and it opened. He took her in and turned around to glare at the two guards who were following him.

"You won't be needed anymore tonight. Get another lift." He wanted her to himself. The doors shut. He slid her down his body and pressed her into the corner of the lift. Their mouths met and savoured each other in a searching and sensuous kiss. His cock felt like it was on fire with a need to be buried within her. He didn't think they'd make it to the hotel bedroom. His hands wandered up her toned thighs, hitching her dress higher and higher. He sank to his knees and moved the flimsy fabric of her white panties to the side. They were soaked with the scent of her need for him. He groaned out carnally and flicked his tongue against her clit. He needed to get her calling his name before they arrived at their floor. With a few more strokes of his tongue, she started to pull hard on his hair, and he knew that her orgasm was nearly there. The lift had cameras, and security was watching him go down on the most beautiful woman in the hotel, no, make that the world, but he didn't care. All he cared about was hearing her breathless moans of climax. He thrust two fingers into her sodden pussy, and she came. It was the most amazing sound. He needed to record it sometime. The lift sounded out their floor, and he withdrew his fingers and lowered her skirt.

"Can you walk?"

"With support."

"Here." He brought an arm around her and guided her from the lift and around the corner towards their room.

He couldn't help but notice the mischievous look in her eyes. This time, she sunk to her knees before him, outside their room, and looked up and down the length of the corridor. She placed her hand on the fly of his tented slacks and looked up at him with glazed eyes; her pupils were still dilated from her climax.

"Please, may I?" She nervously looked around the corridor again.

"Please, may I what?" His angel was growing bold, and this was turning him on so very much. He wouldn't last long in her mouth, not with the way she was looking at him.

"Please, may I suck you off." She hesitated… "Master."

His cock twitched. Master, she had called him 'Master'. He needed to protect her. It had been risky in the elevator, but Matthew would have the surveillance videos destroyed. Here someone could take personal pictures. He got his phone out of his pocket and sent a quick text to Matthew.

'Make sure nobody comes in the corridor of our floor for the next five minutes, maybe ten, but I doubt I'll last long.'

Amy watched him as his phone beeped back with the message,

'I doubt you will last thirty seconds.'

He looked down at Amy who was still staring up at him. Her glazed look was now mixed with excitement and expectation.

"I want you to take me deep. I'll come in your mouth, and then you will lick me to clean me off." He twisted his hands around her hair and pulled her head up until he could kiss her mouth. "Every last drop, I want to taste my cum on your lips when I next kiss them."

"Yes, Master." She undid his zip and carefully pulled his thick length out of his trousers. He already had a drop of pre-cum on the head. She stuck her tongue out and licked it off. He tried to maintain his control and not come at the sight. She pulled his balls out and carefully massaged them. Matthew might be right about his thirty-second estimate. She leant closer and slowly fed him into her mouth. He was too long to fully fit unless she swallowed him, and that wasn't something that he was going to try on her, just yet. Not in the corridor of a Las Vegas hotel anyway. She lightly nibbled on him while her tongue swirled around the head of his cock. He didn't think he could get any harder. He looked down and saw her looking at what she was doing. Most women who had sucked his cock automatically shut their eyes unless he told them to keep them open. She didn't.

"Look at me."

She did exactly what he asked. There was nothing but love in her eyes. She took him a little bit farther so that he hit the back of her throat, and the tip of her manicured nails stroked at the sensitive spot beneath his balls. He couldn't hold back any longer, and his cum shot from his body, deep into her throat, in an explosion. He was sure he would choke her with the amount that kept coming, but she took every last drop. He was certain he saw stars as he slumped against the wall; his torso heaving with exhaustion. She cleaned him up, tucked him back in his trousers, then rose to her feet, and kissed him. He tasted his bitter, salty flavour as it was transferred from her mouth to his.

"Was that acceptable, Master?"

This time, it was his turn to find words hard to come by. He nodded his head and fumbled in his pocket for the key card to the room. He handed it to Amy, and she unlocked the room. The lift around the corner made a noise.

"You decent?" Sophie's giggling voice came from that direction.

"Fuck off, Sophie." He didn't have the energy for teasing. He pushed off the wall and walked towards the suite door.

"Yes, we're decent." Amy bit on her finger with a bright red glow in her cheeks.

All four of their friends strode around the corner. Matthew had his hand on his watch.

"Three minutes and fourteen seconds, by my count. Sonia, you win."

"You didn't bet on us, did you?" Amy was so embarrassed.

"No, we bet on my brother. Goodnight."

"Goodnight, Sis. Come on beautiful. I haven't finished with you yet."

James shut the door on his laughing friends. He groaned when he heard Matthew open a book on the odds of him falling asleep and not having more sex.

SIXTEEN

Amy

Amy untucked herself from James's arm and crept silently across the floor of the hotel room to the bathroom. She did a wee and then reached for her toothbrush to clean her teeth. They'd fallen into bed after a day of relaxation by the pool, champagne and strawberries at La Reve, and a couple of hours dancing at the XS nightclub. James had made love to her in the most tender of ways. It had been slow and searching. He must have tasted every inch of her body until she was crying with a need for them to be joined as one. When he sank into her, he didn't move at first. Instead, they lay together staring into each other's eyes whispering I love you. This was what she loved the most about him. One moment, he was dominant, but the next, he was tender and loving. She never knew which one she was going to get, but whichever persona, James always made sure that she was satisfied before he took his own pleasure.

She washed her face, brushed her hair, and then headed back to the bedroom. She happened to glance at the clock and noticed it was nearly eight am. They had to be ready for the trip to the Grand Canyon at nine am. She pulled the covers off James and paused for a minute to take in his god-like body. It took her breath away every time she saw it.

"Get up. We have to be on the coach in an hour."

He sleepily groaned, opened one eye, looked at the clock, and then shut the eye again.

"I'll get us a helicopter to take us there instead. Get back in bed."

"No. I want to go on the coach. I'll get to see more of Nevada that way."

"Have fun. Take Matthew with you." He pulled the covers from her hand and turned over to go back to sleep.

"James! Get up!"

No response. For a person who was normally an early riser, he was being particularly stubborn. She noticed his glass of water beside his bed, and picking it up, flicked drops of the clear liquid at his head.

"You do that again, and I'll spank your backside so hard you won't be able to sit for a week."

She did it again, and he leapt from the bed and tried to grab her, but she managed to avoid him and ran out of the bedroom and behind the sofa. She squealed as he tried to get round and tackle her to the ground, but she was too quick and again evaded capture.

"Now you're up; you can get dressed. We have fifty-five minutes and counting."

"Bedroom." His eyes darkened. She was in trouble.

"Don't get any ideas. I want to be on that coach, and you're wasting time." She reached for the phone and dialled Matthew's room quickly. "Can you get us some breakfast to go, please? We're running a little late."

James growled and shouted into the receiver, "You better get her an ice pack. She's going to need it to sit down." Before Matthew could answer, James ripped the phone from her hand and slammed it down. He pulled her close, and she could feel his erection through the lightweight fabric of her PJ's. "You're in so much trouble for that."

"Later. I want to go and see the Grand Canyon."

"But on a bus full of tourists?"

"Live a little. It'll be fun."

"Debatable."

She kissed him on the lips.

"Come on, if you're quick we can take care of your morning wood in the shower."

"Sweet talking me isn't going to stop me punishing you later."

She pulled away from him and wiggled her backside at him, and before she could even draw breath, she found herself pinned up against the shower wall with him inside her.

The coach arrived at dead on nine which surprised her because, from her experience, these things were always delayed. She had made James dress down in just a T-shirt and shorts, although they were still all designer brands, and he'd left his Rolex in the safe. She had put on a pair of tiny shorts and a t-shirt which was printed with ethnic designs from their trip to India. She had pulled her hair back in a long braid and topped the outfit off with a sun hat and shades. They boarded the coach and were immediately greeted by an enthusiastic but quintessentially American couple from Alabama who were on their first trip to Vegas and having the best time ever. They were working their way through the shows along The Strip and had won a thousand dollars on roulette last night. James pulled his Armani shades down over his eyes and held her hand tightly. She could almost feel him radiating 'she's mine' pheromones. The tour guide was very knowledgeable and had an excellent sense of humour. On the way to the Canyon, he pointed out numerous places of interest, including the Hoover Dam and the oldest recorded Joshua tree. He also had them all in stitches with his tales of Las Vegas life including many stories about what the Pawn Stars TV show got to sell. Matthew and Sonia sat behind them, and she could hear them both laughing. Despite the fact he was trying to play it nonchalantly cool, she could tell James was also enjoying the guide's speech.

They stopped first at the Skywalk on the western rim. She was told they were in an area that was part of the Hualapai Native American Reserve. They all got off the coach, and the guide gave them half an hour to explore and get a drink.

She and Sonia eagerly went straight to see the Canyon. James and Matthew ambled along behind them, Matthew was very much in stealth protection mode. She was pretty sure beneath his lightweight jacket he was concealing weapons, and knowing Sonia, she probably had an arsenal hidden on her person too. She pulled her phone from her pocket, approached the viewpoint, and snapped a few pictures before just standing still and marvelling. The different rock faces were illuminated by the sun and showed all the different layers which had been carved out by the Colorado River over millions of years to form the canyon. England had its beautiful natural sights, but nothing could compare to this either in scale or drama. She reached out and squeezed her bodyguard and friend's hands.

"Isn't it just amazing?"

"I didn't think it was possible to see something like this on planet Earth. I'm so used to green expanses." Sonia had grown up in the Lake District on her parents' farm. She was used to vast spaces but mainly those covered in grass, trees, lakes and various types of cattle.

She pulled Sonia closer and held up her phone for a selfie of them both. James snatched the phone from her hand and took a much better one of the two of them together before it turned into a round robin of touristy type photos of each couple. She was having so much fun. They needed this, and she could tell that despite it being out of his comfort zone, James was starting to relax.

"How long do we have left?" she asked while they walked towards the visitor's centre.

"About ten minutes." Matthew looked down at his watch.

"Just enough time for some Cactus juice." James clapped his hands

"Some what?" She looked at him a little confused.

"Delicacy in the area. Come on."

She stared at the frothy foam topping the freshly squeezed prickly pear green drink. "I don't know; it doesn't look that appealing."

"Try it." James picked up his cup and drank it in one go. Matthew did the same. Sonia and Amy looked at each other.

"After three?" Sonia volunteered.

"Alright."

"One, two, two and a half, two and three quarters."

James and Matthew picked their drinks up for them, and both men shouted three and forced them to drink it.

She tried not to gag as she swallowed the foam and then the juice. It didn't have much of a taste. There was a hint of watermelon, but it reminded her mainly of cucumber. She was more into her sweet drinks, so it wasn't that pleasant.

"I think that's an acquired taste."

"It's better as an addition to sangria." James laughed.

"I'll take your word for that."

Matthew looked at his watch and led them back to the front of the shop. "We better get back to the coach."

They arrived, and the guide held his hand out to help her up the steps. James pulled her back and snarled.

"You don't touch her."

She turned and frowned at him,

"Manners, James. I'm so sorry." She turned back to the guide and smiled sweetly. "He can be a little protective."

The guide smiled, "Don't worry, Miss. I've seen all sorts."

When they sat down she told James off. "He was just being kind. There was no need to speak to him that way."

"He's not allowed to touch you."

"He was helping me on the coach."

"I was there. I would've helped you."

"Go sit with Matthew and have a think. Because at the moment, I don't want to be next to you."

James reluctantly sat with Matthew, his face like thunder, and she couldn't help but smirk that he looked like a little boy who had had his favourite toy taken away from him. Matthew turned his head, knowing better than to try and make pleasant conversation with his boss now. She called over her shoulder,

"And you better make sure you give him a good tip to say sorry."

She turned back to her seat and noticed the couple from Alabama watching her. The lady smiled at her and turned back to her husband.

By the time they'd reached the location where they were going to get a helicopter to fly over the Canyon, James had mellowed a little. He'd sent her a text saying he was sorry for being a possessive jerk and that she wasn't allowed to orgasm for twenty-four hours as punishment for defying him. She sent him an emoji of the devil back. She loved to tease him knowing that he'd probably break first.

While they were waiting for the helicopters, they divided into groups based on weight and given numbers. The guide came up to their little group with the Alabama couple.

"Howdy folks, gotta request of y'all."

James turned his head. "How can we help?"

"Seems we've oddly balanced helicopters. I know y'all are a group, but I was wondering if we could split you fine couples up just for the flights. Seems you two guys don't overly fit the girls' weights."

"I'm going in the same helicopter as my girlfriend. No arguments on that one. You need to hire another helicopter to do so? We will pay for it."

"Of course, sir, I wasn't gonna split you from yer lovely lady, but I wondered if yer friend and his girl would ride in another 'copter, and this couple here can ride with you?"

She smiled over at the happy faces of the American couple. She placed her hand in James's.

"Of course, that won't be a problem." James tensed beside her. "Will it James?"

"Of course not." He spoke through gritted teeth.

"Thank you."

James pulled Matthew aside, and she saw Matthew give him a gun.

"James."

"Don't Amy. Just don't."

She rolled her eyes. "It's our turn."

They followed another guide out to the helicopter, and she was shown around to the front of the aircraft while James was directed to the back seats.

"She sits with me."

The lady of the Alabama couple came over to him.

"Come on handsome, we won't bite you know. Chill and enjoy the ride. Your girl is perfectly safe, and from the back you can watch her the entire time rather than the canyon, if you want."

She suppressed a little laugh at the way the woman tapped his arm and almost pushed him into the helicopter. She smiled at her.

"My Bill was just the same at first. Once he got my collar on, though, he mellowed a little. Happy to share me now." She pulled down the zip of her polyester jacket and showed her the tattooed cuff around her neck.

"He's your master?"

"Yep, here for the BDSM event on New Year's Eve. You going?"

"Er. Yes."

"See you then."

Amy climbed into the helicopter and was pretty much silent for the rest of the flight. She wasn't sure whether it was because of the beautiful sight of the Grand Canyon or the fact that the relatively normal looking couple would be attending the BDSM club's New Year's Eve bash.

SEVENTEEN

James

James watched Amy while she finished her Eggs Benedict. The breakfast room was a light and airy conservatory which overlooked the swimming pool. The waiters were intently observant, and anything they needed was brought immediately. She had her long, wavy hair pulled back in a ponytail and had applied a little mascara but no other makeup. She was dressed in a white slip dress which accentuated the tan that was slowly developing on her shoulders. The sun brought out lots of little freckles on her cheeks. He still couldn't believe that she had come back to him. At times, he could be a right dick, and still she stayed with him. He was a lucky, lucky man, and he couldn't wait to be her husband.

He was a little nervous about the New Year's Eve ball. He was introducing Amy to something that was predominantly his need, not hers. Control had been an issue between them throughout their relationship.

"Are you sure about tonight?"

She placed her knife and fork down and wiped the edges of her mouth with a napkin.

"Why? Do you not want to go?"

"From the moment we enter that building, I'll need you to be subservient."

She leant forward and took his hand and stared up into his eyes.

"If we were going shopping, and you started picking up anything I said that I liked and placing it behind the counter to buy for me then I'd be angry at you. I know you would be doing it for me because you love me, and you want me to have nice things, but I don't need them. Tonight is different. I'm actually excited. I know you're worried about how I'm going to react to you telling me what to do, but you don't need to be. When I walk into the club, I'll be placing my body and my needs into your hands. I'm willingly doing so because I trust you, and I love you."

"You mean that?"

"Yes, I do but...."

"Yes?"

"The beautician is coming at three to start getting us ready. Until then, I want to spend time just you and me. No bodyguards, no Matthew and Sonia. I want to go and explore the Venetian, have some lunch there, and wander around the shops. Just be a normal couple. We can dress down and look like ordinary tourists. What do you say?"

"I like the sound of that. While you were with the beautician, I was going to go and choose a piece of jewellery to match your dress for this evening. We can choose it together."

"I have enough necklaces and earrings to wear already. I don't need more."

"I'm not talking about those sorts. When we walk into the club tonight, I want everyone to know that you're mine. I want the women to envy you and the men to be upset that they can't touch you."

"You mean a collar? I don't know."

"Not necessarily, you can wear cuffs. Just something that shows you're mine."

"This really means a lot to you, doesn't it?"

"Yes, it does." The waiter began to hover around them before she could answer him.

"More coffee, sir?"

"No, we're good, please have the breakfast billed to our room."

He stood.

"I'll wear with pride whatever we choose."

He kissed the top of her head, and they went upstairs to change.

They walked into the grand opulence of The Venetian about an hour later. It was one of the newer hotels on the strip and included several landmarks such as the Rialto Bridge and the Piazza San Marco.

He stood outside the Banana Republic while Amy was inside browsing the tops. He wanted to give her the space to choose something for herself and not feel pressured from him to buy it. He could see her at all times, and she had promised him she wouldn't disappear into the changing rooms without bringing him into the shop first. He was enjoying this new side to their relationship. His fiancée was fiercely independent, but that only turned him on more. He picked up his phone and flicked through his emails. His lawyer sent him a draft version of a prenuptial agreement. He didn't want to even think about it because Amy would be with him for life, but his parents, even though they loved her, insisted. Miranda had done the same with Sophie and Grayson. He placed his phone back in his pocket when Amy came out of the shop carrying a bag.

"Bought anything nice?"

"Just a top."

"Show me?"

She pulled out a blue lace tank top.

"A little revealing, isn't it?"

"No, it has a camisole under it. I thought I could wear it with the blue trouser suit that you bought me for functions at the school."

"It'll be beautiful. There is a shop up here that I want to have a look in. I think they will have what I want to get you, for tonight."

She smiled up at him, and he waited for the arguments to start. Why did he have to fall in love with the only woman who refused to allow him to buy her anything?

"Come on then. I'm starting to get hungry again, so we better be quick; those pizzas just look so delicious."

"I hope you're building up your energy for tonight. You're going to need it."

She rolled her eyes and gave him her hand, so he could lead her to the shop. He could see the trepidation start to build on her face as soon as she saw that nothing within the window had a price tag on it.

"I don't need this amount of money spent on me."

He put his finger to her lips to silence her.

"This is for you when you're in my domain. I'm the one buying it to show you off as mine. You won't argue with me on this as it's really a present for me even if you wear it."

"Yes. And we all know what happened last time you bought a present for yourself." She fluttered her eyelashes playfully, and his cock began to thicken.

"Get inside the shop before we're arrested for public indecency."

He was sure she swayed her hips that little bit more when she walked through the emporium's door. He'd work that sass out of her later.

"How may I help you?" The plain looking, middle-aged sales assistant stepped forward.

"We're looking for matching twenty-four carat gold bangles, preferably studded with sapphires and diamonds. The diamonds must be VVS or better, near colourless with a very good cut. I also don't wish anything less than three carats. The sapphires must be royal blue, vivid of clarity, and of similar carat to the diamonds. I want the bracelets so that I can thread a twenty-four-carat gold chain between them if I so wish. That will also be purchased in your store if you're able to satisfy my first request. And I think this will prove my credentials for this sale." He held Amy's hand up to show off her engagement ring.

The sales lady momentarily stood there with her mouth-watering. She was most definitely adding up the commission that she'd get from this sale. Amy looked at him with a baffled expression on her face.

The assistant flicked her hand at another lady in the shop who rushed over and pulled out a seat for Amy. Glasses of water were fetched for them while the dumb struck assistant fetched out numerous boxes and lined them up.

"I truly have no idea what you just asked for." Amy held his hand.

"I asked for lovely bracelets for my beautiful fiancée."

"So that is why she's looking like she just hit the jackpot and will finally be able to put her children through university?" She raised her eyebrows towards the assistant now opening the first box.

He ignored Amy and looked at the bracelets. "No. Not right. Next."

"Don't I get a say in this?" She tapped her fingernails against the skin of his palm.

"You can choose from the ones I like."

"Gee, thanks."

The assistant opened a few more. He placed one aside but rejected the others. They weren't exquisite enough.

The final box opened, and he heard Amy gasp. He looked down at the delicately carved bangle. it had a pattern of sapphires and diamonds around it and interlaced winding threads like branches of a tree. It was beautiful. Perfect.

"This one. Sort this out and the chain. I also want a small padlock with one key attached to it. The padlock is to bear the initials JN. I want this all done and delivered to my hotel room by eight tonight."

"Don't you want to know the price first?" Amy enquired.

"You know that doesn't matter."

"I shouldn't even argue with you right now, should I?"

"You can argue with me, but it will delay you getting your pizza."

She looked to the sales assistant.

"He'll take it."

Ten minutes later, they were sitting in the St Mark's Square, complete with expertly painted false sky ceilings, awaiting their vongole pizza and drinking a glass of Pinot Grigio.

"Are you going to tell me how much it was?"

"No."

"Do I need to make sure they're stored in the safe when we get back to England?"

"No, you will wear them at all times so people know you're mine."

"People know I'm yours by the way you growl at them whenever they try to even say hello to me."

"Good."

"Men!" She rolled her eyes.

"Women."

"Cheers." She held her glass up to him.

"Cheers."

Their merriment was broken by a group of people dressed in masks and long robes running through the fake square. A team of security guards chased them, but it didn't stop them throwing leaflets and shouting about God and sinners. They spoke of 'Chastity above all else; Sex for the procreation of the human race.', and they proclaimed that 'All who indulge for pleasure are sinners' and 'This place is full of sinners.'. One of the men chanting the manifesto, who appeared to be the leader, stopped when his eyes landed on them. "This couple," the man continued and pointed at James, "The man is the devil. See how he touches her?" The skin on James's neck pricked up with the words, and the venom of the man's fervent tone. Amy must have sensed his panic and tried to pull him away inside the restaurant.

"Let's go." He refused to move.

The masked man raised his voice, "Missionary is the only condoned position." His throat dried. A security guard tackled the man to the ground and silenced him. He was vaguely aware of Amy still pleading for him to come inside, but he couldn't shake the memories, the pounding agony in his back because the words opened old wounds. The security guards pulled the intruders away, and the square began to settle. Amy came around in front of him. She pulled his face down to hers and met his lips with a heated kiss.

"Look at me. Listen to me. They're just a group of brainwashed idiots. I love you, and you love me. What we do is between us, and we both consent to it. Do you understand?"

He finally allowed her to permeate his darkness, her sweet tones calming his rapidly beating heart. He nodded, and she helped him sit down. She handed him a glass of wine, and he drank it down quickly.

"Sorry. You're right. Come, let's continue enjoying our day." He grinned; more as a way to reassure her than because he actually felt comfortable himself. "And especially our night."

When she went to the toilet a few minutes later, he pulled out his phone and texted Matthew. Something wasn't right, and he wasn't going to let this lie.

EIGHTEEN

Amy

After they arrived back at the hotel, James disappeared into a meeting with Matthew. She had tried her best to calm him, but she could see the doubt lingering in his thoughts. It wasn't that he doubted his own sexual tastes. He worried he was forcing them upon her. She needed to show him that she loved what they did and giving him control in that way turned her on even more. Tonight would be the perfect opportunity to do so.

She made her way down the corridor to Grayson and Sophie's room. The men were to dress and prepare in the room that she shared with James, and Grayson was allowing his room to be turned over to a complete beautician's salon for the ladies. She was excited about this bit. She'd had a couple of spa treatments, and her nails had been beautifully manicured when she was in India, but it wasn't something that she regularly did. She was also excited about spending some time with just Sonia and Sophie. She had few close girlfriends, except Elena, and it was nice to get away from men sometimes and gossip. She also needed to find out a bit more about what was expected of her tonight. She needed to make sure she did everything right for James. It was important to him and therefore important to her.

She knocked on the door. It was swiftly opened, and she was pulled inside. Her lightweight dress was removed from her body and tossed aside. A fluffy dressing gown was wrapped around her, and a glass of champagne placed in her hand.

"What do you want to have done first? I'm going to have a massage. Need to make sure all my limbs are supple for tonight. Grayson says that he's going to use the swing."

"Matthew arranged a shibari master for me. We're still debating who is getting tied up, though." Sonia laughed.

Amy drank the champagne in one long gulp.

"Are you alright?" Sophie came and held her hand. "You look like you're about to run for your life. You know he won't mind if you don't want to go through with this."

"No, I want to. Every time I think about what he is planning for me, I get very... well excited. It's just all these terms. How I should act? What exactly will he expect me to do?"

Sophie pulled her to sit down on the giant leather sofa.

"A swing is basically a large children's swing with strategically placed handles to open you wider to your partner. It deepens the movement between you both. Shibari is the use of ropes and knots in sex. It constricts the movement of the person who is tied up and again can leave them open to their partner's needs."

"Both sound dangerous to me."

"They can be, but that is why we trust Matthew and Grayson to use it appropriately and not hurt us."

"So is James going to do anything like that to me?"

"I think he'll keep things easier for you. You asked for FFM didn't you?"

"Did I?"

"Another female in the room who only you will touch. James and her do not touch each other?"

"Yes. I don't want anyone touching him, but I think he'd like to see me with another woman." She blushed. "And after seeing some of the girls in duo dance acts at the club, I wondered what it would be like."

"You don't have to be ashamed of what you want to try. Last time Matthew and Sonia were here, we pleasured each other for our Masters. We're still at ease with each other afterwards. It's a lifestyle for us, and we feel no shame for what we do. It's all natural. That is why James and I can go to clubs together."

"I wondered about that? Isn't it strange James being there when you're with Grayson."

"James and I have only been to clubs together a couple of times, and each one has been for an important reason. Tonight is New Year's Eve. We will go with you, have a drink with you, and then separate for the rest of the evening. Grayson does not punish me in front of James. He'll take me aside to do that. James understands the life and what it gives me. He knows that Grayson will protect me. I feel no discomfort with him being there."

"So for the start of the evening, it'll be just like going to a regular club?"

"Yes."

"He's going to use someone called Mistress Alexia?"

Sophie squeezed her hand. "Mistress Alexia is lovely."

"I'm a little worried. James has been with her before, but he assures me that by using her it'll be good for me."

"She's a switch at the club. She has several regular men she goes with. She's clean. She has no feelings for them whatsoever. Grayson and I have used her as well. Alexia will enjoy every minute because she loves sex, and if you let yourself relax you will too."

"Okay. Good. I think I feel sick."

Sonia finished having her nails done and came over. "I felt the same the first time with Matthew. But it all seemed so natural when I got in there. My desire to please Matthew just took me over, and I haven't looked back since."

"How do I act in there? I mean do I walk a certain number of paces behind him? Should I kneel at his feet? Can I speak?"

"There will be high protocols this evening because of the nature of the event. However, knowing James, you will walk beside him, almost pinned to his side so that everyone knows you're his. I'm surprised he hasn't got a flashing neon sign for you to wear. For sitting, it depends on the Master. Grayson likes me to kneel at his side, but Matthew has Sonia sit next to him. James will tell you what he wants. And of course you can speak. Nothing will happen that you're not happy with. You've a safe word?"

"Yes."

"Great. You're uncomfortable then use it."

"Have either of you used your safe word before?"

"I have once," Sonia answered, "I was exhausted, and Matthew just made me keep coming. I had to stop him. He stopped that instant and cradled me in his arms as I fell asleep."

"I haven't. But then, Grayson knows my likes and dislikes, so he doesn't push my boundaries too much, now, because we have the rest of our lives together to test them."

"I just need to relax and go with the flow, don't I?"

"Yes," they both answered at the same time.

"Well then, I think I'll start by getting my nails done and then the massage." She wiggled her glass. "Is there any more champagne, and have we ordered snacks?"

At exactly eight-thirty pm there was a knock on the door and as the beautician opened it, in walked James, Grayson, and Matthew. All three had dinner suits on. She was sure her tongue was hanging out, and she was panting like a horny teenager at the sight of James. The black bow tie around his neck emphasised his muscular column, and his shoulders looked even broader in the jacket. He smiled at her as the beautician returned to her side and placed the final few touches to her lipstick.

The dress that he had chosen for her was made of black silk. It had a halter neck collar, adorned with sapphire and gold beads. The beads followed a path down her back into an exposed keyhole design which finished just above her bottom. The dress was tight around her hips before a split to the left side allowed her to show off a beautiful tanned leg which was accentuated by three-inch heeled sandals. She should have probably laid off the carbohydrates at breakfast and lunch time with this dress being so body hugging, but the others assured her she looked amazing. It was now James's turn to look like a randy adolescent. He swept her into his arms and pressed a heated kiss to her lips.

"Let's forget this idea and go back to our room?"

"I have just spent close to four hours getting ready. I want to go out."

"You need a couple of things before you do."

He handed her a mask to disguise herself. It was delicately made of black thread and copied the pattern of the beads on her dress.

"The ball is a masquerade. I have one. Nobody will know who we are. You're only to remove it when in the private room with me."

"Yes, Master." She tried not to laugh and handed the mask to the beautician who placed it on her.

"You have these." He gave her the gold cuffs and helped to put them on her arms. She could hear Sophie and Sonia exhale.

"They're beautiful." Sonia exclaimed and flashed her eyelashes at Matthew.

"Well I didn't get you a bracelet, but you do get a collar to match your dress, if you wish to wear it?"

She turned as Matthew opened a box and showed Sonia a necklace laced with rubies to match her vibrant red dress.

"Matthew, you can't afford this!"

"Seems I can with my winnings the other night."

"Really?"

"Yes." He placed it around Sonia's neck as she watched on. She'd never seen her bodyguard so happy.

"Well, Grayson, what do I get?" Sophie raised a questioning eyebrow.

"You just had a lavish wedding and will be spending the next week in my bed on our own deserted Caribbean Island. I think you've had enough." Grayson stood with his arms folded defiantly across his chest in answer

"Worth a try." Sophie went to him and kissed him. "We ready to go?"

"The limousine is downstairs waiting."

"I just want one moment with Amy, if that is alright?" James held her hand while the others nodded and filed out of the room.

"Is everything alright?"

"Yes, I just wanted to tell you what will happen tonight before we go. I'm sure Sonia and Sophie have told you most things. When we go to the private room, Alexia will come with us. You have my assurances that she will not touch me. If she does, I will remove her from the room immediately and request her disrespect is dealt with."

"I understand. I trust you."

"I want to push your boundaries tonight; it will not only be you trusting me. I'll be trusting you as well. If you don't like something tell me. I'm putting faith in you to tell me. In return, you will be giving me the power to know when something is wrong. That is why you have to give me the control sexually." His eyes had turned dark and focused. "We'll not use a safe word tonight. We're going to use a traffic light system: green, you're happy with everything; yellow, you're feeling a little uncomfortable or nervous; red, stops everything. I'll ask you several times throughout the evening how you're feeling, and you will answer me truthfully. If I do not believe your answer, then we will end. Do you understand everything I'm saying?"

She thought for a moment. It was a lot to take in.

"Yes," she answered.

He smirked.

It didn't take long to get to the club. As the car pulled up, James held her close and whispered,

"How are you feeling?"

"Green. I put my faith in you tonight, and I'll be rewarded." She took a kiss from his lips, and he got out of the car and extended his hand to help her out. She expected the club to be dingy and similar in its facade to how the school had once been, but when she got her first glimpse of it, she was pleasantly surprised. It was sophisticated and looked like a high-class nightclub. She relaxed and took James's arm.

"We have high protocols this evening. You will walk at my side at all times. You don't go anywhere without asking me first. From now on, you may only call me Master or Sir, and Matthew and Grayson are to be treated with the same respect. Remember that they're in control of Sonia and Sophie so be mindful of interaction with them. To touch anyone here, you must ask my permission."

"Yes, Master."

"You may speak to me as you wish but wait for permission with others."

"Yes, Master."

He pulled her close to him, and they entered the glamorous foyer of the club. Grayson was instantly greeted by a throng of guests who obviously knew what mask he would be wearing or recognised him despite it.

James was welcomed and seemed on friendly terms with those surrounding them. They were shown to their VIP seating area.

"Where would you like me to sit, Master?" She wasn't going to presume anything.

He patted the seat next to him. "Always next to me."

"Thank you, Master." She took a seat.

Drinks were brought to them, and the conversation flowed with ease. She needed the bathroom and got to her feet to go.

"Where are you going?" James's stern voice came from behind her. Damn, she forgot she was supposed to ask him if she wanted to go anywhere.

"I needed the bathroom, Master. I'm sorry I forgot I should ask."

His voice grew thick with lust and his eyes darkened. Had he just been waiting for her to make an error such as this? Why did her barely-there panties suddenly dampen with excitement?

"I think you need a reminder. Come here." He stood, and she bowed her head and walked towards him. "Grayson. Turn Sophie away." James pulled her close to him with her breasts against his chest and began to rub his hand caressingly over her pert backside before giving it a hard whack. Again he rubbed and then repeated before growling into her ear. "Ask Masters Grayson and Matthew to do the same to you."

"What?" She suddenly froze.

"Colour?"

Amy pulled back her shoulders and held her head high.

"Green."

She didn't want to go to Matthew first so went towards Grayson.

"Please, Master Grayson. I made an error. Would you help me learn my lesson?"

He nodded and pulled Sophie up to her feet.

"Hold her still." Sophie stood in front of her and mouthed, 'you're doing brilliantly.'

Grayson followed James's example by smacking her twice and caressing in between.

"Thank you, Master Grayson."

"You're welcome."

She could feel her cheeks flushing. She looked over to James and could make out his erection growing within his dress trousers. Her breath hitched, and her clit throbbed. She turned her attention to Matthew, who looked to James for approval. When they had been with the same woman was James dominant over Matthew? She suspected so.

"Master Matthew, please help me learn my lesson?"

Matthew nodded kindly at her and manoeuvred her hands so that they rested on the side of his seat. Matthew did not caress her. Instead, he looked to Sonia and gave her permission to do so. He applied the smack and Sonia's tender hands soothed the pain away.

"Thank you, Master Matthew."

Matthew nodded again.

She returned to James just as someone called to Grayson.

"I need to go and talk to some people. Can you look after Sophie for me please?" the actor asked.

"Of course. Sophie, you will accompany Amy to the bathroom," James replied.

Grayson pulled Sophie to her feet again and pressed a kiss to her lips. "If you're good, I'll reward you with your swing on my return."

"Yes, Master."

Grayson disappeared off, and Sophie took her hand and guided her to the bathrooms.

"How are you feeling?"

"Is it always that intense?"

"Yes."

"I think with the amount I defy James that I'll probably end up with quite a sore bottom by the end of the evening." She laughed, and Sophie joined in.

They did their business and avoided the glares of jealous women when they both strode confidently back to their seats. As they approached, she could see another woman in her position. She was not touching James, but she was near him. Jealousy spiked in her, and her heels got a little louder when she marched towards him and his new companion. Sophie tried to keep a grip on her, but at some point she let go. When she got back to James, she stood directly in front of him with her hand on her hip.

"Yes?" He looked up at her.

"Where do you want me to sit, Master, as there appears to be someone in my seat?"

"She's feisty, Master James. I like her; she's perfect for you."

She turned her head sharply to glare at the woman, taking in her features properly for the first time. She was a little older and probably a dress size bigger. She had her brown hair cut in a stylish bob, and Amy was sure that she had some sort of filler in her lips to make them that pouty.

The woman came to stand in front of her while James stood behind her. "This is your mistress for the evening. You will refer to her as Mistress Alexia."

She bit her lip when he pressed his hard erection into her back and whispered into her ear, "Your jealousy is a big turn on." He pulled back. "Alexia, you may kiss my fiancée in greeting." She pushed back into him, and he came down to her ear again. "I got you beautiful, relax."

She stood frozen to the spot as the elegant woman leant forward and pressed her lips against hers.

Alexia pulled back. "So sweet and delicious."

"Shall we go to our room?" James spoke from behind her.

She just managed to say yes.

NINETEEN

James

Alexia led the way through the slate grey corridors of the club. He held Amy close to him as they followed. She was already breathing rapidly.

"Colour?"

"Green…just"

He had learnt to read her well. She was excited and enjoying everything, even the public display of punishment. He bet the second he pulled her pants from her body that they'd be soaked with the juices of her arousal.

Alexia held the door open for them, and he watched Amy's face intently while she entered the room. It was modern and minimalistic, and the walls were pristine white. In the middle of the chamber was an enormous, circular king size bed covered with fresh sheets in finest black cotton. Along one wall were white cupboards filled with various items that might be required, and there were hooks on the ceiling, should they need them, but he wasn't going to push her too far. He knew what he wanted to use on Amy and had sent Alexia a list so that she could buy new. Even though everything was sterilised, he wouldn't use anything on his fiancée that had been previously used by anyone else.

Alexia walked into the centre of the room and stood with her hands behind her back and head bowed.

"Go and join Alexia. Stand as she does until I give you both instructions."

He went over to the cupboard where his personal toys were stored. He wanted to deprive Amy of as many senses as he could, so she was able to just focus on what he and Alexia would be doing to her. That would be the best way to get her to relax initially. He brought a small MP3 player and a mask over to the bed and placed them down. He then proceeded to take his jacket and bow tie off. He could hear a little purr of disappointment from Amy when he removed the bow tie.

"You like this my little kitten?" He waved the bow tie in front of her, and she looked up.

"I like the way you look in it, Master."

"You want me to fuck you while I'm still wearing it?"

"Please, Master." Her eyes lit up.

"Remove my shirt and put the tie back on me then."

"But I don't know how to tie a bow tie?"

"Do you need Alexia to show you? She won't touch me but merely instruct you."

"Please, Master."

"Alexia, assist her please."

The brunette took the tie from his hands and looked at Amy with a reassuring smile.

Amy undid the pearl buttons of his shirt and slid her hand inside to remove his shirt. She went to touch his chest as she dropped the shirt to the floor. He grabbed her hands.

"Did I say you could touch me?"

"No, Master." She bit her lip.

"Do it again, and I'll chain your hands behind your back, and I won't wear the tie."

"I won't do it again."

He released Amy's hands, and Alexia gave her the bow tie. He watched her face as she, under Alexia's tutelage, tied it around his thick neck. Her breasts already rose and fell on a quickened breath. He wanted to stroke himself when she stuck her tongue through her lips in concentration. He needed to get himself under control, or Amy would find this whole experience wholly unsatisfying.

"Alexia, I want you to undress Amy and help her to lay on her back on the bed." He stepped away from them. "I then want you to put the blindfold over her eyes and the headphones in her ears."

"Yes, Master."

He loosened the buckle on his trousers and slid them down his toned thighs, he watched Alexia undress her with such tender care. Her black silk dress pooled at her feet, and her muscular legs looked even longer in the heels.

"Leave her shoes on."

Alexia nodded and held onto the thin straps on Amy's knickers. She got down on her knees before her and slid them down her legs. Amy didn't take her eyes off him the entire time. The corners of her mouth turned upwards as the cold air hit her pussy. He looked down, and she was devoid of any hair down there. She had always kept herself neat, but everything was gone now. His cock strained for escape.

"Beautiful." He reached out and ran his finger over her saturated labia. "And so wet for us, Alexia."

"May I feel for myself, Master?"

"If Amy allows you."

"She may, Master." He heard Amy whimper when Alexia's slender fingers travelled over her mound. He ran his fingers over her again, and her head fell back. He stood up and with one hand pulled her back up to look into his devouring eyes, and with the other hand, he pushed two fingers between her succulent lips.

"See how excited you are?"

"It's all for you, Master."

"Alexia is a switch. That means she'll be my submissive, but with you, she'll top as well."

"That means she'll dominate me, as well?"

"Yes. She'll give you instructions as I do, but mine will overrule hers at all times."

"Alright. I'm happy with that."

"Good girl. Alexia, please assist Amy onto the bed."

Alexia did as he asked; Amy lay back.

"Put your hands above your head." Alexia spoke, and Amy instantly obeyed. "Master, these cuffs are beautiful. I think we should take away her ability to touch us."

"My thoughts exactly. You blindfold her and put the headphones in. I'll get the chain for the cuffs." He turned to walk back to his jacket but was stopped.

"James?" Amy was suddenly shivering.

"What is wrong?" He quickly came back to her side, his voice full of concern.

"Yellow." Alexia stepped back and resumed her position of hands behind her back and head bowed.

"What I'm merely trying to do is take away your sense of sight and hearing to heighten your sense of our touch upon your body. Alexia and I are going to kiss you and play between your thighs. I'll use no toys here. It'll merely be our lips and hands. We will insert our fingers into you but nothing else."

"That sounds like it would be fun."

"Yellow is a good feeling here. I want you on edge. Besides, I put the Chicago soundtrack on the music player. I know it's your favourite."

She laughed but still hesitated.

"Alexia and I won't touch each other. Alexia will stay clothed and I shall remain as I am now. You've my word on that." He could feel her relaxing again.

"Just make sure you keep your lips on my body at all times."

"I plan on it. You've nothing to fear there."

Alexia returned and placed the blindfold over Amy's eyes and then the music in her ears. He held her hands the entire time. She was tense, but he could stop that in a matter of minutes.

"Alexia, will you fetch the chain from my jacket pocket and attach it? I'll stay here."

Alexia chuckled and swayed her hips when she went to his jacket. He saw Alexia more as a friend than a sexual partner. Yes, they'd been intimate on numerous occasions, but it was never emotional. He'd allowed himself to be guided by Alexia even though he still took the position of dominant. It was from her that he learned the magic of a woman's body, and now he was using her guidance to help him find out more about the body of the woman he would spend the rest of his life with.

When Alexia finished chaining Amy's hands to the bed in a position that pushed her breasts together, she stood aside and waited for his next order.

"Suck on Amy's breasts. She likes an interplay of pain and pleasure, gentle biting and flicking."

"Yes, Master."

He positioned himself between Amy's legs. He started with her feet and alternated kisses and nips up one leg, missing the mound of Venus which she grumbled about. When she tried to thrust into his mouth, he gave her a little tap on her pussy in punishment. He then repeated the kisses and nips back down the other side. His eyes flicked up, and he saw Alexia alternating between her breasts, their colour tinting red as Amy pushed them higher hoping that she'd get more stimulation to them.

"She's greedy, Master."

"Very." He shifted his weight, trying to disguise his movement and bit down with his teeth on her left nipple. Amy arched her back and cried out. "Put a finger inside her but don't touch her clit. Keep one hand on her breast." He continued to pleasure her other breast while he used his other hand to circle her hooded clit which was already plump with her desire. Amy was writhing on the bed from all the stimulation.

"Another finger." He loved how obedient Alexia was: obeying his instructions without question.

"We should use nipple clamps, Master. She has perfect breasts for them."

"I told her I wouldn't use toys while she was blindfolded." He pulled one of the plugs out of Amy's ear. She dreamily moaned.

"I'd like to put nipple clamps on you." His voice was heavy with the desire he was feeling.

"Yes."

He returned the earphone to its place.

Alexia placed the nipple clamps over Amy's breasts.

"Yellow…yellow," she called.

James rubbed her clit and thrust his fingers in and out.

"God. Green!"

Amy arched her back off the bed and almost dislodged his fingers. He placed more weight on her legs.

"Straddle her stomach. We will alternate licks to her ravenous little clit." He had purposely not shaved for this. He wanted Amy to get the different sensation of feminine and masculine teasing her to orgasm. And the fact she had removed all the hair from her mound played into his plan perfectly because everything down there would be extra sensitive. He teased a third finger into her and hooked them to find her G-spot. He first licked her clit, and then Alexia did. It didn't take long before he knew that she was on the verge of her orgasm. The skin of her pussy was flushed red and sodden with her craving.

"Next time, bite down. I want her flying. Keep it going until she multiples."

"Yes, Master." Alexia smiled at him like a proud teacher seeing her student take his rightful place in the world.

Alexia bit down on Amy's clit, and immediately she cried out and began writhing in ecstasy. A rush of her arousal soaked his hand. Her inner muscles gripped his fingers like a vice as his cock strained within his pants to try and get to her. He was sure it would be covered in pre-cum the second he removed it from his pants. He needed to do something to make this last. She began to come down, and he nodded to Alexia to bite again, and instantly, she came again. They did it a third time before Amy whispered, "No more. I need to get my breath back."

He withdrew his fingers and placed one in his mouth to savour her glorious taste.

"Undo her chains and remove the headphones and blindfold. Sit her up."

"Yes, Master." Alexia obeyed his instructions, and he removed his straining cock from his pants. He needed to come now, or he wouldn't be able to last long enough for what he had planned next. He began to fist himself. Amy adjusted her eye sight to the light and saw what he was doing to himself.

"I'm going to come now so that I can continue to pleasure you. That got me a little more excited than anticipated. I'm going to give you a choice. I can come on you and Alexia licks it up, or vice versa. What do you say? Only you get to clean me, though."

She suddenly blushed, and he knew something naughty had crossed her mind. He stopped touching himself and reached out and grabbed her hair and pulled her towards him.

"Tell me exactly what went through your head. Word for word."

"Master?"

"I won't ask you twice."

"I thought that maybe you could come on us both, and we could clean each other up."

He almost came right there.

"Pardon. No, I heard you. I think I have awoken a little demon. Both of you on your knees, on the floor."

Alexia pulled off her top, and they both scrambled to their knees in front of him. He couldn't take his eyes off Amy. She had a mischievous glint in her eye. God, he loved this woman. James fisted himself faster, running his strong fingers over the throbbing head. His orgasm began building deep at the base of his balls. Amy's eyes shifted from his face to his cock, watching every stroke. He saw her grinding her legs together to try to get friction where she wanted it.

"Amy legs apart. You come without me saying, and we will go straight home, and you won't have my penis inside you for at least a week." She instantly split her legs, giving him a better view of her still swollen sex. That was the last straw. He stepped forward and immediately spurted his seed over the welcoming faces and breasts of both women.

"Amy. Clean me."

She leant forward and sucked at the head of his still hard cock. Her warm tongue lapped up every drop.

"You're clean now, Master. May I have permission to clean Mistress Alexia?"

"Alexia?" As a courtesy, he asked her. He already knew the answer from the way the brunette looked at Amy.

"Of course."

Amy tentatively leant forward and brought her lips to Alexia's mouth. She used her tongue to clean her chin, down her neck, and on to where a drop of his cum hung on Alexia's left breast. When she was clean, James motioned for Alexia to clean Amy. He was already getting hard again. Amy wouldn't be the only exhausted person tonight after this.

"Tell me what you're thinking?"

"Master, I'm thinking that your cum tastes delightful mixed with the strawberry flavour of Mistress Alexia's body. Are we finished now, Master?"

"What do you think? Do you say it is fair that we've both taken our pleasure while Alexia is half naked and needing something between her thighs?"

She shook her head. "Alexia, tell Amy what you'd like her to do to you while I fuck her from behind with a set of anal beads inside her."

TWENTY

Amy

It was approaching one a.m. by the time they returned to the hotel. Amy was wrapped up in James's jacket and cradled in his arms. The use of her legs seemed to have failed her ever since she had spent the chimes of New Year with him deep inside her while she sucked on Alexia's clit. It had definitely been a New Year's experience to remember, and she made a mental note that he needed to research a club in London where they could do the same thing. If not, he was to assist Grayson in opening one. She didn't think she would like being treated like someone's property, but it was all about reward, not ownership, and she certainly got her reward with five orgasms by the end of the evening. As James lay her down on the bed, his eyelids were heavy, and she secretly congratulated herself on tiring out her virile lover. He helped her to undress then gingerly walked to the bathroom and brought a cloth to clean her up. He also handed her, her toothbrush to clean her teeth. When he went into the bathroom and shut the door, she pulled out her phone and sent a quick text to Sonia. She had made an important decision tonight, something she had been musing over for a while. She left a message for Sonia to arrange an appointment for her around eleven the next morning and put her phone down. When he came back in, he pulled her into his arms, and tenderly stroked her hair.

"Are you feeling alright? You may be a little sore tomorrow. I was a bit rough with you, and you strained against the chains. I'm surprised you didn't pull your shoulder out."

"It'll be a pleasant ache. One that tells me that I'm loved and adored by the best man in the world."

"And his sidekick."

"Yes and Mistress Alexia. I hope I did satisfy her."

"You did. Alexia doesn't fake her orgasms. I have seen many a man fail to give her one."

"Have you ever failed?"

"Have I ever failed you?"

"No."

"Then, I have never failed with Alexia either."

"There is your ego again."

"Thank you for being willing to experience something that I like. I know how nervous you were and how your past tainted what you thought it would be like."

"I was prejudiced; I see that now. Thank you, for showing me something new that I like. And something that I want to do again...soon."

"Tomorrow night?"

"I think I may need a couple more nights to recover first, but I have a lot of things I want to try. Sonia and Sophie told me about swings and rope tying. That sounded like it could be fun."

"My God. We will never leave the BDSM clubs of London if you get this involved in everything."

Both of them drifted off to sleep in each other's arms. It felt like only a matter of minutes had passed when her phone began to vibrate. James groaned loudly and turned over so his back was to her. He began to snore lightly again. He needed more sleep. He would have normally been up and in the gym way before now.

She crept from the bed and grabbed a pair of clean knickers, bra, jeans and t-shirt. She still had her gold cuffs on but decided she liked them there. She quietly went into the bathroom and jumped in the shower. She was surprised how achy she felt. It was not uncommon for her to dance for hours upon end, but after one night with him, she had more aches than she knew were possible. She dressed, snuck back into the bedroom, and noticed that he was now sprawled out on his back. The sheet was just about covering the lower half of his body. She watched for a few moments the rise and fall of his chest. She was a very lucky woman to have such a handsome man so entirely devoted to her. She took her bag from off the dressing table, popped her phone in it, and silently edged towards the door. She slid her flat Birkenstocks on and opened the door. She was holding her breath the entire time but managed to slip outside unnoticed. Sonia and Matthew were waiting for her.

"Shush. James is still sleeping. I don't want to wake him. I really want to surprise him with this."

"I'll ensure one of Grayson's team remains here to watch him." Matthew yawned and rubbed his bleary eyes.

"Matthew, you look exhausted. You've been trying to manage the security team and enjoy everything we have. Go back to bed. We will take one of Grayson's guards. Sonia, do you have a weapon?"

"I have several." She looked at Amy as though she were mad for even suggesting that she didn't have one.

"That's my girl." Matthew smiled proudly.

"See? I'll be perfectly safe, and James won't need to throw you off the top of the hotel for letting me go out without you."

"I just hope he doesn't throw me off the upper part of the hotel for allowing you to do what you are doing."

"My body. He only rules it in the club. Now back to bed. Let us girls have fun."

Matthew almost crawled back to his room. She had a feeling Sonia would find him fully dressed and asleep on the sofa when they returned. If, in fact, he even made it as far as the couch. She linked arms with her friend, and bodyguard, and motioned for a guard to follow them as they took the elevator down to the waiting car.

"How far is it?"

"Should only be about a fifteen-minute drive although traffic still looks busy even on New Year's Day."

"This really is the city that never sleeps. I wonder if I could persuade James to divert us to a Caribbean island on the way back, just so I can lay in the sun for a few days and not move."

"I'll get Matthew to back you up on that if you do."

The two girls giggled together throughout the entire journey to the tattoo parlour. Amy got out of the car, and a burly man about five times her size with tattooed arms and head came out from the shop. He had several piercings in his nose and ears and one through his eyebrow.

"Miss Jones. A pleasure to meet you again."

"Likewise, Claw?"

"Yes, Miss. My nickname, all folks around here call me that. Come on in, I have everything set up and ready."

"Thank you, Claw, and I'm sorry to get you out of bed on New Year's Day."

"It's alright. My missus would've just had me in the kitchen getting food ready for the BBQ later. You've saved me. Now you still want the design as we discussed before."

"Yes, please. On my collar bone, I want 'James' to be written in a simple Indian Mehendi print. I want it to be seen when I wear halter neck or strappy tops."

"Take a seat. Shouldn't take too long. It's all one colour."

An hour later, she was staring in the mirror at the perfect design on her collar bone. It was intricate but simple at the same time. She couldn't wait to show James. The artist placed Bepanthon over the tattoo and then covered it all with some cling film. He also put a lightweight bandage on top but told her to remove it as soon as she got back to the hotel. She pulled her T-shirt back on as Sonia paid the man.

"Thank you again, Claw. You don't know how much I appreciate this. I'm sure James will be in touch to pass on his thanks, after I show him."

"I think the tip your bodyguard just gave me tells me your happiness. I think I'll get a couple of bottles of the good stuff for the missus tonight. As for Mr North, he has a perfect body for designs, try and persuade him to come back again soon so that I can give him another one."

She picked up her bag and pulled out her phone to see if she had a message from James wondering where she was. There was nothing. Hopefully, she'd be able to sneak back into bed and surprise him with the design when he woke.

A loud crash came from behind her, and she swung around to see the window smash in. A canister landed on the floor, emitting a strange gas. Sonia instantly jumped in front of her and drew her gun. After that, everything seemed to go into slow motion. First, the other bodyguard with them dropped to the floor, blood pooling at his head. Claw screamed. His knee exploded. He fell onto the floor and yelled in agony. Her world span as the gas from the canister flooded the room. She saw Sonia fall to the floor but no blood. What the hell was happening? She tried to reach for her phone to press the key for James's number, but before she could, she was on the floor looking up into the face of the man from the Venetian. After that, she blacked out.

TWENTY-ONE

James

James sat bolt upright in the bed and rubbed his eyes. His befuddled brain tried to figure out where the knocking was coming from.

"Amy?"

No answer. The knocking came again; it was at the bedroom door.

When he opened the door, Matthew stood there and not Amy. His bodyguard looked petrified.

"Amy?"

"No, but we need to go to her immediately. I got the eye scan back from my mate. You were right. It's him."

"Fuck. Where is she?"

"She had Sonia and I arrange a surprise for you." Matthew looked at the ground.

"Where is my fiancée?" His tone was cold and menacing.

"She's with Claw. She wanted to get a tattoo to show you how much last night meant to her."

"And you let her go? Without you."

"She has Sonia and one of Grayson's guards with her, and Claw is a pretty scary bugger but..."

"But what?"

"I just tried to phone Sonia to tell her what is happening, and she isn't answering."

He flew back into the bedroom. He grabbed the nearest pair of jeans he could find and slipped into a t-shirt which was on the chair. "Get my gun from the safe."

Matthew did as he was told. He slipped on a holster, placed the gun inside, and put on a jacket over it.

"Go get a car. Any one, I don't care. If you need to commandeer the vehicle off the fucking manager of this place, do it."

Matthew sped off, and five minutes later, they were on the road to the tattoo parlour.

"Damn that woman. When I get my hands on her, I'll lock her in our room and not let her out without a team of armed guards."

"I'm sure it's nothing. You know Claw likes his music deafening. They probably just can't hear their phones."

"You checked the tracking on them?"

"Yes, they're still at the parlour."

"I guess that is a small mercy. She's still getting punished, though."

"What are you going to tell her about him?"

"I'm not. I'll get us on the first flight back to London and let Grayson's team handle it. We gave him a pretty stern warning last time. He obviously hasn't listened to it."

Both men quieted. They remembered the warning that was given. Three police cars and an ambulance overtook them. His throat grew dry as they turned towards the tattoo parlour. Matthew sped up, and they drew up alongside the police. They all raced to the same destination: the smashed facade of the tattoo parlour with what looked like acrid smoke pouring out.

He looked to Matthew as they both sprang from the car and began running towards the smashed frontage. A burly policeman stepped in front of them.

"You can't go in there."

"My fiancée is in there," he spat back.

"Afraid it's a murder scene, sir. I can't let anyone in."

Murder? No.

He floored the policeman with one punch and barged his way into the doorway of the building. Grayson's guard lay on the floor, his head blown open, his brains splattered against the wall behind him. He couldn't see Amy or Sonia. A gun was pointed at his head.

"Sir, put your hands in the air and turn around slowly."

He did as he was told and his arms were pulled behind his back, and he was cuffed. His gun was removed from its holster.

"My fiancée and her friend. Please, where are they?" he pleaded with the cop.

"What?"

"Two women. They would've been in here. The dead man is a bodyguard." He looked to his left and noticed Matthew talking with another officer. Matthew carried papers which proved they were allowed to carry guns. The cop who held his cuffs pulled him towards Matthew.

"Chief, this one says his girl was in the parlour with a friend."

"Yes, we were just discussing that." He looked to Matthew, wondering how much he had mentioned.

"What has the tattoo artist said?" Matthew asked.

"Not much, but he's in a hell of a lot of pain. The window was blown in, and a gas canister thrown into the parlour. Must have knocked the women out so that they could be snatched."

"Any idea who is behind it?"

"There have been a couple of girls going missing like this recently. They all pretty much fit the description of your two. Cute, early twenties, in a relationship with active young men, enjoying themselves in Sin City. Then we had all those activists from that cult invade the city the other day."

"Is the tattoo artist stable?"

"Yes, they'll bring him out in a minute. Not sure he'll keep his leg."

"May we have a quick word with him? We just want to know if our women are injured. I just want to get my fiancée back." He spoke up as he was released from the cuffs and his gun was handed back.

"Alright. Two minutes. Officer Smith, stay with them please. You go straight back to the hotel afterwards. Any more trouble, and I'll arrest you for assault on a cop and lock you up while we investigate."

He and Matthew went straight towards the medical team as they brought Claw out.

"Ask him questions really quickly while I distract the officer. We need to know the girls' conditions, how many men, anything that was said." Matthew spoke in Karnataka Hindu to him before turning to the police officer. "Officer Smith, can you just explain to me again about these activists? How many girls have they taken?"

He quickly bent down to Claw who was dosed up on morphine but still awake. "Claw."

"Mr North? I'm sorry. I couldn't do anything to stop them taking her."

"Were they hurt?"

"No, the gas knocked them out. Your girl didn't flinch once as I did her tat."

"She's pretty special, but I need you to focus. Do you know who took her? How many? Did they say anything?"

"I saw three men, tall fellas all in black. I have never seen them before. I thought you'd come so didn't tell the cops anything. I'll have to now, though."

"Give Matthew and I as much time as possible to get ahead of them, okay?"

"Will do. I'll ramp up the morphine. Makes me utterly incoherent."

"I'll have my people set up everything for your healthcare. You will get the best service."

"Thanks, Mr North."

He stood to go back to Matthew, but Claw grabbed his arm.

"Wait. There was one thing. Miss Jones… I'm sure she recognised the person, just before she passed out. I saw it on her face. When she was out cold, he said something to her. What was it? "He has taken another angel and defiled her."

"James?" Matthew called from behind him. "We should go back to the hotel and wait there for any news." There was a look of urgency on Matthew's face. He didn't argue and followed Matthew back to the car.

"What is it?"

"Sonia just activated her emergency tracker. I need to get back to the hotel and check the location on my computer and transfer the codes to my phone. It is set up to find Amy's as the primary source, but that hasn't been activated."

"Do you think they're separated?"

"Maybe, I don't know. Sonia will try and activate Amy's as soon as she can. They may be tied up and can't get to each other. I have trained her for this sort of situation. She will protect her. We're going to need more bodies, though. If it is a cult there might be more men than we can handle alone. Their weaponry doesn't look too good either. Claw's wound, the bodyguard's, they're both from sawn off shotguns which is why everything is such a mess. The gas canister is Falkland's war issue."

James pulled out his phone and flicked through for Grayson's number. He answered on the fourth ring.

"I said I wasn't to be disturbed all fucking day."

"Gray. Where is Sophie?"

"Seriously man. I'm knackered."

"Where is Sophie?" This time, his tone didn't leave any room for argument, and Grayson went quiet.

"Right next to me in bed. What is going on?" He could hear his sister's concerned voice in the background.

"Amy and Sonia have been kidnapped. We're on the way back to the hotel now to get coordinates from Sonia's emergency tracker. I need you to get Sophie into lockdown and as many of your men as you can ready to go within the hour."

"I'll do it straight away and be ready to come with you. Any idea who it is?"

"Yeah, my worst nightmare has come back to haunt me."

TWENTY-TWO

Amy

Amy's head felt like she'd been up all night drinking Jägermeister. She tried to remember what happened. She got a tattoo for James and then everything went slightly insane. She lifted her head and opened one eye. The room she was in was dark although it had a small lamp in the corner which provided a little light. She had a gag in her mouth. The rough material was covered in her saliva where she had apparently been dribbling while unconscious. She tried to move her arms, but they were bound behind her. Sonia, who was a bit farther back, was in the same position. Where the hell were they? and what was going on? From somewhere in the room a sermon began to play; a lecture on the sins of man and of fornication for which it was not prescribed. Oh great, as if being kidnapped wasn't bad enough, she had to listen to this. The sound stopped. A key turned in the lock, the door opened, and in walked a man in his early thirties. He was dressed in smart black trousers and a fully buttoned black shirt with a floppy white collar. His hair was cut short.

"Welcome Miss Jones, Miss Anderson. I'm sorry for the need to tie you up, but we couldn't risk you waking and hurting yourselves while attempting to escape." She pulled against the restraints as the man came nearer to her.

"So pretty and so young. How must you have suffered under his touch. Don't worry, you're safe now. You're with the family, and we will protect you for the rest of your life."

She shouted into the gag, "Fuck you, weirdo."

The man lay his finger on her head, and she tried to pull it away from his foul touch.

"Dear child, he has filled your head with so many evils. Untie her." He gestured to two men who walked into the room. They immediately obeyed and removed the ties from her arms. She was pushed onto the floor to kneel before him and held in place by the two men at her sides. She could hear Sonia protesting and struggling behind her.

"Here we don't tolerate language such as that. A lady should be meek. She should only speak when it is requested of her. She should be chaste until she's married, and then her husband will guide her in her way of living. That is what is prescribed. Remove her gag."

The damp rag was drawn away from her mouth.

"I don't know who the fuck you are, but you're messing with the wrong lady. Now if you want to stay alive, I suggest you let me and my friend go. There will be powerful men coming for us, and they won't go easy on you because you are so obviously insane." The man laughed. "Insane and a death wish. Look, why don't you just leave us alone and go say whatever prayers it is you need to before you die?"

"I see so much of his tongue in you."

"He who?"

"Why your fiancé, Miss Jones. Mr James North, the devil himself."

"Look, why don't you go just give your ransom demands to James, and then we can all be home before nightfall. I had a busy night last night. I'm tired."

"There is no ransom demand, Miss Jones. We're here to save you from him. Just like I saved my sister. I thought we'd beaten the devil out of him, but no, it still lives in him. He proved it when he stood there and watched his man do this to me." She froze as the man began to lower his trousers. She caught the sick in her throat when he revealed his dick, but where she expected to see testicles there were none. "See, Miss Jones? Your man truly is the devil. He took away my chance of fulfilling my destiny to be a father to a loyal wife. He violated my sister, and he ordered the murder of my brother. I'll destroy the devil by rescuing you from his clutches."

"He's not the devil. You're the menace with your beliefs, forcing them on others. What he did to your sister was not wrong. It was natural. You started all this by beating him within an inch of his life." She was struggling against the men holding her arms. She lost her common sense against the rage inside of her. "You tried to break him, but you failed." She turned back and looked straight at his groin, "And you're lucky I wasn't there because I wouldn't have left you with a penis." Her head was thrust down on the floor, her cheek slamming against the wooden planks while the man pulled his trousers back up.

"You will learn, Miss Jones. What I do to you will harm me more than you. He has brainwashed you, and I need to cure you." He pulled a large knife from his pocket and prowled towards her. Her life was going to end, and all she could think of was how James would be without her. He'd be broken. The man pulled on the end of her long ponytail and pulled her head up. Sonia struggled against her chair, shouting into her gag in rage and fear. The man stared deeply into her eyes,

"Vanity is sinful. You know you're pretty, so we will remove some of that." He slid the knife into her hair. It fell around her head and jagged edges came over her face.

Her hair had been long ever since she could remember. Her mother always wanted her to have long hair. She had always braided it and dressed it beautifully. Tears swam in her eyes. The man threw the length of hair at her and then put his knife away.

"Eugene, have your wife come in here and dress Miss Jones. I want to make sure that she can't escape. We will marry her to her husband tonight. He won't mind being locked away in the correction room with her while she's made to see the error of her ways."

"What? Married." She gasped out the words.

"Yes, Miss Jones." The man lifted her head again, so he could meet her eyes. His danced with psychosis. "Our mission is to rescue young girls such as yourself. To bring them back to the virtues of being a woman. Your husband will be a good man. You will serve him. You will produce as many children as he requires. You will cook, clean, look after his offspring. You won't argue with him. You will remain subservient just as our Saviour wishes. You will be put back on the path of righteousness." She couldn't believe the utterly warped view of femininity that she was hearing. This man was on another planet. She'd been taken by a cult, and they were expecting her to be a meek and mild wife.

Sonia suddenly crashed her chair to the floor and jumped up. With extraordinary speed, she slit the throats of the men standing either side of her. Sonia pushed her out of their hands and towards the door.

"Run. I'll be behind you."

She did as she was told and headed straight for the door. She got outside and heard the man call for help. Sonia appeared behind her and pushed her along the wall.

"Keep quiet. We need to try and figure a way out of here." Sonia took her hand and pressed the top of her engagement ring.

"What did you just do?"

"Don't get angry, but James has a tracker in your ring. I have one in mine, and I activated it earlier. But they need to have yours too so that they know we're together and can plan their attack accordingly."

"They're coming for us?"

"Of course."

"He's going to be so mad at me."

"He will be relieved to get you in his arms. Now keep low."

"Sonia, what did you do to that man?"

"I stabbed him in the leg. He won't be chasing us anytime soon."

"You didn't kill him."

"James didn't give me permission to do that."

Footsteps came running from behind them as they reached a doorway. Sonia kicked it open and almost dragged her outside. She handed her a knife. "Whatever happens, keep running, get to civilisation."

"Sonia."

"Please. You have to do as I ask."

"Alright."

They were out in the desert. Would there be any civilisation out here? She did as Sonia told her and ran. She reached a small patch of sequoias and large rocks and darted in between them. Her heart was beating so fast. She looked around for Sonia, but she could not see her. She was running on adrenaline, listening out for cars and people talking, looking for any sign that she was reaching somewhere where she could be protected.

She heard her name and froze. It was the man; she recognised his voice.

"Miss Jones. I suggest you stop running, Miss Jones. I know you're nearby. I have your friend, and unless you show yourself to me, I'll kill her." He sounded cold and calculated. She put her hand over her mouth to hide the noise of distress which came from her. She walked towards the voice but kept herself hidden. Sonia was being held down by three men. The man stood next to them. He had a large rip in his trousers and blood oozed from a wound in his leg. He was being supported by another person. "I'm not a patient man, Miss Jones, and I need to have my leg stitched. You've precisely two minutes to show yourself. And to show you I'm serious, I'll give you a demonstration of what will happen to Miss Anderson unless you come on out."

One of the men held Sonia's arm out, another handed the leader a bat, and he swung it down onto Sonia's arm. She held her hand over her mouth to stifle a sob. Sonia screamed, and the bone snapped. Sonia had told her to run, but if she did, they would kill her. What would she tell Matthew? She couldn't do that to him. She couldn't leave her friend.

James and Matthew were coming for them. Sonia was adamant about that. She just needed to gain them more time. She stepped forward from her hiding place and was immediately surrounded by men. Sonia looked at her and shut her eyes before she was hit around the head with the bat and passed out.

"No. You said you wouldn't hurt her."

"She'll have a headache, but hopefully it'll help her see the sense, I think you are now seeing. She's a bad influence on you, and you will be kept separated. Come, we need to dress you for your future husband."

"I won't marry anyone except James."

He grabbed her around the throat.

She spat in his face and was met with a slap to hers. Her arms were pulled behind her back and tied together. Gunshots rang out from the direction of the building they'd escaped from.

"Get her to the car."

"Master?" The guy holding onto her left arm, like a rabid wolf, suddenly looked scared.

"He can't get her. He's the devil. If we allow him to take her back, we will have failed her. We need to leave. We need to get her away and hidden."

"But what about our brothers and sisters? We can't leave them to perish at his hands."

The mind-warped brother pulled a gun from the waistband of his trousers and fired straight at the questioning man. The shot hit him directly between the eyes, and his blood splattered over her face. She screamed.

"Shut her up." A blanket was put over her head, but she continued to shout.

"If anyone else wants to question my actions then say so now, and you can stay behind. The devil is coming for his Queen. She's our salvation. We must save her." The words were muffled by the blanket, but she could still hear them. She was lifted off her feet and carried rapidly. The person holding her stumbled as she tried to struggle and kick out. The blanket came loose, and she was able to shout louder. There was a pickup in front of them. She was thrown into the cab, and the leader climbed in beside her. The man who'd been carrying her climbed in beside them and took the wheel. He started the engine and sped around in a tight circle at great speed and drove onto the main road.

TWENTY-THREE

James

He heard Amy before he saw her. She sounded horror struck. He tore off towards her voice with several of Grayson's team at his side. They ran through the sequoias and craggy rocks of the desert. They reached a small clearing and found Sonia laying on the floor in an unnatural pose. Matthew raced to her, and he held his breath as Matthew checked her over.

"Get the medical team in here." She had a massive lump on her head, and it was evident that her arm was broken. She was barely coherent, but she reeled off things that Matthew needed to know. Amy shouted out again, and he sped off in the direction of her voice. An engine started as he ran out into another clearing. Amy was inside the car, her eyes wide with terror, and next to her sat his ex-girl-friend's brother. He had to stop the vehicle. He raised his gun to shoot at the tyres, but the car began to spin around. If he shot them out, he risked it flipping and Amy being hurt. Matthew appeared behind him,

"Over here."

There was another pickup and the idiots had left the keys in the ignition. Grayson and his personal bodyguard jumped in the back. Matthew floored the accelerator, and they were off, following Amy. He didn't need to direct Matthew. His bodyguard was more than adept at weaving in and out of the traffic on the freeway as they chased after the car carrying her. Anger burned inside his chest.

The driver of the pickup in front of them was all over the road, trying to lose them, and then he suddenly exited. Matthew managed to swerve around a truck and bumped over the kerb and off the freeway. The pickup did a ninety-degree turn down a small road, and he was slammed against the window as Matthew did the same. They skidded to a halt, and he could see Amy being dragged from the car, screaming and kicking out. She had blood on her face, and her hair was cut.

He was going to skin her captor alive. They leapt from the vehicle but ducked behind the doors when a shot was aimed at them. The driver was providing cover so the cult leader could get Amy away. Matthew fired back, shattering the door of the truck where the man hid. Matthew's guns were MI5 issue and went through anything. Before long, the driver collapsed on the ground in a pool of blood.

"Stay in pairs. Stay close. I'll cover James. You cover Grayson," Matthew said to Grayson's personal bodyguard. "No one shoots unless I say. He's unstable, and he could do anything to Miss Jones if we don't get a clear shot."

Amy's screams alerted them of her position. The land was rocky and led to a section of the Grand Canyon. They got closer, and he could hear chants about the devil not tainting this sweet child anymore. That he'd protect her, and that she'd fly alongside him at the hand of God. He planned on taking the pair of them over the side of a ledge. They emerged through some trees, and she was being held around her neck with a gun to her head.

His heart was in his mouth. She looked so tiny and so very scared.

"Stay back, Lucifer. I won't allow you to take her. You took my sister's purity. You tainted her mind with your evil. I couldn't save her, but I won't allow you to take another innocent."

He saw Matthew peel off to the side. The bodyguard would be surveying the scene and working out the weaknesses and how to extract Amy from the madman.

"Jacob, your sister gave herself to me for love. What we did was natural. Your beliefs made her feel dirty. Whatever happened to her was the responsibility of you and your demented brother."

"No," he shouted back, and Amy shrank down. "You defiled her body. She told us what you did. We tried to beat the devil out of you, but he's too strong. Repent James. Fight him. You can be saved, but you will never be able to have this innocent child again. I won't allow it."

"Alright." He placed his gun down on the ground. Amy shook her head at him. "I want to save myself. Let the girl go. I'm Lucifer, she'll obey my instructions. I have brainwashed her to my evil ways. Amy, if Jacob lets you go, you will get straight into the car and go back to the compound. I have done you wrong. They'll save you there." She nodded a 'yes'.

"You're a liar. If I let her go, you will have your man kill me. No. She's staying with me."

Years of oppression and the punishment that Matthew had inflicted on him had left his brain in a different world. He wouldn't have been surprised if Jacob could see him as bright red with horns and with trails of fire surrounding the ground behind him. "Jacob, I want you to save me." He slowly got to his knees, bowed his head, but kept an eye on the man's movements. He placed his hands down on the ground. "I have done many bad things. I ordered the death of your brother. I have forced the lady you hold into sexual acts that have degraded her. I allowed the devil to rule my mind. But with your guidance, I can change. I have finances. We can rid the world of all the deviants and work together to rescue innocent girls and educate them. Let something good come out of all the pain we've both felt." His eyes flicked to where Matthew had taken up position for a clear shot on Jacob. He just needed him to get Amy to step clear. "Please Jacob, let her go."

Jacob dragged Amy farther towards the edge of the cliff.

"No. No. I see what you're doing. You can't fool me. My brother said you did this. You act innocent, but inside you're plotting to take her from me. Not happening." He shouted the last phrase.

" I swear to you I'm not joking. I want to help all the girls you've rescued. I know you've no reason to trust me, but I want to help you." He wanted to rip this man's head off and feed it to vultures, but part of him knew that this was a mental health issue. Maybe, with proper care, Jacob could be brought back to some semblance of sanity.

"No. You don't get it, do you? It'll always be a part of you. It'll always come back. I can't allow you to get near her. It's too risky. She is innocent, and I can't be at his side if I don't stop you. My brother won't allow me to be at his side. He speaks to me and tells me what to do. He always has." He waved the gun in the air.

"No, Joseph. He says he can help us; I can't do that."

"Jacob, is Joseph here now?"

"Yes." He pointed the gun back at Amy's head. "He's telling me I need to rid the world of you." Jacob then pointed the gun directly at him. Out of the corner of his eye he saw Matthew and Grayson cock theirs, ready to fire, but Amy was still too close. He immediately gave Matthew a look to tell him not to shoot until Amy was out of the way, no matter what.

"Jacob, has Joseph always told you what to do?"

"I was his younger brother. He looked out for me." His hands shook on the trigger.

"I'm like that with my sister," he said, "I always tell her what to do. You know what, though. She doesn't listen to me. She makes her own mind up. And she's an amazing woman because of it."

"She's as bad as you. I know where you went last night." He moved the gun and pointed it towards Grayson. "I saw him. Maybe he is the actual devil." Grayson's bodyguard pulled him aside and focused his gun on the sweating and rapidly breathing Jacob.

"No. I told him to do that to her. I'm the devil, Jacob." The gun instantly swung back to where he was still kneeling on the ground. "Alright, you don't want to let the girl go. Why don't you put the gun down? Sit down with her. She looks tired and hot. My man will bring some water over to you. We don't want to hurt the girl, do we?"

Jacob looked at Amy. "I'll put the gun down, but they put theirs down first. "

"Of course. Matthew, do it." Matthew, Grayson and the bodyguard placed their weapons down. Matthew would have another one hidden which he could reach in seconds. "They've done it. Now please, will you put yours down?"

Jacob released his hold around Amy's neck but kept a tight grip on her hand. He leant forward and placed the gun on the ground. As he went to stand up, Amy spun and managed to free herself from his grip. Matthew had his gun in his hand as Jacob toppled backwards over the cliff. Amy began to run, but Jacob managed to shift his weight forward and grab her ankle. He slid back over the cliff and pulled her down and over with him. It all happened in slow motion as if it was a scene from one of Grayson's movies. One moment she was running, and then she was flat on the floor. Her perfectly manicured nails were trying desperately to find something to grip to keep her from falling before she disappeared from sight. He looked beside him and saw everyone else running for the cliff. He looked down at his legs, and they were doing the same. They were running, but he wasn't controlling them. He slid to a halt at the edge and forced himself to look over. She shouted his name. Her bracelet was wedged into some rocks, and she was desperately trying to hold onto another rock. He reached out and grabbed her sweaty wrist. Grayson was at his side doing the same to her other arm. They sought to pull her up, but she was too heavy.

"Get him off me. Don't let me fall."

Jacob still held her legs. He was frantically clawing his way up her body. Matthew appeared at his side.

"Boss?"

He had a split second to make his decision. Amy's hands were too wet to hold her for much longer. He was fooling himself that Jacob could be helped with mental care. He was too far gone.

"Take it."

A shot rang out...Amy was suddenly a lot lighter, and he and Grayson pulled her back up and over the edge. Grayson collapsed. James pulled Amy into his arms. She was crying hysterically. He examined her from top to bottom. She had scrapes and scratches all over her arms, legs and belly. Her t-shirt was in tatters. Her lip was bleeding, and what was left of her hair was covered in dirt. She was almost hyperventilating. Grayson's bodyguard brought over some water and helped Amy to drink it.

"Shush, you're safe. It's over. I have you. You're in my arms, and I'm never letting you out of them again."

She looked into his eyes and moved her filthy and bloodied hand to touch his face.

"I... I thought."

"No. No thinking."

"Sonia?" She sat up alert and looked to Matthew.

"She's with a medical team. Her arm is broken, and she has a pretty severe head wound."

"I'm so sorry. She told me to keep going, to leave her, but I couldn't do it. He would've killed her." She was sobbing.

"It's alright. You did the right thing. Both you and Sonia are safe."

He heard Grayson's bodyguard talking about a clean-up crew. Grayson got to his feet and walked back to the car.

"We have to get out of here. I have a plane waiting to take us back to London right now. Do you think you can walk?"

"No. I want to go and see Sonia."

"Matthew will sort her out and then get our belongings together and bring them home. I need to get you back to London, so you can heal."

"No."

"Listen to me. I'm not going to argue with you about this."

"Will you just listen to me for one minute?"

Grayson put his head in his hands, and Matthew got back into the car.

Even after nearly dying, she was still arguing. "You've two minutes."

"Do you know why I went to get the tattoo?" With everything that happened, he had forgotten about that. She pulled a scrap of her t-shirt aside and lowered what remained of the bandage. Underneath, James could see his name in an intricate Indian design. She had his name on her skin. "People think I let you rule me, and that you control me. But in India you surrendered your control to me when you told me of your past, and here in Las Vegas we have divided our control. Each of us has a role in our relationship. I show you that you're capable of love, and you introduce me to the person I can be. Do you understand what I'm saying?"

"Yes I do, this is all good, but I need to take over the control right now and get you to safety."

"I choose to be with you. I'll be a target all my life because of that. It's what we do about that perceived target that matters. Apart we're weak, but together we're strong. That's what got me through this. I was thinking of you losing me the entire time." Amy looked into his eyes. "Will you marry me?"

"We're already engaged."

"I know we're engaged. But what if I said that you have twenty-four hours, and by the end of that time, I want to be your wife. What would you say to me?"

"I want you to have the fairy-tale wedding. When we get back to London, we will arrange it. We can be married in a few weeks."

"Either you marry me within twenty-four hours, or we will never marry." Despite the dirt, blood, tear marks and rather wacky new hairstyle, Amy had a familiar defiant look on her face.

"Grayson? How quickly can your bridezilla plan a wedding?"

"Twenty-four hours."

"Then call her."

TWENTY-FOUR

Amy

Amy shifted her aching body on the bed, and she instantly felt a hand brush her hips. She didn't even need to open her eyes to know that James would be poised above her with concern all over his face. Had he got any sleep? Or had he sat beside her all night watching her? She opened her eyes and gave them a few moments to focus before she did indeed see her lover. He was all set to jump from the bed to get her anything she needed or kill anyone who tried to come near her.

"Are you alright? Are you in pain? Do you need me to get your medicine?" He helped her sit up and take a sip of water.

"No, I'm feeling alright, just general soreness from everything." She looked at the clock and noticed it was almost ten a.m. "Have you heard anything more on Sonia?"

"Matthew brought her back to the hotel late last night with a medical team. She has a concussion, and they operated to pin her arm, but she'll make a full recovery. I'll take you to see her later. She needs lots of rest."

"Dare I ask how the wedding plans are coming on?"

"I have no idea. Sophie is doing everything. She said it's bad luck my being here with you, but I refused to leave. I need to deliver you to her room at one pm so that you can get ready. She won't let me in, though. Are you alright with that?"

The thought of him leaving her side, even to go the bathroom, terrified her. However, she couldn't get ready for a wedding while being attached to the groom like a limpet.

"Will Grayson be there?"

"Yes, Sophie has asked him to remain near you at all times. I suspect that if you even need a wee, he'll be standing outside the door while Sophie is there inside the bathroom with you."

She smiled, "Will Sonia be able to come to the wedding?"

"I don't fancy Matthew's chances of keeping her away even though she has a broken arm."

She rubbed her eyes again to remove the last trace of sleep and ran her hand through her hair. Tears instantly flooded her eyes. She couldn't help it. She remembered the knife severing a lifetime's growth from her head. He pulled her into him and placed her ear against his heart.

"There isn't time to get you a full set of hair extensions today. I'll do it when we get back to London. It should look alright until your natural hair grows again. We've sourced a top of the line wig, though."

She sat up and pressed her lips to James's. He tasted a little salty. He can't have showered after yesterday; he didn't even leave her alone to clean himself up.

"No. I'm not going to wear a wig on my wedding day. I'm already going to need fake nails." She held her hands up to show her broken and torn manicure. "I want you to be marrying me, not a Barbie doll version."

"I'm glad to see you haven't lost your stubborn streak through all this."

"The world will have to do a lot more than cut my hair, ruin my nails, and drag me over a cliff to make me lose my stubborn streak. Now as for yours—bathroom."

"Why?"

"You haven't showered since yesterday, and you're beginning to make the room smell. Besides, I want to ogle your body one last time as a single woman. Make sure I'm making the right decision."

"Is that right? It will only be fair if I get to check out yours too. I can't be making the wrong decision either."

"You can look but not touch. You gotta put a ring on it first." She burst out laughing and waved her ring finger.

"Seriously. Did you really just say that?"

"I know. I think I might have bumped my head. "

"I love you." He placed a kiss on the tip of her nose

"I love you, too."

He took her hand and led her to the bathroom but stopped when he saw a brown envelope placed on the dressing table. He went quiet.

"What's wrong?" She followed the direction of his gaze. "What is that?"

"Alright, look I don't care about what is in there, please know that. I'd marry you with or without it." James looked into her eyes and held both of her hands. "My lawyer and mother seem to think it's for my best interests, though." She let out a sigh of relief, and letting go of his hands, walked over to the envelope, and opened it. A prenuptial agreement. "I'm sorry. I really didn't want to give it to you. I was probably going to hide it in the drawer, but I suspect my mother would've given it to you this afternoon. It doesn't mean she doesn't trust you. It's just protecting what I've built up. Just throw it in the bin." She picked up a pen, flicked through to where she had to sign and did so. "You need to read that before you sign it."

"Why? I'm not marrying you for money. I'm marrying you for love, and somehow I don't think you will ever let me go anyway. Even when we fight, they're only tiffs, and we spend more time making up than fighting."

"It could say in the event of a break up I'll take sole custody of any children we have."

"It won't."

"How do you know that?"

"I trust that you'd never write that in there. Your lawyers and parents are right we should have an agreement to guard your assets, but I know that the document will be as fair to me as possible because you're too stubborn to let it be otherwise. Now, where were we? Oh yes." She tossed the pen back on the desk. "Bathroom."

A knock at the door spoilt their plans.

James

His father was holding his mother's hand, and James just wanted to rip it from her. He could really do without this now. He just wanted to make sure Amy was alright.

Amy frowned at him when she sat down and spoke to his father. "I know that you gave James the money to set up his business, but what do you do?" She was trying to be friendly and settle them all before the inevitable arguments started.

"I work in the financial industry. I was a city trader for most of my life, but now I tend to work more on the side of advising companies on the policies they need in place. I'm starting to retire."

"That sounds interesting. I bet you've seen some things in your work."

"I have seen many things, but I think the travelling has been the best thing about the job."

"His work allowed me to be a stay-at-home mother to both Sophie and James. I think that's why we have such a close bond." His mother looked over to him as she spoke. "It wasn't always easy not having Pete around, but he was doing everything for his family."

"Shame he didn't keep his dick in his pants." The words came from his mouth before he had had the chance to engage his brain and stop them.

"James." Both Amy and his mother rebuked him sharply at the same time.

"No, Miranda, Amy." Pete squeezed his wife's hand again, and James cracked his knuckles. "This needs to be discussed. We cannot ignore it in favour of pleasantries. Son, say what it is you need to say to me."

How did he phrase this without sounding a complete jerk in front of both of the women now glaring at him?

"I understand that you and Mum were having trouble and that you didn't think you could talk to me about it, but surely you'd a mate you could discuss it with or even marriage counselling. Why did you choose to pay for one of my escorts and take her to the bed you shared with Mum?" He had the first bit off his chest.

His father shifted uncomfortably in his chair. He went to let go of Miranda's hand, but she held it tight, to give him comfort. Amy hadn't let go of James's hand and didn't show any signs of doing it soon either.

"I did speak to someone. I went to see a counsellor on my own, but it didn't work. I met that lady at one of your functions. She gave me her business card which I put in a drawer, and I didn't think any more about it. I never planned to call her. I wish to God now that I had thrown it in the bin. Before your mother went away, we had a big argument. I was searching through the drawers, found the card, and called her. I just wanted some no hassle fun. It was the biggest mistake of my life."

"Why did you do it at the house?"

"I wanted to punish your mother."

"Punish her? You were the one fucking around." His voice raised, and he bashed the table sending a vase tumbling over. No one made any motion to correct it.

Amy interrupted. "Pete. Why were you punishing Miranda?"

"I was jealous."

"Jealous?"

His father looked at him.

"When James was hurt, it didn't just affect his life. It changed mine and Miranda's as well. We nearly lost our son."

"Oh, so you're going to be blaming this on me now." He'd heard enough and went to the bedroom. Amy followed him there.

"Stop it, please," Amy said. "You need to listen to everything he has to say. I don't like it either, but we have to hear his full story. It's the only way all of us can make a decision."

"I'm not going to have him blame me for hiring a prostitute. I can't listen to him saying that I deserved my beating again."

"He isn't. He's just trying to explain everything to you."

"But how do I handle it if what happened to me was the root of their problems?"

Her tender eyes looked right into his, "If that's the case then you don't handle it alone. You'll have me right here with you. And if you want them, you will have your mother and father as well. You need to go back in there and listen to your dad. It's the only way you can move forward."

He took Amy by the hand and solemnly led her back into the lounge area. His father was holding his mother, and it was evident that she was crying.

"I'm so sorry, Mum."

"No, please. I'm sorry we all have to be going through this after everything yesterday, but I need you to listen to your father. As well as Sophie and Grayson, and Amy here, you two are the most important people in my life, and I don't want to lose any of you from it."

"I'll listen," He looked to his father. "You've my word. I'll listen and not interrupt this time."

Everyone took their seats again, and Amy rested her hand in his lap.

"As I said, when James was hurt our lives were also affected," His father continued. "You'll remember nothing of that first night in the hospital. You were too full of morphine, but they took forever to stabilise you. They tried to get us to leave, but Matthew growled at anyone who came near us, so we were able to stay. We stood silently in the corner watching as they cut your shirt from the wounds on your back. Pulling fabric out of the massive craters in which they'd become embedded. All the time, your heart beat went up and down. They were worried about you having a heart attack it was so erratic. Eventually, everything settled, and they put you into a coma to let you rest. I'll always remember the faces of the doctors and nurses: they were ashen. They'd never seen anything like it before. Matthew and I left you with your mother and Sophie, and we went looking for the guys who did it. We didn't find them, but we found Colette. She was shooting her mouth off about how you were a freak that had used her in degrading sexual ways. I'm far from proud of it, but I punched her in the face. Matthew pulled me away before I could do any real damage, but it was too late...I'd hit a woman."

His chest felt like it was caving in as he struggled to reply to his father.

"You hit her?" His father looked down at the table in shame. "You were distraught, tired I should imagine. It was not your fault. You haven't done it again have you?"

"No." His father's adamant answer came quickly. "I have not seen Colette since that day, and I have no plans ever to see her again."

"That makes two of us." He looked at Amy who had tears in her eyes.

"As you recovered, you began to shut down more and more and started to take control of everything around you. The happy, joking son, I'd had, disappeared. Miranda became obsessed with being there for you always, and you seemed to need that. That was what the fight was about that morning. I asked Miranda if we could take a few weeks' holiday away. She said she couldn't leave you that long. She was worried enough about leaving you just for the weekend. I wanted someone just to want me, so I called that woman. She said things to me I wanted to hear."

"She was good at that," James snorted in response.

"I know I made you feel that you deserved the beating. I didn't want to fight with you because you didn't have the strength to fight back, so I just did as you asked. I love your mother so much. Leaving that day is my biggest regret. I was a coward, but I wasn't strong enough to help you. I should have tried to bring you back to life." His father looked over to Amy. "I'm just glad that Amy has come into your life and done it for me." James looked at Amy and ran a hand over her cheek to collect a tear that was tumbling down.

"What happens now?" his mother asked.

"What do you mean?" He looked at her confused.

"I want my husband back in my life. I want my son as well. Can we put all this terrible hurt behind us and try to move forward?"

"I never realised how much what happened affected everyone. I did close down to what was going on around me."

He took a moment of silence to reflect on everything that he just heard. He looked at his father and remembered the games of football on the green that they had by their old home, fumbling lessons on how to shave, and the encouragement when he bought his first property. He saw his real father for the first time in a very long while.

"I won't have you both going into debt to purchase a new house and furnish it. I'll give you the money to do so. You can choose the home yourself, of course, on the proviso it is in Knightsbridge. No arguments, please. It's purely for my selfish needs as I want you both living as close to me as possible, so we can make up for the years that we've lost. "

"Do you really mean that?" His mother began to sniffle.

"Yes, and until we can do that, Dad, I want you to move into my house with Mum. We're going to be a proper family: one that talks about its problems and doesn't shut themselves off to them. That is what I have learned from this beautiful girl here. And I'll love her eternally for that." He pulled Amy closer to him as they stood. His mother and father came around the table, and they all embraced together.

A cough came from the door behind them.

He knew who it was without looking. "Matthew?"

"Sorry to disturb you, but your sister is insisting on having Amy get ready for the wedding."

"I'll bring her there in a minute," he replied as he casually strode over to his father.

"Dad?"

"Son."

He held his hand out, and his father took it and shook it before pulling him into a bear hug. He looked over his father's shoulder and saw Amy standing with the biggest smile on her face. She winked at him.

"Amy doesn't have anyone to give her away. We were going to use Grayson, but I think, and I hope that she agrees, it might be nicer if you accompany her down the aisle to bring her properly into our family." She was nodding her head 'yes'.

"I'd love to."

Amy

Five hours later, she had been scrubbed, polished, made up, dressed to within an inch of her life, and was standing outside the doors of the lilac salon in The Wynn. Surely they could just go to one of the drive-through chapels for the actual ceremony, but no, James managed to secure a beautiful venue for their wedding. He even secured a judge to perform the marriage. She was dressed in a one-shouldered, white, A-line gown with a crystal waistband. Her tattoo was at the crusty stage, so it was better to hide it. She had Christian Louboutin shoes with crystals sewn into them. Her tatty hair had been styled into a sleek short style which reminded her of Charlize Theron in the recent Dior adverts. Her makeup was neutral, and in her ears she had a pair of borrowed sapphire earrings. Sophie had been so excited that she had brought them with her. Even her flowers had whites and blues in them. She had smudged all her makeup when she had first seen herself in the mirror. Amy had no idea how Sophie had pulled this off in twenty-four hours, but she certainly was an amazing soon-to-be sister-in-law.

She was suddenly so nervous, but those nerves were quickly put to ease when she heard Sonia's voice behind her.

"If Matthew expects me to go down the aisle in this chair then he has another think coming." She turned to face her. She could see her friend had her arm in a plaster cast and had a massive lump and lots of bruising to her head. She felt so guilty that she couldn't have done something more to help her. "It looks worse than it feels, honest."

"I'm sorry." She tried not to let the tears flow again. The makeup artist would have a fit if she had to reapply it a third time. "I should have helped you more."

"No, you should have run, like I told you to do." Sonia gave her a stern look. "But I'm glad you didn't."

Sophie and Grayson appeared at Sonia's side and helped her from her chair.

"Make sure you keep hold of me, Sophie, my legs are still very wobbly."

"I will do, and I think my surprise can help to do that."

She raised an inquisitive eyebrow, "Surprise?"

A door to the back of the wedding salon opened, and in walked Elena, dressed in the same sapphire blue as Sophie and Sonia.

She handed her bouquet to Sophie as she tore past her to wrap her arms around her best friend. "How?"

"Private jet all the way. You've got great parents-in-law to be."

"They're great, aren't they?"

"Yep, they've been filling me in on some great gossip on James the entire flight."

"Everything is so perfect. I can't believe you got everyone important to me, here."

"Oh no, you don't. No more crying. It's time to marry my brother," Sophie said sternly. Elena went and helped support Sonia. Pete came to Amy's side and held out his arm for her to take.

The bridal march struck up; the doors opened, and she got her first sight of James. He was clean shaven, and his hair had been styled. He wore full morning dress with a tie which matched the bridesmaid's dresses. She couldn't help but stare at him as she walked down the aisle, and Pete presented her to him. She could tell just by the look on his face that he was amazed at the sight of her. The woman he had dropped off at his sister's suite had looked a complete state, but now, holding his hands before a minister was a sophisticated and elegant bride.

"Dearly beloved, we are gathered here today to join this man and this woman in holy matrimony. If anyone knows any reason that they should not be married then speak now or forever hold your peace." The minister spoke, and James turned and glared at everyone just daring them to say something.

As the minister said the vows, she met James's eyes and never heard a word of the minister's voice. All she heard was James's velvety tones.

"I, James Thomas North, take you, Amy Emma Jones, to be my lawfully wedded wife. Before these witnesses, I vow to love you and care for you as long as we both shall live. I take you with all your faults and strengths as I offer myself to you with all my 'numerous' faults and 'few' strengths. I'll help you when you need help and turn to you when I need help. I choose you as the person with whom I'll spend my life."

The tears did flow now, and behind her, she could hear that she wasn't the only one. He momentarily let go of her hand and wiped one away. She said her vows back to him.

Next, they exchanged rings. They both had platinum bands; his was plain, but hers was studded with diamonds and sapphires. These would always be the stones that she got from him, and at that very moment, she couldn't have been happier. He dropped her left hand after he slid the ring on it, and they both looked expectantly at the minister.

"Amy and James, you have exchanged your vows and made your promises and celebrated your union with the giving and receiving of rings. It is at this time that I now pronounce you husband and wife. You may now kiss the bride."

The minster stepped back, and James drew her to him to seal their union with a kiss.

They'd done it. They were married.

TWENTY-FIVE

James

James pulled Amy towards him as the first cords of the Arctic Monkey's 'I Wanna Be Yours' started to play.

"No treading on my toes alright?"

"I'll just sway from foot to foot while you do the dancing around me. If you feel like dirty dancing, I'm more than happy for you to do so."

"Dirty dancing. But your parents are standing here watching us." Amy feigned innocence. "I could never let them presume that I allowed you anywhere near me before today. No, I'm completely chaste in that regards."

"You? Chaste? You forget I have heard you screaming my name when you come all over my face."

"Well, I never. How vulgar, Mr North. What are you insinuating about your bride?"

He took a tighter grip on her backside and pulled her into him. She gasped continuing her play acting.

"My God. What is that in your trousers?"

"That is a present my wife will be getting very soon if she doesn't quit trying to entice me with her virginal act."

"Not until she has had cake."

She stepped away and let go of his hand when the song ended. She headed towards the table laid out with the wedding cake. How Sophie had managed to get a cake that was three-tiered and in the same colours as Amy's and the bridesmaids' dresses, he'd never know. How she pulled off such a spectacular wedding in twenty-four hours was without doubt a miracle. He owed her big time and was pretty sure she'd remind him on numerous occasions.

"Now don't be letting yourself go now that you're married."

Amy turned back to him; her face illuminated with mischief.

"The sooner we cut the cake...the sooner we can..." She winked and almost skipped in her three-inch heels to where Sophie held out a knife. He casually strode over with his hands in his pockets pretending to show indifference to her teasing.

"I think we should all have another glass of champagne for this moment." He beckoned a waiter, and Amy glared at him. More champagne was brought and toasts made. The cake was cut and photos taken of him and Amy cutely feeding each other a piece. Sophie tugged on Amy's arm.

"Shall we head to one of the bars? Get some food and drinks?"

He stepped in between his sister and wife.

"No. Amy, I want you in our bedroom in five minutes. Don't remove your dress but place your hands behind your back and wait for me."

"Really. Can't you wait for a few hours. We want to party," his sister groaned.

He raised an eyebrow at his sister and looked to Grayson. He didn't need to say anything to his brother-in-law.

"Sophie. They'll join us at the club later. They need time alone as husband and wife. Leave them alone, or I'll gag you."

Sophie pouted, and he laughed. Amy nodded her agreement and took her leave.

"We will come back later, sis. I promise. She's still exhausted after yesterday, and I want her to rest."

"Well, you're definitely married now, big brother. Taking a lady to your bed to sleep."

He snarled at his sister's comment as Grayson removed his tie and placed it in Sophie's mouth. Miranda just looked over at the interaction between her children and her new son and daughter -in-law and chuckled.

"Serves you right for teasing your brother, Sophie. Now let him go and see to his new wife maybe even create a little grandchild for me. Once Grayson has decided you've been punished enough, we can go throw some moves on one of the hotel's dance floors."

It was Sophie's turn to moan now, and his to laugh.

"Enjoy Mum's disco dancing, Sophie."

He left the room and was heading for the lift when Matthew stopped him. He was wheeling Sonia along.

"Do you need me, Boss?"

"For what I'm about to do, no you're alright. Take her back to bed." He turned his attention to Sonia. "You look tired."

"It has been a long day. My head and arm are hurting a little."

"Both of you go to sleep, no offence, but you're starting to look like hell."

"Isn't that what you're supposed to look like after a holiday in Vegas?"

"No, I think usually that's just broke. Seriously, though, thank you for what you both did yesterday. If I had lost her...."

Matthew put both of his hands up in front of him.

"She's family to us. She brought us all together. She will always be protected. Now press that lift button and stop being a sap. I don't think Mrs North wants to see her husband crying. You're supposed to be a tough man."

"That's ok, she saw me crying up close during the ceremony and still said 'yes'."

They all laughed, and he pressed the call button. When they were in the lift and ascending, they all continued to joke amongst themselves. He was glad to have them in his life. Something had happened to Matthew when he was in MI5. He'd never say what it was, but he was aware that it affected him a great deal and had made him the man he was today. Anyone who thought it was easy for him to kill or torture the people he needed to, to protect James, was surely mistaken. He had witnessed that on more than one occasion.

When he opened the door to the bedroom that he shared with his wife, he saw that she was standing exactly where he asked and in the position he requested. He dismissed the guard who was there with her. He still wasn't prepared to leave her alone for any reason and if that meant a man in his bedroom with his wife then so be it. He was eager to continue the role-play that Amy started earlier with him. He liked the idea of pretending that she was completely innocent and only his. Anything previous no longer mattered. All that was relevant was now and their future together.

"My sweet, virtuous wife has anyone explained what will happen now?"

Amy's eyes flicked up and from under her dark lashes. He could see the instant hint of excitement at the words he had spoken.

"No, Sir. All I know is that you will make me your wife in body as well as in soul. I don't really know what that means."

He let out a hum and walked over to her and around her, drinking in every inch and curve. She was insanely beautiful; his perfect woman in body, mind, and spirit. He was broken, and she was lost, but together they had found their way. He stood behind her and slowly lowered the zip on her dress and pushed it to the floor. She wore no bra but had on panties with stockings and suspenders. He rubbed himself against her back.

"Is that my present again?"

"Do you think that you will like this present?" He ran his fingers down her back and found the sensitive spot at the base of her spine. She arched her back and let out a long, sighing breath and opened her legs a little farther apart.

"It seems so colossal."

"Only when you're naked and making that delicious noise." He lowered her panties to the floor but left the suspenders on.

She moved her hips and ground her bottom against his hardening cock.

"I think for all your innocence, my wife, there is a sensuous woman underneath. We will make a good partnership." He trailed a finger between her thighs. She was wet as he had expected. "Turn around and place your hands on the dressing table. Put your head down on the table."

"What? But that will let you see parts of me that are most intimate."

"Exactly. Do it now." His tone turned authoritative, and she obeyed him instantly. He stood behind her. She was fully open for him to take in every inch of her naked sexuality. He took a step closer and slid his fingers over her slit and towards the hooded mound which was already standing proudly. He circled it slowly, exerting a little pressure but then released it, leaving her longing.

"What are you doing to me?"

"It doesn't matter what I'm doing to you because this body is mine now. All that matters is that it feels right for you." He was in full-on Master mode now. He hadn't intended to be like this tonight. He wanted to be tender. She was covered in bruises, and he didn't want to hurt her, but before he could stop it, she had ground her clit against his finger.

"It does feel good. When you touch me there, it feels explosive. What will happen if you keep doing it?"

"You're about to see." He leant over her back and bit her ear gently when he spoke. His fingers swirled more around her clit. She was close. When her breaths became ragged, he pushed a finger into her body and then another, and she gasped out as she came there and then. Forty-eight hours without an orgasm, and she was almost breaking his fingers with the strength of her climax. Her inner muscles clenched and started to spasm. He pulled his fingers from within her and pulled her up to rest against him until she got her breathing back. When she could finally speak, he listened to her words,

"Does that mean we're properly man and wife now?"

He laughed,

"Oh no, my little, naive angel. There is more."

"More." She turned in his arms and looked at him shocked. He swept her up and tenderly laid her on the bed. He was still fully dressed in his suit but that was quickly remedied, and he nakedly climbed onto the bed with her.

"What is that?" She bit her lip and looked at his now stiff cock, standing solidly against his defined stomach."

"That is what binds you to me, forever."

"How?"

"I'm going to put it inside you."

She portrayed the look of horror perfectly. She truly was in the role of the virgin bride. He almost burst out laughing, it was that good.

"Inside me? Where?"

He ran his fingers up the inside of her thighs, still moist with her orgasm, and pushed them inside her again.

"In here."

"But it's so big." She did the terrified, wide eyed look with the hint of interest, astoundingly well. His cock twitched in excitement.

"It will fit you perfectly. We're soul mates, and it's designed for you, and only you, in a satisfying way. Lay on your back."

She did what she was told, but she kept her legs together. He used his strong hands to part them and positioned himself at the entrance to her succulent pussy. In one long, slow thrust he pushed all the way inside her and came down on top of her so that his arms were either side of her head. He didn't move. He just needed to feel the connection between them. When he saw her go over the cliff, he thought his life was over, and that he'd lost the only person who made his heart beat. She moved her hand to brush against the side of his face, and she whispered, all pretence of roleplaying dropped,

"Tell me what you're thinking?"

"You're alive. You're my wife."

"I am."

"You said before that you saved me in India when I told you everything, and you were right. You rescued me. I was dead and going through the motions of a mundane existence. I had people around me, but I didn't allow them to care for me. I controlled them and kept them at arm's length, so I couldn't hurt them, but the irony was that I did hurt them as a result. You saved me and continue to do so every day. I love you so much." At some point in his words, he had started to move within her. He was gently flowing in and out of her, and she was meeting his every movement with a rocking of her hips. She moved her hand and wiped away a tear that he didn't even realise had fallen from his eye.

"You were worth saving. I'd live every moment of our lives together again, if I had to, just so long as each time I get to this moment." The movement between them gained pace now, but it was still tender. This coupling was spiritual as well as physical. They joined together as one forever, and nobody was going to break them apart.

As the first waves of her climax rippled over his throbbing cock, he found his orgasm rush from his balls at a swift pace. They both cried out as they came together; their loving eyes caught in a deep, constant stare. He didn't want to pull out of her when he finished. He needed to still be inside her, but he could see the cuts and the bruises on her front and was terrified of hurting her. He shifted her, so that he could lay with the head of his softening cock just nestled inside her, but she was still cradled in his arms.

"Can I say I love you again, or am I getting soppy?"

"Romantic, not soppy."

"Well, then. I love you."

"I love you too." She nestled a little more into his chest. Her breathing slowed; she was falling asleep. "James."

"Yes?"

"You know I have always disagreed with you spending money on me?"

"Unfortunately, yes."

"And you know we have to fly back to England tomorrow?"

"Again, unfortunately, yes."

"Well, I think we should stay for a few more days."

"You do? Any reason?" He kissed the top of her head.

"Why Sonia of course, she isn't fit to fly yet. She needs a few more days' rest."

"Sonia."

"Yes."

"As you wish," he grumbled.

"James?"

"Yes." His answer was a little tenser this time.

"I thought you and I could spend all of those few days locked in this room with no outside contact except food service. After all, we should be on honeymoon."

His cocked twitched at her playful nature and began to harden again. He had honestly met his match in this woman.

"Get some sleep, 'cause if you plan on spending three days locked in a bedroom with me, you will need all the energy you can get."

Her breathing shallowed, and she fell asleep. He reached for his phone which he had placed on the nightstand. He brought up Matthew's number and texted him,

'Arrange for the rooms for another week please.'

Matthew texted back instantly,

'What about work?'

'I think it's about time I let them do some on their own accords. I've earned a little break. I'm sure they'll figure it out. Besides, my wife needs me, and I need her.'

TWENTY-SIX

James

James dropped down into his seat. His meeting was cancelled at the last minute due to a miscalculation by one of his suppliers. He immediately pulled up his email and sent a sternly worded note to his purchase director telling him to rectify this at once or find a new supplier. He only came into the office this morning for this goddamn meeting. He wanted to stay with Amy. She'd been unwell for a week now. He was sure she was overdoing it. The dance school had taken off, and she spent a lot of her time organising things and not actually teaching dance. He had been on at her to hire an administrator, but she was being stubborn again. She'd also had a meeting with a literary agent. She was doing too much, and it was making her ill. He was determined that she was going to be taking a few weeks off and that they'd be going away somewhere hot and relaxing. He would speak to her about it tonight. He pulled his phone out of his trouser pockets to text her that he was on his way home, but as he slid the screen to open it, he noticed a notification that she had left the house.

"Damn, stubborn woman. If she has gone to work..."

He pulled up the app which tracked her and was shocked to see she was in Harley Street. He jumped from his chair and almost ran to the door, pulling it open rapidly. Marie jumped to attention and gave him a seductive smile. He was in no mood for her games; she had become even more obsessive since he married. He was still determined to let her go. If only she weren't so damn good at her job.

"Where is Matthew?"

She pouted and pointed to a sofa around the corner. He rounded the corner at lightning speed.

"Why is Amy in Harley Street? What is going on?"

Matthew, who was sat quietly reading a book, leapt to his feet. He was normally always calm and collected, but this time he actually stuttered his reply.

"She. Er. She just wanted to get a check."

"You're hiding something."

"Boss, Sonia is with her. She's safe."

"She's at the fucking doctors and has been ill for a week, and you're telling me she's alright and safe. Get the car, I'm going there now."

"Calm done and trust me, alright? Let her do this for herself."

"Either you get the car, or I'll drive it myself."

"Alright. But you won't be the only one that gets their balls busted for this."

"What are you not telling me?"

"It is not my place to say. You need to speak to Amy. I'll get the car." Matthew strode off, and he turned to Marie who was giving him her best 'I would never disobey you in that way' look.

"Cancel everything for the rest of the day. I'll be at home." He stomped back into his office, packed up his laptop, and grabbed his jacket. He had all sorts of things running around in his head now: from a problem with the injuries she received in Las Vegas, to her dying from some awful disease. Why was she so damn stubborn? He got into the car. Matthew put the radio on, but James glared at him and switched it off as they pulled away from his building. The rest of the journey to Harley Street was made in stony silence.

James opened his door and was out of the car before it even stopped.

"Wait. You need to calm down."

Matthew called out from behind him, but he didn't listen. He was at boiling point now. Anyone who stood in his way would get punched. He arrived at the reception, and the petite red headed receptionist looked at him in wonder. He was sure he had steam coming out of his ears.

"Where is she?" His voice left no room for her to try and placate him and calm him down.

"Mrs North is in with Dr Baudin." He ignored her pleading cries that he couldn't go in there and marched off down the corridor to the room. He didn't knock; he was ready for a blazing row with his wife. However, he stopped mid-stride when he was greeted by the sight of her crying.

"James." She turned her head away, and he saw her trying to wipe away the tears.

He came quickly to kneel at her feet. She sat in a chair in front of the doctor. "What is it? We will get the best medical care. I'm sure it'll be alright."

Dr Baudin let out a little cough. "I think Miss Anderson and I better let you talk to your husband for a few moments. We will go and set up."

He watched as Amy nodded at the doctor. Matthew was at the doorway, and Sonia gave him a glaring look and thumped him on the arm. He held his hands out as if to say 'I had no choice'.

"Talk to me, please?" he asked.

"You're going to be so angry with me."

"You know I'm never angry at you. Well, okay that is a lie, but we always have fun making up." She burst into tears. "Please. I'm really worried here."

She reached out and took his hand. "I'm so sorry, I forgot. With everything that happened and then the club opening and the agent. I'm irresponsible. It's all my fault."

"You aren't making much sense. What did you forget?"

"My injection."

"Injection?"

"The contraception one."

"Contraception one." It took a moment for what she was saying to sink in, but it finally did. "Oh."

"I'm pregnant." She placed her hand on her belly. She was carrying his child. Inside her was a life they'd created together. No wonder she had been ill and tired. "Say something, please. Are you furious?"

"Furious?" He entwined his hand with hers "I'm going to be a father. Are you alright? The sickness?"

"Morning sickness, Dr Baudin has given me some tablets to help. My iron is low as well, so I have tablets for that."

"You should have told me. Why didn't you?"

"I wasn't sure. I thought maybe yesterday, and Sonia got me a test. It was positive, so we made the appointment for today. I was going to tell you tonight. I just wanted to ensure everything was alright. That is what the doctor is doing now. She's setting up a scan, so we can see how far gone I am. I really don't have a clue."

"Well, that explains why Matthew was so worried about bringing me here. Sonia will skin him alive." They both laughed together. "So this scan will show us the baby?"

"Yes."

"Let's go then." He pulled Amy into his arms and kissed her. "Are you happy about this?"

"Happy but scared. I like the thought of a baby you and me."

He held her hand, and they were directed to a small room down the corridor. She lay down on a bed and pulled up her top. Her stomach still seemed so flat; she must only be a few weeks. A gel was applied, and he held her hand. The doctor had the screen away from them at first. She explained she was just going to do a few checks and then show them. Amy stared up at him.

"This gel is cold. And I have a desperate need to pee. I had to drink a pint before I came here."

"If what my mum says is true, about me using her bladder as a football when she was pregnant with me, then I think that will continue for a little while yet."

The doctor laughed, "It certainly will. Would you like to see your baby?"

He eagerly nodded.

"I think that is a yes." Amy laughed. The doctor turned the screen, and all James could focus on was the tiny human. It was his son or daughter. Someone they'd made during an intimate moment together.

"You're twelve to thirteen weeks Mrs North. Which is good news because the sickness should hopefully start subsiding soon, but it's probably a bit of a shock that you're three months already."

"It certainly is." She looked at him. "A honeymoon baby."

"Well, we didn't leave the bedroom for three days at your request. No blame on my part there."

"That will teach me for having crazy lust filled fantasies. I shall not be doing that again."

"No, keep having them. Just make sure you set a reminder for your injection on your phone." Amy slapped his chest.

"What happens now? I hope that I haven't harmed the baby in any way. I know you shouldn't eat certain things in pregnancy, and I have been drinking wine."

"You and the baby will be fine. I'd recommend looking at your diet, especially with the low iron, and you should stop drinking wine immediately. I'll print you out pictures of the scan, and you can go share them with the world. I'm sure Mrs North Senior will be particularly excited about this news." The doctor laughed, and he imagined his mother going into full grandmother mode. "I'll schedule regular appointments and a couple more scans. You have the medication. Go home and enjoy your freedom while you have it. Once that little one is born, you will have no control over anything, anymore."

He looked at Amy, and she looked back at him while the doctor sorted out the pictures.

"You've our child inside you." He spoke first.

"I do. Are you sure you're alright with it? I know we hadn't actually discussed children; except to say, we both wanted them."

"No we hadn't, but honestly, this is the best news I could've hoped to hear today."

Amy went quiet for a moment and then laughed.

"What?"

"I just thought, heaven help any boyfriends who try to court our baby if it's a girl."

"She won't have boyfriends. I'll find a suitable man to take care of her. She'll listen to her daddy."

"And complain to her mummy."

"Who will do as I tell her to do."

"James."

"Amy."

They kissed.

THE END

PART THREE
LOVING CONTROL

ONE

James

"James?" Amy called out from where he'd left her collapsed like a beached whale on the sofa. She was tired after spending all day following the cleaner around and making sure the house was spotless. "Can you please get me a jar of pickled onions and chocolate spread?"

He groaned. He had better do as he was told, or his heavily pregnant wife would string him up by his balls. He opened the cupboard to the numerous jars of silver skins and put some out on a plate. He took some cocktail sticks out of a drawer, poured the chocolate sauce into a little dish and put that in the middle of the plate. This craving part of her pregnancy was very odd. Amy was due in less than a month. She was at the stage where she was bored now and just wanted to meet their baby but knew she had to keep it protected a little longer. If he had to help her with prenatal yoga once more, he was going to barricade himself in his office. He grabbed a beer, balanced the plate on his palm and pushed the kitchen door open.

"Here you are, beautiful. Just remember to clean your teeth before you come to bed. You stunk our bedroom out with vinegar breath last night."

She raised an eyebrow at him. "Pass those over here and get on the floor and massage my ankles."

"Er. You do realise I am the Dominant, and you are the submissive?"

"Floor. James. Now." There was to be no arguing with her in this frame of mind. Secretly, he actually enjoyed it. Although as soon as the baby was out she was going to get severely punished for speaking to him this way.

"Yes, dear."

"You're the one that put this baby in me. So you are the one that is going to damn well massage my swollen ankles and feed me onions."

He chuckled. Even when she was grumpy and pregnant, she was still as sexy as hell.

"I actually think it was your fault for not getting your injection, but we won't argue over that." He bowed his head and kissed her ankles. "Do you think it's possible to get started on making baby number two while number one is still in residence?"

"Don't even think about another baby. I'm the size of a house. I haven't seen my toes in months. No more children."

"You may be the size of a house but you are carrying our kid, protecting it, and as such, you are beautiful beyond description."

"You just want in my great big maternity knickers."

He shrugged.

"Seriously, do you think of anything else?"

"I do work on occasion. It isn't my fault my wife is so incredibly sexy. Even if she thinks she isn't."

She groaned and patted her stomach. "Do you think maybe it knows I am going to be an awful mother?"

"You aren't going to be a terrible mother. You've read all the books possible and probably know more about childbearing than the midwives. And we have my mother around to help. I have Matthew doing initial interviewing of nannies to help us out when needed. Stop worrying, everything will be okay. Just enjoy the peace and quiet before we end up with sleepless nights."

She burst into tears. "I want to meet our baby now. It isn't fair. I have been pregnant for far too long."

"One more month and the baby will be here, and you will be complaining you want it back in so that you can get some sleep." He came up to her side and pulled her into his arms. "Our child will come when it wants to. It has my stubborn genes after all."

"James?"

"Yes?"

"Can we play?"

"Play?"

"Yes, make love to me as a Dom?"

"You said that it was getting too uncomfortable. I don't want to hurt you."

"You won't." His wife blushed. "I actually want you to make me come. I miss it."

He shifted her around so that she was looking into his eyes. "If, at any point it doesn't feel right, you tell me, and I will stop. We don't even need a safe word. You say stop and I will."

"I know. You know my body better than I do so will stop before I even realise I want you to."

"Beautiful, I knew what your body wanted more than you did the first time I fucked you."

"That seems like such a long time ago."

"Eighteen months, to be precise. I can probably give you it down to the day, minute, and second as well, if you want."

"Seriously?"

"Seriously."

She leant forward and brought her lips to his. "James North, I want you to take me to the bedroom."

He didn't need to be asked again. They hadn't had sex for a couple of weeks now, and he wanted to be inside her. He got up from the sofa, and despite the extra weight she was carrying, he scooped her into his arms and took her straight to the bedroom. "Mrs North, that will be my pleasure." He lay her tenderly down on the bed and looked at her protruding belly.

"I think the easiest way will be if you go on top? I will support you and help you move."

"If that's what you want to do." Amy removed her clothes and sat up, ready to mount him. "Come on, then?"

"What do you think you are doing?" He frowned, and Amy looked at him with big eyes.

"Waiting for you to remove your clothes?"

"On your back and legs parted." She instantly scrambled to obey him. "You don't just go at it without me ensuring you are ready. I want to eat you first. I am hungry."

"James?"

"Quiet. You are not permitted to speak unless I say." He smirked at his installation of high protocols with his amazingly submissive wife. She wouldn't disobey him. He wasn't able to rip the maternity pants from her body, but he gently slid them down her thighs and off her feet, kissing a path over her soft skin as he went. He didn't know why she thought she was massive. To him, she just looked amazing. There was something about knowing that inside her was their child. He was more in love with her at that moment than he was the day they had married, and that was something he never thought would've been actually possible. He followed his path back up her legs and took a long, slow lick of her labia, teasing each of them between his teeth till Amy was whimpering. He ran his tongue over her clit, exposing it to his tormenting touch. Again and again, he flicked at it until she was writhing under his mouth. Her hands gripped tightly at the sheets, the whites of her knuckles showing. He delved his tongue inside her and lapped up her essence, a sweet honey nectar to his senses. He'd never ever get enough of it. His finger flicked over her clit again. The second he did, she was on the verge of orgasm. He removed his tongue.

"Come."

He increased the pressure on her clit. She exploded in his mouth and all over his face in wave after wave of gratifying delight. Her whole body shook. When she stopped shuddering, he stripped off all his clothes. He opened his bedside table and pulled some fur lined cuffs out.

"I've changed my mind about you on top. Hand's above you head."

He cuffed her to the headboard, checking that her arms would not be marked. Without hesitation, he positioned himself and started to push into her. Amy held her head up and watched him all the time.

"Tell me what we look like together? I can't see."

"When we are together, we look like home." He leant over her bump and pressed a kiss to her lips. "Are you alright in this position, or do you want to go on top?"

Amy was away in the glow of her orgasm, no pain, just the need to come again;

he could read that on her face without her verbal communication, so he began to thrust. He brought one hand in between her legs to massage her still tender spot and balanced the majority of his weight on the other. He hadn't come in the last few weeks either—he wouldn't last long. He could already feel his balls tightening. With expert skill, he stroked at Amy's clit again, and she arched her back with a squeal of delight. James pulled one of her legs up over his shoulder. This lifted her bottom off the bed and that allowed him access to it, to give five quick smacks to her cheek. His hand smarted at his own strength.

"Oh God."

He increased the pressure, his thrusts becoming more urgent, more rough and animalistic. He needed this. She needed this.

"I am going to come again."

"Give me everything you have."

Amy stretched out her body and came over his cock, calling out his name. His own balls pushed his release deep into her. He saw white. Breathless, he removed himself from within her and fell beside her on the bed, happy. "You need to sleep. Come on." He removed the cuffs, and Amy snuggled into his arms.

The next thing he knew, she was prodding him in the chest.

"James, James you have to wake up."

"Urgh.. What is it? It is still dark out. What time is it?"

"Sex. It did something."

"It generally does something, when I do it, now go back to sleep. I really don't have the energy to do it again at the moment." He turned over in the bed and pulled the covers around him. "Why is the bed wet?"

"My waters just broke. The baby is coming."

The words entered his head slowly, 'The...baby...is...coming.' "Shit. Right." He tried to get up from the bed, his feet tangled in the sheets, and he went flying off backwards and landed with a heavy bump on the floor.

"James." Amy appeared on the side of the bed, looking down at him. "Are you alright?"

"Baby."

"Yes, I am in labour."

"Hospital."

"I think that would be wise, it's too early. I'm scared." She grabbed her side and began to pant. "I think some gas and air will be needed very soon."

"Clothes."

"Breathe, please. No falling apart now."

"Breathe. Yes. Oh God. We're having a baby."

Amy turned towards the bedside table and picked up her phone, while he tried to figure out how to put a pair of jeans on. His brain was mush; the baby was coming. He tried to focus on what she was saying.

"Sorry to wake you, Matthew. I think the baby might be coming. James is a little, well...panicking. Would you be able to take us to the hospital?"

TWO

Amy

"How are you doing, Mrs North?" Dr Baudin and a male gynaecological consultant entered the room, along with a midwife.

"Not too bad. I think I'd like some gas and air now, though; the contractions are getting intense." Amy lay on the bed of the deluxe suite of the well-renowned, and very expensive, London Maternity Hospital. If it was good enough for a Duke and Duchess, it was perfect for them. Matthew and Sonia sat at a small table nearby, and James occupied a chair beside her, gripping tightly to her hand.

"Give her gas and air now. She's in pain." James frowned at the doctors.

"Manners." She rolled her eyes at him. Another contraction hit, and her eyes shut to focus on breathing.

"Please." He was sulking at being told off. He still hadn't stopped panicking or worrying. But that was no excuse for rudeness. She wasn't going to let him get away with it.

"We will see to it at once, Mr North." The consultant kept his mood light-hearted. She didn't doubt that he had seen it all before. Dr Baudin nodded to the midwife, and she started to fiddle with something in a cupboard next to the bed. "Let me just check your notes again. No problems throughout the pregnancy, you have no underlying conditions that could cause problems. You're a few weeks early, but the baby's heart beat is strong. It's measuring a good size and weight. We have all the necessary medical equipment ready. I need to see how far dilated you are. Is that alright?"

Before she could answer, the door to the suite flung open, and Miranda, Pete, Sophie, Grayson, and Elena rushed in.

"How is she?" Miranda questioned. The women came straight to her side, while the men all greeted James.

"They're getting gas and air for her now; waters have broken. The doctor is going to check on her dilation." James replied.

The suite, though spacious, suddenly seemed rather full. Everyone chattered. She turned her head away when yet another contraction hit; it was even stronger than before. Matthew caught her eye. He nodded and stood up and whistled into his hands. Everyone turned and looked at him in silence.

"I think we all need to leave Mr and Mrs North to have this baby."

"Yes, everyone out. The doctor needs to examine Amy. We will let you know as soon as we have a baby." James took her hand and whispered into her ear, "Sorry, I lost it for a few minutes. I'm back now. We'll do this together."

Everyone started to file for the door, but she called out.

"Miranda, wait."

"Amy?" Her mother-in-law turned and came quickly back to the bed. "What is it?"

A tear tumbled down her face.

"I always thought that when I had a baby, my mother would be in the room helping out. Please, will you stay?"

Miranda went to answer, and a tear tumbled down her cheek. She looked to James, who nodded his agreement to Amy's request.

"I will be by your side, until you tell me to leave. Thank you."

The others all left, and the doctor set about preparing to examine her. She was flat on her back with her legs apart. Oh, the irony of the way the baby comes out and the way it goes in being very closely linked. The midwife handed her the gas and air, and as soon as she took her first few breaths she started to relax. The consultant pushed his finger inside her to feel at her cervix. James's grip on her hand tightened.

"You are eight centimetres. Not long to go now. I'll leave you with the midwife and come back when you're ready to deliver. I may just have time for a cup of tea." He chuckled. "Now, are you sure you don't want an epidural?"

"No."

"Yes."

James spoke first.

"Yes, I'm certain I don't want an epidural. I can do this."

"Alright. If it gets too much, we'll let the doctor know straight away."

"Agreed."

"I do so love how we negotiate." James laughed.

"Let's hope it continues when the baby is out."

"You two have come far in a short space of time." Miranda brought her a glass of water and helped her drink it. "I'm glad I can share in this moment with you."

"Sophie won't mind, will she?" Had she upstaged her sister-in-law?

"Not at all. I think I'll be long into my retirement by the time she and Grayson decide to have children."

"Good, well I mean, not good for you, but good for me."

"I know."

"Oh God. Another bloody contraction."

She brought the breathing apparatus to her mouth, and the next few hours continued along the same lines.

"Let's see how you are doing now, Mrs North; I am sure we must be nearly ready." The consultant had his rubber gloves on and was placing lubrication on a finger.

"I hope so. I'm getting tired. Nobody told me having a baby required so much energy."

"Just you wait 'til it is born." The consultant chuckled and dipped his head between her legs again. "Ten centimetres. I think it's time for some pushing."

"Oh, thank god." She looked at her husband, who had a massive grin on his face.

"I love you." He was glowing in the fact that very shortly he was going to be a father.

"I love you too." He brought her near and kissed her on the forehead.

"You can do this. I have every confidence in you."

"Mrs North." The consultant's voice came from down below. "When you get the next contraction, I want you to bear down and push. We may have to do it for a while, but we'll get the baby out."

"Alright. I can do that."

"I have you, babe; I'm with you the entire time."

"I'm here as well; you're so very strong, my darling. I'm so proud of you." Miranda, leaned over and kissed the top of her head.

Despite the fact her head was spinning with exhaustion, she shut her eyes. The next contraction came, the gas and air were in her mouth, and she was breathing it down into her lungs, allowing it to flood her body and the pain. With all her remaining strength, she bore down into her pelvis and pushed. Fuck. Trying to get something that size out of somewhere that wasn't anywhere near that big was painful.

The pushing seemed to go on for hours. She could feel every part of her body tying itself in knots of fatigue.

"Why the hell won't it come out?" She turned to glare at James, sweat dropped off her forehead and her teeth gritted as she pushed again.

"You're doing great..."

She cut him off before he could speak.

"Don't give me any of that crap. I am trying to squeeze a small person out of somewhere that barely fits your fucking cock. I swear here and now if you ever tell me to part my legs for you again, I'm going to cut the damn thing off that you want to put in me."

He visibly paled. "Jesus. Get it out."

"I know it is hard, both my children have big heads, and I'm sure your little one will follow suite, but I know you can do it. Focus."

"Miranda, how the hell did you do this twice? I just want the baby out. Ow." Another contraction came, and she pushed down with everything she had, holding both James's and Miranda's hands in hers, confident she was drawing blood. "James. Please."

"Doctor?" James looked helplessly at the consultant.

"Mrs North. You have a tiny frame. It's hard work to push it out, but you're getting tired." He looked at a machine at the side which was attached to the baby. "And the baby's heart rate is going up. I'm going to make a decision soon based on what is best for you both. I'm going to give you a couple more pushes, and if you can't birth the head by then, I'll intervene with suction."

"No." She heard his words and instantly start pulling back in the bed. "Please.

My mother did everything with gas and air. No interventions. Please. I've got to do the same."

"Mrs North, I have to do what is best for you and the baby."

"James, please. I have to do this naturally." Her wide eyes stared pleadingly at her husband.

"I've entrusted the consultants with your care and that of the baby. I'll agree with whatever they say."

"No" she turned away from him and started sobbing.

"Listen to me, though." He pulled her face back to face him. "Since I have known you, you have stood up to your uncle and a man so demented he wanted to throw you over a cliff. You've more strength than anybody I know. We'll get this baby out in the next few pushes, and we'll get it out together. Break my hand if you have to, but use me. Ok. Next contraction. We'll do it."

"Use us both. We're both here for you." Miranda spoke, and she nodded at them both. She could feel the contraction beginning to burn and holding both of their hands pushed down between her legs as hard as she could. The next contraction came about quickly, and she did the same thing.

"Mrs North. Your baby's head is crowning. You're doing it. Pant through the break. I need you not to push yet. Next contraction, we'll birth the head."

"Argh." She was being ripped in two.

James was at her head, whispering in her ear. She found the strength to push again. Suddenly, a baby was being placed on her chest. Miranda was crying, and even James was crying.

"We have a son." James covered her in kisses and placed a protective hand on the baby.

"We did it."

"You did it, beautiful. I'm so proud of you."

Minutes passed as they took in the first moments of their son, his little fingers and toes, his cute little button nose, and the little sucking noises he made. The baby was taken to be weighed and checked. James left her side, at her insistence, to stay with their son. The midwife helped her to bathe while Miranda assisted as best she could. Finally, when they were all settled back into a clean bed, and the room was tidied, she took Miranda's hand and thanked her.

"I felt today that despite losing my own mother, I have another one. Thank you, Miranda." The elegant woman wiped away tears and made excuses that she needed to go tell the others of the safe delivery. They were left alone with their son.

"He's perfect. Just like his father."

"I wouldn't say *that*, but yes, he is perfect."

"We're parents." The baby suckled at her breast again.

"Scary." She shifted in the bed. Her whole body ached, and she could barely keep her eyes open.

"How are you feeling?"

"Sore and sleepy."

"Rest. I'll watch him."

"I love you."

"I love you too."

The door opened, and Sophie poked her head around it.

"Is it alright to come in? I know you probably want some time alone, but there are a few desperate people out here that want to meet the new arrival."

"Five minutes and then Mrs North needs to rest. I mean it."

"Thank you. I will make sure it's not more."

Pete, Miranda, Sonia, Matthew, Elena, Sophie, and Grayson all flooded back into the room. She didn't want to let go of her son just yet, and they all respected that, so they just cooed over him and took photos.

"He is so gorgeous. Almost makes me want one." Sophie snuggled into Grayson.

"Almost?" Her husband looked hopeful.

"Alas, the bags under Amy's eyes put me off."

"I think she looks amazing." Elena interjected, "and this little man is so cute."

Pete thumped James on the back and congratulated them. She was happy to see them getting on so well.

"Do you have a name yet?" Sonia stepped forward and tapped the baby on the head. Matthew remained well back.

"We do. "James looked towards her. "You want to say?"

"Yes. Everybody, I would like you to meet, Thomas Matthew North." She looked towards Matthew as she spoke. "Thomas was my father's name."

Sonia put her arm around Matthew, who took a step back to compose himself.

Thomas let out a little moan, before falling into a deep sleep.

"Right. Everybody out. We need rest. Matthew?"

"Yes, boss?"

"Nobody is to come in until I say."

"I can assure you, boss, on my watch that'll never happen."

As everybody filed out, James took Thomas from her and placed him into his crib. He climbed onto the bed and pulled her into his arms, and as she drifted off to sleep, he whispered reassurances of how proud he was of her. Her world was complete.

James could barely catch his breath as he washed his face in the ensuite bathroom attached to Amy's room. She and Thomas were asleep. Thomas, though appearing to be healthy, had been placed in a special cot with oxygen feeding it. His lungs where still not fully developed, apparently, and it would just help him to get the final bit of strength he needed. He was so tiny. The doctor insisted that at six pounds, Thomas was a healthy wait for a premature baby. The doctor had reassured them numerous times that this happens sometimes, there was no reason as to why Amy had gone into labour early. He knew better though. He'd read about it. Semen contained something which softened the cervix, he'd come in her. And orgasms produced oxytocin which started contractions. He'd given her two of them. And he couldn't forget that he'd been rough. He'd smacked her and cuffed her to the bed; she'd twisted her body all sorts of angles. He had put Amy and Thomas is danger. They could have lost their baby if he hadn't been stronger. Neither of them would have recovered from that. As it was, he was classed as preterm and had to have special care.

He looked into the mirror. His eyes were rounded by dark circles. He failed Amy. He'd allowed his need to rule his brain, and she'd suffered. She'd been so scared and in pain. He wouldn't fail her again. This would never happen again.

THREE

Amy

"Are you going to smile for Auntie Sonia?" Amy watched while her bodyguard, and friend, pulled funny faces at a rather uninterested four-month-old Thomas. "He only smiles at Matthew, never at me."

"Probably because Matthew is always scowling, and he wants him to smile." The lift stopped, and she picked up the carseat.

"It'll take more than that to get Matthew smiling."

"You seem to have a knack."

"I have figured out what buttons I need to press."

Both ladies laughed. The reception of James's office loomed in front of them.

"I'm not looking forward to Marie's comments on Thomas."

"Ignore her."

"What are you two doing here?" Matthew was wearing his usual frown and gave Sonia a peck on the top of her head in greeting before looking down at Thomas. Her mischievous son instantly smiled back.

"See, I told you." Sonia threw her hands up in the air.

"It's the scowl." She smiled at Matthew. "Thomas wanted to see where his daddy works as he has been so busy this week we haven't really seen him."

"He's speaking early, then."

"Don't be flippant Matthew."

"My apologies, Mrs North." He gave a fake bow and took the carseat from her hands. "The boss is just changing after being out on site. You go in. Sonia and I'll take this little man for a tour of his future empire."

"Are you sure? I think his nappy needs changing…"

"Sonia can do that."

"Can I?"

"Woman do nappy, man do protection." He even thumped his chest after. Thomas squealed in agreement.

"Man can sleep on the sofa tonight." Sonia rolled her eyes.

Amy laughed. "There's a bottle of milk in the bag if he gets hungry." With that she kissed the top of Thomas' head, who grumbled at her because she blocked his view of Matthew, and hurried to James's office.

"James?" She called while opening the door. No answer. She hoped he was still in the shower. Not only did her husband have a plush office, he also had a private bathroom complete with walk in shower. "James?" She pushed open the bathroom door. He was indeed showering. His masculine body glistening with the water droplets. A hand wrapped around his magnificent cock as he washed it. She let out a moan. He switched off the water, grabbed a towel, and stepped out of the shower.

"Where's Thomas? Is he alright?"

"Yes." She bit her lip. "Matthew and Sonia are showing him around."

"Is that wise? It's the start of cold season. And this office is probably full of god knows what else. We don't want him getting ill."

"He still has my antibodies, and he's had his first jabs. He'll be okay. Stop worrying. Why don't you lower that towel instead?" She winked at him.

"Don't be silly."

"Wanting to suck my husband off is silly?"

"I'm supposed to be working."

"Like you were working the time you came on my thigh on the sofa? Or the time you had me bent over the desk? Or maybe like the time you licked me out while I sat in your chair and read an important email for you? Which one James?"

"That was different."

"Why?"

"Because our son is out there being breathed on by probably my entire workforce."

"He's with Matthew and Sonia. Nothing will happen to him."

"I still think it would be better if we went and brought him to the office. Go wait in the other room while I dress."

She just looked at him. So she wasn't even allowed to watch him put on his clothes now. Fine. Two could play that game. She stomped out of the bathroom to his desk. She flicked the switch to turn the glass opaque and began to undress. When she was naked, she stood silently and waited.

"What the fuck?" She heard as he walked in the room.

"Let's go get our son." She raised an eyebrow and strode confidently, despite the fact her knees were a little wobbly, towards the door.

"Put your clothes on!"

"Make me." She turned and mischievously smirked.

James's eyes darkened, and he prowled towards her. "I won't ask again." He inhaled deeply, before reaching around her and locking the door. He took her hand in his and brought it to his trousers at the groin. "Is this what you want? You want to take it in that pretty little mouth of yours and suck it hard, until I come all down your throat."

"Yes." She whimpered and bit her lip with anticipation.

"Do you think I should give that to you?"

"Yes."

"Really?"

"Yes."

"You think I should give you the gift of my cock, when you're standing naked in my office when I asked you to wait for me so we could go and get our son."

Well no, not really when he put it that way but what the hell....

"Yes."

"Wrong answer."

She suddenly found herself twisted around and thrust hard against the wall. In quick succession, James landed five hard whacks to her backside. He counted himself.

"Should I give you my cock?"

"Yes." She could take more. She liked being spanked.

Another five followed.

His voice was thick with his rather precise control when he next spoke.

"Last time. Do you deserve my cock?"

This is where she needed to make a decision.

"Yes."

"You know, I think I'm going about this all wrong. You seem to want me to tan you hide so pink that I'll be able to warm my hands on it later. I think, however, I'll try a different tactic." This time he slid his fingers over the curve of her backside down between her thighs and stroked between her sodden folds. "So wet and ready." He stroked her clit with a firm pressure that would bring her to climax quickly.

"Please." She dropped all bravado as she gripped the wall waiting for the earth shattering shuddering to start.

"See, beautiful, you're not as good at this game as I am." He leant over and gave her a lingering kiss on the cheek. "And that is why I will always win." With that, he pulled his hand away and unlocked the door. "You better get dressed, while I'm getting our son."

"What?" She spun round, "You can't."

"I can, and I am. If you touch yourself, I'll know."

She picked up the nearest thing to hand, a book, and threw it at him just as he ducked out the door.

FOUR

James

"Boss?"

"Yeah."

"Tell me to shut up..."

"Shut up."

Matthew groaned.

"What?"

"Are you and Amy alright?"

They had just set off from Knightsbridge towards the city and his offices.

"Why do you ask?"

"She didn't seem that happy with you, yesterday."

He grinned. No, she didn't, not after he left her longing and with an unusually sore arse.

"I've been a bit reluctant to treat her roughly since she had Thomas. I want to make sure she's properly healed. She tested my resolve yesterday."

Matthew chuckled. "Maybe you should have a date night. You haven't done that since Thomas was born. She's probably just feeling more like a mother than a wife."

"Has Sonia said something?"

"No. Just being observant as I am sometimes."

"I'll arrange it. Take her somewhere posh. I would be lost without you, Matthew."

"I think your son would be stuck for entertainment without me."

"I'm starting to worry about his fascination with you."

"He's just learning a proper Dom face for when he is older."

"That is not something I really need to think about just yet."

"Sorry."

The car pulled into the underground parking of the offices, and they both got out and went straight up to the top floor. Marie was already at her desk.

"Morning, Marie."

"Morning, Mister North. I have placed all the folders on your desk for your meetings today." She spoke without barely looking up at them. There was no pouting or flaunting of her assets. Whatever his new Finance Director had done to this woman was amazing.

"Thank you. Can you bring me a coffee please?"

He strode past the desk and put his hand to the office door.

"Oh. I am sorry, Mr North. I almost forgot. A gentleman is waiting for you in your office. He says he's a senior consultant at Maudsley?"

"The psychiatric hospital? Did the doctor say what he wanted?"

She finally looked at him and shook her head. "He said it was confidential. And that he could only speak to you. The guards downstairs did a search of him, and he had ID to prove he was a doctor. Did I do something wrong?"

"No. Thank you."

James beckoned Matthew to join him. His bodyguard dropped a weapon discreetly into his hand, should it be needed.

The doctor was sitting on his couch staring out of the window over the sights of London. He didn't look a threat, and when the doctor turned to face him, he noticed a hospital lanyard around his neck.

"Mr North? You have an excellent view here."

"James, please. The view is what sold the offices to me." The Doctor stepped forward, and he shook hands with him.

"I am Doctor Rahul." His accent was thick with Hindu influence, but he wasn't difficult to understand.

"May I ask why you are here?" He wasn't going to beat around the bush, not when a bad feeling was beginning to knot in his stomach.

"Do you know a Colette Fisher?"

He sucked in a breath at a name he never wanted to hear again. Matthew stepped forward.

"Mr North wants nothing to do with Miss Fisher. She's a part of his past that he wishes to forget."

He held his hand out to silence Matthew. His bodyguard stepped back and stood by the door with his head bowed. He would watch everything, though.

"Why are you asking?"

"Miss Fisher was admitted to our hospital last week. She suffered a severe psychotic episode and tried to take her own life."

"Is she alright?"

"There will be no lasting effects of the attempt. Colette has wounds to her wrists, which will heal. Her mental condition, though, is the reason I am here."

He strode to his desk and pulled a chequebook from his drawer. "You want me to pay for her treatment, as I guess she is blaming me."

He signed a cheque and held it out.

"You misunderstand me. Colette's treatment is covered by the NHS, Mr North. I'm here because as part of her therapy, she asked to see you. She said she needed to face you so she could move on and recover. I'm here to ask you if you will agree to that?"

"No fucking way." He slammed his fists into the desk. "I lived a nightmare for years because of her."

"Mr North, I know exactly what happened to you and why. She's told me everything. I believe that a visit from you will help her considerably."

"She painted me as a devil. "

He turned away from the conversation. "Matthew. Escort Doctor Rahul out." Matthew grabbed the doctor by both arms.

"This way, please."

"I am sorry. I did not mean to cause you such distress. I know the situation must seem hard. Take time to think about it. You know where I am if you change your mind."

"Get him out, *now*."

The doctor shrugged out of Matthew's grip and saw himself out. Matthew followed to ensure he was gone. He sat down at his desk and loosened his tie. It was suddenly scorching in the office. Why now. What couldn't that family just leave him alone?

"Mr North?" Marie appeared at the door. "Your coffee." She left, and Matthew walked back in a few moments later.

"What do you make off it all?"

"I've put out a phone call. My sources confirmed that Colette is there but will get back to me as soon as possible with more details."

"Let me know." He took a sip of his coffee. "Do you think I should go see her?"

"Not my place to answer that boss."

"Alright. I will put it another way. If you were in my position would you see her?"

"If I were in your situation. I would discuss it with Sonia and make the decision together."

James put the mug down and stood. "Go get the car."

FIVE

James opened the front door to hear Thomas squealing with delight. He followed the happy sounds to the lounge and found his father flying Thomas around the room like an aeroplane. He wasn't sure his mum was as impressed with the activity as she followed them around, prepared to catch him.

"Is Granddad getting you ready for my next business trip?" He chuckled as he spoke.

"James? What are you doing home? Is everything alright?" His mother turned to him with a worried expression on her face. He reached out and brought Thomas into his arms and kissed the top of his head. He snuggled down into his arms and cooed contently.

"Nothing to worry about mum. Where's Amy?"

"She looked drained. She said you had a late night, and she was up with Thomas twice. We sent her to sleep."

He used the hand not securely holding Thomas and rubbed the back of his neck. "Yes, it was a little late when we got to bed." He gave his son to his mother.

"What is it?" His mother had always been able to read him.

"Let me talk to her first."

Before heading to the bedroom, he stopped into the kitchen and made Amy a coffee.

"Amy." He called softly as he walked in the door to their bedroom and place the coffee down on her bedside table. She stirred a little but did not wake. He sat on the bed and gently rocked her, feeling guilty at having to wake her after she'd had so little sleep. This needed to be sorted though. "Beautiful, I need you to wake." She stirred again and blearily peered at him through half open eyes.

"James, what time is it?"

"Ten-thirty."

"Ten-thirty? Why are you here? Thomas?" She sat bolt upright in the bed.

"He's fine. Mum and Dad have him."

"Why aren't you at work?" She stretched and yawned at the same time.

"I need to talk to you."

"Okay."

"Here," He held the coffee to her mouth. "Drink some of this first." She did so with his help. He loved it when she was sleepy. It brought out the protective Dominant in him.

"Enough, thank you." She pushed the cup away and lay back on her pillows. He placed the cup back down. "Stop avoiding telling me what is happening."

"Am I that obvious?"

"Just a little."

"Alright." He settled back on the bed next to her. "I had someone waiting for me at the office, this morning. A doctor. Colette was admitted last week after trying to commit suicide. She's having treatment, but she wants to see me."

"What did you say?"

"I had Matthew throw him out of the office."

"But?"

"I started thinking."

"You want to go and see her?" He reached out and took her hand in his.

"I don't know what to do. But I couldn't make a decision without you."

He let go of her hand, cupped her chin, pulled her towards him, and kissed her lips.

"Do you want to see her?"

"Not if it's going to hurt you."

"That wasn't what I asked."

"I feel that if it helps her recover, I should see her. I think I've always held some guilt that I didn't try to rescue her before. It's evident now that her brothers had severe mental issues. Maybe she isn't as far gone as Jacob and Joshua were."

"Then, you have your answer. You go to the hospital." She gave him a gentle smile.

"But I don't want you to get upset. Too many bad memories lay this way for both of us."

"That was over a year ago. Since then, I have married you, and we've had Thomas. I'm happy. I've known all along that what happened in your past may surface again, just like something with my uncle may. But I have also realised that from day to day, we grow stronger together, and anything bad happens we will face it together. Divided control." She shifted on the bed and positioned herself over his lap and nestled her head in his arms.

"I still can't believe you chose me."

"I told you you are the best in bed." She giggled her reply.

"None of that while you're exhausted."

"I will hold you to that later." She playfully rubbed his leg. "When do you want to go and see Colette?"

He cleared his throat. "Now."

She groaned.

"I'll get dressed."

"Why?"

"I'm coming with you. Miranda and Pete have Thomas. I'll feed him before we go, and he'll be okay for a few hours."

"You don't have to come. You're supposed to be resting."

Her frame tensed, but she made no effort to move.

"You don't want me to come?"

"I didn't say that."

"But you don't?"

"No. I want you to come."

"Then, I'll be there to support you, if need be."

"I love you." He kissed the top of her head.

"Go phone the doctor. I will be ready to go in about half an hour."

~

"Why now?" Even though James needed to see Colette, that didn't stop her from being angry that his past was coming back to haunt them again. She supposed at least they had enjoyed a year without any drama. She tapped her nails on the chair. What was taking so long? She pulled the sleeve back on her jumper to look at her watch. Half an hour. Why did she agree to come?

The door opened, and the doctor came out.

"Mrs North. Colette and your husband would like you to join them."

"Is that wise?"

"Mr North and Colette have had a good discussion. She expressed a desire to meet you. She's happy that James has found someone he can be happy with."

"Alright, I'll go in."

The first thing she noticed when she entered the room was the tension. Colette sat huddled on a chair, her frightened eyes flicking between all the people in the chamber. She was pale and looked exhausted. James sat opposite her, one of his legs crossed over his knee, his face tight with worry. He reached for her to sit next to him.

"Colette, this is my wife, Amy."

She held out her hand in greeting, but Colette just regarded it like it was filthy. Alright, this wasn't going well so far.

"She the one you killed Jacob for?"

"Jacob held Amy hostage and, unfortunately, died during the rescue."

"Pretty. Jacob always did like a blonde. Shame he couldn't make babies with her. They would have been cute." Colette turned to her. "Does he tie you up, spank you, and fuck you up the arse?"

"That isn't a polite way to speak to Mrs North." The Doctor reprimanded.

Colette shrugged. "Well does he?"

"Colette," James spoke this time, his voice laced with authority.

Amy took his hand. She wasn't ashamed of what she and James did. "It's alright." She gave James a reassuring smile before turning her face neutral to reply to Colette. "He does."

"You're his submissive?" Colette leant forward on the chair, her eyes wide.

"I am his sexual submissive. In all other aspects, we are equal."

"You enjoy it?"

"I would not be with him, if I didn't."

"He's corrupted you. You don't really like that." She stood up.

"Colette sit down." The doctor warned.

She shook her head.

"What's there to like about it? He degrades you."

"That's where you are totally wrong. He worships me." She kept her voice calm, her back straight and her hand held by James.

"No. You can't." Colette started shaking. "You can't. You just can't."

"Why not?"

"It's wrong."

"Why is it wrong?"

"Because they said so."

"Who said so?"

"My brothers."

They fired their conversation off rapidly at each other. The men in the room observed readily, prepared to act if needed but otherwise remained silent.

"Colette, who taught your brothers to believe such things were wrong?"

She started rocking as she stood.

"I don't know."

"Was it your parents?"

"They're dead. They died when I was young. We lived in foster care most of our lives."

She looked to the doctor, who motioned for her to continue.

"Mine are dead as well."

"Really."

"Yes. A few years ago now."

"Did you live in foster care?"

She shook her head.

"No, I was eighteen when they died. I was looked after by my uncle."

"Did he tell you that the way James treats you was right?" Colette turned the questioning back around to her.

"My uncle was an evil man. He beat his girlfriend to force her to miscarry. He was prepared to kill me to get his hands-on James's money."

Colette froze.

"Family are not always right about what they tell you. Sometimes, it's for their own needs. You listen to them, but you also need to follow what your own heart and mind tell you. Mine tells me that what James and I share is natural."

"No. My brothers were right. They wanted to protect me."

"I don't doubt that. I am sure they wanted to keep you safe. But did that protection make you happy?"

"No." She let out a sob.

She let go of James's hand and stood up.

"What would make you happy?" She dared to place her hand on Colette's trembling arm. The room silenced.

"I read your book."

"You read my book. How did it make you feel?"

Colette's eyes went wild, her tiny fists clenched, and she flew at Amy. Colette managed to get a punch into her face before grabbing her hair and pulling it hard. James jumped to his feet, pulled Colette off her, and threw the manic waif to the other side of the room. He brought Amy into his arms, and Colette started to curse. The doctor punched an alarm button and nurses flooded in. Amy watched from James's arms as Colette shouted names at her, trying to get over to where she stood. Tears formed in her eyes. How could someone be so damaged? One of the nurses injected Colette with a sedative, and she fell still in the arms of another nurse. They carried her from the room.

"We shouldn't have come."

"I'm all right."

"Mr North. Your wife has got further with Colette in a short space of time than any of us have. The book was a trigger point. What's it about?"

"It's an erotic romance," Amy answered, her voice was still a little shaky.

"Please, could I ask you to consent to see Colette again. We are aware of a trigger point and can prevent that."

"Not happening." James took her hand and pulled her to the door. "I'm not prepared to put my wife in that sort of danger."

"I understand. Please think about it, though."

"No. This ends now."

She tried to speak up, but the expression on James's face had grown thunderous. There would be no point now. She bowed her head at the doctor, as they departed.

SIX

Amy

The journey home was done in silence. James wasn't in the mood for conversation, and she needed to work through everything that had happened in her head. Colette had been responding so well. She had the feeling that the poor woman was so confused and didn't know what she wanted in her head at that moment. Reading the book would have confused her even more. If Amy could help her, she would.

The car pulled into the underground car park, and James helped her out of the car.

"Are you going back to the office?" It was one.

"No. I'll work here this afternoon."

"I'll check on Thomas and make us some lunch."

"Wait."

She stopped, and James came over to her and put his arms around her waist.

"I'm sorry for taking you there."

"Don't be. Colette has an illness. She's doing the right thing and talking about her problems. Sometimes, that'll get hard, and she may react as she did. She didn't hurt me." Well, her cheek hurt a little, but she wasn't going to tell him that. "Stop worrying. It'll be alright next time. Let's go see Thomas."

"Amy." The Dom's voice was back again. "You do realise we are not going back there."

"We can discuss it later."

"No. No, a discussion is needed now."

There was no point in talking about this anymore, at the moment. In his mind, all he saw was her being hurt. "I'm going to check Thomas. He probably needs feeding again."

"Don't walk away, when I am speaking to you." James grabbed her arm when she reached the top of the stairs to the living section of the house.

"Go do some work. We can discuss this later."

"We're discussing this now. You're to promise me here and now that you'll not go to that hospital and see Colette again."

Okay, they were doing this now. "Let's go to the bedroom."

"No need. Say you will not go again, and that's the end of it."

"I can't do that."

His brows drew together in frustration.

"I was getting through to her. You heard the doctor."

"She hurt you. She punched you and pulled your hair. If I wasn't that close, she could have done more damage."

"If you weren't near, the doctor would have helped me, or I would have defended myself."

"You still would have been hurt. It is my job to protect you."

"I know." She tried to calm the situation by running her hand along the edge of his sharp jaw. "But I cannot walk away, knowing that she is suffering. She is tiny and frail and needs help. She's not Jacob. She's not going to try and kill me."

"How do you know that for certain?"

She hesitated. She didn't really have an answer to that. It was just a feeling. The vulnerability in Colette's eyes told her.

"I can't."

"Then, you're not going back." He took her arm. "You will not defy me on this. I will have Matthew assigned to you twenty-four a day if need be. I'm not prepared to take the risk that you are injured or worse.

She tried to pull her arm away from his, but it was held too tightly.

"You can cuff me to the bed and spank my arse raw, but I will go back there." Her voice broke.

He flinched back.

"I won't do that."

"Why not?"

"Because your responsibilities lie with being a mother and making sure *my* son is looked after." He snapped out his answer.

Silence.

She was shaking; she was so angry. Was that really all she was to him now? A vessel to feed *his* son?

"I see where I stand."

He tried to bring her into his arms, but she stepped away from his touch. Miranda poked her head around the door.

"Sorry to interrupt. Thomas heard your voices. He's getting hungry, I think."

"Can you put him in his carseat please, Miranda? We'll take him to your house. I'll feed him there." She was trying to hold back the tears.

"Please." James tried to cradle her again.

"No. *Your* son needs me." With that, she left the room, slamming the door behind her.

SEVEN

James

The half-drunk bottle of whisky glistened against the flames of the fire. It was nine in the evening, and he hadn't heard anything from Amy since lunchtime. Sonia had come by in the afternoon and packed a bag of belongings for Thomas and Amy. She'd informed him that Mrs North had decided to stay the night at her mother- and father-in-law's. He didn't argue when she gave him a dirty look and stomped out the house. He poured his first glass and allowed it to burn down his throat.

A door slammed down the corridor, and Matthew's and Sonia's raised voices echoed down the hallway.

"Are you serious?"

"Deadly."

Another door slammed.

"Where are you going?"

"I'm going to take Thomas his favourite teddy. I forgot it earlier."

"He's four months. He's too young for a favourite."

"Amy wants it."

"I'll take it."

She snorted. "Yeah right, and you'll tell her to get her arse home and be a good little wife at the same time."

"No. Okay, I will explain to her that hiding away will solve nothing. A bit like running away from an argument." He could hear the frustration in his bodyguard's voice.

"Fuck you, Matthew."

The front door slammed a second later, and Matthew walked into the lounge.

"Did you hear all that?"

He nodded.

"My fault?"

"She isn't happy with you."

James held the bottle of whisky out.

"I'll get a glass."

A couple of hours later, that bottle was finished, and another was opened.

"Why do we need a woman?"

"Because it's impossible to suck our own dicks." Matthew's answer had them both roll up laughing.

"Yeah, Amy's excellent at that."

"So's Sonia."

"You going to talk to her?"

"Am I overreacting?"

"You said Colette went for her?"

"She did, smacked her in the face and yanked her hair."

"You don't want her getting hurt."

"I think it's more that I'm not allowing her to go back."

"She felt she was getting somewhere."

"Yes."

"We picked ones with kind hard hearts, didn't we?"

"Stubborn is more like it."

"How was Colette with you?"

"Not too bad. She seemed alright." James leant forward and poured another whisky for them both. "She didn't seem to like that Jacob died while Amy survived."

"Do you think she's jealous of Amy?"

"I don't think so. Colette said she was happy I was married. She seemed fine, until she mentioned Amy's book."

"Amy's book about sex? Sex that's been inspired by you and isn't in the missionary position?"

"Yes, that book." He laid his head back against the edge of the chair and shut his eyes. "Why did this have to happen now? Amy's pissed at me, anyway, because I won't go rough with her."

"Yeah, Sonia told me last night. Sorry, mate I lied earlier. Ironically, she told me while I was whipping her arse. A bit of a passion killer."

"I swear those women talk about everything. Sorry again, mate."

"It's cool. We got it back." Matthew also sat back now. "Why are you reluctant?"

"She gave birth early after we'd had rough sex. She was in so much pain. I couldn't do anything about it. I know they say women forget the pain after they have the baby, but what if something I do brings it back."

"Shit. That doesn't sound right. Sonia's never having a baby."

"Good decision."

"And one we should make together. Not you deciding, with our boss when you are apparently smashed out of your head." Sonia stood in the doorway, tapping her foot. James shrunk down into the chair. Another row was coming on. Matthew jumped to his feet, swayed and staggered. He let off a string of expletives. "How much have you drunk? I was only gone a few hours."

"Not much." Matthew tried to walk but hit the coffee table and his leg gave way. "Ok, maybe a little." Matthew actually started giggling like a naughty school boy. James couldn't help but join in.

"You've got to be kidding me." Sonia's brows were knitted together in an exasperated frown. "Matthew, trousers down."

"Babe, James is in the room."

"I want to see if you've broken the skin on your leg. I think sex is slightly out of your capabilities right now."

"Never out of my capa..abila...fuck it. I can always get it up for you, babe."

James got up from his chair and helped Matthew to his feet.

"Cheers boss. Love you."

"Love you too, mate."

"Oh, God." Sonia put her head in her hands.

"Alright, woman. Stop complaining. I'm taking my trousers off." James stepped back to allow Matthew to lower his jeans. "See? No blood."

"A miracle. Take them off completely."

He watched Matthew sway as he did so.

"Sonia, you would make a good Dom."

"Don't fucking go there. I am storing up the punishment in my head for her." Matthew had his trousers off and was trying to get his shoe out from the end of one leg.

James could tell Sonia's patience was growing thin. She'd just spent two hours with Amy. Was his wife crying? Was she angry? The alcohol suddenly didn't settle well in his stomach and a feeling of soberness hit him.

"Sonia, I'll help you get him to the bedroom."

Before they had a chance to assist Matthew, he had whipped his shirt off, waved it around his head a few times, and was heading towards the bedroom. "Come on babe, let's go play."

Sonia inhaled deeply through her nose and turned to James.

He couldn't help it. Matthew wasn't going to get any sex, so he followed. It was like a train crash you just had to watch. When he got to the bedroom, Matthew had his pants off as well. This was nothing new to him. They had seen each other naked before, when they had played pre-Sonia and Amy. He stood against the door frame as Matthew tried to bring Sonia into his arms. She side stepped him, twisted around, and in an instant, had his hands cuffed to a St Andrews cross in the corner of the room.

"Babe. What the fuck?" Matthew's voice showed he couldn't believe what just happened. He'd been bested by his sub. James was impressed with the movement. He gave her a little clap.

"Sush or I will cuff your feet as well and use your whip. You can have the sore butt for once."

"Sonia. Undo me now."

"I said hush."

"Sonia." Matthew's voice had gone dark. James could see Sonia shiver, she played a good Dom, but underneath, she was all submissive.

"You know, when he is sober you are going to get it for that?"

Sonia smirked. "That's what I am hoping. Now as for you. "Go take a cold shower and get a strong coffee. You are going to apologise to your wife."

"Not any of your business."

"I've just spent two hours sitting with her and your mother while she sobs her heart out. She thinks you don't find her attractive anymore and that you only want her to make babies for you."

"You know that isn't true. I worship her."

"I know that, but the point is she doesn't. She is scared. Going to see Colette today was hard for her. She wants her Dom back."

James cracked his neck. He was an idiot. He wasn't being a good Dom. He wasn't communicating with his wife. He was just allowing himself to get lost in his own worries.

"I think I prefer being attached to a St Andrew's cross than a lecture." Matthew piped up, but James could see that he agreed with his girlfriend.

"I'll go shower. I'll need you to run me over there." He nodded to the cross. "You better not leave him like that."

"I know. A good Dom never leaves his submissive tied up without means of escape. I'll get Matthew into bed and come wait for you in the lounge."

"Thanks, Sonia."

"Just don't come home without her."

EIGHT

Amy

Amy laid a sleeping Thomas down in his cot and tucked the blanket around his chubby little body to keep him warm. Not that it would stay there long. She just wanted to sleep herself. It wouldn't come to her, though. The bed was cold and lonely. James wasn't in it. Another tear fell. The aura of being unloved surrounded her. Her body didn't excite her husband any longer. A tear tumbled down her cheek. No, she couldn't sit and wallow. Thomas needed his mummy.

The sound of voices came from the hallway. She got out of bed, pulled a robe around her, and tiptoed quietly to the door.

"Mum. I want to talk to my wife."

"She's your wife again now? Not just a mother to your child."

"I never said that. You're twisting my words."

"That's how you made Amy feel."

Amy opened the door.

"Tell me, then." She tried to keep the emotion out of her voice, but there was a hint of distress and anger.

"Miranda and I'll watch Thomas. You two go in the lounge and talk." Pete appeared from around the corner and guided Miranda into the bedroom Amy just vacated. "Take as long as you want. We'll sleep in here tonight, and you can take one of the other rooms."

"Thanks, Dad," James replied and held out his hand to her to follow him. There was no way she was ready to hold that hand yet. She motioned with her head that she would follow him. When they entered the lounge, James sat on the sofa. She took a seat on a chair.

"Sit next to me on the sofa."

She was about to say she was fine where she was sitting, when she looked him in the eye, and she shouldn't have done that.

"This doesn't mean you can touch me."

"I'll not touch you until you tell me I can."

"Good." She folded her arms.

"I'm sorry for what I said this afternoon. I wasn't listening to you. I allowed fear to cloud my judgement. I want certain barriers put in place so you cannot be hurt, but we'll go and see Colette again. If she lashes out at you again, that'll be the final time, though. Thomas and I both need you, and I am not prepared to risk anything happening.

She went to open her mouth to speak, but James continued.

"I've not finished yet."

She shut her mouth and bit her lip to keep quiet.

"You ever say that I don't want to get in your pants and bury myself balls deep in your pussy, and I'll tan your hide. I want to do it in so many different ways."

"Then, why won't you?"

"I'm scared."

"Scared?"

"You were in so much pain when you gave birth, and it was so early. I was so scared we would loose Thomas. I don't want to inflict that on you again. I couldn't save you from hurting. What if I do something, and it brings all those feelings of pain back again?"

She let out a long cry of relief.

"When I gave birth, I was in pain, and there was a risk to Thomas. But he's fine, he's strong and healthy. And the pain doesn't mean I don't want to do it again. It was a magical experience. Every second of that day was perfect, because it brought us Thomas."

"But I wanted to take the pain from you. To help you in some way."

"You did" She reached out to cup his jaw. "You held my hand and gave me strength just as you always do."

"Have I been a complete idiot and worried about something that wasn't there?"

She nodded.

"Damn it."

"About right."

"Are you still furious with me?"

"You promise we can go and see Colette tomorrow?"

"Once arrangements for your safety are in place. Yes, we can."

"Then, I'm not angry with you anymore. Are you going to be the lover I want again?"

"I'll give you one minute to get into the bedroom, remove your clothes and bend over the bed."

"Er. We're in your parent's house. I refuse point black to have sex with you here."

"Fuck."

He grabbed her arm and pulled her along behind him to the room where Thomas was sleeping.

"Amy you expressed some milk right?"

"It's all in the fridge."

"Then, we're sorted."

"I can't just leave Thomas. What if he wants me?"

"He'll be okay. I told you, Pete and I'll sleep in here with him." Miranda appeared at the door also now.

Walking hesitantly, she went to the hall and wrapped a coat around her PJ's.

"I don't think I can leave him."

"There's a hotel a few doors down. If mum and dad need us, we can be here in a few minutes. What about that?"

She looked down at her feet. Contemplating. She wanted James like never before. She was desperate for him, but what if something happened to Thomas? What could happen? She knew Miranda and Pete. They would take turns watching him like a hawk 'til she and James returned.

She looked towards where Miranda and Pete were smiling at her and gesturing for her to go.

"Ok."

NINE

James

"Walk quicker."

"I only have my slippers on. You seem to forget I have pyjamas on underneath my coat."

James held Amy's hand tightly as he dragged her at almost a sprint out of his parent's front door and towards the boutique hotel on the corner of their Kensington Street.

"You won't even have them on in a minute."

They burst through the door of the hotel, and he strode confidently to the reception desk. He wasn't about to waste any time.

"I want your best room please." He let go of Amy's hand, dug into his pocket and pulled out his wallet. His card thrown onto the desk. "Charge everything to this."

"I..um..Sir."

"What?" His voice was raised. He wanted Amy naked and sucking his cock. He didn't want to be dealing with idiots.

"I'm afraid our best room is taken, Sir."

"Then give me the next best."

"James." Amy's warning came from beside him. He turned and looked at her. She was flushed, but he suspected it was with embarrassment as everyone seemed to be staring at them.

"What? You want it just as bad as me."

The receptionist coughed.

"We've an executive room with a view over Kensington Park."

"I'll take it."

"Would you like breakfast?"

"No."

"Newspaper in the morning?"

"No."

"A wake-up call."

"We don't want to be disturbed unless the hotel is burning down."

She swiped his card, and he entered his pin.

"I'll get a porter to take your luggage up. Is it in the car?"

"My wife is in her pyjamas. Do we look like we have luggage?"

"Er. No." She handed him a key. "Room Fifteen. It is on the top floor."

He snatched the key, grabbed Amy's hand, and dragged her towards the open lift.

"That was rude."

"I took note of her name. I'll apologise in the morning and give her an exceptionally generous tip. Right now, I just want you naked."

The lift reached their floor, and when the doors opened, his lips met Amy's. He needed her. He could already imagine her screaming for him. He would have to improvise, but he wanted to tie her up, blindfold her, maybe some ice play. He would definitely take her from behind. They hadn't done that for a while. Fuck. Why didn't he bring some nipple clamps and a bullet vibrator?

They reached their room; by the time the door shut he had Amy's coat on the floor and her top over her head. She wore a nursing bra, quickly cast away, and he lowered his head to lick around the nipple. She didn't want him gentle, so despite the fact that they could be sore, he bit them. She let out a loud moan of pleasure. He let go and stepped back. God, his jeans were tight. He needed to get them off and quick.

"Remove your bottoms and position yourself over the dressing table. Open your legs and show me my pussy."

His calloused fingers undid the buttons of his jeans while Amy did as she was told. He lowered his jeans to the floor and kicked them and his shoes to the side. He whipped his shirt over his head and threw it in a pile on the floor.

Standing behind her, he slapped her backside.

"That is for doubting that I find you sexy."

He did it again.

"That is for doubting I love you."

She was tinting nicely. He'd missed that colour.

On the desk was a mirror.

"Look at your reflection." She cast her eyes up, they were glossed over with lust. "You are not to take your eyes off the mirror. I want you to see what you look like when I fuck you from behind." He leant down and sunk his teeth into her shoulder. "I want you to see what I see when you come."

"Yes, Master."

The reply made his cock jump.

A full length, free standing mirror in the corner of the room caught his eye. He moved it so it was positioned beside them and gave Amy an image in the dressing table mirror that showed what he was doing to her.

"Perfect."

He ran a hand softly down her back. She arched backwards and pushed her hip into his erection.

"Fuck me, Master."

"I will take you when I want to." He slapped her backside twice more. The beautiful colouring of his hand darkening.

"Please." Her breathless whimper was testing his resistance. He had been such a fool. She was so much stronger and resilient than anyone gave her credit for. She could take him at him most animalistic, and she would get off in an explosive climax.

"Colour?"

"Green." Her reply was immediate.

"If that changes?"

"I will use my safe word."

In one long, agonisingly pleasurable stroke James thrust his rigid cock deep into Amy's welcoming pussy.

"I am not going to take this easy."

"I don't want you to. Fuck me."

He pulled all the way out and slammed back in. Her body jolted forward, but the gasp of lust from his wife's lips had him pulling instantly back out and repeating. He wrapped his hand around her hair and pulled her head up when she let it fall forward.

"I said keep your eyes on the mirror."

Again and again, he banged into her. Why had he held back for the last four months? He was certifiable. He'd missed this so much. She was taking him. She was taking all of him.

"Can you see me fucking you?"

Her eyes flicked to the reflection of the larger mirror.

"Yes, oh god, that's so fucking sexy. I can see your cock sliding in and out of me."

A bead of sweat formed on his brow.

"Master. Please, give me more."

He bent and sunk his teeth into her shoulder. "Come for me."

"I love you...." Her words screamed out when her insides clamped down on him, and she exploded around his body. His hand tightened on her hair again and jerked her head up, so she was forced to watch every second of her orgasm. He couldn't hold back any longer, his balls drew up and propelled his climax deep within her body. Her eyes flicked to watch the expression on his face.

He collapsed upon her sweat-glistened back. He was breathless, and his legs were struggling to hold him up. "I didn't hurt you?"

"Do I look like I am injured?"

He forced himself up and pulled out. A drop of cum dribbled out of her swollen pussy and ran down her thigh.

"That's a beautiful sight."

She snorted a happy laugh, ran a finger over her inner thigh, and brought it to mouth.

"A beautiful taste of you mixed with me." She spoke as if in a dream.

He helped her to stand, pulled her into his arms, and carried her to the bed. She was almost asleep. He tucked her under the blankets, went to the bathroom and cleaned himself off. He brought back a flannel to clean her. She parted her legs and allowed him, but he could tell that she was only partially awake. He threw the cloth back into the bathroom, turned the main lights out, and climbed back into bed beside her. He pulled her into his arms, one hand resting on her breast, the other on her stomach.

"Sleep well."

"Thank you." Her breathing shallowed, and she was asleep.

He really did need to remember that his wife was no longer the fragile little doll he'd first met in Lanzarote. If she didn't like something, she'd let him know. He too drifted off to sleep for a few hours. He awoke, found the dressing gown cord, and tied her to the bed before licking her pussy 'til she came several times. He then fell back to sleep for another few hours before he decided to wake her up with his cock inside her. Damn he loved his wife. And he'd never forget what she could take from him again.

TEN

Amy

After doing the walk of shame through the hotel lobby, Amy had to come face to face with the beaming smiles of her parents in law. They were ecstatic that she and James had made up. She was as well but less enthusiastic about them knowing that she had been virtually dragged to a hotel for a night of wild 'monkey' sex. It was almost certain she walked like a bow legged cowboy. Every ache down there smarted a little, but when James passed her Thomas to latch to her breast, it was all worth it. He had the spark back in his eye, not the worry.

"I just need to speak to Matthew and get things arranged. Are you alright?"

"I'll be okay. I'm going to feed our baby boy and get dressed."

"Why don't you hold off having a shower 'til I've finished my phone call?"

"Because we're going to see Colette, not spend the day passing our son around to different people so we can have sex."

"Just you wait 'til he's in bed tonight. I want you ready."

"Always."

She leant over Thomas and kissed James before he disappeared.

"Your daddy is such a naughty boy sometimes."

After Thomas had been fed and burped, the baby sick all down her shoulder was washed off in the shower, James watched and gave her pointers on where to clean. She puffed out her cheeks in disappointment when he disappeared to greet Matthew and Sonia.

She wasn't entirely sure what was going on with Matthew today. He seemed extra grumpy, and when she asked Sonia to turn her favourite song up in the car on the way to the hospital, he let out a loud grumble that had Sonia in a fit of giggles.

"Are you sure about this?" James leaned over and brought her hand into his lap.

"I can't walk away from her. Her life could have been so very different. She's young. She can turn everything around."

"Not if she actually believes what her brothers taught her."

"She doesn't. Don't ask me how I know that, but I saw it. She's just struggling to reconcile what she was taught to what she wants to feel."

"This will be our last visit to her today. If we can't reach her, she's on her own."

"James." She tried to protest.

"No. Listen to me, please. She's my past. And one that contains a lot of pain and anguish. I'll help her today, but if she doesn't accept that, she's on her own. We've Thomas and our relationship to focus on. That's our future, and Colette's not a part of it. Too much has happened for her to be a permanent figure in my life now."

"I know and I agree with you. I don't want her in our life. I couldn't be friends with her. I would look at her and know that she was responsible for what happened to you. We'll help her see that what she wants isnt wrong, because I don't think she's mentally ill. Then, we need to put her in contact with someone who can help."

"What do you mean?"

"You told me that you once had training to be a Dom?"

"Yes."

"Well, could you speak to someone where you went that will help her?"

"Jesus. We are talking about sex clubs. She wouldn't even let me fuck her from behind."

"Well, not sex clubs straight away, but you must know someone who can help?"

"I don't know."

"Just think about it."

"We're here." Matthew grumbled.

"Thank you, Matthew." She cheerfully replied.

"Why don't you go get a strong coffee from the café over there?" James helped her out of the car and motioned to Matthew at the same time.

Matthew just blew his lips out.

"I'll take him, Sir." Sonia came around the side of the car. "Phone us when you are ready to go."

"Will do." They parted ways.

"What's up with Matthew today?"

"Hangover."

"I thought I smelt whisky on your breath last night. How much did you drink?"

"Not much. Matthew seemed to drink more. I sobered up pretty quickly, when Sonia read me the riot act."

"She did?"

"Yes."

"So I've her to thank for you coming to see me."

"She made me see the light."

"I think Matthew wishes he didn't see the light."

"No, I believe he's just grumpy because Sonia bettered him and cuffed him to a St Andrew's cross."

"St Andrew's cross?"

"They have one in their rooms".

"How did I not know this? And secondly, why do we not have one?"

"You want a St Andrew's cross in our bedroom?"

"Well no, not our bedroom, but we've enough other rooms in the house."

"You want a playroom?"

"Yes."

"An adult playroom?"

"Yes."

"Fuck. You're the best wife ever. I'll get it done straight away."

James escorted her up the steps of the hospital, and a nurse showed them into the room they were in yesterday. Colette and the Doctor were already there. She was scrunched up in a ball, the long sleeves of her jumper pulled down so that Amy couldn't see her hands. She didn't get up from her seat or even acknowledge that they had walked into the room.

"Colette, are you going to say hello to Mr and Mrs North?"

"I don't want her here."

James's hand tightened around hers.

"Go sit down by the doctor."

"Where are you going?" He gave her a quizzical look.

"To talk to Colette." He raised an eyebrow as if to say no. "Please."

"The first sign of trouble...."

"I know."

She got to her knees in the slave position before Colette, and the brunette peered at her from under a tangled mass of hair.

"You read my book."

"It was filth." She spat the words at her.

Amy wiped off her face and continued. Her voice was calm and didn't show any fear. "But filth that you enjoyed?"

"Do you really let him do that stuff to you?"

"Yes, I do. I like what he does to me; it makes me feel alive. It makes me feel loved."

"But it's wrong."

"Is it? Who says it's wrong?"

"It's wrong." Collette turned away her lips pressed into a stern resolve.

"Did your brothers say it was wrong?"

They both shuddered a little at the mention of them. "Yes."

"How did the book make you feel?"

"The way you wrote—-he really loved her. He wanted to care for her so much. Treat her like a princess. What he did to her body was worshipping it." She saw Colette begin to lose herself in her words, but then, she seemed to realise what she'd said. "But that doesn't make it right. It's just formulated into a book. You wanted to sell it to all the other deviants out there."

Colette wrapped her arms around her body.

Amy reached out and took her hand. James leaned warily forward on his chair.

"She consented to it. She didn't fight against him. They both chose to learn about each other's bodies that way. What you read about is physical love. Love that's natural for a man and woman to show.

"It's wrong."

"What happened the night you went home and told your brothers what James did to you?"

"I don't want to talk about it."

"It might help."

"Will you leave me alone, if I tell you?"

"Depends on your answer."

"They were angry and shouted at me. Called me so many different names and said he'd made me his whore. I told them I said no to him. But that didn't stop them. They took me to the shower. Took my clothes off, threw them away. Jacob put me in the shower. The water, it was so hot it burnt my skin. They got these cloth things, like scouring pads." She lifted up the sleeve on her jumper revealing marks on her skin. "When they finished, they took me to my room and told me to do penance. I didn't have anything but bread and water for a week. I had to stay on my knees saying prayers for my salvation. A few weeks later, Jacob came home weak and bleeding badly. He told me Joseph was dead and the Devil did it. I'd brought him into their lives. I was responsible for my brother's death. He threw me out."

Out of the corner of her eye, she saw James had clenched his fists, he got up from the chair and without a word stomped slowly for the door. He was breaking down again.

Colette stood and spoke next. "It isn't your fault. I know that's what you're thinking."

He faced her.

"If I hadn't have tried to do what I did."

"My brothers were insane. Both of them. They were wrong." The room went silent. The enormity of the declaration from Colette's lips resonating with them all. After years of suffering on so many levels for James and Colette, this was their peace and acceptance.

"This will be the last time we see you. Too much has passed between us all for a friendship to develop. I will not be abandoning you, though. When the doctor releases you, I will provide you with funds to get yourself back on your feet. I also know someone who will be able to help you with the other issues you have, and I'll put him in contact with you. Do you agree to this?"

"Yes." For the first time since they'd entered the room, no stammer came from her answer.

"I wish you well, Colette. You're a strong woman underneath. You'll survive."

"Thank you, James."

"I'll meet you outside." James turned his attention back to Amy before leaving the room.

"Just remember to trust what you feel, not what you think, is right. James is right. You have faced so much and are a strong person as a result."

"The person James is talking about?"

"Will teach you everything you need to know. It won't be easy at first, but remain open to him. He'll want to help and protect you."

"That's what they do as well, isn't it?"

"Who?"

"The Doms?"

"Yes. For your faith in them, they reward you with protection and trust."

"That sounds nice. No fear for once."

"Oh, I don't know about that. There's a look a Dom gets."

"I think I read that in your book. Made my knees quiver. I can't wait to see it." Both of them laughed. "Thank you. You didn't have to help me. After what they did to him."

"Shush. That's in the past. We're doing nothing but looking forward now."

She leant forward and brought Colette into an embrace this time.

"Goodbye, Colette."

"Goodbye, Amy."

When she left the room, she found James casually leaning against a pillar

"Can we go home now? I feel exhausted, and I just want to hold Thomas for at least three hours." Her bottom lip quivered when she spoke. He brought his arms around her and kissed the top of her head.

"As long as you plan on holding me for those three hours as well."

"Deal."

ELEVEN

James

James stood at the doorway watching Amy while she tidied up the mess that was their lounge. Toys, books, and a variety of baby clothes were strewn all over the floor. Their six-month-old son had more belongings than he did. "How does something so tiny make so much mess?"

"Just you wait. He was pulling his knees up again today. It will be a matter of weeks before he is crawling, and this mess won't be contained anymore."

"How's the nanny working out?" Amy had recently expressed an interest in going back to the dance school for a couple of hours a week and having one day just to write. They'd interviewed what must have been hundreds of applicants before they settled on five possibilities. Matthew had conducted a final interview with them. Only one survived his scrutiny. James had given her a set of rooms in the house.

"She's great. I think I'd be lost without her. Do you know I wrote three chapters today? The book's nearly done already. I can't believe it."

"Do you have to write tonight?"

"I could take the night off."

"Yeah?"

"Well, I'll have to listen out for Thomas. Mia and Sonia are going out for a drink."

"You don't want to go with them?"

"I have other plans."

"Do they involve me?"

"If you want."

He pressed a quick kiss to her lips and abandoned all care, deepening it. A cough came from behind them. He drew back and frowned. Amy giggled.

"Yes, Matthew."

"Sorry, Boss. I just had the word. Colette was released today."

"Did Peterson pick her up?"

"Yes."

"How'd it go?" He wrapped his arm around Amy's tiny frame and pulled her closer.

"Apparently, he's been going in there for a couple of weeks now. They hit it off straight away. Colette's going to stay with him and see how it goes."

"Is he going to report back to you?" Amy asked this time.

"Do you want him to?" Matthew questioned.

"Yes."

"Then, I'll get him to give reports on a regular basis."

"Thank you, Matthew." Amy smiled at him.

"Will you need me for anything else tonight, boss?"

"Sonia's out this evening?" He replied.

"Yes."

"Good." He picked the baby monitor up from the table and threw it at his bodyguard. "One interruption an evening is enough. Amy, dungeon. You have five minutes. Matthew, you are on Thomas duty. Have fun."

He left his opened-mouthed bodyguard and followed Amy down the corridor.

She was kneeling, naked on the floor, when he entered his dungeon. Her hands neatly on her thighs in slave position. Her head was bowed, but when he came, she looked up at him. Her big blue eyes adoring with love for him. After she had asked him for a play room, he'd built it straight away. It'd been ready for two weeks now, and they'd played in it a few times, but tonight he was going to test her limits.

"What's your safe word?"

"Rose."

"Use it, and everything stops."

"Yes, Master."

"I want to play a lot tonight. I'll use the traffic light system, also, just to make sure. Tell me what that means."

"Green, I feel happy. Yellow, you'll pause, and we'll discuss what I'm nervous about. Red, we stop altogether and will go to our bedroom and discuss why I used an ending safe word."

"Good. Do you remember why we originally got this room?"

"Because Matthew and Sonia had a St Andrews Cross, and I wanted one."

"Cheeky little subbie asking for toys."

"Don't ask, don't get, Sir."

"In that case, what would you like me to do to you?"

"I wish whatever my Master is pleased to give me."

"Doesn't work that way." The banter between them was always so free and easy. She was pressing his buttons because, in the end, he'd get her off even harder. They were very much two halves of the same whole.

"I want to be tied to the cross, Sir."

"And then what?"

"I think I should be spanked, Sir."

"Why?"

"I may have had improper thoughts about another man today."

"Who was he?" His hand was already twitching, his cock rising in his loose track pants from her teasing.

"He's the hero in my new book."

He took a prowling step forward, one of his calloused hands resting under her chin and tipping it up so that her eyes met his rapidly blackening ones.

"Tell me about him." His voice was deep and commanding.

"He's tall, had blue eyes, dark features, muscular, that 'v' that leads to a promised land." She was already breathy.

"Did it make you wet?"

"Yes."

A raised an eyebrow at her evident faux pas.

"Yes, Sir."

"Better. Stand."

She did as instructed, and he turned her around, pulling her closely to him. Running a hand over her stomach and down to the cleft between her legs, she already had her arousal coating her sex.

"Were you this wet?"

"No, Master. I only get this wet when you touch me."

He brought his fingers back up to her mouth and pressed them in so she could taste herself on them.

"Only I will ever do this to you. Make you overflow with desire for me."

She nibbled lightly on the end of his finger. He pressed his mouth to her ear.

"Get on the cross, beautiful. Face me."

He let her go, and she scrambled quickly over to the wooden structure in the corner of the room. He fastened the four leather cuffs to her arms and legs. He could hear her trying to keep her breath calm.

"Colour?"

"Green."

"You sure?"

"Verging on amber but, yes, green."

He dropped a little kiss to her right breast.

"Totally green now." She giggled, and he smacked her thigh.

"I think I will rescind your speaking rights for that."

She pouted.

"I wouldn't do that…"

She pouted deeper.

"I think I need to adorn my mischievous little submissive with some jewellery."

This time she squirmed, and he chuckled, picking up two barrel clamps from a tray nearby. He tweaked a nipple till it budded out with a rush of blood.

"A beautiful colour."

She hissed out a moan of ecstasy when he applied the clip. Her eyes focused on everything that he was doing to her. He loved that attention. It was devotion on his wife's part. He repeated the process with the other clip and took a step back.

"A gorgeous sight, but I believe you need more."

Next, he took a clit clamp, and her eyes widened. It wasn't one they had used before.

"Colour?"

"Does it hurt?"

"It increases pleasure."

"Green."

"Let's find that sexy little clit of yours, then, shall we?" He got down on his knees before her and parted her delicate folds. She still kept herself waxed bare for him, so it didn't take him long to find her clit just peeking out of its hood.

"I sometimes wonder if you are ever not turned on when I am around."

"I can't help it. I only have to feel your breath near me, and I am hot and horny."

"Don't ever change."

"I don't plan on doing so."

He licked the length of her slit, his stubbled jaw scraping against her slender thighs. She whimpered under his touch, and he had to shift his uncomfortable cock.

"I think your little bud is ready for its adornment now."

He applied the clamp, and Amy wiggled with delight. Her arousal was dripping down her legs.

"I seem to remember you fantasising about another man. That means punishment." He lifted a small leather flogger. It wasn't meant to mark her skin, just bring her to the point of orgasm.

"I want a count of ten."

That would keep her focused for now.

Lightly, he flicked the flogger against her skin, and she counted. One against her stomach, only slightly curved now from where she carried their child. One against each side of her breasts, not on the clamps. Back to her stomach again and two on her thighs.

"Six." She counted each time correctly.

His lips twisted this time; he knew where he was heading with the next swish of his wrist.

Thud, and the jangle of metal.

He had brought it down on her left nipple.

Her voice wobbled, and she shut her eyes when she counted seven.

The right breast followed before he whacked the clamp between her legs. He allowed that one to reverberate through her body before allowing ten to come down in the same place.

He could see she was sliding. He exchanged the flogger for a stronger one. I wouldn't mark her skin, but it would give a harder sting.

"I am going to give you another ten. I will count this time."

Her eyes opened, focused briefly, consent given, trust given, control given, so he brought the flogger down in ten more strikes. On the tenth one, she exploded, her screams of orgasm echoing his name around the room. Her whole body was limp on the cross, her eyes shut while she shuddered. He removed the clamp on her clit, and it sent her off again as all the blood rushed back. He brought his mouth to her ear.

"I love you. Fly high, my beauty." A hissed moan greeted the removal of the clamps on her breasts. When he'd done away with the cuffs, he scooped her into his arms and brought her to a sofa in the corner of the room. He shrouded her in a blanket, because she was covered in a sheen of sweat, and he didn't want her to get cold.

Eventually she spoke. "What was that?"

"Subspace."

"I don't think I have ever come that hard before. It just kept going."

"I think you may have a thing for a little bit of pain. I can't wait to explore that."
She shifted on his lap. "Did you come?"

"No. Later."

She slid from his lap onto her knees on the floor.

"May I?"

He nodded.

Amy pulled him out of his pants and took him into her mouth. He put his head back on the top of the sofa. She stopped and looked up at him with tears in her eyes.

"What's wrong?" He pulled her back up onto his lap.

"This is forever isn't it?"

"What?"

"Us. Like this. We can be like this forever now? We may fight, but we will always come back to this."

He rubbed his hand over her still slightly slick hair and brought her lips to his.

"Yes. It will always come back to the bonds we share. The love that joins us together."

"Are you happy?"

"I couldn't be happier. Well, I could, I do believe your lips were wrapped around my cock."

"Oops." She slid back down to her knees.

"I love you."

"I love you too."

THE END

PART FOUR
MISGUIDED CONTROL

ONE

Callum

It hadn't always been this way; dressed in a suit for work. He hadn't really worked. Callum had spent most of his time lounging around, causing trouble for his parents. Sponging off them for whatever he needed. Sleeping with anything with a tight little pussy—he hadn't been fussy. Drinking. Drugs. You name it, and he had tried it.

Now, his life couldn't be further from that. He had a job, an Accountant, one of the most boring in the world. Qualified and everything. He'd worked his way up the ranks and then gone into industry. Today, he was starting a new job. Finance Director of North Enterprises.

This was the big one.

"Callum?" His mother called out. "Hurry up, you'll be late."

Okay. Yeah, he still lived with his parents. He was twenty-nine, but it was safer that way. Well, that's what his father said anyway.

"Coming mum." He grabbed the jacket of his pristine pinstripe suit, took the bag of sandwiches from his mother's hands, as she stood at the door waiting, shoved them in his leather briefcase, and went out the door. He nodded to a policeman outside, jumped into his Audi A5, and tried very hard not to speed off down the road.

North Enterprises was in the heart of the city, and traffic was good, so it didn't take him long to get there. He parked in the underground car park, used the key card he'd popped in to get last week, and went to the top floor where the directors had their offices.

"Callum?" James North's bodyguard came out of the central office. A rather scary-looking man called Matthew Carter. They'd met a few times now, not all in the workplace.

"Hi."

"It's your first day, isn't it?" They shook hands with a very firm grip.

"Yes. James in his office?"

"Nah. His wife gave birth yesterday." Matthew leaned casually against the wall, his legs crossed at the ankle.

"Wow. Congratulations to them."

"Yeah. He's going to take the full two-week paternity."

"He really is a changed man, like the press are saying."

"Don't talk to me about the media. I've already had to chuck one of them out of the hospital for posing as a nurse. They're desperate for a picture of the kid. I only popped in here to drop some papers off, and then, I'm heading back there." Matthew frowned and formed a ball with his fist.

"What did they have?" He was genuinely interested. He'd met James and his wife a few times now and thought they were a wonderful couple.

"A boy. Thomas. Cute as anything but don't tell my girlfriend that."

"Your secret's safe." He held his hands up and smirked.

"Shit, you need someone to run over everything, don't you?" Matthew pushed off the wall.

"You did most of it the other week. It's fine. I'm sure I can find my own way around."

"No, can't have that. Here. This way."

Callum followed Matthew to the main office.

"Marie?" An absolutely stunning woman appeared from behind a section break. Her long jet black hair was pulled back. She wore a teal-coloured sheath dress that showed off a body of a golden age Hollywood star. She had beautiful, bright hazel eyes.

"Mr Carter. I thought you'd gone back to the hospital?" She gasped when Matthew strode into the room.

"I had. I forgot Mr Ashworth was starting today though. Can you look after him, please? He's set up with all the security stuff already, but he needs introductions."

"I need to cancel Mr North's appointments." She gave him a glance and put her hands on her curvy hips. "He can make himself a coffee and sit where you wait while I do that."

"Thank you."

Ok, this secretary wasn't going to be the most fun person to spend the morning with. Shame, she was a stunner. Matthew pulled him over to a Nespresso coffee machine.

"Don't mind her. She is usually politer. She's just a bit pissed off over the baby."

"Why?"

"Don't ask. Make her a coffee and wait quietly. She'll mellow."

"Got it."

"I have to go. I'll try and come back later and check everything is alright. You've my mobile number, if you need me."

"Thanks. Oh, Matthew. How does she take it?"

"Who, take what?"

"Marie."

Matthew snickered, "I wouldn't get any ideas there. I know what you're like. She only has eyes for one man, and he's off limits."

"I only meant how does she take her coffee, but that's just intrigued me."

"White, no sugar. And good luck with day dreaming. It won't last long." Matthew disappeared, leaving Callum alone with the secretary who was using her sweetest voice to apologise to a client. He managed to figure out the rather complicated machine and made himself a black expresso and Marie a flat white. He put it on her desk, and she placed her hand over the receiver of the phone.

"You forgot the chocolate powder over the top."

"You forgot to say please."

"Please." Sarcasm dripped from the word, before she turned her sickly-sweet voice back to whoever was on the other end of the phone. He was starting to relish the challenge of this woman. She'd be good fun to spend the day with. He took a piece of paper and some scissors from her desk. She looked at him quizzically, but he ignored her.

He went back, got the chocolate powder, and quickly cut a shape out of the paper. He could see her watching him, but he just turned his back to her. He lay the paper over, and a heart was revealed. He shook the powder and left a heart shape on her coffee. He was very pleased with himself.

She just rolled her eyes.

A comfortable chair greeted him while he waited for her to finish her calls. He placed one muscular leg over the other and watched her. He didn't know why he was so fascinated with her. She was obviously rude, selfish, and completely delusional. He hadn't failed to realise that Matthew meant she had a thing for James, and that's why she was in such a bad mood today

Half an hour later, Marie finally finished her calls. She came over to him, and in her three-inch heels, she was almost the same height as his six foot three.

"You ready to go?"

"Well, I probably should do some work today."

She led him down a corridor towards another set of rooms, her pert backside swaying. Damn, if his cock wasn't twitching at the sight.

"These are your offices, and this is Sam. Your PA." She motioned to the gentleman sitting at the desk. Sam was about twenty-five, and from the way he was checking Callum out, he was into men.

"Hi, Mr Ashworth. I've set you up on the system; you just need to change your passwords. I've arranged a meeting with the sales and purchase heads for just after lunch, so you can get yourself acquainted with them, and I've emailed you all last month's figures with the explanation for variances. We still don't have the actuals from Rome, but I'll call them again today. I'll let you get acquainted with your office. Can I get you a drink? Tea? Coffee? Cold drink?"

"Black coffee, please."

"You're welcome, Mr Ashworth. I'll get that drink for you right away. Marie, are you staying?"

"Just because Mr North is off, why do people think that I've nothing to do?" She huffed her shoulders and tutted.

"Oh come on, you're so far ahead, and he isn't around for two weeks now. You'll be twiddling your thumbs." So it wasn't just Matthew who knew that this woman had a thing for her boss.

"It's alright, Sam, I think we can find our way alone. Marie here has many important calls to make. She needs to reschedule two weeks' worth of meetings after all." He flashed her his best smile, but she just pursed her lips in reply.

"Thank you, Mr Ashworth." And with that, she disappeared out the door.

The rest of the day went well.

His stomach rumbled. Sam had brought him in an afternoon snack. The sandwiches his mother had made were gone by midmorning. "Sam?"

No answer.

A quick glance at his watch told him it was seven. Damn. Where the hell had the day gone? Sam would've gone home a few hours ago. He shoved the papers into his briefcase and left his room. He was almost to the lift when a female voice echoed in the now quiet office.

"I'm so sorry Helen. It's been one of those days. I should be half an hour depending on the tubes. I know the Northern Line had problems earlier. Is she alright?"

A pause. The person on the other end was relaying a message.

"Oh, thank god. She knows she isn't supposed to do that."

He stepped closer to the voice. Marie had worry lines across her forehead, and the edges of her eyes were damp with unshed tears. She sensed him and looked up.

"I have to go. I'll be there as soon as I can." She hung up and busied herself with tidying her desk and turning the computer off. "I'm sorry about the personal call. It won't happen again."

"It's not a problem, unless Mr North doesn't allow them. Is everything alright?" He was genuinely concerned.

"He doesn't mind. I just don't think I should take them at work." She ignored the question and took her coat off the stand.

"Look at me."

She hesitated but eventually looked up.

"Is it something I can help with?"

She looked back down and shook her head.

"You said you had to get the Tube. I can give you a lift home if it helps."

"No." Her answer a little too frantic in reply. "I mean, it's fine. The tubes won't take long."

He dipped his hand into his pocket, pulled out his wallet, and held out some cash. She didn't take it.

"Get a cab home."

"That isn't necessary."

"It's late. I know you aren't impressed with me, but I'm a gentleman, and I won't see you travelling on the tubes, when it's evident you need to get home. Please take it." He waved the money again. She took it. It was then that he noticed her hands were shaking.

"Thank you."

"You're welcome. Now get home."

He escorted her into the lift, and they descended in silence. When the doors opened on her floor, she turned to him. Her face was etched with guilt. It was horrible to see.

"I'm sorry for the way I was earlier. I've no excuse. It's just been a bad time."

"Don't say anything more. Goodnight."

"Goodnight."

The doors shut, and he was left reflecting on the first day in a new job. All in all, it hadn't been bad. He was going to enjoy it here. Yes, he really was.

TWO

Marie

The walk took her forty minutes. She wasn't going to hang around waiting for a Tube when it could be hours, and the fifty pounds that Callum had given her would come in handy for Owen. After she'd left Callum in the lift, she'd taken another lift back up to her office and changed into a pair of trousers and trainers. They were old and tatty—and the only way to get home safely.

She looked up at the looming, concrete tower block in front of her. It was a home of a sort. Well, as good as it was going to get. Hoxton didn't have much else she could afford. Not that they could move. Even with her job, she had she still had to pay 'them' off. She pulled her bag closer and tried to creep quietly past a gang of teenagers drinking and swearing on the street outside. One of them jogged up to her.

"Got a light?"

"No, sorry." She kept her head down and walked a bit faster.

"I only wanted a light, you bitch. What, you think I want to fuck you? Not likely. I'm more careful where I stick my dick." She rounded the corner and started to sprint up the stairs; her heart was beating so fast. It was always like this. Why couldn't they just leave her and her family alone?

The stench of urine hit her as she approached her front door. They'd apparently been marking their territory again. At least it wasn't shit through the door like last time. That was why the letterbox was sealed up; one day it would be a flaming bottle. Their post always went to her Aunt.

She took a few moments at the door to compose herself before putting the ever-present smile back on her face and walked into the damp and decrepit flat.

"It's just me." Her shout was greeted by the squeal of delight from a now two-year-old Owen.

"Meemee...meemee" He sped around the corner and straight into her arms.

"Hey, my little boy. You have a good day with Nanna and Auntie Helen?"

"Nanna ouch."

"I know. Let's go and see her."

She carried Owen into the tiny lounge area and set him down on the floor with a toy car she'd bought second hand from a charity shop.

"Play with this for me, while I talk to Nanna."

"Brooommmm."

"Good boy."

She turned to her mother and the lump on her head.

"I'm sorry Mee. I thought I could get myself dressed."

"You know you're supposed to wait for Helen to help."

"I don't like feeling so helpless and so utterly useless."

"It will come back, mum. We just have to be patient and keep up with the physio."

Ever since her mother had had a stroke a year ago, they'd been trying to improve her mobility. She'd lost the use of the left side of her body. Thankfully, her speech hadn't been affected too badly.

"I just hate seeing you do everything and working such long hours as well. I should move in with Helen."

"No, Mum, this is your home. It's fine, I love my job and coming home to you and Owen is what I want to do every evening. I just want you to concentrate on getting better."

"See Annie, I told you she wouldn't be angry." Her aunt Helen appeared from the kitchen. "I've just finished the washing up and left your dinner in the microwave."

"Thanks, Auntie. Sorry, again I was so late."

"It isn't a problem. I'll give Uncle Ned a call, so he can come and get me."

"Yeah. Don't go out alone. They're out there again."

"They've been there most of the day. Gave us lip when I brought Annie back from the doctors. Told 'em to shove it."

"I wondered why outside smelled of pee."

"Fucking delinquents."

"You need to get back to the authorities about them."

"Language Helen." Her mother piped up.

"I'll call them tomorrow." She knew her aunt meant well, but it was best just to ignore them. Any reaction fuelled their hatred even more.

"Fish cakes. Meemee says that." Owen added his thoughts.

"You, little imp, are too smart for your own good. Come on. Let's get you to bed."

"No." He folded his arms across his chest and furrowed his brow. The terrible twos had started.

But they hadn't developed so badly that bribery no longer worked. "Not even if I read you 'Whatever Next'?"

This was his favourite book and guaranteed to get him speeding to the bedroom.

"Whoooshhhh." He jumped up, like the rocket in the book, and ran into the bedroom that he shared with her.

Owen wasn't hers, but she loved him just like he was. He'd never know his biological parents, but he had a place with her forever. He was the only thing that kept her going sometimes.

By the time she'd found the well-read book, Owen had climbed into bed.

"Do the voices Meemee"

She read the book in a full splendid performance with Owen joining in the sound effects. When finished, she placed it on the side and ensured he was tucked in properly, a quick kiss on his forehead, and he shut his eyes to sleep.

"Night Night."

When she emerged back in the lounge, Helen had left.

"You look tired, love." Her mum looked up at her with worry in her eyes.

"Just a long day. Mr North's wife had their baby last night, so I had lots of appointments and things to rearrange for him. The next few days should be quieter, though."

"What did they have?"

"A boy, Thomas."

"Lovely."

"Yeah."

"Are you going to get your dinner?"

"I grabbed something in the office." A lie, she just didn't feel like eating. "I'll put it in the fridge, and you can eat it tomorrow."

"Why don't you get me ready for bed now, and then, you can just rest? There's nothing on the TV anyway. I can read."

"Ok, here, give me your right arm, and I'll help you up." Marie used all her weight to steady her mother and helped her to the bathroom. She supported her while they worked together to get her undressed, washed, go to the toilet, and clean her teeth. Eventually, Annie was in her nightdress and tucked up in bed, the iPad James had given Marie for Christmas placed on a support tray so that the pages could be turned.

"I'll check on you before I go to bed and turn everything off. Just shout if you need me. I'm going to change and read for a bit as well."

"Night Mee."

"Night mum."

She turned all the lights off in the lounge and kitchen before disappearing into the small bathroom. They didn't have a bath but a walk-in disability shower, which had taken her months of paperwork to get from the Council. She'd had to blanket bathe her mother for months and months after the stroke. It didn't do either of them any good.

The small mirror in the badly-lit bathroom showed all her worry lines. They were getting deeper. She was only twenty-four and already looked much older than her years. No wonder James had preferred the carefree Amy to her. It was a foolish folly to even think that he'd have loved her and rescued her from the nightmare that was her life. Mind you, he didn't even know where she lived. He didn't know about her mum or Owen. In his eyes, she was a simple annoyance, fascinated with something she couldn't have.

She took a piece of cotton wool from out of the cupboard under the sink and ran it under the tap to take the makeup off her face. She removed her clothes, stepped into the lukewarm shower, and washed the day's worries from her body.

She was tired, probably hormonal. Resigned. The tears tumbled down her cheeks. It wasn't fair. It just wasn't fucking fair.

She finished her shower and got dressed into PJ's. She still wasn't hungry but maybe a hot chocolate? She'd been naughty with regards to the chocolate for the top. She loved the flavour of the one that she had in the office and had stolen one. She made up the chocolate, and when she started sprinkling the powder on the top, she remembered the heart Callum had done on her coffee. She chuckled. God, she'd been such a bitch to him, and he'd still given her fifty pounds to get herself home safely. What was she doing? She wasn't this person. She made a vow to herself to be nicer to him tomorrow. He hadn't been anything but a gentleman. No one else had ever given her money to get a taxi home because they were worried about her.

She finished making her drink and got into bed. Amy's book was on her dressing table. She flicked it open and started to read by the night light she had for Owen. She'd never have a happy ending, but she could always dream of one. Live vicariously through others.

THREE

Callum

"Good morning, Mr Ashworth."

"Good morning, Miss....." He stopped and peered through the open door to where Marie had called him, "What is your surname? Nobody told me yesterday."

"Easton." She smiled.

He took a few steps into the room, stopping by her desk. "Well, good morning, Miss Easton."

"Marie, please."

"Marie." He laughed. "Did you get home alright to sort whatever problem it was you had?"

"I did. Thank you. I have a confession to make, though. I didn't use your fifty pounds. I walked. Please." She held out an envelope from her desk. "Have it back. It was kind of you."

"You were told to get a taxi. It was late." Did she just deliberately set out to disobey people?

"I know. I like to walk. I made sure I was safe."

"Keep the money and get a taxi tonight."

"No, honestly."

His voice went dark and domineering, "Don't argue with me."

She lowered her head and placed the envelope back down on the desk. "Sorry."

His cock was doing that twitching thing again. This woman was stubborn, annoying, and rude at times, but his body still reacted to her.

"I better go see what Sam has lined up for me today."

"That's the real reason I stopped you. Sam was admitted to hospital last night with appendicitis."

"Is he alright?"

"His appendix was taken out during the night, but obviously, he is going to be out of action for at least a week, maybe two. We're trying to get you a temp, but she isn't answering her phone."

"That's ok. I'm sure I can muddle through 'til she does."

"Well." She bit her lip, "Mr Carter suggested that as Mr North is off, and since I supposedly don't have much to do, I can transfer to you 'til Sam recovers."

"And?"

"I have some work to do for Mr North, but I do have time available to assist you. Just until we can find someone else."

"Then, you can start by making me a coffee, and I wouldn't mind some fresh fruit either." He made a dash for his room, before she could reply.

The morning flew by. He finally had the figures he needed from Rome, and he could see why they hadn't sent them over sooner. They were all over the place. Something wasn't right. He picked up his phone and dialled Matthew.

"Matthew Carter." The bodyguard answered on the first ring, in the background he could hear a screaming baby.

"Matthew, it's Callum. You got a few moments?"

"If it gets me away from the baby noise, yes, I've more than a few minutes." The sound of the new-born quietened. "What's the matter?"

"I got the Rome figures. They don't add up. To be honest, they smack of fraud."

"Fuck. James suspected as much. I'll just get him." The phone went silent.

"Hi, Callum. Talk to me." James's voice now, and he wasn't going to beat around the bush.

"The figures are off. They don't tally at all. I think we are looking at, well, at least half a million missing, but that is only for a few months. I am going to look back further."

"Any suspects?"

"Not yet. I am going to get Marie to pull up personal files."

"Marie?"

"Sam is in the hospital. She is covering."

"Right." James went silent.

"What are you thinking?"

"I think I should get on a plane and get out there, now. Sort it in person."

"I agree. Stamp down on it. Find out who is responsible, and I'll send Matthew out to deal with them. Take Marie with you. She is good at what she does and will be an asset."

"You sure?"

"You have my authority. Do what needs to be done. I've got to go. Keep Matthew informed."

"Will do. And congratulations."

"Thanks, Cal."

There was a scuffling as the phone was handed back to Matthew.

"Everything alright?"

"Yeah. I'll call you when I get to Rome."

"Enjoy."

Matthew hung up. Callum grabbed the papers strewn over his desk and put them into his briefcase. He then called for Marie.

"Need more coffee?" She stood leaning against the door frame.

"I would love another coffee, but I need you to do something else urgently."

"Yes?"

"I'm not impressed with the figures in Rome. Can you book flights and hotel for two as soon as possible please?'

"Of course. What's the other name on the ticket?"

"Marie Easton."

Her mouth dropped open in shock. "I can't go to Rome."

"You haven't travelled for Mr North before?"

"I have but not at short notice."

"Mr North asked me to take you. He thinks you will be a great asset. Sit down." He motioned to the chair in front of his desk, and she obeyed. "I think I may have uncovered a theft, and Mr North wants it sorted immediately."

"I can't believe someone has dared to do that."

"They won't get away with it."

"Can you give me a few hours to sort things?"

"I want to be there before the end of day today. To freeze everything in the office but take as long as you need otherwise."

"Thank you." She got up and headed back towards the door

"I will head home now and pack. Text me details, and I will come and pick you up." She froze.

"Um...no it's alright. I will meet you back here, or I could come to you? Where do you live?"

"I live in Mayfair. It's alright, I will come and get you."

"But I live in...in Islington. It seems silly for you to come all the way back."

"I insist." His voice went dark and left no more room for the secretary to argue.

FOUR

Marie

What was it with that damn tone that made her do whatever he asked? She couldn't drop everything and go to Rome! She was sure as fuck not going to let him come and pick her up from Hoxton. Thankfully, she'd said Islington. She could get him to get her from her aunt's house. What was she doing even considering going? There was no way she could leave her mother and Owen on such short notice. What if her aunt couldn't help out? How long would they be away? Why was he staring at her? Did he want something else? Oh yes, he wanted an answer. She was panicking.

"I'll send you the details with the flight information." There, she said it. She was going to give him her address, well her aunt's. Now all she needed to do was sort out the flights and hotel, get home, pack up Owen and her mum, pack for herself, get everyone over to her aunt's and settled in, and get to Rome before the offices there shut. What was the time? She looked at the clock? Nine forty-five. Seven hours. Okay, that was possible. Why was Callum still staring at her? What was his problem? Had there been something else that he had asked her? No, they had covered everything. Her inner monologue was going a bit insane.

"I should get the flights booked."

"Marie."

"Yes, Mr Ashworth."

"Breathe."

"Sorry."

"You look flustered."

He came over to her and turned her around. He put his hands on her shoulders and began to massage. God, he had strong hands. She leant backwards against him.

"Mr North values you highly. He said you'd be perfect to assist me with this job. I don't want you to feel forced, though."

"You're not. It'll be fun...well, the bit that isn't work. Nobody messes with Mr North's money and gets away with it." She gave a half-hearted laugh. Her heart was still thumping away with nerves.

"We can see sights while we're there. I've never been to Italy. We're definitely having a real Italian pizza." He let go of her shoulders, and she stepped back.

"I'll sort everything as quickly as I can." With that, she left. First she phoned Helen and checked it was alright for her mum and Owen to stay at her house. It was, thankfully. Next, she got on the phone and sorted the flights and hotel. She had access to the release codes for James's private jet in the case of emergencies. This was an emergency. She found a boutique hotel near the Pantheon that would suit them perfectly. She booked Callum into an executive room and her into a standard one. Even that would be luxury compared to what she was used to. Besides, it didn't feel right spending money for the sake of it. A standard room was just fine. She picked up her phone to text Callum.

M: Flights booked. Using the private jet from London City. Will leave at one.

C: Thank you. What's your address? I'll pick you up at twelve. Does that give you enough time?

She glanced at the clock. Ten. It was going to be really tight.

M: Can you give me an extra fifteen mins. Still in the office.

C: Get a taxi home. Now. Address?

She took a deep breath and replied back with her Aunt's address.

C: See you soon.

He really didn't take no for an answer. She grabbed her bag, shoved some papers into it, and sped out the door. She could do this. She didn't know how, but she could do it.

FIVE

Marie

It didn't take long to pack her small case and put all of Owen's and her mum's essential belongings in a black bin bag.

The taxi money Callum had given her came in handy, and she was able to get everything and everyone to her aunt's by eleven forty-five. Luckily, Owen saw it all as an adventure. The second he was placed on the floor in Ned's and Helen's house he was off exploring.

"Helen, Ned, I can't thank you enough for this. I'm so sorry it was such short notice."

"Mee, there's no need to apologise. Your cousin's at university, so the rooms are spare for now. Your mum and Owen will be spoilt rotten." Ned took her hand and held it tightly.

"I wish I could tell you how long it'll be, but I don't know. We need to find out about this fraud and take care of it."

"Go, enjoy yourself." Her aunt gave her a warm smile. It set her at ease but only a little.

"I'll just help mum get sorted. I think the journey tired her out."

"No worries. We'll go play aeroplanes with Owen and show him his room." Ned wasn't actually looking too upset to be doing that.

Panicking suddenly gripped her, "He has never slept alone. He might be scared."

"There is another bed in there. If he is upset, one of us will stay in the room with him."

"Thank you." Why did she suddenly feel tearful? Everything was such a rush.

"Go settle your mum. I'll make her a cup of tea." Her aunt headed to the kitchen while her uncle scooped Owen up in his arms and flew him like a plane to his bedroom.

"Come on, mum. Let's get you settled and resting."

"Mee?" Her mother opened her eyes. She had been dozing on the sofa. "I'm okay, honey. You need to get ready. Your boss will be here in a few minutes."

"It's fine. I'll get you upstairs, and you can rest. Uncle Ned can bring you down later."

"That would be nice. I am a little tired."

She helped her mother stand and climb the stairs to her bedroom.

"Do you want to get undressed?" She only had a jumper and loose tracksuit pants on, but she might be more comfortable in her nightdress.

"No, just help me into the bed please."

Marie manoeuvred her mother so that she was comfortably seated and tucked her in.

"Aunt Helen is going to bring you up a cup of tea. Do you want the TV on?"

"Yes, please. I can watch some films."

Marie found the remote and placed it by her mum's right hand. She turned the TV on and gave her mum a kiss.

"Mee, there's a gentleman here for you." Her aunt's voice called up from downstairs.

Oh God, she'd hoped to catch him before he got out of the car. Damn it! Damn it! There would be questions now. He would most likely ask about Owen. Maybe she could just pretend to fall asleep for the entire journey.

"I've got to go, mum. My lift is here. I'll call you when I get there."

"Nice man coming to get you. A real gentleman. Have fun little Mee."

"Bye mum."

Marie left the door slightly ajar. Chatter drifted upstairs and a squeal of laughter from Owen. She'd hoped to get changed, but there wasn't time. They needed to leave to make their flight time. She paused at the door, when she saw Callum, still dressed in his suit, on his hands and knees pushing one of Owen's cars around the floor. Owen was copying him, and they were both making racing car noises. Her heart leapt at the beautiful sight. Owen had very few male role models in his life, bar her uncle, so it was great to see him so free and easy around another man.

"Mee Mee. Man brooooommmmm."

"He is, Owen. You're a good boy for sharing your cars with him."

Callum got to his feet. He looked a little embarrassed at being caught playing with a child's toy car.

"I've got to take your aunt Meemee to the airport now. I'll make sure we take that photo of the plane for you."

"Peas" That was Owen's version of please. Callum ruffled his hair and came to her side.

"Is that your case?" His eyes went to the luggage by the front door.

"Yes, it is."

"I'll put it in the car. We better get a move on."

"I've just got to grab my bag and coat."

Callum turned to her uncle and held his hand out to him. "Nice to meet you Mr West. I'll take good care of her." He kissed her aunt on the cheeks "And you, Mrs West." He picked up her case and disappeared out the door. No questions, nothing? Was he for real? Actually, he was probably saving it all for later when they were alone. She reluctantly got her belongings, kissed her aunt and uncle, and gave Owen a big cuddle.

"I'll phone later when I'm at the hotel. Be good Owen."

"Owen say peas and tank you."

"Don't work too hard, Marie." Her aunt winked at her. "Not with a cutie like that in tow."

"Aunt Helen!"

"Oh, come on. You're telling me you hadn't noticed?"

No, she hadn't noticed.

He *was* handsome, now she did think about it. His jaw was square. His jet-black hair and hazel eyes were enticing, and she wondered if under the sharp suit he had a muscular body. Yeah, he must do. Oh, Shit. She didn't need to be thinking like this.

"I need to go. Goodbye, Aunt Helen. Bye, Uncle Ned."

She stepped outside, and Callum was holding the door open to his car for her to get in. *Not handsome, not handsome.* This was going to be a long trip.

SIX

Callum

Without pomp or ceremony, Callum strode purposefully through the doors of the CEO of Rome's office. Marie was at his side, carrying a case of papers.

"*Sicurezza.*"

"I don't speak Italian, Signore Corvi, but I know you speak English, so we will conduct this conversation in that language. My name is Callum Ashworth; I'm the new FD of North Enterprises. I'm here under the authority of Mr North to freeze all assets of this branch. Here is my ID." He threw his credentials down in front of the shocked, middle-aged man just as two burly security guards ran in. They were quickly shooed away with a wave of a hand.

The CEO had turned white.

"There is money missing from the returns submitted. You are to ask your staff to step away from their desks and leave the building at once. We have security in place who will search them before they go. No-one is to take anything work related with them, laptops, mobiles, papers. They are all to remain on their desks."

"I understand. I need to call my finance manager."

He nodded and watched as the phone call was placed. "The conversation must be in English."

"Giovanni, I've got the company FD here. Can you join us please?"

A few moments later a slimy-looking man entered the room. He wore thick-rimmed glasses; they almost hung off the end of his nose.

"What is this about?"

"Mr Ashworth and his colleague are here to investigate our return. I need you to shut everything down."

"This is crazy. I'm the finance manager here. *Mi piacerebbe sapere se qualcosa stava succedendo?*"

"In English, please." He interrupted

"I said I'd know if something was going on." The irritated man turned towards him with a scowl.

"Signore...?"

"Romano."

"Signore Romano, I'm here to investigate properly." Callum explained again.

The finance manager folded his arms and frowned with contempt. "Alright. I'll do as you ask." The agitated man turned and stomped towards the door.

"Wait."

"What now?"

"Miss Easton will go with you and assist with the closedown. I wish to ask Signore Corvi a few more questions."

"Si."

He leant into Marie. "Keep an eye on him."

"Of course." She gave a brief smile and followed the finance manager.

"Do you have suspicions of who is responsible?" The CEO had stood and was looking out his office window towards the rooms below him.

"No, but I will, as soon as I get into the records."

"Mr North wants to handle this internally. He will send Mr Carter, when I know who it is. "

"Mr Carter? So this is severe?"

"Yes."

"You have my word that I will support you in any way I can. Is my job in jeopardy?"

"That has not been discussed yet."

"*Va bene*. Ok."

The man slumped in his chair. Callum knew from the look on his face that he was not involved in what was going on in the company, but the resigned look of defeat told him that maybe he hadn't been as stringent in looking after it as he should have.

A few hours later, the entire office was clear. The finance officer had kicked up a fuss again, but Callum had politely told him to leave. The CEO was utterly defeated and just quietly slipped away home. Callum and Marie spent the rest of the evening searching through the papers.

He leaned back in his chair, yawned, and stretched out his muscular arms. His back was aching. Talk about a baptism of fire in the job.

"I think I've found something." Marie looked up and came over to him. "These figures don't add up. Callum...there's a couple of million missing."

"A couple of million?" She showed him. "God, you are right. James is going to be livid when he sees this. It's the last thing he needs on paternity leave."

"I think livid is an understatement. Nobody has dared to defy him like this before."

"Any clues as to who it is?"

"No, but it is all signed off by the Finance officer."

"I don't know. I think there is something not right about that man." Callum rubbed his hands over his weary eyes. "Look, it's getting late. Why don't we put this aside for the night and go get some food? I'll give James a follow-up in the morning. We can't give it our full attention when we're half asleep and hungry. This is people's lives and jobs; we could make mistakes. Let's go get some of the real Italian pizza you wanted and then a few hours sleep. Hopefully, in the morning, we will be able to see a clearer picture of what is going on."

Marie agreed. "Where shall we go for pizza?"

"There was a small place by the hotel. Shall we go there?"

"Sounds good to me."

They locked the important papers into a safe and took the short walk to the restaurant. In Italy, people tended to eat later, and the pizzeria, was busy, but the manager managed to find them a table tucked away in the corner. Marie ordered a margarita, while he ordered as much meat as a man could possibly get on a pizza. They ordered a bottle of wine, pinot grigio, after all, they were in Italy.

"So, how long have you been working for Mr North?" Callum asked as he popped the last piece of his meal into his mouth.

"I've been working for the company since I turned sixteen. I started off in the mailroom, doing bits and pieces, and gradually developed 'til I became Mr North's PA."

"Sixteen? You don't have any formal training?"

"Mr North paid for me to do a course to help me learn what I needed to. He must have seen something in me. That's why I like to repay him by working hard at my job."

"You've done well for yourself. PA to one of the richest CEO's in the country."

"I enjoy my job."

"That is the main thing."

"What about you?" She brought her wine to her lips, and he watched as she swallowed a mouthful down. Her lips were like velvet. He wondered what they would be like to kiss. *Jesus, Callum, focus on the job not your libido.*

"What about me?"

"Well, you're an accountant; you must have qualified. Where have you worked before?"

"Yes, I'm qualified. I've worked in lots of different firms, but this is my first FD position. I wasn't really a hard worker in my youth. I liked to party a bit too much. I eventually grew up, though. I know Matthew and James...socially. That is probably why I got the job."

"Oh right. Socially. Does that mean you're...er...how do I say this? I know what Mr North is into... I've read books. Does that mean you're dominant?" She was babbling, and it was so cute to see.

"Marie. I do believe that you're blushing. Yes, I'm a dominant. I know James and Matthew from a local club. You have a problem with that?"

"No, no, not at all."

"Have you ever been to one?"

"No, I don't get to go out much socially."

"Owen?"

"Yes, I spend a lot of my time looking after him."

"He's your nephew."

"Yes."

"What happened to his parents?"

"My sister. I don't want to talk about it." Marie looked towards her watch. "It's getting late. We should get back to the hotel and sleep. Make sure we have our heads right for tomorrow."

"Marie? If there is ever anything you need to talk about…"

She stood.

"I'm fine."

The waiter brought her coat, and Callum paid the bill. "You said you've never been to Rome before?"

"No. I don't tend to get to travel much, unless it's for work."

"Well, maybe when this is sorted, we can visit a few places. I've never seen the Colosseum. I hear it is just breath-taking."

"I would like that very much."

He escorted her to her bedroom door. He wanted to kiss her. Where were these feelings coming from? He barely knew her. He'd been with many girls, enjoyed his time at the club, but had never felt this compelled to feel a woman's skin against his.

His phone rang the caller ID showed it was Matthew.

"It's serious." Callum answered.

"How serious?"

"Millions." There was a sharp intake of breath on the other end of the phone.

"Shit. Do you need me over there, yet?"

"We've not discovered the source, but we're getting there. Hope to have something for you tomorrow. I don't think it's the CEO. He was as shocked as we were. But…" He paused.

"But?" Matthew replied.

"What do you know about the finance manager?"

"I'll get a file on him to your email in the next half hour."

"Thank you." Callum hesitated again, he was unsure how the next part would go down, "Marie."

"What about her?" The bodyguard's voice was sceptical down the phone.

"I know it is not ethical, but can I have a look at her file as well?"

"You suspect she is involved?" Matthew sounded shocked.

"No, no, not at all. She is honest. She respects James too much." He replied quickly to dispel any thoughts of Marie being a thief.

"Then why do you need her file?"

"I honestly don't know, but there is something that isn't right. I don't know what it is. Did you know that she looks after her nephew?" He questioned.

"Her nephew?"

"Yeah, a little boy no more than two. I saw him today. She clammed up when I asked about the kid's mother."

"I'll see what I can do." There was concern in Matthew's voice now. Despite not being long term friends they'd both had a strong sense of understanding of when something was one and implicitly trusted the other.

"Thanks."

Callum hung up and got ready for bed. Something wasn't right with Marie. He just hoped that he could help her. That she would let him in.

He picked up his phone again and brought up the news. His father's name was all over. Thankfully, nobody had put two and two together yet. Only James and Matthew knew who he really was, and they had assured him they would keep the secret. He just hoped he could keep it that way, but he doubted it.

SEVEN

Marie

Marie turned over in the bed. She was cosy and enveloped in a tight cocoon amongst the blankets. She still had her eyes tightly shut. If she opened them, Owen would start talking to her, and she didn't want to wake up, yet. She took a deep inhalation and waited for the musky, damp smell to invade her nostrils. It didn't come, though. She opened her eyes and sat bolt upright. No Owen, no annoying peeling wallpaper, just a plush hotel room. She sank back down into the bed and snuggled against the pure cotton sheets. She was the world's worst traveller. She couldn't even remember where she was. Her phone beeped on the bedside table with a message from Callum asking if she could be ready in half an hour as he wanted to get in early. There was something he needed to check.

The next thirty minutes quickly disappeared when she discovered the walk-in shower with hot water. Yes, actual hot water that didn't run out after two seconds. She could have spent all day in there, but thankfully when Callum arrived, exactly on time, she was nearly ready.

"I'm sorry. I enjoyed the shower too much." She brushed a dab of brown eyeshadow over her lid while he sat on the edge of her bed. He had on a pinstripe suit again, including waistcoat. It framed his muscular body perfectly. Her breath hitched a little as she watched in the reflection.

"I know the feeling." His eyes met hers in the glass. "Maybe we should shrug off what we need to do and spend the day in it together."

She coughed as her throat caught at his words; her shaking hand dropped the brush on the floor.

"I don't think Mr North would appreciate us doing that on his time."

"No, I don't suspect he would." Callum came to her and bent down beside her. He picked up the brush and handed it to her. His hand wrapped around hers as he did and lingered a little longer than it should. "I'll get us some breakfast to take with us. I'll meet you downstairs in a few minutes."

"Alright." She squeaked out. Her body was reacting in all sort of strange ways to this man. Was the room getting hotter? Ok, maybe she should change her panties before she went. This pair suddenly seemed rather wet. Maybe she hadn't dried down there properly.

She traced mascara over her eyelashes and grabbed her bag and jacket. The maid could tidy up after her. It wasn't often that she was allowed to be frivolous and leave a mess.

On the short walk to the offices, Callum told her the Finance Officer invested in a company that went bust and left him with severe debts.

"He has motive then?"

"He does." Callum's answer was hesitant.

"But you're not sure?"

"He could be very desperate, but it's just all too obvious. I feel as though we are still missing something."

"I know what you mean." And she did. Ok, her grasp of financial aspects wasn't as good as his, but she knew that if she were going to steal millions she wouldn't leave a trail so easy to find. "Do you think that he is being set up?"

"Matthew sent me a file on him last night. Apart from the failure of the company, there is nothing to suggest he would do this."

"It could all be a cover to hide who he truly is?"

"It could. Marie, I want to talk to him. While I do, will you do something for me?"

"Of course?"

"I want you to talk to Signore Corvi about him. See what sort of picture you can get from him about the man. I want you to show him what evidence we have as well." He pulled up his laptop and opened a spreadsheet. "I added up all the figures and the dates. They are all dates that he volunteers. He takes the afternoon off to do it."

"I don't understand?"

"That afternoon, Signore Corvi signs any fund transfers."

"Are you saying Signore Corvi is responsible?"

"No, but I think that Giovani might be trying to create an elaborate circle to hide what he has done."

"I'll go talk to Signore Corvi, now."

"Thank you."

The conversation with the CEO didn't shed any light on the innocence or guilt of the Finance Officer for Marie. All it did was make her feel sorry for him. The CEO wanted to take early retirement so that he could spend time with his grand-children, but equally, he loved his job and would be bored without it. He was just waiting for the call from James to tell him that it was time to go.

"I better call Matthew in." Callum placed the file of evidence on the desk in front of them. All paths lead to Giovanni Romano.

"We've done all we can, I think. Matthew has resources I'm not supposed to know about, but given I'm Mr North's PA, I most certainly do." Marie raised an eyebrow.

"I think it's better if both of us forget what you just said."

"I do too."

Callum placed the call on speaker. Matthew would be there in a few hours. They were to lock everything away and get some rest. The shit would hit the fan when he arrived, so he wanted them ready.

"Fancy something to eat?"

"Not really, I'm still full from the antipasto you served up for breakfast." She patted her trim tummy and Callum laughed before blowing out his cheeks.

"Damn women! That was a snack."

"You definitely have a thing for meat don't you?"

"It's what gives me my muscles."

She shook her head this time. "I bet you wear a male girdle under that shirt?"

He took a step closer to her. His warm breath cascaded over her face.

"You want to find out?"

She pushed him lightly away.

"Anyone ever told you about sexual harassment?" She laughed, a sexy little chuckle.

"Anyone ever told you that you have been flirting with me all morning? I've seen the looks."

"Jerk!"

"Oh yeah." Callum grabbed her round the waist and started to tickle her. "Jerk am I."

"Stop." She playfully squealed.

"Apologise."

"Never, you are a jerk," He did it again but harder.

"Please stop it. Mercy. Ok, you're not a jerk." She was so ticklish that she collapsed into his arms. The air grew thick between them when he stopped. She was held within his strong arms, their faces so close. All she had to do was shift forward a few millimetres, and she'd have her lips against his. She turned away, though, and he helped her to her feet.

"Come on, let's go see the Colosseum."

"Ok."

They jumped in a taxi, and she held on for dear life as the driver weaved through the chaotic streets. When the huge Flavian Amphitheatre came into view, it took her breath away. It was a phenomenal sight.

"How old is it?" She turned to Callum, who had the same look of awe on his face as she suspected she had.

"I'm not sure." He pulled out his phone and Googled it. "Says it was started in 72AD but completed in 80AD."

"Wow, that really is old."

They joined the queue of tourists, looking silly in their smart suits, but Marie didn't care. She was too excited to get inside.

Callum brought a guidebook and handed it to her. "Here, a souvenir."

"Thank you, you shouldn't have."

"I'm just all heart when it comes to treating girls."

"Is that why you're single?"

"Who says I'm single?"

"Really?" She put her hands on her hips and looked at him. You've flirted with me, since we got off the plane."

"You have flirted back."

"My body's reaction to a beautiful face. Can't be helped. I don't hold it responsible."

"You know that could go both ways."

"Maybe." What were they doing? They had gone from zero to sixty at the speed of light. She took a step away and opened the guide book.

"Did you know it could hold an average of sixty-eight thousand people? It was used for gladiatorial contests and public spectacles such as mock sea battles, animal hunts, executions, re-enactments of famous battles, and dramas based on Classical mythology." Callum got the message, because he also took a step back.

"And when Matthew arrives, it could very well hold another epic execution."

She stopped mid-step. Callum caught her.

"He..he..wouldn't." She felt sick.

Callum looked around and pulled her into an alcove that was quiet. "Marie, look at me."

She did.

"Breathe. I was joking. I'm sorry, it was in bad taste. Matthew will not hurt Giovanni, no matter what he has done. You have my word on that."

She nodded really quickly. "I need some water, please."

"Alright. You stay here. I'll see what I can get."

"Thank you."

When he disappeared from view, Marie pulled out her phone and scrolled through the pictures. There it was, her and her sister. She was so young, so beautiful. She had so much to live for, but they took her. Blood everywhere. So much of it. She brought her hand to her mouth and stifled a sob into it. She needed to hear Owen and her mother. She dialled her aunt's number. God, it would cost the earth, but she needed them.

"Marie. Are you alright?" Her aunt answered with worry in her voice.

"Hey. I'm good. I just wanted to check on you all."

"We're alright. Your mum is asleep. Owen is helping me bake cookies."

"How did the check-up go?"

"They're a little worried about her blood pressure. It seems a bit high, so they've put her on more tablets to try and lower it, but other than that, she is fine."

"That is great news. Is Owen being good?" A clash of pans echoed in the background. She suspected Owen was playing drums on the saucepans.

"He's a little angel. How's Rome? And that man you're working with?"

"Rome is beautiful. I think we should be back tomorrow, maybe. We've discovered everything and are just waiting for Mr North's bodyguard to come and finalise the issue."

"That's good. We miss you." A shadow came over her, and she looked up. Callum was back.

"I have to go." She hung up.

"Here, drink this. Is your family alright? Do you need to go back?"

"It will be all right."

"All right. If you need to fly home, just say. We should get lunch, now and get back to the office. Matthew will be here soon."

"Yes, I think I have finally digested the antipasto, so I really want some pasta now."

He did a theatrical bow in front of her.

"Your wish is my command." He helped her up, his warm hand wrapping around hers as he guided her back through the Colosseum. He didn't let go 'til they were safely in the taxi. She knew she should probably try and shrug him off, but his gesture made her feel safe. Comforted. It was probably the first time she'd felt anything like that since the day her sister died.

EIGHT

Marie

Matthew Carter walked into the room with a no-nonsense air about him. Marie sometimes forgot just how imposing James's bodyguard was. No wonder people didn't mess with them. Giovanni Romano was in big trouble.

"Good to see you both. Have you got the evidence?"

Callum pulled out a folder from amongst the papers in front of him. Matthew flicked through it, while she watched in silence.

"Is this it?"

"It's all we can find?"

"Are you a hundred percent certain it's him?"

Marie wasn't certain. Something still niggled at her. "Mr Carter, I do believe that Giovanni is involved, but the answer is too obvious. We found it too quickly, and I don't think he's a stupid man.

"Callum, do you agree?" Matthew swiped his hand over his brow.

"Yes, I agree." They both looked at her. "Marie, in the safe in the CEO's office, there is another folder. I'm sorry I didn't tell you about it at the time. Could you get it for me please?"

"What do you mean another folder?"

"Marie, please will you go and get it for me." He looked down at the desk. This was odd.

"Ok, I won't be more than a few minutes." She huffed and left them to their male machismo. She entered the CEO's office and noticed that the room was just as well laid out as James's. It had a large desk, a table for meetings, sofa, drinks table, and even a personal bathroom. She wondered if it had a shower in it just like Mr North's. She opened the safe, using the combination Callum had changed it to when they first arrived. There was indeed a folder in there. She pulled it out and opened it. It was empty?

"What? What's going on?"

From behind her, she heard the clicking of a gun.

"Miss Easton, I want you to turn around. Drop the folder on the floor, put your hands where I can see them, and turn around, *adesso*, now." The heavy Italian accent laced through all the English words.

She inhaled sharply and slowly raised her hands into the air. "Signore Romano, please you don't have to do this."

"*Si*, I do, Miss Easton. I do. It isn't my fault."

'What do you mean?"

"It's his fault. He told me to do it. It was supposed to be the only way."

"Who told you?"

"Oh, you won't believe me." He began waving the gun around in the air. "I'm going to take all the blame for this. There is only the one thing that can happen." He was shaking, his entire body trembling as he took a step closer to her. "It's not fair. I only wanted to help people. I only want *salva I bambini*" He broke down.

"Giovanni, listen to me." She took a step forward, but he brought the gun back up and pointed it directly at her forehead.

"No. No. Enough. He said you would try to do this. Play the sweet little innocent."

"Who said?"

"Over here, get over here, do it now." He waved the gun in the direction he wanted her to go, and she quickly scrambled to where he wanted her. "I don't want to do this. I really don't, but I have to. You've gotta to make them see it wasn't my fault."

"What are you going to do?"

He opened a container, and the overwhelming fumes of a solvent washed over her.

"Oh, my God. No, please."

"We have to stop them. This is the only way."

"I wouldn't do that if I were you, Mr Romano." Matthew Carter's stern voice came from behind them. He had his gun drawn and a worried-looking Callum at his side.

"No. You're trying to blame me for something that isn't bad. I was trying to help people. *Sono innocente.*"

He quickly picked up the can and threw it at her. She screamed as the liquid drained into her clothes. Callum took a step forward. Matthew remained calm and held him back.

"One wrong move, and she'll burst into flames." He had the gun pointed at Matthew and Callum, now.

She looked at Callum, who had guilt all over his face, his hand clenched tightly at his sides. That's when it hit her. This was the plan. The folder was empty for a reason. She'd been used as bait.

"Mr Romano, put your gun down and step away from Miss Easton."

"No, you've got to not blame me. Blame him!"

"Who is him?" Matthew's voice was commanding.

"Him, *lui*, him." Giovanni's eyes were darting all around the room. He was becoming increasingly agitated.

Marie watched as he pulled a lighter from his pocket. Her legs were barely holding her up she was so terrified "I'll do it. I'll do it to her. I promise you. Let me go. Blame him. Go after him. I only wanted to help people. I don't care for the money. I don't want it. He told me it was for helping others."

"Signore Corvi."

Giovanni spun on his Versace heels. His finger flicked on the lighter and brought it into flame. "He wanted to retire and get out. He didn't have enough money, though. Mr North had treated him like dirt. He took all the money for himself and never helped anyone. If we did this, he could retire, and I could help people. He set me up."

"Yes, yes he did. Mr North regularly donates to charity, and Signore Corvi is paid a very handsome salary. Giovanni, Mr Carter and Mr Ashworth know you were not behind it. You did it to help people. Let them deal with Signore Corvi. Put the lighter away. You do this, and you will be in so much trouble. You will never be able to help anyone again. All of us. We'll all speak to Mr North. He will be lenient and help you. He isn't the evil man Signore Corvi has made you think he is. Please. Put the lighter away."

"Giovanni," Callum spoke this time. "Put the lighter away. I knew you weren't the sole person behind this. That's why I made you feel guilty yesterday. That's why I told you what Matthew Carter would do to you if he found out. We are clear on the whole story now. Matthew will not hurt you. He just needed to find out what happened. Signore Corvi will be the one in trouble. You have my word on this. You have Marie's word on this, and you have mine."

Matthew lowered his gun.

"You won't hurt me? You won't kill me?"

"I won't kill you. You won't even go to prison. None of this will happen."

"I'm going to lose my job, aren't I?

"That's negotiable. I need a full declaration from you of what happened. That way, I can see that you are not the one to be held accountable. Without it, I cannot help you. If you put that flame to Miss Easton, your life really will be over. Prison won't be able to protect you."

Giovanni looked down at the flame, rocking on the spot. Marie had never seen a man so distraught and broken. He shut the lid and dropped the lighter to the floor. Matthew came over quickly and removed him from the room. Callum came towards her but did not touch her. "We need to get those clothes off. We need to get you washed."

He led her toward the private bathroom. It did, indeed, have a shower.

"You knew this was going to happen?" Her voice was shaky when she spoke.

"I'm sorry Marie. Matthew and I made the plan. We didn't know it would turn out this way. We thought we'd have you protected at all times."

"Protected. I'm covered in flammable liquid. One mistake, and I would be..."

"Please. You were protected. Come, in the shower."

Her legs wobbled when she walked. Callum still didn't touch her.

She took her clothes off. Slowly. He threw them into the shower. She wouldn't wear them again. He could throw them away.

She stood in her bra and panties before him.

"You should leave."

"I'm not leaving you alone."

"But?"

"I'm not leaving."

His eyes had turned dark.

If she was honest with herself, though, she didn't want him to go. She undid the clasp of her bra and dropped it to the floor. He averted his eyes, but she knew he could sense every movement she made by the way he gripped the sink. She reached for the waistband of her pants and pulled them down.

"Can you get in the shower alright?"

"Yes, I can."

He turned the water on when she got in. Warmth washed away the filth of what could have killed her. She scrubbed her skin while tears fell. She slathered herself in the soap that he handed her. She'd nearly died. She'd really, really come close to dying. Oh God. Her mum. Owen. Guilt washed over her as she cried and cried. The entire time Callum stood outside the shower. He no longer averted his eyes. He watched as she sobbed and sobbed. She didn't want him to look away. She wanted him to watch. He needed to be close. She wished he could be in the shower with her; inside her. He could take away the pain of her life, but she couldn't. She had to be strong.

When she finally got out of the shower, he wrapped a towel around her and rubbed her until she was dry.

"I don't have a change of clothes for you. But." He took off his jacket, tie, waistcoat and shirt. "Take my shirt, it will cover you. My coat will keep you warm." He put the waistcoat back on.

"You don't have a girdle." She wasn't sure where those words had come from. All she knew was that she had looked at his muscular torso and that was what had popped into her mind. She let out a little giggle.

He took a step closer to her and wrapped the shirt around her. She dropped the towel to the floor, and he did the buttons up. He stopped after a few and rested his forehead against hers.

"I'm so sorry. I've never hated having to do anything as much as I hated putting you in that position. It was the only thing we could think of. Signore Corvi had hidden things too well."

"It's ok. Everything worked out."

"Mr North will be very pleased with you." Callum hesitated on the words.

"And with you."

He brought his lips down, so they hovered just above hers. "Marie, may I kiss you?"

She swallowed. "Yes. Yes, please. Kiss me."

Their lips met, and she savoured his heady, spicy scent. At first, the kiss was soft, a tentative searching. He brought his arms around her waist and pulled her closer, as he deepened the kiss. It felt like hours were passing as they stood in the silence of the bathroom tasting each other. When he pulled away, she looked up at him. Any chance of her being sensible had disappeared. For once, she was going to do something she wanted.

"Let's go back to the hotel."

NINE

Callum

Callum didn't think Marie's lips left his once on the journey back to the hotel. Not that he wanted them to. He pushed her against the wall just outside his hotel room, as he searched for his keycard. His right hand massaged her perfect-sized breast through the fabric of his shirt. His left fumbled with the card in the lock.

Marie giggled into his throat. His already rock-hard cock jumped even further to attention.

"Do you need help there, Mr Ashworth?" She pulled away and helped steady his hand to open the door. "I hope you're going to be more dexterous when I allow you in my panties."

"You've got nothing to worry about on that score my little kitten."

"Kitten?"

"Mysterious, and I'm pretty sure, deadly when provoked."

"I like the sound of that. Now, where were we?"

"Right here."

He bent and scooped her up into his arms. In a matter of seconds, he kicked the door closed behind them and made it across the bedroom to the bed. He placed her down and stepped back. She looked up at him with her bright blue eyes.

"I want you to remove my shirt from your body. I'm going to watch."

All the nerves in his body sprung to attention as she knelt before him, her eyes never leaving his. She had her legs slightly parted, but the cotton hid all that she had to promise. Slowly, her fingers started to undo the buttons. It was agony. She nibbled on her lip, when the last button popped free. With even more of a playful attitude, she lowered the sleeves of the shirt and left herself naked before him.

She was stunning.

Her perfect breasts were covered in freckles. Her pussy was shaved and ready for him. She wasn't one of those skinny girls who fashion seemed to love. She had a curvy arse, and he couldn't wait to grab hold of it while he rode her into ecstasy.

"Is everything alright, Callum?" Her husky voice broke through his appreciation of the vision before him.

"I've never been better. You're beautiful." He leant over her and wrapped his hand around her hair, pulling it a little until she was less than an inch from his face. "But little kittens that deliberately tease me will get punished."

She gulped, and a flash of panic waved over her eyes. He let go of her hair. What was wrong with him? He was getting far too ahead of himself. "You say you are aware that I'm a Dom and that I like a particular sexual lifestyle. Do you understand what that means?"

"I do."

"Tell me."

"You will control me in the bedroom. I mustn't come until you say. You may tie me up and spank me. I'm not sure how I feel about whips. I don't really want to be hurt. Do I have to sign one of those contracts?" He tried his hardest not to laugh at her naïve explanation of what he expected. She'd taken all the bits from the most famous novel on the lifestyle and assumed that was everything. "Did I say something wrong?"

"No. That's the aspect of the lifestyle frequently publicised, but it's a lot more than that. What we're going to do today is about trust and me giving you something to take away the fear that you felt earlier. I'll discuss more of the finer aspects of the lifestyle in the future. I think you've had enough to deal with today, and I want to get my mouth on your pussy."

Her breath hitched. "I'd like that."

"I know you will. If at any point you want me to stop, you just say stop. None of that safe word business just yet."

"Alright. I feel very naïve."

Fuck it. Enough talking. He brought his lips back down against hers and pushed her up the bed 'til she was laying naked underneath him. She could undoubtedly feel how rigid his erection was as he ground it slightly into her thigh. She let out a lingering moan of longing.

"What do you want me to do to you, Marie?" He lowered his voice to a full command.

"Touch me."

"Where?"

"Down there."

"Down where?"

Her cheeks flushed a little. "My...my pussy."

"Say it again. Beg me!"

"Please, Callum. Please, I need you to touch me between my thighs. I need something inside me. I need to come."

"Excellent." He shifted his weight so he could reach a hand between the apex of her thighs and through the delicate petals that glistened with her arousal for him. She was soft, soaking, and goddamn sexy. He ran the tips of his fingers either side of her clit, and she whimpered. "You said you wanted something inside you." He arched his middle finger and eased it into her tight channel. "Damn, you're drenched. So warm. Tight and ready for me to finger fuck you."

"I've think I've been this way since you put that heart on my coffee."

He threw his head back and laughed.

"What? Nobody has ever made me coffee before."

"I'll remember that in future. To get you ready for me to fuck you. I just need to bring you coffee."

"With a heart on."

"Always with a heart on."

He added another finger inside her and scissored them a little to test her stretch. It would be tight, but she would accommodate his girth. Damn, he couldn't wait to sink inside her. He hooked his fingers to reach her sensitive spot inside and massaged with a consistent pressure. This was going to be a slow build up, not a wham bam thank you, ma'am.

"I want to know what you taste like."

She nodded, and he brought his tongue out to lick at her core. She was sweet, like honeyed nectar. A subtle flavour of absolute femininity. He curved his tongue and flicked at her clit, which was starting to peek out from under its hidden cover. After a few more touches of his tongue it was proud and pulsating, begging for more. Marie had been watching him all the time, up to this point, but now she tipped her head back, arched up on the bed, and gripped tightly to the sheets. He thrust his fingers and lathered her clit with attention. Her breathing quickened, groans of imminent release louder and louder.

"You don't come until I tell you that you can."

"Fuck you." Her back undulated against the bed as she tried to create more friction. He withdrew his hand and tongue completely.

"Pardon?"

She let out a sobbing cry. "Please, Callum. Please?"

"When was the last time you came? I mean with the assistance of a man."

A fine sheen of sweat covered her body as she still rose and fell on the bed. She whimpered again. Tears fell from her eyes. Shit.

"Marie?"

"Since before my sister died. Over two years. I haven't even touched myself in that time."

He impelled her with his fingers again.

"Come for me, but I want you to watch me giving you your orgasm the entire time. Open your eyes. Look at me!"

Her eyes opened wide and met his, as he brought his mouth back down on her clit. He sucked hard. She gasped, and her body convulsed around him. She gripped his fingers inside her like a vice. She never once let her eyes leave his. He didn't ease up on the pressure and sent her over again with a small bite on her clit. She called his name, tears streaming down her cheeks as she shook.

Breathlessly, she asked him to stop, and as promised, he did so. He came up beside her on the bed. Her hair was everywhere, so he brushed it back behind her ears. She looked up at him, and her eyelids were heavy. She had been through so much today. He turned her around so they spooned and brought the blankets over them.

"Sleep."

"What about you?"

"We have plenty of time. You need rest."

"Don't leave me."

"I won't."

She shut her eyes, and within moments, her breathing shallowed, and she slept. His mind drifted back to the file that Matthew had given him. Her sister had been killed in a drive-by shooting. It was suspected that it was gang related, but it could never be proven. Her mother had had a stroke soon after, and Marie looked after her and her sister's son now. Matthew had been shocked. He hadn't really paid much attention to her. On the surface, Marie portrayed the bimbo secretary, but underneath was the side she kept hidden. The side that cared for those around her. The side he'd seen that had a thirst for knowledge and a wicked sense of humour. He wanted to see that side more often. The stresses of the day caught up with him, and despite the fact he was still hard, he drifted off to sleep as well.

He wasn't sure how much later they woke to the sound of a phone ringing. It wasn't his. Marie shifted on the bed and reached for her handbag, which had been dumped in amongst the pile of clothes on the floor.

"Aunt Helen. Hi. We solved it. I'll be home soon. How's mum?" He could just about hear the voice on the other side of the phone.

"Marie. I need you to come home now." Her aunt's voice was trembling, barely able to get words out without it cracking.

"Mum?"

"No. Owen. He's in the hospital. They think it's meningitis. Please hurry."

TEN

Marie

Beep.

Beep.

Beep.

Marie wasn't sure how such a simple noise could be so annoying, yet so comforting at the same time. Owen was so tiny, covered in red spots all over his little body, tubes coming out of his nose and mouth. Patches stuck to his body monitoring various functions. He'd been put into an induced coma to allow his body to fight the disease. He'd been so happy and carefree when she'd left for Italy. How could things have changed so much in just a few days? At some point, she didn't have a clue when, they'd been transferred to a private room. She was told her employer was meeting all costs, and she was not to worry. She should phone James and thank him. Her aunt came back into the room and took a chair on the other side of the bed.

"How's mum?"

"They've admitted her for observation. She's sleeping."

"What happened, Helen?" She tried not to let her voice waver.

"I don't know. It all happened so quickly. He was playing, and then, he was sick and crying. We noticed the rash and brought him straight to the hospital."

"I shouldn't have gone away."

"You had to. It's your work."

"It wasn't all work." Callum chose that moment to enter the room, a cup of coffee in his hand. It wasn't until he handed it to her she noticed there was a heart on top.

"There is a relative's room next door, why don't you have a sleep?" Callum placed his hand on her shoulder.

"I'll stay with Owen until you come back." Her aunt added.

"I don't need a rest. I'm fine. I just need to stay here until Owen wakes up."

"He's not going to wake up of his own accord, Marie. The doctors will wake him when they feel that he is improving."

"Well, I'll stay here until then. He's young and probably scared. They say that you can hear the people around you when you're in a coma. Well, he'll be able to hear me."

"And when he does wake up, he's going to need you even more, and you'll be exhausted and unable to help him."

"You're not going to let up, are you?" Right now she'd be glad if Callum would just go home. She didn't need comforting because this was all her fault.

"No. I'm not."

"You won't leave him alone even for a minute?" She queried of her aunt.

"Even if I have to pee. I'll hold it."

"Alright." She allowed Callum to help her up from the chair and into the relative's room. Her back was aching. In fact, her whole body was a bit sore. Callum sat on a bed and stretched out.

"This room is for use only by us. Come and lay with me, and I'll hold you while you sleep."

'There's no need. You probably have better things to do. You should go home. I'm sure Matthew needs your help on the fraud case."

"Matthew Carter is able to deal with that on his own. I'm not going anywhere."

"Callum, really. This should be just family. We aren't even dating. Yesterday...last night. How long ago was it?"

"Yesterday. It's Thursday now."

"Ok. Look, what happened shouldn't have. You're my boss."

"No. I'm your boyfriend."

"You can't call yourself that. We've not even been on a date. Last night was just you pleasuring me. We'd had a stressful day. That's all it was."

She still wasn't going to lay next to him on the bed. He sat up.

"No, Marie. Last night was me marking you as mine."

She put her head in her hands and tugged on her hair to release some stress. She really didn't want to do this now. She just wanted to get back to Owen.

"Look, Callum. I can't date you. My life is a bit of a mess. I have to look after my mother and my nephew. I owe more money than you can imagine possible and to all the wrong people. I will only marry a millionaire, because I want to be rich and disappear from all this. What happened yesterday will not happen again. Please, will you just go."

He stood up and walked over until he was directly in front of her. He held his arms rigidly at his sides, his eyes dark and foreboding. She'd pissed him off. Great. Could she do anything else wrong? Ok, she thought, just get the abusive backlash over and done with. She wasn't allowed happiness. Trust her to turn the only chance she had against her.

"On your knees."

"What?" She tried to push past him, but he blocked her. He'd slowed his voice down when he spoke again. It had lowered a couple of octaves as well.

"On your knees."

She was tired, felt so guilty about leaving Owen first to go to Rome and now to not be at his side. She wasn't going to take this shit from anyone.

"You said being a Dom was control in the bedroom. I am tired, and I don't need you to control me. Go home."

Callum simply replied, "This is a bedroom."

There was something about his tone that told her she shouldn't mess with him any further. Why, she had no idea, but she lowered herself to her knees. Her head bowed and she looked at the floor.

"First of all Marie, what happened yesterday will happen again, because whether you like it or not, your body responds to me. I own you now, and that will never change. Secondly, you will not be allowed up from that position until you explain to me what you mean by you owe money to the wrong people." He placed his hand under her chin and tilted it, so she had no choice but to look at him. "Do you understand me?"

"Yes." The words came out. She had no intention of telling him anything. She would escape before that.

"Yes, what?"

"Yes, Callum." Escape, yeah, that wasn't going to happen. She was on her knees in a hospital room. She tried to get up, but Callum didn't move. She made the mistake of looking into his eyes again. They were full of fire, almost black with a mixture of lust and defiance.

"Answer me now."

"I can't. It will put you in danger."

"Your trouble is mine. That what comes from me owning you."

"You can't own me. They do."

"Who are they?"

"Please."

"Who are they, Marie?"

"The people who killed my sister." She slapped her hand over her mouth as she spoke. She couldn't, no shouldn't talk about this. It was too dangerous. They had eyes and ears everywhere. "Please, go. Turn around. Walk out that door and never look back." She felt a tear drop from her eye. This was her life, the one her sister had left her with.

Callum came down to his knees in front of her. He took both of her hands and leant in. He kissed the tear away. She let out a sob.

"I'm going nowhere. Now talk to me." His voice was softer.

"It started about five years ago. I was almost nineteen and had just become Mr North's assistant. My sister, she was younger than me. She'd always been a bit of a wild child. Messed around at school. Got suspended from school for drugs and smoking. Even got caught having sex in one of the classrooms. She didn't actually leave school with GCSE's but found a job anyway. She said she was a delivery courier. We didn't think anything else of it. She had her own money. Mum, let us do what we wanted within reason. My dad left when we were babies. Never seen him since. I heard he remarried and had two more kids, but I never tried to see him. One night, my sister came home crying. She'd been with a couple of boys and was pregnant. She didn't know which one was the father." Her voice caught in her throat. Her sister had been a mess. Callum wrapped his arms around her shoulders and pulled her into his lap, so that they cuddled together on the floor. She'd not felt this close to a man ever. She could tell him anything, and she just knew he wouldn't judge her for it.

"We set about preparing for Owen's birth. She was adamant she couldn't go through with an abortion."

"Your sister died in a drive-by shooting. Was this related to the father of the baby."

"How do you know that?"

"Matthew."

"What else does he know?"

"That is pretty much it. He says you're a hard person to research."

"I did something right, then. Yes, she died in a drive-by. It was a few days before Owen was due. She'd gone out to get some nappies ready and was shot seven times. She didn't die instantly, though. They took her to the hospital; every shot had missed Owen. He was in distress, so they did an emergency caesarean. The second they removed him from her she died. She'd held on so he could be born. She never saw him." Again, the tears started to flow. Callum held her and patted her back as she shed so much sorrow for the sister she'd lost. Eventually, when she had composed herself, he spoke.

"I'm sorry Marie, that is heart-breaking. But it doesn't explain the money."

She looked up to the heavens. She should hate her sister for this. For leaving her to deal with it all, but she loved her so much and blamed herself. She should have known. She should have stopped it. She'd become so wrapped up in being the perfect PA. She was the one who'd failed.

"I was given custody of Owen along with my mum. We have to have regular checks from Social Services, but they seemed to forget about doing that a couple of months after he was born. I guess they found he was being looked after well. It was a week after we brought Owen home. There was a knock at the door. When I opened it, two men carrying guns barged through the door. I was terrified they were going to take Owen. I still had no idea who is father was. One of the men looked at him. I'll never forget his words. 'The sins of the parents are shown in the innocence of the son.' I knew he was one of the possibilities, but he wasn't there to be a father. He didn't have a paternal bone in his body. He explained why my sister was killed. She'd stolen from him and his gang. She'd been his girlfriend since she'd started running drugs for him at the age of sixteen."

"The courier job."

"She stole seventy-thousand pounds worth of drugs from him. And he wanted payment. Her death wasn't enough of a statement not to mess with the gang. He said he'd accept down payment of Owen to sell, but I refused so he stated that until such time as the debt was paid, he owned my arse. I'd pay him every last bit of money I could afford. I don't think I've even repaid twenty percent of it. He keeps trying to get me to sell my body to pay it off quicker. I can only keep him happy with payments from my salary so long."

"Why didn't you go to the police?" Callum asked.

"Fear of retribution. It's going to take me a lifetime to pay that money back. "

"I can help you."

"You have that sort of money laying around?"

"No. I'm sorry. What about the house? It's in a good area. If you sell that, and move in with me. All of you. Your mum and Owen."

"It's not my house to sell." She reluctantly answered.

"What?"

"Where you picked me up. I don't live there. I'm from the tenements in Hoxton." This time it was Callum's turn to go quiet and pale. "Social housing, I don't own anything. Not that they'd let us move while we owe them money. They have us right where they want us, to continue the shame and make sure we pay."

"Shame?"

"Let's just say I walk a gauntlet every time I go home."

"You're not going back there." The Dom's voice was back again. It would not work this time, though. All the fight had gone from her.

"Go home Callum. This is not your battle. I'm not your woman. You can't own me. I've already pledged my life to this. Please. Will you just go? I'm going back to Owen." She got to her feet, smoothed out the wrinkles of her long jumper, and she left the room.

ELEVEN

Callum

The smell hit him first. Damp and piss. Its foul stench was everywhere.

"How the hell could she live here, and I not know?" Callum watched as Matthew stepped over—well he wasn't entirely sure what it was—but it didn't look healthy. It hadn't taken Matthew long to find out Marie's actual address after Callum called him. The door to the flat had already been busted open, when they arrived. The apartment was ransacked and disgusting abuse had been painted on the walls. No matter what she thought, there was no way Marie was coming back to this flat.

"I think Marie has been far too good at hiding the truth about herself. And I should know, I'm the master of that."

Matthew threw a knowing look at him. Matthew Carter knew exactly who he really was.

"Do you think there is anything salvageable?"

"Mementoes. I don't think much else." He picked up a picture of Marie, her mother and another girl that had been smashed on the floor. He assumed it was her sister. They both had the same vibrant black hair.

Sonia appeared in the doorway. She had a black sack in her hand. Her gun was visible in its holder.

"This is bad." Her face screwed up in revulsion and anger. Callum knew a little bit about Sonia's past. For her to be so upset said a great deal.

"We're going to salvage what we can. I'll get onto James about sorting them out new accommodation when I get home." Matthew started to sort through the broken trinkets.

"No need." Callum picked up a few more photos and placed them in the black sack. "I've already spoken to my father. He's launched an investigation. They'll have somewhere different to live by the time Owen wakes up."

"You sure about that? It could cause him trouble." Matthew questioned.

"It could also cause the people that allowed this to happen a hell of a lot more trouble. Questions should have been asked. Visits should have been made." He was livid.

Matthew nodded. It didn't take them long to pack up the rest of the meagre belongings. Callum placed them in the boot of his car just at two young lads on a bike rode past. They watched him with suspicion.

"Lookouts?"

"Wouldn't surprise me." Matthew pulled his phone from his pocket and dialled. "Jasper. I need a favour ASAP. I want guards put at the Royal Free. I need them assigned at all times to Marie Easton, her mother, and nephew. They are not to be let out of their sight. You will also need to include her aunt and uncle in the protection. Make sure your people know that this is drug- and gang-related so that they will be prepared for anything." Callum breathed a sigh of relief that Matthew was here.

Sonia gave him a little embrace while Matthew continued to relay his orders. "She'll be fine."

"I think she's more likely to be angry at me for interfering, but I know what you mean."

"Go home and get some rest. When Owen wakes, and she realises what is happening, she's going to need you to explain."

Matthew hung up his call.

"Guards will be there within fifteen minutes. Sonia and I'll go straight there now and check on them. Do as the wise, and very sexy woman says and go get some rest."

"Thank you. Both of you."

The boys rode back again on their bikes.

"We'll follow you out. Sonia, you drive. I want a clear shot if needed."

Thankfully the shot wasn't necessary, and twenty minutes later, he arrived home. His mother greeted him at the door with that concerned parent look. He would be fed a home cooked meal and a brandy any minute now. Mind you, he probably looked awful. He still had on the clothes he'd travelled in and hadn't shaved in over thirty-six hours.

"Your father's in the dining room. Come and sit down. When was the last time you ate? You must be starving." His dad stood up and handed him a brandy when he entered the room.

"You mother had it ready for you. She's been pacing the foyer since you called. How was it?"

"It was...it was like nothing I've ever seen." He could still smell the odour of the worst of humanity on him. "I hope heads will roll, dad."

"They already have." His father reassured.

"Good."

"Hopefully, they'll have new accommodation tomorrow as well."

"If not, I'll be buying them somewhere myself."

"Callum." His mum placed her hand on his wrist. "Your father will sort it. Just be patient."

He shrugged her off. He wasn't in the mood for placating. In the space of a few days, he'd held Marie as she'd had her first orgasm in two years and then held her as she broke down and told him of the harrowing life that she'd been living. She'd near enough said that he had to leave her, because they couldn't be together if he couldn't pay off her debts. She'd sacrifice her own happiness, and his, to protect her family. She was that caught in a mindless trap these drug pushers had created for her. He'd wanted to tell her there and then. He'd wanted to tell her the truth about who he was, but he'd taken the coward's way out. Too many women in the past had wanted him for what he could give them. He wanted to trust Marie, but there she was, saying she would only marry someone rich. Well, fuck it! He was rich! He'd inherited a trust fund on his twenty-first birthday that provided him with millions. He hadn't spent all of it, when he went crazy and started drinking, smoking, and gambling. The women he'd met, then, had used him, so he used them back.

That was, until he needed to change.

The day his father went to meet the Queen. The day his father had become Prime Minister of the United Kingdom of Great Britain and Northern Ireland.

TWELVE

Marie

"How is he doing?" The instantly recognisable voice woke her from a daydream. Callum stood at the door to the hospital room.

"They've taken him off the drugs keeping him asleep. They're hoping he wakes soon. They'll be able to do more tests and know more then." The night had been a long one. Between her and her aunt, Owen hadn't been left alone.

"That's good news. Can I come in?" He pushed off the door frame but didn't enter the room.

She smiled. "Of course, you don't need my permission. Or are you a vampire as well as a Dom?" Without warning, Callum pulled her up and sat in her chair. He arranged her so she sat on his lap and leaned against his broad chest. She didn't argue. She knew she should, but she needed this. She needed him. "I'm sorry about last night."

"You were worried about Owen. It's understandable. I'm still here. You don't get rid of me that easily."

"I don't know whether I should fear that or be grateful." She nestled her head into him.

"You should probably reserve judgement 'til you hear what I've done."

"Done?"

"When I left here last night, I spoke to Matthew."

She pushed off his lap.

"You told him what I said?" Her hands started to flap as she began to pace. "Oh God, are you crazy? They'll come for Owen. We have to go. We have to run. You've no idea what you've done. You've made everything so much worse." Years of pent up frustration suddenly surfaced and brought itself down on Callum's chest. Her hands stung, but she didn't let up. She just kept punching. "You come into my life and try to control it. You've no idea. Go, leave me alone. I *never* want to see you again!"

Callum grabbed her hand and spun her around. He flipped her over his shoulder.

"Put me down!"

"He flung the door open with his free hand. "Helen?" Her aunt appeared and paled.

"Helen, call the police. I want this man arrested."

Nobody moved.

"Helen, stay with Owen." Callum finally spoke. Her aunt just pathetically nodded in reply. "Jasper." A stunningly muscular man stepped forward. Where the hell did all these men keep appearing from? "Any change in Owen's condition, send someone to get me. I'm taking Marie on a little field trip."

"You aren't fucking taking me anywhere." She started to kick her legs as best she could. If she could just move her left leg a bit more to the right, she stood a chance of getting him straight in the balls. Callum shifted her a little and used his other hand to secure her legs. Fuck it!

"You need a hand to the car?" Jasper asked.

"I've got it. Thanks."

A hospital security guard came running up.

"Help me." She bellowed.

"I'll deal with it, you go." Jasper got between them and the security guard.

Callum walked her through the hospital still screaming and shouting for help. People looked at them, but nobody made any attempt to stop them. What was wrong with these people?

They emerged out into the sunlight. She blinked repeatedly and squinted against the light. A car drove up in front of them, and Callum pushed her into the back. She was in trouble. Serious trouble. She could sense someone beside her; Callum took a seat in the front and the car started to drive away. Her eyes were shut. She was terrified to open them. What if Matthew worked with them? What if her whole life had been one great big lie?

"Marie, sit back and put your seatbelt on please, the alarm is really annoying." A familiar voice permeated her panic. She opened one eye. James North sat next to her, a seat belt in his hand. She sat back, and he helped to put it on.

"That's better." He smiled.

"Are you going to kill me?" Her voice came out so small and trembling it was barely loud enough for a mouse to hear.

Callum turned in his seat. "You think we're working with the gang that killed your sister?"

"I don't know what to think anymore. I'm tired. I'm scared. I just want this all to end."

Callum reached around his chair and placed a hand on her knee.

"It will. We're about to send a statement."

"A statement?"

She looked out her window and saw her tenement home looming before her.

"No." She shook her head. "Please. You can't come here."

"We've already been here." Matthew pulled the car to a halt, and all three men got out at the same time. Callum came and opened the door for her.

"Out."

She huddled further into the seat.

"Now." Callum whispered in her ear, as he protectively placed an arm around her shoulders. "Good girl."

She just glared at him. She could hear James and Matthew laugh.

"Who are your friends, Marie?" They all looked around to where the voice had come from. She didn't know his name, but everyone called him D.

"Who's asking?"

James stepped forward. Marie wanted to jump in front of him. She'd seen these young lads with guns before. Callum must have sensed it and held her tighter so that she couldn't move.

"I asked the first question."

"They're just here to help me get a few clothes for Owen." She found her voice. "He's in the hospital."

"Three men to assist for a few kid's clothes." Two more lads, slightly bigger, appeared beside him. "If you ask me, they look more like pigs."

"Police! No way. You know I wouldn't go there."

"You know what would happen to Owen if you did." D sneered.

Matthew took a step forward. Callum still held her.

"We're just here to get clothes." She reached up to Callum's cheeks. "He's my boyfriend, and these two are his mates."

"I think the boss will be interested in hearing you have a boyfriend and pals who own an Aston Martin."

No one made a move. The tension in the air was thick. Her billionaire boss stood to her left, his bodyguard, who was ex- MI5, to the right. She was pressed into Callum, who, well she didn't know where he came from, but as much as she hated him right now, she didn't want him to get hurt. D clicked his fingers, and all the boys disappeared.

Matthew pulled his gun out.

"We don't have long. Callum, do what you need to do. I'll stay here as look out."

Callum nodded and picked her up and put her over his shoulder again. What was it with him and the caveman attitude? James pulled his own gun out and flanked Callum as he brought her up to her flat. He placed her down outside the door. It had been kicked in. Her heart deflated. It wasn't the first time they'd broken in and stolen the little things that she managed to hide. Owen's toys, her mum's iPad. They would all be gone. If it could be sold, it would be. Not that it would be deducted from the debt she owed.

"We don't have to go in here. Callum please, you know where I live now. Can we go back to the hospital?"

James ignored her and pushed the door open. The smell hit her, and she saw him screw up his face. He'd probably never seen anything this bad.

"You live here?" The billionaire's brows furrowed.

She nodded.

"Is this why you flirt with me?"

"What?" She hadn't expected that.

"You wanted me to fall in love with you, marry you, and take you away from this?"

"Yes." She timidly answered.

"Marie, I love Amy. I won't be leaving her, but I won't be leaving you here, either. Matthew will pay the debt off today. I am loathe to give a drug runner money, but he will not destroy your life anymore."

"You can't do that. I can't ask you to do that."

"You're not. I'm telling you I'm doing it." She wanted to shrink away, but Callum stood directly behind her. He hadn't spoken since they entered the flat.

"May I touch her?" James's eyes flicked to Callum.

"Yes."

James lifted her chin up. His dark blue eyes bore into her. "Throw the books away Marie; this is real life. No amount of dreaming would ever have saved you from this." He spun her around so she faced Callum. His arms were folded across his chest. His gaze was deeply intense. She felt her insides clench. "Real life is standing right in front of you. Don't risk losing it." With that, Callum stepped aside and let him pass.

"What are you going to do to me?" She asked Callum.

"Place both your hands on the wall. I'm going to make you see sense as a Dom would."

She tentatively did as he asked.

"What are you going to do to me?"

"Do you trust me?" He asked.

"Yes. But I still want to know."

"I'm going to spank you. Now, James doesn't own you, but you should have asked either him or Matthew for help. I own you, and you lied to me. You want me to stop you say Rome."

"You can't do that. You don't own me. The gang does."

"Not anymore."

He brought his hand down on her backside in a whack that shook her very core.

"I think I prefer them owning me. Pissing in my hallway is a lot less painful that you smacking my arse." Her catty remarks didn't get her any respite as he hit her twice more, quick successive punishments that left her smarting.

"Who owns you?"

He hadn't tied her up or anything. She was able to move, but why couldn't she.

"Answer me." Another wallop on her bottom.

"One last chance, Marie." The next hit almost had her legs buckle.

"You do." Her lips moved involuntarily, and she screamed the words he wanted to hear. "You do." Tears started to fall down her face. An emotional outpouring of relief.

"Yes, I do. Last night, I removed all your personal belongings from this place. You will be moving to different accommodation effective immediately. It's over. They don't own you. I do, and I protect what's mine."

"It's not that simple." She implored through water stained eyes.

"Yes, it is."

"Owen?"

"Matthew has methods. We'll find out who is his father, and he'll be signing away every right he has to that little boy. He's ours now."

"Ours?" She queried.

"Mine and yours. You come together. Your mum, too. Do you understand me?"
He was adamant in his answer.

"I think so. My brain is taking a bit of time to catch up."

"Say goodbye to this flat."

She looked around the damp, rotten room. She wouldn't miss it.

"Goodbye." She breathlessly uttered.

Callum swept her up onto her feet. "I would like to give you better aftercare than this, but I'm afraid we need to get out of here."

She shut her eyes.

"Hospital?"

"Yes."

"Wake me when we get there."

James's and Callum's chuckling was the last thing she heard, as they descended the stairs. Her brain allowed her a moment's peace, and she used it to sleep.

THIRTEEN

Callum

"Could I get you another drink, Mr Ashworth?" Marie winked. He sat opposite James North in the Chairman's office. Callum had been discussing the latest management accounts for the last three hours. With the corrections to the Italian balances, everything was looking in order.

"Yes, please. Coffee."

"I'll have another coffee as well, please," James asked.

"You don't need another one. I'll get you water." She swayed her hips walking out of the room.

"I'm not sure whether I should be offended or laugh." James shrugged.

"Jealous your affections have been replaced?" Callum chuckled.

"No, I couldn't be happier. How are things going?"

It had been a month since the incident at Marie's old flat when Callum had earned her trust. Owen had woken later that day, and within a week, he was up and running around as if nothing had happened. Marie and her family had moved to Kensington, to a small house with a separate lounge, kitchen, and dining room and three bedrooms. Callum suspected that somewhere along the lines James had been involved with the location and choice of the house, but he didn't question it. Marie was happy, and she was safe. Matthew had paid off the drug dealers and sent a harsh message to them to leave Marie alone. Again, Callum hadn't asked.

"It's good. We're taking things slowly. She's had a horrific couple of years and needs time to just breathe and feel free."

"Not planning to take her to the club just yet, then?" James raised an eyebrow.

"No way but we do have a date tonight. I hope she enjoys it."

"So long as she's happy."

"I think she is. Especially since you get water and I get coffee."

James rolled his eyes.

Marie came back with his coffee. "I got you biscuits as well. It's been a while since you had breakfast, and I don't know when you'll break for lunch." She placed the cookies in front of him. James reached out to grab one, and she slapped his hand. "Matthew has your food outside. Mrs North will not be impressed if I let you eat biscuits and not the food she has prepared. I'll send him in with it, if you're hungry."

"That won't be necessary. Callum, are we done here?" James pushed back his chair.

"Pretty much. Why?"

"I think I'm going to take the rest of the day off. You two can go home as well. Spend the day together as well as the evening." This time she looked down with a grin. Had his naughty little kitten been playing a game with her boss?

"If you insist, Mr North. I'm sure Mrs North will enjoy having you home to help with your son."

"I suspect she will. And Marie, as I'm nice to you, I want coffee and biscuits tomorrow."

"Of course." She looked up, and guilt was written all over her face. He would have to watch this one. Callum just shook his head. He said his goodbyes to James and met Marie at her desk. She was already packing up.

"That was a very naughty game you were playing."

"I don't know what you mean. If he has biscuits, he'll get fat, and too much coffee will keep him awake. I'm looking after his health like I always have."

"So it doesn't matter if I have a lot of caffeine and sugar?"

"Oh, it does. I just need you to have a lot of energy tonight." She looked at him coyly. "I asked the carer if she'd be able to stay overnight to care of mum and Owen. I thought maybe we could go to your place."

He pulled her against him so she could feel the effect that her words had had on him.

"I've a few things I need to finish here." He growled into her ear. "I want you to go home and get ready. I'll text you before I pick you up." He stole a breathless kiss from her.

"Try not to fuck her over her desk, Callum. She has important papers I've got to handle on there." James emerged from his office with a laptop carrier over his shoulder and a wicked grin on his face.

Marie pulled away from him and in a fluster finished packing her bag.

"You're telling me you and Amy haven't done anything on your desk?" Callum retorted.

Matthew appeared from wherever he hid during the day. "I wouldn't start that argument. As he keeps telling me, he's the boss, so he can do whatever he wants."

"Maybe I should ask cleaning to disinfect your desk?" Marie added.

"You know what Marie?" Matthew stepped forward. "I like this new you very much."

James frowned and folded his arms across his chest.

"Matthew, take me home. At least my wife is kind to me."

"Only when she wants sex. The rest of the time, you're under her thumb."

Callum pulled Marie back towards him. "Get a taxi home. Take a bath and don't touch anything that's mine while you get ready."

"My body..." He cut her off with a kiss and a smack on her pert little bottom. "Alright. I'll behave. What do I need to wear?"

"Something warm and casual. Jeans and a jumper are fine."

When she had left, Callum pulled out his phone and dialled. She wanted to stay at his house. Well, considering he lived in number 10 Downing Street, that wasn't going to happen just yet. Not until he told her who his father was.

There was a Sofitel hotel in St James that he liked. He phoned and booked an executive room. It wasn't too far from the location of the evening he had planned. It would be a little different, but he hoped she liked it.

It didn't take him long to finish the rest of his work and get home to change. He packed a bag and dropped it off at the hotel on his way to Marie's. He wasn't driving so it was taxis all the way. The cockney driver spent most of the journey telling him about how he was off Essex way for the evening to a party with his family. They'd move out of Romford to the coast and had a beautiful house overlooking the Blackwater Estuary. Callum thought he knew everything about this new house by the time he changed the conversation to a discussion on the fact that he'd had Adele in his cab the other day. He got the impression it was going to be his claim to fame now. The driver even showed him a selfie on his phone, as they stopped outside Marie's house.

He knocked on the door, and Marie's mum answered. He handed her the bouquet of flowers that he'd been carrying for her. "Hello, Mrs Easton."

"I've told you before, it's Annie."

"Hello, Annie, then." He gave her a peck on the cheek in greeting. "You're walking even better than last week." He followed her back into the lounge.

"Yes, now we have no damp house, my bones aren't aching as much, so I can do a lot more of my physio. Marie?" She called out, "Callum's here."

"I won't be a few minutes, mum."

"She's been trying on different clothes for an hour now. I think not knowing where she's going is making her worry."

"I want it to be a surprise. I'll tell her if she needs to change. Casual will be good, though. I've told her that."

Eventually, Marie appeared, wearing a pair of skinny, black jeans that looked pretty much painted on, a thick blue jumper that emphasised her breasts, and knee high three-inch heeled boots.

"Is this alright? You said casual." He couldn't keep the little growl of appreciation from slipping from his throat. Annie laughed, and Marie flushed.

"I think that is a yes, Meemee. You've rendered the man speechless."

"You'll need gloves, a scarf, and hat if you have them? We're going to be walking for a bit as well. Are you alright in those boots?"

Annie laughed, "Marie has been wearing heels since she was out of nappies. She could probably run a marathon in them if you asked her."

"Mum." She grabbed gloves and a scarf from in the hallway and put them on along with her coat. "Ready to go."

"Do you have an overnight bag?"

"I've got the essentials in here." She pointed to the bag over her shoulder. That was another thing he adored about Marie. Anyone who knew her from the office would probably think that she was high maintenance, but she was far from it. He was willing to bet that the only things she had in that bag were mascara, her tooth-brush and paste and a change of knickers.

"Let's go, then."

"Let me just say goodbye to Owen; he's eating in the kitchen." He watched as she said her goodbyes. When they emerged into the now dark sky, he put his arm around her.

"So are you going to tell me where we're going yet?"

"We are going to watch the fireworks."

"Fireworks. I forgot it's the fifth of November. Guy Fawkes."

"Yes. Time to celebrate someone wanting to blow up the Houses of Parliament." Oh, the irony.

They rounded a corner and the warmth of the fire hit them. The guy was already burning away at the top. Children were jumping and screaming excitedly, shouting at their mummies and daddies 'When will the fireworks start?' He bought them both a warm cider, and they stood and watched the flames dancing for a little while. She leaned into him and shivered a little.

It was then that it hit him. He'd brought her to see a body (albeit fake) burning. That could have so easily been what happened in Italy.

"Is this alright? It's not too much. Memory wise."

She looked up at him.

"It did cross my mind, but no. There is a story behind this, and it didn't happen to me."

From behind them, there was a whoosh followed by a bang and a colourful explosion in the sky. The fireworks started.

"I haven't seen fireworks in years. How did you know about this?"

"My dad always used to bring me, when I was younger."

"You lived around here?"

"No, he worked nearby and had a flat here. He liked the display and the food stalls, so mum and I often came up to meet him."

"Are you an only child?"

"Does it show?"

"No. I just wondered."

"Yes, my parents tried for more children, but it never happened. My mum called me her little blessing. I wasn't always good as a youngster. In fact, I'm pretty confident I'm the reason my dad went grey early, but we get on really well. I still live with them."

"You still live with your parents?"

"Not exactly the flash lover you wanted?"

"It just surprises me. I thought you would have a shag pad."

He laughed. "I probably did have what you call a shag pad, but circumstances changed, and it just seemed easier to move back in with my parents."

"Do they need your help?"

"No. They're both perfectly fit and healthy. Mum's constantly going to one social function or another. Anyway, enough of my parents. Do you want something to eat?"

"Just one final question, please."

"Alright?"

"Do you think it is wise me coming back to yours tonight? I mean they haven't met me, and I coming back so we can have sex."

"I booked us a hotel room for the night." His heart started to beat faster at the thought. "I want you all to myself."

"Ok," She bit her lip. "In that case, yes I'm hungry. Can we get hot doughnuts?"

"Doughnuts?" She nodded quickly. "Whatever the lady wants."

"Well, *I* wasn't eating biscuits all morning. I need some sugar to give me energy. Especially if I have a full night in a hotel with you...and it is Saturday tomorrow so no work."

"Wait here." He kissed the tip of her nose and with deadly purpose stalked towards the doughnut van.

"I want twenty-four hot doughnuts."

FOURTEEN

Marie

Callum pushed open the door for her, and Marie preceded him into the hotel bedroom, rubbing her hands together to try and get them warm. After finishing the doughnuts between them, without being sick, though she wasn't sure how, they'd decided to walk to the hotel to burn some of the calories. It was late in the evening, and a frost had developed in the air. Her nose tingled as it began to warm up. She sneezed.

"You didn't get too cold, did you?" Callum immediately looked concerned.

"No, I just seem to feel the cold a lot lately. I think it is from finally having heat after so many years."

He pulled the cover off the bed and wrapped it around her.

"Warm up. I'll get us some drinks. I won't be long."

He disappeared out of the room. She was starting to get the heat back into her body. A quick bathroom visit to wee and refresh her breath with mouthwash and she was back in the room waiting for Callum. It was time to get comfortable. She took off her jeans and jumper, making sure to leave on the sexy Victoria's Secret underwear she had treated herself to, climbed under the sheets, and waited for Callum. It wasn't long before he returned with chocolate covered strawberries and a bottle of Prosecco.

"I found us a treat."

"Hmm.. strawberries." She rose to her knees and allowed the covers to billow down around her waist. "Do you want to eat yours off me?"

He placed the food and wine down on the solid oak dressing table. "As tempting as that offer is, right now, no. For our first time together, I just want you and me. No props, if you know what I mean. I just want to learn that beautiful body of yours, inside and out."

He leant forward and kissed her, his teeth lightly gripping her lip and tugging it when he pulled away. This time, she chased his mouth.

They'd been dancing around each other for over a month now, and it was way past time for two to become one. He was a dominant though. Could she touch him without his permission? She reached for the hem of his t-shirt, brought her eyes to meet his, seeking permission. He placed his hands over hers and helped to discard the offending navy garment. His skin was smooth. He seemed to sense that she wanted to explore him first, so he lay back on the bed, placed his arms under his head, and with a welcoming smile allowed her. She met his lips again before travelling over the apex of his collar bone towards his well-defined pecs. She bit lightly at one of his nipples, and he groaned. Slowly she lowered herself down his body, kissing and savouring the salty taste of his masculinity. His spicy essence added to her lasciviousness, and she was quickly pooling with desire between her thighs.

"Lower," he ordered, and she dared to undo the zip of his pants. Holy fuck! He was commando and sprung out like a rigid flagpole before her. He was also bloody massive, not just in length but also in girth. He was never going to fit that inside her, not without leaving her unable to walk for a week. She pulled his trousers down. His heavy balls hung tightly below.

"You wanted to explore all of me. Tell me what I taste like."

She took her tongue and licked the whole of his length. He was fresh but tasted like pure sex. The tip held a bead of pre-cum, and she lapped it up.

"You taste amazing. I can't wait to swallow your cum one day." She took him fully into her mouth and worked him in and out. She could barely fit even half his length in. She made a mental note to work on her gag reflex.

"Fuck. I need inside you now."

He threw her over so she was flat on her back, and he was between her thighs.

"Are you particularly attached to this underwear?"

"Would you be angry if I said yes?"

"Damnit."

He shifted her again and undid the clasp of her bra. When he revealed her breasts, they instantly pebbled. Damn those smouldering eyes of his. They could melt the panties right off her. He made short work of said panties, sliding them down her legs. Leaving them both naked together.

"So wet already. Did you like sucking my cock?"

"It's something I plan on repeating again rather soon. I want to swallow it all."

"Patience, kitten." He reached over to the nightstand, grabbed his wallet, and pulled a condom out of it.

"I'm clean and on the pill." She blurted it out before she even realised what she said. She tried to quickly qualify what she said. "I mean, I have regular physicals as part of my healthcare plan with North Enterprises, and I had heavy periods as a child, so they put me on the pill to stop them. We don't have to but if you would prefer to use a condom. I just trust you, and if you own me, then, neither of us will be going anywhere else."

He placed his finger against her lips and threw the condom on the floor. "I'm clean as well. Same medical plan." He thrust inside her, taking his time so that he didn't hurt her.

"If I can have you bareback, then, I'm damn well doing it." He pulled out slowly, teasingly, agonisingly. "I'm clean as well. Tested regularly at the club, not that I've been there since I met you."

"Maybe that could be our next date." She closed her eyes as mild panic started to set in. He was dominant. Would he expect her to wear a collar and crawl around on her knees like a cat? Oh God, he'd called her kitten. She had read a book before where the dominant did that.

"Open your eyes." He withdrew from her. "What were you thinking? You tightened up and not in the right way. Did I hurt you?"

"No. No." She brought her hand behind his neck and pulled him back down to her lips.

His eyes darkened, and this time not in a good way. There was fury behind them. He pushed off the bed and pulled on his trousers, struggling somewhat to get his still hard erection to go back into them.

"I'm not doing this, until you tell me what went through your head."

She huffed down into the bed and pulled the cover over her head. It was the act of a petulant child. She was horny and needed to come. He was a stubborn arse. She screamed into the duck down duvet before pulling it down and rapidly firing off her thoughts.

"I thought that maybe you'd want me to wear a collar when we go to a club and crawl around on all fours like a kitten. I heard that there are butt plugs that have tails and everything. I didn't like it, and I think if you want me to do that, we're going to have issues."

He let out a laugh.

"What?" She flushed red, part with anger and part with embarrassment.

He lowered his trousers again, came back over to the bed, and climbed on top of her. She tried to push him away, but he used his strength to pin her in place.

"I think I'm going to have to give you some new books to read." He went to kiss her, and she turned away.

"Well, I'm sorry I'm not as clued up on BDSM as you are. Maybe the only place that I can read about it is in books. There is no need to make fun of me."

"I'm not making fun of you. I'm sorry. I just think it is, I don't know, sweet. Marie, I can honestly say to you I will never stick a butt plug with a tail inside you and make you crawl around on all fours. Yes, I will ask you to wear my collar if we go to a club, but that's only to show everyone in the place that you are mine, and they need to keep their fucking hands off. I'm not a lifestyle Dominant. The only place I will expect you to submit to me is in the bedroom but only when you are ready to. I may also use techniques like I did with your spanking in the flat when I need to get through to you about something. But believe me, if I put you in a room with Sonia for a few hours, you would learn a lot of submissive tricks to put me in *my* place when I'm stubborn or an idiot." He stroked down the side of her face, a tender gesture that had her heart melting again. "I love the feisty you. When you told. James he couldn't have coffee and biscuits today, it was all I could do not to jump you and fuck you on his desk."

"You call me kitten…"

"I told you why before. You're spirited and I love it. I'm also beginning to learn that you purr a lot when you're horny."

"I don't."

He ripped the sheets back, thrust her legs open and bit down on her already sensitive clit."

She purred.

"See."

"Damn you, Callum Ashworth. Make me come, please."

"Whatever you ask for my little kitten."

He thrust back inside her, the ache surging through her entire body as he found a rhythm that had her almost singing like an in-heat cat on a hot tin roof. He shifted, and the tip of his cock ground against her g-spot. Within seconds, she was panting for air as she exploded around him. People had said to her before you know when you've found the perfect partner. They just fit. And Callum sure as hell fit. He found her clit, squeezed it, and she climaxed again, her legs spasming as he continued to ride through her orgasm.

He still hadn't come.

"Damn, you're gripping me like a vice. I'm never going to want to get out of you."

She was breathless, and a sheen of fine sweat covered Callum, as his thrusting became more urgent. He flicked her clit, and she went over the zenith again. This time she screamed his name, and he called hers as he seemed to endlessly empty himself inside her. He collapsed, manoeuvred her so he was still inside her, but was able to bring her into his arms.

"'I. I er." She couldn't seem to get even a single word out.

"That good huh?"

She nodded.

His cock was still twitching inside her. Every time it did, she let out a whimper of satisfaction.

"I think it is only fair to tell you, Marie."

"What?" She questioned.

"I'm going to want to go again in about half an hour. I hope you didn't plan on getting any sleep tonight."

"Seriously? That long?"

His cock started to harden inside her again.

"Well, shit. That has never happened before. I think Marie Easton my body has decided you're the perfect woman."

FIFTEEN

Callum

Callum rolled over in the luxurious, super-king bed. A hint of daylight flooded through a crack in the curtain. Marie was not in bed with him. He sat up and rubbed his tired eyes. They'd only got a few hours' sleep after making love three more times. On the final time, he had 'kinked it up' as Marie had called it, and tied her to the bed, blindfolded her, and made her come with his only his mouth.

"Marie?" She popped her head around the bathroom door. There was a pink toothbrush in her mouth, and he noticed she had on his t-shirt. She held a finger up to tell him one minute before disappearing, and he heard her spit the tooth-paste out. He needed a wee. It was still early stages in their relationship, but she was going to have to get used to this. Without bothering to cover himself up, he strode buck naked into the bathroom and started to do his business. Marie stood there, stunned, the toothbrush hanging out of her mouth.

"Get used to it. We're in a relationship. Now are you coming back to bed?" He shook himself off, flushed, washed his cock and hands and left her still standing silently in the bathroom. "Kitten?" He called.

She popped her head around the door again. She raised her finger and opened her mouth as if she was going to say something but stopped and gave the biggest smile he'd ever seen. She took a run for the bed, jumping on it and into his arms.

"What was that for?" He asked.

"You were normal around me."

"Normal?"

"Yeah. You needed to pee and went. I was afraid things might be awkward this morning. That was why I was cleaning my teeth, so I could leave quickly if I needed to." She wrinkled up her nose.

"Do you feel awkward?" He responded.

"No. I loved last night. It's just..."

He lifted her chin back up, when she looked down.

"It's been so long since I've done anything like this, and before, it was nearly always one night stands."

"Well then, every man you've been with before is a stupid idiot. How sore are you?"

"A little, but I'll be alright." She shifted as if testing down there.

"Good. Cause we never did eat those strawberries."

She laughed, one that spoke of pure unadulterated happiness.

He flipped her over and slid inside her, knowing she would be wet for him. He was falling for her so quickly. She was everything he'd ever wanted. Kind, funny, beautiful, feisty, but most of all honest. The niggling doubt in his head that he was lying to her about who he was surfaced. He pulled out and got off the bed. His dick protested. He ignored it.

"Callum?" She sat up; concern etched on her face. "What's wrong? Did I do something?"

"No. It's me. Get dressed." Her face deflated, tears pooled in her eyes.

"You want me to leave?" Her lips quivered as she spoke.

"No, no. I need to show something. Please."

"Is this the end?" She wiped a tear away when it fell.

"What? No." He hesitated. "This is I love you, Marie Easton. I need to tell you who I really am. I want to be honest."

She climbed out of bed, wrapping her arms around him.

"Can you tell me here while I lay in your arms?"

"Not possible. Please." He's voice was beseeching in its urgency. He didn't even consider using his Dom's voice; it was far too important.

"You're scaring me a little." She let go of him and searched the room for her underwear. He grabbed his jeans and pulled them on.

"I don't mean to. I just have resolve at the moment, and I really need to go for it while I do."

"Ok, now you're really scaring me." He saw her shiver as she put her bra and knickers on. The painted-on jeans skimmed her thighs, covering up the pussy he would rather just sink back inside. He was suddenly very nervous. Jesus, he was a big bad Dom who could intimidate mischievous little subs, or erstwhile employees, who wouldn't meet his exacting specifications, but this woman in front of him was nearly bringing him to his knees with worry.

"Let's go. We'll grab a coffee and danish on the way."

"Callum." She reached out and touched his arm. It was a tentative, timid touch. So different from the passionate interaction between them, previously. "It's not drugs or gangs is it?"

"What?" He turned and pressed a searching urgent kiss to her lips. He needed to reassure her. "I promise you it isn't."

They picked up the remainder of their belongings and checked out. He held Marie's hand the entire time, squeezing it reassuringly as much as he could.

The morning was overcast when they emerged from the hotel. It wasn't raining, just dull, the nip of the frost still lingering in the air.

"It's about a ten-minute walk. Are you alright with that, or would you rather a taxi?"

"I'm good to walk." She let go of him to pull her gloves and hat out of her bag. Slid them on and resumed their hand holding. "Which way?"

"This way, towards The Mall and Horse Guards."

Before they walked anywhere, though, he leant in and gave her another kiss, a lingering one that allowed him to savour her taste.

"Well, well, well, Mr Ashworth. It's been a long time since I've caught you sneaking out of a hotel." A flash went off. Shit. He'd know that voice anywhere. It had plagued him for most of his early twenties.

"Miss Bridgewater." He shielded Marie from the nosey reporter. "I would say it is a pleasure, but I'm sure you know I would be lying."

"Of course. Who's the young lady? A conquest?"

"Nothing of the sort. She's my girlfriend. Now if you'll excuse me, I have to be somewhere."

He held Marie's hand; she frowned at him.

"Has she met your father? Should I ask him for a statement?"

He was trying to placate the temper that was boiling inside of him. It got the better of him, though. This woman had made his life hell. She was responsible for every news feed that had come out about him when he was just trying to grow up. She was there when he stumbled, drunk, out of clubs with women on his arms. He wasn't a fucking celebrity; he was an accountant for fuck's sake. He just happened to be the son of the Prime Minister. Nobody needed to know what he was up to, unless it was illegal. And drugs had never been his thing.

"Leave my father out of this." He was in her face now. Marie kept her hand in his.

"Callum, let's go. I don't know who this is, but we need to walk away. Please." Marie pleaded/

"All you need to know, Miss Bridgewater, is that Marie is my girlfriend. Nothing more, nothing less. There is no story to be found here so go stick that filthy nose of yours elsewhere, or I will have a harassment order out on you."

With that he pulled Marie out across the road, a stunned cyclist swerving to miss them.

"Can I have a second name, Mr Ashworth? It will make this so much easier?"

He rose his middle finger in the air behind them.

At a pace which was akin to almost running, he sped into horse guards via the royal society building. His other fist was clenched. He wanted to punch something, anything, and a nearby wall seemed a great victim. He let go of Marie's hand and struck out. The wall won, though, and he was left with nothing but bleeding knuckles. Marie screamed and stepped well back from him.

"Fuck" He called. It wasn't supposed to all come out like this. Damn he was losing it.

"Callum." Her voice was laced thickly with alarm.

"I'm sorry."

"Who...who was she?"

"A journalist."

"Journalist." He took a step towards her, but she took another two quick ones back. "Stay there."

"I was a bit wild in my youth. I was often caught stumbling out of clubs.

Normally by her. She was a junior reporter then. Looking to get a story wherever she could. I provided her with them."

"I don't understand." A young couple jogged past them with a dog in tow. They both stepped back to give them space. The dog barked as if to say thank you. When they'd gone, he took steps closer to her and held his hand out again, the left one this time, not the grazed right. She refused it.

"Come with me, and I'll show you. It's just at the end of Horse-guards."

"But there's nothing there except Downing Street." Her mouth fell open, the penny dropping. "Callum Ashworth. You're the Prime Minister's son."

He took her hand, and thankfully, she let him. He suspected it was more as a result of the daze she was in than willingness, though.

"Let's get inside."

She followed him. One foot going slowly in front of the other.

They got to the gate and the guard recognised him. "Morning, Mr Ashworth."

"Morning. This is my girlfriend, Marie."

"I need to have her searched before she goes in."

"Of course." He turned to Marie. She still hadn't spoken. "Marie. Do you consent to an officer searching you and your bag?"

She nodded.

"She alright?"

"We had a run in with Sally Bridgewater on the way over. I suspect she'll turn up at the gates asking for a statement before long."

"Piece of trash, that reporter. She'll get nothing from us."

"I know."

A female guard searched Marie's bag and person.

"I'll put her on the clearance list, so she doesn't have to be searched again."

"I should have done it earlier."

"No worries. We've been told your dad is off to Parliament soon."

He took Marie's hand again, but she dug her heels in.

"I can't go in there." The guards gave them some space.

"Why not?"

"I'm a nobody from the worst part of town. Oh God, does your father know everything? The gangs? My sister?" She started to take steps backwards. "This can't be happening. You lied to me. You told me you were nobody. You're the son of the fucking Prime Minster."

He tried to bring her into his arms, but she pushed him away. It was at that moment his mother and father appeared at the famous door.

"Callum." His mother called and waved, and they both started over to him.

"Marie, please listen to me. I want to take you inside, so I can explain everything. You said you needed a billionaire to save you. I was scared. I've been used that way many times in the past. I needed to know that it was love for the right reasons."

"You think I'm a money-grubbing whore like everyone else." Tears welled in her eyes.

"No. Not at all. Please come inside let me explain."

"Callum, is everything alright? Who's your friend?" His father patted him on the back while his mother walked over to Marie.

"Is everything alright dear?" She placed her arm around Marie's shoulders. "Come inside. I've just put the kettle on."

Marie started to shake.

"I can't. I'm sorry. I shouldn't be here."

And with that, she fled out the gate leaving him rueing his stupidity.

SIXTEEN

Marie

It had been a week since the incident outside Callum's home. Well, no it came with his father's job, so it was the British public's house. She'd cried for hours. Her mum tried to comfort her, but nothing worked. He hadn't told her who he was because he thought she would only want him for his money and fame. When he'd said that he loved her, her heart had leapt. She loved him too. It had happened so suddenly, but she never wanted to be apart from him. Well, until she found out the truth.

She'd taken a few days off work. Mr North had been worried and had sent Matthew round to check on her. It had taken a bit of reassurance, but eventually, he had realised she just needed a few days to recover. Callum had consistently phoned at first. He'd banged endlessly on her door the first night, but she never wavered and let him in. At work on the first day, he'd tried to talk to her, but she disappeared into the ladies' toilets and stayed there until Matthew had told Callum to return to his office. Matthew had offered her a sympathetic look when she returned and that had her breaking down in tears.

The next day, there had been a file on her desk; it was all the articles about Callum from his youth. That night she read it all. None of it mattered to her. It wasn't his past, or even who his parents were, that upset her. She was more confused and disappointed in herself. She had allowed herself to become the parody of a gold digging bimbo. No wonder he didn't want her. Nobody would ever want her.

She hadn't had much of an appetite the last few days but as time went on her body called out for food. It was a cold day. She didn't fancy the sandwiches she'd brought with her, so she grabbed her bag and headed out for soup. It was only mid-November, but Christmas was already in full swing. Band Aid blared out in the coffee shop while she ordered butternut squash soup with ginger and chilli croutons. That would knock the cold away. She took a seat in the corner of the room facing away from the door. She just wanted peace and quiet. While the steam cleared from her soup, she pulled out her new Kindle and it opened to the page of her latest mummy porn novel. It was a particularly juicy passage, not that she felt in the mood for it.

"I wouldn't think you'd have a need for that, dating Callum Ashworth, Miss Easton."

She looked up. Miss Bridgewater stood peering at the Kindle over her shoulder.

"I've nothing to say to you."

"Come on; I just want to eat my soup like you, and there's nowhere else to sit." She looked around, at least the journalist was telling the truth about that. "May I?"

"If you must."

The woman took a seat opposite.

"So what is the book about? I don't think it's one I've read. She's a good author, though. I met her at a convention once. Really shy, didn't really talk much."

"Do many people talk to you?"

"You've got me there. No not many people do. I can't think why."

"Maybe because it will be in the paper the next day." She raised an eyebrow at her.

"Like your story will be?"

Marie dropped her spoon.

"What do you mean?"

"Where do I start? Junior in North Enterprises, raises up the rank, possibly by giving Mr North sexual favours. Gangbanged, pregnant sister gunned down in a drive-by after it was found out she'd stolen from a local dealer. Revenge, suffering —all until you found the Prime Minister's son and now miraculously all your family debts are paid, and you live in Kensington. Do you want to add anything else?"

"How do you know all that?"

"I have my sources. I shall not be revealing them, though." The reporter reached into her bag and pulled out a piece of paper. She threw it at Marie, nearly landing it in the soup. "That will be in my magazine tomorrow. If you have anything to add to it, my details are on the card attached. This soup is disgusting. I think I'll eat elsewhere." She stood up. "Have a nice day, Miss Easton."

The tabloid reporter left Marie sitting alone at her table.

Gold-digger from London slums ensnares Prime Minister's son.

Is this the type of trash we want living in Downing Street? Marie Easton has no qualifications but managed to work her way up North Enterprises to become PA to the leading man, James North himself, in less than eight years. Was it sexual favours that did it? Judging by her sister's experience, it wouldn't surprise me. She was passed around between lovers and pregnant at the age of sixteen, before dying in a drive-by shooting. Will the great British public allow this type of woman behind the sacred doors of Number 10? Callum Ashworth seems to think so."

. . .

What could she do about this? This would drag everything back up. She yanked her bag off the side of the chair, shoved the paper into it, and sped out of the café. Her heels clicked rapidly as she fled back to North Enterprises. Stumbling, she swiped her ID card through the turnstile and jumped into the lift. Frantically, she pressed the button for the top floor.

"Come on, Come on." She bashed the button again, and the doors finally closed. It was the longest ride to the top floor. Only pretentious men that liked to mess up people's lives would have the high level. Make everyone else feel beneath them. When the doors finally opened, she ran out towards the accounting department. Sam was at his desk.

"Hello, you look spaced. What's wrong?"

She ignored him and thundered into Callum's office. He wasn't there.

"Where is he?" She screamed at Sam when he appeared in the doorway.

"Ok girl you need to calm down."

"Like fuck! Where is he?"

"He's in the boardroom with the directors."

She stomped down the corridor, pulling the bit of paper from her bag while she moved. Without knocking, she kicked open the door to the board room. All the directors of North Enterprise, including James, Callum, and Matthew, turned to look at her.

"This is your fault." She stopped in front of Callum and thrust the bit of paper at him. "Well, I hope you had your two minutes of fun, 'cause now I have to deal with the consequences."

Callum looked down at the paper, scanning it quickly. "You think I did this?"

"Well, you seemed to know each other well and even said that you gave her stories. What. Did she pay you to find a 'sap' to get a good story for her? Well, you certainly found one in me, didn't you?" She fumed.

"Marie." James stood up. She just glared at him, but in a few steps, he and Matthew were in front of her. Matthew took the paper from Callum. He scanned it and nodded an uncommunicable message to James. "If you'll all excuse us; we'll adjourn the meeting for an hour." There was no mistaking the tone of her boss' voice.

What had she done?

"I'll go pack my belongings up. I'm sorry."

"Sit," Matthew spoke this time. She froze.

Callum took her hand. "Do as he says."

She sat. The three men continue to stand around her. She felt severally intimidated.

"Where did you get this?" Matthew asked

"Miss Bridgewater."

"She actually gave it to you? Did you meet with her?" Callum came down on his haunches before her.

"I was in the coffee shop. She came in and gave it to me." Marie turned away. She couldn't bear to look at his traitorous face.

"You think I gave her this story?" Callum asked.

"Well, there are only three people in this room that know everything. Two of them I trust not to lie to me." She spat out.

"Damn it. I didn't lie to you. I gave you a chance to fall in love with *me*, without the preconceptions of what you thought you had to do." He stood back up.

"You didn't tell me who you were."

"And why should it matter? It doesn't matter to James that I'm the Prime Minister's son. As far as he's concerned, I'm his accountant."

Both their voices were raised. James and Matthew made no attempt to give them privacy.

"Because you should have told me. How can we have a relationship when you lie to me?"

"I didn't lie."

"You didn't tell me the truth either."

"What would you have done? Would the pound-signs have flashed?"

"See you do think I'm a gold-digger." She was indignant.

"No, I don't. Damn it Marie. You needed to find yourself before you found me. By not saying anything, I allowed you to do that. As soon as I realised how much I loved you, I told you."

"You didn't tell me. Miss Bridgewater finding us made you say. I don't think we were even going to go to your home that day."

"Don't bullshit me Marie. You know full well I was about you tell you before she met us."

"I don't want you to be his son. I want you to be my Callum. Everyone will always hate and question me. Nobody will ever believe that I fell in love with you just for who you are. For the way you make me feel, make me laugh, make me feel worshipped and protected. They'll all think I want the fame and fortune because of who I am and where I come from." She could barely get the words out she was crying so much. "I'm just a bimbo. I couldn't even save my sister."

He came back down in front of her, his hands reaching out and bringing her down on his lap. She struggled, but her strength was no match for his.

"Nobody could've saved your sister. She was too far gone. But Owen is a precious blessing that you protect and care for. As for people hating you, my mother and father were so worried about you. Mum was nagging me to take her to your house to make sure you were alright. She's been badgering me every day since. Honestly, if I don't go home and tell her soon that we're back together, she *will* be knocking on your door. They know everything, and they adore you. I've told them so much about you. The good stuff and the bad. Dad is so impressed at how brave you are. He thinks you'll make me a good wife one day."

"Wife?"

"Yes. When we're ready."

"What about the public? Especially when they read this?"

"Miss Bridgewater smells a good story and takes it to the extreme. She did the same with Amy when we first got together." James interrupted. "Matthew, what do you think?"

"It's written in an entirely scandalous manner and revealing that they've moved to Kensington is dangerous to the family, but the bulk of it is based on facts. And ones she shouldn't have access to. That is what worries me the most, at the moment. Sorry, Marie. I'm going to review all our security protocols. If I were you, I'd get onto our press office and see what they can get them to change." Matthew left the room. James took the paper.

"I'll deal with this. Callum, do you want to take Marie back to your office and wait there? I'll message as soon as I hear something. I think as you two have started talking you should probably do some more."

"What do you say?" Callum moved her off his lap to stand and held his hand out to her."

"I would like that very much."

SEVENTEEN

Callum

"Sam, can you bring Marie and I a coffee please? I want you to hold all my calls unless they're from Mr North or Mr Carter. We are not to be disturbed."

"Of course, Mr Ashworth. Is she alright?"

"Had a bit of a shock. She'll be fine." Callum directed Marie into his office and to the comfortable chair. She hadn't spoken since they'd left the boardroom. She was shaking, even though, she still had a great big, thick coat on.

"Marie, I need to take your jacket off. You're going to get too hot."

He was hanging it on his coat stand when Sam brought in the drinks.

"I popped a drop of brandy in Marie's. She looks like she needs it." Sam whispered.

"We have brandy in the kitchen?" He was shocked.

"We have a fantastic selection of spirits in the kitchen."

"Is Mr North aware of that?"

"Given he asks Mr Carter to keep it stocked, I suspect so."

"Alright, I won't question it, then."

"You're going to take a mouthful, babes. You had me terribly worried with that tantrum."

Sam lingered.

"Sam, I'll take it from here. I've that meeting at three that you'll need to cancel."

"Alright boss, if you need me, though, just call."

Callum brought the cup to Marie's quivering lips again.

"Here, drink some more."

She did, her big eyes looking up at him.

"I've missed you." She finally spoke.

"I love you. Please tell me that we can work through this."

"We can. I'm just scared."

"I know." He knelt down in front of her. "It was never my intention to hurt you. I know I withheld a vital truth about myself, partly for selfish reasons, but it was also to help you. I haven't known you long, my little kitten, but I know how that brain of yours works. If you'd known the truth at the start, you would have doubted yourself. Doubted your feelings for me because of the life you'd lived for so long. I wanted you to step out from that life and feel free to make a decision without thinking about the consequences. I just didn't bank on me being the first one to admit to being in love with you. I didn't realise how hard I would fall for you. We may come from different lives, but I will never feel ashamed of where you've come from, because it has made you the person you are. You needed to know that as well. Despite your fears, I think you do. We've both been stupid and chosen misguided paths in our lives but not anymore for me. I know what I want, and I hope you want it also."

"What do you want?"

"You, a family, a happy ever ever." He shifted, so he knelt on only one knee before her. "Marry me?"

"What?"

"Marry me?"

The corners of her mouth turned up into a smile.

"Yes." Her answer was confused but adamant. "I love you. I think my body has always loved you since the moment I first met you. It just took my mind a little while to catch up. Yes, I'll marry you. I love you. I love you. I love you."

Their lips crushed together, as the emotion of the declarations took over. He pulled her off the chair and down onto the floor with him. Her mouth parted to allow his searching tongue admission. A blazing heat met his thrusting.

"What did you have for lunch?"

"Chili and ginger croutons."

"Explains a lot."

"Well, I expected to be avoiding you for the rest of the day. Maybe we should send Miss Bridgewater a thank you note. She got us talking again."

"We'll give her the exclusive on the engagement."

She pulled away. "Seriously?"

"Joke. Do you think I'm nuts?" He chuckled with with deep timbre.

"Maybe a little."

He growled. His voice reverberating around the office. "Oh, my little kitten. I really need to teach you that it isn't good to tease a Dom. Especially one who is going to take you somewhere quiet and secluded for a month for your honeymoon. I want you on your knees."

Her eyes flicked to the door. "James?"

"James will deal with the press release. You have nothing to worry about. But if it makes you feel better." He got up, went to the door, and locked it.

"I want you on your knees. Palms face upward on your thighs, head upright but eyes down." He could see her flush when she realised what was happening, but she obeyed him without question. He would enjoy discovering the submission side of Marie's personality as much as he was finding the side that made them equals and lovers.

He strode confidently over to her and stood before her. "You look beautiful at my feet. Whenever we are playing this is the position you will assume. Understand?"

"Yes, Callum."

"Good. Now how would you like to serve me?"

"I would like to make you come."

"How do you wish to do that. Inside that sweet little pussy of yours? On those beautiful tits? Or maybe in that naughty little mouth."

"In my mouth. Please, Callum."

"I like that idea very much. But first..." She'd been eating chilli and ginger. He may enjoy a little bit of pleasurable pain with his sex, but he wasn't a masochist. He retrieved a toothbrush and paste from his drawer and handed them to her. "Clean your teeth. We may have to keep a better eye on what goes in your mouth in future."

"Again, I didn't expect to be talking to you, let alone sucking your dick this afternoon."

It didn't take long for her to clean her teeth and return.

"Take me out of my trousers. Don't put me in your mouth, yet, though."

"Yes."

"Yes?"

"Yes, Callum."

He watched as she undid his belt and fly. The button holding his suit pants up was unhooked, and she slid them down his toned thighs. His cock was so hard already that she had to be careful not to catch on it on the way down. He was commando, as always, and sprung free, almost hitting her face. She took him in her hands and massaged up and down his length. Damn, she was good.

Her eyes never left his cock. He could see her studying the throbbing purple head with each stroke. The veins on the underside pulsated with the stimulation she was giving him. He groaned, and she looked up at him.

"May I take it in my mouth now please?"

"I want you to lick him slowly, up the length and over the crown."

She did, and he fisted his hand into her hair to pull her head to the side a little so he could watch what she was doing. She looked amazing with his cock in her mouth. Heat was building at the bottom of his shaft already. He was going to come like a virgin getting sucked for the first time.

"Suck my balls."

He planted his feet squarely on the floor and gripped the desk with the hand not entwined in her hair. She took a testicle sac into her mouth. He looked to the heavens, thanking whatever God had sent him this angel. She returned to his cock and took as much of it as she could into her mouth. Her throat vibrated around him. With the hand in her hair, he guided her to pace, and for a few moments, he just felt everything that was happening to him. The wet noises of her sucking and the feeling of being deep in her throat. Her teeth lightly scraped his length again, and he hissed out a growl. He was going to come.

"Marie, if you don't want to swallow me, you need to stop now."

She didn't, and within a second, he was exploding down the back of her throat. She was trying her hardest to keep it all inside her mouth, but a little tumbled out and ran down her chin. When he finally pulled out with a pop, she licked around to clear up the escaping essence.

"I knew you'd taste fantastic."

He shut his eyes and lost himself for a few seconds longer. When he opened them, she had gone back to slave position awaiting her next request.

"I want you over my desk. Tits flat to it, arse in the air." She hurried to her feet and lay over the desk exactly as he'd asked. She was a vision, a perfect spectacle laid out for him. He knelt down behind her and, without ceremony, ripped her panties from her body.

"Hey, I might need them."

"I'll get you more. Actually. New rule. No knickers in the office."

"I do believe I'm Mr North's PA not yours." He smacked her hard on the back-side, and a flawless red handprint appeared.

"Ouch!"

He smacked her on the other cheek and stood back to admire his handy work.

"You know; I think I'll get a framed picture of that for our bedroom one day."

"You will not. I'm not having Owen coming in and asking why you have a picture of my bottom on the wall."

"That boy has been mollycoddled by females most of his life. It's about time he had a male influence."

"You are not giving him pointers on being a Dom."

"No." He laughed. "I did actually mean he needs a man to teach him about foot-ball and stuff like that. I'll wait till he's a little older for the lady bits." He met Marie's eyes, they watered tears again. "What's wrong?"

"Nothing. Everything is perfect. You'll be a great father figure to Owen."

"I hope so."

"I know so."

He ran a hand over her silky folds. They were sodden with arousal for him. His cock hardened again (so much for the thirty-minute wait), and he pushed slowly into her. He wanted to savour every moment of her pussy clamping down on him in welcome.

It didn't take either of them long to reach orgasm. Afterwards, when they'd dressed, he sat in his chair with Marie in his arms. She was half asleep, and he stroked her hair. It had been over an hour since James had disappeared with the press release, and he hoped that it wouldn't be long before he came back with it changed. He couldn't prevent the world knowing that this amazing woman was his, he couldn't stop the world from judging her past, but he'd damn well make sure that, until his dying day, he would love and protect her.

EIGHTEEN

Marie

"Owen, no. I just tidied that up." The pile of toys came crashing down on the floor. Marie sighed with frustration.

"I want Mr Red." The little boy was searching for his favourite red car.

"Callum!" He poked his head round the door. "Please. Can you take Owen, wash his face, and put the tie on?"

"I don't want a tie." Owen pouted.

"You need it to look beautiful. Please, for MeeMee."

"Don't want a tie, want cars. Brooooooooooommmmmmmm." Cars littered all over the floor, and she put her head in her hands.

"Why don't you go check on your mum while I tidy this up and sort Owen out." Callum appeared, put his arms around her waist, and pressed a line of little kisses to her neck.

"You'll put him in the tie?"

"He doesn't need it." She wriggled out of his cuddle.

"Please. I want everything to be perfect for your mother and father. They're used to visiting the Queen. Not a crazy family from Hoxton without an ounce of good breeding. Oh God, he's going to hate me. He won't allow us to marry. I can see it now." The breath was suddenly very short in her lungs.

Callum brought her into his arms and kissed the top of her forehead. "Breathe. They will love you, just as much as I do. Trust me. Owen doesn't need a tie. Am I wearing one?"

She looked down at the black t-shirt and blue jeans he was wearing.

"No but..."

"No buts. Owen is fine as he his. You're sexy as you are. The house is spotlessly tidy. You've prepared enough food to feed the entire Protection Department for a month, and I love you for it. Now. How about we open that bottle of champagne in the fridge and get this engagement dinner started?"

"I'm totally freaking out aren't I?"

"Just a little. There was no come back from the article. Everything will be all right." Miss Bridgewater's article still contained all the facts about Marie's time in Hoxton and the death of her sister, but Callum's father's press secretary had put out a statement stating she and Callum were engaged, and she was a strong and resilient lady to take the responsibility of looking after her family under such adversity. It had detailed how public services had failed to help her, and an investigation had been started to ensure that they were not failing any other families in the area. She'd been hailed as a heroine in the press' eyes, and they were all calling out for photos of her and Callum together.

Callum had been by her side the entire time.

Owen had questioned why Uncle Callum got to sleep in with her, and he didn't anymore. She'd told him that he was a big boy now, and he was allowed his own room because he was very brave. She couldn't help laughing afterwards when Owen asked Callum if he wanted to borrow his night light as Callum wasn't brave enough to sleep on his own. They'd discussed Owen's future as well. Marie was his legal guardian. She'd wanted to adopt him, but it hadn't been possible up until now. Callum had stated that as soon as they were married, they would look to do it in both their names; making sure to keep the Easton in there somewhere so he could remember his mother.

The doorbell rang just as Callum popped open the champagne.

"Oh my god, they're here." Her hands holding the flutes started to tremble. Callum grabbed them from her.

"Well go open the door, then." Her mother demanded, while placing some nuts in a bowl. "You can't leave them standing at the door all day."

Callum took her hand and led her to the front door.

"You sure they're not going to hate me."

"Only if you don't open the door and leave them standing out in the cold."

She took a deep breath, checked her appearance one final time in the ornate hallway mirror, and opened the door. Callum's parents smiling faces stood the other side. His father had a bouquet of pink and purple flowers and a bottle of red wine. They were not dressed as she expected in a full dinner suit and an evening gown but in casual attire. Callum's father was not even wearing a tie.

"Mr and Mrs Ashworth. Please come in."

"Marie." His mother pulled her into her arms and held her tight. "It is so lovely to finally meet you properly. Callum has told us so much about you. I'm Elizabeth, but everyone calls me Betty for short, and this is my husband, David, but we just call him Dave."

"Dave?" Marie tried not to laugh. The Prime Minster was known to friends and family as Dave. And his wife was Betty.

"I know. Not what you expect a politician to be called."

She moved onto hugging her son while *Dave* passed Marie the wine and flowers he carried.

"Please take a seat. Callum was just opening some champagne. I'll just put the flowers in a vase."

Owen chose that moment to speed from his bedroom into the lounge, flying his car. He ran straight up to Callum's parents, jumping on his father's lap.

"Owen. No." She almost dropped the flowers and wine as she scrambled to get to Owen. "You mustn't jump on our guests without asking. Remember your manners."

"Sorry, MeeMee." He pushed his bottom lip out and pouted.

"That looks like a good car. How fast does it go? Have you got one I can play with?" Dave got down on the floor next to Owen. Owen looked up at her as if asking if he could play. She nodded.

"Marie," Betty spoke. "You make Callum happy, and he wants to marry you. That's all we need to know about you to know you are a good person. Relax around us. We don't bite. Just because we are who we are doesn't make us any different from you or even that cute little nephew of yours."

Callum kissed her on the cheek. "Don't worry Kitten. You're stuck with me now."

Everyone laughed.

"Well, are we going to get this celebration started?" Marie turned around and saw her mum carrying out a tray of drinks. It was the most she'd carried since the stroke.

"Mum, careful." She leapt forward to try to take the tray from her.

"Hush, child. Let me do it. I'm not as weak as I once was." Marie helped to hand out the drinks, and after introducing her mother to Betty and Dave they all stood to toast the engagement.

"To the future."

Everyone raised their glasses. Owen raised his car.

"To the future."

At that precise moment, the lights flicked and went out in the entire house. Everything was pitch black.

"MeeMee," Owen screamed.

"It's alright, I've got him," Dave spoke.

"I've got some candles in the kitchen. I'll just get some matches. Callum, can you help me?"

Before she had a chance to move, the front door was kicked open. Several masked men rushed into the lounge, carrying flashlights and guns. Callum rushed to pull her behind him.

"Well, well, well. It seems I wasn't invited to this little party. Such a shame considering I'm practically family."

The lights flicked back on, they were obviously being controlled by the gang and in the centre of the room stood her sister's ex-boyfriend, Freddie. The drug dealer who ordered the drive-by shooting and was possibly Owen's father.

One of the masked men pulled Dave to his feet and snatched Owen out of his arms.

"Hi, son. Well, I can only assume you're my son. After all your mother was a slut." Owen was still crying when Freddie took him into his arms.

"Please. Let him go." Marie pleaded.

"Why?"

"You're scaring him."

"What is it you want?" Callum finally spoke.

"So you're the boyfriend. Or should I say, fiancé? Which must make these your parents. Tie them all up."

"No. Please." Marie cried.

Freddie thrust a still-screaming Owen towards a man standing nearby and prowled towards them. "You have to be made an example of for what your sister did. She *stole* from us."

"You punished us enough when you killed her."

Callum placed a hand on her arm. "He's just trying to antagonise you. Ignore him. In a few moments, officers of the Protection Department will invade this building, and he'll be dead or carted off for a long future rotting in prison. The former is preferable to me.

"What? You mean the officers that are outside? Dead." He cackled. "All dead." Marie felt Callum tense. His father's and mother's faces paled. Freddie pointed his gun in Callum's face." Now, I could punish Marie by blowing your brains out all over her or I could hold her down and fuck her while you are forced to watch. But you know what? I think I'll stick to the original plan. It's so much more blood-thirsty." Freddie whipped the gun back, and she could only watch as he brought it down on Callum's temple. He groaned and slumped to the floor, blood flowing from a large gash on his head.

Marie flew at Freddie. Her nails dug into his face as she clawed at him.

Someone grabbed her from behind, and she was flung through the coffee table onto the floor next to Callum. A searing pain ripped through her side like a piece of the wooden furniture had just shattered into her body. Her mum screamed.

Freddie laughed. "I said tie them up. Miss Easton here just provided us with the firewood we need."

NINETEEN

Callum

The muffled voices echoed in his throbbing head. Callum tried to remember what was happening but everything was so confused. He wanted to sleep but couldn't move to turn over. Why was Owen screaming?

Recollection flooded back.

He opened his eyes. The bright light stung his eyes. The metallic taste of blood was at the corners of his mouth. And what the hell was that smell? Petrol?

"Well, I didn't expect you to wake up so soon. You must have a pretty thick skull." Freddie loomed over him.

"You won't get away with this."

"Jesus. You're really boring. Honestly, Marie. We could've been so much better together. Shame you prefer limp dicks rather than a real man."

"You a real man? My sister had to go elsewhere to get pregnant and a find a decent fuck." Marie rolled her eyes to match the venomous retort.

Callum struggled to try and get up as he watched Freddie jump at Marie. The increasingly sinister drug dealer pulled her up, so her head was just by his cock. She screamed as whatever pain she was in ripped through her body.

"If I didn't know what a slapper you are; I'd feed every inch of my serpent into the fuckable little mouth of yours. But we don't have time for that. I have a buyer for my son, and he's waiting, so let's get on with this." He threw her back down onto the floor. Callum wanted to rip this man's fucking head off. If he could get just a hand free, this would be over in a matter of seconds. Callum seethed. He shouldn't have let Matthew handle this his way. He should've insisted that this shithead was killed at the start.

"Take the pictures and post them. It's time to start a fire." Flashes went off from the phones around them. "You know; I feel I need a theme song for this. Let everyone know that if they mess with me, I'm going to go crazy on their arse."

"'Avenged Sevenfold, Shepherd of fire'?" One of the guards added.

"Not crazy enough."

"What about that Eminem song with that sexy chick in it. The one where she keeps singing burn."

"Nah, too sissy. I think Prodigy, 'Firestarter'. Get our vibe on while we fuck people up."

Callum's head was thumping again. He could feel the darkness starting to wash over him. In a dreamlike state, he watched Freddie pull a box of matches out of his pocket. He swiped one, and it burst into flame. It mesmerised Callum.

The screams of the women around him drowned out as he watched the match fall to the floor, fluttering down in slow motion 'til it caught on the pool of petrol and raced towards the firewood. Footsteps echoed through his dreamlike state when the gang started to file out of the room. His eyelids fluttered. He could hear Marie screaming his name, but he couldn't focus on her. Freddie's demonic laughter reverberated around the edges of his consciousness. A loud blast rang out. Freddie's eyes went blank. A trickle of life giving blood fell from the hole in the centre of his forehead. The dealer gurgled. The haze around Callum's brain dissipated.

Silence.

Nobody moved.

"I knew I should have killed that bastard the first time I saw him."

Everyone's heads whipped round to where Matthew Carter stood with a smoking gun in the doorway. Specialist police flooded in the door and started to help everyone free. Matthew came to him.

"Can you walk? We need to get out of here. The fire brigade is on the way, but it's going to explode soon."

"Yeah. Help Marie."

"She's alright. Sonia's got her."

"How did you know?" Matthew had his arms free, and they were both working on his legs. He could feel the heat of the now-burning pile of debris.

"No time for that now. Out." Matthew helped him to his feet. His legs were wobbly, but he managed to stand. He was almost at the lounge door when Marie screamed. He turned quickly to see her running towards the fire. What the hell was she doing? Sonia tried to go after her but was quickly beaten back as the fire spread and started to engulf the curtains.

"We need to get out of here." Matthew held him tightly.

"Marie."

"We have to wait for the fire brigade." Matthew was shaking his head.

"I can't."

"Callum no, you're in no fit state."

"I'm sorry." He pushed Matthew away and sped off through the rapidly swelling flames towards where Marie had run. He could hear his mother scream behind him. Then silence, nothing but the crackle of the fire as it feverishly engulfed everything in its path.

"Marie?" He coughed. The blaze was rampant now, dense smoke started filling the room. He got down low; the oxygen was at the bottom. He needed to stay close to the ground. All the safety training they'd gotten when they'd moved into Number ten came in handy for something. His head thundered the effects of the pistol whipping, a terrible migraine distorted his vision, but just in front of him, he could see Marie. She was frantically trying to get a box out of a dresser. The edges of the wooden piece of furniture were ablaze.

"Marie?" He called again. She turned to look at him. She was crying inconsolably.

"My sister." She coughed into the suffocating air. "This is all I have left of her. We need to get it out. They're mementos of her. Please Callum, help me. I can't lose her completely; it's all I've got left. She's my sister. My baby sister. I miss her so much." Tears appeared, running down through the sooty covering on her face. "Please. I can't have *nothing* of hers. *I have to.* I have it for Owen, for mum…for myself. I know this is stupid but help me." She was bordering on hysterical with the grief and need. She been a fool, but she had reasons. They would discuss it later.

He yanked the box out of the dresser and pulled her to him.

"We need to get out of here. The ceiling could fall in at any minute. Get on the ground and crawl. Try to keep a hand over your mouth to stop the smoke." They turned to go back the way they'd came, but an explosion forced them back.

"The kitchen." They sped as fast as they could into the kitchen. He held her close. They could see barely a foot in front of them due to the smoke. There was a window that faced out onto the street. He grabbed the nearest thing which happened to be the microwave and threw at it to smash it. He wrapped a kitchen towel around his hand to move the jagged glass so they could escape.

Matthew appeared at the window with Sonia.

"Pass me Marie." He shouted in. Callum could feel the darkness coming again. The smoke, the head wound.

Matthew pulled her out, still clutching the small box of photos, covered head to foot in soot and blood. Callum swayed. His eyes shut, and he started to fall.

"Oh no you don't!" Matthew was there. Next thing he knew; he was on the grass outside the burning building. A paramedic ran to him, an oxygen mask placed over his face, and he shut his eyes again. Marie's voice whispered into his ear.

"I love you."

It must have been a few hours later when he woke in the hospital. Marie sat on one side of his bed holding his hand. His parents on the other.

"Owen and your mum?"

"At Downing Street," Marie spoke. "Apparently Owen likes the cat and wants one."

"As long as I can get a dog." He managed a little laugh but winced when it hurt his head.

"Just rest, son." His father spoke. "You have a concussion and smoke inhalation."

"And there was me thinking I'd got severely drunk after one sip of Champagne."

"I wish." Marie winced in the chair next to him.

"What happened?"

"Freddie threw me into the table. I've got some stitches but nothing too bad."

"Freddie?"

"Dead" Matthew stepped forward from the shadows.

"You still lurking?"

"Always. He's at the morgue. We got him out. Should've let him burn, but I wanted to make sure he was dead. Makes a better example to the gangs of London that way."

"Let me guess. His photo has been released on the Internet to replace ours."

"I can't confirm or deny that, Mr Ashworth," Matthew smirked.

"How did you know?"

"Our friend, Miss Bridgewater. She was found at her flat this morning."

"Dead?" Even though that woman had threatened to destroy her life, Marie sounded worried about her.

"No, but she won't be doing any reporting for a while. She'll have to wait for them to unwire her jaw and fix her broken arms first."

"Ouch." Marie shuddered.

"I can think of a few people that have wanted to see that happen to her for a long time."

"Callum." She lightly thumped him on the arm.

"I'll leave you to family time." The bodyguard grinned.

His father said, "We'll go with you. I'm supposed to be going to Buckingham Palace tomorrow."

Marie sunk down into her chair. "I'm sorry. This is all my fault."

"Oh, honey don't be so silly. Despite the nearly dying, we had a great time. Welcome to the family." His dad pulled his fiancée up into his arms and gave her a big, big hug.

"Yes, welcome to the family. Your mother and Owen have already decided on rooms at the house. I'll spend tomorrow tidying Callum's, we can't have you staying in a pigsty."

"Mum! My room is not a mess."

"It's not suitable for a young lady to stay in either. Needs more femininity. Now get some rest. "I'll pop back with some clothes in the morning for you both," his mother added.

Callum and Marie were left alone.

"It is over, isn't it?"

"Yes. Freddie's dead. The message has been sent that you are protected and to leave you alone."

"Owen? Matthew did a rush DNA test. Freddie was his father."

"It's all biology. You've been a mother to that little boy since he was born. You've earned the right to be called his mother. I would like him, when he's ready, to call me father. We'll build a family around him. Give him brothers and sisters to play with when we're ready. Your sister had her faults. She caused a lot of trouble. But she produced an amazing little boy. She lives on in him. We'll never forget her."

"I love you, Callum."

"I love you too."

"I've been so confused all my life. I lost my way completely. You saved me. You've made me whole again." She brought her lips to his. They shared a kiss. It wasn't just one of passion, of love, of friendship, of hope. It was home. Marie was his home, and he was hers.

TWENTY

Marie

"Something old?"

"I've got nanna's old pearl earrings." Marie double, no triple checked the backing was securely fastened. These earrings had managed to survive a war, things she didn't want to know about what her mother got up to in the sixties, *not* being sold to pay back drug dealers, and a fire which burnt pretty much everything else. She wasn't going to risk losing them on her wedding day. Her mother marked 'old' off the checklist.

"Something new?"

"My necklace from Callum." She was planning on using the five-inch wedding shoes that Amy North and Sonia Anderson had insisted on taking her shopping to buy, but before they parted last night, Callum had presented her with a delicate heart pendant. She had cried with joy of course and presented him with a reminder of what she was willing to do as his wife when she sank to her knees.

As for Amy and Sonia, there was a time when she didn't think it possible but they were probably her BFFs now. Strange, so very strange.

"Pay attention Marie, you're daydreaming again." Her mother brought her out of her reverie with a jolt.

"What's next?"

"Something borrowed?"

"My tiara from Callum's mum. It's one she's worn to a function with the Queen, you know."

"You've only told me that about a hundred times now."

"But it's something the Queen has seen, and I'm wearing it."

"I took you to see the crown jewels when you were little, and the Queen sees them all the time. I seem to remember you yawning and asking when we could go home."

"That's different."

"How?"

"I'm wearing the jewels this time."

They both laughed.

"Do I need to even ask what your something blue is?"

She lifted her skirt up and flashed the garter belt on her thigh. "My underwear is blue as well, but I'm saving that for Callum."

"Too much information."

"Sorry, mum."

He mother stopped in front of her. A tear trickled down her cheek.

"I'm so proud of you. Callum's perfect, and you'll be so happy together. I thought there was a time when we wouldn't see this. I thought you'd get dragged down by everything and wake up one day and realise that you'd wasted your life."

"I thought that'd happen as well. I never dared allowed myself to actually imagine marrying someone I loved. At best, I thought it would be someone who was willing to care for us financially so we could get away from Freddie."

"Don't think about him today. He's out of our lives permanently. Rotting in hell."

"I won't. Oh God." She wiped under her eyes. "We need to stop with the emotional stuff, or I'm going to have mascara running down my face and look a fright, when I greet my husband-to-be at the altar."

"He'd still marry you. I wouldn't worry."

"Mama?" Owen had been sitting playing quietly in the corner of the room. She wasn't sure when it had started, but recently he'd been calling her mama all the time. She felt bad—the words should have been for her sister—but Owen was her child, in reality.

"Yes, my little monkey?"

"You look really pretty."

"Thank you. You look rather fine yourself in that suit."

Today was a big day for him as well. Not only was Marie taking Callum's last name, Owen was going to take it as well. It would unite them all as a family.

"Am I Owen Ashworth, yet?"

"Not yet."

"Oh."

"Do you remember what you have to do first?"

"I have to be a really big boy and walk Nanna down the...I forgot the word." His speech was really developing. Dave—and she chuckled every time she said his name—had been spending time with him reading.

"Aisle."

"I have to walk Nanna down the aisle, and then, you will come down and marry Daddy. Then, I become a Ashworth."

Marie's breath caught; he'd called Callum Daddy. It was the first time. She wished Callum was with her to hear it." Her mum turned away.

"Yes, when mama marries daddy, we are all Ashworths."

"And then, we can have the cake?" He smiled hopefully.

"You're a little rascal, aren't you?"

"I like cake. The top bit is chocolate all for me."

"I think you may have to share it."

There was a knock on the door.

"Who is it?" She called out.

"James." The voice from behind the door replied.

"And Matthew."

What were they doing here? Alright, they were guests at the wedding. Notable guests she'd seated at the same table as her family, because let's face it, that consisted of only her mother and Owen.

"Come in?"

The door opened, and they both stood there open mouthed, admiring her in her princess wedding gown.

"You look fantastic." James came over and kissed her on the cheek.

"You scrub up well." Matthew did the same.

"Is Callum alright?" Had he changed his mind? He didn't want to marry her. He'd finally realised he was too good for her. She started to breathe far too rapidly in the tight-fitting corset.

"Calm down." Matthew handed her the half-glass of champagne she'd been sipping throughout the morning. It was warm now, but she drank it down in one long gulp.

"Callum told us you're walking yourself down the aisle?"

"Yes."

"Well, that is not going to happen."

The two large Doms crowded her.

"You'll have two escorts. We're not giving you away, cause you work for James, and he never wants to get rid of you. I think, even when you have a baby, he'll want you back at your desk the next day." Matthew held out his hand.

"Hell yes, she's not even allowed a day off sick, 'cause I can't find anything. Look at it as...us bringing you to the man we see good enough to marry you." James held out his hand.

She took both of their hands and burst into tears.

"Oh god, her makeup. Marie stop crying."

James and Matthew looked terrified as her mother sprang at her with tissues and a mascara wand.

"I'm just...so happy." She sobbed. "Thank you. I know I was a pain, but you don't know how much this means to me."

"You weren't a pain." James kissed the top of her hand.

Her mum stepped back.

"Right. I think it's time I got married."

∼

Amy

"Thomas. Come back here." Chasing a crawling, almost one-year child around was not going to make for a fun day, especially in a tight dress, high heels, and a sore backside. Ok, she had asked for it by being a naughty little submissive in the playroom.

"Oh no, you don't." Sonia grabbed Thomas and flew him around her head.

"He's getting heavy now." Thomas was quickly handed back to Amy, when he started to fuss. He was going through a clingy phase.

"Excuse me, ladies." One of the ushers came up to them. "Can I ask you to take your seats? The bride is on her way down."

"Of course."

"Do you want me to take Thomas out?" Sonia looked at her.

"We'll see how it goes. I think once he sees daddy and Matthew he'll be okay."

They took their seats at the front and looked towards where Callum was fiddling with his cuffs. He looked nervous, glancing towards the door all the time. When the bridal march started, you could see him visibly relax.

Marie's little boy entered first, his tiny hand held by Marie's mother. They took their seats, and Thomas stared at Owen. He smiled at him, and Owen smiled back. Thomas' gaze shifted to Marie and his daddy and Matthew leading her down the aisle.

"Dada dada da."

"Yes, daddy."

He held up his chubby little arms to try and get to him.

"In a minute." She tapped him on the nose.

"Dada dada da."

James winked at him, and Thomas burped.

"Beg pardon, you." She turned to watch James as he and Matthew proudly handed Marie over to Callum and came and took a seat with her and Thomas. Thomas instantly went to his daddy and settled down in his arms to nap. Matthew and James had developed a good friendship with Callum, and that had brought her closer to Marie as a result. Initially, she had thought she was a gold-digging bimbo, but as they had got to know each other, she learnt that Marie had a wicked sense of humour. And she could rap on a par with Nicki Minaj.

Amy and Sonia had helped Marie prepare for her first night at the local club with Callum. She'd been so anxious and on edge that they were surprised she'd even been able to enter the club doors. By the end of the evening, though, she was completely relaxed and asking if they could go the following week again.

They'd seen Colette with her new partner, Micheal Larson. When Michael had seen them, he took Colette away out of courtesy to James, but Amy had noted that the one-time waif was looking stronger and happier than she had in a long time. Something still remained hidden behind her eyes, though; she just hoped one day Colette would be able to finally place all her demons to rest.

Amy snuggled into James as they both watched the marriage take place. James kissed the top of her head, and she looked up at him with loving adoration.

"What are you thinking?" he whispered.

"The last time I was a guest at a wedding, I had a clit clamp on."

"You're insatiable."

"That's why you married me, and Callum is marrying Marie."

"We're doomed. I must tell Matthew never to get married."

"Don't you dare. I think Sonia is getting impatient for a ring."

"That's why I told Marie to make sure Sonia catches the bouquet."

"Cheeky."

"Sometimes Matthew needs a push."

As if sensing his name, Matthew looked their way.

"James."

"Yes?"

She looked towards Thomas as he lay sleeping in his daddy's arms. It was the cutest sight ever. Her heart fluttered with contentment.

"I'm due to get my next injection on Tuesday. I've booked the appointment, but I'm wondering about cancelling it. What do you think?"

"Are you asking me what I think you're asking me?"

"Shall we have another baby?"

"Do you feel ready?"

"I do. I was an only child, and I don't want that for Thomas. I want him to have lots of brothers and sisters. I don't want them to be too far apart in age either. Thomas will be almost two by the time the next baby is born. I think that is a nice gap."

"I do as well. Similar to Sophie and I."

"Does that mean yes?"

"That means that were going to have a lot of fun over the next few weeks."

Amy kissed James's lips just as the registrar pronounced Marie and Callum husband and wife.

∼

Matthew

"Would you care for a dance, Mr Carter?" Matthew Carter looked up to where his stunningly beautiful girlfriend, Sonia Anderson, stood hopefully in front of him.

The music changed to a slow song.

"You know that's going to totally kill my street cred."

"I think you can handle it."

He wrapped his arms around her slender waist and pulled her closer. Their feet started to move in time to the romantic beat.

"So you caught the bouquet?"

"I did. Although I suspect Marie threw it straight at me."

"I've no doubts about that. Do you want to get married?" He knew she was his forever. They'd even discussed starting a family, but marriage worried him. Why?

"I won't lie and say I haven't thought about it. I would like to be your wife, but only, when we're both happy with that decision. Now isn't that moment, and I'm content with being your girlfriend."

"You mean that?"

"Even if we never marry, I'm with you until death."

"Hopefully, that is when we're old and decrepit."

She laughed.

"What's so funny?"

"I just imagine you as an old man. Using a cane to walk around."

"As long as you can still get on your knees to suck my cock and I can use that cane to redden your then-saggy backside, I'm happy."

"Hey, even when I'm ninety, I'm going to do butt clenches to keep everything in place."

A commotion in the corner of the room caught his eye. He looked over the heads of the guests drinking champagne and eating little burgers.

"Shit!"

"What is it?" Sonia turned as well.

"Sally Bridgewater."

"Trouble?" James asked.

"I doubt she was on the guest list," Matthew replied with a sigh, and they all headed over to support Callum.

"You're not welcome here." Callum had his fists clenched as he spoke.

"Leave," Marie added in a snarl.

"I'm not here for you two. You're last year news. Nobody cares that the Prime Minister's son is marrying a nobody. No, I'm here for someone else." Miss Bridgewater quipped back quickly, scanning her way around the room till her eyes landed on him.

"Mr Carter. I knew your day would come. Always there when a story is about, but seemingly hidden from any scandal."

James stepped in front of him and motioned for one of the stand in bodyguards to take Miss Bridgewater away.

"I believe this is a private function. By invite only. And you're not on that list. Therefore, Mr and Mrs Ashworth, I'll have my guards escort her out."

"I think Mr Carter and Miss Anderson will want to hear what I have to say. After all, this story has been cleared by my lawyers and will be posted tomorrow in its entirety."

"Let her speak. I've got nothing to hide." He was growing tired of this woman's fascination with their lives.

Miss Bridgewater's lip curled up into a malicious grin.

"I don't think that is true, is it Mr Carter? No, in fact, I believe that it is far from it." He watched as she pulled a piece of paper from her bag and thrust it into his hand.

"My headline tomorrow."

He looked down at the paper.

James North's bodyguard is an ex-MI5 agent with a story to tell. A story that will leave you wondering how such a man can be trusted. After all, he was responsible for the death of a colleague. ~Beth Parks.

He swallowed down the flood of memories that came rushing back. Sonia had come to his side and was reading the article as well. Her arm went around him as his world started to crash down.

"You might want to read on a bit further, Miss Anderson. You see, Miss Parks had another name." The reporter pursed her lips in a triumphant stance. He knew what was coming. "She was also Mrs Carter."

THE END

PART FIVE
CONTROLLING DARKNESS

ONE

Sonia

"Mummy? Mummy, wake up." The little girl crawled closer to the still body on the floor. "Mummy?" Minutes turned to hours. Nothing changed. Her mummy didn't wake up. Sirens filled her head, and a policeman rushed in.

"Come on, little one. Shall we go find a teddy for you to cuddle?"

"Why won't mummy wake up?"

"She's very tired. The doctors will come and look after her." His anguished face looked to the cold figure on the floor.

"Oh. I'll get my toy cat; it's called Mr Whiskers." The little girl took his hand, and as he led her from the kitchen, she called back over her shoulder. "Have a good sleep, mummy."

~

Sonia sat up on the bed, sweat drenching the tangled mess of sheets. No, not again.

Why tonight? Tomorrow was the first day of her new job. She'd trained so hard for it. Sonia tried to straighten the sheets and padded into the kitchen to make hot chocolate. Too many memories stirred after that dream.

Why? Why did her stupid subconscious have to remind her now?

"Mummy" echoed through her head.

She'd only been seven when she found her mother, twisted and bleeding on the kitchen floor; dead, though she hadn't realised it at the time. Her life changed dramatically that day. It derailed, and she was finally getting it back on track. *Come on Sonia. You're stronger than this. Don't let him win!*

Her hands stopped shaking, and she picked up the hot chocolate and drifted back into the bedroom. The next thing she knew, her alarm clock shrilled out, waking her with a jolt.

It hadn't taken Sonia long to dress in a smart suit, grab a breakfast of croissants and a skinny Americano, and travel the short distance, across London from her one-bedroom flat in Hackney, to the Central London offices of North Enterprises. The massive, shimmering structure loomed up skywards in front of her. Okay. She could do this. She had been through a rigorous training regime and had been selected from candidates she thought far superior. But the man-mountain who told her she had the job seemed to empathise with her past work. She had originally trained for the police but had quickly become jaded with all the bureaucracy. After that, she moved into a branch of the Metropolitan Police's Protection Command for a year and, then, transferred to guarding private clientele. She had travelled to lots of places, protected an assortment of people, and enjoyed every minute of it. This was most definitely the career for her.

Sonia was escorted up to the top floor of the building and into the expansive office of Mr James North. Behind him stood the man who'd interviewed her, Mr Carter. Mr North stood and held his hand out to her.

"Miss Anderson, a pleasure to meet you. Please take a seat. Matthew has told you of the job specifications?"

Sonia sat on the offered seat, her legs to the side and hands folded neatly in her lap. She so wanted to make the right impression to her new boss at this first meeting.

"He has, Mr North. I am to ensure Miss Jones' safety at all times, but at present, I'm to stay back and not allow her to know that she has a bodyguard. Mr Carter will accompany her when you don't need him, and I'll report back to him for all instructions. Under no circumstances am I to acknowledge you. I'll maintain this cover, unless I feel it necessary to break it to protect Miss Jones from either physical or emotional harm."

"Superb!" Mr North looked up at his bodyguard. "I have a meeting, but after that, I'll be taking Amy shopping. Matthew, provide Sonia with everything she needs. Please give her the keys to the Lexus." Matthew nodded at Mr North as the latter left the room. He hadn't spoken the entire time she'd been in the office.

She'd learnt about him during the training phase. He was often silent; it gave him an allure of mystery and power. Sonia'd first met him when he'd just finished a workout. He was wearing only a pair of shorts. He was toned and muscular in all the right places, and even his shorts looked as if they could barely contain his statuesque thighs. His hair had been messed by the towel he had been drying himself with. Sonia must have looked like one of those cartoon characters whose long tongue rolled out and along the floor when they saw something that sexy. Matthew'd given her a pleasant smile and gone into business mode.

"Miss Anderson, I hope you're not prone to daydreaming when on duty."

Matthew's voice broke through her reflections. She bit her tongue and looked guiltily down at the ground.

"Sorry, Mr Carter, just a little nervous after meeting Mr North. He's overawing."

Matthew laughed, "Give him a week, and you'll see he's a pussy cat. Miss Jones has the measure of him already."

"Is that why he isn't telling her she has a bodyguard?"

"The relationship between Miss Jones and Mr North is still in the early stages. Mr North understands that he needs protection to ensure his safety, but Miss

Jones is independent and somewhat naive. They tend to clash a little as they sort out their differing opinions. I am sure you'll see that this afternoon."

"I think I understand. Miss Jones thinks a bodyguard will take her independence away, but Mr North knows she'll be a target because of her association with him and his wealth?"

"Not just that. Miss Jones has an unpredictable uncle. Mr North's just shown Miss Jones several things about him she was unaware off. We aren't sure if Mr Jones will try to talk to his niece again. This isn't to happen for any reason. He's a very dangerous man. Do you understand that?"

"Yes, of course. Do you have a photo of him?"

Matthew strode towards a safe, punched in a combination, and pulled some papers out. He also retrieved a gun. He brought them back to the desk and handed Sonia a picture.

"This is Stephen Jones. No criminal convictions but he's suspected of murder, grievous bodily harm, human trafficking, and pimping. He's a nasty piece of work and recently ordered his own girlfriend have their child beaten from her stomach and joined in himself 'just for fun.'"

No wonder Mr North wanted Miss Jones protected from him. "I'll make sure he gets nowhere near her."

"Thank you. This is for you as well." He handed her the gun. "You're aware of how to use it?"

"Yes, Sir."

"It's for emergencies only. Here, if you're caught with it, this will give you a reason." He handed her a piece of paper.

"MI5?"

"I used to work for them. Still have contacts."

Sonia hadn't used a gun much in the past for her work, but she's trained with them and had spent a lot of time on the shooting ranges and hostage simulations perfecting her technique. It was a powerful emotion, when she was able to hit her targets with one hundred percent accuracy.

"I better show you your car, and then I need to go and collect Miss Jones. I don't think she's looking forward to this shopping trip, but most of her clothes have been ruined, and she needs lots of clothes for the upcoming trip to India. Not that she knows about that yet."

"India?"

"Yes, which reminds me. I'll need your passport so that I can sort out the visa for you to come as well. Can you make sure you bring it tomorrow, please?"

"Of course, Mr Carter."

"Mr Carter is my father, Sonia, please call me Matthew."

"Matthew it is, then." Sonia smiled. This job was going to be complex, but she was already relishing the excitement of it. The last man she'd protected had been an eighty-year-old ex-banker. He was still in his heyday when local London mobster's wanted to see him destroyed for financing the wrong gang. It had been a pretty boring job, she spent most of her time walking him around in his wheelchair and trying to avoid his wandering hands. No, this job was going to be vastly different. She was certain of that. It was going to be a breath of fresh air, and one that got her away from all the fears that she was trying to suppress from her past.

After what seemed like hours of driving around London, they pulled up at the shop on Oxford Street, and Miss Jones actually agreed to get out of the car. They'd been to Bond Street and Regent Street, but each time the car pulled away. Mr North and Miss Jones got out of the car and headed into Topshop, the former with a heavy frown on his face. Sonia followed Matthew to park the vehicles. Within minutes, they re-joined their already bored-looking boss. Amy had a couple of items in her hand, and James was showing her other things, but every time, she looked at the price tag and said no. Sonia was impressed. Sonia'd seen plenty of gold diggers. Eventually, however, Miss Jones caved under her boyfriend's pressure, and Matthew stood with his arms piled high with clothing. Sonia tried not to laugh at him, as he looked over and rolled his eyes. She ducked behind a mannequin and dug through the pile of jeans as if she were looking for her size.

When Amy went into the changing rooms, Sonia went into the next cubicle. After about an hour, and lots of arguments later, they all went back to Knightsbridge, and Sonia followed in the Lexus. It was a nice car, and she was beginning to love driving it. It was going to be difficult leaving it to get the Tube home.

Sonia went into the car park and waited for Matthew. Eventually, he strolled down into the garage, one hand in the pocket of his tailored suit, and a glass of water with ice and lemon in the other.

"Here, this is for you. You need to make sure you've a bottle of something with you in future. Rookie mistake getting dehydrated on the job, especially in the summer. It slows the reflexes. I should've asked you this morning if you had anything."

Sonia took the glass and drank it down quickly. "Thank you. I normally always bring water. What do you need me to do now?"

"You can take off for the night. He has to cook Miss Jones dinner as punishment for making her spend too much money. So, they won't be leaving the house again." The bodyguard laughed as his spoke. His voice was gravelly and reverberated around Sonia's body, causing nearly every hair to stand on end. No man had done that to her in a while, in fact, no man had ever done that to her. Men only caused trouble and destroyed lives. She'd had no need for one, both for companionship or physically. Her hand and a friendly rabbit were just as good. And for companionship, her four-year-old tabby cat, called Mr Whiskers, was perfect. Matthew was standing in front of her, awaiting an answer. She had drifted off again in thought.

"Sorry. I'm not normally so spacey. I was nervous and didn't sleep too well last night."

"No worries, I get it. This probably isn't like any assignment that you've had before. Mr North's slightly intense, but once you get to know him, and he's able to tell Miss Jones about you, I'm sure it'll be easier."

"Thanks."

"Look, I'm going to head to the gym. I generally use Mr North's, but I'm also a member of one down the road. Do you want to come with me? I can sign you in as a guest."

"Is that okay? Doesn't Mr North need you to protect him here?"

"He has a way of contacting me, if he needs me. I'm not at his beck and call. That would drive me insane. Inside the house, he's perfectly safe."

"Ok, I would like that. My gym is a bit dodgy, but all I can afford. I suspect a Knightsbridge one is the height of luxury by comparison."

Matthew laughed again. "I wouldn't bet on that!"

TWO

Matthew

Matthew hunched over his knee and pulled the twenty-five-kilo weight into a bicep curl. His workout had been somewhat disjointed as he found himself watching Sonia pound out mile after mile on the runner. He couldn't fault her cardio strength. That would definitely come in handy. Matthew was getting too old for that shit. Which reminded him, he needed to collect a present from Harrods James had ordered for Amy.

He returned the weight back to its holder and strode to the front of Sonia's machine. Matthew wrapped a sweaty towel around his shoulders after stripping off his sleeveless vest. He couldn't help but chuckle when Sonia's run began to stutter, and she pressed a button to slow her pace down.

Sonia's run slowed to a stop "Everything okay?"

"Yes, I just remembered I need to collect something for Mr North. You fancy driving me home? And you can take the Lexus home for the night; it'll save you having to use the Tube. We can get something to eat, as well, if you don't have any other plans. I can fill you in a bit about the next few weeks."

"Sure, sounds good to me."

"I'll go grab a quick shower. See you out front in ten minutes."

"Give me fifteen. I will need to tame this wild hair without a hairbrush."

"I've probably got a spare in my bag; I'll send it to you."

Sonia looked at him in confusion but also with a little dejection behind her eyes. "Won't your girlfriend mind me using her hairbrush?"

"No girlfriend, so that will not be a problem. Mr North likes me to be prepared, so you'll be surprised at what I keep on me."

"Really?"

"Yeah. Since Amy became a client, I have some weird stuff in there. The day after she moved in with Mr North, I gave her this questionnaire regarding details of items such as her favourite brand of lipstick, perfume, toothpaste and hairspray. She was a little shocked when she got to the question of sanitary products, but my job is to make sure she's never caught short of anything."

"That actually is being prepared. There've been numerous occasions where I've been caught short without a tampon." Sonia blushed at the direction of their conversation. Matthew liked the way even the tip of her nose went pink. "I'll have to make a copy of the bag so I can be ready should she need anything as well."

"I'll get one made up and put in the boot of the Lexus."

"Thank you."

"Right. Showers. If I don't get this present, my balls will be chewed off!"

Before freshening up and changing, Matthew got one of the reception ladies to take a little collection of items to Sonia.

Matthew headed to the car and climbed into the passenger's side. Now was as good a time as any to check Sonia's driving skills. She'd done core competencies during the training, but Matthew wanted to see if she needed any further work. Sonia got into the driver's side after about five minutes and Matthew handed her the keys.

"Mr North's driving is awful. If I can get away with it, I am always behind the wheel." The corners of Matthew's mouth turned up into a laugh. "I won't tell you where we're going. You just have to follow my instructions."

Sonia started the engine and Matthew directed her. At one point, he asked her to overtake in a terrible situation which, if her reflexes weren't good, could have caused problems. She managed it with ease, though.

As they pulled into the Harrods' car park, Matthew was pleasantly surprised at how well she'd done.

"Not bad. I want to get you on a motorway soon, but your reflexes are good. Once James tells Amy about you, we can share the driving."

"Thank you." Sonia had a beaming smile on her face. Matthew hadn't really noticed before, but she was gorgeous. Sonia'd pulled her brown hair down from the ponytail that she wore all day, and it framed the delicate features of her face. At twenty-six, she was seven years younger than him, but she was so fresh faced she only looked twenty. Her dark brown eyes were echoed by naturally long lashes, and he could see that she didn't wear much makeup. Sonia Anderson was a natural beauty. He turned away as she coughed softly. He'd been staring at her.

"Sorry, I was distracted. As a reward, you can choose what we eat. And don't worry about the cost. Mr North is paying."

"The steakhouse here is good enough for me. I went there once before with this actress I was protecting. She was a diva, and near enough anorexic, I was surprised she met a man there. Mind you, all she ate was lettuce. Such a waste of money. What's Mr North like on that score? Does he like restaurants and eating out?"

"His mum tends to cook for him a lot. He eats out when necessary. He's an easy boss, really. The best I've ever had. He has issues like most people, but he has his head in the right place."

"He's pretty scary at first sight." They both got out of the car and walked towards the store as the valet took the car to park it. "What is it you need to collect?"

"Mr North has purchased a bag. Miss Jones doesn't really like lots of money spent on her, but he's desperate to please her. The issues with her uncle have left her a little mistrustful, but I've never seen my boss so happy than when he's with her."

"He looked comfortable but a little stressed today. I liked the fact that she didn't let him get his own way all the time."

"Yeah. He wouldn't have liked that." Matthew's face soured. "Look, Sonia, there are issues with Mr North. I can't talk to you about them without his permission but understand that everything that he does is for the best for Miss Jones. They may only be early into their relationship but he adores her. I would even go as far as to say he's in love with her."

"I understand. Don't worry. I saw the looks between them today. They are both lucky to have found each other."

"How long have you been working for Mr North? "Sonia enquired at the steak-house, later, as she sipped her non-alcoholic Raspberry Crush, and Matthew took a sip of his beer.

"About six years now. He was my first private client. We clicked, and I've just stayed. He wasn't a billionaire then, but he was up-and-coming."

"He's definitely very successful. He seems very intense, though."

"Again, I can't talk about that. Your detail is to Miss Jones, not Mr North. But don't worry, his past shouldn't affect her future. Her uncle's the problem."

"Yeah, he doesn't sound like a nice man. Would Mr North ask you to make sure he didn't come near her again...?" Sonia looked up at him.

"Have you killed anyone before Sonia?"

"No, but I have seen a lot of death."

"Before this, I worked for MI5. I've been in places you can only imagine in your worst nightmares. I've killed people. To survive, I've killed more than I care to count. Mr North understands that and leaves those decisions to me. I'll only make them when I believe they are necessary. At the moment, Mr Jones is trying to save face. He lost a lot of money when Amy choose James over him. He's trying to do whatever he can to repair that reputation." The steak arrived, and they both sat back at it was served. Matthew could see that Sonia's head was full of questions. When the waiter disappeared, she leant forward.

"This isn't an ordinary security detail, is it? You have killed for him before, haven't you?"

"You know I can't confirm or deny that, Sonia. All I will say is that you need to be prepared. You need to be ready for the unexpected, because no, this isn't stan-dard protection." Matthew put a piece of steak into his mouth, and it melted away. "But I wouldn't have it any other way. Let's change the subject from me. I should be interrogating you. Tell me about yourself?"

Matthew knew about Sonia anyway—she'd had a full security check with MI5, before he even considered employing her. Some of the stuff had been hard read-ing, especially the part where her father had killed her mother.

"Not much to tell really. I grew up on a farm in the Lake District. My mother died when I was young, so my aunt took over my care."

"I am sorry to hear of your mother's death. That must've been hard. How old were you?"

"I was seven."

"Very young." Matthew kept his face neutral but welcoming, to invite her to open up to him.

"You don't need to do the interrogation techniques on me, you know. I make no secret of the fact my father killed my mother. He's in prison for life without parole as a result. I don't see him. I don't want to see him. I have no father, as far as I am concerned. But I suspect you probably know all this, and more, about me." She brought the steak up to her mouth again and swallowed it down.

"I'm sorry, that was rude of me. Yes, my spy training took over. It's all I've known since I left school. Sometimes I let it rule me a little. You must tell me to shut up, if it happens again. This working with a partner is new to me as well. I spent a lot of time alone, when I was on duty." Matthew cursed himself as he spoke. He was opening himself up to interrogation. He didn't do this. This is the reason he kept away from women. They made him talk. Yeah, when James had gone to clubs in the past, he'd joined him and enjoyed the company of the ladies there. He and James worked well as a duo of Masters, but Matthew was glad that James had found Amy now and that his boss had become effectively celibate since Lanzarote. It meant Matthew could just focus on the protection side of things. But this woman here, in front of him, was destroying that. He knew Sonia'd seen the way into changing the conversation around to him. Despite all her first day nerves, she was as excellent in her techniques as he was. That's why he'd chosen her. Matthew pulled his phone from his pocket and pretended he'd received a message.

"I'm really sorry. James wants the bag now. I'm going to have to go." He pulled out his wallet and threw a hundred pounds on the table. "Order yourself dessert as well and then take the Lexus home. I'll get a cab. See you tomorrow." Without letting her reply, he stood and took a coward's retreat as fast as possible. He couldn't trust another woman. Last time it had almost gotten him killed. He wouldn't make that mistake again.

THREE

Sonia

Sonia jumped into the passenger seat of the Bentley Matthew was driving, and they exchanged weary glances. Sonia'd just broken cover and revealed herself to Amy. The poor woman was being hounded by the press for comment on her relationship with Mr North. She was on the edge of the Diana Memorial Fountain and being pushed further back, in danger of falling. Sonia'd had no choice. Matthew'd been with the car.

As the car pulled under the house in Knightsbridge, Miss Jones got out and stomped off without a word.

"Is he going to be mad at me?" Sonia got out of the car and looked at Matthew. She'd been working with Mr North for a month now and had seen his temper on more than one occasion. Amy seemed to be the only one who could melt it; however, given the mood, she was in, Sonia doubted that would happen anytime soon.

"You did what was necessary to protect Miss Jones. Mr North'll understand that. It was his choice not to tell Amy about you, and he needs to deal with the consequences of that decision." Matthew locked the car and headed for the stairs. "Come on, you might as well come with me. I have my own rooms; I'll make you a drink while we wait for the fireworks."

Sonia hadn't spoken to Matthew about anything other than business since she told him about her parents. She couldn't blame him—he wasn't the first, and he wouldn't be the last. The thought, however, of trying to make pleasant conversation with him while worrying if she had a job filled her with dread.

"It's okay; I should go and get my car. I'll do that while we're waiting."

The warmth of his fingers wrapped around hers, and he pulled her to him. Shivers of electricity flooded her body.

"Stay."

Sonia pulled her hand away; she was still angry with him.

"It's okay; you don't have to be polite just because things are messed up. We can stick to business mode." She pulled the strap of her handbag over her head and made for the exit to the garage. Before she knew it, though, Matthew was in front of her, his broad arms folded across his chest and a stern expression on his face.

"Upstairs, now!"

"No!"

"Sonia, I'll not ask you again!"

"Look I get it. My father killed my mother. It makes you uncomfortable around me. It's nothing new. Just let me go."

Matthew didn't move. He studied her, and she felt so small. Slowly, he stepped aside, but as she went to pass him, he grabbed her, tossed her over his shoulder like a rag doll, and pinned her so she couldn't move. She was better trained than that. How had she allowed him to get her into this position? Matthew went up the stairs, and his big boots clomped on the marble floor.

"Matthew put me down!" She tried to thump his back. If she could reach her gun, she would shoot the bastard in the foot. "Matthew!"

"No!"

"Damn it. You may be my boss, but you can't manhandle me!"

"Who says!"

"Err...government rules on sexual harassment in the workplace."

"I told you, Sonia, this's no standard job. The rules don't apply here."

What the hell did he mean by that?

Matthew dropped her to the floor without any grace or ceremony, when they stopped outside a doorway in a long corridor. From nearby, she could hear James and Amy shouting at each other. Sonia got up and tried to escape again, but Matthew just pinned her against the door with his muscular body. Damn. All her fantasising over his taut abs and six-, no make that eight-, pack.

"Stay still. You don't move!" Matthew turned his attention back to the door. Sonia just stood still. Jesus. God complex or what. She bet his dick was tiny, and he was making up for it with the attitude. When the door was open, he stood back, releasing her and motioned for her to go in.

"Why?" She clenched her teeth and glared at him.

"Because I want to talk to you."

"I want you to learn some manners, but I'm not sure that's going to happen. I can see why you and Mr North get on." Matthew growled. God, the man was an animal. Suddenly losing her job didn't really seem to bother her. She wasn't sure she wanted it anymore. She went into the room. Before Matthew knew what was happening, Sonia swung around, kicked her leg out, and sent him flying onto the floor. She pulled the gun out of its holster and pointed it at his head.

"Now, I still have the safety on, but unless you tell me what's going on, I'll take it off. And I don't care what you say about that breaking your stupid rules or being irresponsible. I happen to think you swinging me over your shoulder and demanding I go into your bedroom is pretty fucking stupid as well!"

"This isn't my bedroom!" Matthew didn't flinch, although he did look a little surprised to be flat on his back on the floor. "When I asked you here it was to explain." Matthew started to get up from the floor. Sonia let him but didn't holster the weapon. "I don't find it uncomfortable that your father killed your mother. In fact, if you ever want to talk about it, I am here for you. I have issues, Sonia, they stem from my Secret Service work. I'm so sorry if you felt that my silence was your fault. Please, put the gun away. Let's go sit down and talk. This is obviously a big issue for you. The fact you've drawn a weapon on me for saying it does worry me. It would seem a little bit of an overreaction."

"I drew the gun, because you're a prat who picked me up and carried me over your shoulder!"

Matthew got to his feet and started laughing.

"I'm sorry Sonia." He took a step back and held his hands up. "I know the details of your parents' case and a lot of what happened to you afterwards. I made it my business to know when James agreed to your employment. It's the only way I can protect him."

"You know everything?"

"I don't know your feelings, but I know the facts."

Sonia retracted the gun and placed it on a table beside her.

"He was an alcoholic."

"Your father?"

"Yes."

Sonia sat down. She'd never spoken to anyone about any of this. Matthew sat beside her on the sofa. He didn't touch her, but she could sense his presence.

"Did your parents argue a lot?"

"Always. Every night, he would come home drunk and complain about something. He didn't have the right dinner, or it wasn't warm enough. She hadn't washed his favourite clothes for the morning. I was being too noisy and needed to be quieted. He would spend all his days on the farm and would get off around seven and would disappear to the local pub. He never drove—just walked across the fields. One night, I remember him being brought home by a couple of the farmhands. He'd fallen in the snow and slid down an embankment. He had bruising and blood all over his face. He was swearing and shouting at my mother. Do you know what she was doing?"

"I don't."

"She was trying to clean him up. I remember him smacking her across the face, stumbling into the bedroom, and locking the door. She spent the night in my room with me. We woke up to blood from her lip on my pillow." Sonia looked up at Matthew. She never even talked to her counsellors like this. Damn him. "I really need to go and get the car." Sonia stood up and walked away from him towards the door.

"Sonia, what happened the night your mother died?"

She turned to face him. "I'm not ready to face that."

Matthew came closer. She could smell his spicy cologne.

"Okay, I'll not ask any more questions. Sonia, there's something you should know. The file I got about you said you could be a liability, because you don't talk about your feelings. You keep them bottled up inside you like a ticking time bomb. I know that only too well. It's one of the reasons that I chose you for this job. James, Mr North, he's a man with many issues, and I'm the same. I don't know Amy that well, yet, but I see the same with her. Together, I would like to believe that we can heal each other."

"That's a rather optimistic view of life." Sonia leant in, breathing in his scent again.

"I need to have some hopes of humanity, or I may as well take my gun and go for a rather long walk."

"Please don't do that."

"Why?"

"I think Mr North needs you. You're a good 'south' to his 'north'."

"Please, I've heard enough of the psycho drivel to last me a lifetime." Matthew wrapped his arms around her waist and pulled her towards him. "Use me, Sonia, I want to help you get over this. I may have only known you a month, but you're a wonderful bodyguard, and you could do some great things with your life. Don't let the past hold you back."

"Says the man who has barely spoken to me the last month, because I am a woman and turned the conversation around to him and not me."

"No, because I'm a man, and as such, I'm a stupid fool. Ignore that!" Matthew leant further over her so that their lips were only inches apart. What the hell was happening here? She could feel her lady parts beginning to flutter with excitement. Hello, get a grip, this is your boss. He's just trying to find out what he wants about you to manipulate you. That's what men do. "Sonia, one final question for tonight. Will you answer it?"

"That would depend on what it is."

"It's about your parents."

"Then I can't guarantee that I'll answer it. But you can try."

"Did you see your father murder your mother?"

The world went quiet. The dreaded question. Everyone always asked her that: her aunt, the police, the counsellors, even the children at her school. She pulled away from Matthew. She wouldn't let him be the same.

"It's the one thing missing from your records. The one question that you've always been asked, but you never answer."

"Matthew, please."

"Sonia, answer me."

A knock came at the door of Matthew's apartment. Sonia breathed a sigh of relief. What happened that night was hidden behind closed doors.

"Matthew, is Sonia with you?" James' voice came from the other side of the door.

"Yes, boss." Matthew gave her a look that said this isn't over before striding to the door and opening it. Both James and Amy stood the other side. They stepped into the room and James pushed Amy forward.

"Say it," James spoke with stern authority. Amy looked ashamed.

"Hello Sonia. I want to apologise for my behaviour earlier. If James had told me about you, I would have been a little bit friendlier when you interceded with that nasty reporter. I hope that you can forgive my rudeness. I am sorry."

"That is okay, Miss Jones. I am sorry to have given you such a shock as well. I hope that in future we are able to work together with fewer problems." Sonia stepped forward, still shaking from her encounter with Matthew. She needed to sort herself out. No weakness—she couldn't afford to show that; it would only lead to pain.

FOUR

Matthew

The flight to India reached cruising altitude, and the seatbelt sign flashed off. Matthew undid his belt and got up. He leant over to Sonia, who already had her headphones on, lying back on the seat with her eyes shut, her half-drunk glass of champagne was in her hand. He touched her gently, and her eyes sprang open. She lifted the ear of one of her headphones off. "Is everything ok?"

"I just need to go and speak to the stewardess. Do you want anything?"

"No, I am going to stick to a movie until dinner. Or do I need to check on Miss Jones?"

"You're fine. Rest. We will have a full day, when we arrive in India. Mr North booked out the whole of first class so they could be alone."

"Oh. I better leave them to it then." Sonia blushed.

Matthew nodded to Sonia and headed off to the find the stewardess who was looking after the first class. After finding her, and parting with a considerable sum of money, Matthew was safe in his knowledge that his boss could get up to whatever he wanted to and wouldn't be disturbed. And it wouldn't be reported in the newspapers tomorrow. He returned to his seat, and Sonia pulled her headphones off.

"Did you find the stewardess?"

"Yes, everything is sorted. We should have a peaceful flight. What are you watching?"

"The latest Renegade film. I saw it at the cinema when it came out."

"Good choice. What do you think of the lead actor?"

"Grayson Moore? He is good. Needs a bit more realism in some of his stunts. They sometimes feel too staged. A side effect of the job, I guess."

Matthew let out a barking laugh. "I thought you might have known. I was testing you. James' sister, Sophie, is engaged to Mr Moore. They are marrying at Christmas."

Sonia's mouth fell. Matthew couldn't help but laugh again. "Seriously? Please, you mustn't tell him I think his stunts aren't that good."

"Oh no, that's too priceless not to tell him. He'll tease you rotten!"

Sonia went bright red. She looked cute, when she was embarrassed. He guessed that was why he had taken to teasing her whenever he had the opportunity.

"It's okay. I've told him the same thing before anyway. He blamed the stunt coordinator. Apparently, he needs everything to look a specific way for the film. If Grayson had his way, he would just go for it and figure out the fight with the other guy on his own."

"Now that would make the films a lot better. Maybe you and I should take over as his stunt coordinator!"

"What, and miss listening to Amy and James having sex in an aeroplane bathroom." Matthew laughed but right on cue came a carnal giggle from Amy and a slam against the wall from within the toilet.

"Has he done this before?"

"What?"

"The mile-high club?"

"No, that's a first for him actually. I like to be one step ahead of him, second-guess what he'll want."

"You're good. How did you learn everything?"

"I see what you're doing."

"What?"

"Turning the conversation around to me."

"I wasn't."

"Don't lie. Your nose crinkles when you do." Matthew pulled his foot stool down and saw Sonia watching him as the stewardess brought him another glass of wine. "So are you going to tell me?"

"Tell you what?"

"Did you see your father kill your mother?" Matthew kept his voice calm.

"Matthew, please, I don't want to talk about this. Not here at least."

"Now is a good as time as any. We have ten hours stuck on this plane together. I don't watch films, so you're going to talk to me."

"Has anyone ever told you that you're really bossy?"

"I get told most days, but I know you like it, really, just from the way you obey me." Sonia blushed again, and Matthew felt a strange stirring. "Come on, answer me."

Sonia looked away and out of the window for a few moments, and Matthew didn't speak. When she turned back, she had tears in her eyes.

"Yes. Yes, I did." Her words were quiet, and she faltered but continued. "It was his birthday. My dad had been down at the pub most of the day. Mum made a special meal for us so we could celebrate it together; however, it was late when he got home. He asked why I was still up, and mum explained. I just stood there cowering. My dad actually smiled and told mum that was very thoughtful. He took a seat at the table, and I tentatively brought him a book over to read. He read it to me, one of the things he always did, drunk or not. His voice was slurred, and he stank of beer, but I loved the closeness with him. Mum brought the food over to the table. Pie and chips. His favourite." She turned away again. After a few minutes, she turned back again, took a sip of her champagne, before pushing it away as if it were poison. "Everything was perfect. Until my dad cut into his pie. It was chicken instead of beef. He began to shout at my mum, calling her names which, as a seven-year-old I shouldn't have known but were already second nature to me. Mum started to cry. I got down from my chair and went to her. I looked up at my dad and said he wasn't very nice, mummy was only trying to make his birthday special for him, and she had spent all afternoon making the pie. I will always remember the look on his face."

"Sonia, you're doing so well. I know this is hard, but I am here to listen."

She nodded, "He flew at me and smacked me in the face. He was about to kick me, but my mum jumped at him and began to hit him on the back. He turned and punched her in the stomach. He was shouting at the top his voice, calling us both names. I scrambled into a corner of the kitchen. My mother, she should have just laid there and taken the beating, but she didn't. She fought back and told him she was leaving him. She would never let him hit her daughter." Tears were tumbling down Sonia's face, now. Matthew sat at her feet, holding her hand. "Dad picked one of the sharp knives up off the table. When he finished, blood covered his shirt. He looked at me, turned, and ran. I haven't seen him since. He was sentenced to twenty-five years in prison. I know he'll be eligible for parole soon, but I don't think I can ever face that." Sonia slid off her chair and into Matthew's arms. He enveloped her, while she cried.

FIVE

Sonia

Sonia shifted on the sun lounger so that she was more in the shade. Amy was swimming lengths of the infinity pool at the top of the hotel, while James was with the hotel's manager, completing business before they flew to the Maldives tomorrow. Sonia wore a lightweight trouser suit. It wasn't designer, but it was tasteful. Amy had told her she didn't need to wear suits at all, but it was all she had ever known as a bodyguard. Maybe they could go shopping when they got back to London and find something Amy felt was more suitable.

Sonia was planning for this job to be long term. She never did that. All her previous posts were short and sweet.

The door opened to the roof top pool, and Sonia's hand instinctively went for her Glock. She relaxed, when she saw it was Matthew. She smiled across at him, and he winked back and took a protective stance, which meant he had been dismissed by Mr North and would take on responsibility for Miss Jones.

Amy noticed him as well and pulled up to the side. She placed her arms on the edge of the infinity pool and started to tread water.

"Do you think I can get James to build one of these on the roof of the house in Knightsbridge?"

Sonia took off her sensible shoes and jacket, rolled up the end of her trousers, and dipped her toes in the water.

"Would he be getting some of the lovely weather back to England as well?"

"Unfortunately, he keeps telling me he isn't God, even though he acts like it, and he can't control that sort of thing. Yet."

"I don't know what you see in him, Amy. He can't control the weather. He's useless."

"He's just so incredible in bed. I guess I will have to settle with that for now."

"I am not sure I need to know that about my employer!"

"Oh come on. I think you've heard us the last few nights!"

"Ear plugs. It's the first thing you get given at Bodyguard school!"

"Bodyguard school? You mean there's such a place?" Amy looked at her with mocking shock.

"No, but James employs Matthew for a reason. I was thoroughly put through my paces to get this job. I think his requirements are stricter than those for the Queen herself!"

Amy looked over to where Matthew stood, and he did a little theatrical bow. She then quietened her voice as she spoke to Sonia.

"So, Matthew?"

"Yes, Miss Jones? Mr Carter, he's yours and James' bodyguard and my boss."

"I've noticed the way he looks at you…"

Sonia prayed that Matthew couldn't hear what they were saying. He was sexy, but she wasn't going to admit that about her boss. All he was doing was looking after her and making sure she was able to do her job properly. He'd already made it clear to her that he kept himself to himself. "Matthew's probably looking at me because I don't do everything the way he likes."

"No, I think he wants you to do lots of things the way he likes them and not just as a bodyguard!"

"Amy!"

"Hey, I'm in love, and I know the signs."

"It's just a working relationship. He helped me overcome something that was holding me back. That's all. Besides, we wouldn't have time to protect you and James from mishaps if we were making lovey-dovey eyes at each other all the time."

"True. And James can really get himself into trouble. Okay. I'll leave it for now!" Amy pushed off the side and swam to the steps to get out of the pool. Sonia picked up her dressing gown, ready to hand to her, but before she could, the door to the pool area opened again, and James' voice bellowed out.

"Amy. What the fuck are you wearing?"

Sonia looked towards Matthew and could see him sigh.

"It's called a bikini James." Amy reached out to take her dressing gown. With her back to James, Amy rolled her eyes. Sonia tried not to laugh.

"It's a strip of fabric that shows off your body. Your body is for my eyes only!"

"And that's why the pool was only available to me while I was swimming. Sonia and Matthew ensured it."

James looked towards Matthew.

"Why didn't you tell me that she was swimming half naked?"

"Sorry boss, I did as she asked—cleared the pool and had Sonia stand guard so nobody could see her."

"What you should've done was buy her a swimming costume that covered her from head to foot. They have them here."

"Yes, boss."

"James, I'm not wearing a burkini!"

James turned back to Amy. "Get in the bedroom now!"

"James!"

"NOW!" His angry voice echoed against the wind protected area.

"Fine. Matthew, Sonia. Thank you for carrying out my request, even if Mr 'I have a stick up my arse' doesn't agree with them."

"Amy!" James glared at his girlfriend, but Sonia couldn't help but notice the tenting in his trousers, which indicated how Amy was to be punished for flashing her flesh.

"You're such an annoying old man sometimes!" Amy walked through the door, allowing it to bang behind her.

"Matthew, I've finished all the work I need to do here. I'm going to spend the next twenty-four hours with my girlfriend, reminding her of my rules and how she's punished if she disobeys them. We'll not leave the bedroom. Arrange for guards to be placed outside. You and Sonia can have time off for your own leisure."

"I'll arrange things at once, James."

"Have fun." James looked over to Sonia and smiled. Sonia controlled her urge to roll her eyes.

James disappeared through the door, and Matthew took a few steps closer to her.

"Is it me or are they trying to match make?"

"I thought you might be worried about them arguing and what James would do to Amy."

"Arguing's foreplay for them. I'm not stupid. It's nothing like what my parents used to do. Anyway. Back to my question."

"Yes, they are matchmaking. But this doesn't have to be anything more than you want it to be. Look, I'll be honest. I'm not a relationship type of guy. I'm married to my job, and I always will be. If you want to have fun while we have some free time together, I'm more than happy to do so. But love and all that stuff? It isn't going to happen."

"Ok." Sonia wasn't ready for a relationship either. She still had things hidden from him. "So, this friendship, fun thing. What are you thinking about?"

"You ever been on a motorbike?"

"A few times, why?"

"It's one of the fastest ways to travel in India. Do you fancy going cross-country for the day? There're a couple of things you need to experience before we leave."

"Sounds fun. What do I need to do?"

"Go back to your room. I'll organise some leathers and get them sent up."

They walked into the air-conditioned hallway, a welcome relief from the already hot day outside, and Matthew pressed the call button on the lift. The elevator arrived, and they stepped in. Sonia only had one floor to go, but the rooftop could only be accessed by special cards inserted into the lift control pad. Apparently, this was a security precaution and meant that room keys only allowed access to a particular floor. It was normal and put in place in hotels of this quality after the Mumbai terrorist attacks.

"It's a place called Pondicherry. It's where the French settled when they came here."

The lift dinged for Sonia's floor, and she spoke as she got out.

"How long does it take?"

"Five hours the way I drive."

"Five hours!" She spat out her answer!

The lift doors started to shut.

"Pack an overnight bag."

"Wait. What!"

The doors closed.

Sonia drifted back to the suite she occupied with everyone else. She could already hear Amy being punished by James. Sonia opened the door to her room and sat down on her bed. She was in a bit of a daze. All she could hear was Matthew saying pack an overnight bag, his gravelly voice promising something. They were going somewhere alone together. He'd said he didn't want a relation-ship, just fun. Did he mean sexual fun? Maybe with all the teasing, he thought that's what she wanted.

Oh God. Could she change her mind and say she didn't feel like going now?

Sonia laid her gun on the dressing table, undid the buttons of her shirt, and let it fall to the floor. She then kicked off her shoes, lowered her trousers, and folded them back into the suitcase. Her room had an ornately carved full-length mirror in it. She hated mirrors. She had a small solitary one in her flat back in England that she used to put makeup on and do her hair, but other than that, she avoided them wherever she could. She forced herself to open her eyes as she stood in front of this, though. She was being foolhardy. Matthew would never want her. Nobody would ever want her in that way. She was damaged. The ugly red scars that marked the top of her thighs and her buttocks were all that she could see when she looked at the full reflection of her naked body. This is why she avoided physical intimacy. Nobody wanted someone as grotesque as she was. It was the lasting legacy of her father and the way he killed her mother.

A gentle knock came to the door, and she pulled a gown on. As she opened the door, Matthew stood there with biker's leathers.

"That was quick." She forced the happy tone into her voice. She could tell that Matthew was not fooled, though. He instantly frowned.

"Is this too much?"

"Pardon?"

"Going away for the night? You must still be tired after the plane journey. Maybe we could just go for a little ride and then have dinner in the city. The Bangalore Palace can be beautiful." That would be the safer option and definitely the most sensible the way she was feeling, but something snapped within her at that moment

"No, this might be the only chance I get to see India, so I want to see as much of it as I can. I'll be ready in half an hour."

"Okay." He put the leathers down just inside her door and rested his hands on her shoulders. A sudden heat surged through her body. "I promise you, nothing will happen that we both don't agree on together. I won't hurt a woman again."

Sonia tilted her head. "Again?"

"Again?"

"You said you won't hurt a woman again."

"Sorry." He pointed towards Amy's and James' room where the bed was now ramming against the wall, and Amy was screaming. "I can't think straight with that going on. Half an hour, and we'll get out of here and can explore. You happy with that?"

"Yes."

"Good." Matthew let go of her and walked off to his room.

Again? Why had he said again?

SIX

Matthew

Matthew felt Sonia's slight arms tighten around his waist, as he pulled the brand new Triumph Street Twin to a halt. One good thing about working for Mr James North: if you wanted something, it was given to you. In a matter of minutes. Matthew stopped at a Hindu temple.

They both removed their helmets and placed them on the bike.

"We won't stop here long, but I wanted to show you something."

"We can stay as long as you want. It's a fantastic place. Nothing like the English churches. It's all so colourful."

Matthew looked up at the unusual statue of the deity Ganesha, which dominated the entrance of the temple. It was indeed very different to the bland churches in the UK. The four-armed and elephant-headed god was painted in vibrant pink with gold accents. On either side were two worshipers who had gold all over them. The temple itself was decorated in blues, purples, greens, and yellows. It was a spectacular sight.

"Come," Matthew reached out and took Sonia's hand, "I want to show you inside, but we need to take our boots off and leave them outside. It's polite." Matthew pointed towards a pile of sandals that were scattered on the floor.

"How do they actually remember where they put their shoes?"

"I have no idea, but they do. Chaos works in India!"

"It certainly does."

They removed their boots and left them by the bike rather than on the mound of flip-flops.

"Ganesha is the god of wisdom and intellect, isn't he?"

"Yes." Matthew looked at Sonia as she questioned him.

"Are you hoping that maybe this visit gives me more wisdom to follow your high intellect and rules?"

"I think you might need to stay here for a month for that to happen."

Sonia whacked out a hand into his hard bicep.

"Hey!" They walked into the temple together, and the hum of people worshiping filled their ears. Matthew looked over to Sonia and saw a look of wonder on her face. She often looked so lost, but when she smiled, she was the most beautiful woman on the planet.

"Do you think they will mind if I take a few photographs?" She pulled out her phone.

"Of course not. I will make a substantial donation when we leave, so we can do anything we want here within reason." Money still talked in India.

"I left my rupees in my bag on the bike."

"It's fine. You can pay me back later."

"Thank you." Sonia smiled again and turned to take her photos.

Matthew stepped back against the wall and tried desperately to focus on something other than her tight backside in her skin-tight leather trousers as she wiggled away.

"Oh my God. There's an elephant in here." Everyone stopped what they were doing and stared at Sonia, who instantly turned a bright shade of red. Matthew just shook his head before pushing off the wall.

"Sorry, the first time she's seen an elephant." The staring crowd murmured and returned to their worshipping. "You want to go and see the elephant. It's actually the reason I brought you here." He held his hand out to her, but she didn't take it. Instead, she buried her head in his broad chest. Matthew felt his breath catch.

"I feel so stupid."

"It's okay." Matthew stroked her hair. "They're probably used to it. They don't advertise the fact there's an elephant in the Temple!"

Sonia, lifted her head, and he met her questioning eyes. He wanted to lean in and kiss her. Her lips were so inviting, so tempting.

"Sorry." Sonia pulled away from him and nervously fiddled with a strand of her hair. "Yes, let's go see the elephant. What's so special about it?"

Matthew coughed as he stepped back to try and draw air back into his lungs. He reached into his pocket and pulled out some rupees.

"Go up to him and wait. Hold this flat in the palm of your hand."

"Seriously?"

"Seriously."

"Okay, but if I get trampled, I'll come back to haunt you."

"Go!" Matthew laughed, the unease of moments earlier lost as they both strode over to the elephant and Sonia stood in front of it as she was told to. Matthew watched as the elephant brought its enormous trunk up and swiped it over Sonia's face. The elephant then took the money, gave it to its handler, and turned its head to the next patron. Sonia turned back to him, a baffled expression on her face.

"Ok, what was that?"

"You were just blessed by an elephant."

"Blessed? I thought he was giving me a wash."

"He's only slobbery with the ones he likes."

"That's good to know." She laughed and wiped her face on the cuff of her jacket. "Do they do this in many temples?"

"Sometimes elephants, sometimes cows. Animals are sacred and worshipped here."

"I actually think I enjoyed that more than my holy communion."

Matthew just shook his head again before calling over one of the priests.

"Hi, I have a new bike outside. Can we get a puja for it please?"

He pulled out his wallet and handed a wad of rupees to the priest.

"Of course, Sir. I'll arrange it at once." The man scurried off.

"Um. What's a puja?"

"A way of making sure we get back to Bangalore in time for the plane tomorrow. James can be rather stressed if I make him late. Follow me."

Sonia followed, as Matthew grabbed her hand again, and he led her back outside the temple. A man was placing a flowered garland over the front of the bike. He then threw a handful of petals over the rest of it. Matthew pressed his hands together and presented a courtesy Namaste greeting to the priest. Matthew felt Sonia tense beside him as the priest picked up a coconut shell and set it alight. He then chanted as he waved it over the bike. He blew the flame out and smashed the coconut on the ground.

"This is the fun part." Matthew handed Sonia her helmet and boots and put his back on. "Back on the bike." Matthew manoeuvred the bike to ride off but waited until the priest had placed limes under the wheels. "Hold on!" He switched the engine on, and the bike sped away, crushing the limes. He could hear Sonia chuckling behind him.

"That was mad!" She spoke into the microphone in her helmet, and it echoed in his.

"It's bonkers but very important. Did you enjoy that place?"

"I loved it. I can't wait to see more of Pondicherry."

Matthew turned the bike on what would probably be a B road in England into the French District of the city. He pulled up outside a whitewashed villa neatly erected on a set grid place. The French Quarter was formally laid out.

Matthew stretched and flexed his neck, as he got off the bike. It'd been a long ride, and he needed a warm shower. He grabbed his bag and handed Sonia's to her.

"I feel like I'm in France, not India."

"It really does feel like that doesn't it?" Matthew guided her towards the entrance to the hotel.

"Ma'am, you must go this way, please."

They both looked up to the attendant dressed in traditional dress.

"Of course, you have to go with the woman. It's only for the start. They need to do a quick security check, and then, we can meet when we get in there." Matthew had forgotten about the segregation in some places in India.

"Why can't we go together?"

"Women are respected for virtue in this country. Their dignity is maintained when they have to be searched. It isn't done everywhere, but this hotel apparently chooses to do so." He pointed towards a little curtain. "I'll wait for you just the other side. Please, don't worry."

"Okay."

Matthew breezed through his security check. He'd left his gun back in Bangalore. He felt naked without it, but he didn't need it here. His hands were more than a capable weapon. And the knife that he'd hidden in his boot wasn't picked up. He strode to the desk and gave them his name. He might as well get the keys to their rooms. Sonia might be a while, stuck behind a woman with three children in the queue. He always felt it a little unfair that the children frequently ended up with the woman while she was trying to get herself checked and them. Surely her husband could have taken one of them.

"Welcome, Mr. Carter. Can I get your credit card, please? I've put you in your usual room."

"Merci Sabine. Where's Miss Anderson's room?"

"Miss Anderson's room?" Sabine looked confused. "I had the message that you wanted one room. I'm so sorry. We're fully booked."

Sonia appeared behind him.

"I can phone around a few hotels for you, Mr Carter, but there's a big festival on tonight, and the city is very busy."

"Does the room have a sofa or twin beds?" Sonia asked

"It has a sofa."

"I'll take the couch."

"You'll not!" His protective side came out. "I'll take it."

"You won't fit."

"I could see if we could get an extra bed put in the room, Mr Carter?" Sabine interjected.

"See to it at once, please." Matthew picked up the key card and stomped to the elevator.

"Matthew, I don't snore, you know. And I'll even wear PJ's, so I don't give you a fright."

"I'm sorry. I didn't plan this."

"I know. It's just an error. We didn't exactly know we were coming here 'til a few hours ago."

"Thanks for offering to share. If they can't find a bed, I'll take the couch." Matthew was going to be adamant on this. He was responsible for her safety while she was here, and he wouldn't allow her to sleep on a couch.

"If they can't find a bed, we can share the double together. Come on, let's get changed, and then, I want to find some French food. I've had enough of curries for this trip!" Sonia swiped the key from his hand and ran ahead to the bedroom. Matthew let out a long exhalation of air. It was going to be a long night. A very long and very tortuous night.

SEVEN

Sonia

Sonia stepped out of the walk-in shower and wrapped the fluffy, white towel around her body. After five hours on the back of a motorbike, in often very dusty and hot conditions, she really needed to have a wash. She hadn't minded the journey, though, as she'd seen so much of India. This area was famous for its old ambassador cars, and she'd definitely seen a lot of them. The poverty in the country had struck her, though. It was everywhere. There was an immense divide between the rich and the poor. She wondered if it would ever really change.

Her ears pricked up, as she heard Matthew on the phone. Matthew hadn't been joking. He really was married to the job. He was obviously talking to James, on the phone, from the nature of the conversation. Even when he was given a day to himself, he was still checking on his boss and making sure everything was safe and in place for him.

Sonia took the purple A-line dress from the coat hanger on the back of the door and put it on. She really didn't know why she'd let Amy talk her into bringing it. She shoved her feet into a pair of high heels. She put a little bit of blusher on her cheeks and some mascara over her eyelashes. A quick towel dry of her hair and a comb through, and she was ready. Tentatively, she opened the door, Matthew turned his head to her and stopped speaking.

"James, I have to go." Matthew hung up. "You look beautiful."

"Amy made me borrow it. I should have just brought some trousers and a top. I feel silly."

"Why?" Matthew was dressed in a pair of tailored black casual trousers and had a short sleeved shirt on. As he stepped closer, Sonia could smell his spicy aftershave, filling her nostrils. She loved that smell. It was quintessentially Matthew.

"I don't really wear dresses."

"You should. Honestly, you look beautiful." Matthew was directly in front of her now. Sonia bit lightly on her lip, as she felt Matthew's eyes travel all over her body.

"I'll just get my bag, and I'll be ready to go."

"Yeah." Matthew almost ran back over to his side of the room and grabbed the room key and his wallet. "The restaurant's a couple of minutes' walk. It's called the Hotel Du L'Orient and is set in a little courtyard. Very typically French."

"I'm looking forward to it; however, if the menu isn't in English, then, you're telling me what's on it!"

"No worries. Je vais vous assurer que vous mangez les escargots." Matthew smirked at her.

"Ok, what did you say?"

"I'll will make sure you eat the snails."

"I think I'll ask the waiter to translate instead!"

"Fine, if you want les cuisses de grenouilles."

"Oh God. What's that?"

"Frog's legs!"

"Ok, I think I might ask for a curry."

"Honestly the food's good. They have fantastic steaks."

Sonia's stomach rumbled at the thought of a steak; its juices oozing from within a pepper sauce.

"Let's go. I'm starving!" She grabbed her handbag and stamped her foot impatiently as Matthew messed around with his shirt.

"Patience. It's still early!"

"Unless you want me to start gnawing your arm off, I suggest you hurry up!"

"Women!" Sonia watched as Matthew tucked his wallet and his phone into the back pockets of his trousers. "Come on, then!"

Matthew was indeed right about the restaurant. It had food that melted in Sonia's mouth and tantalised all her senses. For her dessert, she had a Pineapple Ravioli with a salted caramel crumb. She felt like she was floating away in a warm hug of deliciousness. Matthew laughed as she moaned her satisfaction and questioned whether she was acting out the scene from *When Harry Met Sally*.

As well as the mouth-watering food, the company was pleasant, and Sonia was extremely surprised to find the normally closed-book Matthew opening up. He was still very cagey, but she managed to learn that he had grown up in Hampshire with a father who was a lawyer and a French mother, who was a teacher in the local secondary school. He had one brother, Christopher, who was a lawyer like his father. She had the feeling Matthew was a bit of a black sheep in the family. She asked him about his time in MI5, but he became more reserved, so she changed it to their hobbies. Both of them were big Star Wars geeks, and when Sonia found out James had taken Matthew to watch the last one being filmed, and even got him a small part in it, she was extremely jealous. The closest she had ever gotten to anything like that was a Star Wars convention in London where she had dressed up as Princess Leia and had a photograph taken with an Ewok.

As they returned to the room for the evening, another bed still hadn't been set up.

"I'll get on to the reception." Matthew picked up the phone, with an angry frown on his face.

"Matthew, honestly don't worry. We need to be up early in the morning to get back to Bangalore in time for the flight. It's already gone ten. If you call them, it'll take another hour at least. The bed is more than big enough for two. We can put a pillow in the middle. I trust you with my virtue!"

He put the phone down. "You trust me, but I'm not sure if I trust you. I mean, look how sexy my body is." Matthew turned and wiggled his backside at her. Matthew was always so imposing and stern when on duty, but this relaxed version was really tempting.

"Oh God. I don't know if I can sleep in the same bed as that gorgeous arse and not want to bite it." She pretended to roll her eyes.

"You can eat all you want, babe!" Sonia gulped as she saw Matthew's eyes darken. She wasn't sure if Matthew sensed her nervousness, but he bowed his head and handed her the pyjamas she had left on the bed earlier. "I have some calls I need to make to check everything is ready for Mr North in the Maldives. You head to sleep. They have a work area. I can make the calls there, so I don't disturb you."

"Okay." She turned towards the bathroom. The door silently clicked behind her.

In silence, Sonia got ready for bed, trying to understand what just happened. Did she want Matthew? Had he really sensed she was worried about being alone with him? Or was she just not his type? Sonia was the daughter of a murderer. She had lank brown hair, which just hung there, and she could do nothing with it. Her bottom and hips were too big, and her breasts were almost non-existent. She wasn't as beautiful as Amy was. She was plain, and then, there were her scars.

Yes, just one look in the mirror told her that she was someone Matthew could never be interested in. She climbed into bed and cried. She must've fallen asleep, because the next thing she knew, Matthew was tapping her lightly on the shoulder.

"Sonia, I'm sorry to wake you, but I want to show you something. This is one of the main reasons I come to Pondicherry."

She turned over and rubbed her eyes, still sore from crying. "What time is it? It is still dark."

"It's just before six. We have to leave at eight to make sure we get back. Are you okay to get up?"

"Yes, it's fine, I'm just a bit achy after the bike ride yesterday. Been a while since I have done that. What is it you wanted to show me?"

"Come to the window." Matthew got out of the bed, and all he was wearing was a pair of tight boxer shorts. Every other inch of his muscular body was on display. Sonia felt that view right between her legs. He did indeed have a backside she wanted to sink her teeth into. "Come on, you don't want to miss it!"

She pulled the blankets back, swung her legs out of the bed, and strode to the window. The hotel was on the seafront, and the sun was coming up, its pink, purple, and amber tones appearing over the horizon. It was vast and unimpeded by clouds like it would be in England. It felt like she could almost reach out and touch it. In fact, she brought her hand up against the window pane. Matthew moved in behind her, and she felt his warm breath on the back of her head. His hand slid over the curve of her hip. His pressed his body into her, and she could feel his cock starting to twitch awake against her back. She turned in his arms and looked up at him. Neither of them spoke.

Matthew brought his lips down on hers. Sparks of electricity surged through her body as she parted them slightly. Matthew lifted her off her feet, and she wrapped her legs around his waist. Jesus. His cock was rock solid underneath her. He laid her out on the bed and climbed on top of her. He made sure not to bear any weight on her, but his lips never left hers, not until he pulled back to look into her eyes again.

"You're perfect, Sonia. You're so beautiful. I want to make love to you. I don't ever want to stop."

Perfect? She wasn't perfect. She was far from it. Fear washed suddenly over her, and she pushed Matthew away as hard as she could.

"No!" She leapt from the bed, her arms wrapped around her body trying to protect herself. "No, I can't do this."

"Sonia." Matthew reached out to her, and she could see the worry in his eyes. "Sonia, it's okay. I won't hurt you. We don't have to do anything you don't want to."

Sonia turned on her heels and fled into the bathroom. She locked the door behind her.

"Sonia, please. Talk to me."

"Look, give me half an hour. I want to shower and get dressed. Go and get us some breakfast."

"Sonia, that isn't going to happen. I'm not leaving you."

"Matthew, please." She needed him to leave so she could think this through. "I promise you I'll be okay. I won't be able to calm down while I know you're out there." Or do what she had to do.

"Okay. I'll go to a place nearby that does croissants and come straight back here. If you haven't opened the door by then, I'll break it down."

"I will have. I promise."

Sonia heard the door close. She quickly scrambled to her feet and started to rifle through his shaving bag. He had an old-fashioned razor, and she'd never been so grateful. She pulled her PJ bottoms down. Her heart was beating so fast; it was like it was trying to escape her chest. She'd gone six months without doing this. The first time had been just after she had been transferred to her fourth foster home. None of her foster parents could cope with her. She was a loose cannon after her mother's death. She could be sane and sensible one minute then climbing off the walls and smashing things the next. She got into fights and swore and shouted at her foster parents 'til they shipped her out to the next one, and it all started again.

Scars littered her legs. This is why she could never have sex with Matthew. She was broken. She took the blade and brought it down on the biggest scar, breaking it open again. The pain surged through her veins, and she relaxed her head back against the wall as the blood dripped onto the floor. The rush of anxiety flowed away, and she went to her safe place and became the girl who had everything.

This time, the girl of her dreams had a man: Matthew. And she was allowing him to worship her body.

EIGHT

Matthew

Matthew tightly gripped the fence that surrounded the hotel. He tried to calm himself, but it was no use. He pulled his arm back, balled his fist, and sent it smacking through the wooden panel, causing it to shatter and splinter all over the floor. He was a goddamn fool.

She was fragile. He'd known that from the moment he'd met her. For all her bravado, underneath, she was delicate. Matthew'd seen her files, never more than a year with one family, until she was fifteen.

He'd pushed her too far, too fast, too soon, and he needed to take a step back.

After leaving MI5, he'd retreated into himself. The thought of having a relationship, and having a woman depend on upon him for safety, scared him. Even though he was fond of Amy, it was his job to look after her, and he was able to keep his feelings purely business. With Sonia, however, since the moment he'd first met her, he wanted to look after her.

Matthew pushed off the fence and headed back to the hotel. He stood outside the door to their room for a few moments, contemplating what he would find inside. He really didn't want to have to break the door down. As he placed his shaking hand on the handle, he took a deep breath and opened the door. Sonia was sitting on the bed. She was brushing her hair and pulling it back into a ponytail.

"I hope you like croissant and Danish."

"Sounds fantastic. I made our coffee."

"I hope mine's strong, it's going to be a long drive back."

"Two spoonfuls, just how you like it."

"Thank you."

Silence descended, and Sonia turned away. She fiddled nervously with her brush, before placing it back into her bag. He watched her every movement. He had to say something, to show her everything was okay, but he couldn't. She turned and looked at him, and the edges of her eyes were red-rimmed from crying. "Please, I know you probably don't want to, but we need to talk about what happened."

Sonia lowered her head, "I'll see if I can get a flight back to England tomorrow."

"What?" He took a step closer to her, and she scrambled back. He held his hands up and went over to the desk and sat down on the chair. "Sonia, I'm going to sit here, and I'm not going to move, but you're going to talk to me. Why do you think that you would need to fly back to England?"

"Miss Jones can't have a bodyguard who suffers from panic attacks."

She wasn't telling him everything again. By rights, yes, if James knew of her having panic attacks, he wouldn't want her to protect Amy.

"When was the last time you had an attack?"

"Sorry?" Clearly, Sonia hadn't expected that question.

"When was the last time you had an attack?"

"Six months. "Sonia got to her feet, and she seemed to be walking a little gingerly. Maybe she'd taken a bit of frustration out on the bath? He leant forward in his chair, his large hands resting on his open thighs. He kept his face blank, any emotion hidden away, but he gave off the aura that nobody was leaving the room 'til she spoke to him, and he was satisfied with her answers. Sometimes, he was glad for the Dom training he and James had undertaken. Shame it didn't work, though, 'til he found Amy.

"Sonia, I'm waiting for an answer."

"I can't remember."

"Try harder!" Even his voice was commanding.

"Matthew, please!"

"Was it because the person you were protecting was hurt?"

"No, I've never failed in my duty."

"Okay, was it because you were hurt?"

"No."

"What was it then!"

"I received a letter from my father." Sonia slapped her hands over her mouth as the words left it.

"You had an anxiety attack, because your father sent you a letter? What was in it?"

"He sent me a visiting order."

"Did you visit him?"

"No. I tore the thing up and threw it in the bin. After I calmed down, I went to work."

"Did anything bad happen at work that day?"

"No, I seem to remember it being utterly boring. I followed my detail around the shops and stood beside her while she lunched in the Ivy."

"So nothing bad happened, and your panic attack was not related to the job?"

"No." Sonia looked down, her hands twisted together in front of her.

"Then, I'll not be telling Mr North of what occurred here this morning."

"You would lose your job, if Mr North were to find out."

"Mr North trusts my judgement, and Miss Jones'll not be in harm's way. Your problems don't relate to the job."

"Matthew, please. I can't do this."

"No. Sit down Sonia, and I'll have my say. You've had yours." She instantly sat on the edge of the bed, her eyes wide.

"When I was in MI5, I saw a colleague killed right before my eyes. She didn't have half the strength that you do, and it led to her downfall. She shouldn't have been in the position that she was, and that was my fault. That's why I don't talk about my time there— I am ashamed of it. And it's why I haven't had a relationship since then. I'm not a saint; I got my kicks from women.

But you're different. I want a relationship with you. I want to protect you. I want to show you that you're a wonderful woman and worthy of so much more than you've been given in life. It won't be easy. We both have pasts which are dominating our present, but I think that together we can change our futures." Matthew took a deep breath, as he finished his speech. He'd never laid his heart on the table like that.

"Matthew." Tears filled her eyes, and Matthew longed to be able to hold her in his arms and wipe them away, but he couldn't move. He needed her to take the first step. As if on cue, she got off the bed and dropped to her knees before him.

"There's only ever been one person who told me she loved me and that I was beautiful. My mother, it was her dying words to me. I'm scared to hear you say them to me. I want to believe them. You're the first person to get me to admit what happened and make me feel good about myself. Since I started this job, I've never felt as happy as I do now. I feel like I belong. I've never had that before, and it's all happening so quickly for me. I feel like I am losing control, and it puts me back there in that day. Everything going on around me, chaos, people everywhere. Matthew, what I'm trying to say is I am scared to admit that...that I think I want a proper relationship with you as well."

Matthew let out the breath that he had been holding. He reached forward and dared to take her hands and pull them onto his lap. "I need to prove to you that I want you. That I'm not going to reject you when you're a little bit of a brat or do something I don't like. We're going to take this slowly. Neither of us is ready for anything physical, yet, but, that doesn't mean that I'll not want to put my arm around you and cuddle you if I have an opportunity. It also doesn't mean that I'll not compliment you if you look lovely. A compliment that you'll take. And it certainly doesn't mean that I won't kiss you if I get the chance. In fact, there'll be lots of that, but we'll not go any further 'til we've revisited this discussion, and we're both completely comfortable with it. Do you understand?"

"Do I get a say in this?" Matthew was sure he could hear a little chuckle in her voice. It lit up his heart.

"Right now, no, you don't." Matthew leant forward. He needed to kiss her, needed to taste the sweetness of her lips again. They were like the best sugary treat he'd ever had. "If you don't want to do something then you tell me 'red', yes?"

"Okay. Should I inform you that I'm green, bordering on amber, at the moment?" This time, it was Matthew's turn to look shocked.

"You know what I want?"

"I've known since the moment I met you, Matthew."

He smiled, leant in, and pressed his lips to hers. She met them and hummed a moan of satisfaction into his mouth, and he could feel himself getting hard again. His poor cock had been rigid for most of the last twenty-four hours and without any chance of even being able to touch himself, until he was safely tucked away in his room in the Maldives, it would just have to go on wanting what it couldn't have.

"Come on." Matthew stood and pulled Sonia in to nuzzle into his chest. "We need to get back to Bangalore."

NINE

Sonia

Sonia looked across the bed to the man sleeping with her. So much for taking things slowly. The night they arrived in the Maldives, Sonia decided she didn't want to be alone and tiptoed from her private cabin to Matthew's. She had expected him to be asleep, but he was sitting outside reading a book on his Kindle. He had been shocked to see her at first, but he put the Kindle down, pulled her into his arms, and lead her to the bedroom where he tucked her in his bed and climbed in beside her. He kissed the top of her head, wrapped an arm around her, and within minutes, they were both asleep.

Sonia did the same every night after that.

It was hot, but she was still wearing her body-covering pyjamas. There was no way she could let Matthew know about what she had done in the bathroom when he had gone to get breakfast. Once it was healed, she would tell Matthew, and she would be able to say she did it in the past when she was in the foster homes. He would never need to know that in times of high stress it was the only way she could calm herself.

She didn't feel like she would need to do it again. She was relaxed and happy and enjoying herself. She was even starting to believe Matthew's comments about finding her beautiful and sexy. The fact that he seemed to get an erection every time he was near her helped. She wondered what it would feel like to have his cock in her mouth. Would he be delicious in his taste when she swallowed him? Her few forays into sex had been mostly blow jobs. She had discovered that getting a man off that way would satisfy him, and she wouldn't need to take her clothes off. God, she was pitiful. She was a twenty-five-year-old virgin. There she had said it. She had never had sex because she was scared that any man that went down there would call her a freak, because she must be for harming herself. If Matthew really did love her enough, he wouldn't reject her. Would he? She hoped not. In the mean time, she had to be careful. Amy didn't need to cover her body. She was slender, muscular, and wasn't covered in scars. She wandered around in just a skimpy bikini. Although, James did still try to cover her up whenever the staff of the hotel appeared. Sonia was actually surprised Amy could sit down. She had seen James take her over his knee one time when she had refused to put her sarong on and spanked her backside. Sonia tried her hardest not to look, but she couldn't help but wonder what it felt like. It certainly wasn't painful or degrading in Amy's eyes. She was thoroughly enjoying it. When James had whispered into Amy's ear afterwards that she was so wet and had better get in the bedroom, Sonia had looked to Matthew and his eyes were dark with lust. He wasn't watching Amy and James, though; he was completely focused on her. Sonia wondered what it would feel like to have his large hands punishing her that way. The wetness between her thighs told her all she needed to know, and she scurried off to the bathroom to relieve her sudden aching urge.

"Sonia!" Amy called out to her as she got off the boat. "Oh my God that was incredible. I got in the water and looked at the fish. You so have to do it!"

"I'm sorry to have missed it. I drew the short straw." Matthew strode off the boat behind James. He winked at her.

Amy pouted at James. "Sonia should've been able to come with us."

"Next time. I'll leave Matthew behind. He's far too moody anyway." James kissed Amy's nose as Matthew just grunted and hauled all the bags off the boat.

Sonia laughed, as she took a bag from Matthew, and he growled at her in reply. This time, it was Mr North's turn to laugh.

"Oh Amy, I think Matthew may have to punish Sonia the way I do you!" James patted her on the bottom.

"Fuck off, Boss!"

"Tetchy, Matthew."

"Mr North, I can assure you that Mr Carter has no right to punish me like that."

Matthew stood behind her, his erection pushing against her, and suddenly, she felt a lot hotter. She coughed, and James burst into a fit of laughter.

"Yes, Sonia. I can see that if Matthew took you over his knee for your sarcasm, the first thing on your mind would be requesting an employee tribunal. Congratulations, Matthew. I'm happy for you."

Sonia turned and looked up at Matthew. She wasn't ready to have people thinking that they were having sex. A relationship. Oh God. That was serious. She could feel her heart starting to beat faster, and she was getting hotter and hotter. Matthew stepped away from her and turned a frown face on James.

"We're good friends, boss. If it develops into a relationship, I'll let you know. Please don't tease either of us about it. It doesn't impact the job that we do for you."

"Of course. Please accept my apologies."

"Of course." Matthew answered him, Sonia couldn't look up from the floor. She was beginning to feel sick.

"Sonia?" James' voice cut through everything.

"Sir, it isn't a problem. I'll help Miss Jones back to the room with her belongings. I've placed some paperwork in Mr Carter's room that was faxed over for you to sign."

No more was said. Sonia held Amy's bag to her chest and followed her to her room, while Matthew went off with James. By the time they entered the villa Amy and James shared, Sonia was on the verge of tears. Amy walked straight over to the mini bar and pulled out a shot of brandy.

"Here, drink this. It'll help."

"I'm fine Amy." Sonia still couldn't look up and into the eyes of the woman she now thought of as her friend.

"I know you're not. Sonia, I know nothing of what's happening between you and Matthew, but if it is something that you don't want to happen, you must tell me, and I'll have James put a stop to it."

"What?" Sonia panicked and looked straight at Amy. "No. I mean. I. We aren't sleeping together. Well, we are, but not sexually. Why is this so hard?"

Amy came straight up to her and wrapped her arms around her. "It doesn't have to be. Talk to me Sonia."

"Matthew and I have feelings for each other, but because of issues in both our pasts we are taking things slowly. I've spent the last few nights in his bed, but nothing's happened. I like him a lot, but I'm not ready for more."

"I'll talk to James and tell him to stop taunting you both."

"No, it's okay. James and Matthew are friends. It should be normal to tease each other."

"Not if it's going to upset you. Matthew'll not want that."

"Amy?"

Her friend stepped away from her and took a seat on the bed. She patted for Sonia to come and sit beside her, but Sonia chose to stay standing.

"Do you think that Matthew'll want more from me now? How long will he wait?" Sonia almost felt like giggling. This was such a silly conversation for a twenty-five-year-old to have.

"He's a man, Sonia, and he obviously thinks you're sexy." Sonia shook her head and screwed her face up a little bit. "As for how long he'll wait... I haven't known Matthew for long, but I think he'll wait for as long as you need."

"I think I could fall in love with him, but I'm scared as to what that means."

"Physically or emotionally?"

"Both."

"Emotionally, you'll deal with him. Come on, my relationship with James hasn't exactly been dull so far, but we get through it by keeping open lines of communication. Physically, well, what have you done so far?"

"We've kissed."

"And?"

"We've kissed." Sonia could feel herself blushing. She was sure she was actually sweating under this interrogation.

"Okay. What've you done in the past?"

There was no way getting around this.

"I'm a virgin. I've sucked a guy off before, but that's it."

"Okay, you can try that with Matthew. I'm sure he'd like that. Most men seem to, if it's done right. What about letting Matthew touch you, get you off?"

She shook her head.

"Why?" Amy looked at her quizzically. It was as though she were an alien.

"I don't know. I can't explain it." It was all that came to her head at the time.

"Okay. James is into something called BDSM. It doesn't always involve sex. I'm sure Matthew knows something about it as well. You could talk to him about that? You just need to learn to relax and trust each other."

Sonia spun on her heels. She needed some fresh air. This was all happening so fast. So much information in her head, and the bloody cut on her leg kept tugging against her cheap polyester trousers causing her pain.

"I'm sorry, Amy; I need to get out of here. Sorry." Sonia sped out the door, Amy calling after her. Her head was thumping and swirling. She could feel the sweat now dripping off her. All of a sudden, she bent over and emptied the contents of her stomach onto the sand beneath her feet. What the hell was going on? She really didn't feel well. This was more than just embarrassment.

"Sonia." Matthew's voice called out. She looked up, and he was standing there with James, a look of concern on his face. He took a step towards her, but all she could feel was herself falling. Her head hit the ground, pain shooting through her body as she blacked out.

TEN

Matthew

"Are you sure you're ready for this? She's different from the girls we've played with before." Matthew watched as James signed the papers and handed them back to him.

"As sure as you are that you're ready for marriage."

"Point taken. I won't interfere anymore. I like her, Amy likes her a lot as well. We both know that she has issues, and you aren't exactly Mr Sunshine, but I think you'll be good for each other. Just make sure Amy's the number one priority."

"You know I'll always do my job!"

"Good. I want to get back to my girl. I think I have a couple more things I want to explore with her."

"I'm surprised you both haven't got chafing!"

Matthew strode out of his villa with James in front of him.

"Jealous?"

"You may be my boss, but I don't think Amy would mind if I smacked you in the face for disrespect. We all know she wears the trousers now!"

Matthew turned his head and saw Sonia stumbling out of James' and Amy's villa. She was deathly pale and shaking all over. She bent over and was violently sick everywhere.

"What the.... Sonia?" The last word was shouted out.

She looked up at him, before she collapsed right in front of him. Matthew's legs were moving before his brain had even engaged. James was beside him as they both leapt over the small fence separating the villas. Amy ran out and straight to Sonia, but Matthew pulled Sonia into his arms.

"She's burning up." The unconscious form in his arms felt like fire.

"I'll get a doctor. Take her to her room. Amy, help Matthew cool her down." James jumped up and sped towards the reception.

Matthew scooped Sonia up and ran towards his villa. Amy followed and turned the air conditioning up higher to cool the room. Matthew's head was scrambled. What was going on?

"What did you say to her?" He snapped at Amy.

"Just a little advice. Nothing to cause this. Matthew, this is a fever. We need to get her out of these clothes."

"I can't!"

"Then go and wait for James and the doctor, because I'm going to!" Amy didn't wait for Matthew. She tried to pull Sonia up to remove her jacket. She was struggling.

"I'll hold her up." He took Sonia and held her still as Amy removed her jacket.

"Matthew, I'm going to remove her shirt as well."

He nodded and averted his eyes. "Amy, tell her I didn't look."

"I will Matthew. Don't worry. Once she's cool, she'll be all right."

"Thank you."

"You can lay her back down. Keep facing the other way. I'm going to take her trousers off."

Matthew did so, and as Amy covered her top half with a sheet, he turned away. He wouldn't see her in the flesh until she agreed to it.

He waited till Amy said he could turn around, but all he heard was a loud gasp.

"Amy?"

Sonia must have woken up, because he heard her scream.

"Get off me. Get out!"

"Sonia. You're awake? Are you okay!"

"Get out, both of you get out!"

"What?" Matthew wasn't keeping his back to her anymore; he turned around. She was huddled up and had pulled the sheet all around herself. She was still sweating, but this time, she was paler. "Amy?"

Sonia was looking straight at her friend. Matthew could see the absolute terror in her eyes. Amy was moving her mouth, but nothing seemed to be coming out. The door opened behind them, and James and a doctor ran in.

"Miss Anderson?"

Matthew pointed to Sonia.

"I understand you fainted, and Mr North tells me you've a fever. Can I take a look?"

"No!" Sonia scrambled further up the bed. "I got hot. It's hot out today, that's all. I feel much better. Please, an hour's rest and I'll be all right."

"You won't." Amy whispered the words, but Matthew heard them.

"Amy, what's going on?" James came to Amy's side and wrapped his arms around her.

"Sonia, I have to tell them."

Sonia was crying now.

"What's going on?" He shouted and thumped his fist down on a nearby cupboard. Sonia startled and turned her head to him. "Show me?"

She didn't say anything, just let the sheet fall. Her eyes went blank. Matthew looked down to her legs. Criss-crossed patterns of scars rose from both her thighs. One of them looked red and angry. It was new. And it was infected. Matthew's mouth went dry.

Pondicherry. The bathroom. It all hit him. He left her, and she'd cut herself. He stumbled backwards, bumping into the wall, and sliding down it. Sonia shut her eyes and let the tears fall.

"Amy." James' voice cut through the silence. "The doctor'll see to Sonia. Come on. We should go back to our room and let him work." Matthew watched them both leave. He got to his feet as the doctor came over to Sonia.

"Was the razor blade clean Ma'am?"

"It wasn't sterile." She looked over to him, "Mr Carter'd used it for shaving." The bottom fell out of his world. She'd used his razor.

The doctor placed a thermometer into Sonia's ear. "Your temperature isn't as bad as I expected it to be. I suspect the heat contributed to your fainting. You do have an infection, though. I'll clean up the cut and give you a shot of antibiotics. When do you leave?"

"Tomorrow."

"You should be fit to fly. I'll come and check on you before you do. When you return home, you must go straight to a doctor and get it checked again. Ma'am—you need to look at counselling as well. That's important."

"I have a counsellor."

"Mr Carter, you're responsible for this woman?"

Matthew was listening to the conversation but struggling to take everything in. "Yes, I am."

"She'll need rest and plenty of fluids today. Try to keep her cool but don't use cold water on her. It can do more harm than good."

"I will."

They sat in silence as the doctor did his work. When he was finished, Matthew placed the sheet over Sonia and followed the doctor out.

"Will she heal?"

"She has lots of old scars. She's been doing this for a long time. The one she opened is probably her 'go to' cut. The one she uses when desperate. Do you know why she did it?"

"I have a good idea."

"Talk to her about it. It's all you can do, at the moment."

"Thank you, doctor."

"If she gets worse, call me. I'll sort the bill with Mr North."

Matthew nodded and went back inside.

"Sonia." She looked over at him. "Start explaining."

"Should I go back to my room?"

"You even go try to go back to your room, and I'll tie you to that bed, and we'll remain here 'til you decide to talk!"

She made sure the sheets covered every inch of her body. "I cut myself. I've done it since I was a kid. I'm a freak. Don't worry, I know what you're going to say."

"How do you know what I'm going to say?"

"Because I've heard it all before."

Matthew pursed his lips together. He grabbed the end of the sheet and pulled it off her.

"Matthew!"

"Quiet. You don't have permission to speak. You'll listen to me."

"I don't have permission to speak?"

"Silence, or I'll put you over my knee and spank that beautiful little arse 'til you can't lay on your front or back. I've seen the way you watch James do it to Amy. I know that every time you do, you disappear to get yourself off."

She didn't say anything, just made herself small like she was trying to hide.

"You were passed between different foster homes, told you were a trouble-maker, and you believe it. It caused you to feel pain, so you decided to start cutting yourself to get a pain of a different kind. Am I right?"

"Yes." Her voice was mouse-like in reply.

"You're not well enough now for me to show you a different way of releasing pain when you're stressed, but when we return to England, and the doctor has given you all clear, I'll be showing you. And Sonia, don't think I mean that I'll have sex with you. I'll not do that 'til I believe you're ready for it and you agree." It suddenly hit him, of course, it made complete sense. "You're a virgin."

Sonia whimpered and placed her head in her hands.

"Yes."

Matthew couldn't help but feel a little bit excited by that thought. He would be the first one to be with her.

"Okay, we'll discuss correcting that when you're better. I have to show you what you've been missing out on."

"Matthew, you don't have to do this."

He let out a gravelly breath. He was at the end of his tether with her self-deprecation.

"Lay back on the bed!" The commanding tone was back, and though Sonia hesitated at first, she did as commanded. Matthew pulled his shirt over his head and climbed next to her on the bed.

"Don't move." She swallowed down a gulp as Matthew brought his lips down to hers. She was the best taste he'd ever had. Slowly, he moved his mouth over her jaw, down the slender column of her neck, and across her shoulder blade. He lowered her bra strap and pulled her right breast out of her bra. Her nipples were the perfect mix of pink and brown. He pinched the tip, and she moaned.

"Pain can also be pleasurable. Remember red if you want me to stop."

She nodded at him.

"I need to hear that you understand, Sonia."

"Yes, Sir."

"Good girl."

He lowered his mouth again, travelling down her body, savouring every inch of her flesh. He stopped at her thighs and looked back up at her. Sonia's eyes were wide.

"Every inch of you is beautiful." And he pressed delicate kisses to her scars. He put his nose against the delicate fabric of her panties and took a long inhalation. He carefully pulled them down. She was completely shaved. His cock leapt.

He parted her labia and ran a finger down from her clit to the entrance of her moist pussy. She instinctively shut her legs.

"I know you've brought yourself to orgasm before. This will be no different, just more intense."

She opened her thighs, and he traced his finger over her again. This time, he tested her entrance and pushed a finger slowly in. She was so tight. He circled his thumb over her clit, teasing the sensitive nub from its hood. She was fantastic. Her breath quickened. He flicked his finger over her clit again as he pressed another finger inside her and bent his head to kiss the scars on her legs again. She arched her back and exploded around him. Her pussy clamped down on his fingers as she rode her waves of pleasure.

He was her salvation, and she'd be his. In that instant, he knew it.

As she came down from her climax, Matthew withdrew his fingers and brought them to his mouth. She tasted so sweet, just a hint of tanginess. He pulled her knickers back up and corrected her bra. Sonia was exhausted. The fever and the orgasm had wiped her out. He placed the sheet over her and sat beside her on the bed as she settled herself and closed her eyes.

She drifted to sleep, and Matthew stayed by her side.

ELEVEN

Sonia

Three months later.......

"How was he today?" Sonia entered the bedroom that she now shared with Matthew and placed her bag down on the oak table.

"He managed to shave this morning and then locked himself in his office to work. I took him a tray of food, but when I went back an hour later to collect it, he'd only taken a little bite of the sandwich," Matthew replied to her as he lay on the bed, his arms propped behind his head. The look of boredom on his face told Sonia everything she needed to know. Ever since Amy'd left James, Matthew'd become increasingly frustrated with his job. It'd taken a month before James even left his bed after he was shot, and he still wasn't the same man. Sonia and Matthew had discussed finding Amy and talking to her, but they agreed it was probably best to leave them to sort out everything for themselves.

"Miranda's anxious about him. She was quiet when we were shopping."

"I know. Sophie should be here later today, so hopefully, that will help. He always seems to brighten up when his sister's around."

"I hope so. Do you want to watch over Miranda tomorrow, and I will stay at home with James?" When Amy'd left, Sonia'd been assigned to protect Mrs North instead. She suspected it was James' way of making sure she still had something to do. "I can't promise you it will be a thrilling engagement, but she does have the talk at the art museum tomorrow. Some of the attendees always make me chuckle."

"No, I'll stick with James. I'll try and force him into the office tomorrow for an hour or so. At least that'll get him out. I'm sure I can make up some excuse to get him there."

Sonia removed her trousers and placed them in the linen basket that she'd brought to try and tidy up Matthew's room a little bit. For such a disciplined man, he had a terrible habit of leaving his worn underpants on the floor. She reached for a pair of yoga pants. "Are you forgetting the rules?"

Sonia stopped with half a leg into the pants. "Sorry?"

"We're alone in our rooms."

"Your body and your soul are both beautiful. When we're alone, you know you're not supposed to wear clothes so you can realise that."

"I thought you would want dinner."

"Depends on what you're serving?" His voice turned gravelly and dominant.

She stepped back out of the pants and placed them on the side, her shirt, bra and knickers joined them.

"That's much better. Come here." He moved to the end of the bed and opened his legs wide, as he beckoned her.

Sonia couldn't argue with that look, when his eyes went dark, and he looked at her like she was a delicious dessert to savour.

She came between his legs, and he pressed his head against her breasts. He didn't move. She could just hear him inhaling her scent and felt his warm breath against her tender flesh. He pulled back and ran a hand over the healing scars on her leg and dropped a kiss on them before letting out a long sigh.

"He's dying on the inside. I don't know what to do to save him. I feel useless."

"You're doing all you can. Mr North and Amy just need time. We'll give them another few months, and then we'll spur them along a little bit." Sonia got down on her knees and leant her head into his lap. He stroked her hair, his thick digits running through the soft tendrils.

"I love you, Sonia. Don't ever leave me."

"I have no plans to, Matthew. Who else will, or even could, make me feel beautiful like you do?"

"Are you doubting again?"

She shook her head." I know what happens when I do. Although maybe...."

"Deliberate antagonism doesn't get you a spanking, my dove."

"Why a dove?" She looked at him with a querying expression.

"Because you're learning to fly."

She liked that idea.

"Matthew, Sonia." A knock and Miranda's voice at the door.

"Get on the bed and in position. I'll be back in a minute."

Sonia jumped eagerly onto the bed as Matthew disappeared. She listened to the voices coming from the hall.

"I'm sorry to disturb you. Sophie and Grayson are here already. His bodyguard's asking for you, and James won't come out of his office. Can you help?"

"Of course. Give us five minutes, and we'll both be there."

"Thank you, Matthew."

"No worries, Mrs North."

Sonia got off the bed and put her clothes back on as Matthew returned to the room.

"You heard everything then?"

"Yes. Why won't he come out of his office?"

"I don't know."

Sonia grabbed her navy jacket off the side as Matthew swapped his Led Zeppelin t-shirt and jeans for a formal suit.

"Do you want me to deal with Grayson's security detail, while you sort James?"

They left their rooms together and headed down to the main section of the house in Knightsbridge.

"I better sort them. His bodyguard's a good man, but he can be a bit self-important. You go in and meet Sophie. You'll like her."

"Okay. Call if you need me."

Sonia went to walk around the corner to the lounge, but Matthew grabbed her arm, her back landed against the wall as his body pressed against her, and he drew a kiss from her lips.

"Matthew Carter. You have a girlfriend?" The excited shriek came from behind them, and they jumped apart. Matthew grunted out a cough, as Sonia flushed.

"Miss Sophie. May I introduce Sonia? She's your mother's bodyguard."

Sonia raised her head and smiled as a woman jumped towards them and threw her arms around Matthew, first, and then Sonia.

"Oh, my God. Come tell me all about yourself. How long have you been together?"

Sophie linked arms with her and dragged her into the sitting room. Matthew winked a goodbye and headed off towards James' office.

"Sophie, leave the poor girl alone." Miranda rolled her eyes as they entered.

"How can I, mum? I mean, Matthew has a girlfriend. Sit, Sonia."

A man with long black hair and American-Indian features came into view.

"Sophie." His gravelly voice sounded just like Matthew's when he was in dominant mode. "Come sit with me, and you can question Miss Anderson without making her feel like it's an interrogation."

"You're no fun." Sophie pouted at the man Sonia surmised was her fiancé.

"Put your bottom lip away and sit, or I will show you just how much fun I can be."

"Will you spank me?"

"Sophie, please." Sonia was sure Miranda turned green. "There are things a mother doesn't need to know."

"Sorry, Mum." Sophie finally sat down next to her fiancé, and he wrapped a protective arm around her shoulder.

"Miss Anderson. I am Grayson Moore, Miss North's fiancé. It's a pleasure to meet you. Miranda's been telling us about how you've become a valued member of the protection team. How long have you been here now?"

"Only six months."

"You helped rescue Mrs North when she was taken?"

"I did."

"Thank you on Sophie's part for that."

Sonia found it a little strange that Sophie was no longer speaking and Grayson was dictating the conversation. She was sure she could say thank you on her own.

"I'm just sorry that I couldn't prevent Mr. North getting shot as well."

"It was a difficult situation." Sophie squirmed beside the imposing man. "You may ask your questions now Sophie."

"Thank you." She winked at him and turned her head to Sonia.

"Is it true you're dating Matthew?"

"I am, yes."

"Oh, I'm so happy." She brought her hands to her face in a joyful prayer.

"We're taking our relationship slowly. Mr. North isn't doing too well." Maybe she could divert the attention away from her.

"He needs to just get out and have a night in the club. That'll sort him." Grayson tried to mumble under his voice.

"Club?"

"I don't need more babysitting. I just need to catch up on all the fucking work I've missed while I was in the hospital." James' angry voice shattered through the door before Grayson had a chance to answer her question.

"She's your sister, and you'll get your arse in there and say hello, or I'll smack you in the face 'til you pass out, and I can drag you in there."

"You know you aren't so indispensable that I can't fire you."

"I am. Nobody else would put up with your shit."

"Go fuck your girlfriend before she walks out on you like mine did."

"I'll let that one go. Now get the fuck in there!"

The door opened, James stumbled in, and Matthew blocked the exit.

"There's the welcoming brother I know and love." Sophie stood and held her arms open to him.

"You didn't have to come, Sophie. I'm fine. I just have lots of work to catch up on." James made no effort to embrace his sister. He stood with his arms folded and glared at everyone in the room.

"You're a mess. Stop lying to us and yourself."

"The woman I love left me. Sorry, I'm not a happy clown at the moment."

Sonia was getting scared.

"You lied to her. She needs time to calm down, and then, you can talk to her."

"I didn't lie."

"You did!"

"I was protecting her!"

Sonia looked over to Matthew and could see how much this was hurting him. James was his best friend, as well as his boss, and there was nothing he could do for him. She coughed, and they all looked at her. "Mr North, if I may, Miss Jones loves you. She just needs time to understand what happened. She used her safe word—that doesn't mean she's finished with you. Matthew taught me that it means a break for reflection and understanding."

Sonia looked back over to the figure that loomed large in the doorway. Matthew had an adoring smirk on his face. It made her heart leap.

"Miss Anderson's right," Grayson spoke next, and everyone turned their heads to him. "Matthew, how far is my club from here?"

"Half an hour, Sir."

"Miss Anderson is trained?" Grayson raised an eyebrow as he spoke. Why did he need to know if she was trained? She was a bodyguard. Of course, she was trained!

"She's learning."

"Sophie, take Miss Anderson and help her dress. You as well. Wear my favourite outfit. Mr Carter will send any requirements he has to you both shortly. James, Matthew, both of you get changed as well. I think a long shower is required for you, James."

"I'm not going to the club!" James folded his arms across his chest as Sophie got up and came over to Sonia.

While the men continued to argue, Sonia leant in and whispered to Sophie.

"Why are we going to a club? Are we going to try and find James another woman?"

"Nothing of the sort. Gray asked about you being trained?"

"Yes, I'm a bodyguard. I had training."

"Not that sort of training."

"What sort then?"

"BDSM. I have a feeling my fiancé wants to remind my brother of the rules of being a dominant lover."

"Miss North? How will this help Mr North?"

"Please, call me Sophie. We all have issues that we keep inside." She looked towards the men as James finally, and very reluctantly, agreed. Matthew allowed him out of the room to change. "It takes a certain knowledge to find it and help guide someone to overcome it. That doesn't only work between Dom and submissive. It works on all levels."

TWELVE

Matthew

Matthew pulled Sonia closer, as they walked into the club. She may not be collared, but she was his, and nobody was going to get close to her. James went straight to the bar and ordered a large whisky. The two-drink rule was going to be a problem later on.

James had made it clear he was not here to play, and as soon as Matthew and Grayson disappeared into rooms, he was out of there. Matthew wasn't entirely aware of what Grayson was trying to do. He just hoped he did it quickly and that it worked.

Matthew took a seat on a plush, black leather sofa and motioned for Sonia to sit beside him. She hadn't spoken since they entered the club, but her eyes had been flickering between various scenes that were going on around them. Sophie took a seat at Grayson's feet.

"So, what're you planning? He won't scene."

"He might not have a choice." Matthew wasn't sure he liked the look that crossed Grayson's face.

"Sophie. While I talk with Matthew and James, why don't you take Sonia and show her around? Stay with her at all times. If she gets into any trouble, your punishment will be denial. Do you understand?"

"Yes, Master."

"Do you want to go, Sonia?"

"I'd like to look." She bowed her head as he took her hands. She raised her eyes up from under her long lashes. He slid his hand under one of the slashes in the sleeveless top she had on. The top was covered in them and gave an illusion to her breasts being covered. In fact, if she moved in the wrong way anybody would be able to see them as she had no bra on. Her nipples were hard already as he alternately took them in his hand and twisted.

"Stay close to Sophie. You don't have permission to speak except to her."

He removed his hand, and she whimpered from the lost contact.

"Yes, Master."

Matthew watched them walk away.

"When are you going to let me in on the plan? Especially since it seems to involve my property."

"Have you whipped her before? I appear to remember that's your forte."

He had, a few times. She enjoyed it.

"Yes."

Grayson shook his head, and James took a seat near them.

"Your club's rules are shit. Tell them I want another drink."

"The two-drink maximum is for everyone's protection. There are no exceptions to the rules."

"I might as well go home then."

"You'll stay. We're just starting the evening."

From behind them, a commotion started up. Several women screamed, and a loud thud echoed around the vaulted ceiling. It was the direction Sophie and Sonia had headed in. Matthew jumped to his feet. Grayson stood a little more casually. James didn't move at all.

A muscular man dressed in only a leather loincloth rushed over to them.

"Master Grayson. Master Noah needs you at once."

"Of course. James, Matthew, would you care to join me? I suspect I need to officiate something. I could use your input."

Matthew stomach sank. He clenched his fists, because he was very close to smashing them into Grayson's face. He followed Grayson, and as the sea of observers parted, he saw Sonia being held back by Noah from a Dom who was laid flat out on the floor. He rushed over to her and pulled her away.

"Hands off her."

"Is she yours?" Noah said as he bent down to assist the beleaguered Dom up from the floor.

"She is."

"Is she not collared?"

"Not yet!" Matthew gritted his teeth as he searched Sonia for signs of injury or distress.

"She shouldn't have been left alone, then." The man who'd been on the floor brushed himself down as he spoke. Matthew glared at him as he turned his attention to Sonia.

"What happened?"

"I was watching a couple on a cross, and he started speaking to me. I couldn't answer him, as you said I couldn't talk. I didn't want to disobey you. I turned to Sophie to get her to talk to him, but she was talking to someone else. When I did, he tried to grab me. My instincts kicked in, and I flipped him onto the floor. I'm sorry. I didn't know what else to do."

"Shush. It's okay." He pulled her into his chest in comfort.

"How was I supposed to know she couldn't speak? She wasn't collared and was standing alone. This isn't my fault. When I touched her, she should have dropped to the floor. I demand punishment for her." The man turned to Grayson. "You have rules here, after all."

It suddenly dawned on Matthew what was going on. Grayson had set this all up.

"Not happening!" He wrapped his arms around the shivering woman nestled against him.

"Master Grayson, if he's her Dom and doesn't allow the punishment, I want his membership revoked."

"Revoke it?" Whatever game Grayson had in his mind, Matthew was playing along correctly, judging by the smirk on the owner's face.

"I don't think I can do that. After all, his employer requires it for his job." Everyone turned to look at James who was casually leaning against a spanking horse.

"Doesn't bother me. Not if it means I can go home."

"But what about when you need to bring clients here, James? Your bodyguard wouldn't be able to carry out his job."

"Just do it Matthew, and then, we can go home." James let out a frustrated moan. Sonia clinched harder to Matthew's chest.

"I'm sorry, Sir, but I'll not punish my woman for something that's my fault."

"It would seem we have a stalemate then. No one will be leaving anytime soon. Not until we can sort this out. I suggest we all take a seat and allow others to continue their scenes."

Sonia lifted her head and looked straight into Matthew's eyes. Her dark eyes were watery with unshed tears. Matthew shook his head again.

"Oh, for fuck's sake. What punishment do you want? I'll do it." James stepped forward and spoke to the man who'd been wronged. So this was Grayson's game.

"I think ten lashes with a bullwhip. James, you've trained on them?"

Matthew clenched his fists. He wasn't sure he could watch this, let it happen.

"Yes, I have. Matthew, put Sonia over the bench."

"Are you not going to ask my permission to do this?" Matthew asked.

"Do I need it?"

Matthew met Sonia's eyes and leant to whisper in her ear.

"Sonia, you can use your safe word at any time if you don't want to do this."

"Can you stay with me?"

"I'm going nowhere. You're going to need to remove your clothes."

"People will see…"

"At this moment, no woman in this room can match you."

Matthew kept Sonia as close as possible and helped her remove her top and trousers. Small gasps came from the crowd, when they saw the marks on her legs.

"At least no one's looking at my breasts or vagina." She let out a little giggle before looking down at the floor. Matthew led her over to the bench and placed her so her back was facing James, who already had the flogger in hand, twisting it in practice.

"Keep your eyes focused on me. James'll want you to count. I'll help you. It'll be a bit more painful than we have used before, and he doesn't know your body as I do but…"

"It's okay." She interrupted him. "I'm ready," Sonia spoke to Grayson but kept her eyes on his.

Grayson addressed the crowd, " Miss Anderson has consented to punishment for disrespecting a Master. She'll be given ten lashes by Master James. Master Noah, you speak for this gentleman. Does he accept the punishment?

"Yes, he does."

"You may begin then." Grayson nodded to James who pulled his arm back.

"Maybe you should think that she's Amy." Sophie spoke just as James started to bring the flogger down. The world seemed to turn in slow motion to Matthew as he saw James stop his movement. The recognition dawning on James' face as the tendrils fell gently onto Sonia's back. Her eyes went wide. He was around the side of the bench, and she was in his arms before the flogger even hit the floor. James sagged to the ground. Sophie wrapped her arms around him as Grayson stood over them.

"Matthew, take Sonia to my private room upstairs. Noah, let him in please. Anything they want ensure they have it. We'll look after James."

Matthew could hear his heart almost beating out of his chest as the adrenaline flooded him. Noah led them away.

"They broke him." She whispered so softly that Matthew barely heard it.

"He'll be better now."

"Did you know what the plan was?"

"I guessed it the second I saw the Dom on the floor."

The door to a velvety, plush room was opened. A king-size bed lay in the middle, and mirrors adorned several of the walls and ceiling. Grayson had good taste. Matthew set Sonia on the bed and tucked her into the Egyptian cotton bedding to keep her warm. He went back to the door to talk to Noah.

"How did you get the Dom to agree to that?"

"He owed Grayson. He didn't have much choice. Your woman has good moves."

"Don't get any ideas."

"Grayson says you can have the room for the night. He has men outside to watch the family. You won't be disturbed. Ring if you need anything."

"Thanks, Noah." Matthew shut the door on the outside world. It was just him and Sonia alone together in the room. He sat on the bed, and she reached out to him. He couldn't help but stare at her.

"What? Do I have something on my face?"

"Sorry. I can't believe you didn't use your safe word."

"I didn't need to. I knew that you would take me out of there if it meant I would be hurt."

"That flogger isn't a lightweight one."

"Show me?"

"Don't be silly."

"I'm not." She dropped the sheet, and it pooled around her knees as she knelt on the bed with her seductive curves displayed. "When I removed my clothes, I thought of how horrible my scars looked."

"You did?" He raised his eyebrow. "Well, that does deserve some sort of punishment."

"Please, Master."

"Bend over, Sonia. It's time to play."

THIRTEEN

Sonia

Sonia managed to hide the trembling in her hands the entire time, but now she was alone with Matthew she didn't have to. As she knelt before him naked, it wasn't fear causing her shivers but more the anticipation of what was to come. He'd used soft floggers on her before. The sight of the one that James had held up had sent an electric pulse of desire down her spine.

"Sonia, I'm not going to use the one James was about to employ on you. I'm not prepared to go that far yet. What I'll use, though, will leave marks. Are you sure you're ready for that?"

She nodded.

"I need to hear you say it."

"I'm ready, Master."

"Good girl."

"Would you've stopped James if he went to hit me?"

"He isn't just my boss, Sonia. He's also my closest friend. I want nothing more than for him to be back to the man he was rather than the shell he's been the last few months, but there are limits. I had to let Grayson's little plan run its course as much as I could. But I promise you, James North wouldn't have left a mark on your skin. That's my job. I don't share my responsibilities, when it comes to you."

"I think I like that answer." And she did. Matthew broke her from her thoughts with a kiss to her forehead, stopping her in front of a wall that contained a St. Andrew's cross.

"I'm going to strap you to this. How are you feeling?"

Sonia looked at the strange contraption. "Green."

"Place your arms in the loops, and I'll secure you."

Sonia did as instructed. Matthew wrapped the soft leather cuffs around her wrists and ankles. This was a little nerve-wracking, but excitement was also beginning to build, a heat coiling within her. She couldn't see what Matthew was doing, but she could hear him remove his jacket and shirt. Suddenly, his fiery breath was on the back of her neck, and the hairs on her arms stood like a salute to their master.

"I'm going to use a knotted flogger on you. It'll leave marks, but I'll take care of you after. Ten, for doubting your beauty again. I want you to count. I need you to stay with me."

"I'll count."

"Pardon?" Matthew's brought his large hand down hard on her pert backside, the reverberation of lust pulsed through her.

"I'll count, Master." Her answer was breathless.

His closeness was gone. She heard the swish through the air, and when the pain exploded over her buttocks, she realised he already had his tool of choice in his hand.

"One."

"Louder. I need to be able to hear you clearly." The knotted tendrils came down again.

"Two."

"Do you understand you're being punished because you doubted your beauty?" The leather met her flesh twice more in quick succession as he spoke.

"Three. Four. You tell me I am beautiful, and I shouldn't doubt your judgement."

The next four lashes came with only the count spoken between them. Sonia's mind was fading into the realm of pain and the oh-so-beautiful pleasure she was feeling, but her consciousness of the number brought her back. The heat of her arousal pooled between her legs, and the tender spot between her legs ached for his touch. This was more intense than any of the previous play they'd engaged in. The final lash came down, and as she screamed out ten, she heard the flogger drop to the floor, and Matthew's lips met her inflamed skin. He trailed lower, caressing her body. He massaged her buttocks.

He dipped two fingers inside her and angled the rest to circle the engorged nub of her sex. Within seconds, she was screaming out his name as she came in an explosion. As she slowly came down from her high, Matthew withdrew his hand and eased her into his arms as he undid the cuffs binding her to the cross. He laid her out on the bed on her stomach and reached over to the bedside table to take a bottle of oil. Silently, he smoothed it into her body. She let out a moan of contentment as he returned the bottle to the table.

"How are you feeling?"

"Like I am floating. I found it so hard to count. I just wanted to drift away."

"Subspace."

Sonia turned onto her side to face Matthew.

"Do you want me to help you dress, so I can take you home?"

Sonia opened her eyes wide and looked at Matthew in confusion.

"Home?"

"Yes. It's where we live. Big House, Knightsbridge address. Owned by a grumpy boss."

"But I thought?"

Matthew got up from the bed, Sonia couldn't help but notice the rather visible bulge in his leather trousers.

"It's too soon."

Sonia sat up, her bottom smarting a little as she did so.

"Too soon. But earlier you said you were going to take my virginity? What has changed?" There was an angry tone to her voice. She couldn't understand why not more than half an hour ago he wanted to sleep with her, but now, he didn't. Maybe she wasn't what he wanted? But the tent in his pants? It was probably just the flogging that turned him on, not Sonia herself. Matthew turned away towards the door.

"I'll wait outside."

"Don't bother. I'll get a taxi back."

Before she could collect the rest of her clothes, she was thrown back against the wall, one of Matthew's large hands massaging a naked breast. His erection grinding into her still thigh as he growled.

"Is that what you think? I want to go out there and fuck someone else?"

"Well, you won't fuck me, despite promising. I obviously did something wrong." She turned her head away, as he tried to kiss her. She wanted nothing more than to kick him in that hard swelling, inching closer to the cleft between her legs, but her stupid body betrayed her as the moisture of her arousal started to flow again. He twisted her around and landed a hard smack on her inflamed skin.

"I told you never to doubt yourself. Doubt again, and I'll tan this rosy rear so that you really won't be able to sit tomorrow. I want you so much, but I don't want to hurt you. I don't make love. I fuck. I can't guarantee that I won't hurt you, and that scares the shit out of me!"

She didn't know where it came from, but she let out a little laugh. He smacked her arse again.

"I don't think that's funny."

"I don't either." She tried to shift in his arms, but he was holding her too tight. "I don't want tender love-making, Matthew. I want you to fuck me 'til I am raw and marked as only yours."

"I can't do it. I can't hurt you on your first time."

"Unless I have a first time, you'll never be able to fuck me."

"I am scared I'll break you."

"You saved me. You can never break me."

Sonia dropped to her knees before him as she spoke.

"Please Master, may I suck you?"

"What?" He looked up from whatever point he had been studying on the floor.

"You won't fuck me, but I won't leave you like this." She placed her hand over the tented trousers. "Please."

He nodded his head in agreement, and Sonia reached to undo his belt. Slowly, she moved onto the buttons and undid them before lowering his trousers to the floor. She slipped her hand under the cotton of his tight boxer shorts and freed his cock. It was the first time she'd seen it. Everything they'd done in the past had been for her. It was a beautiful length and certainly wide. The purple crown stood proudly, searching for a much-needed relief. She leant in and licked the tip of her tongue up the shaft.

It was salty to taste. She murmured her delight to finally give him pleasure.

Matthew placed his hand on her head. "Flick over the head and back down to my balls. I love my balls being sucked."

Sonia did as he asked. She took one at a time into her mouth, and he groaned. "Oh God. Your mouth was made for this. For doing this to me. Take my cock in."

She opened her mouth wide, and slowly, she brought him as far in as she could. He touched the back of her throat, and she gagged a little.

"We can work up to that, my little dove. For now, just be comfortable. It still feels like heaven for me." That gave her confidence, and she began to move up and down his rigid length.

"Play with my balls."

She obeyed, cupping the sensitive jewels.

"Yes, oh yes. That's it." His hand tangled into her hair as he started to lose himself to the feeling. He was controlling her pace, now, but never pushed her further than she could go. Perspiration beaded on his head.

"I'm going to come. Pull back if you don't want to take it."

.Sonia made no move, other than to continue her assault on his cock.

The first spurt hit the back of her throat, and she watched as he thrust his head back and closed his eyes in ecstasy. She swallowed as much of him down as she could. When he was finished, she released him with a pop, and he sunk to his knees beside her.

"That was. That was the best feeling ever."

Sonia secretly felt very proud of herself, but she needed to follow through on the second part of her plan.

"Matthew, take me now, please."

FOURTEEN

Matthew

Those words, that plea, the eyes staring at him full of longing. How could he deny her what she wanted? He flipped her onto her back and thrust straight in. So wet, so tight, she was constricting him like a vice. Sonia cried out as he pierced the barrier to her purity.

Shit.

What was he doing?

Not like this.

He withdrew quickly and threw himself away from the bed. His head banging against the wall in rhythm with his curses. Fuck, Fuck, Fuck. He should leave. He should get out right now. He couldn't look at her.

"I'm sorry." Sonia's voice finally broke the air of tension in the room.

"You're sorry?" He looked up at her.

"It was only a moment of pain. I shouldn't have cried out like that."

"Don't you apologise for what happened. That was completely my fault."

"But I asked you to do it."

"And I should have done it better, taken my time, been gentle."

"Matthew, I don't want careful. I want you, not what you think you should be to me. I'm a big girl, now." She smiled at him. "I can handle it, and if I can't, I'll tell you."

"Trust."

"Trust. Now, where were we." He let go of her chin, and she reached out to touch his now deflated cock. It thickened instantly.

"I need to stop letting lower brain take over."

"No, the exact opposite. Switch your brain off and let him do what he needs to do."

He raised an eyebrow at her and watched her melt into the bed with desire. "Lay down."

She gripped the cotton sheet. Her legs parted, giving him a view of her sex, already flushed and glistening for him. He stood before her and stroked the full length of cock, working from the tip all the way to the trunk, which joined to the rest of his body. He bent and pulled a condom from the pocket of his trousers. She watched him tear it open with his teeth and cover his massive length.

Placing himself at her entrance, he risked a look at her face. Her fists were scrunched so tightly he could see the whites of her knuckles.

"Matthew?" The words were breathless and pleading. Taking his time, he pushed slowly inside her again. Her heat was a welcoming cocoon with each inch that he pressed in. Finally, he was in to the hilt. He stilled, waiting for her to adjust to his size.

"So full. Move. Please." Her head fell back against the pillow, and she let out a long moan that reverberated through her body to his cock.

He leant forward and brought his mouth to hers, their lips and tongues tangling together at a frenzied pace. He was lost in her. Sweetly innocent but the vibrant tang of hunger invaded his nostrils, adding to the blood pumping rapidly around his body and into his dick. He quickened his pace while moving his mouth over the line of her chin, nibbling his way down her neck, across her collarbone and to her breasts. The small peaks were hard, and he flicked at one with his tongue before sinking his teeth into the deep red nipple.

"Fuck." His balls tightened.

She dug her nails deep into his skin, when he shifted and hit the tender spot inside her. He bit down on her shoulder, his teeth sinking into the tender flesh marking her as his and his alone.

"Get there Sonia, touch yourself. I can't hold on much longer."

He felt her tiny fingers slide between them and stroke her clit. He quickened his pace. His balls slapped against her arse with every thrust.

He met her eyes. She flew over the edge; he watched her. It wasn't until the last second that her eyes rolled back in her head, shuddering all around him. It was all he needed, and he followed her over. Growling out her name while filling the condom to bursting point. He could barely breathe. His heart beat so fast that he could hear it ringing in his ears. She whimpered, when he gently withdrew. With wobbly legs, he got to his feet, tied off the condom, and threw it into his bag on the floor. He would dispose of it later. There was a bin for that sort of stuff, but he'd never left his DNA behind. Force of habit from the job.

In the corner of the room stood a sink and fresh towels. He turned the water on, tested its temperature, and wetted the cloth. Sonia still laid on the bed, her chest lifting and falling rapidly trying to catch her breath. He wiped her clean. This room was equipped for most eventualities, and he took some ice from the fridge's freezer and wrapped it in a fresh towel. Tenderly, he placed it between her legs, but she winced.

"Keep it there for a while. It'll help with the discomfort."

He climbed into the bed next to her and lay her gently out on his chest.

"Thank you," She murmured, half awake, half asleep.

"What for?"

"The best night of my life."

"I think I should be thanking you. You talked me down this time."

A knock at the door. He pulled the sheets over them.

"Yes?"

It opened slightly, and Sophie stuck her head in.

"Sorry to disturb you, Master Matthew, but James wishes to return home soon. Do you want Master Grayson to see if he can allocate one of his guards to him for the night?" Despite protocol in the club, James asked that Sophie never called him a Master. As Grayson owned the majority of it, nobody argued with him.

"Tell your Master that Miss Anderson and I'll escort James home. We'll dress and be out in a minute."

Sonia rose her head and looked towards Sophie. As she was slightly in front of him, Matthew couldn't see the look on Sonia's face, but he saw the wink and smile from Sophie.

"Return to your Master Sophie, or I'll have him enact a rather unfulfilling punishment on you."

She rolled her eyes.

"I was just checking on my girl. You're a big man Matthew."

Sonia laughed and laid back down on his chest.

"Your girl's fine. Now go."

She shut the door. Thankfully, the rooms were well sound proofed, or he was sure he'd have heard her telling everyone that they'd finally done it. There were never any sexual secrets between them all. He liked that, though. Lord knows he kept enough other secrets. It was nice just to be honest for once.

"I don't know if I have the energy to get dressed." Sonia hummed into his peck while tracing an imaginary circle around the other. "I wish we could just stay here."

He got out of the bed and looked around for his clothes.

"I'll help you dress in a minute and undress again when we get home. You just rest. You're off duty."

"I can dress myself." She moved the covers back and laid the iced towel down on the bed.

"Listen to your Master, little Miss Stubborn."

She bit her lip.

"Maybe I should let you dress me. It seems my legs have gone to jelly."

"Told you." He retrieved a bottle of water from the fridge and handed it to her. "Drink this."

"Thank you." She took the water, and he put his shirt back on. Sonia watched him the entire time. He picked up her clothes and went over to her.

"Arms up."

He pulled her top over her head. He leant forward and kissed each of her breasts before lowering the silky fabric. Her legs dangled over the edge of the bed, so it was easy to pull her trousers on. He supported her while she stood again and secured them at her waist. She started to shiver. She'd wear no jacket 'til they got outside, so he pulled the blanket from the end of the bed and wrapped it around her shoulders. "Keep that over you, 'til I can get your coat."

"Thank you, Master."

"No more Master, now. Just Matthew."

"Thank you, Matthew."

A little tear tumbled down her cheek.

"What's wrong?"

"Nothing. I'm happy. I feel..." She hesitated on the final word. He searched her, waiting for the answer. "I feel normal."

He brought her chin up and laid a tender kiss on her lips.

"I love you," she whispered. The words were there. They were on the edge of his lips. He opened his mouth to speak. To say them. "I know there's still more to learn, and you'll tell me when you're ready. I know until then that you can't reply to what I just said, but the look in your eyes, just then, told me everything I need to know." She kissed him this time, and he let out the breath he didn't realise he'd been holding.

"We'd better go, before Sophie's sent back in to see if we have gone to sleep. I don't want to be responsible for my cheeky friend being denied an orgasm. Not now I know how good they can be."

"Move into my apartment with me? I don't want to spend any time away from you if I can help it." The words flowed from his lips, before he even realised.

"Let's get home and get some sleep. We can talk about that in the morning when we're not in a blissful post sexual haze."

He nodded then scooped her up into his arms.

"As long as you stay with me tonight."

FIFTEEN

Sonia

Sonia rolled over in the bed. The ache between her thighs reminded her of what had happened last night.

"Do you need more ice?"

Matthew pulled her into his arms and kissed the top of her head.

"I think I'll be okay."

"I didn't do my job properly, then. I'll do better tonight." He chuckled, and she patted lovingly at his chest. See looked over at the clock.

"We better get up. James'll want to go to the office soon."

"He knows you stayed the night. Don't worry, he'll work from home 'til I'm ready to take him." He still hadn't opened his eyes.

"What? You're supposed to be at James' beck and call."

"You're worried. Tell me."

"My position here is rather precarious. Miranda doesn't really need me, and with Amy gone..."

"And coming back soon if I have my way."

"Let me finish."

"James doesn't need me, and I like this job. The family." She lowered her voice, "You being around daily. I don't want to lose it by doing something mundane like staying in bed with you if James doesn't like it. That's why I need time to consider you asking me to move in here."

"You're anxious about this aren't you?"

"I feel settled for the first time in my life. I'm so scared of losing that. I'm torn, Matthew. I want to wake up every morning with your arms wrapped around me. But I'm so afraid of losing what I have."

He let out a long sigh and threw back the sheets. Getting out of the bed, he pulled on a pair of jogging bottoms, which were over the back of a chair in the corner of the room. Next, he went to his wardrobe and pulled out a t-shirt and shorts.

"Put these on." He handed her the clothes. The t-shirt would be a dress on her; the shorts were probably not needed.

"Why?" She took the clothes and started to dress.

"Breakfast."

"How's that going to solve my worries?"

"You'll see."

"You keep saying that."

"That's why I'm the Dom, and you're my very willing submissive."

She huffed.

"Who knows as many fancy moves as you to lay you flat out on the floor."

"Try it." He held his arms up welcoming her to attack him.

Matthew followed her out of the bedroom and led her into the kitchen. James was sitting at the breakfast table, studying The Times intently while sipping his coffee. Matthew escorted her to the table.

"Wait there." He left her alone and disappeared into the lounge.

James looked up. She was suddenly very nervous at being dressed in only Matthew's t-shirt and oversized boxer shorts in the middle of her boss' kitchen. James smiled at her, and she embarrassingly returned the greeting. Matthew returned with a cushion, pulled an antique wooden chair out from the table and put the pillow down on it. "Sit."

"If she's sitting on a cushion, I don't need to ask if you two had a good evening."

Matthew took a seat next to her and growled at James in response.

"James Thomas North, you leave them alone." Sonia jumped a little when Miranda suddenly appeared from inside the walk-in larder. "Good morning, Matthew, Sonia. What can I get you?"

"Coffee, please," Matthew grunted then looked over to her.

"Um. I."

"She'll have a coffee as well, Mrs North, a splash of milk, no sugar." Matthew reached out under the table and took hold of her leg. She almost jumped out of her skin. "It's okay." His tone was soft and calming; though, his eyes conveyed so much more. Her heart stopped beating like it was a freight train on a collision course and returned to a more natural speed.

"A coffee would be good. Is there anything I can help you with Mrs North?"

"Not at all. You relax. If I need help, James can get up. You're a guest here."

Matthew cleared his throat, James furrowed his brows and looked between them.

"Actually, that's something I wanted to talk to you about."

"You didn't win." Grayson's deep masculine voice complained while he led his fiancée into the kitchen.

"I did, too."

"Morning everyone." Sophie breezed over to a seat and Grayson pulled it out for her. Sonia watched as the youngest North sibling smiled up at her fiancé. He took a bowl from her place setting and piled it with fruit from the exotic salad in the centre of the table. He was careful to make sure he took no blueberries. Sonia remembered that Miss North didn't like them. Grayson placed the bowl down in front of Sophie and handed her a croissant.

"Make sure you eat it all. We had a good workout last night."

"Please, I don't need to hear that when I'm eating my toast." James took a bite and made fake gagging noises.

"He meant at the gym big brother. We went before the club."

Grayson and Miranda took their seats, and everyone started to help themselves to food from the table. Sonia had never seen such a spread, fruit, croissants, pancakes, cereals, toast with various homemade jams, yoghurts, there were even sausages, bacon and eggs. She sat there feeling a little awkward. Should she just help herself? Grayson had given Sophie her food. This wasn't her home. Matthew leant forward and handed her some toast. He smiled and told her if she wanted anything else to help herself.

"Matthew, you had something you wanted to say?" James spiked at a sausage while his gaze remained firmly fixed on her.

"I hope it's that he's going to take poor Sonia shopping later to get her some decent clothes for when she stays. I remember the first time I stayed at Grayson's. He offered me his dirty pants to put on. They better be clean clothes she's wearing, Matthew Carter."

She wished the ground would open up and swallow her at everyone's comments. She'd spent most of her life just having a bowl of cereal alone in her flat, to have everyone chatting and knowing that she spent last night in Matthew's bed was just utterly embarrassing.

"Sophie, quiet." Grayson silenced his fiancé with one word. "Let Matthew speak."

Matthew moved his hand from her thigh and took her shaking hand in his. "Boss, I was wondering if it'd be okay if Sonia moved into my rooms with me?"

"We'll all help her pack and move her belongings in today. It's about time." He popped the sausage into his mouth while continuing to grin.

Miranda came around to Sonia's side of the table and cuddled her.

"It's about time. I'm so happy for you both. You're a proper part of the family now."

Sonia could feel tears starting to form in her eyes. She snuffled.

"Oh no, no tears. This is happy news. Well, it will be, when you get out of those clothes and into something a bit more stylish!" Sophie laughed then clapped her hands together in excitement. "I know! We can go back to the club tonight and celebrate. Master?" Sonia's eyes widened in fear of what was going to come out of the excitable Miss North's mouth. "Could Sonia and I scene together with you and Master Matthew? It's been so long since we've done a scene with anyone."

"I don't think in front of your mother and brother is the place to discuss that." Grayson rose an eyebrow.

That was all Sonia could take.

"I'm sorry. I need the bathroom." She jumped up from the table and fled back to Matthew's room. He appeared at the door a few seconds after she'd thrown herself on the bed trying to catch her breath.

"Breathe in for four and out for four. Slowly. Focus on your breath." He sat down on the bed next to her.

"Did that just happened?" she spoke through gulps of air.

"Normal breakfast in the North household, I'm afraid."

"They're so open. With everything."

"Yes. For a family that hid behind so many secrets for years, they're pretty casual. What do you say?"

"To what?" She finally had her breathing under control. Well, as controlled as it was going to be with Matthew moving his hand up and down her leg in reassurance.

"To all of it. Moving in. The club bit if you fancy it."

What did she say to all of that?

She then looked over to Matthew, who sat calmly on the bed, his eyes focused intently on her. "Yes to it all."

SIXTEEN

Matthew

"How about this one?" Sophie held up a tight, and incredibly short, leather dress. Sonia shook her head furiously, so the young Miss North threw the garment onto the ever-growing pile of discarded clothes. Grayson, standing in the corner and supported by the door frame, groaned and went back to texting on his phone. Matthew had been sitting in the same comfortable armchair for an hour now. He, Sophie, and Grayson were dressed and ready to go, but Sonia was still in a dressing gown.

"Grayson, Sophie, can you give us a minute please? What's wrong with the dresses?"

"Nothing."

"You know what happens when you lie."

"I didn't. I didn't lie."

"Sonia."

"I didn't lie, I promise you. There's nothing wrong with the dresses. They're perfect for Sophie, but there just not me."

"Wait here." He strode out of the room and called for James. His boss appeared from his study where he was working late after spending the day helping with the move. James had decided that last night had been enough at the club.

"What's wrong?"

"I need a favour. It's a big one. Please say no if you don't feel up to it."

"I don't want to go to the club."

"No, it isn't that." Matthew ran his hand nervously through his hair.

"What is it?"

"The clothes you had me buy Amy—I remember a bright red corset and matching leather leggings."

James swallowed.

"I'm sorry. Forget it. I'll sort something else." He turned to go back to where Sonia was.

"Matthew. Take them."

"I can't."

"Red isn't Amy's colour, anyway. I don't know why I suggested it. Red suits Sonia much better."

"Amy will return. You two—you're meant for each other. I'll go check on her, talk to her. Or I could send Sonia."

"No. I know you know where she is, but I don't want to know. When she's ready. When we're both ready. It'll happen." Matthew thought he could see tears forming in his boss's eyes. "Anyway. Enough of the girly stuff. Go get the clothes and dress up your woman. Have a great night and try not to think of me slaving away at work."

"Yeah, don't worry. I won't think of you at all." He fired back.

After collecting the clothes, he took them back to Sonia. "Are these better?"

"I love you. They're perfect. They're me. I know I'll get naked in the club, and I can handle that, but when I'm just there, I need to hide my scars. They're a part of me and what makes me beautiful. I know that, so I don't need a flogging to remind me, but I don't know. I just feel more comfortable in trousers than dresses or skirts."

"Get dressed. I'll send Sophie back in. Grayson and I need to plan."

"That sounds worrying." She picked up the leather leggings and put one foot in the hole.

"No, that sounds promising." He turned to leave.

"Matthew?"

"Yes?"

"I'm going to like living with you. Having someone."

He smiled. He was going to like it also. It had been a long time since he had someone like that. Ever since...no, not tonight. This was Sonia's time. He wouldn't make the same mistakes again.

∼

"Master?" Sophie asked Grayson, "Are Sonia and I both bottoms tonight or is one of us topping?" They'd just finished a discussion on safe words and had installed the traffic light system.

Grayson shrugged his shoulders, "Matthew, what do you think?"

He didn't know. Sonia definitely had the makings of a switch, but the fact that her hand was trembling in his worried him that she wouldn't cope with Sophie's mischievous nature. She tugged on his hand.

"Master."

"You may speak." They'd been sitting in the bar area of the club for around an hour, now, just watching the scenes going on around them. A Dom was whipping his sub over a bondage bench. Another was strapping her rather excited sub into a cock and ball strap. He shuddered. It would be a cold day in hell before anyone did that to his balls. Well actually, when he was training, he allowed it to happen, but nobody dared look him in the face or say one word to him while it was attached. Sonia's voice drew him out of his disturbing reflection.

"If I top Sophie, that means I can be her Mistress doesn't it?"

"It does."

She looked thoughtful.

"Does Sophie like to be topped by women?"

"You may ask her."

"Sophie, do you like to be topped by women?"

Sophie looked up at Grayson from her kneeling position at his feet. "May I answer her, please?"

Grayson let out a belting laugh. "That tells you the answer there, Sonia." Matthew shook his head. He knew that his friend's fiancée was behaving for a particular reason. "You may answer her."

"I'd like it very much if you'd top me."

"I don't believe that was the question you were asked, but you're trying so hard to be good that I'll let it go." Sophie turned to look at Sonia again.

"In answer to your question, I'd like to be topped by a woman very much."

"Shall we take this discussion somewhere a little bit more private?" Matthew put his arm protectively around Sonia's shoulders.

"Yes, please, Master, may we?" Sophie was now almost bouncing on her knees.

Grayson led the way through the throng of spectators, watching the scenes.

"We'll go to my private room. I think Sonia was on display enough for your liking last night."

She certainly had been. He was glad this was going to be done in seclusion. It was still a steep learning curve for his young sub, and he didn't want to scare her off.

Grayson opened the door to his room. He tended to work with James in clubs, although he'd witnessed several of Grayson's and Sophie's scenes before. Grayson was a true Master of his art. The room was tastefully decorated in natural fibres with a definite Native American vibe. Despite his past, Grayson was very close to his native roots. He was born into the Navajo tribe, and for many years was known as Gini, or Hawk, as it was translated. Matthew didn't know the full reasons behind why he left and became the famous actor he did, but even though Grayson never spoke of it, he always adhered to his ancestral beliefs.

"Sophie, undress Sonia please," Grayson spoke, but Matthew nodded his approval. They'd had a brief discussion earlier on how the evening would go. It wasn't going to be about the men. It was going to be about worshipping the two perfect women they had. The girls had agreed with much enthusiasm.

"Yes, Master."

Grayson and Matthew took seats on leather chairs in the corner.

Sophie helped Sonia off with her corset. He was surprised to find her not self-conscious but proudly standing before them. Her trousers and thong were removed next, and she stood naked, her head held up high. Sophie folded the clothes up and placed them on the side. She returned to Sonia.

"Go back to your Master, please, so we can wait for his next instructions."

"Yes, Mistress."

He couldn't help but chuckle at the bright smile that washed over Sonia's face.

Matthew beckoned Sonia to him with a finger.

"On your knees before Grayson, but I want your back to him."

She obeyed.

"Sophie," Grayson spoke. "I want you to remove your clothes and kneel in front of Sonia."

"Yes, Master."

Matthew shifted his chair so that the two kneeling women were sandwiched between their seats. He could see Sonia's face and Grayson could see Sophie's.

"How sensitive are Sonia's breasts?" Grayson questioned him.

"What are you thinking?"

"Nipple clamps? Sophie looks so beautiful in them."

"Sonia." Grayson allowed him to take over.

"Yes, Master."

"If you would like to wear nipple clamps then you're to ask Sophie to put them on you. I want you to put them on Sophie, though. If you're not sure what to do then you're to ask Master Grayson. Do you understand?" He sat back in the chair, his feet placed firmly on the floor but his legs parted. He took a long sip of his warm brandy. Grayson handed the clamps to Sophie.

"Yes, Master. Sophie, I wish you to put the clamps on me, please. If you do me first then I'll assist you. Make us pretty for our Masters."

"Yes, Mistress. I like to be decorated for Master Grayson."

"Less chatter, more clamping."

Sophie lowered her head to Sonia's breast and circled her small tongue around the stiffening peak.

"Sweet like sugar. You smell of lavender."

"My favourite perfume."

Sophie ran the nipple through her fingers and placed the clamp over it. Sonia let out a moan. The second clamp was applied, the glazed look already washed over her face. He bet she was already dripping for him.

"Is she wet, Sophie?"

"Touch me and show my Master how much I weep for him already." His cock rammed into the zip of his leather trousers. His little lady had turned into a sex kitten.

"She's sodden. So ready for your cock already." Sophie brought her fingers up to show him where they glistened with arousal.

"Give your fingers to Master Matthew. Allow him to taste his submissive's desire for him." Grayson shifted forward in his seat, his massive forearms resting on his muscular thighs. Sophie brought her fingers to his mouth, and he twisted his tongue around Sonia's honeyed taste. Damn it was the best ever. His cock throbbed. He adjusted, and Grayson curled his lip in a playful smirk at the suffering Matthew was so obviously experiencing.

"My girl tastes so sweet. I think I need more."

Sophie pulled her fingers out of his mouth and went back to Sonia.

"Not yet. Wait."

"Sonia, turn around and get on all fours. I want to see my pussy. Sophie's clamps will have to wait."

"She'll be rewarded for her patience. She likes to give more than receive anyway." Grayson brought his lips down onto Sophie's in a promise of what she would get later.

Sonia adjusted her position to that which Matthew had asked her. Her most intimate parts were displayed for everyone in the room to see.

"Ask Master Matthew if you may taste his girl? On your knees, crawl to him. I want to watch your pussy while you do." Grayson gently threw her down.

Sophie crawled to Matthew, but he could barely pay attention to her when Sonia was on all fours.

"May I use my mouth on Sonia, Master."

"Yes." Her eyes darkened.

"Thank you."

His breathing became more rapid watching Sophie lick at Sonia's clit.

"She tastes so sweet. Best woman I've ever licked."

Sonia writhed under the touch. Small little groans floating from her lips, every one signalling how much she was enjoying what was happening to her.

"Anal?" Grayson asked. Sonia tightened, her eyes widened.

"I'm prepping, but we're taking things slowly."

"Plugs?"

"Yes."

"What size?"

"Slim."

"Sophie, get me some lube and the slim plug."

"Sophie. Grayson and I get hot when two women kiss. I want you to keep Sonia's mouth entertained. Sonia, I'm going to fuck you. Grayson's going to put the plug in your arse and play with it. We want you to feel full."

"I want all of that, please, Master. Especially your cock."

"May I play with her breasts and the clamps as well, Masters?"

"Good idea, Sophie. I'm in agreement if Grayson is."

"Yes." Grayson was busy rubbing the lube around the plug. "Do you want to put it in?"

"No, I'll go suit up."

"Condom?"

"We need to have the doctor's appointment."

"Go there tomorrow man. That pussy needs fucking bareback."

He pulled down his trousers and glided his hand up and down his rigid length a few times before placing the condom on. He was listening the whole time to Sonia, moaning as her puckered hole swallowed up the plug.

"Ready?" Grayson asked.

He nodded and placed himself at her entrance. In one long, slow thrust he pushed inside. He could feel the plug against his cock.

Sophie leant forward and tugged on one of Sonia's clamped nipples. Their mouths crashed at the same time, feminine delicacy abandoned to a burning desire. Boy, was that hot. He started to thrust. Grayson took the end of the plug, and as Matthew pushed his cock into her pussy, Grayson pulled the plug almost out of her anus. The three of them worked together, driving Sonia towards a rapid and explosive climax. Just as she came down, they sent her over again. She was thrashing, screaming so loudly, that despite the soundproofed walls, he was sure people would hear. On the third orgasm, he followed her over.

SEVENTEEN

Sonia

"Sonia, are you ready to go?" Matthew called out. She was busy searching through her chest of drawers.

"Five minutes. I just need to get Miranda's leaflets for her coffee morning." Where the hell were they? She'd been living with Matthew for a month now and had gotten far too comfortable already. There was nothing for it. She'd have to empty the entire drawer. Pulling it out, she turned it over and let the bits of paper, hairbands, random coins, odd cables, and a selection of keys and sweets tumble onto the floor. Frantically, she searched through the mess. "Where is it?"

"Sonia. What are you doing?" Matthew appeared at the door. He sighed and frowned at the chaos she'd created.

"What!" She exclaimed. "Everyone has that one drawer you put everything in for safekeeping. You have a whole cupboard." She waved her hands in the air towards the direction of his wardrobe.

"You can't find what you're looking for because I gave the leaflets to Miranda earlier. You put them out on the bed this morning."

"What?" The words spat out disbelievingly. "I don't remember that."

"Probably because you did it just after I'd had my tongue in that beautiful little pussy of yours."

She snarled at him. "You could've told me you were taking them. I've just spent the last ten minutes searching."

"What's this? Her Majesties Prisons?" The flushing receded at a dramatic pace to be replaced by a chill so cold she felt like she would freeze. He held up a piece of paper she knew only too well what it contained. "Sonia?"

"It's nothing." Everything was back in the drawer. She wanted to snatch the paper back from Matthew but knew better than to do that. She stood and started to put the drawer back.

"Drop the drawer now. Turn around and get on your knees. You're lying." Damn, Dom sixth sense. She was risking it, but she ignored him. This was foolish, and she'd never done it before, but now wasn't the time. They both had jobs to do. Shoving the drawer roughly back into place, she grabbed her bag and stormed from the room. Matthew stalked behind her down the corridor. She could feel the heat radiating off him. His nostrils were probably flaring that he had been ignored. She was so going to end up with a bright red arse and not in a good way. She couldn't talk about this, though. It was her past.

"Come on, Miranda. Let's go. I don't want you to be late for your meeting." She smiled cheerfully.

Mrs North senior went pale and swallowed. Miranda looked behind Sonia and took a step backwards.

"James, I think you better take me."

"Matthew?" James enquired.

"She's lied and isn't telling me something."

"I'll take mum and stay with her 'til you show up. Take as long as you need."

"Will do. I'll text you when we leave."

James and his mother left her and Matthew alone. Silence. Nothing except Sonia's heart trying to beat out of its chest and the aura surrounding Matthew threatening to explode. He prowled around her so that he stood in front of her, not behind her. She quickly looked down to the floor. He grabbed her chin and tilted it up so that she had no choice but to look at him.

"What is this?" He waved the paper at her.

This was nothing to do with him.

"I asked you a question."

"You have eyes, read it for yourself."

"Don't make your punishment worse. You're already at twenty for walking away from me."

"You can't spank me for this."

"Who's talking about spanking? I'm talking the whip."

She inhaled sharply.

"Last chance. What is this?"

Punishment with the whip meant that he wouldn't allow her to drift into subspace. He would make her count. She didn't like it when he did that.

"It's a visiting order."

"This was for last week. Did you go?"

"No." She looked back down to the floor.

"Lift your head and look at me." She was defeated and in the space where her brain had no choice but to tell her body to obey his commanding tone. Her head wouldn't move to look away, but she managed to shut her eyes.

"Open them." The darkness in his voice gave no leeway. The frustration she was feeling bubbled over. Her voice raised, and she spun round, storming back to the bedroom. "This is none of your business. I don't want to visit him, even if he sends me a hundred orders." She paused at the entrance to their bedroom. Her bag fell off her shoulder and slipped to the floor.

Her legs started to burn, the cuts calling her to open them. Matthew brought his muscular arms tightly around her. Sheltering her from the pain she was feeling. She struggled against him. Needing to get away. Needing pain, not comfort.

"I'm here." He whispered into her ear. "I'm here."

"He killed her."

"I know."

"I saw it all. The glass the way it cut her. The screams of agony mixing with his angry yells. His eyes, they were dead the entire time. Glossed over with the drink. He didn't even realise what he was doing."

"It's okay. I'm here."

"I can't visit him. I can't. How can he be my father? I can't even go back to the house, but I can't bring myself to sell it."

"Sorry?" His voice was confused.

"The house was signed over to me when I turned eighteen. He said he wanted me to have money should I need it. I was going to go there and clean it out before selling it but I couldn't. As far as I know, nobody has been there since the day my mother died."

"Twenty years ago."

"Yes."

"You're running away from your past. Trying to bury what happened in the sand. You'll never get over it until you face it. Sonia, you need to see your father and go back to the house."

She knew that she shouldn't feel this way, but that comment angered her.

"I'm running away from my past." She pulled out of his arms. It was a bit of a struggle as he was reluctant to let her go, but he seemed to sense the change in her mood. "Can you get any more hypocritical. At least I faced up to what happened in my past. You can't even admit you love me to my face, because you hide behind yours. You want to talk about burying the past then look no further than yourself." She stomped over the bed. She wasn't going to let him touch her. The bastard, one rule for her and another for him.

"There's a difference."

"How." She screamed at him.

He came forward and knelt at her feet. "I admit I hide behind my past. I know I can't say I love you, yet, because of it. But I don't want to bury my head in the sand any longer. Sonia, allow me to help you with this and then together we will work through what happened to me."

"Let's sort you first?"

"You know how stubborn I am. It has to be you first. I have to know that you'll be able to handle everything that I throw at you when I tell you what happened."

"That's just your male ego speaking. Fix the women first."

"I wish it were the case. But it isn't."

"I don't think I can see my father."

"You don't have to make that decision, yet. How about we go to the house first. See how you feel when you're there and see it again."

"I should sell it. Mum would hate her precious kitchen not being used for cooking. It's probably a wreck by now. I'll have to get someone in to decorate and check it all out structurally. It has been severely neglected for twenty years."

"I think we might know someone who can help us with that."

"Hand it over to James? Great idea. He can go and sort everything out instead of me."

"No, you need to go. You need to find closure."

"Damn you." She slid off the end of the bed and into his lap. "When do you want to go?"

"I'll arrange with James for us to go tomorrow."

"So soon."

"We have a lot to face. We need to do it before we change our minds."

"Ok, but no more talk of my father. I'm not ready to face him."

"Okay."

"We should get to James and Miranda."

"Not yet."

"Matthew."

"You lied, that requires punishment."

"Seriously?"

"Yes. Besides, I think Miranda'll absolutely love showing James off to all the lady friends. I can just picture all the cheek pinching he'll get. It'll do him good."

Sonia couldn't keep in a little chuckle at that thought.

"I'm sorry for not telling you about the visiting order. I've always just ignored them and put them in a drawer 'til I threw them away."

"We've both lived separate existences, insular in our needs, for far too long. It's going to take getting used to. We'll fight. I'll stomp and shout. You'll throw tantrums and slam drawers, but ultimately, we'll come back to this." He wrapped his arms around her and pulled her in for a kiss. "Now remove your clothes. I think I made it a count of thirty for disobedience."

"Really." She pushed back from him, her bottom smarting at the thought, but her core clenched with the knowledge of the pleasure it will bring. Matthew's voice turned dark.

"Now, Sonia."

This time she obeyed.

EIGHTEEN

Matthew

"I think I'm going to be sick." Matthew slammed on the brakes of the Harley-Davidson Lowrider. Sonia jumped off and whipped her helmet over her head. She flung it on the floor and bent over, the vile vomit projecting from her mouth onto the floor. He secured the bike, took a bottle of water along with some tissues, from in the storage compartment, and helped settle his poorly girlfriend. She was white as a sheet.

"I'm sorry." He could see that she was fighting back the tears.

"You've nothing to be sorry about."

"I'm so nervous."

"It's a big step you're taking. I'll be with you the entire time, though."

"I don't think I can do it."

"Do I need to give you a reminder of how strong you are?"

"No."

"Drink this." He passed her the water and wiped her forehead.

"Let's go." Before he could help Sonia to her feet, a Land Rover pulled up next to the bike. A tiny lady jumped out. Her mouth dropped, eyes wide she stumbled over to them.

"Aye, it be a ghost." The woman started to drop down to the ground, but he jumped up and caught her. "Sonia?"

"Yes."

"Thee be the spitting image of tha ma. God rest 'er soul."

"I know you?"

"Yer did. Mary Scott, I live on the farm next to yours. Thee going tha?"

Sonia nodded.

"I knew tha'd come back one day. Me husband and I've been looking after it.

Tha Ma would have hated to see it fall into disrepair. I can't believe how much yer look like 'er."

Sonia looked down. Matthew helped Mrs Scott to stand.

"I'm sorry. I don't know yer."

"I'm Matthew Carter, Sonia's partner."

"Pleasure to meet tha, Mr Carter."

"Matthew, please, Mrs Scott."

"Then, tha call me Mary."

"I will do."

"I'm just going to clean up a bit more. I won't be a minute. You head back to the car and bike. I'll follow."

"She okay, love?" Mary lowered her voice and leant into him to whisper her question as they returned to the vehicles.

"Nervous."

"Tha knows everything."

"I do."

"Poor child. I remember when they brought 'er out. So much blood. She just thought 'er Ma was sleeping."

"You've been looking after the house?"

"Her father sent me a letter from prison. He's such a wazzock. I 'ad a key to the house already. Told me 'e would sign it over to Sonia as soon as 'e could. Asked if we could look after it. Sell what we needed to cover the costs. We ran it as the farm it was. My son was sixteen. He's taken on most of the running of the place. We wondered about 'im moving in there, but it didn't feel right. I tried to find where she was, but I just couldn't. Is she 'ere to sell it?"

"I don't know, yet."

"I'll go ahead and unlock for thee. Then get out of the way. Come over to our place afterwards, love. 'I'll give thee tha tea an' tha's welcome t'stay"

"Thank you. I really appreciate that. But we can easily find a B&B. I don't want to trouble you."

"I'll get a bed med up for thee. It's no trouble."

"Thank you." Mary drove away. Sonia reappeared.

"I don't really have any photos of my mum. I have my memories of her, but I never thought I looked like her. I hope there are some at the house."

"I'm sure there will be. It sounds as though Mrs Scott and her family have really looked after the place."

"I'm glad of that."

"You ready to go?"

"As I'll ever be."

It didn't take them long to reach the house.

"It seems so much smaller than I remember."

"You were only seven when you were last here. Everything always seems smaller as an adult than to a child. You ready to go in?"

"If I said no, would we get back on the bike and go home?"

He gave her a look that told her the answer to that question.

"I didn't think so."

Matthew opened the door for her. The décor on the walls could do with a bit of a re-vamp, but the place was clean. He'd not been expecting that. Sonia stepped over the threshold and let out a long breath.

"Where do you want to go?" He cooed, not wanting to scare her or make her run.

"I need to go straight in, don't I. Face the demons?"

He nodded.

"This way." She led him down the corridor towards a closed door and opened it. He watched her carefully as her eyes fell to a particular spot on the floor. She let out a deep breath before chewing on the edge of her lip.

"I thought there would still be blood."

"I believe Mrs Scott has cleared it all up." The room looked spotless. He suspected that the generous lady came and cleaned at least once a week.

"I sat here for ages. I thought she was sleeping. She looked so peaceful. Why did this happen?"

"It isn't an excuse, but your father had an illness. It wasn't understood then as it is now."

"She was barely older than I am now. It wasn't fair. I can't even accurately remember her." A tear left Sonia's eye and tumbled down her cheek. She wiped it away. This time, he brought her into his arms. He didn't speak. She needed to do that. "I can smell her in here. She always wore jasmine perfume. It was funny, because at the end of the day, it was mixed with the smell of baking. That was my mum's smell." She turned to nestle further into his arms. "I remember the day before she died, well I think I do. I don't know if it's true or not. Dad was out on the farm. He was having a good day. We'd had a massive Sunday roast together, and he'd gone out to tend the animals. Mum and I made fresh soup from vegetables from the garden, onions, carrots, leeks, a bit of garlic, stock and herbs. I was seven, soup seemed like the devil's food to me, then, but I still helped. We made fresh bread to go with it. I remember her showing me how to knead the dough. We both ended up throwing it around the table." She paused and sniffed. He ran a hand down her hair. "I remember we sat down that evening as a family. We laughed. Dad even read me a story. I guess it was the calm before the storm. I'm glad I have that memory, though. Shows I did have a normal family sometimes. Why does it hurt so much, Matthew?"

"I wish I could take your pain away from you. Make it easier at least. Only you can do that, and that's why it hurts so much. You love both your mother and father."

"I don't love my dad."

"Did you not love him, when he ate the bread and soup you helped make. When he read you the story?"

"I haven't loved him since he killed my mother. He doesn't deserve it anymore."

"Sonia."

"I'll never forgive him. Please don't ask me to." She stood, shoulders slumped by the door. "I'll never get the image of her laying on the floor out of my head. It haunts my dreams. I have no father." She pushed him away and got up. "I'm going to get a few bits, and I want to see my room."

He sighed, as she left the kitchen. She was stubborn but understandably so. He just knew from experience until you forgave you couldn't move on.

"Matthew?"

Sonia called out. She was distressed. He quickly got up and ran to where the sound of her voice was coming from.

"It hasn't changed."

"What hasn't?"

"My room." He peered in the door, which she held open. "My toys are still here. My bedcovers." She opened a wardrobe. "My clothes. It's like time stood still."

"I never figured you as being a pink girl." It was a very girly room. "I thought you'd have action men."

She laughed at this one before breaking down in floods of tears. He just held her. He didn't know for how long, but it was what she needed. His warmth, his love, his reassurance.

"John, get yer feckless arse in 'ere. Supper's up." Mary called out as Matthew and Sonia took their seats at the table a few hours later.

"I'm coming." Mary's husband replied and ambled into the kitchen. "Parkin, me favourite. Good lass."

"Don't yer good lass me. Sit down so I can serve yer. Where's Jack?"

"On 'is way. Was just finishing up the feeding."

"Well, 'e better hurry or tha be nout left with yer appetite."

"Ere." Mary slapped her husband's hand when he reached out for the cake." Guests first. Matthew, Sonia?"

"Thank you, Mary." He took a piece of the gingerbread tea loaf for himself and served Sonia. After the afternoon, she was weak and drained. He just wanted to get some food into her and then get her to bed. They'd made the right decision to stay here the night rather than travel back.

"Ma? Dad?"

A deep masculine voice came from the hallway.

"In 'ere?"

Matthew knew that he was big, but the man who entered the room barely fit through the doorway. He was a ball of pure muscle.

"Well feck me, little seesaw came home." Everyone looked towards him. Sonia, who was mid-bite of cake, dropped it to her plate.

"Jack, manners." His mum chastised.

"Sorry, ma." He replied and took his seat.

"Little seesaw?" Matthew asked.

"It was what I used to call Sonia."

"I remember," Sonia spoke up. "Jack called me it because whenever I came around here, he had to spend hours playing with Harry and me on the one in their back garden."

"It's still out there yer know. Ma's hoping one of us eventually give her grandbabies."

"You're not married?"

"Disgrace ain't it. Thirty-six and still living at home."

Matthew wrapped an arm around Sonia's shoulder. He'd never felt jealousy before, but these two remembered each other, and Jack was a big man. He wasn't a part of this conversation.

"I almost forgot. Jack, this is my partner Matthew. Matthew this is Jack. He's the one who's been looking after the farm."

Jack wiped his hands on his trousers and reached over the table to shake Matthew's. He returned the greeting

"Pleasure to meet yer."

"Your accent isn't as broad as your parents."

"I took a year out in London with my brother, Charlie. He lived down that way. Lost a bit of the tongue then. Lots of southerners up 'ere now that I deal with so easier for 'em to understand."

"Yes, we are a simple bunch who prefer our language just as we're used to it."

"I 'ad a great laugh watching Charlie trying to chat this lass up once in a club in London. She didn't have a clue what he was saying. Needless to say 'e didn't get owt that night."

"Poor Charlie. Is he still in London?"

"He moved back last year. Works in York."

"What about Harry, George, Sam, and Ellie?"

"How many siblings do you have?" Matthew spluttered into his coffee.

"There be five of 'em." John smacked his lips together as he spoke, "My lass did 'er duty."

"More like you couldn't keep yer 'ands off me."

"Ma. We don't need to know that." Jack put his head in his hands. "They're all still around the area. We went separate ways for a while, but all came back."

"The place has that pull. Even if you want to get away, you can't." Sonia put her head down. Her eyes watered again.

"I'm sorry about what happened. If I could've done anything to 'elp."

"You've done so much. Your mum said you've been looking after the farm."

"I 'ave. It's a good little earning. Yer Dad asked us to set up an account to pay the profits into after I took a wage and costs."

"And then, he used the rest trying to buy alcohol in prison."

"No, lass." Mary interrupted. "Yer dad stopped drinking shortly after 'e went to prison. E's been writing to me. I'm not saying 'e didn't slip at first, but e's been dry for ten years now. 'E loved yer ma; 'e 'ates himself for what happened. Yer can't punish 'im more tha 'e is 'imself." Mary pushed her chair back and went to a drawer in an old style dresser. She pulled out a wad of papers. "This be 'is letters. Read 'em, lass. Please. Before yer made any decisions."

NINETEEN

Sonia

"Is it really time to go? I barely feel like I've slept." Sonia rubbed at her tired eyes.

They'd been awake most of the night. Matthew'd the letters to her.

"I'm glad I read them. I can see that he's truly sorry. The first few letters he still blamed my mother, but the ones when he stopped drinking showed his real remorse. He misses her. He'll never forgive himself for what he did. I think the next time he sends me a visiting order I'll go and see him. I can't guarantee that I'll go through with it when I get there, but he's my father. I owe him a chance to explain." She looked down at the floor, moments of thought drifting through her head at the words that she'd read. He'd spoken of their courtship and how much they'd fallen in love. The drink wasn't an issue at first, but it became so when he started to drink far too much, and the farm began to suffer.

"That's a brave decision." Matthew reached out his hand to assist her onto the bike. "You don't have to wait, though."

He hadn't gotten on the bike, yet, but stood in front of her. She narrowed her eyes at him.

"What do you mean?" She stepped off the bike again.

"Are you certain you want to see your father?"

"I think I owe it to us both to put closure to this."

Matthew pulled his phone out. He held a finger up to silence her and placed the phone on speaker so that she could hear.

"Jasper."

"Mr Carter, what can I do for you? Or are you going to do something for me?"

"Haven't I done enough?"

"Probably. What is it? I can't talk for long. The head honcho wants us ready for a briefing in five minutes."

"It won't take long. I need a prison visit today."

"Which one?"

Matthew placed a hand over the phone.

"What prison is your father in?"

"Wakefield."

He removed his hand.

"I need to get into Wakefield. My girlfriend wants to see her father."

"Does he want to see her?"

"He's been sending visitor's orders."

"Can't she use one of them?"

"She destroyed them."

"Give me his name."

"Simon Anderson."

"I call you back ASAP."

"What about your meeting?"

"I've got a pressing matter I need to deal with now. His Highness will have to wait."

Matthew chuckled. "He always did act like he was God. I can't imagine what he's like with their real Highnesses."

"I can only imagine. I won't be long."

The line went dead.

"Today. Now." Her heart was suddenly beating rather rapidly and her palms moistened with nerves. "Surely we have to give more notice?"

"Not when your ex-MI5 and your contacts still are." He pulled her close to him, his warmth soothing her fears. "I'll be with you the entire time. I'm proud of you for making this decision."

"It's the right thing to do, isn't it?" She lay her head on his solid chest.

"You hold so much guilt inside you, blaming yourself for something that wasn't within your control. An innocent bystander. No matter how many times you replay it, you couldn't have changed the outcome. Destiny is the darkness that engulfs us." She pulled back from him and looked up into his eyes. They'd gone blank; he couldn't see her movement. He was lost in a world of his own pain.

"Matthew." She whispered. "You lost someone."

"Yes." The phone rang, and she could've cursed. He pushed away from her and answered it.

"Matthew Carter."

"You're in. Get there as soon as you can."

"Thank you. I owe you one."

"I actually think we're probably about even."

"Give it a week."

Matthew hung up and got on the bike. "You ready?"

∼

The door opened and a guard walked in, behind him stood an elderly man, his face sunken, and the shadows around his eyes thick with regret. Lines marked his battered face, each one telling a story.

"God help me." He exclaimed when he saw her and staggered back against the wall. The guard moved to his side and helped him to his seat. She remained glued to her seat, her eyes transfixed on the man who was once her father. "Of all the punishments, this is by far the greatest. Your mother, you're like her twin. She wouldn't have been much older than you when she died." He paused, "When I killed her."

With those word's Sonia's regard flashed back to her father. Sorrow filled his eyes, guilt and penitence echoing in the dull green irises. A colour that matched her own.

"You admit it?"

"Yes. I alone am responsible for the death of my wife and your mother. Lost the two people who meant the world to me."

"I survived." It was all she could answer.

"But I lost you from my life. I missed all the happy moments of seeing you grow up because I was drunk or in prison. Your first day at school, your first lost tooth, date, graduation. I don't even know what you do for a living. Is the man you're with your husband? Do you have children of your own? The demons that I thought I lost at the bottom of a bottle robbed me of that."

"And my mother." She was not going to let his self-pity control her emotions.

"I'm sorry. I wallow on my own grief. I deserve none of those first moments, because I took them away from you and your mother. What I did was wrong."

"It was. I'll never be able to fully forgive you for it. You know that, don't you."

"I would never ask you to."

A silence descended on them both. This was harder than she had thought it would be. The man in front of her might be her father, but he was also a stranger.

"Mr Anderson. I'm Matthew Carter."

Her father smiled at Matthew. It seemed such an effort for him, though physically not in a bad way.

"It's a pleasure to meet you, Mr Carter." He tried to raise his hand to shake Matthew's, but the guard, still in the room, barked "No touching".

"Why did you keep asking me to come and see you?"

"To apologise." He ran a hand over his bald head. "But it seems so insignificant and worthless now that you're here. Apologies will not change what happened."

"Nothing will change what happened."

"Why'd you decided to come and see me now?"

"I went to the house yesterday. I saw Mrs Scott. She gave me the letters that you had sent her. " She pursed her lips together. The bitterness built inside her, bubbling in a manner that threatened to explode. He killed her mother. He should die, painfully, preferably. "You killed her." She screamed so loudly the noise startled even her. "I watched the bottle. You kept plunging it into her; she was screaming in agony. She hadn't done anything wrong except love you. I hadn't done anything wrong except love you. You're a monster. You deserve to die. I want you dead. Not her." Tears flooded down her cheeks. She crumbled to the floor. Matthew was instantly there, his arms surrounding her in a comforting cocoon.

Her father huddled over in his chair and started to cough.

"Oh God," Matthew whispered above her head.

Two other guards appeared. They had breathing apparatus and were hooking him up to it. That's when she noticed it. The blood, red, a wine of life ebbing out of her father.

"Daddy?" The child's innocent phrase slipped from her lips. "What's happening?

What's going on?"

"Miss Anderson, please take a seat. Let us stabilise him."

"Stabilise?"

"Sonia." Matthew took her hand and wrapped his arms around her again.

"Why is he like this? What's going on?"

"Wait a moment."

"You know what's wrong?"

She searched him.

"I have my suspicions."

"Tell me." She pursed her lips angrily together.

"Sonia." He father's voice broke through the gasps for air. "I know you'll never forgive me." He stopped to catch his breath again when it caught in his throat. "God has seen fit to enact his own judgement on me. You wish me dead...it will happen. Soon."

"What?"

"I'm riddled with cancer. I have a few months left at best."

"Cancer. What treatment have they given you?"

"None."

"That can't happen."

"It can and it has."

"No." She turned to Matthew. "Can we speak to James? Get his doctor to look at him."

Matthew shook his head. "This is your father's decision."

"I died the night I took your mother's life. My body has just taken a long while to catch up with my soul."

"I don't want you to die. I didn't mean what I said." Her voice sounded so small.

"I know. This is what must happen. I'm just glad I got to see the amazing woman you've become. You make sure he looks after you." His eyes flicked to Matthew who was standing against the wall.

"He'll always do that."

"She's safe with me, Mr Anderson."

"I'm tired. I need to sleep. Go live your life. Enjoy every moment of it. The past has shaped you but don't allow it to destroy you."

"I want to see you again."

"No. We have made our peace with each other. Allow me to die and reconcile with your mother."

The guards returned and helped her father to a wheel chair. They supported all his weight. She tried to keep her composure. To allow him to see her for the last time as the strong woman, he was proud of.

"Sleep well, daddy."

He turned his head, the corners of his mouth turning up into a smile.

Sonia's father died two days later.

The funeral was a very quiet affair. James and Miranda had joined them at the graveside along with the Scott family; he was buried next to her mother. Jack was in the process of buying the farmhouse from her. It was another memory she wanted to put in the past.

TWENTY

Matthew

"Matthew, can you put that box of cupcakes over here please." Miranda's instruction brought him out of his reflection. "James, they are macaroons. They go over here. Please be gentle with them. They're so delicate, and I don't want to have to discount them."

"Yes, mother."

"Yes, Mrs North."

Both men did as they were told.

"Please say your mother isn't really considering doing this more than once a year?"

"I can't tell a lie to you, my friend, you know that." James started to put the macaroons out on the stand but not before rolling his eyes in annoyance.

"I think we need to seriously discourage her. There must be some sort of security threat I can worry her with. Cakes can easily be used to hold bombs?"

"She makes most of the cakes herself, and she would just have you scan them."

"Any of those attending could injure her?"

"The event is ticketed, and you've examined the guest list in detail?"

"Cakes lead to cholesterol and heart attack?"

"James," Miranda shouted before his boss had a chance to reply. "You don't lay them out like that. In circles, alternate the colours. Make them look attractive to those buying them. I thought that you were supposed to be good at design?" She tutted.

"I'm not. I pay people to do it. Just like we should have done for this."

"I can't pay people!" She looked horrified at the suggestion. "It's for charity. We need to be seen to be doing all we can. Only last week Mrs Morgan held a charity dinner in her home, and she actually waited on the tables herself. What would it look like if I hired people to do it instead of doing it myself?"

"Sensible," James mumbled under his breath, and Matthew tried not to smirk. "Mum, we don't need to compete with the likes of Mrs Morgan. I give at least double what her husband gives to charity a year in just a month. We help as many people as we can and in lots of different ways. A little extra help wouldn't be frowned on."

"I'm being totally over the top aren't I?" His mother slumped down onto a chair.

"Just a little, Mrs North." Matthew couldn't stop the answer from coming out of his mouth.

"Mum, you want this event to be a success, and it will be, but one macaroon out of place will not be a disaster and asking for a little help won't be either."

"I won't be able to get assistance at such short notice. It's going to be a disaster." The matriarch of their little group placed her head in her hands.

"Should ask all the Dom's from the club to help. That would get all the patron's talking and definitely make it an afternoon tea not to forget." Sonia appeared at the doorway, partially hidden by an enormous croquembouche. I know I wouldn't mind being served cake by a topless hunk." She winked at him, and he made a mental note to collect a few leftovers for later.

"That isn't a bad idea, actually." Miranda had lifted up her head, and he could feel her also measuring him up as a topless cake serving waiter.

"Is this what it feels like to a woman when we stare at her boobs?" He queried of James.

"I'm just glad they're all staring at you and not me."

"James, do you think you could arrange it?"

"I'll have to call in a few favours."

"But you could do it. You and Matthew can help out as well. Such good boys." Sonia placed the croquembouche down, and he watched her laughing, thinking she had hidden behind it. He raised an eyebrow at her, which told her in no uncertain terms she was being tied up and flogged tonight.

"I'm not wandering around here topless mum, but I'll see if I can get some people to help." James pulled out his phone. His mum shoved him out of the way and proceeded to organise the macaroons.

"I'm not going out there like this." Matthew growled.

"Shouldn't it be me telling you that you're not allowed to flash your body to other women?" Sonia ran a hand down his bare chest and stopped at the waistband of his trousers. She pressed a kiss to his left nipple.

"Fuck, now I'm going out there with a hard on."

"Too much information, Matthew." Callum, one of the Doms from the club, called out while pumping his pecs.

"And I don't need to watch you flexing those weak arse excuse for muscles."

"Jealous."

"Yeah right."

"I donna know what ye lads are worried about. I'm wearing a kilt!" Blair interrupted their protestations. "I goona end up flashing me hooded bandit."

"Hooded bandit?" Callum questioned. Matthew laughed, knowing full well what the Scot was referring to.

"You know, me willy."

"Come on boys. Showtime." Miranda stood in the doorway sniggering. They filed out, each taking a tray of cakes as they went. Matthew watched the Mayor of Kensington's wife pinch James' bottom.

"Mr Carter?" A hand tapped him on the leg.

"Mrs Hurlington-Webb. It's good to see you again."

"It's good to see rather a lot of you." He chuckled and handed her a chocolate cake.

"Did I guess right?"

"Of course."

"Miss Anderson's looking somewhat enervated."

"She's had a death in her family recently. It's caused her a lot of stress."

"You must take her on holiday. Replenish her puissance."

"I was thinking the same thing this morning."

"Don't just think it, young man. Just thinking will do that poor girl no good."

"I'll talk to James later about time off."

"I'll phone Miranda tomorrow to ensure that you have." She gave him a small wink, and he placed the cakes on the table. A pinch to his bottom, elicited a low growl.

"Mrs Morgan, if you're going to pinch my backside." He hesitated while leaning closer to her. "At least give it a good grab." The ladies all started to laugh again as he turned and presented his backside for closer inspection to the now red-cheeked woman. All the women now came over to have a feel. Out of the corner of his eye, he caught Sonia watching him, a hand resting on her heart. Her lips parted, and she ran her tongue over them. They were going to have a good night. He pulled away from the ladies, and they returned to their gossip and cakes. James was standing over by the drinks table. He had lipstick kisses all over his chest.

"I don't think I want to ask what happened to you."

"I don't want to relive it either."

"Is your mother happy?"

"Ecstatic. They doubled the funds raised last year. We're going to be a regular thing, apparently."

"Damn it."

James handed him a beer.

"I was wondering if Sonia and I could take a week or so off?"

"When?"

"As soon as possible. I'm going to take her to France. Meet my parents. Then, yes. I'm going to tell her everything. It's time."

TWENTY-ONE

Matthew

"What do you fancy next?" Sonia unlocked her phone. They'd been listening to Matthew's choice of music since they'd left Poitiers three hours ago, and it was time for something different.

"I don't mind. You can choose."

"I thought my taste in music was spectacularly wrong?"

"When you play show tunes it is."

"What's wrong with the Wicked soundtrack?"

"Do I even need to answer that?" Matthew smirked but kept his eyes on the road in front of them.

"Just for that, and the fact that we're in France, Les Miserables soundtrack it is." She giggled as the thunderous beat of 'Look Down' beat out the car stereo.

"You know you'll suffer for this."

"Only after your ear drums have." And she turned the volume up. He used the controls on the wheel to turn it back down. "Spoilsport."

They'd borrowed James' Aston Martin for the journey, at their boss' insistence, so she reached over and used her credit card to pay the toll and the barrier rose.

"They should charge on the M25, might lessen the amount of time I have to spend sitting in traffic, when Miranda's off on one of her excursions to the gardens with the other ladies."

"It probably won't make much difference, actually. We're just too small a country for the number of vehicles on the roads."

"France has definitely been easier to travel in. How long have you been coming here?"

"My parents moved here after they retired, but we've come here since I can remember to see mum's family. I've spent many a summer helping out in the winery."

"Do they still crush the grapes with their feet?"

"No, my family have a machine that does that now. My *grand-père's* feet weren't exactly hygienic. There is a festival during picking season, though, where they still do some by feet. I'll have to see if I can bring you to see it."

"I'd like that very much."

The expanse of symmetrically laid vine plantations loomed in front of them as they drove further and further into the countryside, leaving behind the alternating fields of vines and asparagus they had been seeing for the last thirty minutes or so.

Matthew turned a corner, and a sea of sunflower heads, illuminated by the vibrant afternoon sun, revealed themselves to her. "Oh my God. So many of them. What do they grow them for?"

"Oil mainly."

"Can we stop, please? I want to take a picture."

"Of course." Matthew pulled the car over.

She jumped out of the car and stood beside the field. Matthew turned the engine off and joined her. He wrapped his arms around her waist pulling her against his hard body.

"They're beautiful."

"Tu es belle. Je t'aime." He whispered into her ear and pressed kisses against her cheek.

His hands lowered over her hips, pulling her tightly against him.

"Je pense que ta mère préférerait que tu rentres à la maison d'abord." A masculine voice came from behind them, and she jumped back.

"Putain. Oncle Henri. I'll go see my mother soon."

"I don't think that's any way to speak to your Uncle." The two men drew each other into a warm embrace, kissing each other's cheeks in a traditional French greeting and thumping each other's back in a not so traditional one. "Your aunt Lourdes and your mother have been cooking all your favourite dishes since first thing this morning. It's been such a long time and to be bringing such a belle femme with you." Matthew's uncle reached over and brought her into the traditional greeting now. "As my nephew isn't introducing me himself, allow me. I'm Henri Bresson. My sister is Matthew's mother."

"I'm Sonia Anderson. I'm Matthew's girlfriend. It's lovely to meet you." Henri had come from the direction of the sunflower fields. "Are these your fields?"

"Yes. From the *Chateaux* to as far as the eye can see."

"Wow. Matthew told me his family had a winery, but I didn't realise you grew other crops. The sunflowers are just stunning."

"Do you want to come back on the tractor with me?"

"She'll be safer in the car," Matthew answered before she could.

"Tres bien. A bientôt."

"See you later, Uncle." Matthew led her back to the car. He opened the door for her, but before she got in, she stood on her tiptoes and kissed him.

"What was that for?"

"For being you."

"Get in the car before I change my mind about going to the house and find the nearest hotel and fuck you 'til morning."

That took the breath out of her chest.

It didn't take them long to get to the winery. The driveway leading up to it meandered through a forest before the horizon opened up to expose a large farm-house, surrounded by neatly organised vines.

"This is your family's?"

"Yes. Welcome to the *Chateaux Maison Du Bresson*. My mother's ancestral home."

A small woman with jet black hair and a dark tan threw herself at Matthew, when he got out of the car. "It's so good to see you, mon petit. It's been far too long." Matthew greeted the woman, who Sonia assumed was his mother. A tall gentleman, who could only be described as pale looking and British, greeted him next.

"Hi, Dad. Mama. Aunt Lourdes. I'd like to introduce my girlfriend, Sonia Anderson."

"Right, inside everyone. We have cheeses and bread ready to be eaten. I'll serve dinner later, but I know that it's been such a long journey for you both, so you must be hungry.

"That would be lovely, Mrs Carter." Despite stopping on the way down, her tummy started to rumble at the thought of a snack.

"Phillip, I hope you opened the vintage 2010 when I told you so that it could breathe. I'm sure they're both in need of a drink as well. "

The bottle was not only opened but had been decanted, and a selection of cheeses was laid out before her.

"When are you two marrying?" Aunt Lourdes hovered over Matthew, filling his plate with more food.

"I think that's a bit premature."

"*Zut alors,* Matthew. You're not getting any younger. This isn't the first...."

"Aunt." Matthew's abrupt interruption made Sonia jump. "Sonia and I'll discuss marriage when we are ready to. At the moment, we still have a lot to learn about each other. A lot to learn." He stressed the last few words, and that confused her. Henri reached out and took his wife by the hand.

Sonia took Matthew's hand and noticed a little look pass between him and his mother. She couldn't place what it meant, but it made her uneasy.

"Matthew, why don't you take Sonia on a tour of the house? I've put you in the guest quarters out back. I thought maybe you'd like some privacy."

"Good idea. I think we could do with a lay down."

"I should help your mother tidy away first."

"No need, you're a guest here Sonia. I know how hard you and Matthew work for Mr North. Please, this is your holiday. Rest and relax. Take the bottle of wine and glasses with you. I'll call when dinner's ready." Matthew's mother took her plate from her hands, and Matthew led her from the room. They got outside, and she dug her heels in.

"I was happy for you to keep whatever secrets you wanted 'til you thought you were robust enough to tell me, but I'll not sit in a room with a group of people who obviously know everything. That's disrespectful to not only me but also our relationship. I'll not be made a fool of."

"Sonia, please. Give me time."

"We've been together for six months. What is it? Do you not trust me? I've told you everything there is to know about me. I've opened my heart, let it bleed truths.

Now is the time, Matthew. Now or never. Your decision." She turned around and stomped towards the guest house without looking back to see if he was following.

TWENTY-TWO

Matthew

His world was shattering in front of him.

"Sonia." It was all he could say, and his voice wavered.

"Your choice Matthew. I'm going to lay down."

She slammed the door to the guest house, leaving him outside.

"Give her a few minutes to calm down and then go and tell her everything."

His father appeared beside him and placed his hand upon his shoulder.

"I don't know if I can."

"Do you love her?"

"More than anything."

"Then, you can."

"What if she hates me?"

"You did nothing wrong, Matthew."

"Dad."

His father stopped him.

"You did nothing wrong. It was her choice. She made the decision to die. Not you."

"But I could have stopped it."

"I wasn't there, but I know when someone's determined to die, nothing will be able to stop them. You can't watch them twenty-four-seven."

"I should've done something."

"Matthew, she's the past. Sonia's the future. Don't lose her."

His father was right. He needed to face what he always tried to hide.

"Thanks, dad."

"No worries. Now go and sort everything before dinner. If your mother's meal is spoilt, she'll be a nightmare for weeks."

"I will."

With rather hesitant steps, he trudged towards the guest house.

"If you haven't come to talk to me, you can turn around and go back the way you came." Sonia turned the water off, dropped the towel that encased her body, and got into the bath. She didn't even look at him. He took a seat on the toilet. His long legs crossed in front of him and an arm resting on the cistern. To an external viewer, he may look relaxed, but he was far from it. Sonia looked over to him and ducked under the water to wash her hair. When she surfaced, he'd finally managed to find his voice.

"I did many different assignments when I was in MI5 and also when I was seconded to MI6. I travelled to lots of different countries. I always returned home to England or came back here afterwards. I took time out and broke from the intensity that each assignment brought." He was staring in front of him, not really at anything, not even at Sonia. The chill of the memories surrounded him. This was why he hated to say anything, to go back to those places. Sonia thought his parents knew everything, but the reality was he'd never told a living soul all that happened on his last assignment. "I was given a commission by MI5 to Paris; it wasn't to be a short one. I was told from the outset that I could be there at least a few years. I had an American woman from the FBI as my partner. I was given a new identity, *Matthias Durand*. The American agent was supposedly my wife, Jennifer. Jen as I called her. I'd left the south of France at a young age with my family and made my fortune and name in England and America as part of the Milieu or mafia branch there. I'd met Jennifer when she'd started working for my firm. We'd apparently fallen in love and married. I'd grew tired of the hatred for foreigners in England though; the discrimination only worsening. Especially when Jen was assaulted for being married to a Frenchman. We left and moved to Paris to start afresh in a country that would welcome us both and our money. My task was simple, to infiltrate a particular section of the French mafia and help eliminate human trafficking in the UK and USA." He paused. He could vividly remember his first meeting with Francois LaFont, the leader of the Corsican gang of the same name. "We were able to get in, and I started off as a soldier but soon became a captain."

"After I became a captain, an opportunity came up that brought me in direct contact with the boss, Francois Lafont. I was his consigliere. It was the connection we needed, and I started to take the firm down from the inside."

"What about Jennifer? Or...what was her real name?"

"Beth."

"What about Beth?"

He sighed heavily. "Beth and I got close. Eventually, we became lovers. She inserted herself with the wives and girlfriends of the gang and used that to help with bringing them down. I had to travel to England for a deal and took her with me. We made an on the spot decision, went to Gretna Green, and were married." Sonia let out a pained breath.

"You're married?"

"No."

"Divorced?"

"No."

"Dead." The word caught in her throat.

He nodded.

"Oh God."

She put her hand over her mouth like she was going to be sick.

"Shortly before the assignment was due to end, Beth was lunching with LaFont's wife and several other women attached to the gang. The restaurant was attacked. LaFont's wife had her throat slit in front of everyone. Beth had a knife plunged into her stomach."

"She died, because they thought they were killing the wife of the consigliere?"

"She didn't die from that attack."

"What? I don't understand."

"She did, later. Francois had a son, Jean-Claude. He'd arranged the hit. He'd told the attackers to kill his mother but only injure Beth."

"His own mother?"

"He knew it would weaken his father and make him vulnerable. What he didn't know—Beth was carrying our child. The baby died, and she had a hysterectomy to save her life."

Sonia had tied him down to his story this far, kept him from falling deeply under the spell of his memories but no longer. He was back there the day of her death. The sounds and smells of the vibrant city of Paris invaded his nostrils as he looked around to see Beth's final moments.

"Are Jasper and the others on the way?" Beth moved slowly over the sculptured lawn of the LaFont mansion's gardens.

"They'll be here within the hour. They have enough evidence to take down Francois and Jean-Claude. They'll rot in prison forever."

"And we'll go back to our regular lives."

"Isn't that what you want?"

"I don't think life will ever be normal for me again."

She held her hands over her stomach where stitches still marked the effects of the knife that had stolen their child.

"I love you, Beth. This changes nothing." He took her hands and kissed both of them before kneeling before her and kissing where the baby had grown.

"I'm not a proper woman anymore."

"You're all the woman that I need. Child or not. We'll always be together."

"I should go see Francois. He wants me to help pick out clothing for his Elise's funeral dress."

"I'll come with you."

"No. There's no need. You go get everything ready for Jasper."

"I'll at least walk you in. Francois may be an awful man, but I can't deny how much he loved his wife. I owe him condolences for that.

"Five minutes. Then you go."

"Okay, bossy."

Matthew followed her into the house. Monsieur LaFont was sitting shrouded by the darkness of thick drapes in his grand sitting room. He looked like he hadn't slept in weeks, not just days.

"Francois?" She cooed. He didn't answer. Just beckoned for her to come to his side. The old man looked directly at him.

"Matthias. You'll find who did this and bring them to me." Francois spoke in French, but the words entered his head in English.

"They'll die painfully. You have my word on this."

"You're good. I'm glad that you're here with us. Even if it means suffering to your beautiful wife. When the funeral is over; take a break, go to Corsica. You can stay with my friends."

"That's very generous of you, Francois." Beth placed a blanket around the old man's shoulders.

"I'm going to go and speak to my sources, see what I can find."

Francois took Beth's hand. "Let's go choose a dress for my wife."

"Au revoir, Matthias." Beth kissed his cheek.

Matthew watched them go.

"Matthias. Where's my father?" Jean-Claude called from the doorway.

Jean-Claude had always been a bit of a mystery to Matthew. He appeared loyal to the LaFont's, but there was always a question mark in his mind as to how far that allegiance ran.

"Do you know who did it yet?"

"Not yet, but I'm working on it."

"Work quicker. I want answers by the end of the day."

"You'll have them." Just not the answers that he wanted.

"How's Jen? Should she be up and around already."

"She's stronger than she looks."

"I'm sorry she was involved."

"So am I for her sake and the baby."

"Baby?"

"She was pregnant."

"What?" Jean-Claude's face paled. "You hadn't said?"

"It was early stages."

"Fuck."

"That's putting it mildly."

"I should go check on my father." Suddenly, the younger LaFont couldn't wait to get away from him. Matthew didn't care, though. His phone rang.

"You here?" His screen flashed up the code name for Jasper.

"Yes."

The next thing Matthew knew, he was thrown through the air. A massive explosion ripped through the mansion in a violent crescendo of flames and flying debris. Hard stone rained down on him, bruising and bloodying his skin. He fought to remain conscious.

"Matthew?"

"Explosion." It was all he could manage as dust starting to settle all around him invaded his lungs. The coughing started.

"We'll be there in five minutes."

Matthew turned to look at what remained of the mansion. Nothing.

"Beth?" Was the last word he'd managed before the darkness claimed him.

"Who was responsible? Jean-Claude was in there. It couldn't have been him."

"Beth did it."

"What?" She shook her head disbelievingly.

"I found out afterwards. She'd rigged the mansion to explode. That day, she took the detonator with her. She destroyed herself and Jean-Claude but allowed me to live."

"I'm so sorry, Matthew."

"I've never told anyone as much as I've said today. James knows bits."

"You lost your wife and child in the space of a few days and in a violent manner. No wonder you've wanted to keep that buried so deeply within you." She leant into him, her warmth surrounding his body. For once, she was giving comfort, and he was taking it.

"The darkness is locked away where it can be controlled. If you let it out, it destroys you. That's the reason I left Paris the day she died. My father dealt with the funeral. He hadn't even met Beth. He had her buried in a small graveyard near where we'd lived."

"Have you been there?"

"No."

"But you can't hide from what happened forever. You taught me that."

"I was never one to follow my own rules." He kissed the top of her head.

Sonia shifted so that her deep brown eyes looked up at him. "You forced me to confront my past, so we're going to do the same with you."

"What?"

"We're going to go to Paris so that you can say goodbye."

TWENTY-THREE

Sonia

"Do you know what plot she's in?" Sonia looked around at the old mementoes to those that had been lost to heaven.

"No. I don't." Matthew looked down at his feet in shame.

"It's ok." She squeezed his hand reassuringly. "I'll go and ask."

"Slight problem."

"What?"

"You don't speak French."

"Damn it. You go."

Matthew disappeared into the church. She took a seat on a bench to wait. Her eye was caught by a man watching them. His face was thunderous. Matthew reappeared with a map, and the man was gone.

"The priest has marked the map."

They meandered through the rows of ornamental graves and sepulchres. Ornate crosses and angels decorated them all. A mournful lament came from behind a large stone carving. Sonia surmised the elderly woman she spied was mourning the loss of her husband. She, herself, had grown so close to Matthew that she could image herself doing the same should anything happen to him. She couldn't think about that, though. Everything he'd told her had been a massive shock. It was an entirely different life that he'd lived before he met her. But in many ways, it was what had defined the man who she'd fallen in love with. It was responsible for his caring nature and the strength that he showed her. That first time he knelt before her on the plane, while she told him the story of her parents, that was who Matthew was as a result of his past. She never wanted him to change that.

"This is it." Matthew's voice broke her out of her reflection. She looked over at the grave in front of her. She'd been expecting to see the name Beth Carter, but her breath was taken away when she read, 'Jennifer Durand'.

He knelt in front of the grave and placed his hand on the soft earth that would have been at her feet. "She had no family. Nothing before the assignment. I never fully became Matthias Durand, but she did become Jennifer." He stood and turned away from the grave. "I don't think I should have come. I destroyed her life. She carried my child and lost the ability to have anymore because of who I was."

"Stop." Sonia stepped forward and placed her hand on Matthew's chest. "You looked out for each other. You cared for each other. You were blessed with the child as a result. That child will be in heaven with its mother now. They'll be caring for each other. Watching over you as you live your life and be the good guy you are. Beth made her own decision to end things her way. She set you free, because she knew what a good man you are."

"Sonia, please. I killed people while I was undercover. I helped with trafficking women."

"And you saved as many as you could." She bit back at his self-pity. "And you've continued to protect people. Beth sacrificed herself because you're one of the good guys who'll always put others before himself."

"I should've protected her. That's what a husband does."

She pointed towards the grave. "You did. You gave her peace for eternity."

"But I didn't give her life."

"I don't know why Matthew, but she didn't want life. You couldn't have stopped her."

He slumped to the ground. A heavy sigh leaving his resigned lips.

"I couldn't have saved her."

Sonia shook her head.

Matthew made the sign of the cross, while he repeated a prayer in French. When he was done, he stood and held out his hand for her.

"Thank you."

"For what?"

"For making me come here. You were right. I should've followed my own advice years ago. I feel calmer already. She was a strong and brave woman who made a terrible sacrifice at a time where her emotions were destroyed. I'm lucky to have had her love, even if it was such a short period."

He leant forward and gave her a kiss.

"You said something about the Eiffel Tower, didn't you?"

"I did."

Matthew turned back to the grave, took one last look, put his arm around her shoulders, and she nestled her head against his chest.

"I love you."

"I love you too."

～

The Eiffel tower loomed large before them, and Sonia craned her neck so she could look all the way to the top. The metal structure was a feat of modern engineering. They purchased their tickets and travelled to the observation deck top. It was late in the day, and the eager tourists had already been, so it wasn't that crowded.

"Wow," That view is stunning," Sonia exclaimed as she looked about over the city of love. You can even see Sacre Coeur in the distance that way and Notre Dame over there.

"I've never been sure whether I prefer this view or the view from the London Eye."

"You've been on the London eye?"

"You haven't?"

"No."

"You live in London and have never been on it!"

"I've never been one to spend my money on frivolities."

"Actually, true. I didn't pay for my trip."

"James."

They both laughed, and she leant forward against the railings. A gust of evening wind blew around the top, and she shivered. Even though it was a hot day, it was getting late in the day, and they were high up. Matthew sensing her cold pulled the rucksack off his back and removed a long shawl she'd put in there earlier. He wrapped it around her shoulders and pressed the warmth of his body into hers. They were overlooking the Louvre. There were a couple of other tourists and a guard up with them.

"I'll be back in a minute."

Matthew walked over to the guard, and they conversed quietly. The guard walked over to the other tourists and started to engage with them by leading them off in the opposite direction of the tower to her and Matthew.

"What did you do?"

"You'll see. Turn around and admire the view. No sound whatsoever." Matthew said it in the tone that made shivers run down her spine. She obeyed and looked out back over the view of Paris. His hand circled around her breast. The nipple peaked instantly.

"Matthew." Her voice sounded a little panicked.

"Colour." His voice rumbled in her ear.

"Green." She was nervous, but no way in hell did she want him to stop.

"Part your legs sweetheart."

Her breath quickened with each step she took to comply. Matthew bunched up the bottom her of dress and delved underneath to flash across her already damp knickers. He pressed his body harder into hers, and she could feel his cock hardening against her bottom. She couldn't help but wiggle against it.

"Don't tempt me. I'm not able to fuck you here, but you'll get off."

With that, he slid a finger under her knickers and across her clit. Fuck, she was on fire. He worked his fingers over her slit and slid one inside her. She tried not to moan.

A second finger joined the first, and he angled his hand so he could rub her clit at the same time. Her eyes blurred, and she struggled to maintain the sense of where she was, the fire building between her thighs engulfing her. Matthew's voice growled into her ear.

"Come."

And she did. She exploded into a powerful orgasm there on the top of the Eiffel Tower. Her body shaking with waves of pleasure flooding through it. The scream formed in her throat, and she slammed her head quickly into Matthew's shoulder and bit down on his t-shirt and flesh to muffle the noise.

The evil bastard actually chuckled.

TWENTY-FOUR

Matthew

After a couple more days in Paris, spent exploring the sights, it was time to return to Bordeaux. They didn't visit Jennifer's grave again despite Sonia asking Matthew if he wanted to. He'd stated that part of his life was over, and for the first time, he felt it. There also hadn't been a public repeat of sexual deviance, although behind the bedroom door they'd swung from the chandeliers in the hotel. James would be proud to know his precious antique lights had been used for such a purpose, and the ceiling hadn't caved in. Sonia'd had a fit of giggles when they'd seen the dying slave statue of Michelangelo's in the Louvre. He'd later found out it was because of his small penis, and she imagined the disappointment of his lovers. He guessed the old adage of it isn't the size, it's what you did with it was lost on his girlfriend. Although he was quietly intrigued by her suggestion, they could get a sculpture made of his for when he was away with James, so she didn't have to miss him too much.

"What time do we get back to Bordeaux?" Sonia put her hand over the copy of La Monde newspaper that he was reading.

"Vingt minute." His brain was so focused on reading in French that he answered the same. She just looked at him. "Twenty minutes."

"Time for a quickie in the toilets?"

"You're insatiable."

"You've brought out the sex goddess in me who loves a public place."

"Wait until later. I've got a better idea for a public place for you."

"Where?"

"You'll have to wait and see." He raised his eyebrow, and she pouted. "You know what that gets you."

"Well, not fucked in a train toilet that's for sure." He pulled his paper back up, and she let out an exaggerated groan.

"What I have planned is much better."

Forty-five minutes later, they were in the car speeding up the A10, her hand resting on his thigh as he drove. They hit a small road and travelled along it, the car bouncing around. Not the best for the suspension but the place where they were going was worth it. A medieval chateau appeared before them.

"Whoa." Sonia let out an astonished breath. "A Chateaux. Look at the turrets. It's stunning."

"And mine."

"What?" She spluttered out the word.

"James bought it for me. He's been helping me do it up, so should I ever want to leave him, I can retire here."

"It's yours." He could tell the words were still sinking in.

"Yes. In fact, it was actually another ancestral home. During the Revolution, it was taken away from us, though, and passed to Republicans. My family went the way of most aristocracy then and met the guillotine."

"I'm sorry. That must've been hard to find out, but at least you've got this back now."

"There was a lot of damage inside, after World War II. You can still see some bullet marks on the walls from where a fight took place here. It's not had the best history, but I plan on changing that. Make it the seat of the Sawyer generations for years to come."

"Sawyer generations?"

"When the time is right." The thought of Sonia getting pregnant scared the life out of him, at the moment, but there would come a time. "Work hasn't started inside yet, or I would have brought you here to stay, rather than go to my parents'."

He weaved his way around the building and led Sonia through a white stone arch into the garden. This was the part he wanted to show her, and this was the part where her sudden love of public display would come to fruition. "Remove your clothes."

"What?" Sonia went from admiring the gardens to open mouthed and staring at him in two seconds flat.

"I said remove your clothes, my little submissive."

"But your gardener?"

"Is not here today."

"Can anyone see us?"

"This from the lady who orgasmed at the top of the Eiffel tower." He rolled his eyes. "Last chance or I'm getting back into the car."

Sonia slowly began to remove her clothes and dropped them all onto the ground.

"Turn around. There's a little something else you need."

"Matthew?"

She arched her back when the first drop of suntan oil hit it.

"Can't have that beautiful skin of yours getting burnt, now, can we?" He rubbed the lotion into her skin, making her a little slippery. Part of his plan. He paid particular attention to her breasts and the shaved cleft between her legs. "Especially these parts."

"What happens now?"

"You run."

"What?"

"You run."

He slapped her backside, and she took off over the green grass of the manicured lawn.

He waited a couple of seconds while removing his clothing before moving over the grass after her.

"Sonia." He called, his voice low and full of desire. She'd disappeared into the forests, surrounding the chateaux. "You know you can't hide from me. I can smell your need for me even from here."

He twisted and turned among the trees of the forest before he spotted her naked backside flash between the sturdy old wooden trunks. Silently, he prowled, the scent of her need for him inveigling his nostrils.

"How do you like my hands between your thighs...strong and hard or soft and gentle? You know I can get you off with just one look."

A streak of brown hair darted between the trees before him, and he sped, quickly, towards it. He caught her and wrapped his arms around her body. Her slippery suntan oil caught him off guard the first time, and he lost his grip, but on the second time, he managed to catch her and pulled her to the floor. His hands roamed over her body, searching out the seductive flesh he had so often marked as his own. She let out a wanton moan that went straight to his dick.

"You're mine, my love. Forever more."

Quickly flipping her onto her back, he surged inside her, his rigid length pushing the boundaries of her tight haven so that she called out in ecstasy.

She was his. He thrust harder and harder while she lay upon the sun-warmed ground.

"Come for me, sweetheart."

He didn't need to tell her twice. On the final word, she exploded. She was his present, his future, and in many ways, his past. She defined him. She surrounded him. She gave him everything that she was, and nothing would ever change that. This was the future that he would always live. His cock buried deep inside the warmth that only this one woman could give him. He groaned a final release and collapsed upon her.

"I love you always." The decision had been made. His heart made it for him. Love. It was here. Digging into his heart like a vine surrounding a fence in its beautiful floral nature.

"I love you forever more."

They lay there, entwined, for what seemed like an eternity. His cock hardened again, and he took her again. This time more slowly, savouring every inch of her body. They didn't often make love like this, just simple in its pleasure. Frequently, they 'kinked' it up because that's what they both enjoyed, but here and now, this felt right. The sun started to lower on the horizon, its glow turning beautiful hues of red, orange, and pink.

~

It was almost dark by the time they pulled up the driveway of the winery. Flashing lights illuminated the night sky. Sonia looked towards him, her face paling.

"Matthew?" He put the car into park and automatically opened the door and got out. He didn't answer Sonia, he just needed to find out what was going on. His legs took him towards the police surrounding his family's home. He could sense Sonia running alongside him to keep up.

"Mama, Papa?" He called and the police turned to him. They barred the way.

"Mr Sawyer?" A portly gentleman stepped forward.

"Yes."

"I'm Inspector De Ternay. I'm afraid you can't go inside. There has been an incident."

It suddenly clicked in his brain that they were speaking French when Sonia wrapped her hand around his. "Can you speak English?"

The Inspector switched his language. "We were called an hour ago to reports of gunshots."

"No." Sonia's worried response caught in her throat.

"We're still trying to investigate what happened."

Matthew pushed past the gendarme, sitting in the doorway, in one fluid motion. The door to the hallway opened, and he saw a medic working on a prone body on the floor. Blood flowed in a circle around the person. The medics stepped back and called the death. Sonia took hold of his hand again as the identity of the dead person was revealed. Guilt and relief washed over him; it was one of the farmhands and not his family. That guilt quickly turned to anger, a fierce rage directed at the inspector who had followed them.

"Where are my family?"

"Matthew?" He spun quickly around at his Aunt Lourdes' voice. She ran to him. Blood covered her cream shirt, She slammed her body into his, and he wrapped his arms around hers.

"What happened?"

"It was awful. So awful. He shot them." His aunt's voice broke. He knew he should be comforting her, but instead, he pushed her back and started to shake her.

"Shot who?"

Tears streamed down his aunt's cheeks.

"Your parents."

TWENTY-FIVE

Sonia

Shot.

The word rumbled around Sonia's head.

"Lourdes, where are they?"

Henri staggered into the room. "They're at the hospital. You need to take Matthew. Get him there quickly. He needs to be with them before..."

"What happened?"

He looked over to where the Inspector had his back to them now and then to Matthew. From his pocket, he withdrew a small box and handed it to her.

"What's this?"

"Get Matthew to his parents first. He needs to say goodbye. He'll know what to do after."

"What about the police?"

"There's nothing they can do. Go, Sonia. Please hurry. For Matthew's sake."

"Matthew. We have to go to the hospital. Your mother and father are there."

"You drive."

Matthew's hand hovered over the doorknob. She could see he was willing himself to turn the handle. The door pushed open, and the beep of machines hit them first. Matthew's mother lay attached to a device. A bandage covered her head, and there was a stump where an arm had once been.

Matthew put his fist through the glass of the door.

"Matthew." She tried to comfort him.

"The box, what was in it."

With the worry over his parents, she had forgotten the box.

"I don't know. I haven't looked."

"Give it to me." He growled the words, not with any passionate intentions. She was used to that particular noise coming out of his mouth but with pure venom.

"Mr Sawyer?" A man in scrubs interrupted them. "I'm the doctor who's been looking after your parents."

"Where's my father?"

"He's in recovery. We'll have him brought down here soon. He's critical. The next few hours will let us know more. At present, I can only give you a fifty-fifty chance of survival for both your parents. To be honest, with the wounds they had, they are lucky to be alive now."

"My mother's arm?"

"She was shot twice in it. I'm sorry. There was just no way we could save it. Your mother was also hit over the head, hence the bandage, but Mr Sawyer, I must tell you. Your father was shot in the head. I can give you no guarantees of what'll happen if, and I remind you that's a very big if, he wakes."

Sonia brought her hand to her mouth to try to keep quiet the cry that was threatening to leave her lips. She had to be strong for Matthew now. She couldn't think of the suffering that his parents must have experienced. She had to focus on keeping Matthew all together and not allowing him to lose his sense of control. He was a trained killer. This could end badly.

"I want my father in the same room as my mother. If this room isn't big enough, find one. I'll pay whatever you need."

"We'll see to it at once. There's nothing you can do for now. I would suggest you get some rest, but if you want to stay, I'll have a nurse bring you some drink and clean clothes."

Matthew turned away from the doctor and pulled his phone out. The doctor was dismissed. The doctor left them alone in the room, and she took a seat next to Matthew.

"The box." His voice was far too controlled; it was scaring her so much.

She gave it to him and watched as he opened it. Inside were two rings and a crest. The crest bore a furred Phoenix holding a fleur-de-lis with the writing Vincit Omnia Veritas' below it.

"Truth conquers all things." Matthew shut his eyes. "Did my aunt and uncle say anything about the man who did this?"

"No."

"These are my wedding rings. I didn't wear mine. Jennifer had it around her neck. They were never found after the explosion."

He pulled out his phone and dialled. The phone was on speaker.

"Where are you?"

"Outside the hospital." Jasper's voice answered.

"We're in room two four five."

Matthew hung up. "You have to leave. Jasper will take you."

"What?" She scraped her chair back and stood up. "I'm not going anywhere; I'm staying right by your side."

"You need to get back to England and into safe custody. You have to do whatever Jasper says."

Jasper came through the door. "I'm so sorry. I got here as soon as we got the alert from your parents."

"Is it him?"

"From the description your uncle gave to the gendarmes, and the fact they are backing off the investigation, I would say so."

"Have you got everything in place for Sonia?"

"Yes. I've got a car outside, and the airfield is nearby."

"Good, I want guards put on this door. I've asked for mum and dad to be kept together."

"Already in place. They came with me."

"Ok, take her. Keep her safe for me." Matthew sat back down at his mother's bedside and took the hand that was still there into his.

"You're not coming?"

"Neither of us are going anywhere." She sat down next to Matthew and folded her arms across her chest.

Jasper raised an eyebrow towards Matthew.

"Pick her up and carry her. Watch her left leg, though, she looks to go straight for the balls." Matthew spoke without even taking his eyes off his mother.

"What the fuck!" She spat the words out, Jasper took a step nearer to her. "Come any closer and they'll be needing a third hospital bed in here, and if you don't stop shutting me out Matthew Sawyer and giving me answers, they may as well add a fourth."

"Shall I wait outside?" Jasper stopped advancing and looked towards Matthew. Sensible man, she would render him unable to breed for the foreseeable future, if he tried anything.

"No, it's okay, I should've known she would be this stubborn."

"I'm not stubborn. I'm trying to care for the man I love. Although, I'm seriously starting to wonder if the words he spoke to me this afternoon were all a bunch of lies."

Jasper withdrew to the corner of the room, and Matthew got to his knees in front of her.

"I'm sorry. Sonia, I love you, and I'm scared. I am facing the possibility that my mum and dad are going to die, and if I don't get you into protective custody, he'll find you and try the same thing."

"Who will find me? Please, I need to know so that I can protect myself."

He took a deep breath.

"Jean-Claude."

"But he died in the explosion?"

"That's what we were led to believe. Please, I need you to go with Jasper and get back to England. He'll make sure you're safe, while my former colleagues try to find Jean-Claude and bring him down."

"What about you?"

"I can't leave my parents."

"Let me stay the night. You said there were guards outside the door. Nobody'll get in here."

"I can't, I need to know you're safe to be strong. Please, sweetheart, go with Jasper."

"I don't want to leave you. What if he comes for you? I can help you fight. I can't lose you."

"You won't. You'll see. You'll wake up in the morning, and I'll be there beside you in the bed. My parents will be under armed guard and recovering." It was easy to see that he was trying to reassure himself.

"I want to know the second your parents wake or Jean-Claude is caught so I can come back here."

"I promise. Jasper will stay with you the entire time."

"I love you."

"We need to get going, if we're going to make our flight clearance." Jasper interrupted.

"Okay." She pushed herself out of the chair and took hold of Matthew's hand. He came with her to the door and then let go; she walked out. She turned around to see him take a look at her before closing the door. There was too much finality here. She could almost feel her heart breaking. He wasn't leaving her, but she wondered if she'd see him again.

"Matthew isn't going to be a part of the investigation is he?"

"He'll be at the hospital under our protection."

"And when Jean-Claude is caught?"

Jasper slammed the door shut. He climbed in the other side.

"Jasper?"

"Please don't ask me that question again."

"He won't be the same man when I see him again will he?"

"I think you should prepare yourself for the worst."

Jasper pressed a button on his wheel, and a call started ringing before she answered.

"We'll be there in a few minutes. Start the engines."

"I'll be ready."

From out of nowhere, a car skidded to a halt in front of them. Jasper swerved, but they clipped it, which sent the car into a spin. It flipped, rolled, and slammed to a halt against a grove of trees. Her head bumped hard against the dashboard. Jasper groaned beside her, and she looked over to see him hanging from his seat-belt. Smashed glass littered his side of the car where the window had broken. His face was covered in little cuts. They needed to get out of the car. She released her seat belt and fell onto the roof of the car. Her body ached from the force of the impact.

"Jasper. We need to get out." She tried to release his seatbelt, but it was stuck. He groaned again but didn't stir.

Jean-Claude was coming for her. She needed to think. Jasper must have a gun. The door behind her was ripped open, and large hands grabbed hold of her legs and started to pull. She tried to find something to anchor herself to, but nothing helped. She was pulled cleanly from the car and onto her knees before an imposing dark haired man.

"Jean-Claude."

TWENTY-SIX

Matthew

It seemed like days since his mother and father had been placed side by side in the hospital room. It'd only been a few hours though. His phone rang. He answered it without looking at the caller ID.

"Hey, sweetheart."

"I didn't know you cared that much." He heard a scuffle over the phone.

"Matthew." Sonia's voice.

"I don't care how you get there, but meet me where this all started. You have three hours."

"I'll be there. You hurt her, and I won't be responsible for what I do to you."

"Matthew, don't come. Stay with your parents. You know it's a trap."

A hard slap resonated through the phone.

"Shut the fuck up, bitch."

"Go to hell." He heard his woman spit at Jean-Claude.

"Sonia, sweetheart. Try to leave something left of the man for me to beat on please."

"I'm not making any promises." They both chuckled despite the intensity of the situation.

"That's enough." Matthew heard Sonia scream. Jean-Claude had obviously pulled her away from the phone again. "You've three hours Matthew. Don't waste them."

The line went dead.

Jasper appeared at the door. Dried blood had formed a clump over his eye. Matthew prowled forward and smacked his fist hard into his friend's jaw. The agent stumbled backwards against the wall. Matthew stormed out of the room.

"Are you going to tell me where you're going?"

"What do you think?"

"You know doing this alone is suicide."

"If Sonia dies, I've got nothing left to live for."

"She isn't Beth."

"No, she's not."

"We'll follow discreetly. The first sign of trouble, and I'm giving the order to go in after you."

"Nobody kills him but me."

"I'll give you that."

"Give me your gun."

"Please."

"Give me your gun, or I'll punch you in the face again."

"You always were so polite."

"I'll never change."

Jasper handed him the gun, and he placed it into the back of his trousers.

"Bullets."

Jasper handed over a few clips.

"I've seen you shoot before. You only need the one. Don't get dead, Matthew."

"I don't plan on it."

With a deep breath, he strode purposefully from the hospital. Clicked the keys to his car and climbed in. This would end today, with Jean-Claude La Font suffering.

TWENTY-SEVEN

Sonia

"Hey, I need to pee." Sonia shifted in her chair and glared at Jean-Claude.

"*Merde*, Pierre. Take her."

The heavyset man, with a face like a pit-bull, stood up.

"My pleasure." Pit-bull un-cuffed her from the chair.

"You want to wet yourself instead then be my guest. I like it when little girls do that right before I fuck them. Shows them just who their Papa is."

"Pierre. Just take the bitch to the bathroom. I need to concentrate on this." Jean-Claude was losing his temper as the time for Matthew to arrive approached. This was good. If she could play on that stress, she could force him into making errors.

"Come on, bitch." Pit-bull pushed her into the small bathroom--a hole in the ground like many public French toilets.

She gave him a death stare. "Turn around."

"What, so you can bash me on the head? I don't think so."

"And there was me hoping to get a better view of your cute backside." She gave him a wink and subtly pushed her breasts together.

"Nice try."

"Damn, and there was me thinking that you had the brain of the ugly dog you look like." He slammed her up against the wall, his hand around her throat.

"I guess you never got the memo."

"What memo?"

"Never get me in a position where I can connect my left leg with your balls." With a swift knee-jerk, she slammed hard into his groin. Pit-bull let out an agonised scream and fell to the floor. She slammed her foot into his face, knocking him out cold and breaking his nose for probably the third time. Then, she made a run for it.

The commotion behind her told her Jean-Claude was after her. She jerked to the right and behind a pillar. Silently, she waited for them to run past and outside looking for her, but they never came.

She held her breath and silently tried to creep closer towards the door. This would be so much easier if she had a weapon. She nearly made it to the door when it opened, and Matthew walked in.

"Run," was all she managed before taking off towards the door again. Matthew was right behind her, his hand reaching inside his trousers to take his gun out. A shot fired, and Matthew stopped; his leg gave way.

"Matthew." She stopped running and came to his side.

"Go."

"You know that isn't going to happen."

It was too late. Jean-Claude and his associates were upon them and surrounded them.

"Nice of you to join us, Mr Sawyer."

"Pierre." Pit-bull appeared with blood caked all over his nose, he snarled towards her. "Why don't you take Miss Anderson and tie her up again. This time try not to let her hit you in the balls."

"Get the fuck off me." She screamed and tried to kick out. Jean-Claude stepped forward and straight onto Matthew's leg where he had been shot. He reluctantly let out a yell of pain.

"Shut up, bitch, and do as you're told."

He stepped off Matthew's leg only when she became placid and allowed herself to be led back to the room. Turning back to see what was going to happen to her lover, she watched in horror as Jean-Claude took the gun and whacked it hard over Matthew's head knocking him unconscious.

"No!" She screamed so loudly that Jean-Claude looked at her. His lip snarled upwards in an evil motion that sent shivers through her body. It was a look she'd only seen once before, and that was the night her mother died. That night was fuelled by alcohol and poor decisions, though. What was happening right now was the direct result of a man who wouldn't stop until she and Matthew were begging for mercy. He stepped forward towards her and grabbed her by the chin.

"Strip them and tie them both up naked. It's time they both learned some truths."

TWENTY-EIGHT

Matthew

His head hurt like a bugger, and his leg wasn't much better.

"Well, it's nice of you to join us."

Matthew just kept his attention squarely focused on Sonia in front of him. She was shaking.

"I see you're just as delusional as my father if you think you're going to get out of this. Your life will end here today, and this un-classy bitch you call a girlfriend will be joining you as you rot in hell."

"We won't be the ones rotting in hell. We'll be off happily living our life." This time Sonia spoke, her eyes flooded with darkness. She'd regained her composure and strength from knowing that he was near.

Jean-Claude pulled her hair tightly, her head pulled backwards. Matthew pulled at the ropes binding him, furiously trying to rip them so that he could wrap his bare hands around the man's throat 'til his eye popped out of his head.

Sonia spat into Jean-Claude's face. He'd been right above her so that she could see the gloating on his face. In one quick swipe, the Frenchman hit her square across the face sending her chair flying onto the floor.

"Fucking bitch." Jean-Claude kicked her in the stomach, and she let out a pained scream.

He couldn't watch anymore.

"Are you so much of a coward? Why don't you untie me, and we can sort this man to man?"

"You think I'm scared of you?" Jean-Claude was facing him now. "You were a fool back then, and you're a fool now."

"A fool, I'm not the one who had my mother's throat slit." He fired back an insult that he knew would rattle.

"She deserved it. She never supported me over him. I'd still be running stupid little errands if my mother and father had, had their way. Giving all the top jobs to a bloody spy and then wondering why they kept going wrong."

"They gave you the crap jobs because you were no good at the important stuff. It took a real man to do that."

"What just like it took a real man to get your wife pregnant."

"Jean-Claude." It couldn't be. "Now that's no way to talk to my husband, is it?"

"Beth."

The slender form of his wife appeared in front of him. He could barely look at her, gone was the sweet catholic girl he had known. She was replaced by a gangster's wife, dripping in the finest jewellery, designer clothing, and coiffured hair.

"No, I chose the right side. It just took me a while." Jean-Claude wrapped his arms around her waist. Any love or remorse for her death, which once had sat like a putrid wound in the pits of his stomach, was gone

"Who were the other two in the explosion."

"Who cares," Jean-Claude replied with a nasty sneer. "They did their job."

"At least the lady got a proper burial."

"Not that you would know. The other day was the first time you'd even been to my grave."

Sonia gasped.

"The man staring at me. It was you."

"You led me right to him. Pierre, why don't you sit Miss Anderson up. I want to have some fun." Before he could prepare himself, Matthew found his stomach clenching up in agony when Jean-Claude swung a fist into it. The pain ripped through him, but he refused to let out a noise. He was almost biting down on his tongue to show nothing. That was one of the first things he'd been taught for situations like this. Give nothing away. Show no pain, less it shows a weakness. An ugly looking man with an obvious broken nose righted Sonia in her chair. He punched her in the stomach; she was prepared and didn't even flinch. She definitely was his girl.

"Seems the woman is better at this than you."

"Well, he always was a bit of a girl. I always used to beat him in training." Beth had taken a seat, her long legs crossed showing off her Jimmy Choo shoes.

"I'm not going to play your games, Beth, so don't even bother trying. And dickhead," He faced the guy who'd punched Sonia. "You hit her again and I'm going to break most of the bones in your body before I put you out of your misery permanently."

The bastard dared to do it again. He took a deep breath, calming himself. The time would come.

His eyes narrowed to slits when Jean-Claude picked up a bat. This wasn't good. Sonia may be able to withstand punches from a hand, but with a bat... It would break every bone in her delicate little body. He needed to protect her. Meeting her apprehensive look, he calmly gave her reassurance, hope, the knowledge that help was on its way.

"Why him, Beth?" He turned to look at the woman he'd thought dead.

"He's going places."

"What prison?"

"You know that'll never happen. They couldn't capture me before, and they won't capture me now." Jean-Claude was far too certain of his own name. He was going to enjoy wiping the smile off his face.

"We've followed your career, Matthew. You caused a lot of damage. I think when the news of your violent death comes out, there will be a lot of people who will be only too happy with it." Beth was like a changed woman. He couldn't believe that he once loved her. She had none of Sonia's class and warmth.

Broken nose man punched Sonia in the face. Jean-Claude swung the bat hard into his stomach. He'd had time to clench, but it still hurt. He did it twice more, and Matthew heard the crack of his ribs breaking. He tried to keep his focus squarely on Sonia, but the anger inside of him flared, when he saw broken nose man rub his hands over her breasts. He was heading lower; no man would touch his girl that way. They hadn't tied his legs down so he kicked out. Without shoes on, it wouldn't cause much damage, but he had strength, and the man collapsed to the floor.

"That was stupid." Jean-Claude swung the bat again, straight into his balls. A low blow that had his eyes watering and his brain failing to hold in the scream.

Sonia kicked out, catching Jean-Claude.

"That was a big mistake, bitch." Matthew summoned all the strength he could and strained against the ropes. They didn't give, but the chairs weren't made of the stuff that could withstand a 6 foot 5 giant in a berserker fury, and the back of the chair shattered. The wooden splinters fragmenting all across the floor. His hands were still tied but he could move. He head-butted Jean-Claude, who stumbled backwards. Beth screamed and lunged for him, a knife in her hand. He deflected her first thrust, but her second caught him and ripped through the flesh of his shoulder.

≈

She was free.

Matthew was still holding his own with Beth and Jean-Claude, but the wound to his shoulder wept blood, and it wouldn't be long before he needed help.

"Told you I'd get to fuck you in the end. I'm going to enjoy this." Pit-bull slammed into her, knocking her to the floor. He squeezed her breast. Stupid man. She'd kneed him once in the crotch, and he hadn't learned anything. When her knee met his balls, she sniggered at the shocked expression on his face. She rolled out from underneath him and grabbed a jagged piece of the broken chair. He jumped to his feet and lunged for her again, but before he knew what was happening, she thrust the piece of wood directly into his stomach. He gurgled and blood came from his mouth. She spun to face Matthew just as Beth sunk the knife deep into the cavity of his clavicle.

≈

The pain was excruciating. He struggled to maintain consciousness. The world spun, but Sonia was at his side and removing the bindings at his wrists. He pulled the knife out of his shattered clavicle with a sucking noise. He would only have one arm to fight with but that was better than none. Turning the knife around he struck a line down Jean-Claude's face. He swung the bat out in retaliation but both he and Sonia jumped back in time. Sonia was on the attack this time and managed to knock the smug smile off Beth's face when she caught the side of her face with the chair leg she held as a weapon. It ripped off the lower half of his wife's ear and sent her no doubt expensive earring flying across the room.

"I'll find that after you're dead and pawn it to pay for the next grave stone. Believe me, it won't be as flash and respectful this time."

"How does it feel knowing that you're sleeping with a married man. I'm the reason he wouldn't marry you, because he still loved me." Beth covered her ear but still rolled off a load of venom.

"I think "still loved" you is the optimum word. Sonia is about fifty times the woman you were. And a loads better submissive as well."

"Thank you, handsome." Sonia advanced forward again so did he.

"Maybe you're just a crap Dom. Ever thought of that Matthew? Too wrapped up in saving the world when it doesn't need saving." Jean-Claude aimed for his damaged shoulder, and the pain of the bat connecting with the broken bone caused him to bend and vomit all over the floor. Sonia flipped over Beth and smacked the chair leg over Jean-Claude's head, but Beth was just as quick and had another knife pulled out and sunk into Sonia's leg. She cried out and struggled to stay on her feet. They were losing this battle fast. If they didn't do something soon, they would die. Jasper must be here now. He needed to get a sign out to him. Jean-Claude came at him again, but he caught his arm and thrust his head straight into the wall.

"Jean." Beth called out, Matthew rounded on the battered faced Frenchman to try and slam him into the wall again, but he was too slow, and Jean-Claude took his feet out from under him and sent him sprawling onto the floor. He kicked out and sent Jean-Claude to the floor this time and leapt to his feet in an elaborate back arc. That's when he saw it. The window. He looked to where Sonia was still in arm to arm combat with Beth. She was holding her own despite the fact her left leg was weak. Jean-Claude was still down, so he made a beeline for the window. Wooden boxes where piled up next to it. With dwindling strength and a hell of a lot of pain, he picked one up and threw it through the window.

"You know she came to me after you two had fucked, completely unsatisfied and needing me inside her, showing her what a real man could do."

"You don't get it do you? She'll cast you aside when the next person comes along."

"She helped kill my father so I could take over. She has supported me all these years, and I've supported her."

"She had you kill a baby who could have been yours."

"She made a sacrifice for the sake of the future."

"She's been playing you all along."

"She loves me."

They were circling each other, now. Matthew turned and caught Jean-Claude off guard. With his damaged arm screaming at him to stop, he flipped Jean-Claude over his back and out of the window. He landed with a thud on the ground. His body jerking as the last embers of life left it. It was a shame he died so easily. Matthew had wanted to make it painful.

Matthew turned to see Beth stab the knife through Sonia's body. She fell to the floor.

"No." He rushed for them, jumping straight at Beth. She was startled and couldn't escape him. He had her by the throat. His bare hands tightening around the tiny column that was her neck.

"You bitch. I'm going to drain every inch of your life to make sure that you're definitely dead this time."

"You don't have the guts to do that. You were always weak and self-sacrificing. Besides you forgot Jean-Claude."

"What the Jean-Claude I just threw out of a window."

He had to give her some credit, a look of grief crossed her face for a second.

"Doesn't matter. His replacement is already lined up. And with you dead, I don't have to keep putting off a proposal this time."

Jasper burst in, gun's cocked and ready to fire.

"Beth." Jasper's face turned white. "What the..."

Before anyone else could move, Beth had a knife at his throat and began to press. Time seemed to pass so slowly.

He felt nothing, though. No pain. Surely he should be gargling his last breath. Why was he not dying? Beth went limp. Sonia. She was standing, holding a knife in Beth's heart. She stumbled, and he grabbed her. She tried to speak, but nothing came out. Sonia collapsed. He couldn't move. He was frozen to the spot. He saw people mobbing around him. One checking on Beth, the other on Sonia. He heard the words alive coming from the man checking Sonia. He wanted to kneel down and help the medic who had rushed in, but he couldn't. A blanket was thrown around him, the weight of it sending sparks through the knife wound to his clavicle. He couldn't breathe. He had to get out of here. He staggered in a weaving pattern towards the door. Jasper came up beside him and wrapped a supporting arm around.

"Let's get you to a medic."

"No."

"I'm not taking no for an answer."

"Okay. But not here. I need to disappear."

"Sonia's alive, man."

"I know. But she's injured. My dad could be dead, and my mum lost her arm. It's all because of the decisions I made. I need to leave."

"You sure?"

"Yes."

TWENTY-NINE

Sonia

"I say we go with the blue petunia theme."

"Petunia's are so 2016."

"I agree; Mayfair have gone with Gerbera's. They look fabulous in contrast with the white backgrounds that they used."

"But they don't last that long. We need our display to be the best. We need to get this title back again."

"Sonia what about you? Do you have any ideas?" Miranda turned to face her. The warming smile on James' mother's face had her searching her brain for an answer. She didn't know anything about flowers for goodness sake, let alone how to turn them into an award-winning display for a late summer fair. The fields of sunflowers she had seen in France filled her memory. The ever-present tears of late started to well in her eyes.

"I don't know much about flowers, but in France, they had fields of sunflowers. They looked so very pretty."

Miranda smiled and brought her attention back to her friends. "That could work, you know. The yellow and the black plus there are so many other varieties now. We could use it like a sunset."

"That's a brilliant idea."

"Oh, I like the sunset theme."

The women's voices faded out, as she retreated inside her head. Ever since Matthew had disappeared, she had lived there. James had flown to France later that day and brought her back to England when she was fit enough to travel. She had asked him to take her to see Matthew's parents before they left, but he felt the journey would be too much for her. Instead, he had set up a Skype call with them. Eleanore was doing well and adjusting to having only one arm. Phillip had eventually come out of his coma. He was alive but struggling with memory loss and his speech had been affected. He was fighting it, though. Henri and Loudres were doing everything possible to keep the winery running smoothly for the family. When she was fully recovered from the stab wound to her stomach, Sonia was adamant that she was going to travel back to Bordeaux to see them.

James had brought her back to his home in Kensington and had installed her as a house guest to be mothered by Miranda as much as possible until she decided what she wanted to do next. Her job was there if she wanted it. He would never take it away from her. All she could think about, though, was Matthew.

She got to her feet and informed Miranda she was going to lay down as she was tired. Miranda nodded and offered to assist her to the bedroom, but she refused. Her wound was heeling well, but sometimes, it still pulled a little when she moved quickly or stretched.

"Sonia." James called out when she walked pass his office. "The flower discussion is getting a little heated."

"Just a little. I'm afraid that I'm not really a flower person."

"I have to agree there. I leave that sort of thing to my mother." He chuckled. "How are you feeling?"

"Getting better. I was thinking maybe I should start looking for somewhere to live. Right now, I'm not sure I want to go back into being a bodyguard." At the moment, all she wanted to do was curl up in a little ball and lay there. Not knowing where Matthew was, was killing her. Was he even alive? He'd had some pretty bad wounds. They could have got infected, or he could have bled out. She'd been told he left with Jasper, but she had no way of contacting him, short of storming down the Agency's door and demanding he speak to her. She didn't think that would get her very far, though, and would probably land her in jail more than anything.

"Why do you want to move out? You have your own room here."

"I have Matthew's room."

"It's your room as well."

"I'm sure he'll come back soon, and he's made it perfectly clear that he doesn't want me in his life anymore."

"Have you spoken to him, then?" James, who had been sitting at his desk, now stood and came around to perch on the front of it beside her. His long muscular legs crossed at the ankles. He wasn't her Dom; he was her boss, but he still gave off those vibes that made her shiver with a need to do as she was told.

"No. I haven't." She put her head down like a naughty school girl.

"Then how do you know he doesn't want you in his life anymore?"

"He left me."

"No, he took the coward's way to try to sort out his head. His father and mother had been shot. He didn't know if his father was still alive or not. His mother had lost an arm. You had been taken, and he had to watch guys strip you naked, touch you, hit you, and stab you. Then, to top it all off, his wife, who he thought was dead, reappeared and tried to kill him. He lost his mind. I'm sure the blood loss he was experiencing didn't help that. He'll find it again and be back. Matthew has always been a tower of strength since the first day I met him. He rigidly controls everything. Do you know in MI5 his nickname was 'The Machine'? Because he never faltered, never failed, and never showed he was human. What he's done, taking the cowards route, shows that he's a human after all."

"You've spoken to him?"

"No, I have not. I have a private investigator searching for him, but Matthew is trained by MI5. If he doesn't want to be found, just yet, he won't be."

"Have you tried Jasper?"

"Jasper is loyal to Matthew. I'll not get an answer from him."

"So we're none the wiser to where he is." Her heart deflated.

"But I'm not going to give up."

"Thank you for trying."

"Look, I think we both need a little bit of fun. Why don't we go to the club? You don't have to participate in anything. They have a demonstration night next week. We can go and watch."

"I don't know." She knew that James wouldn't try anything with her. She was Matthew's submissive to him and always would be. He would be like a protector. She couldn't hide away all the time. It wouldn't do her any good. She was just getting into a deeper and deeper mourning for the loss of her future.

"I'll try. I can't promise anything, though."

"That's all you can do." James placed his hand on her shoulder. "Sonia, I know what you're going through. I can't believe Amy isn't in my life. Every day, I want to run screaming through the streets, find her, and carry her back here and fuck her 'til she sees sense and tells me she loves me. But she used her safe word with me. I need to give her time. If we are meant to be together, we will be brought back together. Damn fate and all that. Matthew didn't use his safe word but his walking away means he needs space. I know that it's so incredibly hard for you, because it's virtually impossible for me, but you need to give him time."

"What if time doesn't heal him? What if he loses the love he has for me?"

"Then you'll deal with it, because you are a strong woman. You can survive this."

"It hurts so much." She tried to stifle the tears that were now threatening to swamp her.

"I know." He pulled her into his arms, and his warmth gave her some comfort. "Look. I'm not in the mood for working. I say we order pizza, ice cream, and wine. Put on soppy movies and watch 'til we pass out?"

"Isn't that what girls do when they are miserable?"

"I hate to point this out, but you are a girl."

"That's a nasty rumour I'll thank you not to repeat." A little chuckle left her lips.

"That's better."

"It happens occasionally."

"Just not when my mother and her cronies are talking about flowers."

"Yeah, that was a little tedious. I'm not really a lady who does lunch."

"Alright. We'll go to the gym and lift weights like men, come back, and cry into our ice cream. How does that sound?"

"Perfect!"

THIRTY

Matthew

She looked so happy. Couldn't have been missing him at all.

Who was he kidding?

He could see the sadness behind her eyes, as she followed behind Miranda towards the house. He'd been in hiding for weeks, recovering from his injuries. His arm was still in a sling, the broken bone in his clavicle healing nicely but slowly. The slash down his back had melded together, and the stitches were starting to dissolve. Yes, his body was healing well. His mind, however, was still full of torment.

His wife, believed dead for so long, had reappeared and tried to kill him.

The last few years of his life had been a lie.

But the woman he now watched hadn't been. She'd been the truth, and he'd walked away from her when he should've held her hand and reminded her he loved her. He didn't deserve her. He'd hurt her.

He needed to get out of here. He held his uninjured arm up for a taxi, but it drove straight past, when an Aston Martin pulled up beside him. It was a car he knew well. The door opened.

"Get in." James spoke, his face lined with concern. "If you don't, I'll back up and drive forward again to break both your legs so I can get you in the car."

"You know I can still beat you with just one arm?"

"In your dreams. It's why I hired you, I'm too lethal with my bare hands."

"Good to see you have your humour back."

"Well one of us has to make jokes, or we are just annoying, slightly aging men."

His boss laughed at him; Matthew knew he had no choice but to get in the car.

"How long have you known I was back in London?"

"My sources called me the second you caught the train at Paris. I was going to give you a week to contact us, and then, I was going to storm down the door of your Mayfair hotel. I own the building so don't think I wouldn't."

"It's why I chose your hotel. It would be the kick up the arse I needed if I didn't come and see you of my own accord."

"Plus you knew you'd never have to actually pay the bill."

"Well, that helped."

"Although, I'm considering deduction of the mini bar expense from your wages. I think the hotel sold out of whiskey."

"Helps me sleep."

"I don't have to tell you that Sonia should be helping you recover."

"I know."

"Then why did you walk away."

"Because I was a complete idiot."

"No, you just proved you are mortal after all. I think I like you better for it."

James put his foot down on the accelerator and weaved through the traffic. Eventually, he pulled into Kensington Park and put the car in neutral.

"What are you going to do about it?"

"What do you mean?"

"That girl's barely holding on. She doesn't even know if you are alive or dead. She put all her trust in you, and you shut the door to her. You're her Dom for god's sake. You may have broken the link between you forever."

Matthew shrugged. "I should've known I wouldn't get any sympathy from you."

"You're lucky I'm not kicking your arse for what you did. I understand that you got messed up, but we talk through these things. You hurt me as well, man, disappearing like that. Come on. We're like brothers."

During his time away, Matthew'd wallowed in guilt. He'd never loved Beth, not as much as he loved Sonia. When he saw Beth stabbing Sonia, and her lifeless body fall to the floor, it'd destroyed something within him. At that moment in time, he felt failure, like he'd not protected the greatest person in his life. The one who'd made him the man he was. He couldn't breathe. He couldn't think straight. All his brain had told him was to run.

As time had gone on, he knew Sonia would be angry at him, and he found it harder and harder to return. But he had to see her. He had to know how she was. Had he deliberately made himself visible to James so that he could end the nightmare of his own making?

He smelt like a bloody whiskey distillery. He couldn't remember the last time he'd shaved. He was turning into the man of Sonia's nightmare. The man who he'd helped her see wasn't a demon but weak. Weak, that's exactly what he was.

"I know it doesn't help, but I'm sorry."

"You're coming back?"

"I guess that depends on Sonia. I'm not going to make her life more difficult. She loves this job, and if she doesn't want me in her life, I'm not going to take it away from her. I'll make sure you're adequately covered, though."

"That sounds like you are giving up and not even going to fight for the woman."

"I honestly don't know if I can fight for her. I did the one thing I promised I'd never do to her."

"How far are you prepared to go to try?"

"Why?"

"Because I have a plan."

Matthew shifted uncomfortably in his seat. That expression on his boss's face could be scary. He didn't make billions without being a genius at the art of manipulation.

"Are you going to let me into this plan?"

"Soon. All you need to know for now is to be at the club on Thursday

THIRTY-ONE

Sonia

The bustier looked all wrong. With Matthew, he'd always adjusted it so it showed off her breasts to the best her athletic body could show them. When she put it on, it just looked wrong.

Jesus, why was she even going to the club with James. Would he expect her to scene with him? Maybe they should scene together. It would give them both the Dominant/submissive pleasure they needed.

This was just crazy.

Matthew was just a man. One man.

And she missed him so much. The bedroom seemed so big without him. Argh! She needed to get a grip. She was one of those wimpy women she always vowed she wouldn't be. She was going to go to the club with James, and if he wouldn't scene with her, she would find someone who was willing. She was attractive if she kept her trousers on so nobody could see the scars. She flinched, Matthew would give her ten lashes with a whip for that thought. She was pretty; she was beautiful; she was so fucking sexy he nearly came in his pants when she walked into a room. It'd all been lies. Great big, fat, ugly lies. She picked up her bag and threw it at the door just as James opened it. It hit him square in the face.

"Er...sorry." She bit her lip and looking guiltily at the floor.

"No, I'm sorry. I was knocking for a while, and when you didn't answer, I got worried. I shouldn't have barged in."

She'd been so lost in her thoughts that she hadn't even heard him.

"It's ok, I'm..."

"Do I need to give you ten lashes like Matthew would for doubting you look good? I prefer blondes, as you know, but you look beautiful."

"Do I really look alright?" She did a little twirl for him.

"May I do something?"

"What?"

He went to her cupboard and pulled out a short skirt. It was frilly, teal and black lace. Matthew had bought it for her. It was her favourite. Why did he have to pick that out?

"I want you to wear this."

"Boss." She hesitated, her hand over the skirt.

"Tonight you will call me James or Master when in the club. I'm not your boss. If you want to scene, and you cannot find a partner, which will not happen, we can discuss it. We'll have certain proviso's put in for both of us to ensure we're happy."

"Do I have to wear the skirt?"

"You don't have to, but I honestly think it suits you."

"Ok, I'll wear it."

She changed, and they headed for the club.

She stopped by a scene of a St Andrew's cross and flogger. She and Matthew had once scened on this spot. She watched the rhythmic motion of the whip and felt herself getting warm between her thighs. The memories swamped her. Her heart started to beat faster. She couldn't breathe. She shouldn't be here. She turned on her feet and headed for the door but slammed straight into a solid wall of masculine chest. The scent of him engulfed her, warm, spicy—Matthew.

"Shh. Calm my sweetheart."

That voice.

Was she drunk? She pushed away from the familiar chest without even looking up to the face and began to run towards where she knew her boss was. But a booming voice echoed out, silencing the whole club.

"Sonia. On your knees." Her body jerked, and she found herself dropping onto the floor. "You'll stay there until I tell you to get up."

She shut her eyes trying to block out everything, but she could still feel the heat of everyone's glare upon her.

"Sonia." James' voice permeated her brain. "I need you to open your eyes and look in front of you."

She opened one eye and saw the kind and reassuring face of her boss. Everybody else faded into the background but her boss.

"He's gone. He left me to die."

"You know that isn't true."

"How can I know anything?"

"Here in this place, we work our differences out differently."

"What do you mean?"

"Your Master did not protect you as he should. He did not respect you as he should. You have the right to punish him."

"Punish him."

"Here, on the club floor."

"You're talking in riddles." She was so confused. She was a sub; she didn't punish her Master, did she?

"Sonia."

Matthew, her Matthew. He was alive, and he was here. He smiled at her, but it was a tentative one. He was nervous. He still had his arm in a sling, and he looked tired, but he was clean-shaven and seemed to bear little ill effects of the torture he'd suffered. Inside her, somewhere, a burst of anger exploded. She'd been stabbed, and he'd run away like a coward. Jumping to her feet, she launched herself at him and sent a hit direct into his jaw. He staggered a few steps back as she wiggled her hand to try to get the pain now throbbing through it away. Damn, that man and his strong jaw.

"Fuck, Fuck, Fuck."

"Some ice," James called out, and the bartender was there in mere moments with a cold compress. Matthew stood back while James applied it.

"I should hit you as well for setting me up."

"Matthew'll accept any punishment you chose to give him. I believe he once gave you a count of ten on this very floor for disobedience."

"He needs more than ten." She huffed.

"Then give it to him. Give him as many as you want. He'll take it to prove he was a complete idiot. He wants to earn back your trust by placing himself in your hands."

She looked over to where Matthew stood to rub his jaw.

"I made the biggest mistake of my life running away. I broke the faith you had in me. This is the only way I think I can win it back."

"I don't know if I want you in my life anymore. Did you even care if I was still alive?"

"I received constant updates, but I became a chicken."

"Why now?"

"Because I realised the woman I was mourning for wasn't the one who was dead."

She swallowed. His words hitting her hard.

"Twenty."

"Twenty. What whip?"

She didn't know. She let Matthew choose them, generally. Whips were kind of his thing. Their thing.

"I suggest this one." James handed her one from Matthew's bag. "It's lightweight for you to swing, so it doesn't injure your stomach. It'll still punish him though."

"He can't go on the cross with his arm."

"The bench is free."

The sea of people watching them parted and lined the way to the bench. Matthew'd already started walking there.

"Wait. Your shoulder. I can't do this."

"I trust you to aim where you'll not hurt me." He was back at her side and had taken her hand.

"Amber." She said the word and then clasped her hands over her mouth. She was trusting him again. James stepped away and bowed his head reverently.

"Why?"

"I don't want to hurt you." It was the most honest answer she could ever give. "I know what it's like to hurt, and I don't want to do that to you." A tear fell from her eye. Matthew looked around, and she saw James motion to a side room.

"Come with me."

She took his hand and followed him into the small room. It was the one in which he had taken her virginity. Her heart constricted, as the memories of that night flooded back.

"I still feel the moment you gave yourself to me every time I walk in this room."

"Don't."

"I'm sorry."

"For the comment? Or for running away?"

"Both. I have no excuse for what I did. I was a coward. I thought I'd failed you. I gave you my word I would always protect you, and when I saw you go down, I lost it."

"You should know better than that. A knife wound won't stop me."

"I was a complete fool."

"Yes, you were. Are coming back?"

"If you'll have me. James's pretty pissed off as well. I'm thinking you may be my boss now."

"I like the sound of that."

"Do you ever think you can forgive me?" Matthew fell to his knees before her. He looked so lost. He'd made a mistake, and he was grovelling for her forgiveness. Her tears were flowing freely now. He'd let the darkness win at first, but then, in the end, he'd controlled it and come back to her. She wasn't going to let her own darkness fester inside her. Matthew was her life; he was her future.

"Kiss me." The words left her mouth as the weight of the last few weeks flowed with them. She was free. His lips didn't hesitate to press against hers, and she was home.

He groaned. "I've missed that taste. It's uniquely you."

"Matthew."

"Yes, sweetheart."

"Make love to me."

"How's your stab wound?"

"Healing. Yours?"

"We might need to be a bit gentle on my arm. They had to pin it together."

"Ouch."

"Enough talk, Miss Anderson, more removal of your clothes, please."

Within seconds, she was naked, him close behind her. His lips were at her body, remarking every inch. He kissed over the knife wound.

"Another scar." She sounded downbeat.

"Another mark for me to worship as a part of you." He kissed her wound again before going higher to her breasts. His tongue swirling around the tips as they peaked to hard nubs. She lay back on the bed as he worshipped every inch of her. She'd missed his touch so much. He completed her. They didn't speak. He just slid inside her. Home. He was home.

Their eyes met. She held him in her gaze, and he thrust gently.

"I can't promise you marriage and children. I'm still so scared of that."

"I don't need them. I just need you and your love."

"You have that forever."

The heat started to build inside her.

"I love you."

"I love you too."

The first wave of her orgasm hit her. She couldn't take her eyes off Matthew. The shaking of her body matched his, when he let out an elongated groan of pleasure, and she felt him flood her insides with his seed.

Home.

The word just kept reverberating around in her head.

"May I take you home, Miss Anderson?" Matthew pulled out of her; she whimpered at the loss of his warmth. She wanted him back inside her for at least a week before she would allow him out of her bed. James'd better not plan on needing them for a while.

"You may, Mr Sawyer, but first." A wicked grin spread across her face. "I do believe you owe me a count of twenty."

THIRTY-TWO

Sonia

Marie and Callum's Wedding

Sonia looked around at everyone as they all watched Sally Bridgewater. What had their little group done to anger this woman? She was becoming a thorn in their sides. This time, however, she wasn't going to get a rise out of them.

"She wasn't just known as Mrs Carter. She was also known as Mrs Durand, Matthew's wife, or should I say, Matthias Durand." Miss Bridgewater continued her diatribe. The intrepid reporter thought that she was pushing her buttons.

"I believe a lot of that is classified information, Miss Bridgewater." Matthew stepped forward. He had his serious look on his face. He was ready to destroy the woman. Sonia was instantly back at his side. She linked her arm with his.

"Your lawyers cleared this story?"

"It was from a reliable source."

"A reliable source who's been playing you." She gave a smug smile.

"Pardon." The reporter didn't look so confident of herself now.

Sonia pointed to the part which stated that Jennifer Durand, or Beth Parks, had died in an explosion at the La Font mansion. The woman had no idea.

"Your source has given you misleading information. Either they don't know the full story, or they are wanting you to get sued for publishing misleading information."

"I don't understand." Sally flustered under the gaze of the wedding party.

"Matthew never killed his wife. She faked her own death."

All eyes went to Matthew, and he nodded his agreement.

"I thought for a long while it was my fault she died, but alas, I'm the innocent party. She was working for the other side."

"You're making it all up to make yourself look better. You sent her into that building. You knew she wasn't coming back out."

"I watched a woman I believed to be my wife walk into that building. What came out the other side was a monster." Matthew wrapped his arm around Sonia's waist.

"And if you publish that story, you'll be posting information on a top secret MI5 mission. I believe that even you are aware of the implications of that for anyone still working undercover. I don't think your editor will be impressed. I see the headlines now. 'Reporter responsible for hundreds of women being sold into slavery—all because of some personal vendetta.' You'll never work again."

"Not with a formal complaint about harassment against my wife on your record as well." James stepped forward, Amy at his side.

"Publish away, Miss Bridgewater. As you can see, I have no secrets from my girlfriend or my boss, so your story will do little to harm me. I care not for what the public think. I didn't go into MI5 for that. I saved people during my time there. Yes, there may have been sacrifices, but people survived because of me. That's all that matters."

Without a word, Miss Bridgewater turned on her heels and stomped off.

"I'm proud of you." Sonia stood up on her toes to kiss Matthew.

"People will always try to spoil love," Callum spoke this time. He had Marie in his arms and was kissing her.

"Yes, it's just jealousy on their part. I think Miss Bridgewater needs to get seriously laid and soon." Amy was kissing James in between all her words.

"Talking about getting laid, I think it's about time I escorted my wife to the bedroom." Callum patted Marie on the backside.

"Hey, not in front of my boss." Marie scolded her lover.

"I think your boss is having similar ideas for his wife." Sonia looked over to Amy and James. James was well on his way to getting his hands under Amy's long dress.

"We've got no child for the night. We're are going to make the most of it. Besides, we want to make another one." Amy smiled.

"Amy, beautiful, they don't need those details."

Both couples disappeared to their respective rooms.

"Do you want another drink?" Matthew took hold of her hand and started to lead her back to the bar.

"I'd rather something else?"

"Something else?"

She pulled on his hand until it rested on the cleft between her thighs.

"Thank God for that. I thought you'd want me to dance 'til gone midnight. I've wanted you out of that dress all day." Matthew scooped her up into his arms and carried her at a rapid speed towards their bedroom. She couldn't stop laughing.

"Matthew, put me down. I need to tell you something."

"What." He did as she asked and searched her face for signs of anything being wrong. "What is the matter?"

She took his hand again, but this time, she placed it on her stomach.

"I did a test this morning. I was late."

"Late for what?" She chuckled. For such a smart man, he looked thoroughly confused.

"I'm pregnant."
"Pregnant?"
"Yes."
He went silent.
"How do you feel?"
"I feel fine. I need to pee a lot, but it's still early days. I'd like to see a doctor soon, though. I want to check everything to give me peace of mind."
"I'll get one arranged for tomorrow."
"Matthew."
"Yes."
"Are you alright?"
"You're pregnant."
"Are you angry?"
"Angry? Why would I be mad?"
He dropped to his knees in front of her and started to roll the hem of her dress up so that her stomach was exposed. "I'm taking in the emotion of the moment."
"What does that mean?"
He kissed her belly.
"You have a part of both of us growing inside you. I thought after everything with Beth, I never wanted children. I couldn't look after my wife let alone myself, but right now, right now, my life is complete. You're going to have to cope with me being more protective than James was with Amy, but you're pregnant with my kid. I'm ecstatic." He was quickly onto his feet and twirling her around in the air. "I'm going to be a daddy."
"Put me down." She squirmed.
He instantly lowered her to her feet.
"Did I hurt you?"
"No. I'd just rather you make love to me as opposed to swinging me around the room."
"Isn't that the same thing?" He sniggered.
"Dork."
"You're a dork. Now get that sweet little arse on the bed, Miss Anderson. It's time for me to put myself back home."

Sally Bridgewater

"Well, that was quite a show." The slow rhythmic clap alerted her to his presence.
"You set me up." Sally Bridgewater turned venomously on the man in front of her.
"All part of the plan."
"And when are you going to tell me what your goal is?"
"Soon. Real soon but for now, I think you've earned what you wanted."
"What I wanted?"
"A chance at the man who destroyed your life." She rubbed her hands together in glee. "I want you to fly to Los Angeles. All expenses paid of course. There's someone there I'd like you to meet."
"Who is she?"
"I didn't say it was a she."

"If it involves that man, it will be a she. It's always she and normally not just one."

"Boy, we do have it bad for him."

"I hate his fucking guts and can't wait to destroy him."

"Tut, tut, tut, that bad in bed was he?"

She curled her lip.

"We both know I'm the best fuck you ever had."

"Yeah, you were, until you broke my jaw."

"An accident." He stroked his hand down her cheek.

"One I won't forget." He roughly grasped her breast and started to knead it. His hard cock pressed against her thigh. What was it about the bad boys she couldn't resist?

"How about I take it a little more gently this time." His hand moved from her breast down to her pussy. She was gone. He would have her again tonight. And tomorrow, she would fly to Los Angeles. Her prey was in sight. He maybe a Hawk in his native roots, but Grayson Moore was a pesky fly she was going to squash.

THE END

PART SIX
CONTROLLING HERITAGE

ONE

Grayson

One year ago

"Why don't you come here and sit on my face?" Grayson lowered his leather pants and pulled out his rigid cock; the tip was already dripping with pre-cum. "And you two can suck my dick." Blonde 'one' dropped her lacy thong down her slender legs and straddled over his body and slid up to his face. He could smell how ready she was for him. It was a pretty cunt, but you could tell that it got a regular fucking. But then that was what these girls were for. Brought in to satisfy his basic needs and to get off on the fact they had a movie star's dick inside them. Basic human instinct really. He was always working so didn't have a chance to find a date on his own, and any woman he did meet…well he could never be sure they wanted him for Grayson Moore the actor or person. It was a downside to the career that he loved doing.

"How do you like to be sucked, Master Grayson?"

Blonde 'two' inquired, while twisting her hand up his shaft.

"Show me what you know, and I'll tell you if it is wrong."

He was jaded. Everyone liked to play the submissive since Fifty Shades of Grey, but very few had their heart in it. He wanted a real submissive. Blonde 'two' flicked her tongue over the tip of his cock. He wasn't as hard as he should be. That would make for good reading in the online gossip pages these girls used to discuss how good an actor was in bed. Yes, such things did exist. He better up his game and get his head on straight. The last thing he needed was to be labelled a dud in the sack.

"Take me deeper. I want to feel the back of your throat."

"I don't know if I can." She twilled in her bimbo's voice. "You're so big."

"Then move aside and let your friend try. You can suck my balls instead." She pouted and her friend, blonde 'three', eagerly took over. She had his cock in her mouth and at the back of her throat in a matter of seconds. Blonde 'one' wiggled her hips against his chin. He smacked her fat injected backside.

"I say when you get off babe, not you. Spread those legs further."

She gratefully obliged, and he dragged his tongue up the length of her slit and drove it into her hole. Maybe he could get into this. There was nothing like a juicy pussy to make everything right in the world. His hands slid up her body to grab a handful of her breasts. As expected they were rock hard. Un-natural.

"Fuck this." He lifted blonde 'one' up and threw her unceremoniously on the floor. Blonde 'three' paused midway down his dick. Her scarlet lipstick smudged over her face. "Get off me and get lost."

"What?" The sound of Blonde 'three' reverberated around his rapidly shrinking dick.

"But your PA promised us five thousand dollars if we spent the night with you." Realising her mistake, blonde 'two' made a rapid retreat to her clothes.

"He did what?"

"He pays us to fuck you."

"And I will pay you the same to get the FUCK out of here. Double, if you get out in the next two minutes." This time he pushed blonde 'three' off the bed and stepped over blonde 'one' who was still leg's akimbo on the floor. He yanked his jeans off a chair and put them on. A Rolling Stone's t-shirt was whipped over his head in seconds. His sneakers were next; he couldn't be bothered to tie the laces so just slid into them. Without so much as a glance over his shoulder at the naked, medically enhanced Barbie's in his luxury trailer, he slammed the door on the way out.

"Jared?" He bellowed at the top of his voice. The set was a hive of activity, but everyone stopped and looked at him.

"Grayson." The slimy git of a PA appeared from up the director's arse. He was obviously butt licking again.

"You're fired." Grayson pulled back his fist and sent it flying into the shocked ex-PA's face.

TWO

Sophie

"James, I can't believe you've put me forward for this." Sophie moaned into her iPhone.

"Suck it up sis and get on with it. If you stay working for me forever, we are going to end up killing each other."

"You know I hate you right now." She rolled her eyes at big brother over the FaceTime call.

"Love you too. You'll kill it."

"I'm so nervous." She worried.

"He's a movie star. How hard can being his PA be? It's not as though he does anything of importance." James responded peevishly.

"Given his last PA is suing him for an assault that is what I'm worried about."

"His last PA was a complete dick. I'd been telling him for years to get rid of him. The assault case will disappear. Matthew is working on it." James winked at her.

"That doesn't make me any less nervous."

"Get out of the car, Sophie Isabella North and go do what you're good at. Sort that man out." He frowned.

"Thank you for getting this job for me."

"Not a problem. Phone me in the morning, UK time not LA time. I don't want you calling in the middle of the night."

"Night. Sleep well." She blew a kiss to her brother over the screen

"Night." He waved at her.

Sophie pressed the end button, and her billionaire brother disappeared. She thought a call with him might have relaxed her a little, but it hadn't. Her palms were sweating, and she developed a nervous tick in her eye. She'd been in Los Angeles for a week now preparing for her new role. Since she could remember, she'd always been a part of James' building company helping out where she could, but a secretary was not what she wanted to do. When her brother suggested the role of personal assistant to the world famous actor, Grayson Moore, she jumped at the chance, but now that she was over five thousand miles from her family, it didn't seem like she'd made the best choice.

She opened the door of her rental car and slid her long legs out of it. She was wearing her favourite Victoria Beckham cut out back dress. It was a vibrant red, which matched her brunette hair and tanned skin. She especially liked the zip all the way up the back of the dress. It gave her that sexy edge. Mind you, it was probably a mistake to wear this dress given Grayson Moore's reputation.

"Miss North?" A security guard greeted her at the gate.

"Yes." She replied

"Mr Moore is currently out running. He asked me to show you to the pool area. He has everything set up there for your meeting. I will arrange for your car to be parked inside the grounds."

"Thank you." She smiled sweetly.

She followed the guard, noticing the modern mansion with a high vaulted ceiling and acres of glass. She was used to properties of this size, but James had a flair for antiques. It was a change to see minimalism in play. Well, minimalism except for the occasional picture of odd symbols. It wasn't a case that she needed to work. James would look out for her. It was a matter of her wanting to find her own place in the world and achieve something for herself.

Her breath caught when she saw the view from Grayson's pool area. The infinity pool stretched out to encompass the Pacific Ocean; formal gardens surrounded an outside kitchen and bar. The gardens were covered in succulents not plants, such as roses that she would expect to see in England. As she found later, there was even more to the mansion with an enormous grand foyer and a drive-through garage with its own breath-taking view of the area. There was even a window from a basement room looking into the depths of that infinity-edge swimming pool, also bathrooms with heated toilets, which also act as high-end bidets with cleaning and blow-drying services

However, this was her first sight of any of it, and the pool was fantastic.

'Wow' was the only word she could think of to describe it.

"It's the reason I bought this place." The deep American voice had her spinning on her Louboutin. Her breath caught again. Grayson Moore stood in front of her. He was topless, and his muscular chest glistened with a fine sheen of sweat. His marbled thighs rippled in tight shorts. She opened her mouth to speak, but the bulge in his shorts caught her attention. It hardened; she shuddered in desire before forcing her eyes to look up into his face. His lip was curled in a knowing smirk. He pulled a towel off a chair and wrapped it around his waist. She wanted to slap herself. He probably thought she was an airhead, standing there opening and closing her mouth like a fish.

"I...err."

"Drink?" He asked

"Please." She scrambled for a reply.

"Throat dry."

"Yes." She squeaked.

"Sit." He commanded.

She sat down on the nearest chair immediately.

She could hear him chuckle to himself. Come on Sophie. Get it together.

A butler appeared, as if by magic, with two bottles of iced water. He went to put the water beside her, but Grayson took it from him. The Butler retreated. Grayson unscrewed the lid and held it to her lips.

"Drink."

She obeyed.

"Good." He placed the bottle on the table beside her and opened his own. She watched his throat muscles working to swallow every gulp. She needed more water, maybe a cold shower? The pictures in the magazines and the films didn't do justice to just how good-looking Grayson Moore was in the flesh, especially when he was showing so much of it. His features were symmetrical perfection, and even his hair, wet with perspiration, looked like it had been coiffed for hours. Now she understood why he topped so many eligible bachelor lists.

"Did you read through all the documentation I sent you?" Grayson asked.

"I did." She found her voice, the one that made her sound like an adult, not a drooling toddler. "I brought the signed copies of the non-disclosure contract that you requested. James had his solicitors read through it."

"I expect nothing less from your brother. He's an astute businessman."

"He did have an appendix added to it. He wanted you to sign a non-disclosure for anything that I may mention to you about him. I told him that it wouldn't be needed, but he insisted."

"And that is why your brother is known as a tough negotiator in the business world. He even covers his ass with long-time friends like me." He laughed.

Grayson placed his bottle of water down and took a seat on the chair opposite her. "I'll sign the contract and have his sent back to him later."

"Thank you. I know it's not normal. But he did ask that you fax him a signed copy immediately". She squirmed slightly having to say this to her new boss, but she knew what her brother was like when thinking about his business empire.

"Don't worry."

"Where would you like me to start?" She asked.

"Have you reviewed my itinerary for the next few weeks." They were both sitting, looking out over the pool to the hills of Hollywood.

"I have. There are a few bits that I'm not sure on the timing of, but we can look into it when I've learnt a bit more about how things work here in LA."

"Perfect. That's enough work talk for the moment. Do you fancy some breakfast?"

The butler appeared again. Seriously, was he telepathically linked to Grayson somehow?

"Fruit, Miss North?"

Her tummy rumbled. She was unable to eat anything this morning due to her nerves. Now, she found herself relaxing, and she was getting hungry.

"What are you having?" She asked Grayson.

"Bacon and Eggs. After a run, I require something a bit more substantial."

She bit her lip.

"Would it rude to ask if I could get some Pancakes? I think they have become a weakness of mine."

"Not at all Miss." The butler smiled and retreated to wherever he materialised.

"Well, you can tell you are new to LA. It is novel to see a woman actually request something with carbohydrates."

"Sorry, should I have just had the fruit?" she winced.

"Not at all. I will make sure pancakes are ready for you whenever you have breakfast here."

"I think I really would stand out in LA if I ate pancakes every day."

They both laughed. She noticed Grayson had a beautiful smile. It warmed her heart with its pure nature.

"It's refreshing to find a woman whose curves are natural. Don't ever change that. Look. I'm going to be honest with you about why I fired my last PA."

"The rumours said that he was stealing from you, and you punched him on set."

"I punched him; that part is true, but he was not stealing from me. He wanted to take me along a different direction in my career than I wanted to go. And when I say career I mean reputation."

Their food arrived, and they quieted, while it was served. The pancakes were massive and covered in strawberries and cream. She would need a good run later.

"What do you mean a different direction?" She popped a mouthful in after she finished speaking. Her stomach was telling her that her throat had been cut.

"He wanted me to become more entrenched on the action hero side, not only in films but reputation as well."

"The womaniser."

"You've done your research."

"Actually, Matthew Carter presented me with a file. I just read it."

"Sounds like him. One day, I'm going to get a file on him." He took a mouthful of his bacon and eggs. They smelled delicious.

"You didn't like that reputation? I thought that helped build the franchise and made you famous?"

"Would you like the reputation of being a slut?"

"It's a bit different between men and women. You would have the reputation as a stud not a whore."

"I don't mind having the reputation of being a stud but not when the woman that give it to me are sluts. The reason I punched my PA is that he offered five thousand dollars, of my money, to three women of scant morals to make sure I got off."

"Sounds like a nice man. I can see why you punched him." She rolled her eyes.

"I will have to buy him off to get him to go away, and it sickens me that I have to give him money. I never asked for those women, but for a long time, I accepted them. I was as bad as he." He placed his knife and fork down before rubbing his fingers through his hair. "I left a lot of my culture behind; I betrayed it."

"Your Native American roots?" Grayson was an Indian, the type who wore feathers on a crown and danced around a fire in Westerns but were now often clever business people. It wasn't always obvious from looking at him as he'd inherited a lot of his British mother's features.

"Yes, they mean a lot to me, and I've betrayed them in many ways. I want to get back to them, but I also want to keep true to certain aspects of myself."

"What do you mean?"

Grayson put down his knife and fork.

"Now is probably not the time to talk of this. It's probably getting a little in deep for a first day." He tried lightening the mood with a chuckle, but she could tell that there was something deeper to his thoughts. "I've got a documentary being filmed back in my Navajo lands in a few weeks. We can discuss it more then."

"If that makes you happy." She finished her last mouthful and put the cutlery together on the plate. "I'm not sure I feel like work after that, but I better get started."

"I hope you find me a good boss. I know the reputation that I come with probably makes it a worrying prospect, but I would like to think that I can be kind."

"I'm sure everything with be fine." She gave him her most reassuring smile. He reached out and touched her hand. A spark of electricity shot up her arm. She pulled her hand away and got abruptly to her feet. "I'll call if I need anything."

She knew he had an office for her to work in, so headed back inside. The heat of his eyes burned into her back; he was watching her. It couldn't be helped; she turned back and met his eyes. Was there such a thing as an instant attraction, because there was certainly some strange mojo going on right now. This was going to be an interesting job to say the least.

THREE

Grayson

"When you get there, you'll be greeted the Mayor of Los Angeles, and he will direct you to where you make your mark in the concrete. He is the emcee for the event. He is new mayor as the position was vacant for many years. There will be several other dignitaries from the Chamber of Commerce as well. I'll tell you their names before you shake their hands." Grayson was trying to listen to Sophie tell him about what would happen during the ceremony to put his star on the Hollywood walk of fame, but she had on another tight dress that showed off all her curves. It was rather distracting. Maybe he should have a discussion with her about suitable attire when around him. It is hard to be erect most of the time when she was around. A black trash bag should be okay. But then, it probably didn't help that he hadn't had any naked time with a woman since the three blondes' incident. Time to get his head in the game.

"Do you have a towel for afterward?" Grayson asked.

"Of course. Wouldn't want you all dirty, now, would we." Sophie replied.

She can dirty me up at any time. Fuck. His mind was straight back in the gutter again.

"Are you alright Grayson? You look a little flushed."

"Just a hot day in LA."

"It is. So different from the UK, I'm going to need to go shopping again. Most of my clothes from England are jumpers. You don't need them here."

"I can have a personal shopper come around the house later if you want?"

"You don't need to do that. I can do a "Pretty Woman" act on Rodeo Drive."

"I think your brother may have you on the first flight home if you wore a hooker outfit in Beverly Hills." After he, himself, peeled her out of the outfit and licked every inch of her body. Damn it, he was going to hell. He couldn't seem to have a decent thought.

Her cheeks pinked. "I didn't mean that part."

"I know." He interrupted just as the car pulled to a stop outside East town on Hollywood Boulevard.

"After you Mr famous movie star."

He got out the car to the flashing of paparazzi bulbs. The screams of his young fans grew to a crescendo. "Grayson, Grayson." They all chanted, "show us your muscles." Later, he mouthed at them, and a couple took a swoon. Despite the chaos of the situation, he enjoyed the admiration that he got for his work.

"Mr Moore, it's a pleasure to meet you." The mayor held his hand out, and Grayson confidently shook it.

"Likewise. This is my assistant, Sophie North."

"We've spoken already. A pleasure to meet you as well, Miss North."

She shook the mayor's hand. He was younger than Grayson expected for a mayor and he couldn't help feel a pang of jealously as Sophie gave the mayor a seductive smile. That was his smile. Jesus, was he going insane? He wasn't this type of man. He wanted Sophie in his bed, and he wasn't going to stop till he had her.

The emcee started his introductions, and the ceremony began. He placed his hands into the cement and signed his name. That would be turned into a plaque and put elsewhere at a later date. Next was to reveal his star. Since he'd been a child on the plains of Monument Valley, he'd wanted to be a movie star. He didn't envision action films; he liked the old cowboy and westerns that they shot around his home. He'd love to do one of them, but also he loved drama. Unfortunately, he was told that with his looks he was better suited to action movies. That didn't mean that now he'd made it he couldn't do what he wanted. This was what his trip back to Monument Valley would allow him to do.

He pulled the cover back off his star, and the paparazzi went mad again. He flashed his perfect smile and enabled them to get all the shots they needed. When the ceremony finished, he spent some time talking to fans and signing autographs. Sophie approached him.

"Sorry, Grayson. We have to get going now. Your lunch meeting is scheduled for half an hour." Sophie pointed out.

"Thank you." He signed a final few autographs then placed his hand on the small of Sophie's back. It was a natural gesture, and he didn't think anything of it until the cameras around them started flashing.

"Are you two dating?" A reporter's voice called out. Sophie realised his mistake and pulled herself away.

"Sophie is my personal assistant; I'm just a gentleman." He winked at the reporter. Out of the corner of his eye, he couldn't help but notice Sophie look timidly down at the ground. There was a look of regret on her face. Was it from the loss of his touch or the mistake he'd made? They walked in silence to the car, and that awkward reticence continued until they reached the restaurant for his meeting with a possible co-star for his new project.

"Tessa is already inside apparently. She arrived five minutes ago. The maître d escorted her to her seat and provided her with champagne. I'll wait in the car for you." She didn't look at him when she spoke, simply rifled through a folder of papers that she had on her lap.

"You're not joining us?" He asked.

"I thought you would be better able to sell your ideas to Tessa without me there." She replied not taking her eyes off the papers.

"Oh. I would like you there though." The words left his mouth before he really had a chance to think about what he was saying. She looked panicked. "You've read the script and know it back to front like me. You can give a woman's point of few."

She nodded happily. "Alright. I'll join you."

"Thank you. Sophie, is everything ok?"

"Just a little homesick." She lied. He saw that flash quickly over her eyes.

He couldn't help it. He took her face and gently brought it up to meet his. Her eyes could not look away from him.

"You just lied to me. If you were mine, I would punish you."

Her breath hitched. He'd heard it.

"Do you know what that would entail?" His voice was low and commanding.

"Yes." She expectantly whispered.

The car door opened, and she was able to break the spell that he had her trapped in. He'd never seen someone scramble out of a car so quickly and still managed to maintain dignity and pose. He followed and strode past her.

"This is not over." He pointedly whispered.

The maitre d showed them to the table, which his vivacious actress friend was sitting at. She tapped out a message on her phone but placed it down when she saw them.

"Grayson, Darling." She stood and flung her arms around him, kissing him feverishly on the cheeks.

"Tessa. It is good to see you again."

"And you. I'm sure those arm muscles of yours grow every time I see you. I bet you could bench press me with just the one arm now."

"I wasn't far off in Renegade Two." He retorted.

"No, you weren't actually." Her eyes looked behind him at Sophie. "And who is this lovely lady?" She winked.

"Tessa, this is Sophie North, my personal assistant." He introduced Sophie.

"Just personal assistant? She is far too gorgeous for that."

"Just personal assistant." He growled.

Tessa repeated her over the top greeting with Sophie. He couldn't help but notice that she lingered a little longer with her hold though. He and Tessa had become good friends while filming Renegade Two. Unfortunately, her character died toward the end of it, and she hadn't been in any more of the movies. They had had so much fun. Especially one night at a club when they had both topped a submissive. Tessa was a switch but preferred to only top women. She would have instantly sensed Sophie's passive nature and be interested in the dynamic of their relationship. Even if it was technically still classed as a working one.

He assisted both ladies to sit and handed them menus. The restaurant was one of his favourites, because it served a lot of Native American dishes. Home cooked food presented in a 'posh' way.

Sophie coughed

"Is everything alright?"

He looked over to her.

"The menu's a little bit alien to me."

Tessa leant forward.

"Don't worry, darling, the first time I came here, I had no idea what I was eating. Grayson, why don't you order for Sophie."

There was no mistaking the meaning behind her tone of voice. As a Master, he wanted a twenty-four-seven submissive. That would mean he would order food for her.

"I'm sure I can explain the menu to Sophie, and she can decide what she wants to eat herself." He frowned at Tessa. She just sat there with a smug smile on her face.

"No, that is fine. Please choose for me, Grayson. I don't have any allergies, and I like most foods except for mushrooms. They are the devil's food." She even stuck out her tongue and gagged at the mention of them. He couldn't help but laugh.

"Mushrooms starter followed by main mushroom course and mushroom ice cream for dessert. How does that sound?"

"Like I might throw up in your lap?"

"Maybe I'll get you Goat's milk pancakes, roasted mutton, and then, yucca fruit salad for dessert. How does that sound?"

"Much better." She gave him her cheeky smile. That was better to see. Shame when he turned to Tessa she just raised a knowing eyebrow. He was screwed and not on the level that he wanted.

The lunch meeting went well, and he convinced Tessa to join them in the new project. She was to play his love interest. Sophie excused herself to go to the bathroom while he paid. Tessa leant forward on the table.

"So?"

"So what?" He tried to play dumb.

"She is perfect. Where did you find her?"

"She is an exceptional PA; yes, I agree." He signed the bill and handed it back to the waiter.

"Don't play dumb with me Grayson. I know you too well." Tessa tapped her long talon fingernails on the table.

"Back off Tessa. She is my PA. That is all."

"You want more?" She asked.

"PA." He replied in frustration.

"She's a submissive."

"She is the sister of a good friend of mine."

"She's a twenty-four-seven submissive." Tessa was chuckling now.

He placed his hand on his head and ran his fingers through his hair.

"I know." He almost cried.

"Have you spoken to her about it?"

"No."

"She is what you have been looking for, for years?"

"You don't have to remind me." He pushed his chair sharply back and stood. "Just leave it, please, Tessa."

"Is everything alright?" Sophie was behind him.

"Yes." He answered a little too quickly.

"Tessa?"

"Everything is fine, darling. Just teasing Grayson here."

"I took the liberty of requesting both our cars. They should be out the front."

"You are a God send. If you ever tire of Grayson, I would love a new PA."

"I'll bare that in mind." Sophie giggled. "It was lovely to meet you, Tessa. I look forward to seeing you again soon."

"The feeling is mutual." He watched both women hug and then stepped forward to embrace Tessa himself.

"Thank you for agreeing to the project."

"No worries. I'm looking forward to it."

"I'm sorry for shouting." Sophie walked off in the direction of the entrance to check on the cars.

"I'm sorry for bringing it up, but Grayson, hear this though. Don't waste this opportunity. It will be your biggest regret."

He looked toward Sophie as she shook the hand of the maître d.

"I know."

FOUR

Sophie

They set off from Grayson's LA home early that morning to fly to the private airport close to the Navajo lands. The Jeep Grand Cherokee that waited for them was brand new. Sophie felt a little guilty that its shiny exterior was probably going to be ruined in a few hours by the sandy landscape, which surrounded them. It might be barren, but it was beautiful. A terracotta red, it shimmered in the hot sun. Boy, was it hot!

"Make sure you keep drinking." Grayson motioned toward a bottle of water, which had been placed in the car for them. She had arranged a driver for them, but Grayson had stated that he wanted to do the driving, so they travelled alone. His bodyguard travelled in a car behind, even though he said he didn't need him either. She wasn't going to take any risks on her watch. The bodyguard had been told to stay back and not disturb Mr Moore. Just keep watch.

"And there was me thinking LA was hot." She fanned herself with a piece of paper.

"Told you to pack lightweight clothing." He countered.

"I am glad you told me to change out of the designer dress and just put on a maxi dress. I would be melting already if I didn't."

"See, Grayson knows best." She saw a big cheeky smile spread all over his face. They developed a great working relationship where they spent most of the time teasing each other.

"Sometimes. I'm your PA remember. I'm the one who knows best about where you have to be and when."

"That is very true."

The smile turned to a fake frown. "I'd probably still be back in bed scratching my head wondering how I was going to re-arrange my flight if you hadn't have set my alarm this morning."

"See, talented PA."

"Very smart." The words rolled off his tongue with velvety innuendo.

He had backed off since the day of his star unveiling, and she was a lot more relaxed around him. She knew that she had feelings for him. Every day that she spent with him, she found something else that he did that she liked. She just couldn't risk a relationship with him though.

They pulled through the gate of Grayson's ancestral home. They would be staying at a hotel tonight, as it was easier, but he still wanted to see his parents. His house was nothing special. She learnt that he offered to upgrade his parents on so many different occasions, but each time, they refused. They like the simplicity of the native way of living. In the four walls, they had all they needed. That didn't mean that they weren't the best dressed on the reserve, apparently. His mother had a weakness for fashion and jewellery. She made her own but always made sure she purchased the best stones to do it with.

"Yá'át'ééh."

"Giní" A woman ran out of the netted front door. Grayson was over six foot in height, but the woman was only five foot so looked so strange next to him. He picked her up and swung her around in his arms.

"Shimá." She'd done some basic research on the Navajo language and knew that this meant mother. So this woman was Grayson's mum. She saw it now. She had the same eyes as he, although his colouring was purely native.

"We weren't expecting you for another few hours."

"My PA is a slave driver and wanted to get travelling early, so we can scout out some locations for the filming."

His mother peeked behind his shoulder

"And is this beautiful lady your PA?"

"She is. Shimá, please meet Sophie."

Sophie stepped forward and offered her hand to his mother, but she grabbed her and pulled her into her arms.

"We don't stand on ceremony here, girl. We give big hugs."

"I think everyone I've met in America, so far, does. I think we British folks have far too much of a stiff upper lip."

"No, my mother is just a very huggy person." Grayson placed his arm around his mother's shoulder."

"Be nice Giní or there will be no cactus pudding for you."

"Giní?" She'd heard that word twice, now. It wasn't one she recognised.

"It means Hawk in my native language. That is my spirit animal."

"Suits you. Always watching."

"You better believe it, Miss North."

"I wondered why you were preparing so much food?" A younger well-set woman strutted up the pathway like she owned the place. "Brought another one of your LA slaves for us to supposedly fawn over, brother?"

"Déélgai." Grayson's mother admonished. "Sophie is Grayson's personal assistant."

"And what exactly does she assist him with, I wonder."

"Swan, if you got nothing nice to say them, maybe you could crawl back under your rock and allow me and my friend to have a nice dinner with mom and dad."

She was named after a swan; that was a big irony. She was nothing like the graceful and beautiful bird. From the death stare vibes coming off Grayson, she wondered if the young girl's heart was made of pure venom.

"You think I'd actually sit at a table with someone as filthy as you and your whore. Not likely." A bead of sweat appeared on Grayson's temple. He was controlling his rage, but he was reaching the end of what even he could take. She'd seen him explode once since she'd been in LA, and it hadn't been pretty. She wasn't really in the mood for a repeat.

"Do you have a habit of insulting all guests that come to visit your mother or is it just me, because I'm white?" She'd had just about enough insults to last her a lifetime. She wasn't stupid. She knew what this woman meant by her comments.

"Don't flatter yourself, princess. I couldn't care less what the colour of your skin is. It's the what you let this man do to you that concerns me."

"What pay my salary to organise his schedule? I personally can't see anything wrong with that."

"I think I mean more the fact that he ties you up and beats you up."

"Enough Swan." Grayson's mother stepped up this time. "I will come over tonight to see you, but for now, I want to have a pleasant lunch with my son and his friend. Leave."

"I've no idea why you even still associate with him. He turned his back on us. You'll regret it one day." With that final retort, Swan left.

"I'm sorry you had to witness that, Sophie. I'm afraid my daughter doesn't agree with my son's choice of occupation. Hopefully, one day, we will be able to build some sort of bridge between them."

"It's not a problem. Please, Mrs Moore. Don't think anything more of it." She reassured.

"Thank you, dear. Grayson why don't you show Sophie around a bit. I'll have your dinner ready in two hours. I know you wanted to look at locations for your film."

"Will do. Love you, mom."

"And you." Grayson looked pensively at the floor, as his deflated mother walked back into the house. The elation of their arrival replaced with worry and strain.

"It's not because of your film career is it?" Sophie asked.

"Sorry?"

He looked up at her.

"It's because of your dominant and submissive beliefs?"

He nodded.

"Let's go and look at the locations. I want to know more about where you grew up." She held out her hand to him. He took it. She led them back to the car.

"Take me to see the monuments."

"Sophie."

She put a finger to his lips.

"You know my brother's past."

"Yes."

"Give me time."

FIVE

Grayson

The journey to Monument Valley was made in relative silence, just the sound of the radio for company. Sophie spent most of her time looking out the window, lost in her thoughts. Her brother was one of his friends. He was beaten and scarred for life because of his beliefs in the BDSM world. Sophie was a teenager when it happened. It must have left its scars. She had her left hand on her lap as she sat. He reached out and wrapped his fingers around hers. She turned her head and looked up at him. There were unshed tears in her eyes. Painful memories were flooding her mind. He squeezed her hand, and she smiled. They made the rest of the journey this way. Hand in hand.

"I can drive around the resort if you want, or we can take one of the tours. What would you prefer?"

"I would actually like to take the tour if that is alright. Do something proper touristy. But won't you get recognised?"

He nodded to the cap and sunglasses in the back. "I should be fine."

"The ever-faithful disguise." She laughed.

"It hides a multitude of sins."

"If only it were that easy." She quietened again. They pulled up to the tour stop. He put on the hat and glasses

"No more frowns. Come on." He hopped out the car with a spring, came around to her side, and helped her out with an over the top theatrical bow.

"What was that for?" She looked at him quizzically.

"To see that smile back on your face."

"You're an idiot." She rolled her eyes.

"And you love it."

"Hawk?"

A voice called out from behind them.

"Wolf." Grayson replied.

His friend approached, and they bear hugged, slapping each other hard on the back. Wolf had been his best friend for years.

"What are you doing here? I hope you're not going to start a stampede, Mr famous movie star."

"I hope not as well, hence the disguise."

"Yeah. Not that convincing mate. I saw through it in a minute."

"Yeah, but your ugly mug spent most of its life looking at my stunningly handsome face, so it should recognise it."

"I see you haven't acquired modesty yet." Wolf shook his head.

"Never." They bear hugged again.

"Who's the chick?" Wolf flicked his head in acknowledgement of Sophie.

"Wolf, this is Sophie, my PA and friend. She wants to do the tour, if you can squeeze us in somewhere." Without thinking about, it he put his arm around Sophie and brought her close to him. It was a protective gesture, but it was also a keep your hands-off warning.

"Of course we can. Come on. I'll get you on the next bus. Follow me."

They followed Wolf through the sea of people to the front of the queue. Several grumbled curses under their breath. Grayson dropped his hand from Sophie's shoulder to her hand and gripped it tightly.

"If they only knew who they were complaining at." Sophie giggled into his ear.

"Don't give away hints." He winked at her then helped her into a rundown bus, which they used for the tour.

"I'm so excited about this."

The bus started up. He learnt from experience to hold on, but Sophie hadn't. She went flying at the first bump and landed across his lap.

"I'm sorry." She pushed up, and her hand grazed his groin. He swelled within his jeans. She blushed.

"I should have warned you; it's a little bumpy."

"I'll be sure to hold on, this time."

She quickly tried to scramble back to her her side of the seat, but he placed his arm around her shoulders and brought her into his chest.

"I'll keep you safe." The words were loaded heavily with his meaning. He wanted to protect her in so many different ways.

"I know." She whispered back to him before focusing her attention on the 'Mittens' and buttes. The magnificent, monumental sandstone landforms seemed to connect the ground to the sky. This was where the ancestral spirits of the Navajo Nation were infused with the rugged landscape, which seemed so alien, yet so, oh so, familiar due to its constant use in Hollywood films.

The trip lasted no more than half an hour. He watched Sophie's excited face the entire time. She was happy. He always felt that she held a little something of herself back around him. She wasn't now though. She felt the magic of his ancestral lands. He knew it.

He helped her from the bus. She didn't drop his hand but held it tightly as they walked around the booths, which some of the Indian women had set up. They sold wares, trinkets, sandstone pictures, and some beautiful jewellery, made the traditional way.

"How much is this, please?" Sophie picked up a silver bangle with a natural turquoise stone.

"That'll be ten dollars," the lady selling it replied.

"I'll take it please." She reached into her strap over bag to produce her purse.

"I'll pay." He placed his hand over hers.

"You don't have to." She replied.

"I want to."

"Thank you." She smiled and placed the bangle on her wrist. He handed over a twenty and told the seller to keep the change. They resumed holding hands while returning to the car.

"Grayson." Sophie stopped at the door of the car.

"Yes?" he cocked his head her way in reply.

She went up on her tiptoes and pressed a soft kiss to his cheek. It warmed his body, especially when she lingered close. "Thank you for today."

"It's not over yet. We have dinner and then let's go to the hotel."

SIX

Sophie

The words 'it's not over yet' hung heavily in the air during the forty-minute drive to the Desert Rose Inn, after a fabulous dinner with Grayson's parents. She was sure she should've been looking out the window as the sights, but the true meaning of those words left her confused. It hadn't been the words necessarily; it was the way he said them. The purpose behind them. She was probably reading too much into it, and he simply meant to sleep. She was so stupid. Yes, he was implying to sleep. Time to focus on the landscape; she scolded herself.

"We're almost there." A few moments later, they pulled up to the modern looking, wooden lodge hotel. It was beautifully set against the red landscape. "It's not a fancy hotel; I'm afraid. We don't have a lot of them around here, but I like its quirky style. Reminds me a lot of home."

"I'm sure it is fine. If not, I'll get my brother to build one here for next time we visit." Grayson helped her from the car, and a porter ran out to take their luggage. The middle-aged manager of the hotel appeared and shook Grayson's hand warmly.

"It's a pleasure to have you at our hotel, again, Mr Moore."

"It's good to be back. This is my PA, Sophie North." He pushed her forward, so she could shake hands.

"I believe we spoke when I booked the hotel."

"We did. Such a beautiful accent and an English rose to match."

"Flattery, just what I like." She replied with a smile.

"I've put you in the family suite. It should be quieter there. We have a conference going on, so most of the King rooms are booked. Everything that you requested is in the chamber already, if you'd like to follow me." They followed the slightly greying man through the grounds to a small log cabin.

The second that the door was opened, she knew why Grayson liked this place.

The stunning rooms were furnished just as she would have imagined. Colourful and cosy, like an Indian chief's headdress. It was a piece of Grayson. His flair painted on the walls of a log cabin.

"Do you like it?"

"I love it. How did you find this place?"

"I used to stay at my parent's when I visited, but with my sister's attitude, it became more difficult. This place was recommended, and I've stayed here every time since."

Grayson stepped away and tipped the manager and concierge. She kicked her shoes off and padded through the entranceway into the kitchen. Opening the fridge and pouring two glasses of chilled water, she set them down on the counter. Grayson came into the room and drank his in one long swallow. She couldn't help but watch his throat working as he did so. It was one of her favourite things to do. It was so masculine in its motion. She turned away before she dribbled her desire down her chin.

"I'm going to make a few phone calls. Check the schedule for tomorrow."

She hurriedly picked up her bag and started for the door.

"Stop." Her body froze to the spot. Grayson's demand rendering her limbs immobile. She was a puppet, and he was pulling all the strings. "Face me." She willed her body to keep walking. She knew that if she turned around, she would be lost. She wanted him. He wanted her. "Sophie." Her bag fell to the floor, and she pivoted. Her feet caught in the straps and she stumbled. He was there to catch her. The concern in his darkening eyes boring into her.

"Tell me no." His voice wavered for a moment; his mahogany eyes continued boring into her.

"I can't."

He brought his lips down onto hers. Gentle at first then firm with passion. Demanding entry to her mouth. She opened, and he invaded her mouth with his skilful tongue. Her head was spinning. This shouldn't be happening. Her betraying body preparing itself for the pleasure it needed from the handsome man cradling it. He was her boss. She was his personal assistant. A job that required she make sure he showed up to a meeting at the right time not drop her knickers to satisfy his carnal needs. Drop her knickers. Shit. She was already planning on getting naked. It was getting hard to breath. She pressed against his chest. He pulled back, and she scrambled to the other side of the room.

"I'm sorry. I shouldn't have done that." She looked at the floor, hoping it would swallow her up. "I'll hand in my notice and find a taxi out of here."

Grayson growled. He actually growled. What the fuck! Like the domineering man he was, he prowled across the room in a few strides. He was in front of her and lifting her chin up, so their eyes met.

"Why are you so scared, my little one?"

"I'm not scared." Her reply was barely audible.

"Do you want to fuck me?" The intent in his tone went straight into her pants.

"Grayson." She pleaded.

"Answer me."

She wavered on her reply. He had her captured. She couldn't look away, even if she wanted to.

"Yes."

In a swift movement, he bent down and scooped her up into his arms. They were leaving the kitchen and entering the bedroom, before she could even whimper a protest. He laid her out on the bed like a delicate piece of china. Tender and full of affection. Then, the animal appeared again. Her dress was over her head, leaving her in just her knickers; she hadn't needed a bra with the dress. His ravenous gaze drank in her body. He licked his lips when he reached her breasts. She wasn't a virgin, but no man had ever made her skin heat the way Grayson's stare did.

"Lower your panties down those long legs of yours." Her hands went to the lace top of her black Victoria's Secret knickers. They seemed to be dropping all on their own without her even thinking about it. "Keep your eyes on me." She pulled her pants off over her feet and held them up in the air. He took them, brought them to his nose and took a long drawn out inhalation of her scent. "I'll be keeping these."

"Grayson." She squirmed on the bed, rubbing her thighs together to get friction where she so desperately needed it.

"Legs apart. You know how this works." She did. When her brother was beaten for his sexual beliefs, she did a lot of research on BDSM. Even if she hadn't known Grayson's sexual persuasion, she could just feel the essence of Dom he eluded. She opened her legs to display her glistening sex to him. She was ready.

"How many lovers have you had?" Grayson removed his t-shirt and shorts while he spoke.

"Who says I've had any?" She coyly replied. Her mind was in other places, like the muscular chest in front of her leading down to a rippled stomach and a that 'v' of promise. So much promise judging by the bulge in his designer boxers.

"I know you had at least one. The fact that you're almost salivating at what has captured your attention in my pants and not looking worried tells me that. I think we'll have your eyes on my face for now."

She grumbled while working her eyes in reverse up his body. "I've had two lovers."

"Tell me about them?"

"Seriously?" This was not what she wanted to be doing right now. She wanted his boxers off and what she suspected a massive cock pushing into her.

"I want to know everything about you, Sophie."

"Can't we just have sex and then I can tell you?"

"No."

"Damn." She pouted. "Alright, I lost my virginity at sixteen to the first ever boyfriend I had. We are school sweethearts. It was nice."

"Just nice?" He was still standing at the foot of the bed. She had to look at his face, but every now and then, his gaze would travel elsewhere on her body."

"We didn't really know what we were doing. It got better, but then we went to different university's and split up."

"Who was next?"

"A mistake." She was embarrassed by this one.

"Keep going."

"I went out with my girlfriends one night, and they set me up. I got drunk, and the guy and I had fumbled sex against a toilet wall in the pub. He zipped up afterwards and left without even saying thank you. I was so ashamed."

"When was this?"

"I was seventeen...so five years ago."

"You've not been with anyone since?"

"No. James was attacked shortly afterwards, so I swore off men and focused on my career." Those thoughts about whether she was doing the right thing suddenly flooded back.

"Stop." He demanded of her.

"Stop what?" She questioned.

Grayson climbed over her on the bed, his large frame swamping her.

"Doubting what is about to happen. I'm not going to zip up and walk away afterwards. I plan on coming inside you a lot more than once. And, it's going to be a lot more than nice."

She let out a little chuckle. "I guess you know that from your vast experience in the field of play?"

"Is that a subtle way of asking about my lovers?"

"I didn't think it was that subtle." She shrugged her shoulders.

"It's not as many as you think." And with those words, he silenced her thoughts with another kiss. His lips tasted at the corners of her mouth, travelling over her jaw and down her chin in a mixture of kisses and bites. He reached her breasts and brought his hand up to massage the left while the right was treated to the expert talents of his tongue.

"Oh God." She murmured, her voice husky with lust.

He went lower still, parting her legs with his hands to display her neatly shaven femininity. His tongue worked its magic down there as well, flicking over her clit, withdrawing it from its hood until she thought she might burst. He pressed a finger inside her, then two, stretching her out ready for him. It was all she could do to stay in her body.

"Please." She pleaded. Her hands gripped the sheets, talon nails embedding into the luxurious fabrics. She never climaxed this quickly, even when fondling herself. "I'm going to come."

"Come." He didn't need to tell her twice. She climaxed all over his tongue and fingers. So much pleasure. Fuck. She was high. Her body shuddering so violently. She started to come down, but he flicked inside her with his tongue, and up and over, she soared again.

"Grayson!" She screamed out his name. Her voice was hoarse. Her body red hot from desire but sated by his actions.

He had withdrawn his fingers from her body and was dropping his pants. When he said she didn't look scared of what was in his pants, he'd been doing himself a disservice. Now he was exposed in front of her, he was massive. The thickly veined member, with a slight curve to the left, standing proudly. He bent to ruffle in his jeans. Retrieving a condom, she watched as he covered himself.

"We will need to look into birth control and examinations. Tonight will be the only time I take you with a condom."

"You're rather confident that I will want you to take me more than once."

"How many times did you just orgasm?"

"Twice." She shrugged, the juices still trickling down her legs reminding her of the ferocity and pleasure of both climaxes.

"Can you feel your legs?"

He had a point there. She suspected if she tried to walk she would end up in a heap on the floor.

"Put yourself inside me, and then, we'll talk."

He shook his head. "Miss North, I can already see you're going to change my life completely." He pressed a kiss to her forehead, gently easing past her swollen folds and into her warm and very welcoming pussy.

He filled her just to the edge between painful and erotically painful. Her skin inflamed, and she came again. Her head thrown back in wonderment. Gulping breaths of air swallowed down into her lungs between screams.

"Fuck. I can feel you clamping down on me. I'm going to come as well."

Grayson pulled back and thrust in hard. His balls hit her arse, and his pelvis stroked her clit. He quickened his pace, his control a feathered piece of string. She couldn't not again. Not another one. Oh yes, she could. Grayson slammed into her one last time and spilt his release into the condom. She climaxed again. A fourth time! Her spent body collapsed like a puddle of jelly on the bed. Her new lover withdrew, and she whimpered at the slight tenderness.

"Lay there and don't move."

"I don't think I could even if I wanted to."

She watched him stride off into the bathroom. He pulled the condom off his deflating cock, wrapped it in tissue and placed in the bin. He then brought a damp flannel back to her.

"Lay still. I'm going to clean you up." He placed the warm cloth between her legs and gently wiped away the evidence of their coupling.

"I can do that." She tried to take the flannel from him

"No, it is my job."

"Your job?"

"To look after you."

"I thought it was my job to take care of you. Isn't that what PA's do?"

He turned around and sighed. His shoulder slumped.

"I knew that you should have stopped me."

"I don't understand."

"I want a relationship with you."

"I want that also." She sat up on the bed and pulled the sheet over her body. A sudden chill in the air made her want to cover herself.

"I thought you knew. Knew what I'd want. Damn, I thought James would've told you." He paced away from her. His hands in his hair tugging at the ends.

"I know you're a Dom." She called after him. "I know what that means; in the bedroom, I will submit to you, and in return, you will give me lots of pleasure. I want that as well. Especially if what just happened is anything to go by. That was the best sex I've ever had."

He turned around to face her. "I don't just want you submissive in the bedroom. Sophie, I want a twenty-four-seven submissive."

SEVEN

Grayson

He'd made a big mistake. His dick had ruled his head. And there he was trying to dispel the myth that action heroes didn't have brains.

"Twenty-four-seven?"

"Yes." She sounded so confused.

"I don't understand."

Sophie had wrapped the sheet around her body, but he'd memorised every inch of it. He was getting hard again just looking at her. Time for clothes. He grabbed his trousers and pulled them on, taking a great deal of care with the zip due to his freshly re-aroused state. He padded back along the tiled floor to the bed and perched on the end.

"You're correct about what a submissive in the bedroom is. You place your trust in me to dominate you, and in turn, I'll give you everything I can. However, I want one step further than that. I don't just want to be your Master in the bedroom. I'll control all aspects of your life. I'll tell you what to wear, what to eat. I want to feed you that food. Most times, I'll have you by my side on the sofa or at a table, but if I feel you've misbehaved, I'll make you sit at my feet. I want you to give up daily control to me to know what is best for you."

She shuffled on the bed, he could tell that she was uncomfortable with his needs.

"So basically, I'll be a slave to you."

"Far from it. You'll be treated like a princess. Worshipped and adored. Respected and loved."

"But if I'm naughty, you'll make me sit in the corner like a child." She pouted.

He needed to take a gamble. He could see the submissive in her. It screamed at him to be let out. He turned his voice dark.

"Red stops everything, Amber if you feel uncomfortable, Green for happy. Do you understand?"

"What?" She scrunched her face up in confusion.

"Do you know what I mean by that." Grayson's voice was such that an answer had to be given.

She nodded.

"I have to hear the word."

"Yes." She replied.

"On your feet."

The frown adorning her face belied the decision she was making within her head. She slid from the bed; the sheets still wrapped around her like a Greek Goddess.

"Drop the sheet."

He saw her take a sharp inhalation of breath. She made no movement.

"Drop the sheet." His voice was a deep reverberating rasp.

A moment more hesitation then the white Egyptian cotton billowed to her feet.

"Good girl. I want you to stand in the corner of the room." He pointed where. "Face the wall with your hands behind your back. I'm going to go and fix us some food. You will not move until I come back. If you do, there'll be punishment." She shuddered but didn't go to the corner. "We're in the bedroom Sophie. You've stated you want to submit to me here."

"Amber."

He handed her back the sheet, and she quickly wrapped it around herself. "Talk to me."

"I'm scared. My heart and body are telling me to go and stand in that corner. To do it because I want to. I know that you will not hurt me. I don't fear that. I am afraid of others."

"Your brother's assault?" Grayson knew Sophie's brother well. He was a Dom through and through, even if he denied it now. He tried to get slightly kinky with a girlfriend, and she had her crazy brothers beat him half to death. James had had a massive angel tattoo done over the scars, but in the right light, you could still see how much he must have suffered. Ever since that day, he'd only played in clubs under pseudonyms and often masked.

"Yes." Sophie's fearful voice interjected into his reflective thoughts. "I was only seventeen when he was attacked. Sex had still been an experimental thing at that point. I already knew from my previous encounters that I needed more than was probably normal. When James was beaten, I started reading about the lifestyle. It was what I needed. The instant I read about submission, I just knew. But I couldn't do it. I was watching my brother lying there dosed up on morphine. His back was covered in stitches from how viciously he was beaten. I'll never forget the colour of his skin. It was almost like an alien from the movies. Purples, greens, blues." He reached up and wiped away a tear that tumbled down her cheek. "His wounds eventually healed. Slowly, with physio, he learnt to walk again. But his mind... James had always been so carefree; he was witty and loving, so, so loving as a brother. He'd hold me when I cried over a bad test result at school or a fight with a girlfriend on something as mundane as who was going to marry what member of N Sync. If I had bad period pains, he would bring me a hot water bottle and chocolate.

It was little things, silly things. But he stopped them all. All he did was work, go to the gym, eat and sleep. He shut down. I watched the brother I love become nothing. He's still like that. I don't know if he will ever change. I know he goes to clubs to see women. I'm not stupid. I'm glad he does that, but I just want him to be happy."

He scooted around on the bed until he held her in his arms. One hand stroking her hair in comfort.

"Your brother suffered a significant trauma. I know he is working through his issues; I've seen it, but it'll take time. He's still your brother underneath; he adores you."

"But he was made what he is today because of something he believed in. Something he craved in his soul."

"You're scared that the same thing may happen to you?"

"I am. That is why I've stayed away from sex for so long. I was scared of not being able to be normal when everything in me was screaming to be dominated. With you though, I can't control it any longer. I'm conflicted."

He inhaled deeply. His beautiful girl knew what she wanted but was terrified of the consequences. Her mind and body were in a fight for superiority.

"I can't promise you that you won't be beaten for your beliefs. No matter how much I want to. But I can no more promise a homosexual, a ménage, even different religions. I'm native American. I've suffered in the world of LA because of that. I'm one of the lucky ones who have broken through despite my heritage, but not all make it. Dreams are taken away from us every day. But having those dreams is the important part. You need to have faith in what you want. Tell me little one. What does your body say it wants?"

"It's telling me to go and stand in the corner."

"And your brain?"

"That it will only lead to pain and ridicule."

"Which one do you want to win?"

She shifted and looked up at him. Her big brown eyes filled with honesty. "My heart."

It was enough to break him. He ran a finger from the top of her forehead, down her nose and to her lips. She kissed it tenderly.

"Now, here. We try. If you decide you cannot do it, we walk away tomorrow. We will both always hold our regrets, but at least we tried. You have my word that I will never speak of what happened here. I will protect you in all aspects forever.

Sophie brought her hands up to her eyes and wiped away her tears. She then pushed out of his arms and dropped the sheet. With a soft look over her shoulder at him, she walked to the corner of the room.

He let out the breath he didn't realise he'd been holding for her actions. She was beautiful, accepting the punishment. Her hand's resting gently at the top of her pert bottom were neatly entwined. Her head bowed. He brought his hand down to the fabric of jeans and rearranged his growing, hard masculinity.

"I won't be long." He tried to keep his voice low and commanding. "You're not to move or talk. I will only be in the next room. If you need me urgently, call out ha-glade. It means mine. I will come straight away. For I will always protect what is mine. You may answer me to confirm that you understand."

"Yes…yes, Master."

"Good girl."

He left the room on shaking legs and rested his forehead against a wall. He took several deep breaths to centre himself. Damn, he was so used to control, but right now, he felt wildly out of control. What was this woman doing to him? He was rock hard; his jeans would probably be leaving an imprint on his cock. She was terrified beyond belief but was still submitting to him. He had one chance to get this right, or she would be out of his life. That would be it. He would never find a more perfect mate. He would be alone for life. His heart pained at the thought of that. It took him a few minutes to quickly throw the food, which had been left for them, onto a tray. He warmed up some of the items that needed to be so then headed back to the bedroom. Sophie hadn't moved at all. She'd obeyed. He lowered his jeans as he could no longer cope with wearing them any longer. Jogging bottoms were going to be the way to go when his little one was around.

"Lower your arms to your side and turn around to face me." She did as instructed even keeping her head bowed without prompting.

"Why did I ask you stand in the corner?"

She didn't answer.

"Sophie." Had he upset her?

"Forgive me Master, but you told me I could not speak unless it was to call ha-gade." She looked up, and the sparkle in her eye showed she was playing with him.

His heart leapt. In two longs strides, he was across the room, and she was over his knee.

"You know what cheeky little submissive's get?"

"A spanking?" She said with a wink. He'd unleashed a monster. He ran his hand between her legs, she was wet. There would be time for that later. "Count me ten." He brought his hand down on her bottom in a quick smack.

"One." She squirmed.

"Still or I double it."

"Sorry, Master."

He continued his assault on her beautiful posterior. It looked rosy pink, so hot, with his hand prints on both cheeks. On the final count, he ran his finger back over her folds. She was drenched with desire.

"I think someone enjoyed her spanking. Now answer my question, and then, you can eat."

"I would rather do something else than eat."

He smacked her again. She whimpered at the shock and tried to rub her thighs together. He brought his large hand in between her legs to stop that.

She huffed. "I doubted what you wanted from me. I thought you wanted me as a slave but being a twenty-four-seven submissive is so much more and oh so pleasurable."

"Right answer."

He brought his thumb up against her clit. It took no more than a few seconds of stroking before she came violently in his arms. He held her tightly while she came down.

"Thank you, Master."

"Unless we are in public scene or I direct you otherwise, you'll still call me Grayson."

"Grayson." She hummed dreamily.

He helped her to stand and directed her to the bed. Her legs were barely able to keep her upright.

"Lay down on your stomach." While she settled herself, he retrieved his toy bag and pulled out the Aloe ointment he used for aftercare.

"What's that?"

"It'll sooth the ache. I'm afraid you've pinked up well. It may be a little difficult to sit down tomorrow." He pulled out a bottle of paracetamol from his bag also. "Here take this as well. It will help you sleep. It can be uncomfortable the first time. You're not used to it." He rubbed the ointment in with tender care

"I'm sure people would say I'm mad. I enjoyed you spanking me so much that I need to take painkillers to sleep."

"But the point is you enjoyed it, and I'm taking care of you. I don't hide what I am, Sophie. If people ask about my sexual orientation, I will admit I'm a full-time Dom. I'm the owner of a club. There are always people who call me filthy for what I like. I'm not a masochist for pain. There are certain limits we need to talk about. We cannot go into this blindly if it is what you choose. There may be things I want to do to you that you don't want."

"Fisting; Anal or vaginal. I don't like the sound of that." She interrupted him with a screwed up facial expression. It was so cute he couldn't help but laugh. He helped her to sit up on a cushion. He handed her one of the warmed up goat's milk pancakes. A staple in life.

"Eat." She took it and ate. "That is something I have experimented with before. I can see that it brings some women great pleasure. At the moment though, it is not something I would even consider doing with you. You're too tight. And an anal virgin?" The last part was a question.

"I asked my boyfriend to try it, but it didn't work. He used his finger, but his cock was too painful. Maybe I should add no anal to those limits as well. This feels weird talking to you about this stuff. My mind is saying I should be embarrassed, but I'm not."

"I'm glad you don't feel ashamed talking of these things. It's a good start. As for the anal. Would you allow me to try? I suspect that your boyfriend was not aware of how to prepare you for that type of sex."

She bit her lip as she thought. It did nothing for the erection he still had.

"Ok, but if I don't like it, we add it to the no list."

"Of course. I'm not into blade or fire play. I would like to use whips and floggers on you. How do you feel about that?"

"I'm glad about the blade and fire play. Nervous of the whips and floggers but willing to try."

She finished her pancake and reached out to take another one. He could see the moment it suddenly dawned on her and how she withdrew her hand before it touched the food.

"May I have another please?"

He smiled.

"In a minute. I'm not going to be able to concentrate on anything until I get rid of this." He pointed at his groin. "I want you to ride me."

He stroked himself a few times while Sophie moved the tray to the floor. She straddled him.

"Condom?" He whispered into her ear.

"I'm clean and on the pill."

"I was checked after I fired my last PA."

"Please let me have you in me bare."

His answer came in the form of pulling her down on his cock. Relief, he was sheathed within her tight pussy. It was home. She clenched down on him, and he helped her to start moving up and down his length. Every time she swallowed him whole, it must have been banging her sore backside down on his legs. She proved to be the kinky little girl who he thought she was when she brought herself down faster and further. They were in a steady rhythm now. He was lost in her eyes; they were joined as one. His perfect woman. His. She was his. And as he emptied his seed into her warm havens, he knew he'd fight tooth and nail to keep her.

"Yes."

She uttered breathlessly, drawing him from his post orgasmic haze.

"Sorry?"

"I'm yours. Twenty-four-seven. I am everything that you need, because I'm already half in love with you."

"I think I'm already fully in love with you." Was his breathless reply.

EIGHT

ONE YEAR LATER

I now pronounce you Mr & Mrs Grayson Moore. You may kiss the Bride.

Er...Mr Moore I think maybe you should remove your hand from under Mrs Moore's dress and your tongue from her throat. I do believe there are lots of guests watching.

NINE

Sally-Bridgewater

Three Years Later

At least the plane journey had been in first class. It seemed to take forever to fly to Phoenix from the UK. Sally had never been one for travelling. Shame it was part of her job, an intrepid investigative journalist for the London Daily Magazine. It might sound like a cheap little rag, and well, to be honest, before she arrived, it had been. She got the big stories that helped it grow. Many of them were thanks to her kind benefactor. But enough of him for now. He finally gave her the go-ahead to go after Grayson Moore, and she was going to do everything within her power to destroy the arrogant movie star once and for all. He deserved no kindness from her, and he wouldn't get it. He would be penniless and alone in the gutter when she was done with him. That was how much venom she felt towards him.

The car pulled up to the run down shack of a house in the middle of the red sandstone desert. So this was where the poor little Indian boy, who made good, originated. She wondered if they would let him back into his homelands after she had finished destroying him. Judging by the emails that had led her to this place. She very much doubted that and, boy, did that feel so perfect.

A raven hair woman opened the door to the house. Sally got out of the car, grabbed her bag, which contained her laptop, recorder, and notebook and went to greet her.

"Hello. Swan, isn't it?"

"Yes, Miss Bridgewater." They shook hands. Grayson Moore's sister was tiny. She couldn't have been more than five foot three, if that. Sally knew that Grayson's mother was white and only his father was Native American. But Swan, as she was called in her mother tongue, looked pure Indian.

"Please call me Sally." She responded politely.

"Sally, come in."

She followed the young girl into the house. It was little more than a kitchen and seating area with room to the side that held mattresses on the floor for beds. It was spotlessly clean though.

"I'm sorry. My home is basic. I'd rather die than accept any of my brother's money."

"I understand." Sally motioned to a chair. "Shall we sit, and you can tell me more?"

"I'll get you a drink first. You must have had a long trip. I've never been out of Navajo lands. I choose not to, because I don't like the world I've seen in print and on the TV beyond our borders. But I know how long it takes to travel anywhere, and I looked on a map, and London is so far away."

Sally tried not to roll her eyes. This girl was going to be easy to manipulate. She was a complete simpleton.

"It has taken me almost twenty-four hours to travel here."

"That is a long time." Swan handed her a drink. It was a putrid green in colour.

"What is this?" She inquired with genuine interest.

"It's cactus juice. I make it myself."

"I can't say I've had that before. Thank you." She took a sip. It was the most disgusting thing she'd ever had in her mouth, and she'd had some pretty revolting things in there to facilitate a story. She tried not to pull a face.

"It's delicious." She placed the glass down on the table. "You don't mind if I record everything that we talk about, do you? It just makes it easier, and I write everything up later."

"Of course not. There's nothing I'll tell you that I'm ashamed of. My brother is a disgrace to his ancestry."

This naïve girl was going to be perfect for her plans.

"I know little about him." The massive lie quickly left Sally's lips, "but what I do know makes me sick." She turned on her recorder.

"That is the horrible part. He was such a lovely child. So caring as a brother. Willing to do anything for me. Prominent in the community as a whole. He volunteered whenever it was needed. Then he got that job offer. He changed overnight." Swan rested her elbows on the table to help aid her thinking process it seemed.

"The part in the first Renegade movie?"

"Yes. We didn't even know that he auditioned. He told us that he was going away with a couple of his friends for a week. When he came back, he said he was going to be a movie star. Mom and Dad were happy for him, but I was sceptical. He's a more sensitive soul than an action movie star. I've seen some of those films. All they do is run around and kill people. Rescue the girl. That sort of thing. Where is the side of Grayson that I know? Or knew." Swan spat out bitterly.

The Indian had finished her cactus juice and was pouring some more. The bottle was held out to Sally.

"I'm fine thank you." Sally took another sip of the juice to look polite. She hoped that it wouldn't make her sick later. "Have you watched his films?"

"I watched the first one. Mom and Dad had a massive party for the premiere of it. Every time he was on the screen people were applauding. I didn't enjoy it though. Too much of my brother on display. And that scene at the end, when he rescues the woman and they fornicate on the beach, it's disgusting. The way he tells her what she can and can't do. That isn't romantic." Swan shook her head in disgust.

"Critics have applauded that scene, saying it is good to see an action hero with a bite finally." Sally happened to enjoy it as well. Despite hating Grayson, she had to admit he had a pretty perfect body, made for the big screen.

"The critics know nothing." The young girl's face turned red with anger, "That film made a mockery of my ancestry. They purposely chose Grayson because he is half Native American. They are vile creatures who drew him into their web of lies and deceit. Manipulated him into someone, no something, I no longer recognise. And he allowed it to happen."

"How did he change?"

"Sexually."

"What do you mean?" Sally asked.

"He was virgin when he left here. My mother brought us up to be good people. To save our purity for when we are married. But they turned him into the wrong sort of man."

"What do you mean by the wrong sort of man?" They were getting to the good stuff now. That bit that could destroy Grayson's reputation; he was known as a womaniser, and people didn't care because he appeared to be a nice person.

"The kind of man who turns his back on his ancestry just so that he can get sex."

"Turn his back?" Sally was almost rubbing her hands in glee, an evil cackle stuck in the back of her throat desperately screaming for release.

"Yes. You've seen the reports. He always has a different woman on his arm, sometimes more than one. His ex-PA said he would pay them to have sex with him. He gave away his money to sluts so that he could get his kicks when we, his family lived in poverty."

"I thought you said that you wouldn't take a penny from him?" She needed to make sure the story was cast iron tight so that Grayson's solicitors could do nothing to stop it reaching worldwide.

"I don't want a penny." Swan snapped back. "I like my home. We're a big community though. People are suffering here. Individuals on whom he could have spent that money. We need a new town centre hall; the old one is damaged and may not last long. The Chiefs need respect; they cannot have it when that is their base." Swan shifted in her chair when she spoke

"Has Grayson been asked to donate?"

"He shouldn't need to be asked. He turned his back on his family. He knows nothing about what is happening here anymore. He should still keep in touch with us and aim to help. Do you know that last time he came back here?" Swan's voice was raised in great fury.

"No."

"Two year's ago. He brought his slut of a wife here. The two of them dripping in gold and designer clothes. Her with a dog collar around her neck. It's disgusting watching them together. She walks behind him, only speaks when he allows her to. She isn't allowed to eat anything that he doesn't let her or feed her himself. It's sick. Grayson Moore is not the great film star he makes himself out to be. He is a traitor to his blood. He neglects his family and treats his wife like a pet." Swan lowered her head towards the Dictaphone as she spoke. Each word was coming out with such revulsion and vehemence.

"As well as the money he's spent on the woman of ill repute; where else do you think he's neglected the community." It was time to go in for the killer blows.

"Those clubs he bought." Bingo! She had Grayson's career in the palm of her hand and was about to squash him like the bug he was.

"You mean…" She lowered her voice so it looked like she was repulsed as well. "The clubs that he bought?"

"Yes. Those clubs. He would rather buy a sex club than help out his family." Swan's rage was so potent that it bubbled over in a display of aggression that saw her pick her cup up and throw it at the wall. The green slime slid down the wall and mixed with the sandy dust that appeared to be a feature in the house and everywhere else in this barren place.

Swan's hatred of her brother was pure gold. Sally was finding it so hard not to jump up and hug the girl. This would be her finest article yet.

"I'm sorry." Swan got to her feet and grabbed a cloth.

"It's alright." Sally took the cloth from her and made a show of wiping up the cactus juice. "After hearing everything you have to say, I'm as angry as you are. He can't be allowed to get away with this."

"You're going to destroy him?" Swan looked at her hopefully.

"It seems to me as though he wants to forget who he is. I'm not going to allow that to happen. Mr Moore has ignored his roots for far too long now. It's time that he was reminded of his upbringing and the family that gave him the skills he needs to be who he is today." Sally came back over to Swan and pulled the now crying girl into her arms. "Yes, Swan. I'm going to demolish your brother's life as he knows it."

TEN

"It's beautiful." Grayson watched Sophie wipe away a tear. She was lounging on a plush leather sofa in their LA home, reading the script he had written with his screenwriter friend. It was five years in the making, but they finally finished it.

"Really?"

"Yes. The way you work your ancestry into the story is incredible. I can really feel your heart in it." She giggled. "The Academy really needs to get this on the Oscar nominations."

"I'm not sure it's that good, but I'm happy to settle for critical acclaim and maybe the highest grossing film of all time. It's about time Avatar stood down from that."

Sophie took the script and whacked him gently with it. His heart leapt. Even after four years together she knew how to get him going.

"I think someone is looking to be a naughty little imp doing that to her Master."

"I...er..." She licked her lips.

"On your knees before me." His wife quickly obeyed and settled between his open thighs. Her long brown hair cascaded over her shoulders like a waterfall over a rocky cliff. "You know what happens when you sass me."

"I have to apologise."

"You do. And how do you apologise to me."

"By sucking your cock till it explodes down my throat." Fuck! The words out of her mouth were like the most beautiful symphony. Grayson made quick work of freeing himself from his jeans. He stroked his length up and down while Sophie sat back on her heels and waited for him to allow her to begin her part in this.

"You want my cock little one?"

"Yes, please." Her words were breathless.

"How much do you want it?"

"I'm desperate for it. To taste your desire, to choke on your size."

He moaned his response.

"Lick me from the base to tip." He sat back to watch.

Sophie poked her tongue out from between her ruby red lips and brought it down on his length. He gripped the chair as she repeated the movement.

"Sod going slow." He took the back of her head and thrust it down on his length. She gagged at the surprise; recovered and swallowed him into the back of her throat. He was controlling the movement now. Using her mouth to get himself off. They both liked it this way, because it was the trust that she had given to him. His hands twirled tighter in her hair pulling on her scalp.

"Damn baby, that feels so good. You really are good at apologising to me. I think I like you being a naughty little girl."

Sophie purred in the back of her throat at the praise. It sent tremors right down his dick. He was going to come. Grayson pushed her head back down his length one final time and held it there as he emptied himself into his wife's mouth. She took everything he had. He was spent and released Sophie and collapse back onto his chair.

"Clean me up." He still had a little bit of dominating tone in his voice, although most of it was covered by contentment. Sophie licked him clean and then popped him back in his trousers. She went back onto her knees in front of him.

"Into my lap little one." Like a puppy who being praised, she wiggled her backside and scrambled up into his arms. He stroked the collar around her neck. It was a simple necklace made of gold with a diamond encrusted 'G' and 'S' woven together as a pendant.

"I love you, Master."

"I love you too." He smiled. "I think after that you've earned some play time. Do you want to go to the club later?" The club had been one of his first purchases when he had enough money to buy it. He'd been taken to it when he first entered the world of showbiz. The Fifty Shades of Grey film was popular, and an unscrupulous pimp decided to jump on the bandwagon of the Dominant and Submissive lifestyle. Shame the services he offered were from women who had been sold into slavery to pay off debts. He'd been so disgusted that the second he had the money he bought the club and shut it down. He helped the women find new lives away from the pain and fear they had been living under. What shocked him more was that several had become so ingrained in the lifestyle that they didn't want to leave it. That was when he decided to turn the club into a proper BDSM one. Membership, health checks, pension plans, the works. The girls were employed to waitress and scene with the club's highly trained masters, if they wanted to. Several told him he saved their lives. They no longer feared what would happen to them. They enjoyed sex once more. He couldn't have been prouder of his decision.

Sophie bounced on his lap, and it brought him back to the here and now. "Can we please? You promised me a violet wand the next time we went. Please." She was giving him the puppy dog eyes, which meant he could deny her nothing.

"If you can be a good girl for the rest of the day, we can. Go do your PA work."

"Thank you." Sophie got off his lap and went off to their home office. Grayson got to his feet and went into the kitchen. He needed a cold drink after that climax. His legs were still a little wobbly. He grabbed a Coke from the fridge and picked up his phone that had been charging on the counter. Thirty-eight missed calls? Several texts and voicemails. He'd put it on silent when they'd been reading the script, as he didn't want anything to disturb Sophie's concentration as she finished the last act. He'd even turned off the house phone. Grayson used his touch identification to open his notifications. They were from his agent and several other identified sources. There were some from James and Matthew as well. What the hell was going on? He pressed the call button to his agent, but before there was an answer, an ear-piercing scream came from Sophie. He dropped his phone and found himself running through the house to the office.

"Sophie." He slammed the door open to find her crying at her desk. "What's happened?"

She pointed at the screen of her computer. His mouth fell opened as he read.

Multi-millionaire movie star, Grayson Moore, leaves his ancestry behind to run a string of sex clubs.

What the fuck was going on? He read on.

Grayson Moore, the star of the Renegade films has left the Chiefs of his tribe to fend for themselves in squalor while he purchased, Infinity, a club that has been involved in sex slavery. The twenty-eight-year-old movie star even takes his wife to these clubs and leads her around on a dog collar. Sophie Moore, nee North, is the sister of British billionaire James North who is also well known for his warped views of women. Moore's sister, Swan, lives in a one-bedroom hut in the Navajo Desert, stated that she was appalled at her brother's behaviour. She called him a disgrace to his Native American ancestry. Swan feels that he was corrupted by the glittering lights of Hollywood and that there is nothing of the caring brother left. He hasn't even visited his family in two years."

That was enough; he couldn't read anymore. Grayson picked the computer up off the desk and threw it hard at the wall. Sophie screamed again.

"Grayson." She called out in fear. It permeated his brain, which was filled with anger and fury.

"My fucking sister. That's the biggest pile of crap I've ever read."

"I know. We need to get onto your agent?"

He picked up the phone and dialled.

"Grayson. Thank God. Have you seen the news?" His agent sounded harassed when he answered the phone.

"Just. What the fuck is going on?" Grayson placed the phone on speaker so that Sophie could hear everything that was being said.

"Sally Bridgewater of the London Daily apparently did an interview with your sister. I've no idea how she got access to her. We've always kept her out of the press for this reason exactly."

"Sally Bridgewater?" Sophie exclaimed. "She's been after my brother and his friends. She's playing a game with us."

"Can we get the story dismissed as a bunch of lies?" Grayson added.

"You're not going to like what I'm about to say but no. Everything she had printed is accurate as far as we can tell." His agent replied.

"Accurate." He yelled into the phone. "The article accuses me of neglecting the Chiefs of my tribe. I've given loads of money to them; four years ago, I gave them half a million to build a new community centre."

"Um." His agent hesitated on the other end of the phone.

"What?"

"Maybe Mrs North should leave the room."

"Sophie and I have no secrets."

"You gave the money to your last PA for the community centre. The audit trail shows it never got there. It went straight to the women who were employed to bed you." His agent went quiet.

Sophie turned away from Grayson's touch, a loud sob ripping from her throat.

"I've been a complete idiot."

"I think we all have been. I've got the solicitors working on what we can do and say now. I'll call you back later. Stay home. Don't go out. Make sure Sophie stays home as well. The article talks a lot about your lifestyle and not in a good way."

"Ok." It was all he could say before he hung up and replaced the phone. "Soph?"

She came into his arms with genuine love in her eyes.

"I'm scared." She whispered into his chest.

"I know. We've got a good team around us now. We'll let them sort it. We know the truth. That is all that matters."

"You should phone your parents. Warn them what is happening. They'll probably have more press arriving to ask questions."

"I'll get one of the guards to bring them here for safety."

"For Swan's safety as well, I think your dad will go mad when he finds out."

"She's created her own problems. I'm not going to waste any time on her." His sister could go to hell, as far as he was concerned. Alright, he hadn't been back to his Navajo lands in two years, but his parents and friends had visited them loads. He'd even hosted some of the Chiefs. He picked up the phone to call his parents, but it rang in his hands. The caller ID showed it was the club manager, his good friend Wolf.

"Wolf?"

"Hi mate. I know you're probably busy with the fallout of the article, but we've got a bit of a situation down at the club?"

"What is it?"

"A riot."

"A riot." Sophie gasped.

"Hawk, the club. They set fire to it. We managed to get the girls who live there out, but a couple got hurt in the process.

"I'm on my way." He threw the phone back in the holder.

"We were told not to go out." Sophie grabbed his hand.

"You stay here. I'll get a guard to sit with you."

"No." She urged.

"I have to see and help the girls."

"Then I'm going with you." Sophie was defiant.

"It's too dangerous."

"The girls will be distressed. They know me." She was right about that one. Some of the girls had been through so many horrors. He and his wife looked after them and gave them a home and a life.

"You stay with me at all times."

"Yes, Master."

He touched the collar at her neck again.

"You are a good man Grayson. Don't listen to words in the article."

"As long as I have you by my side and you believe in me, I won't."

"You've got me always. Till death do us part, remember." Sophie replied.

The closer to the club they got, the busier the streets LA streets became. Grayson had clubs in LA, London, Las Vegas, and Florida. He was a silent partner, up until now. All the clubs were used to hurt and degrade women in the past all in the name of so-called BDSM. He turned them around to be places where people could happily live the lifestyle without fear or punishment that they didn't want. None of that was talked about in the article.

He turned his car onto the road where the club was. The red and blue lights of the troopers, ambulances, and fire engines flashed. Shit. He wondered how severe was this fire? The answer was given to him straight away when the burnt out remnants of a building loomed in front of him. Sophie gasped beside him and grabbed his hand.

Wolf ran up to greet them as Grayson showed his ID through the window of the car to pass through the police cordon.

"I'm sorry, but I thought I had to call you."

"It's ok, where are the girls?" Grayson jumped out the car and went around to Sophie's side to help her out. He kept a tight hold of her hand. The car that contained his bodyguards stopped behind him, and the two burly men filed out to stand beside him and Sophie.

"Jane and Callie are in the hospital. Smoke inhalation and minor burns. They were sleeping upstairs and had to be rescued by the firemen. Alexia is with Gina and Becky in the cafe. She was visiting for Jane's training."

"Burns." Sophie squeezed his hand. It was the only word that he'd heard as well.

"Wolf, will you take Sophie into the café? Carl, go with them." One of the bodyguards nodded. "I'm going to talk to police." He could feel Sophie tense beside him. He pulled her aside.

"It's ok. I'll be just over there. You know Wolf and Carl. They'll protect you."

"Ok."

"Good girl. I love you."

"I know. I love you too."

He reluctantly let go of Sophie's hand, but he knew she would be safer in the café than out here in the open. He could already see the crowds of onlookers that had formed. The flashes of cameras from reporters dying to get the best picture of the unfolding situation. The high from his earlier climax was well and truly gone.

He strode over to the police officer who appeared to be in charge, but before he could get there, a commotion appeared in front of him. A large crowd of people were after him. Waving banners in his direction and shouting insults. The guard with him grabbed him and tried to pull him away, but it was too late. The crowd surrounded him. Flashes of cameras blinded him.

"Pervert!" A woman slapped him hard on the face.

"Sicko." Another kicked out at him. His bodyguard tried to get in front of him.

"Mr Moore, do you have any answers to the fact you've neglected your family so you can have sex with whores?" A reporter thrust a microphone into his face.

"Is there to be an investigation into the women who work at the club. Have you been involved in human trafficking?"

Grayson stared at the reporter who had posed that question. Where had that one come from? He was involved in nothing of the sort. Everything seemed like it was happening in slow motion. The world that he knew was falling apart, and he felt like he was standing there just watching it.

"Grayson." Sophie's cries echoed out above the crowd. She was nearby and not in the café. He looked around to see her fighting her way through the crowd. The other bodyguard, Carl and Wolf with her. She reached him the same time as the police started to push the crowd away. He grabbed her and pulled her to him.

"Move," Carl shouted at him. He nodded and started running for his car. He had Sophie's hand and was pulling her with him. The crowd followed still shouting the insults. "Faster." The bodyguard was pushing them along now. Sophie's hand slipped from his, and she fell. He tried to turn back to get to her, but Carl pulled him away. The crowd surrounded her. He couldn't see what was happening. Grayson punched Carl square on the jaw, and he was free. He went back to Sophie, pushing people away from her. The police did the same and formed a cordon around them. He pulled her into his arms, checking every inch of her for signs that she was hurt. Her hands and knees were scrapped. He would clean them up later. He got to her neck. Her collar, it was gone. Sophie let out a pained cry and opened her hands. In them was her collar...broken.

ELEVEN

Sophie

Sophie turned in the bed to face Grayson. He'd finally fallen asleep an hour ago. It was the early hours of the morning; mind you, she wasn't really sure what time it was as they were somewhere over the Atlantic on their way to England. After the incident earlier that day, her brother phoned and insisted that Grayson bring Sophie to England for protection. Neither of them had had the strength to argue. Grayson's face was covered in lines of stress even in his sleep. He had a black eye forming where he was hit by one of the protestors. Sophie touched her neck. Her collar was gone, ripped from her body by the crowd who proclaimed her free of the monster. Its remnants lay in a box in her suitcase. Grayson assured her that as soon as they got to England, he would look for someone to fix it for her. It wouldn't ever be the same though. It was tainted now.

The plane hit a bit of turbulence; it did little to settle her stomach. Maybe a glass of water would help. Throwing her legs out of bed, she grabbed a robe and tied it around her waist. Carl and Damian, their bodyguards, were sleeping in their seats when she stepped into the galley kitchen to find a bottle of water. The stewardess jumped to her feet.

"Mrs Moore what can I get for you?"

"It's alright. I just want a bottle of water."

The stewardess was at her side and pulled out two bottles before she had a chance to think.

"Still or sparkling."

"Sparkling please."

"Is there anything else you want?"

Sophie ran her fingers through her hair.

"The ability to sleep."

"I wish I could pull that out of the cupboard for you." The stewardess smiled sympathetically. "Mr Moore is a good man no matter what they say. And I can see that you really love him. That's what counts."

"Thank you. That means a lot."

"Goodnight, Mrs Moore."

Sophie nodded her reply and pushed the door to the bedroom open. Grayson was sitting up on the bed rubbing his eyes.

"What's wrong?" He queried.

"I needed a drink."

"Damn, I'm sorry. I didn't get you one before we settled down."

"That's ok." She reassured. "You had a lot on your mind."

"No, it's not." He snapped at her. "I'm supposed to be looking after you."

"Hey." She climbed into the bed and rested her hand on his strong jawline. "You are looking after me. Don't doubt that because of what is happening."

"I let your hand go." He looked so sad.

"You were being pushed along by Carl and Damian. I had high heels on. It was a dangerous situation. It was going to happen, and there was nothing we could do to stop it. I'm just glad they got you to safety before anything worse happened." She gave him a kiss to show she was not upset about what had happened.

"Worse, they broke your collar."

"Which can be fixed." She'd been distraught about the collar. She loved having the symbol of being owned and cared for, but there was something that she was more worried about. "When I saw the crowd around you I was so scared. I knew you told me to stay with Wolf and Carl, but I couldn't. I had visions of them beating you like my brother. All I could think about was getting to you and protecting you from that."

"You were terrified that what happened to James might happen to me?"

"Yes. When that woman hit you, I wanted to rip her hand off." She quieted; the thoughts she had in her head were all jumbled up. She needed to collate them before she spoke. "I love our life, and I don't want anything to change."

He pulled her close to him.

"You're not scared of physical violence to me, it's the emotional scars it will leave." He understood her perfectly.

"Yes. I'm scared that you'll become like James and stop being who you are. You've done nothing wrong, yet you are being reviled because of it."

"I'm not James; the situation is different. I was scared out there today. I will admit that. But not because of who I am. As you say, I've done nothing wrong, and I'm not going to change. You misbehave little one, and I'm going to pink that backside of yours until it glows. What upset me most is that the reports criticise me for neglecting my roots. I need to reflect and reconcile myself with that. Maybe I have done my ancestry wrong. They never got the money for the community centre; I didn't follow it up.

She had to interrupt him there. "You can't be held responsible for that. You gave the money to your PA in good faith to help out the Chiefs. You were not to know he paid women instead."

"But I should have checked." She could see that there was no point in discussing this further. Grayson had made his mind up that the blame lay partly with him. He would see it right though. That was the sort of man that he was.

"We can think more on it tomorrow. I think we should get some sleep."

"Sleep in my arms?" He asked.

"Of course." She would never deny him.

The plane landed four hours later, and they were whisked away to James' country mansion in Yorkshire where she crawled into bed for almost fourteen hours of sleep. Sophie felt awful. Lack of sleep and tears had left her with puffy eyes. She had scrapes on her hands and knees, and every time she tried to eat something, she felt sick. Grayson made her eat, of course. He seemed more relaxed this morning and focused. They were both in the kitchen with a lavish spread of breakfast laid before them. Grayson was on the phone to Wolf for an update on Jane's and Callie's conditions when James popped his head around the door.

"I hear someone needs a cuddle from her big brother." Emotion hit her, and she burst into tears.

"James, you're not supposed to make her cry." Amy pushed her husband out of the way and came to give Sophie a hug. Grayson held his finger up to show he would be a couple of minutes and left the room to finish his call.

"Sorry, Sis." Her brother wiped away her tears.

"It's alright. I'm a little emotional."

"I think you'll find that James thinks all women are emotional." Amy patted her stomach. She was five months pregnant with their second child.

"Where's Thomas?" Sophie asked

"With mum and dad. They wanted to spoil him before his little sister arrives and takes all the attention." James poured himself a coffee. "Where is Mrs Aimes?" Mrs Aimes was the housekeeper of James' country home. She and her family ran and lived in the house even when the North family wasn't there.

"She and Mr Aimes have gone to town. They needed more supplies for dinner."

"I hope she is cooking her beef dish with the pepper sauce." Sonia came into the kitchen with an even bigger belly. She was six months pregnant, Matthew, her partner and James' bodyguard, entered behind with the suitcases. "I'm so hungry and craving red meat all the time."

"I got some red meat you can have it you want it, my little dove." Matthew Carter joked with Sonia.

"Oh, I'm craving that as well."

"Oh thank God I'm not the only one." James' PA, Marie, appeared as well. Sonia was starting to wonder how many people had travelled here.

"Please don't tell me you want it again. I must be getting old, but I don't think I've recovered from twice on the plane yet." Callum, her husband and finance director of North Enterprises, poured a coffee when he walked in before collapsing on a chair.

"Welcome to the world of pregnant women you two. It will slow down soon when they can't see their toes and have to be hoisted off the sofa." James laughed and took a seat next to her at the table.

"Slow down, she's only four months. I still got five to go!" Callum replied.

"Hi, Marie, Callum, Sonia, Matthew. Is there anyone else coming?" Sophie was a little in shock at the sudden invasion.

"Just us," Amy replied and sat next to her husband.

"When we heard what was happening we all had to come and support you. That woman is a nuisance." Marie took a croissant from the pile on the table. "I hope that you are going to cut her off this time, Matthew."

"Believe me," Sonia answered before Matthew could. "If I get my hands on her, she won't be writing any more stories anytime soon."

"Ladies, let the gentlemen deal with Sally Bridgewater. You three concentrate on the babies inside you." If looks could kill, Matthew Carter would be flayed alive.

"It's alright. Grayson has his lawyers on the case. We just need to prove that he helped out the girls in the club not force them into anything. They are also trying to show he had the intention to fix the community centre."

"What about all the lies concerning your relationship with him?" Amy questioned.

"We had a chat about that on the plane. We know the truth, and that is we're in love. That is all that matters." Sophie smiled at that thought. Her first smile since the article had been published.

"Oh. I think I'm going to cry." Sonia snuffled. Matthew handed her a tissue.

"Another thing you've got to come to Callum."

"Already there mate." The accountant handed Marie a tissue from his pocket; she also had tears streaming down her cheeks.

"Woah." Grayson stepped back in the room. "We having a party?"

The men all stood and shook hands.

"Not a party. Not yet anyway." James folded his arms across his broad chest. "Someone has tried to mess with my sister's life. The same person who has messed with all our lives recently. Enough is enough. Tomorrow, the girls go for a ladies' day, no arguments about that from any of you when three of you are pregnant." Amy went to open her mouth but shut it straight away again. "We are going to figure out how to bring Sally Bridgewater down once and for all."

TWELVE

Grayson

"Mr Smith will see you now gentlemen." Along with James, Matthew and Callum, Grayson stood and followed the secretary into the opulent boardroom. It was decorated with the finest wooden furniture. The glass panels of the windows had excellent views over the whole of London; no wonder there was a restaurant on the roof that offered afternoon tea with Champagne at a hundred pounds a time.

A portly gentleman sat at the head of the boardroom table. He stood when they entered.

"Mr Moore I expected a visit from you when I heard that you were in the UK but not Mr North and friends as well. I hope I don't need security." It was time to rub the smug smile of the editor in chief of London Daily. James stepped forward.

"I think you'll find that I'll be the one calling security or just having Mr Carter here remove you from the premises." Mr Smith's smile faded especially when he looked up at Matthew who cracked his knuckles.

"You can't do that." Mr Smith tried to be stern, but the underlying fear in his voice showed. Grayson was pretty sure that the man was about to piss himself.

"I think you'll find I can. You see, at eight am this morning, I became the owner of London Daily." James stood back with a smug smile on his face. "It was a brilliant idea of my Finance Director actually. He's been on me to diversify for a while now. And when an opportunity presented itself, I had to take it."

"You can't just walk in here and spout lies like that." Mr Smith banged his fist on the desk.

"Matthew," James called his bodyguard forward. Matthew pulled a document, which Grayson knew to be the contract for the sale, from inside his jacket and thrust it at Mr Smith with a grunt before stepping back.

"I'll think you'll find that everything is in order. In future, I would appreciate it if you speak to me with respect I demand as your boss." Mr Smith picked up the paper and turned white as a sheet when he read it. Grayson smirked, and James winked at him.

"What do you want?" The editor's demeanour had slumped, and he fell back into his chair. James' reputation for sharp business acumen was well known.

"The first task Callum undertook for me was to bring up all the personal files of the company. There will be lots of changes there, but I have one pressing one. I'm sure you can guess what?"

"Sally Bridgewater."

"Exactly." James reply was laced with menace. "Callum, would you care to explain?"

"My pleasure." Callum stepped forward and placed a briefcase on the table. He opened it and pulled out a file before putting it in front of Mr Smith. Grayson watched everything with glee, because he knew what was coming next.

"This is the file of complaints against Miss Bridgewater." The file had to be at least an inch thick. Some of which were still not settled. Callum opened the file and put five pieces of paper on the table. "These are currently in court, and our solicitor is not confident of a settlement in favour of Miss Bridgewater. Also, as I understand it, Mr Moore here will be releasing a statement later today to repute Miss Bridgewater's allegations in the latest article that the magazine published. He will also be issuing his intention to sue the magazine and Miss Bridgewater for defamation."

Mr Smith looked towards Grayson. His response was to scowl; this was the man who gave that bitch the go ahead to publish that article. Callum pulled another piece of paper from his briefcase.

"This is my calculation of the cost to the company now owned by Mr North. I'm sure you will agree that doesn't make good reading."

"It certainly doesn't" James interjected. "And I'm not about to suffer those losses. The way Callum tells me we have two alternatives. Firstly, liquidate the company making everyone redundant to pay the legal costs. Of course, top management, like yourself would suffer greatly from this alternative. Editor in Chief of an international magazine and it went under during your time in charge. I'm sure that would make it hard to get any future jobs." James paused there for dramatic effect. "Or we could get rid of the culprit. Show that we do not support her. Issue apologies for articles and offer cursory damages to those involved. What alternative do you suggest Mr Smith?"

"It will not be legal. She's done nothing wrong."

"These court cases prove that is not true." James pressed his finger down onto the documents that Callum had laid out. Mr Smith looked between them all.

"I'll call her in immediately. She'll be gone by lunchtime."

Grayson let out a long breath. Retribution was his.

THIRTEEN

Sophie

"I think I'm actually bored of being pampered." Amy stretched out a long limb and wiggled her toes to check the turquoise coloured varnish that was just painted on. Sophie leant forward to admire it also.

"I know the feeling." Sonia moaned from under a face mask. "Matthew won't even let me go to the gun range anymore. Apparently, the noise is too loud for his son's delicate growing ears. I did tell him that it would be nothing but a mute pop to the baby." Sonia told Sophie the night before that after weeks of arguing over finding out the sex of their baby they'd made the decision, and it was a boy. Sonia laughed when telling her and had even did a display of a strutting peacock. Apparently, Matthew walked around that way for days afterwards.

"Callum and I have no hope of peace and quiet. Owen thinks he is a lion, at the moment, and spends most of the day roaring." Marie added. Owen was Marie's and Callum's adopted son. He was Marie's sister's boy, but unfortunately, her sister died under horrific circumstances when she gave birth.

"This is why Grayson and I don't want children yet," Sophie added with mocking supremacy.

"You'll have to have a baby soon, or your mum and dad will expect me to keep having more to make up the numbers. They want lots of grandchildren." Amy shifted from her seating position. "I've got enough stretch marks to last me a lifetime."

"And my brother worships every one of them. You keep pushing them out for the North repopulation team." Sophie was laughing this time; Marie and Sonia joined in. The pampering was indeed becoming tedious. They could only sit around and drink tea for so long when worried about what their husbands or partners were up to.

"You know what? Let's go to Betty's in York. I haven't been there for ages. I want afternoon tea and fat rascals." Sophie stood up.

"Custard tarts." Sonia joined her.

"One question first." Marie held her hand up, "What is a fat rascal?"

"A scone made with lard, fruit, sugar...everything that is not good for you really," Sophie answered.

"I'm in." Marie picked her bag up. "Amy?"

"I don't know. James said we should stay here." Sophie could see the reticence on her blonde sister-in-law's face.

"Carl and Damian are here. I'll make sure they come with us. But we have the best bodyguard in Sonia with us anyway." Marie replied, and Sonia smirked proudly.

"You know James is going to spank me for doing this."

"I'm hoping Grayson does the same." Sophie chuckled.

Sonia let out a lascivious moan.

"Oh God. You've got her dreaming about the whipping she will get now." Marie laughed.

"Let's go and be naughty little Subbies before our Dom's realise." And with that final word from Amy, they were all out the door.

Carl and Damian moaned most of the journey to York, but as they all walked through the streets of York towards Betty's, they settled down and relaxed. There had been a phone call to one of the bodyguard's mobiles when they'd left the house. They all knew it was James or Matthew, as they were the ones who had their significant others 'chipped'. The phone was passed to Sonia who informed the person on the other end of the line that pregnant women needed cakes and afternoon tea. They surmised it was Matthew when she told the caller they had bodyguards, and she was deadly, as only he well knew, and that they would be perfectly safe. They would go for tea and come straight back. She confirmed that she would accept her punishment later and looked forward to receiving it, before hanging up and throwing the phone towards Damian. When it rang again a few seconds later, she glared at him until he put it back in his pocket and turned the music up so it couldn't be heard.

"Please, can we go in here?" Sonia clapped her hands while looking hopefully at a shop. Sophie looked up at the sign above her. The Armoury. Of course, of all the places that the bodyguard wanted to visit, it would have to be this one. Sophie herself looked lovingly at the cocktail bar across the road, but she knew with three pregnant women that was never going to happen. "I really want to get Drew a present."

"Drew?" Amy asked.

"The baby. Matthew and I decided on the name last night. Andrew James Carter. Already shortened to Drew."

"Oh, I love it," Amy exclaimed, and they all hugged in the middle of the street. "James is going to be so proud." Her sister-in-law wiped away a tear.

"Enough sappiness. Let's go look at knives for a baby." Marie raised an eyebrow. "I can't believe I just said that."

"Surreal isn't it." Sonia laughed, and despite being six months pregnant skipped into the shop.

When Sophie entered, Sonia already had several knives out and was looking at them. Marie went over to assist. Amy threaded her arm through Sophie's and pulled her aside.

"How are you feeling?" Amy asked.

"I'm ok." She replied.

"And now tell me the real answer."

"Honestly, I'm just tired. Jet lag. I know whatever the guys are doing will make everything alright. I'm just hoping it isn't murder." Sophie rubbed at the wedding ring on her finger while she spoke. She was sure they would be sensible, but even she knew that in Matthew they had a great and very deadly weapon.

"You know; James doesn't always have Matthew murder everyone. Just a few people and they were trying to kill either him or me at the time."

"Justified killings then." Sophie chuckled.

"Of course."

Sophie had developed a close relationship with her sister-in-law. They spoke to each other on the phone several times a week and used What's App to ping messages all day. She hated not being around Thomas all the time, but thanks to Skype, she saw and spoke to him lots. LA was her home now, and that would never change. She loved it there. Well, she did until the article broke. Would it ever be the same again?

"Do you know what James is doing?" She asked Amy.

"I know bits. Trust them. It'll be alright." Amy took Sophie's hands and squeezed them when she replied.

"I do." The two of them embraced.

"Hey, can we get in on the love-in." Sonia wrapped her arms around the two of them.

"Girls rule," Marie giggled out and joined.

"Girls are in a lot of trouble." Matthew's gruff voice came from behind Sophie. They all jumped apart and stood in a line. James, Matthew, Callum and Grayson all filed into the shop wearing frowns that had Sophie's bottom smarting already.

"We...er..." Sonia tried to answer, but the growl from Matthew silenced her.

"Carl, Damian." Grayson stepped forward.

"Yes, boss." They both cowered.

"You are relieved of your duties for the day. You may go back to Mr North's home."

"Yes, Sir." Both men couldn't get out the place quickly enough.

"Sophie." Grayson turned his attention to her. She stepped forward. They were still in the armoury. Everyone around them went quiet. "Do you remember your safe word?"

"Yes, Master." The games were about to start

"Ladies, how about you?" Grayson addressed Marie, Amy, and Sonia.

"Yes, Master Grayson." They all replied in unison. Grayson nodded at the other men. They all had that look on their faces that meant by the end of the night Sonia, Marie, Amy and herself would be left thoroughly sated.

"Good because we have four very disobedient little submissives to punish."

FOURTEEN

Grayson

"Slave position. Now." The tone of Grayson's voice left Sophie, Marie and Sonia in no doubt of what was about to happen. He couldn't believe that Sophie had gone out with the girls and was even more incredulous that it was her idea. He told her to stay in James' mansion, and she defied him. James took Amy to his London home, they had their playroom there, but Grayson, along with Matthew and Callum came to the club that Grayson owns in London. At least that one hadn't been destroyed by a rioting crowd. The club was empty, apart from them; a definite benefit to owning such a place.

All three women knelt before them naked with their heads bowed.

"The club safe word is red; you all have your individual safe words. If you are not sure about anything to use them. Do you understand?"

"Yes, Master Grayson." A chorus of female voices replied.

"Sonia, you are more experienced with play of this nature and Sophie you're a full time submissive. Would you help Marie with anything that she does not understand?" Callum stepped forward. Grayson knew that the Prime Minister's son was an expert in the art of Domination and Submission, but his wife was relatively new to it and still learning.

"We will do all we can to help her." Sophie and Sonia agreed.

"Do you know why you are to be punished?" Matthew spoke this time.

"Because you told us to stay in the house, and we went shopping for Drew," Sonia replied. Matthew stepped forward and twisted his hand around Sonia's ponytail. He pulled her head up until she was looking at him. "Nothing to do with Rascal's cakes and filling that beautiful belly of yours."

"Maybe." She pouted at him.

"I don't think my girl is remorseful for her actions at all, Grayson. She seems to think that she isn't my pet to do with what I like."

"I have a feeling Sophie and Marie feel the same way. Don't you Callum?" Grayson smirked. The play was underway and the skin on his arms pricked up with the allure of what was to come. They decided together what they would do with the women on the way to collect them.

"I think we need to remind them." Callum turned and pulled a length of hemp rope from his bag. This had been Grayson's idea; he was a shibari master. They would dress their women in the beautiful ropes, restrain them so that they could do whatever they wanted.

"Amber," Marie called out. They all stopped, and Callum knelt beside his wife. "Talk to me."

"I'm worried about the baby."

Callum looked up at Grayson to answer this question.

"We will not be tying ropes in any way that will harm the baby. Only Sophie will be suspended." His little submissive wiggled her bottom in delight to hear that one.

"You won't leave me alone the entire time?" Marie looked up to Callum. Her soulful eyes wide with wanting to try but fear for the safety of her unborn.

"Darling, I'll be in you most of the time, so believe me, I'm not going anywhere." Callum's reply brought a chuckle to Grayson's lips. He planned on being the same with Sophie.

"Ok." The brunette smiled. "Let's do it."

Callum rewarded her with a kiss on the lips.

Grayson turned to Matthew. The bodyguard was standing behind Sonia and was already binding her arms together. Matthew was also an expert at this. They had both worked together in their training and had taken turns in tying each other up. It wasn't something they spoke about between them. Although Grayson did have to admit he felt less on edge around the big man when he was restricted.

He took his own length of rope.

"On your feet little one."

Sophie stood up. She placed her palms flat to her thighs.

"I've taught you well. Let's see about securing those hands so they can't play. He made a loop and thread it around her hand. The fabric of the rope was soft to touch; she would feel it against her skin, but it wouldn't cut her. He pulled the rope around her body and then fastened the other hand.

"That should keep you from pleasuring yourself for a few minutes." Grayson looked over to Matthew and Callum; each had withdrawn to a corner of the room. Callum was already building an intricate pattern of beautiful knots between Marie's thighs and up her backside.

"I think my little one needs ties in those places." He caught Sophie watching also. "You always were a voyeur. I think I'm going to have to blindfold you to keep that concentration on me."

"I'm sorry, Master." Sophie smirked with delight.

He pulled a silk scarf from his bag and tied it around her eyes. "That should focus your attention a little better. Next, he worked his knots between her thighs and bottom. He paid particular attention to her clit with a beautiful rose adorning it.

"You smell amazing already." He inhaled deeply and then blew out. The little gusts of air from his breath sending waves of dancing delight over her highly sensitised skin. He needed to taste her. To sup at the glistening desire that was evident between her thighs. The wet tip of his tongue traced her inner folds, flicked over her clit and then swirled around her opening.

"Mmm." She moaned and dug the tips of her fingernails into her hips.

"You like that?"

"Yes, Master."

He wasn't going any further just yet though. He still had a lot of rope left and his wife needed to be suspended for the next part of his plan. She was placing a lot of trust in him, and he would reward her with his complete devotion. The rope was looped around and ankle and back up her calf. He brought it back down the other leg then straight back up to her breasts. The fibres of the rope bristled together in the silence of the room. None of the other couples made a sound as each man concentrated on adorning his woman with the most beautiful of natural tethers. He knew that Sophie had a sensitive spot just above her bottom, so he finished his knots there. She wiggled with the feelings pulsating through her body. He placed a hand over the knot on her back, and she let out a long lust filled moan.

"It's time to string you up."

"Please Master." There was a very keen edge to Sophie's voice. Grayson loved how she embraced her submission when she was with him. There was no hesitation or worry. She trusted that he would not hurt her; she trusted him to bring her great pleasure. Since the day he first saw her looking out at the Hollywood hills, he knew she would always do that.

He reached above them to where two chains dangled down from the ceiling. They both had hooks on the end of them which he attached to strategically placed knots on Sophie's ropes. One at her shoulders and one between her legs by her knees.

"Brace yourself." On the wall behind him was a button. He pressed it, and the chains shortened lifting his stunning creation into the air. He needed out of his jeans at the vision before him. He created his very own goddess. Sophie breathlessly mewed. The tension of the rope was pulling on each of the sensitive spots dotted around her skin. She swayed; her head fell forward as she became enveloped in the feelings flooding through her body.

"Oh, no. Time to bring you back to consciousness." He took a vibrating butt plug and smothered it in lubrication. He made a design in his ropes that allowed him to pull on the end of a length, and it would adjust Sophie's legs to just how he wanted them. He pulled it. She gasped. She was now splayed open for him to do with as he wished.

Matthew and Callum brought their woman back over to where they were.

"Please Master, when Drew is out can we do that?" Sonia's eyes were wide open with envy.

"If I can flog you while you're up there." The bodyguard raised an eyebrow.

"Have you got your toys?" Grayson asked both men.

"Already in." Callum smacked Marie on the back side, and she let out a loud groan where Grayson guessed her butt plug was already situated.

"On all fours on the chair my love." Matthew held up Sonia's toy, and she obliged him. Grayson ran his hand over Sophie's glistening folds and brought her juices back to her puckered hole. He then tenderly pushed the lubricated plug in. She shuddered with the intrusion.

"Tell me how you are feeling?" He whispered into her ear.

"Like I need more, Master."

"More?"

"I want you to fill me everywhere. Show me that you are the boss, and I need to do as I'm told. Use my body. It's yours to take."

"Fuck. You'll be the death of me one day."

"I hope not, Master." She giggled.

"You disobeyed my order today. That means you don't get my manhood inside this tight little pussy." He stuck a finger inside her for emphasis. The ropes swung her so that she was fucking his finger. "You'll get to suck me till you swallow all my cum though. This cunt is getting a substitute." He pulled a thickly ridged vibrator from his bag. Matthew and Callum did the same. Sophie and Marie gasped. Grayson was in charge now. He was dominating the group towards their inevitable climaxes. This was the role he took over the others. He relished it. He'd wasted so long in mindless sexual escapes, just to get his kicks, when all he needed to do was play tutor to Dom's with his special little goddess.

"Master, please, I want to see. I promise to pay attention to only you." Sophie whimpered out. He placed the vibrator down and came to Sophie's head. He pulled her head up and whipped the blindfold off.

"Me, you focus only on me."

"You, only you." Her eyes gave him the promise he needed. He picked up the vibrator; she followed him with her gaze. She gasped, and the ropes shook again. The tight knots heightened the absolute pleasure in her body.

"Please. Please." He loved it when she begged.

In a tantalising thrust, he settled the vibrator into her tight haven. She cried out at the intrusion.

"Full. So full." He smirked at her passionate retort. Marie and Sonia were also panting with their thirst for climax.

"Matthew do you have the other jewels that I asked for?"

"More?" Marie called out.

"Always more," Callum replied to her. "No more words unless it's you screaming my name."

"Yes, Master." The brunette was new to BDSM, but she was well trained already. A natural when she forgot her nerves.

"No clit is complete unless it is adorned with a beautiful little butterfly." Matthew handed Grayson and Callum clit clips. Grayson applied his to Sophie and stood back to watch his bejewelled beauty. The toys were all highlighted by the rope. All he needed to do now was turn them all on.

"Do you think out ladies have learnt their lesson yet?" Matthew chuckled.

All three women nodded.

"I'm not actually sure they have." Grayson held up a remote and pressed the on button.

"Fuck!" Sophie called out as all the devices attached to her started to vibrate at once. She jerked, and that sent her swinging on the ropes. "Oh God!" She let out a loud out on a long, long sob.

"No, just your husband." Grayson laughed as he observed Matthew and Callum press their buttons, and the other two girl's eyes lit up.

"Now, we have two holes filled. But I do believe that there is a third. And that is the one that got them all into so much trouble. That is the one that does all the talking about disobeying us." Matthew mused.

"That is the one that would have eaten all the cakes," Callum added.

"So that is the one that gets to eat something else." Grayson was already pulling his jeans to the floor while he spoke. His cock rejoiced at the freedom it was being given. He stroked up and down his length which brought a welcoming whimper from Sophie's lips. "Time to pleasure your Master."

All three men now had their dicks out and were feeding them into the warm and welcoming mouths of their partners. Sophie's mouth was always delectable. He instantly went to the back of her throat as he knew she could take him. She licked around the rim, around the length and backed down again. He didn't need to move. All he had to do was give the ropes a gentle push, and everything was done for him. His wife was swinging backwards and forwards, and her mouth was caressing up and down his cock. He pulled out when she swung back again.

"You don't come until you feel me come down your throat; do you hear me?"

"Yes, Master," Sophie replied; her wide eyes darkened with desire, looking directly up at him. Sonia and Matthew, Callum and Marie were all lost in their worlds of euphoria. It was time for him and Sophie to lose themselves in theirs. He turned up the button on the vibrator, Sophie screamed out his name, and he rammed his dick back in her mouth. This time he wasn't gentle. This time he needed resolution. He fucked her mouth like it would be the last thing he ever did. He was using her as a toy to get off, and he saw in the flushing of her face and vibrations of her throat around his cock that she loved it. She loved giving herself over so completely, perfect trust, perfect pleasure. His balls tightened, and the warmth of his orgasm rushed through his body and out into his wife's mouth. She detonated around his dick; her entire body was convulsing as she shook so violently with her orgasm her eyes rolled back in her head. She was flying high; he'd taken her to subspace. The pride settled well on his shoulders. He watched her, another press of the button and she came again. His legs collapsed when he released himself from her mouth with a pop. He fell to the floor trying to catch his breath. Sophie hung limply in the ropes. She was completely out of it. He gathered himself together. In an instant, he had stopped the vibrators and removed them. He lowered the chains so that she was resting on the floor. He unhooked them and took a pair of scissors from his bag. The ropes were snipped, and she was in his arms in less than a minute. Matthew and Callum took their women to quiet corners for aftercare. Grayson pulled Sophie on his lap when he sat on a sofa. A blanket rested there, and he covered them both with it.

"Talk to me little one." He needed to check she was ok and coming back into her body alright.

She let out a contented moan.

"Thank you, Master."

"Thank you for trusting me."

"Always." Her words sounded so dreamy, as she began to drift off to sleep.

"Will you go out again when I've asked you not to?"

"Not this week?" She laughed before drifting off.

FIFTEEN

Sophie

Sophie placed the magazine article down. No matter how many times she read it, she never tired of taking delight in the content and especially the photograph that accompanied it. The loathsome Sally Bridgewater being thrown out of the London Daily headquarters. Apparently, she created a storm of colourful language when fired and threw things at the Editor in Chief. She had to be ejected from the premises. Sophie thought that it couldn't have happened to a nicer person.

"Mrs Moore." Sophie looked up to see Mrs Aimes, the housekeeper, standing before her.

"How can I help you?"

"I was just about to start preparing dinner, but I need a few things. I'm going to head to town. Do you need anything before I go?"

"No. I'm going to have a little sleep before Grayson gets back."

The sun was rising by the time they got back to the mansion after the club scenes the previous evening. Grayson had a few hours sleep and then headed back to London for business meetings. Sophie's body ached pleasantly. Their scene was so intense but just what they needed after the tension of the last few days.

Mrs Aimes left Sophie alone. She threw the newspaper article in the bin. It was time to move on and forget that woman. With a spring in her step, she leapt up the stairs to her bedroom. The room was decorated in princess style. She had antique French furniture with light pink accents on the wall. The room was dominated by a massive chandelier. It was the bedroom of her dreams; James had always said that he would make her such a room one day. He had kept his word. She lay on the bed and instantly drifted off to a peaceful slumber.

A short time later, Sophie woke by her bedroom door opening. She glanced at the clock, three pm. Grayson was home early. She sat up and rubbed her eyes. The figure at her bedside emerging from the hazy sleep though was not her husband; it was Sally Bridgewater.

"Miss Bridgewater." Sophie leapt from the bed and reached for her phone on the nightstand. However, before she could get it, Sally grabbed it and threw it across the room at the wall.

"I don't think so." Sally spat out. The droplets of saliva hit her in the face. "You and I need to have a little talk about your husband. Sophie noticed that Sally had red rims around her puffy eyes; she'd either been crying or hadn't slept. She imagined it was both.

"Any questions you have need to be addressed directly to Grayson. Get out! There will be people here soon."

"I don't think so. Your husband is in London, and the estate steward had to leave to assist his wife who strangely seemed to get a puncture. The bodyguard left behind really needs to watch what he drinks. I don't think he'll be waking anytime soon." Sally cackled.

Sophie gulped; her whole skin prickling at the apparently insane woman's words.

"Sally, I know what happened yesterday, but you being here will only make matters worse. If you leave now, I won't tell anyone you were here."

"Not enough," Sally screamed while rocking on the spot. "Over here...NOW." Sophie didn't want to aggravate the woman anymore. It was evident that reasoning was not going to work; she feared Miss Bridgewater's brain was too far gone for that. She followed Sally's direction and sat down at a little table that had been rescued from a French Chateaux before it was demolished. It was placed by the window with two chairs. Sally let out a bellowing laugh.

"So this is what it feels likes for Grayson when he is bossing you around. I think I like this power. I wonder what else I can get you to do." The evil smirk on Sally's face brought bile to her mouth. "Don't worry. I'm not into women. That is the whole reason I'm here and ready to destroy your husband." Sally said before taking the seat opposite her. Sophie hadn't seen it before but on the table was a folder. She really didn't want to know what was in it but had a feeling she was about to find out.

"Just tell me what it is you want and then leave."

"Sally pushed the folder towards her.

"Open it."

"You open it." She retorted.

"Open it or things are going to get interesting." With a shaking hand, Sophie reached out and pulled the file towards her. She opened the front cover to reveal a baby.

"Who is this? She asked.

"My son."

"So that's what you want, to guilt trip us. You went after my husband with lies." She didn't need to hear this, so she slammed her chair back and stood up. "Get out."

"That was my son as a baby." Sally ignored her and flipped over another page. "And this is my son, now five, a few weeks ago."

The bottom fell out of Sophie's world when she looked down at the piece of paper. The eyes, the hair colour, the face that stared back was that of Grayson.

"No." She wrapped her arms around her body to try and shut out the pain.

"Yes, my son is also Grayson's."

"You're lying."

More pages were turned and a birth certificate was revealed. Sally shoved it in her face. Sophie's heart told her not to believe all the evidence, but her brain rationalised everything and said she had to believe it. She sat back down and picked up the picture of the little boy.

"How?"

"I played a groupie for a scoop on Mr Moore's sex skills. I'm sure you already know I will do anything for a story. Unfortunately, I was not as careful as I should have been with my pills; the flights messed me up, and the condom broke. I didn't want to believe I was pregnant at first. Me, pregnant that couldn't be happening." Sally shifted in her chair as if the memories of her disgrace were more painful than anything else. "By the time I admitted it, I was too late for a termination. I had to give birth to the bastard. Thankfully his new family took him straight away, so I didn't even have to look at him. Unfortunately, I got sent that photo."

"Why didn't you tell Grayson?"

"He had just announced his relationship with you, including the whole leading you around by the collar thing at that party. I was disgusted. That was the man who had put this thing inside me. But do you know the worse part? Mr Smith won't publish my article on Grayson. I told him that we could really get a good story out of it. I could see the headline." Sally's eyes glazed over as she held her hand up to her chance at stardom. "Renegade star doesn't use protection. How many more bastards does he have out there?" It was shut down, and I was sent away to have the child. It was the one time in my life that I messed up, and for what, a quick fuck that wasn't even that good?"

"We would've helped you if you'd come to us." Sophie offered.

"I don't need your pity." Sally slammed the folder shut. "That article was mine; I should have been allowed to publish it. I was punished for your husband's misdemeanours. He was the one who should have been lambasted for fucking anything that walked. He is a disgrace to his roots. I'm glad I did that article with his sister."

"You don't know Grayson well. He isn't the man you paint him to be."

"And you are blind." Sally interrupted her when she was about to try and defend her husband. "And I'm not going to rest until I destroy him. It will make me the greatest reporter there has ever been. Your brother's little plot will fail. I will expose the lot of you for the freaks that you are." Sally grabbed the folder back from her and jumped to her feet.

"I won't allow you to do that. Sally, you need help. I can help you." It was evident now that somewhere along the line, Sally had lost her mind." Sophie made her own attempt to retake the folder of the fast retreating woman.

"Get the fuck off me." Sally pushed her and Sophie stumbled backwards against the table. Her hip caught on it, and a pain ripped through her left leg. Sally made a beeline for the door. Sophie knew that she needed to keep the women in the room. If she got out, if she got out then their lives, Amy's and James' lives, would all be exposed. Would Sally find out that her brother had killed people? He would be sent to prison. Grayson could be hurt; she could lose him. She couldn't allow that to happen. In a quick movement, she ignored the pain in her leg and was on top of Sally before she reached the door. She ripped the folder from the shocked reporter's hands and threw it across the room. The contents spilt out everywhere.

"You bitch." Sally turned and sent a punch straight into Sophie's face who managed to recover from it quickly and returned her own punch.

"You are not going anywhere. You need help, and I'm going to make sure you get it."

"I need to destroy anyone involved with the North family. I know what you are like. You all use your money to think you are above the law. Grayson, your brother, his bodyguard, and the Prime Minister's son." They were both grappling together on the floor. "I'll destroy everyone." Sally sent a kick to her stomach, and before Sophie had a chance to react, the reporter was on her feet and racing for the door. She managed to reach her hand out and grab Sally's trailing leg though. The reporter went down straight onto the edge of a sturdy wooden dressing table. Her head cracked with a sickening thud, and she slumped down onto the floor unmoving. Sophie got to her to check. The reporter had blood pouring from a wound to her head.

"Sally?"

Nothing.

"Sally?" Sophie couldn't see her breathing. She'd killed her. It was an accident, but she'd killed her. What should she do? She looked around the room. Furniture was upended, and the paper was everywhere. The evidence of Grayson's misdemeanours with the reporter. It was accidental. She hadn't meant to do it. She just wanted to stop her from leaving. The police, she needed to call them. No, an ambulance, maybe she wasn't dead. She was going to be sick; air, she needed air. Without actually thinking, Sophie left the room, her brain a maelstrom of confusion. Had she just killed someone? She was shaking. Stepping into the ornate porch of the mansion, she bent over and was violently sick everywhere. Heaving again and again 'til nothing was left. She was going to go to prison. She murdered someone. The mother of Grayson's child. She heaved again. Think. She hit herself on the head, trying in vain to get her brain to start functioning. It didn't work so she slumped down and curled up into a little ball. Her life as she knew it was over.

The sound of a car engine brought her consciousness back to focus. She instantly recognised that car as the one that James used when in Yorkshire. Matthew slammed on the brakes and skidded to a halt as the car got to the entrance to the house. Matthew and James both leapt out.

"Sophie." Her brother called. Matthew pulled a gun from his pocket and primed it. James was at her side checking for injuries. "Where is she?"

"You know what I did? How?" She looked at him through now fatigued eyes.

"Matthew has been tracking Sally. As soon as we saw she was on the way here, we got here as fast as we could."

"She's inside," Sophie replied. James looked at Matthew, a quizzical eyebrow raised.

"Sophie. What happened?"

"She's dead." The emotion in her voice was flat. She felt as if she were in a dream. That nothing happening around her was real. Matthew disappeared into the house.

"Sophie, let's get you inside. You can't stay out here."

"No." She didn't want to go back to her room. Her nails dug tightly into James' hand.

"It's alright. You don't have to go to your room, but I do need to get you into the house. It's getting cold out here, and I don't want you to get sick." She nodded at her brother, and he picked her up and carried her into the house. He settled her on a chaise lounge in the hallway. Matthew appeared at the top of the stairs. He coughed, and they both looked up at him. The bodyguard shook his head.

"Sophie, I need to know that happened?" James focused her attention back on him.

"We fought, and she fell. She was going to destroy us all." She was almost hyperventilating, trying to get the words out.

"Alright. I need you to stay calm. Matthew will deal with Miss Bridgewater."

"I'm going to go to prison. I'll be charged with murder." She was the opposite of calm; she was terrified. She clung to her brother's shirt.

"Little sis. You know I won't allow that to happen." Matthew came to the top of the stairs again and whistled for James to join him. "I've just got to speak to Matthew. You stay here. When I get back, I'll get you a stiff drink." He rubbed her shoulders; she was still shivering. "And I'll get a blanket to keep you warm."

She nodded, and her eyes followed James up the stairs and to Matthew. They lowered their voices so she couldn't hear them, but she knew exactly what was being said when Matthew passed the photo to James. He put it in the pocket of his suit trousers before disappearing into her bedroom. He reappeared a few minutes later and descended the stairs to wrap the blanket around her shoulders. He pressed a kiss to the top of her forehead then went into the lounge to pour a huge glass of brandy. He helped her to drink it down. The warm liquid calmed and centred her.

"Thank you."

"That's alright little sis. I don't employ an ex-MI5 agent for no reason. You won't go to prison. Matthew will make her death look like a suicide."

"But I killed her."

"She was never here Sophie, so how could you have killed her?" The look on his face told her that she shouldn't argue with him; he was protecting her.

"Alright. But what do I tell Grayson?"

"I'll talk to him for you. As far as he will be concerned, she committed suicide on our premises. You found her, and it upset you. Matthew moved her body away from here to avoid a publicity circus. It's what has to happen Sophie. Do you understand that?"

"You won't tell him that I killed her?" She bit her lip with worry over the lie.

"I think it's best not to." He reached for the photo in his pocket. "Does he know?"

She shook her head.

"I only found out when she came here and showed me the photo. She was about to expose the story to the press. I tried to stop her from leaving the room. She hit me; I hit her back. We fought, and she fell onto the table. I didn't mean to kill her." She had her brother's hands held really tightly, so tightly, in fact, that his knuckles turned white from the pressure. "I just knew she couldn't leave the room. I was trying to lock her in so I could call you and Grayson."

"I know. Shush. Don't worry. It will be alright."

"What should I do about the boy?"

"We need to find him and check that he is Grayson's."

"Look at him." She pointed at the picture.

"I know, but looks can be deceiving. Sally Bridgewater did anything for a story. That's been proven a million times. I will have Matthew find the boy, and we can do a DNA test. We can then break the news to Grayson, when we know the truth. He is apprehensive about the slur on his ancestry and neglect of culture. He needs to come to terms with his thoughts on that first. Finding out he has a child could send him spiralling even more."

"I want to protect him. I love him but to lie to him?" She didn't think she could do that.

"Sophie, you have to trust me on this. We will tell Grayson eventually. We just need to ensure that everything is alright first."

What could she do? Her brother was rescuing her from prison on a charge of murder. She wasn't in control of her situation anymore. That little boy would haunt her for the rest of her life. Grayson had a child with another woman, and Sophie had murdered the mother. She shut her eyes and let the tears out. She let them flow for the end of her life as she had known it. She'd been protected and sheltered, carefree and alive. Something inside her died today; it would never be replaced. It would never be the same.

SIXTEEN

Grayson

A month later

Grayson slammed his fist into the boxing punch bag. He'd been hitting it for an hour now and still didn't feel like he had expelled all the anger that he held inside him. That damn woman. Even in her death, she was still haunting them. That day, when he returned from London, he found his wife broken and distraught. Sally Bridgewater had put a gun to her head where she knew that Sophie would find her. He'd insisted on seeing the body to know that she was indeed dead. There wasn't much of her head left given she'd used a shotgun. He hoped she rotted in Hell.

Sophie came into the gym in their LA mansion. She had on her gym gear; day after day, she seemed to just run on the treadmill for hours. His wife withdrew into herself. He offered to get her a counsellor to help her through the worse of her emotions, but she'd stated that she was fine and that she was reconciling them on her own. He used his Dom voice to try and convince her, he even brought a counsellor to the house, but she still refused help. The only person she seemed to talk to about everything was James. The dynamic of their relationship had changed. She had to blame him. It was the only reason she was shutting him out.

He watched her build up to a fast pace. The bones were jutting out on her back she had lost so much weight. This shell wasn't his wife anymore. He pulled off his boxing clothes and put them away. He was covered in sweat from all his efforts. A cold shower was just what he needed. And he made the decision that his wife was going to join him. He went to the front of her running machine. She looked up at him and pressed the button to slow down.

"No exercising for you today little one. I've got other things planned for you."

She brought the machine to a halt but didn't stop. "I want you naked in the shower in five minutes. I'm going examine every inch of your body to see how much weight you have lost. I'm then going to fuck it until you remember I'm your master. After that, we are going out for food, and you will eat all that I tell you to. Do you understand?"

She looked at him and bowed her head.

"Red." The word from her lips took him aback. He reached out to a cross trainer behind so that he didn't fall.

"Red?"

"Red." She repeated.

"To all of it?" He sounded like a complete idiot, but he was utterly bewildered.

"Yes."

"Why?"

"I want to run." That was her reason. She wanted to run.

"You do too much running. Sophie, you are losing to much weight. I'm worried about you." Despite the fact he was sweaty, he pulled her into his arms to show her his affection. She didn't relax into his comfort. Instead, she remained rigid like a statue. "I know this is my fault. My past made that woman do what she did. You need to let me help you so I can make it up to you." Sophie wriggled out of his arms.

"I'm going lay down. I don't feel well." With that comment, she left the room at a run. It was as though she couldn't even stand to be near him. His marriage was breaking down before his very eyes, and he didn't know how to fix it. He loved her so much; he wanted his wife back. Damn his male slut ways. They were the reason for this. He managed to convince his Native American heritage of his true intentions to help them, and the new community centre was halfway completed already. Had he lost his wife in the process though? He needed to speak to the one person who knew Sophie just as well as he did. Her brother.

Grayson quickly showered and entered his study. He shut the door so Sophie couldn't hear him. She'd curled up in their bed and had fallen asleep so that shouldn't be a problem anyway. He dialled.

"James North." His brother in law sleepily answered.

"Hi, it's Grayson." He replied.

"What's up. It's two am here." Shit, he forgot about the time difference.

"Fuck, I'm sorry man. I'll call you back tomorrow." He could hear Amy murmur in the background, and James tell her to go back to sleep.

"It's alright." Grayson could hear James get out of bed and walk to a different room and shut the door. "It's not like you to forget the time difference, so you obviously need to talk."

"I'm worried about Sophie." There he had said it. "She just safe worded."

"Safe worded. Do I want to hear about this?"

"I asked her to shower with me which would have led to…"

James interrupted him with a 'la la la'.

"Sorry, I told her after the shower we were going to head out for food."

James went silent for a moment.

"She safe worded because you wanted to shower and eat with her?"

"Yes. James, if you saw her… All she does all day is sleep and run. I've tried to feed her like I normally do, but she only has a few bites before she ambers. She's lost so much weight. I called in a counsellor, but she wouldn't speak to them. I know she talks to you a lot; has she said anything?" He felt a great weight lift off his chest as he confided in some else his fears.

"She's said a few things. I know what happened has affected her. She probably just needs times. Sophie's always been a sensitive soul. You knew that when you married her. She's probably still just petrified that you're going to get hurt." James' reply was reassuring, but he was at the stage that he needed more.

"I think there is more to it. She's not even really spoken to me about what happened that day. What has she said to you?"

"Look, Grayson, how about I talk to her? I'll give her a call tomorrow and see what she says. If I think there is something major wrong then I'll fly over, and we'll stage an intervention together. I know you're worried about her that makes me concerned."

"That would be great. I have to head to Navajo territory tomorrow. I have a photo shoot for the community project I'm doing there. I did ask her to come with me, but she said no. She'll be home all day." Grayson was actually worried about leaving her, but he really wanted to be involved with the projects, he had going on in his homelands, as much as possible. They accepted his reasons for not being seen to be helping in the past, and he was building many bridges in the area.

"I'll call her and have a long chat then."

"Thank you, James."

"Not a problem. Leave Sophie for today. We'll get this sorted. Night."

"Night." Grayson hung up and relaxed back in his office chair. For the first time in weeks, he felt the tension evaporate from his shoulders. He let out a long breath. On his desk was a picture of him and Sophie on their wedding day. He picked it up and stroked his wife's face. She was his saviour, his angel. She got him and his needs and wasn't ashamed of her own. They were a match made in heaven. He wouldn't allow Sally Bridgewater to drag them down to her type of hell. He placed the picture back down on his desk and rubbed his eyes. Maybe it was time to join his wife for sleep. He wouldn't pressure her into anything. He just wanted her to know that he was there for her to help her. He ambled into the bedroom and stood against the door frame. Sophie was on her back with her long blonde hair fanned over the bed. She looked like an angel, peaceful and sleeping. She moaned and thrashed to her side. Her little face scrunched up.

"Stop it." She called out.

"Sophie." He stepped forward in concern. She didn't wake but threw herself onto the other side of the bed.

"I didn't mean to do it. It was an accident. I had to stop her. Please." She called out.

"Accident, stop who?" Grayson was getting more and more worried by the minute. He placed his arms on Sophie's shoulders and shook her. She startled awake, took one look at him and scrambled from the bed. She ran into the bathroom, and when he followed her, he saw she was sick in the toilet. He took a facecloth from the side and wet it. Sophie was covered in sweat and shaking.

"Little one what happened?"

She burst into tears, and his heart started to break. He hated to see her like this. His past had harmed her in ways that he could never stop from hurting. Damn that reporter. He was her master and was supposed to be protecting her, but at the moment, he was weak and not able to do that. He was failing.

"Bad dream." She sobbed.

"What about?" He questioned.

"I...I..." She hesitated. "I don't want to talk about it."

"Sophie. What was an accident?" He stroked the hair back from her face to calm her down.

"I'm sorry." She blinked up at him.

"You were calling out in your sleep. You said you didn't mean it to happen. It was an accident, and you had to stop her? Who was her? Please tell me what is going on."

His wife went as white as a sheet, sobbed 'I can't' and placed her head back into the toilet to be sick again. There was nothing more that he could do. She shut him out again, but he stayed with her just holding her hair back. All he could do was pray that James could get some answers.

SEVENTEEN

Sophie

Her stomach hurt so much from where she spent hours being sick. Nothing stayed down. She felt dizzy where her body was so weak. She was living in a nightmare and couldn't escape. Every time she shut her eyes, she saw Sally's face looking up at her. Her eyes dead pools of nothingness. She, Sophie had done that. She'd killed someone, and now she was lying to her husband. She would burn in the afterlife for this. Grayson reluctantly left her earlier that morning to head to the Navajo territory. He left the phone beside her and told her to call him if she needed him at all. She could see the guilt on his face. He blamed himself for the way she was. She was cruel to him, but she needed to listen to her brother. Why wouldn't this pain go away?

The phone rang, she looked down at the caller ID, it was her brother. She answered and immediately burst into tears.

"Sophie?"

"Yes." She cried.

"Put the phone on a video call. I need to see you."

"No." She replied.

"Please, little sis." There was sadness in her brother's voice. She switched the call and held the phone in front of her. "Fuck," James exclaimed when he saw her face. She knew she looked awful. Her eyes were sunken in, and her skin was ghostly pale. She had bags under her eyes from where she was so fitful in her sleep. "What have I done?"

"You've done nothing. I'm the one that did this when I murdered Sally Bridge-water." Her reply was devoid of all emotion.

"No, listen to me. That was an accident."

"Matthew shot her in the head."

"She was already dead; she didn't feel anything." He tried to reason with her.

"They had to use fingerprints to identify her." She shuddered at the thought. In most of her dreams, Sally morphed from the woman who she had tried to reason with into a horrific vision of blood and torn flesh. An eye dangled by a thread from its socket taunting her for her crimes. Then, the little boy would appear, calling for his daddy.

"Sophie, it needed to be done to save you. I'm not going to let you feel guilty for what happened after you left that room. That was my and Matthew's decision. Any guilt is Matthew's and mine."

"That is easier said than done when she haunts my dreams," Sophie screamed into the phone.

"I know." James' voice was kind, but the underlying tone was one of control, "But you have to move on. Matthew is on his way to you now. He's bringing my doctor. You're to listen to whatever she says and take whatever medicine she gives you. No arguments. Do you hear me?"

"I don't need pills, I need answers."

"And we are getting them," James shouted down the phone at her. She could see he was getting frustrated. "Look, I'm not just sending Matthew to see you. He has found the boy. Matthew is going to do a DNA test to ensure that he's Grayson's. Then we can tell him. The waiting is nearly over. You just have to get it together and hold steady for a few more days. Be the strong girl I know that you can." James paused. He ran his hand through his hair. "Be the one who supported me after I was beaten. Do you remember that Sophie? At the hospital. I remember you talking to me when I was sleeping. Telling me that you loved me, and I wasn't to listen to what I'd been called. I was a great brother and a good person. Kind and so helpful. I only got through those first days because of you. If you hadn't been there, I would have probably killed myself.

"Please don't" She wept.

"Yes. You are a real person, Sophie. None of this is your fault. It was an accident. Sally was not a nice person; she was deranged. She gave away her child, Grayson's child. She never allowed him to know of his son. The more digging I've done on her, the more I've found out what she was willing to do for a story. Sleeping with Grayson seems angelic compared to some. Sophie, she injected her own mother with heroin to watch her die from an overdose. You have rid the world of a menace. Grayson's son would have been in danger as long as she lived."

"What?" She silenced her crying, her voice caught in her throat as she tried to find words for what she was hearing. "She...she killed her own mother?"

"It could never be proven. She was clever but yes. Matthew is hundred percent sure of that."

"I'm losing my mind over a person who had no heart."

"Yes. Neither a heart nor a soul, she sold that to the Devil years ago" Her brother's face softened.

"Grayson is anxious about me isn't he?"

"He phoned me yesterday in the middle of the night. He said you safe-worded. As much as I don't like to know what my little sister gets up to in her sex life, I know you've never done that before. It worried us both."

"He wanted me to be normal. I got so scared the way he was looking at me. I've been lying to him."

"To protect him. He'll understand."

"Will he?"

"Sophie. He loves you. We did what we needed to do at the time to protect you. He will know that when we can all sit down and explain. I'm getting a plane over tomorrow. Amy and I had a check-up at the doctor's today, so I didn't want to miss that."

"Is everything alright?" Her worry turned instantly to her pregnant sister-in-law.

"Yes, just a regular check but I like to attend them."

She could feel herself calming down and centring. She'd been so stressed with everything, but now she actually felt like she could cope. And maybe even eat something. Some goat's milk pancakes. She wondered if Grayson would make them for her when he got home.

"What are you thinking?" James asked. She must have completely spaced out for the call.

"Pancakes."

"That sounds like the sister who I love."

"Does the boy have a name?" The question suddenly popped into her head from nowhere.

"Grayson's?"

"Yes."

"His adoptive parents have called him Ashkii, Ash for short. It's a Navajo name that means boy. I guess that they knew he had a Native American father."

"I like it. Ash. Suits him. Ashkii Moore."

"Sophie." James interrupted her train of thought. "Don't start thinking of him as yours and Grayson's. There is a long way to go yet. Remember, he believes that the people he lives with are his mother and father."

"He'll never be mine; I know that. I just want Grayson to know about his son."

"He will." Sophie heard Amy call over the phone for pickles. Her sister-in-law's cravings were obviously in full force again. "I better go. Last time I ignored her, I spent a week grovelling."

"Give her and Thomas a cuddle from me." Sophie smiled at her brother's roll of the eyes.

"Bye sis."

She placed the phone down on the bed; she could do this. She could survive. But when she looked up, all she could see was Grayson and thunderous fury written all over his face.

EIGHTEEN

Grayson

It was all that he could think about. Getting home to see Sophie. It was the quickest interview he'd ever done and then took the helicopter he rented straight back. He didn't want to leave her at all. She'd cried all night. His wife, helpless, and there was nothing that he could do to help. It wasn't right. He had approached their bedroom and heard her talking. He guessed it was her brother when he heard James voice talking about how she saved him after the attack that left the older North sibling scarred both mentally and physically. That would turn his girl around. She just needed to realise how special she was. The next words out of his brother-in-law's mouth left him reeling though. His world was spinning. The entire conversation between James and Sophie happening in slow motion. He had a child. A son. Ashkii. What the fuck! He'd slept with Sally Bridgewater? Sophie ended the call with James; Grayson stepped forward, and she saw him.

"How much did you hear?" It was the first words from her lips.

"Son." It was all he could say. He needed to sit down, or he was going to fall. He staggered towards the bed. Sophie scrambled across it and tried to touch him. He reeled backwards and chose to sit on a chair instead.

"Grayson, I can explain. Please." She fell out of the bed and onto her knees on the floor in front of him. Her palms rested on her thighs. It was a beautiful slave position. So perfect. But it did not excite him. No, too much was falling into place.

"Accident. James used the same word as you did. What do you mean by it? What was an accident?"

"You have to trust me. Matthew is on his way here. I'll explain everything then."

"No, you won't." He shouted at her. "You will tell me now. You are my wife, and I demand answers."

"Grayson, please. You are in shock at what you heard."

"Your brother said I have a son with Sally Bridgewater. I think I have a fucking right to be shocked; don't you?" He wanted to know what the hell was going on and he wasn't going to rest. "Maybe I need to phone your brother." He stepped over Sophie on the floor and went for her phone.

"No." She was up on her feet and with him. Both of them fighting over the phone. He pushed her away, and she fell down again her dressing table hitting her head in the process. When she sat back up, she had a line of blood falling down her face. She touched it and looked at the crimson life force colouring her hand. Grayson covered his ears when she let out a blood-curdling scream. He was there at her side. Holding her down when she started thrashing wildly around. She was screaming, crying, pleading for mercy.

"I didn't mean to do it. It was an accident. Please, you have to believe me. You have to understand what was happening. She was going to destroy you. She was going to destroy James, Matthew, Callum. All of you. I didn't mean to hurt her."

He shook her to try and snap her out of the fit she was in, but it did not work.

"Sophie." He called. What the fuck was going on? He had a son, Sophie had hurt someone. Sally Bridgewater. He'd gotten her pregnant. He had to calm Sophie down as she was the only one who could tell him what was going on.

He pulled his hand back and slapped it hard around her face. She froze. The blood from her wound was all over them both now.

"You hit me?"

"I needed to do it to calm you down so you can tell me what is going on?"

"I can't." She was pleading with him. Her big brown eyes were scared.

"Sophie, I'm your husband. We have no secrets from each other."

"I can't tell you, Gray. Please, you have to trust me."

He was done pleading. He wanted answers. He grabbed her by the hair and dragged her to her feet.

"Red, Yellow and Green. Remember." He waited a moment for her to answer.

"Yes, Master."

He had his reply. Without another word, he pulled her through the house to the small playroom that they had installed a few years back.

"Remove all your clothes and lean over the bench."

Sophie did as he asked.

"I want answers, little one, and you are going to give them to me."

"I can't."

"You don't speak unless you are answering my questions." He smacked her hard across the backside. "Understand?"

"Yes, Master." He selected the tool for his task. A wooden paddle. Neither he nor Sophie were masochists. Not like Sonia and Matthew but he needed something strong.

"Sally had a son." He lightly tapped the paddle on her backside, so she knew what was coming if she didn't answer his questions.

"Yes, Master." She replied.

"I'm the father?" He hit her again, this time a little bit harder.

"Yes, Master."

"How?" He hesitated this time, the pain would only come as a reward for an answer.

"She acted a groupie, seduced you for a story on your sex life. She said that the

condom broke, and she was remiss with her pill after she'd flown to LA specifically for the story." He rewarded her with a whack.

"Why didn't she tell me?"

"She didn't want to believe she was pregnant until after the time for a termination. We had just begun our relationship then. She had the baby and gave him up
for adoption." Sophie was getting more and more breathless with each word. This
was the punishment that she craved for all the lies and deceit. He didn't reward
her with another paddle this time but just massaged the ache he knew she would
be feeling.

"Where is my son. Where is Ashkii?"

"I don't know, but Matthew is on his way to ensure that he is your son."

Thwack.

"What do you mean?" He replied

"Matthew is going to do a DNA test on the boy to ensure that she was not
lying. But I know she wasn't. The picture showed me that." Whack

"What picture?" His beat increased.

"She showed me a picture of him. James has it."

His paddle came down hard, this time, as he fought against his temper. They
had seen his child, and he hadn't. Sophie screamed out. Grayson placed his hand in
between her thighs and pressed down on her clit. She exploded in a violent
orgasm. He wasn't finished with her though. He kept his thumb on her now
swollen and tender bud.

"When did she show you this picture?"

"The day she died."

"The day she died. She came to see you? You spoke to her?" It suddenly dawned
on him. Accident. She didn't mean to. Fuck! "You killed Sally Bridgewater."

He stepped back. Sophie sprung up and covered her body with a nearby towel
they used for cleaning up.

"Yes." She tried to flee, but he grabbed her. She'd killed Sally Bridgewater. He
must be sick, but the thought made him hard.

"How?"

"She was trying to leave the house. She was going to tell the world you abandoned your child. She said she had proof James was a killer. She told me she was
going to bring down anything related to our families. She'd gone insane." Sophie
struggled in his arms.

"Colour."

"Green." He needed to check. This was a game but a deadly serious one. Her
reply had him rock hard. He yanked her back onto the bench and lowered his
jeans and underwear.

"I'm going to fuck you now."

"Please, Master." She whimpered.

"You are going to tell me exactly what happened while I do." He kicked her legs
apart and surged firmly inside her. She cried out and clamped down on his cock.
Fuck. He was going to come straight away. "Tell me."

"She tried to escape the room. She hit me, and I hit her back. We ended up
rolling around on the floor of my bedroom. Sally got the upper hand and kicked
me in the stomach." He withdrew and then slammed back into her. "She got to her
feet and tried to run. I had to stop her, so I grabbed her ankle. She fell and hit her

head on a wooden unit." Grayson's pace was getting quicker and quicker now. "When I looked at her, she had blood all over her face. She wasn't moving. I panicked and left the room. James and Matthew appeared. Apparently, they were tracking her. They took over and told me what to do." She barely got the last words out before she exploded on his cock, her juices bathing it. He reciprocated and thrust in deep to fill her with his essence.

He collapsed down on top of her. "Including lie to your own husband. Make him feel guilt for something you had done." He pulled out of her. She'd lied to him.

"Grayson." She turned and grabbed his hands. "Please." He pushed her back on the bench.

"You stay there." He pulled up his trousers.

"Where are you going?" She cried, tears filled her eyes.

"I'm going to get my son." He spat back.

"You can't."

"Watch me." He threw the door to their playroom open. Matthew Carter stood the other side. Grayson saw him survey the scene before him. Sophie covered in blood, her ass red raw and cum dripping down her legs.

"Wait." But he never got the rest of the words out before the body guard's big fist knocked him out.

NINETEEN

Grayson

"I'm sorry I hit you." Matthew was driving Grayson up the coast of California to San Francisco to meet his son. "I didn't realise you and Sophie did sado-ravishment."

"We don't normally," Grayson replied and continue his embarrassed stare out of the window. "I'm Sophie's, Dom. I needed to do what I did to bring her out of her depression."

"You did well. Although, you're lucky it wasn't James as the door. I think I would've been hiding your body right now. Particularly, since it looked like you were leaving without administering aftercare." Matthew kept his eyes directly ahead of him but raised a telling eyebrow of rebuke.

"Fuck. I was." He groaned. "I guess I got lost in the emotions of the scene as well. I would have left her, if you hadn't had been there. All I could see was that she lied to me."

"Sophie is a full-time submissive, Grayson. I was there after she killed Sally. She was looking for someone to tell her how to act and react. James did what he had to at the time. What he thought was best."

"But to not tell me about my own kid and lie about my wife?" Matthew felt wrong that they had done that. Both should have confided in him straight away.

"James isn't God, although don't tell him I said that. He does make the wrong decisions sometimes. At the time, he was concerned with making sure that his little sister didn't go to jail. I hate to say it, but you probably didn't figure in his decisions." Matthew pulled them off the freeway, as he spoke, and down into the cosmopolitan city. "Sophie couldn't cope with that though. Even though she was just following orders. It's obvious she knows her loyalty lies with you, and it was destroying her. You have got a good one there."

"Have I?" At this point, he wasn't so sure. The woman who loved him had murdered someone and kept that and the fact he had a secret child from him. He wasn't sure that their relationship would ever be the same again. Would he ever actually trust her again? He hadn't even had time to think about Sally's death. How did he feel about that? His wife murdered the mother of his child? He only had Sophie's word on what went on in that room. What if she killed Sally because of the child? Jealousy had consumed her, and she'd struck out? No, that was not the sort of person that Sophie was. He knew her well enough to know that. They had talked about having children, but neither of them were ready yet. With the lifestyle of a twenty-four-seven submissive, it would be difficult. Matthew was right when he said that Sophie needed people to make decisions for her. His wife was the best PA he'd ever had; she was perfect at her job, but she needed him to control her day to day life. She could not do it herself.

"Sally Bridgewater was out to destroy you. I did a sweep of her flat. The woman was obsessed with your destruction, but you weren't the only one. The woman had an obsession with whatever would get her the biggest story. Some of the things that she'd done to get it would have landed her in jail or worse. This was the inevitable end to that woman's life. At least it was quick and merciful."

"You're so practical with death." Grayson watched the straight-faced Matthew as he spoke.

"You mourn her?" Matthew asked

"She's the mother of my child," Grayson replied.

"She's the woman who slept with you for a story. She's the woman who kept the fact she was pregnant with your child. If she hadn't been so blinded, there wouldn't have been a child because she would have aborted it. And when she did finally have the baby, she gave it up without a second thought."

"She must have been scared though?" Grayson couldn't help but try and put himself into Sally's shoes at that time. Matthew pulled the car up to a beautiful Victorian house on the edge of the city. It looked a nice neighbourhood. Cute picket fences and all the gardens were well maintained, houses painted in traditional colours, and neighbourhood watch signs in the windows. This boded well for the life his son had had so far.

"Before you start feeling sorry for her, there is something else you need to know about Sally Bridgewater." Matthew turned the engine off and faced him. His face, usually devoid of emotion unless Sonia was in the room, was covered in anger. "Your son was never officially adopted. This is a foster home. He's been here for a few months now. Before that he was at his adoptive home. Sally didn't want any paperwork that could lead the child back to her, so she sold the kid on the black market. The family he was living with had four other children, all of them were brought up as slaves to the cunts who had bought them. They barely had any food; the clothes that they had were dirty and too small. The eldest, a girl of fifteen, there was evidence of sexual abuse. There was none with your son, but he has seen some horrors. The woman you are worrying about sold him into this and went to the Seychelles on holiday with the money. Do you still feel any remorse for her death?"

The anger flooded through Grayson. He gripped the side of the car so tightly that the whites of his knuckles showed.

"If she weren't dead already, I'd kill the bitch myself." He gritted his teeth together when he spoke. "I hope that the people who dared to do that have been suitably punished."

"They will be."

Grayson's humanity kicked in. "Maybe Sally didn't know about the family."

Matthew snorted a laugh.

"I sometimes forget that you and James have souls that I lack." He reached for his phone on the dashboard and brought up a copy of a document. Matthew handed the phone to him. "That proves that she knew when the kid was two. She must have had a crisis of conscience, because she searched him out. Did she go to the police with her findings though? No. She planned a story on it. Her only concern was how to make sure nobody found out that the boy was hers. It's why she didn't publish the article, in the end." The last words had barely left Matthew's mouth before Grayson was out of the car. He yelled out and sent his fist into a nearby tree. Curtains twitched and a couple of car alarms started ringing out such was the ferocity of his temper. Matthew was beside him and caught his hand as he went to punch the tree again.

"Your boy is in that house. If he hears you like this, he'll be wary from the start."

"Fucking bitch." He growled

"She'd dead. Sophie did that. She did that for you." Matthew was forever the voice of reason. "You need to pull yourself together."

"You still going to do the DNA test?" He took deep breaths to calm himself down.

"I think we both know the result, even if he isn't yours, but for the sake of the child I will."

He nodded. "I have a son."

The front door to the house opened, and a well-dressed lady stepped out.

"Let's go and meet him."

Grayson brushed the bark from his knuckles. Somehow, he hadn't broken the skin on his hand, but it still stung like a motherfucker.

"Mrs Portillo." Matthew extended his hand to the lady who greeted them. "I'm sorry for the little scene. I'm Matthew Carter; we spoke on the phone. This is Grayson Moore."

The woman blushed. "It's alright Mr Carter; I know who Mr Moore is. I've had enough kids come through here now who love the Renegade films. Many despite the fact it has an age limit." She extended her hand to Grayson, and he shook it. "Please call me Judy; I'm Ash's foster mother. Come in, we are just finishing lunch. It is one of my kid's birthdays, so we have cake."

"It's lovely to meet you, Judy." Grayson stepped inside the door. "How many children do you have here?" He was genuinely interested in this angel of a woman.

"Five, Ash has been with me for eight months now. I was hoping that his mother would come for him, especially after I sent her the photo, but I heard nothing back. And then I saw the report about her suicide." He followed Judy through the house to the kitchen. Matthew was behind them. "He may be shy at first; I don't like to get the children's hopes up, so I only told him that a man was coming to do a test on him." Judy went to open the door, but he stopped her.

"Was he damaged?" The question was asked in a very shaky voice.

Judy placed her hand on his arm; the middle-aged woman gave him a reassuring smile. "Ash was lucky; I think the older girl helped look after him. She taught him to walk, talk everything that a baby needs. He was the youngest but had to grow up quickly. Those people." She spat out the word, "Hadn't even named him. He was called four because he was the fourth child. None of the children thought anything of that. When he came here and found the other kids had names we spent a lot of time deciding on one for him. We chose Ashkii because of his native looks. I can't believe that we got the right tribe. Fate I think. He is obviously behind in a lot of aspects, especially with his learning, but he goes to a pre-kinder-garten here one day a week which has helped with his social ability. He is an adorable little boy, Mr Moore." She quieted and then opened the door. The noise of cheering and sounds of happy birthday being sung greeted him. He stepped into the room, and five pairs of eyes turned to face him. He only noticed one though. The ones that were the same as his. His breath hitched. Matthew stepped up behind him.

"You got this," Matthew stated supportingly.

"Hi everyone."

One of the older boys squealed; he guessed that the boy must be about four-teen. "It's Grayson Moore. Tilly, Judy got you Grayson Moore for your birthday."

The girl, Tilly, he assumed by the big birthday cake in front of her, jumped to her feet and ran to hug him. Her hugged her back. "Can you do that flip kick thing you do, that is so cool?"

"Tilly let Mr Moore go. I'm sure he'll do the kick for you later. He's had a long drive from LA, so let's get him a drink and a piece of your cake first."

"How far away is LA?" A boy of about eight asked.

"I would say about four hundred miles, I think," Grayson replied.

"Don't you know exactly?" The boy looked perturbed.

"I'll find out the exact miles for you later, Evan." Judy interrupted. "Evan is autistic; he likes to know exact details on things."

Matthew stepped forward and pulled his phone out, "I will Google it with him." He handed Grayson the DNA kit.

"Ashkii, why don't you come and sit next to Mr Moore?" The little boy looked up at Judy with his dark eyes.

"Is he the man who will do my test."

"He is honey."

The little boy slid off his chair and came to sit next to Grayson.

"It's nice to meet you, Mr Moore. I don't know your films. When the others talk about them, I always say I want to see them, but Judy always says in a year or so as I'm a bit young to watch them right now. But the others have told me the good parts."

"That's ok. So how old is Tilly?" He couldn't take his eyes off the little boy, his affection for the child was already ingrained into his heart. He knew then that he was leaving this building with him

"She's fifteen."

"A big girl."

"Yes."

"It's three-hundred and eighty-one miles, exactly, and it's taken them almost six hours and forty-seven minutes to drive here." Evan ecstatically called out.

"Such a long drive." Ash looked up at him.

"Don't tell Evan, but we got a helicopter most of the way, so it didn't take us that much time," Grayson whispered to the boy.

"You've got a helicopter?" The boy's eyes went wide.

"I do. You can go in it one day if you want."

"Can I?" Luxury had become standard for Grayson now; he didn't think much of it. It was a part of his lifestyle, but this boy, he'd had none of that. He hadn't even had clothes and food. His heart ached.

"Of course, you can."

"Judy says you have to do a test on me?"

"I do. Are you alright with that?" DNA didn't matter to Grayson at all, at that moment.

"I am. I have to open my mouth, and then you'll rub something against my cheek." Ash opened his mouth.

"Good boy." Grayson pulled the test out, took the swab, and wiped it around the kid's mouth. He placed it into a sealed container and handed it to Matthew when he appeared behind him.

"This is where being ex-MI5 comes in handy. I'll go speak to Jasper and have the results for you in half an hour."

"I already know the results," Grayson exclaimed as Matthew left the room.

"Alright, kids, who's for cake?" Judy called out and started to cut pieces. Ash waited quietly until he was passed a piece then devoured it in super speed.

"I want a paw patrol cake for my birthday." Ash splattered crumbs all over the table when he spoke.

"I don't know paw patrol. I'll have to look it up." It suddenly dawned on him that he didn't know the first thing about being a father. The house wasn't even set up for a family.

"It's brilliant. I want to be Chase when I grow up. He's the police officer."

"Maybe we can watch it together later?"

"It's not my day for watching what I want; because it's Tilly's day, she gets to choose."

"You have to take it in turns to watch the TV?" Grayson was confused.

"Miss Judy can only afford one, so we have to share. We can watch it tomorrow, but then I guess you won't be here." The boy looked down into the last crumbs of his cake. Grayson looked over to Judy; the helpful lady was watching them together. He could see that she had tears in her eyes.

"Tell me more about Paw Patrol. What other characters are there in it?"

The next half an hour passed in a flurry of information on talking dogs who had special vehicles. Grayson was actually excited and wanted to watch the show. It sounded like a kid's version of the Renegade films. Ash had moved onto his lap at some point, and Grayson had his arm around him. The other children disappeared to play with a new toy that Tilly received. It was a small karaoke machine, which allowed them to sing songs at the tops of their voices. The floor upstairs vibrated with the fun they were having. Judy was busy trying to tidy the kitchen. He could see that she held great affection for the children but was struggling financially. In the past, he had been accused of not helping those in need, but he was going to make sure that for the rest of her life this woman had what she needed to continue to help these children.

Matthew appeared at the door. Grayson tilted his head at him in question.

"Positive."

He let out a long breath. In his heart, he already knew what the the outcome would be, and it wouldn't have changed the decision he was about to make, but it was nice to have the confirmation.

"Ash?" The little boy looked up at him.

"You know the test that we did."

"Yes."

"That showed that I'm your daddy." Judy stopped her cleaning and came back to the table just in case Ash got upset.

"My daddy?" Ash frowned.

"Yes."

"Does that mean I can come and live with you in LA?" He could see the little boy's mind working behind his eyes. He hoped that whatever it was saying was good.

"What you like to?"

"Do you have a TV?"

"I have five."

"Five!" The little boy exclaimed and bounced up on his lap. "So I can watch Paw Patrol whenever it is on?"

"Yes, of course, you can?"

"What about Miss Judy?"

"What about her?"

"I'll miss her."

"Whenever you want to see her then you can. I'm going to buy Miss Judy a bigger house and all your friends their own TV so they can watch whatever they want." Judy gasped.

"Can you buy her house near yours?"

"If she wants to." Grayson looked at Judy who had tears streaming down her face. He smiled at her, and she brought her hands together in front of her in a gesture of thank you. "So do you think you like to come and live with me?"

"Um." He hesitated again.

"What is it?" Grayson asked.

"Do I have a mommy?"

How was he supposed to answer that one? Yes, she's dead, but you don't want to know her 'because she is the reason that you had to be in that place you grew up in. His thoughts turned to Sophie, his little one, his life, his love; she was at home alone. He'd asked her not to come here. He was still trying to work through his thoughts on her and what she'd done. Tears came to his eyes. He wished she was a part of what he was experiencing now. They should be doing this together. He had his answer.

"Yes, you do have a mommy. Her name is Sophie, and she is going to be so excited to meet you."

Ash wrapped his little arms across his broad chest.

"Let's go home, daddy."

TWENTY

A watched phone never rings. That was certainly what was happening to Sophie. She had been staring at the phone for hours now and nothing. Maybe it was broken. That had to be it. She swiped it on and tested it with a call to the home phone. It rang. Damn it! It was working. Why was this taking so long? She opened the folder that Matthew had left with her on Ashkii; she was barely been able to read the words with the tears that she shed after learning what had happened to him. Any guilt she had for killing Sally Bridgewater evaporated. The woman was evil scum and deserved to burn in Hell. If she could kill her again, she would and make sure it was much more painful this time. Sophie picked up the photo of Ashkii; he was such a beautiful little boy. The spitting image of his father. How much he had suffered. She just wanted to hold him and help him. Who knew she had a maternal instinct, but for this little boy, it was on full display. She just hoped Grayson would allow her to be a part of their lives. When he left, things were still very much up in the air. He had saved her from the pit of depression she was falling into. He'd known what she had needed despite his fear at what she was involved in. She was in every way possible a full time submissive. He'd seen that and used it to his advantage.

The Butler appeared in front of her.

"Mrs Moore, your brother is here." James strode confidently into the room.

"James." She jumped to her feet and ran into his big burly arms.

"Hi, little sis." He embraced her back; tapping her back to check on how much weight she had lost. "You look a little bit better than you did on the call yesterday."

"Grayson and I worked through a couple of things."

James raised a disgusted eyebrow. "So Matthew told me. I hope you are applying the balm regularly today, and he did get that cut checked, didn't he?" He turned her to examine the small abrasion on her head.

"Yes, he had a doctor come and put a couple of stitches in it."

"It was an accident?" The protective big brother was asking this.

"Yes, it was an accident. Everything was consensual."

"Good, because you know I will have Matthew kill him if he ever hurt you without consent."

"I'm kinkier than I thought, but you knew that even if I didn't." She shrugged and laughed.

"I did not need to know that. I think I may bring up my plane food." He brought her to his chest again. "Have you heard from them since they went to San Francisco?"

"No. I'm getting a little worried."

"I'll phone Matthew." James pulled out his phone and called. He did not put the phone on speaker though. "Hi Matthew, I'm with Sophie. What is happening?"

Sophie listened to the one-sided conversation for any hints as to the state of her marriage and Grayson's relationship with his son. She could guess nothing from her evasive brother's side of the conversation though.

"I'll get her packed, and we'll be there in a few hours," James said into the phone.

Were they going somewhere? Where? Was it to meet Grayson?

"I managed to find my way here safely. I think we'll be alright without a bodyguard."

Matthew replied to James' comment, and Sophie could guess what that comment was.

"Alright. I'll take one. Jesus, you are worse than Amy and Sonia. I'm a grown man; I think I've proven I can take care of myself on enough occasions."

Matthew repeated something, which she couldn't catch.

"That was one time; I got confused because I was tired. At least I had a nice few days' relaxation in the Maldives instead of working hard in India."

This time she caught most of the reply which was full of expletives.

"I said I was sorry for not telling you. There is no need to bitch at me again." James laughed. "I'll see you in a few hours." Her brother hung up and put his phone back into his jeans' pocket.

"By the end of today, I'm going to have no idea what time zone I'm in. You're lucky I love you, little sis."

"We're going somewhere?"

"Yep."

"Where?" Her tone was maybe a little too impatient.

"To meet your husband and son in Navajo Nation."

TWENTY-ONE

Grayson

"Shimá, Shizhé'é" Grayson called out for his parents when he walked through the door of their home. His heart had told him that this was the first place that he needed to bring the boy.

"Giní." His mother replied and raced out of the kitchen. She stopped dead when she saw the little boy beside him. His father appeared beside his mother and caught her when she began to fall, having fainted at the surprise.

"Mom." He stepped forward and helped to assist her to a chair. Ashkii remained where he was just looking around the big house. Grayson motioned for him to join them.

"How, when, I...?" The torrent of questions tumbled from his mother's lips.

"I'll explain that later but first, Ashkii." His son stepped forward and wrapped his arms around Grayson's legs. He was nervous. "I want you to meet your grandparents."

"Hello." He stuttered nervously.

"Hello." They both replied. His mother was sobbing.

"Giní, I can't believe this?"

"He's mine, mom." His son looked up at him.

"Why does Nanna call you *Giní?"* His mom whimpered a little happiness at the use of an affectionate term for her.

"That is my native name. It mean's Hawk."

"Mine means boy." He said proudly.

"It does. We'll teach you lots of our language." Grayson's father responded.

"I can't wait." Ash let go of his leg and went to his grandfather's arms. "Thank you, Grandpa."

Matthew coughed in the doorway.

"Sorry to interrupt. Swan is outside, and she's not saying the most pleasant things about you. I didn't think your parents would appreciate me hog-tying and gagging her to shut her up, so I figured it best that I tell you."

His mother let out a little cry of shock at the bodyguard's blunt words.

"That was an excellent idea. Mom, will you look after Ash for me."

"Giní, let your father speak to her, please."

"No, I need to put an end to her tainting of me. It has to stop." He was a father now; he was a husband, a good person, and he wasn't going to let his sister's warped views run him out of his ancestral home. He would always support his family, promote his culture. Yes, he had lost his way, but he was home again now.

"Daddy." Ash was at his side.

"Yes."

"You're coming back?" He got down onto his haunches in front of Ash. The fear in the little boy's eyes ripped at his heart.

"I'm just going to be outside for a little while. You stay with Nanna and Grandpa, and then, when I come back, I'll take you to meet the Chiefs. Would you like that?"

"Yes, please. Do they have the big hats that Evan said they do?"

"They do, and if you are a very good boy, I'm sure that they will let you wear one."

"Can I, can I? I promise that I'll be good."

"Of course."

"Ash." His mother came and took the boy's hand. "Why don't you come in the kitchen with me. I made cake earlier. Shall we get you a piece?"

"Two pieces of cake in one day. I can't believe it." Ash and his grandmother disappeared off into the kitchen. Grayson's father stepped forward. "I think I've been too lax with Swan."

"It's not your fault dad. Swan is independent and feisty. She has a role on the Council and uses it."

"A lot like her mother was until I married her. Maybe that is what is needed to mellow Swan."

"Heaven help the poor guy." Grayson laughed. He helped his father out of the house by holding the door open. They went to the courtyard outside the front of the building. A large crowd had gathered. Swan stood on the bonnet of his car preaching her sermon.

"Another visit, two years we heard nothing from him. That article is published, and he is here all the time. This time, he comes with a child who looks just like him." How had Swan known about that? Grayson looked around and saw his parents' neighbour amongst the throng of people. She gave him a smug smirk. Eyes everywhere. "That child is the product of the ways he fell into. The ways that are not of our people. He does not show any respect to us to bring that thing here."

Matthew cracked his knuckles next to them.

"It's alright. She'll come out of this looking the fool."

"You sure I can't gag her?"

Grayson shook his head.

Swan continued, "If that thing is indeed our blood, then, we need to rescue it from him. Mould the child to our culture. Get it away from its father's material-istic nature. The money appears now for fixing up the community centre, and Giní with it. Photo shoots in magazines to show what he does help his family. But that is only because I took a stand and did that article. Showed the world who he truly is. His club is destroyed; the angry people of Los Angeles burnt it down. They don't want him, and neither do we. Grayson Moore is the devil. I say we ban him from the Navajo Nation. Cast him out forever. Who is with me?"

A few cheers went up, and several of them looked around at him chanting 'Out, Out, Out'.

"I think I've heard enough. Time to put this crowd right." Before he could push his way through the crowd to the front, a tiny figure, that he instantly recognised, stepped forward. Sophie jumped onto the bonnet and pushed Swan off.

"Swan has had her say; now, I get mine."

TWENTY-TWO

Sophie

Sophie couldn't believe what she was hearing. The world was full of delusional women when it came to her husband. He'd made mistakes in the past, they both had, but they were good people. Grayson had never forgotten his culture; it was a part of him. It was always there. James tried to drag her into the house, but she was having none of it. Swan had had her say on her brother; it was Sophie's turn to now defend her husband. She pushed James off her and jumped up onto the car. Swan had quickly toppled from the bonnet with a firm shove.

"Swan has had her say, and no I get mine." The crowd quieted. Shocked at her sudden appearance, a few started to heckle her, but she silenced them with a stare. "You are good people and need to hear both sides of the story. I know that you will listen."

A hush fell over the crowd. Swan was up on her feet to protest, but her father appeared by her side, and Sophie heard him tell her to be quiet. She looked up, and Grayson stood next to his father. She wanted to run to him, but he gestured for her to continue. She coughed to clear her throat.

"I know what a lot of you think of *Gini*; he was seduced by the fame and fortune. That I'm nothing but a slave to him. He mistreats women and couldn't care less about his heritage, but none of you know the man who I love." She raised her voice even higher. "He is a kind and caring husband. Yes, we don't have a traditional relationship. I'm a twenty-four-hour submissive to him. That means that he dresses me, feeds me, and if I'm naughty punishes me. But that doesn't mean he treats me like a slave or a child. I'm a grown woman. I make decisions myself. I'm a successful PA; I manage his career. I have a brain. All our relationship means is that I trust him. I trust him in ways that not everybody will understand. I know that when I fall apart, he will be there to put me back together." She looked down at Grayson, and he placed his hand over his heart and mouthed always. As if it was the confirmation that she needed that he still loved her, she tried desperately to fight back the tears.

"I've lived with *Gini* for a long time now. The first meal I had with him was Goat's milk pancakes. I was hooked; and whenever I want them, he makes them for me. Most of the food that we eat originates from recipes that he learnt when growing up here. When he wakes in the morning, the first thing that he does is pray to the Sun God. He spent ages teaching me the incantations, and I join him as well. The native culture has entwined with mine. Our home is full of indigenous artefacts that he has rescued from being sold off to foreign buyers to be lost forever. We have a room that we painted with just symbols of your culture. We sing and dance to Navaho music. We buy rugs from those woven with loving care by the people who we meet. I know that we have not visited as much as we have wanted to, in the past few years and that I took him away from you all to England to marry him. I wish in some ways I could have combined the two cultures more, but I was the selfish one and wanted the princess wedding I'd dreamed of since a little girl. Grayson, *Gini,* is not to blame for that. All he did was give me what I wanted."

The crowd had fallen quiet around them. Several of the women were crying as well.

"I don't deny that he went through a wild phase. Neither would he. LA is a city that does that to you. I've not met the little boy, yet, but yes, he brought his son here to meet his grandparents." She hoped Grayson didn't mind her admitting that they'd still not had a chance to discuss everything or anything. The big smile he still had on his face said that he was not angry. "We did not know of the child until recently, and the second *Gini* knew, he went straight to find the boy and bring him home." Her voice broke again. "Home as in here, Navajo, not LA. He brought Ashkii back to his people. If he were ashamed or wanted to forget his heritage, he would not have done that. We would be in LA and not here to show you a new member of your family. He does value his ancestry; he wants to help you all. He wants to help everyone. A large part of Grayson's income is donated to projects around LA, and though he has been remiss in seeing that his donations reached his tribe in the past, he is ensuring that now." She wrapped her arms around her body. "If, after the things I have just said, you still want to ban him from his home then we will leave, but we will take his son with us and ensure that he is taught all about his culture and heritage. Even if he cannot visit it. Thank you for listening to me." She went to the edge of the car and jumped down into Grayson's arms. He brought his lips down to hers and kissed her as though he had been starved of her sweetness for eternity.

"I love you." He whispered into her ear when they parted.

"Forever." She replied.

A massive cheer went up in the crowd. They were calling Hawk. "What's happening?" She asked

"I think my people have decided they want me to stay." Grayson smiled.

"They are idiots; you will betray them again." Swan stood up to her brother.

"He never betrayed them in the first place; you did when you did that article." Sophie didn't like her sister-in-law.

"Swan, I think it is time to let your jealousy of your brother go." Grayson's father interjected.

"Jealous. I'm not jealous."

"Hush. Enough. I think it is time that you learnt about the real world. Now we have a grandchild, we are going to be spending a lot more time in LA, and you can join us. Who knows? We may even find you a husband to shut you up."

"Dad."

"Don't dad me. You may be on the Council, but family comes first."

"Fine." Swan stomped off like a petulant teenager.

"She'll sulk for a few days, and then we'll talk to her again. The people have spoken, and you are part of the family again, son." Grayson and his father embraced, slapping each other on the backs. Some of the other people, who had been in the crowd, came up and congratulated Grayson on becoming a father, saying they couldn't wait to meet the boy, and he must join them for supper soon.

Matthew handed her a tissue to wipe away the tears.

"Thank you, Matthew."

"You're welcome Mrs Moore."

"So where is my nephew then." James was there beside her.

"Nephew."

Grayson took Sophie's hands.

"We may have to make a decision to tell Ashkii the truth in the future, but he asked me today if he had a mommy. I said that it was you. He can't wait to meet you." She looked at him with her mouth open.

"Grayson. I. I can't. What I did. I killed his mother." She didn't deserve to be a mother to that boy.

"You killed a vile piece of garbage who didn't not deserve to be called a woman let alone a mother. She lost any right to that boy when she chose a newspaper article over him. You did him a favour."

"Are you sure?" She was holding onto a little bit of hope.

"Let's go meet your son."

The group dispersed, and she took Grayson's hand. Matthew and James followed them. When they got to the door, it opened, and Ashkii came running out. He was so much like Grayson that she instantly fell in love with him.

"Mommy." He called and jumped straight into her arms. "Daddy said that you were on your way. You're so pretty."

She had a lump the size of Texas in her throat.

"I think Mommy is very happy to see you." Grayson took the little boy from her. "You're still weak; I don't want you to exert yourself too much." That wouldn't stop her from wrapping her arms around them both though.

"Yes, Master." She bit her lip at the use of the normal word for Grayson.

"Why did you call him Master?" Ash asked.

James and Matthew chuckled behind them.

"I think these two are going to have a swift introduction to having a child around."

Sophie glared at them. "It's just a term of affection for him." Parenting 101 success. She stuck her tongue out at her brother.

"Master, can we have some more cake please?" Ash asked his father.

Sophie and Grayson looked at each other and burst out laughing. It was a Parenting 101 fail.

TWENTY-THREE

Grayson

"I never realised how energetic a five-year-old boy could be." Sophie collapsed onto the bed in Grayson's parents' spare room.

"He's certainly going to keep us on our toes."

Sophie sat up and wrapped her arms around his shoulders while he removed his shoes.

"I like it but are you sure about him calling me mummy."

"Never surer. If we have to tell him about Sally, we will, but I want him to know that he is loved by the two of us."

"He certainly is." He suspected his wife was as in love with the little munchkin as much as he was. "We'll have to change the dynamic of our relationship."

"Why?"

"Er...how would you explain to him me eating my dinner off the floor for example." She raised an eyebrow at him. That was true. Could they still have a twenty-four-seven submissive relationship with a five-year-old child living with them? Why couldn't they? As long as they gave him a healthy appreciation for women as equals and explained the relationship minus the sex bits; because he would never be ready for that at such a tender age, they could be as they always had been. Ok, Sophie would have typically eaten her dinner naked; that may have to change, but the essential elements of their relationship didn't have to.

"I would tell him that mommy had been naughty and she needed to think about what she had done. It's no different to us telling him off when he has been naughty."

"You do realise that he may ask why daddy never gets to eat on the floor."

"Because daddy is never naughty." He retorted with a chuckle.

"Mommy begs to differ on that. I think he's very naughty in the playroom sometimes."

"Only when I need to be." He twisted her around and laid her out on his lap. "I owe you an apology. I was going to walk out of a scene without any aftercare."

"Don't" She reached up and pressed her fingers to his lips.

"No." He kissed them and pulled them away. "This needs to be said. What happened between us was very intense. You didn't mention a safe word. I just need to check that you are alright with it."

She entwined her hand with his and brought it down to rest on her breast through the sleeveless top she wore.

"You saved me that day. I was drowning. I'd become someone who wasn't faithful to her beliefs. You brought me back. It's what I always trusted you to do. To know what I need better than I know myself. That is the dynamic of our relationship. So to answer your question, yes, I'm alright with everything that happened."

He leant down and kissed her. It felt like forever since they had been like this.

"I was thinking. My parents have a lot of lands out back. I'm going to ask them if we can build a place on some of it. Nothing fancy, just a place we can bring Ash and stay every now and then."

"I was thinking as well." She laughed, "We live in the modern world. Communication with everyone is secure via a computer or phone. We don't need to be in LA all the time. Why don't we make our permanent home here? What Ash needs more than anything now is family."

"Are you serious?" He didn't think that she'd want to leave LA, to immerse herself even more in his culture. He'd made enough money to last a lifetime and then some. He didn't need to work all the time. He wanted to spend more time at home with Ash and Sophie. Maybe even take a turn on the Council.

"Yes, this is where we belong. I still want to go to LA; a lady needs clothes, and once the club is repaired, we have to scene in it again. But I feel happy and content here; more than that, I feel free."

"I better talk to your brother in the morning then. Get him started on drawing up the plans."

Sophie sat up on his lap.

"Master, will you make love to me?" He studied her, not saying a word. "You are making me self-conscious now." She shivered.

"No words." He replied before pulling her top over her head. He removed her bra and nestled in between her breasts. Slowly, he took one nipple into his mouth and sucked it to a hard peak. He then repeated the same with the other one. "Perfection."

She laughed and wiggled her bottom over his hardening cock. "Perfection."

"You know what naughty little subs get don't you?"

"A spanking." She looked hopeful.

"Normally, but I'm afraid you will still be too sore after the paddle. So for tonight you just get this."

He picked her up and threw her onto the bed. She squealed. He was going to have to gag her. Damn it. He didn't have his bag with him. The belt of his jeans would have to do. He pulled it through the loops of his trousers while Sophie watched from under hooded eyes. She knew what was coming, and he bet she was practically dripping wet inside her shorts. He looped the belt around her face and brought it down to rest over her mouth. "That should keep you a little quieter. The whole Navajo Nation doesn't really need to hear you screaming my name."

She grumbled behind the belt.

"You tap me twice on the left shoulder to stop everything or even anything." It was something they had worked out before during play where she could not speak openly. She tapped him once on the right shoulder. This was her confirmation that she understood. "There is something that I've really missed recently, and that is the taste of your succulent pussy. I bet you are wet for me already aren't you, little one? Are you ready to accept your Master's tongue?" He licked his lips while undoing her shorts and pulling them down her legs. Her tiny panties followed. He sniffed them. "Sweet as always but with an added element of danger. I think it makes you even more delectable. And indeed more fuckable, not that my dick ever wants to leave your pussy." The dirty talk was flying from his mouth tonight. It had been so long since they had been able to just be Sophie and Grayson. They'd allowed others to interfere in their relationship. It had brought them to the point of destruction, but they survived it and were stronger than ever. His woman parted her legs for him, and he nearly came in his pants. She was dripping for him. The aroma was heady. He buried his head between her thighs. Her naked sex open and waiting for him. He used his fingers to unfurl her labia and went straight for her clit, teasing it, tantalising it, drawing it from its hiding place. She was his favourite meal, and he would worship it every day forever. He eased a finger inside her. She must have been sore from the other day. They had been very rough, and he didn't want this to cause he any more discomfort

"More." She mumbled around the leather gag. His goddess had spoken; he gave her what she wanted. He curled his two fingers, which were inside her, up to stroke at the sensitive spot within her. He could hammer nails with his cock it was that hard, but this was about Sophie. About his job as a Dominant to take her trust and reward her for it. He flicked over her clit again, and she came, washing his face with her essence. He licked up every last drop. He would never get enough. He pulled his fingers out, and she groaned at the empty feeling.

"I will make you feel full again soon."

He pushed off the bed and dropped his jeans and pants. His cock sprang out. It was fiercely ready for taking Sophie. But tonight wasn't about fucking, it was about making love. It was about showing his wife that he adored her, and they would be a fire together. He sat on the bed with his legs out in front of him.

"Come here." She obeyed and knelt before him. "I want you to sit on my cock and then place your bottom on the bed." She had to still be sore from the paddle so having her on his legs would hurt her bottom. "Put your legs over my shoulders and join your feet behind the back of my head. I'll do the rest." Sophie settled herself exactly as he'd asked. When she slid onto him, he let out a loud moan of pleasure. Maybe he should have gagged himself as well. This was his wife, and he was worried about his parents hearing them making love. The sooner he got the house built, the better.

"This is going to be a slow burn little one. I want to watch you as we make love. I want to see the moment that my cock hits the parts inside you that make you come. I want to look at you as your pussy clenches down on my cock and milks me for all I can give you." Sophie had tears in her eyes again. He didn't want her gagged for this. He wanted this natural. Just the two of them joined together. He dropped her legs and reached around to remove the leather belt.

"I might scream." She whispered.

"Scream all you want. I'm not ashamed of what we do."

He started to rock his hips, and Sophie pushed against the bed in perfect rhythm with him. They were slowly moving themselves to orgasm. He lifted his head to take her lips. Seal the love and affection that they had for each other. Their tongues twisted in a passionate tango; sweat glistened over their bodies in a beautiful sheen of arousal. They were moving as man and wife, as two lovers who were moving as one, who were one in ecstasy. They both pulled back from the kiss as they felt their combined climaxes approaching. He held her ardent stare, neither of them blinked as simultaneously he thrust in one final time and gave her everything he had while she clenched down on him and bathed him with her love.

He pulled her down beside him. He would stay inside her, as long as he could, as long as he stayed hard and long.

He never understood the actual value of heritage until this moment and the need to control it and hold it close. Heritage was the past, present, and more importantly, the future. It was in him. It was in Sophie. It was in Ashkii. It was what defined them, guided them, and guarded them. What he and Sophie did together would leave a legacy for generations to come. The Navajo people worshipped the natural; they embraced it and nurtured it. He had been blinded by the materialistic. He'd forgotten his true roots, and it had taken the tragedy to return him home. But now he was here, he would never leave again. For he had his wife, his son, and his family by his side.

TWENTY-FOUR

Ryan

He watched the wooden coffin lowered into the ground. He wasn't going to shed any tears for this malevolent woman. He knew that she was planning to double cross him and had already started planning her story. Sally Bridgewater lived for a story, and she died for it as far as he was concerned. She wasn't a pleasant woman, and Grayson Moore had fallen into her trap because of his overactive libido.

He watched the few mourners dressed in black over coats, to protect against the coming cold of winter, throw their handfuls of dirt on top of the black coffin. She was in Hell now. Just where she belonged in the fiery pit of pain. She made a good toy for the Devil. He rejoiced that he had put her there. Sophie really wasn't the most intelligent of the North siblings; he guessed that came from her over whelming need to have everything done for her. She was a child who had never grown up. He was there that day and listened to the entire conversation between the two women. She even walked past him hidden in the shadows when she left the room where Sally fell. It presented him with the perfect opportunity. He went in just as Sally came back to consciousness. She tried to get up, but he held her down and cut off her ability to breath until she spluttered her last breath in his arms. He had to be careful. Matthew Carter was on his way. The bodyguard was ex-MI5 and was trained to know if something was wrong. He made sure it looked like Sally died from the head wound. It wasn't as if they were going to do an autopsy to diagnose the cause of death. Not in the current location she was in anyway. James North was that obvious and controlling. He would do anything to protect his sister, and that had played right into his hands.

He left the graveyard with the other mourners. Exchanging pleasantries and saying inconsolable condolences for the tragic loss as he went. This was the part of his job that he loved; tying up the loose end towards the finale. His time was coming; he would have his revenge. Years of wondering why he was cast aside had twisted him into the bitter shell that he was today. Nothing made sense. Why him? What was wrong with him? What was so special about James and Sophie North anyway. They were rich kids who thought they could get away with anything. Well, the stack of evidence was mounting against them. Everything they knew would soon crumble.

He climbed into his black saloon car, paid for by his highly skilled job, with all the latest gadgets. They meant nothing to him except a means to an end. He tapped a button on his dashboard and a touch screen computer screen popped up. With a press of his thumb to the screen, two faces he knew well appeared on it. His mother and father. Not that they deserved that loving title. Not after what they had done to him. Abandoned him for no apparent reason. He stroked his mother's smiling face. He saw elements of himself in her, the slight wave at the corner of his mouth. The green hue that tinted his eyes. However, it was his father who he resembled more. His well built structure, his square jawline, and the set of his eyes. Thankfully, prosthetics hid that most of the time. They'd even made him hate his own face. That was how much they damaged him with their rejection. He pushed the screen away and started the engine.

Thanks to Sally Bridgewater, he had the evidence to destroy his brother and sister and all their friends. James, Sophie, and their families would have nothing in this world, just like him. The world would see them all for the monster's they really were. The people who controlled all around them on the belief that they had the right to murder and defile. All he needed for his revenge was the final pieces of the puzzle to crush his parents. He was ready to demand answers to so many unanswered questions that he had. Miranda and Pete North's time on planet Earth was limited. Death was coming and he would bathe in their blood.

THE END

PART SEVEN
CONTROLLING DISGRACE

ONE

Colette

THE PAST

"Jacob? Joshua?" Colette called out. She shivered as she ran through the door of the home she shared with her brothers. The three-bedroom house was in a quaint little village, surrounded by the Surrey countryside. It was the sort of place you saw on postcards sent around the world to best represent quintessential England. Her home was Tudor in style: with an ingle-nook fire place, wooden beams, with fairy tale features throughout. She adored it and loved living there, but at this precise moment, the dread of her situation and the punishment this house could offer filled her with fear.

"Joshua? Jacob?" she called again.

This time, Jacob's head appeared from around the corner of the main living area. He had a sullen expression on his face, which told of his displeasure at being interrupted.

"Do you have to be so noisy? I'm trying to pray," he snapped at her, but she needed to urgently verbalise what had happened.

"James did bad things to me," she blurted out.

"What?" Joshua's head also appeared around the corner.

"He, he…" She hesitated.

"Spit it out. We don't have all day." Jacob clipped her around the ear.

"We laid together as man and wife, despite not being married," she spat out nervously while rubbing her ear.

"You did what?" Jacob's eyes darkened. Joshua stared up at his elder brother and took a step backwards.

"We had intercourse. We've been doing it for a while. I believed I'd marry him, but now, after what he's just done, I realise I can never do that. I've made such a terrible mistake."

"Whore!" Jacob snarled and grabbed her by the collar of her floor length, black dress.

"Wait, brother." Joshua stepped in. He was always a bit more reasonable, only a little though. "What did he do?"

Jacob still had her by the collar and was grinding his teeth in front of her. He was like a rabid wolf ready to pounce if she said the wrong thing.

"Brother." Joshua placed his hand on Jacob's shoulder. "She knows she's done wrong with giving herself before marriage, but it sounds as though she believed Mr North's affections to be real. We need to ascertain what he's done to her. Can you not see that she's distraught? Please let her sit and explain further."

Jacob let her go with a loud huff. He stomped into the lounge, and she heard the creak of his favourite wingback chair as he, no doubt, threw himself into it. Joshua motioned for her to follow. She put her head down, shuffling into the lounge. Joshua followed. It would be wrong for her to sit down, so she went to Jacob and knelt before him.

"Talk," he demanded.

"James has been asking me for a while if we could try something else other than missionary position." She kept her head bowed while speaking. "I relented tonight due to the pressure he exerted on me to agree."

Jacob hissed but didn't say anything.

"He placed a blindfold over my eyes and asked me to go on my hands and knees like a dog. I knew it was wrong, but I thought he would realise half way through and beg for forgiveness," she whimpered. "He didn't, though. It excited him to degrade me that way. He finished while smacking my backside."

She dared to look up into her elder brother's eyes. They were black as jet. The shaking of his hands, the redness of his face, told her of his fury. She quickly placed her head even lower, sliding her body down, cowering submissively at his feet.

"I'm so, so sorry. I've done terrible things, and I allowed him to defile my body. Save me, brother, please." Her body hugged the ground in a desperate need for forgiveness.

"Get up," Jacob ordered. "I'll not have you in my house in your current state. You're a vile, dirty creature who isn't worthy of being called my sister. I want you out." She shot up to her feet, and Jacob grabbed her by the collar again.

"Brother," Joshua cried, "You can't throw her out. She's begging for mercy. She's made a mistake and needs help."

"Quiet!" Jacob ordered. "I'm the elder; therefore, I get to make the decisions here. Under the sink in the kitchen are steel pads. Go and get them."

"What are you going to do?" Joshua asked.

"Do as you're told, stop questioning my authority," he thundered as Joshua scuttled away.

"Strip!" Jacob turned his attention back to her and commanded with a level of threat that made her not question the instruction. She quickly divested herself of the maxi dress, letting it billow to the floor. She stepped out of it and was left standing in a pretty bra and panties James had bought for her. "What are they?"

"J…James bought them for me," she stuttered, "He said he liked to see me in nice clothing."

"Take them off."

"But?"

"Do it!" he shouted.

She was wrong. She'd committed many sins, and she needed cleansing. That was why her brother was doing this. She needed to remember that. He was the only person she had in this life, apart from Joshua. He was being protective, looking out for her. She'd gone off and done things that degraded her. They made her worthless. Now, her brother was going to bring her back into the folds of righteousness.

She swallowed and removed her underwear. Joshua returned to the room with a cardboard box containing the steel pads she used for cleaning dishes with stubborn stains on. Oh God!

"What's going on?" he asked.

"She even dresses up in the devil's clothes. Women have no need for these frivolous things." Jacob tore the underwear from her hand and stepped closer to the fire. He threw them straight into the dancing flames, and she watched as the gossamer silk caught alight, disintegrating in the heat. She'd liked the way the underwear had made her body look. She wasn't tall, only about five feet five, with a curvy body. Her long chestnut hair trailed down her back to her bottom. She always wore it pulled back in a braid. She had green eyes that, in the sunshine, glimmered like emeralds. She wasn't a classic beauty, but James had always made her feel beautiful. All her clothes were black or grey. She possessed a special dress for church, which was cream in colour. Other than that, all her clothes were plain and dull. They didn't flatter her body, but it never occurred to her to be worried about it. Jacob and Joshua provided her with new clothes as she grew or the old ones became worn out. She didn't wear a bra, except when seeing James, and all her knickers were plain white, covering large parts of her from her waist down to almost her knees. This was her life, and she didn't think to question it. Watching the beautiful teal bra set burn in the hypnotic flames, she wondered why she couldn't have such things.

"Bring her." Jacob's stern command drew her out of her reflection. Joshua took her arm, and they both followed Jacob towards the bathroom. "Colette, in the shower."

"We're going to clean her?" Joshua asked.

"She has his vile venom all over her. We need to get rid of it. It'll taint her and draw the devil into our home. I won't allow that to happen. Turn the water on as hot as possible."

She stepped back.

"It'll burn me."

"The pain will be a lot less than the flames of the devil when he drags you down to hell," Jacob snapped back at her. She flinched. Joshua turned on the water and placed his hands under it. She saw him recoil back from the heat.

"In," Jacob ordered.

She whimpered a plea.

"Ungrateful bitch. We're trying to save your soul, and all you do is defy us. Do you want to sit on the devil's knee? To be his concubine?" Jacob grabbed her arm, pushing her into the shower.

The water was scalding, and she instantly felt the burn to her skin. She screamed and jumped out of the way of the tumbling waterfall.

"Hold her down." Her older brother ordered the younger sibling.

"But the water will burn me," Joshua replied with a frown on his face.

"Do I have to do everything myself?" Jacob moaned and pushed into the shower with her. If the burning water affected him, he didn't show it. He grabbed her again and positioned her directly under the head of the shower. Her skin heated under the scalding water. She wanted to escape but couldn't. She had to take her punishment. Jacob was right; she was evil, and if he didn't save her, then she'd sit at the devil's side. She didn't want that. She wanted to experience Eden and Heaven. She was a good girl; she really was.

The hot water in the tank must have been low, or she'd blacked out from the pain on her skin, because the torture only felt like it lasted a few moments before the water turned tepid. She breathed a sigh of relief.

"Look at yourself," Jacob told her. "See how the water cleanses your body. Rids you of his filth."

She looked down and saw nothing different just a red tint that covered her whole body. She could still feel where James's hard cock had been inside her. She was small; he was big. Every time they had sex, she felt him between her thighs for days after. She rubbed her thighs together.

"It isn't enough," Jacob cried as his gaze travelled to where she squeezed her legs together. "He's still there. Joshua, the pads."

Oh god, she looked towards where her younger brother stood, still clutching the pads she used to clean dishes.

"We must cleanse her skin thoroughly. Give me one. Take one yourself and help me. The water's cooler now."

"Yes, brother." Joshua opened the packet and dropped all the pads to the floor bar two. He stepped into the shower with them, which pressed her against the wall.

"Please. He's gone from me. Give me another punishment not this." Her skin was already raw from the scalding water. If they used those pads on her, they'd tear it apart.

"You're nowhere near clean enough. You need to pay further for being James North's whore. I won't let the devil have you. He'll smell him on your skin. We must drive him from you."

Jacob took a pad from his brother and scraped it down her back. She cried out as the metal dug into her raw flesh and pulled it apart.

"Please," she begged, though her words fell on deaf ears, as Joshua took his own pad and started to scrape the front of her body. She wasn't sure how long they scrubbed, but by the time they stepped back, her entire body was covered in inflamed skin and blood. Some of the cuts were deep, and she'd scar. Her body ached, and she wanted to curl up into a ball and cry. She was such an evil woman. She'd allowed herself to be sullied. She deserved everything that had just happened. She bowed her head, allowing the now freezing water to wash the blood and filth away.

"There's one place on you that I won't clean. Unfortunately, it's the place that needs the most cleansing." Jacob held the pad out to her. She snapped her head up. "You'll clean your female parts."

She tried to speak, to protest, but no words came out. She deserved this. She'd lain with a man out of wedlock. She'd allowed him to place himself inside her while in a position that was proscribed. She took the blood soaked pad, parted her thighs, and wiped down between them, the bristles of the wire catching her sensitive flesh but not ripping it.

"Harder," Jacob demanded. "That won't get rid of his poison."

She'd been strong to this point. She hadn't cried once, but now a lone tear tumbled down her cheek. She braced herself against the pain and did as her brother ordered. She screamed, as she felt herself ripping and tearing. This healing would take a while. She'd never be the same again.

She dropped the pad onto the floor.

"Am I clean now?" she asked.

"In body, yes you are. We now have to work on your mind."

Her legs almost gave way. She couldn't cope with anymore. Jacob grabbed her braid and pulled her out of the shower. She was dripping water and blood all over the floor. Her skin was burning from the scalding water.

"Jacob, please," she begged, but it was to no avail. Her brother pulled her out of the bathroom, through the house.

"I knew there was a cellar in this house for a reason. I didn't realise before, but I do now. It was the Divine's way of showing me how to punish you."

"What?" she stuttered.

"I'm glad I never did anything with it. I was going to put lights in there and remove the damp, but this will be the perfect place for your reflection time."

Damp, light, punishment. The words scrambled together in her numbed brain.

"I don't understand. What are you going to do with me?"

Jacob halted outside the cellar.

"You'll spend the next week down there in the dark, reflecting on your indiscretions. In that time, Joshua and I will deal with James North. You'll never see him again."

With those final words of menace, Jacob opened the cellar, pushed her, still wet and naked, into the black room, and shut the door on her.

TWO

Michael

Present

Dear Colette,

My name is Michael, and we have a mutual acquaintance in James North. He's asked me to write to you, having told me of your current situation.

I feel silly writing this letter. I don't know what it'll achieve, but I wanted to send something to you. I don't know you. I've not met you, but I can tell you're a strong woman, from all I've heard.

Don't be angry at James for telling me of your past. He did it in good faith. He's a decent man. One of the best I've ever met. Everything I'm writing is so jumbled. I can assure you I'm normally more controlled and coherent in my writing than this. I should just get to the point.

James believes you have questions in relation to the BDSM world he can no longer answer for you. If you'll permit, I'd like to visit with you; you may ask any questions you wish. Your doctor has already cleared this as a good course of treatment. If you wish to meet me, let your doctor know, and I will come.

Yours,
Michael

~

"Mr Peterson, if you'd like to come this way." Dr Rahul indicated for Michael to follow him. He still wasn't sure he was doing the right thing, but he knew he needed to try. When Colette had written back to him, her letter had been short, the penmanship shaky. She'd asked him to contact her doctor, nothing more, nothing less. "Miss Fisher's very jumpy today. She's suffering with her nerves. All of this is very new to her. To think of a relationship with the opposite sex has been frowned upon her entire life. The last time she tried to explore something physical, she was brutally beaten. Colette's a frightened and confused woman. She's almost thirty, but in many ways, she's still a child."

"Are some of her issues related to any special needs she may have?" He needed to ask the question.

"No. Not at all. She's an exceptionally intelligent woman. She was home-schooled by her family. She knows of modern technology although has barely used a computer or mobile. Her use of the TV has been confined to religious programmes. She was allowed to watch the news to warn her of the evil in the world, and that was it. She doesn't even know what reality TV is." Dr Rahul held his hand on the door handle.

"You say that last bit like it's a problem. I know many a person who'd be grateful to not have reality TV in their lives."

"I'm with you there." The doctor chuckled. "What I'm trying to say is that everything is scary for her. Her world has suddenly expanded and opened up many new avenues. We can't tell how she'll react to you, so that's why I'll be with you. Take things slowly. I know Mr North believes this will be the best course of action. It's a new and novel treatment for me to agree to, but I'm running out of ideas for anything else."

"You have my word. The second I sense she's becoming distressed, I'll cease. It's not my intention to see her worried. I want to help her." He nodded to the doctor who, being reassured, opened the door.

He peered inside the room to see a slight woman sitting on a chair. Her long, brunette hair billowed around her face, blocking him from seeing her features. He stepped into the room, and her head shifted, so behind the long hair, she could see him. At thirty-five, he was five years older than her, but he'd looked after his body. His blonde hair, which he normally wore natural, had been brushed back with a little gel for this meeting. He had on a formal shirt and black trousers. In comparison to her, in leggings and a tatty t-shirt, he looked respectable for once. He was a casual sort of man. He was often mistaken for a surfer, despite the fact that he'd never touched a board in his life. Dr Rahul followed him into the room and took a seat to one side.

"Colette, this is Michael Peterson. Will you say hello?"

Nothing.

"Colette."

Still nothing.

He held his hand up to the Doctor to silence him.

"It seems Miss Fisher has taken a vow of silence. That doesn't matter. What matters is her position. She leaves me at an unfair disadvantage, because I can't see her face or her eyes. She sees all of me and can make her assessments, but I see nothing of her."

He positioned himself in front of the woman. She still didn't look up at him or make any effort to move. "You've been treated with strict discipline all your life, and that won't change with me in it." Colette shivered. "You'll also learn with discipline can come pleasure."

"No!" From under all the tangled hair came the retort.

"It speaks," he offered.

"It bites as well," she countered.

"Intriguing." He brought his finger to his lips and pondered his next move for a moment. "May I touch her, not sexually?" He addressed the doctor and not the girl in front of him. He was a trained Dom with fifteen years' experience. Before him was a brat, a broken brat, but a brat nonetheless.

"I don't think anything about this meeting is orthodox, so I'm just going to say, yes." The doctor turned away to look at a pad of paper he was holding and began to write.

"Do you know the one thing a good Dom should always carry with him?" He paused for an answer, but nothing came, so he reached into the pocket of his trousers and pulled out a hairband. "Something to tie hair back. It's not fair when a Dom can't see his submissive's face." Without pomp and ceremony, he grabbed Colette's hair and pulled it back into a ponytail. "See, much better." He stepped in front of her to survey who he was dealing with. He hadn't expected the large, sultry, green eyes, which stared back at him. They were full of terror but also sensuality. She took his breath away. Her lips were full, and her face, although in need of a good meal to fill it out a bit, was stunning. He held his hand out.

"Nice to meet you, Miss Colette Fisher."

She looked down to his outstretched palm and back up to his eyes.

"Will you hurt me?" she asked.

"My intention, as stated in my letter, is to answer any questions you may have. Nothing more, nothing less. Only what you ask." As he spoke, he already knew he wouldn't be able to let this woman leave his life. She called to him with a need for affection and love.

"I don't know if I can do this?"

"How do you know until you try?"

He watched as the young woman wrestled with her emotions. She was desperate to try and escape from her past, but the ingrained trauma left her feeling weak and insecure. His hand was still outstretched, and he felt her tiny fingers slowly curl around his brawny ones and squeeze.

"Be gentle with me," she whispered.

"I promise." He let go of her hand and took a seat on a nearby chair. The soft, black leather of the chair wrapped around his masculine frame. "I want you to get down onto the floor on your knees."

"What?" Colette gasped.

"The first thing a submissive learns is how to pose for her Master." He placed his hands on his thighs and stared down at her.

"My brothers made me sit on my knees for hours praying for salvation." The corner of her eyes welled with tears no doubt from painful memories.

"Did they make you sit on a hard floor?"

"Yes."

He reached around and pulled a cushion out from behind his back. The room was clinical, given it was in a hospital, but it was also designed for giving comfort to all who were in it.

"Use this." He threw the pillow onto the floor.

"You...you still want me to kneel?"

"You still want me to teach you about BDSM?" he countered to her comment. He wasn't going to give any leeway.

Slowly, Colette rose from her seat. He could see her legs were stick thin. How they held her up, he'd never know. The strength of the human body was astounding. Gingerly, she sunk to her knees before him. She bowed her head, and her hands instantly went to a prayer position in front of her.

"No."

Her head came up.

"Am I doing it wrong?" she sounded scared.

"For the most part, it's right. We don't hold our hands like that, though. We place them on our thighs. Like mine."

Colette moved her hands so the palms lay flat on her upper thighs. "Like this?"

"Yes. Good girl." He felt the need to praise her, because she sounded happy to have her hands in the correct position.

"Why do we have to sit like this?"

"It shows your willingness for what comes next. You're prepared to place your body into my trust."

He saw Colette suddenly swallow deeply.

"What is it?" he asked.

"You don't expect me to do anything with you, do you? I just want to learn about BDSM. I don't want to partake in it."

"No. Not at all. I want you in this position to ask me your questions, because it will help free you in the end."

She snorted a little laugh.

"Why do you laugh?" he questioned.

"Because nothing will free me, now. This is more about broadening my horizons, should we say? My history's too ingrained in disgrace to allow me salvation." Colette looked back down at the floor.

He didn't reply to her comment. What could he say? He could reassure her everything would be alright, but neither of them could see into the future. She may never leave the hospital where she currently resided, and a normal life for her would remain a dream. Just like it had been for him after the tragedy that had touched his life. He couldn't think about that, now. He needed to stay strong for the broken woman in front of him.

"What are the questions you have about my lifestyle?" He moved one of his hands to his chin and rubbed at the light stubble, which peppered it.

"Amy's book, she had the Dom do things to the woman that shouldn't be done unless the woman's a prostitute. Sex isn't for enjoyment. It's for a man and woman to create a new life. How can a woman not be a prostitute and, yet, like those things? You shouldn't enjoy sex. All this BDSM stuff is about loving it."

"Hush." He interrupted her when he saw her starting to get flustered with her own thoughts.

"But..."

"No. That's a lot of questions, already, which I need to answer. Let me do so."

"Ok," she whispered.

"In some cultures, you're right, sex is for procreation only. It's what's needed to make a baby, but BDSM isn't all about sex. That's a part of it but not all. Let me tell you a little about myself. That may help you understand more."

"Ok."

"As you know, I'm Michael Peterson. What you don't know is I'm a widower."

"You were married? You don't look old enough to have lost a wife. I'm sorry."

"Death can occur at any age, as you well know."

"My brothers?"

"Yes."

"Bethany and I'd been together since school. We were childhood sweethearts. She was a teacher, and one day, she went to work and never came home. One of the pupils had been dumped by his girlfriend, and he didn't take kindly to it. He brought a knife to school and tried to stab the girl, but when Beth stepped in to save her, the blade pierced the femoral artery in her thigh, and she bled out within minutes. There was nothing anyone could have done to save her. She was a hero, and the young girl survived. The boy will be lucky to see parole before he's fifty. If I get another chance to make an impact statement, then I'll see he's never let out." While he was speaking, Michael had clenched his fists into a tight ball. He was still angry about his wife's death. She'd been so beautiful and had been his life. There wasn't a day he didn't wake and reach over to the pillow beside him, hoping and praying he would wake from the nightmare, and she would be there. He saw a lot of her in Colette. The innocence Bethany had had was exactly the same. It was an amazing thing people could retain, despite the cruel world they lived in. His wife had only been twenty-nine when she died. He knew this to be the same age as Colette was now. He'd been thirty, older by a few months, but now, as he approached thirty-five, the wounds had started to heal.

Colette took her hand off her thigh and reached out to touch his shoe. It was a gesture of comfort that travelled up his leg and straight to his heart. He could see how hard it was for her to undertake the small motion, in the shaking of her fingers. The kindness that dwelt, hidden within her, pushed her through the barriers of fear.

"I'm so sorry. I wish I could offer you comfort for your loss. She'll rest at God's side for her heroism. I know that for certain. Your wife was a brave woman who gave selflessly. She'll be rewarded." A tear tumbled down Colette's cheek. He wished he could reach out and wipe the grief from her face.

"Would you still say those kind words if you knew we practised BDSM together? We did scenes together in clubs, and she was my twenty-four hour submissive."

Colette lowered her head but didn't remove her hand from his shoe.

"You think I believe she died because she was sinful?"

"Isn't that what you'd say to me, if you truly believed? I didn't love her, and she wasn't godly."

"I...I...I don't know." She hesitated.

"Bethany attended church every Sunday. It was the only thing we argued about. I liked to have my Sundays in bed. I was the selfish one who wanted her with me. She wanted to pray. We came to a comprise and would have breakfast in bed when she returned."

"Maybe, you didn't do all the bad things Amy's book talked about."

"Bad things?" he asked, knowing full well what she meant.

"I mean...I mean the whips, positions, taking her in a place a man's appendage isn't designed for."

He laughed. "Anal sex?"

Colette blushed.

"Yes."

"Anal was one of Bethany's favourites. She liked to be full."

"Oh." Colette nibbled at her lip. "God wouldn't have taken her for that. She was a good woman. I can see that just in the love you have for her."

"So, why do you believe if you choose to explore and understand BDSM, you'll be taken for the devil's property?" They were getting to the root of the problem now.

"It's in my blood to be sinful and wrong. I have to stay good and obey all the rules. When James did what he did to me, I had to pray for forgiveness. My brothers scrubbed me until I bled. They saved me, but then, they died. All these feelings have resurfaced, and I'm scared. I'm scared the devil will take me." He fell to his knees in front of Colette and brought her into his arms. He held her tightly as she broke down and sobbed.

"I want to be normal and to feel these things. To know that, when my body feels a certain way, it's alright. It's not wrong. I want to go to the cinema like a normal person and see a romantic film. I've never been. I want to know what a disco is. I'm fixating on BDSM because of everything to do with James, but the truth is I don't know how to be a normal twenty-nine-year-old. I've never even been to a pub to have a drink. I'm a naïve child." She pushed at his chest to try and get away from him. He refused to let go, though.

"Hush." His warm breath flooded over her head in comfort. "You're not a child. You've had an alternative upbringing. That's all. Colette, now is the time you can make decisions for yourself. You can hide away and be what your brothers wanted you to be, and you can run scared of the devil for the rest of your life. I can tell you, now, you have an inquisitive mind, and it won't allow you to obey all the rules. There's nothing wrong with that. What your brothers taught you isn't necessarily wrong. I wish I could condemn them. Their morals were different to mine, and in my eyes, they're the evil of your situation, but I know they believed what they preached. They couldn't see any other way, and they thought they were protecting you, but they're gone now. You have to be brave and make your own decisions."

"How will I know what's right or wrong?" she whispered into his chest.

"You won't for certain. You just have to follow what your heart tells you."

This time, Colette pulled back. He allowed her to, so he could look into her green eyes. They were still wet at the edges with her tears, but they were no longer full of fear. Excitement sparkled in them.

"I can make my own decisions?"

"Yes," he responded, and she looked over to the doctor then blushed.

"What is it?" he asked, lowering his voice.

"When I read Amy's book, one of the scenes in which they made love, well, it made me..." She looked over to the doctor, again, who seeing her hesitancy turned away. Dr Rahul could still hear what she had to say but was giving Colette the semblance of privacy she needed. "It made me feel funny down there."

"It got you wet?" Michael smirked.

"I...I...yes?" she reluctantly admitted.

"Did you touch yourself?"

She adamantly shook her head in the negative.

"Why not?"

"It's wrong."

"No, it isn't. I touch myself, most nights in fact, because I have a high libido. Do I have horns? Do you have a copy of the book here with you?"

"Yes, but I've not read it again."

"Do so, tonight. Don't think as you read. Just see where the book takes you, and don't think anything is wrong. I know this will be hard, but don't punish yourself. You're free to make this decision about your own body." He stroked a stray tendril of her hair from her face. Electrical energy fizzled through him. In that moment, he wanted to place his lips on hers. He hadn't kissed another woman since his wife had died, so the feeling was alien. He'd been with other women at the club his friend Grayson Moore owned, but he'd never done more than just scene with them. He was lonely. He missed having someone at home to care for and worship.

"I would like to come and see you again." He wasn't sure where the words came from, but they seemed to come out of his mouth. "If that's ok with you?"

"I don't know."

"Sorry, it was a presumptuous question." He interrupted and got to his feet quickly. She placed a hand at his feet again to stop him from walking away.

"I don't mean it in a bad way. I mean, will you give me a chance to get through tonight? I have a lot to digest from today. Right now, my mind is doing somersaults at the thought of reading the book again. I'm terrified of making a decision like that on my own, but I need to. I know that. I just can't make two decisions at once. It's too much for me."

He reached down and helped her to her feet.

"I completely understand. I'll leave my address with the doctor. You may write to me, if you want me to come."

"Thank you for understanding." He'd still been holding her hand and let it go, so it fell back to its natural position at her side.

"Remember, listen to your heart. Switch the brain off for a while. Your body will tell you what it needs." He stepped forward and pressed a little kiss to her cheek. "Goodbye, strong lady. Have faith."

THREE

Collette

Dear Mr Peterson,

I want to thank you for visiting me the other day. You gave me a lot to think about, and I have been doing nothing but that, since then. I've had ups and downs with it. Some of the memories I hold within me are very painful. I remember one time when I was sixteen. My tutor (I was home educated by a teacher whom my brothers deemed suitable) gave me Pride and Prejudice to read. We had to write an essay on the virtues of a woman within the novel. I was very foolish and spoke well of Lydia Bennett. I tried to say that she just wanted to be loved. When of course, she's nothing but a big flirt. I was struggling with my own sexuality at the time. I had feelings I shouldn't entertain for men who visited our house. They were part of my brothers' prayer group, but I sometimes imagined them touching me, and my hand would go between my thighs. I wasn't touching myself; I was just trying to stop the ache there. I don't know why I did it, but I used that as an example in my essay. My brothers went mad. I was forced to stay on my knees for twenty-four hours praying for my soul. I wasn't allowed to eat or drink. I wet myself at one point because I'd become so desperate for the bathroom. Sorry, you probably didn't need to know that. By the end of the time, I knew I'd never have those thoughts again, and I didn't. That could also have been because I met James North shortly afterwards.

I went off on a bit of a ramble, there, but I think from meeting me the other day, you've already discovered I can do that. I apologise. My real reason for writing is because, ok courage don't fail me now, I did as you said and read the passage again in Amy's book. I got those feelings, and I did what you said. I can't describe the feeling that came over me. It was like a choir of angels singing inside my body. That must mean it isn't a bad thing, right? My face is so hot writing this. I must look like a beetroot.

Having said all that, if your sentiments towards visiting me are still the same, then I would very much like to see you again.
Regards
Colette Fisher

~

"What is that?" Colette stood up from the chair she always sat in, in the doctor's interview room. She'd taken care with her appearance today and had pulled her hair back. She had on leggings and a comfortable jumper. It was her favourite attire, now that she wasn't forced to wear those long, grey dresses. Michael had arrived a few minutes ago and wheeled a TV attached to a black box into the room. She was excited to see him again but intrigued as to what he had brought her.

"It's a game console."

"A what?" she asked.

"We're going to play a computer game on it."

"Oh, my brothers let me play one of them before. It was a quiz on the Bible. I did really well. I think I only got one wrong. I remember the answer to that question to this day, though. I had to repeat the passage over a hundred times to make sure I knew it."

Michael winced, and she knew she'd said another one of those things that wasn't normal for a twenty-nine-year-old woman who'd had a sensible upbringing.

"I think you'll find this game a little more fun. It's not questions but a platform game. I'm a big Star Wars fan, so this is a Lego Star Wars game."

"Star Wars? Lego?" These were two terms she'd never heard before, and she had no idea what he was talking about. Actually no, that was wrong, now she thought about it, she'd heard James talk about Star Wars once. He'd wanted to take her to the cinema to see a re-run of the first few episodes. She knew her brothers would never have allowed her to go, so they'd stayed at his home, instead. She'd cooked him a meal, and they'd watch television. It had been a wrestling show which she didn't really enjoy.

Michael's reply drew her out of her reflection.

"They're a film franchise I like, and I'm bringing Lego next time I come. That's the best toy in the world."

"Toys. I had a doll when I was growing up, but that was it. My brothers didn't really have toys, either." Michael pressed a few buttons on the box while she spoke, and it sprang to life. The screen lit up with dramatic music and lots of little yellow figures. He handed her a strange looking contraption.

"What's this?" She looked down at the thing in her hands with 'x' and 'o' printed on it.

"That's the controller." He smiled. "You press the buttons like this, and you can control the characters on the screen with it."

She watched the screen while he pressed the buttons. There was a little character dressed in a white costume, holding what looked like a blue shining stick, that jumped up and down and waved the stick around.

"What's he holding?"

"A light sabre."

"What's one of those?"

"It's a Jedi sword."

She paused.

"What's a Jedi?"

Michael let out a little chuckle, and she blushed. She felt silly not knowing anything.

"One step at a time. Let's see if we can get you playing the game first. You have a go at pressing the buttons, now."

She reached her index finger out and pressed the 'x' button. The little character jumped. She squealed.

"It moved."

"Yes, it did."

She pressed another button, and the character spun around in a circle before running off to the side and falling off a cliff.

"What happened?"

"You died, I'm afraid."

"Died?"

"Yes, you're supposed to stay away from cliff edges."

"Oh," she sighed. "Is it over?"

"No, watch." He pressed a button, and the little character rebuilt itself. "This is a fictional world, a game. You can't properly die in it. You play it until you get bored or finish the game."

"Ok, I'll give it another go." She pressed the buttons, and this time, the character moved but didn't walk off the cliff. "I did it."

"Well done." Michael sat back in his chair, and she continued to play. Time disappeared, and the next thing she knew, she'd been playing for an hour. Michael stretched in his chair.

"I'm sorry." She placed the controller down. "I've taken far too much of your time, today. I apologise."

"Don't. I've enjoyed watching you play. I'm sure, if Dr Rahul agrees, we can leave this here for you to play when you want to."

"I'd like that, thank you."

"I want you to answer me something, first." Michael looked over to the corner of the room where Dr Rahul sat with a pen in his hand. She knew her doctor would be writing down anything of interest that occurred during their conversation. The doctor nodded encouragement to her companion. Something was going on?

"You've been asked to question me?" She looked at Michael, with her mouth wide open. She was shocked. She trusted him, and he was obviously working with the doctor.

"I have been, but you don't have to answer me if you don't want to." It was Michael's turn to look at the doctor, this time, with a stern expression on his face. "I can ask questions. But, unless you feel comfortable talking to me about the answers, I don't want you to give them. No matter what anyone says.

"Ask me?" She dropped to her knees in front of him and placed her palms flat on her thighs. It seemed such an alien thing to be doing, but in truth, it felt right. It was how she could convey to him her trust.

"You don't have to." He motioned with his hand to encourage her to stand up. She refused and bowed her head. He hissed.

"I'm to ask you, who your parents were?"

She hadn't expected that question. It wasn't the hardest one she feared being asked, but it was the one she wanted to bury deeply within her memory and never allow to come to the forefront again. It was destined not to happen, though.

"I don't really remember my mother. Jacob and Joshua did. They told me all sorts of bad things about her. Apparently, I had the same hair colour and eyes as her. They said they needed to give extra protection to my virtue because of how much I looked like her." She raised her head and looked into Michael's inquisitive eyes.

"You don't have to tell me," he responded, regretting his line of questioning.

"I want to. I don't want to keep anything hidden anymore. If I'm to be a normal person, whatever that may be, considering my past, then I can no longer hide the truth." He motioned for her to come and sit next to him on his chair, but she stayed kneeling. It felt right. "My mother was a prostitute, for want of a better word. She and my father were married. Joshua, Jacob, and I are genuine brothers and sister. When the family needed extra money, after I was born, my father started to pimp my mother out to his friends. They'd both always been into drugs, but her addiction got worse as she tried to cope with the things the men made her do. Eventually, she took a drug overdose." A tear pooled in the corner of her eye and trailed a path down her pale cheek. She never cried for her mother. The drugs had addled her brain, and the woman was never the loving mother she'd dreamt of whilst growing up. Joshua and Jacob had been mother and father to her for a long time.

"What happened to your father?"

"He was arrested for supplying the drugs that killed her. He attacked a policeman and was sentenced to prison. We never heard from him again. He may be alive, or he may be dead. I don't really care. He was never my father. Just a sperm donor."

Michael ran his hand through his long blonde hair.

"You were taken into care?"

"No. We fell through the system and lived on the streets for a while. I was ten. My brothers got lots of offers for me, if you know what I mean." The thought of the older men who threw large amounts of money at her brothers, all for the chance of one night with her, made her feel sick. Michael obviously sensed her repulsion and reached over to get a drink of water which he brought to her lips.

"I don't see how social services could just let you go?"

"Paperwork was passed the wrong way and got lost."

"How did you get off the streets?"

"That's how my brothers became unquestionably religious. They started to attend this makeshift church they found. Eventually, the leaders took us in and taught us their ways. I was always getting into trouble for not fully believing all the silly rules. Joshua and Jacob embraced them, but I didn't. As we got older, they sent us out to spread the word. That's how we came to Surrey, and how I met James. I was sixteen."

She saw Michael clench his fist then cover it with his other one to prevent it shaking. He was trying to control his temper. She shuffled a little further back in her position. It caught his attention, and his gaze dropped to where she was focused on his hands. He instantly flattened them.

"You've been wronged on so many levels."

"I didn't have the best start to life, but I'm hoping that can change now. Just this…" She pointed at the game console and the TV. "…is a start for me."

"Have you thought about what you'll do when you get out of here?"

She hadn't, and the thought of leaving the hospital caused her to shudder. It was her safety net, and she didn't want to even consider stepping outside the main entrance.

"I guess I'll go back to the house in Surrey. It's the only place I know." She shrugged her shoulders.

"What about a job?"

"I've never worked before. I just looked after my brothers. The last few years, with them gone, I've done little bits around the village, cleaning and helping people out where I can. I don't have the best education, so I couldn't work in an office or anything. All I really know is domestic service. I was trained to be a wife, mother, housekeeper. I don't know anything else."

Michael rubbed his hand against his chin.

"What if I said I was on the lookout for a housekeeper?"

"For me? You live in London, though. I would have to travel everyday from Surrey. That would involve the trains, and I'm not sure I could do that. Or afford it." She couldn't help but rub her hands down her legs with nerves.

"What if I wanted a live-in housekeeper?"

"A what?" Her mouth dropped open. Was he talking about a housekeeper or someone to have sex with?

"I'm phrasing this all wrong. My current employee handed her notice in two weeks ago. She wants to spend more time with her grandchildren, and at sixty, I think she's starting to find the house a bit too much. You'd have her quarters and privacy. I'd expect nothing from you except for keeping the house tidy and feeding me. I'm completely incapable of cooking anything. I even burn toast. I was thinking, during the day when all your tasks have been completed, you could study for a qualification in something that interests you." He chuckled. "Although, after seeing you with the game console today, I suspect you'll fill your time with that. What do you say?"

"I would be an employee, that's all?"

"Yes, or actually no. I feel like we've built up a friendship here, and I'd like to help you achieve whatever it is you want from your life. I want to help you, as a friend, but I also need a housekeeper, or I will starve. So, I am abusing our nascent friendship, a little, to meet my needs. I hope you don't think me too selfish."

"I don't know." She was unsure how to take the offer. Nobody had ever given her a chance like this, not without wanting something in return. Plus, he was a man, a handsome man, and she would be living with him. "Will you give me some time to answer?"

"Of course. We aren't sure when Dr Rahul will release you, anyway, so take all the time you need."

"Thank you."

Michael looked at his watch.

"You know what? I don't have a meeting for another hour. How about we play a bit more?" He held out the controller, and she took it.

"Michael?"

"Yes?"

"You're the kindest man I've ever known."

FOUR

Dear Colette,

I wanted to apologise for my impertinence the other day. The offer I made to you was done with honest regard, for your future, and my need for someone to try and prevent me from living in a pigsty. I really am that messy when left to my own devices. I hope it didn't offend. To confirm my intentions, I include a copy of a contract my previous housekeeper signed. I have detailed a few of the important points below:

- *The position is full-time live in.*
- *You'll be expected to work every day but Sunday.*
- *Breakfast must be ready at 7am.*
- *Lunch at 12pm (should I be working in the office I require a packed lunch).*
- *Dinner at 7pm.*
- *Other duties will be cleaning, laundry, and ad hoc (as agreed between us, dependent on my needs at the time).*
- *I don't like mushrooms.*

I hope this confirms my intentions were honourable. Should you have any questions, please don't hesitate to write back. I look forward to meeting you again on Tuesday. I have a book I'll bring with me and leave with you. It's similar to Mrs North's, but it's been made into a film, which you may like to watch.

Regards,
Michael

FIVE

Dear Michael

Thank you so much for your letter. Please, don't worry. I didn't doubt your intentions in offering me the job were honourable. It was just a shock. I'd not even thought about what I was going to do when I left here. It's a scary prospect. I've been thinking very hard about it, the last few days. Dr Rahul says I'll have to continue counselling, but he doesn't see why I shouldn't try to live my life. He likes your idea of a job, as well. He thinks it will give me something to focus on rather than returning to Surrey and worrying about whether I'm behaving normally or not. I am considering your offer. I have a few questions, though, as follows:

1. *What accommodation will I have? Where is it situated? Will I have to provide furniture and furnishings?*
2. *I'll still need to attend counselling sessions with Dr Rahul. May I, therefore, be allowed a half day on the day of the counselling and a half day on Sundays?*
3. *Please can you clarify what you mean by 'ad-hoc'?*
4. *I hate raw tomatoes.*

I look forward to seeing you on Tuesday. The book sounds exciting, please bring it.
  Colette

SIX

Dear Colette,

Thank you for your reply. I can't tell you how happy I am you're considering the position. I clarify your points below (I'm sorry we didn't talk about them when we met last. I felt it was better to just enjoy the short time I had available for my visit.):

1. *The accommodation is a self-contained apartment. It includes your own kitchen/dining room, bathroom, two bedrooms, and a lounge. It has a shared entrance with my place, but the door connecting them will be kept locked at your discretion. You won't need to provide anything for the apartment except for any personal possessions you wish to bring. I can take you to your home in Surrey to retrieve anything that you may wish to have with you.*
2. *You may take the full day on Sunday and the half day for your counselling. Should you need me to assist you with getting to the appointment, please let me know. I have a car that will be made available for you to use, so you may drive, if you feel up to it.*
3. *By 'ad-hoc' I mean, for example, if I were to entertain clients and needed you to cater for the function (no more than six people, normally). Additionally, if I attend external functions as part of my work then, in agreement with you, I would love you to accompany me, on occasion. All clothing required will be provided.*
4. *It is the texture of mushrooms that I do not like. I can eat it, if pureed.*

I hope you're enjoying the book.
Regards,
Michael

SEVEN

Dear Michael,

Thank you for the clarification. I respond as below:

1. That's a very generous offer to take me to Surrey, but I have so little I'd want to bring with me. The memories I have of that place aren't ones I'd want to be reminded of. Maybe, you could assist me with having the place cleared and rented out?
2. You're, again, very generous. I accept your offer and have annotated the contract to reflect this. In relation to the car, my brothers didn't believe a woman needed to, or even should, drive, so I was never taught. I'll be fine on public transport.
3. This will probably sound like a silly question, but what do you do? If the functions are to be held at clubs like the one in Amy's book, I'm not sure I'll be able to attend with you, just yet, but I'll try.
4. I've noted that. It's the seeds that I don't like in tomatoes. Once they're cooked, they're fine. I use them a lot in my cooking, and it isn't a problem. As regards to, the food I cook, will I be expected to cook separately for me, or can I eat the food I prepare for you?

The book is very, um what's the word...interesting. I like the main male character. He was a bit creepy at first, but I see that he has the lady's best interests at heart.
Colette

EIGHT

Dear Colette,

See below: (sorry the note's quick. I'm heading out to a meeting and wanted to reply straight away – Dr Rahul told me you're to be released next week.)

1. *Of course, I'll assist you in clearing and renting your property.*
2. *You won't use public transport. I'll arrange for a driver for you.*
3. *It's not a silly question. I should've told you ages ago. I'm the CEO of a public relations company. Grayson Moore is one of my clients. That's how I met him and was introduced to James North.*
4. *If you feel happy to, I thought it'd be nice for us to eat together occasionally? Other than that, you won't need to cook different food for yourself. All meals will be for both of us.*

I hope you have been allowing your hand to explore yourself while reading the book. Embracing the side of you that needs freeing.
~M
X

NINE

Dear Michael,

Firstly, yes, I let my hand explore.
  Secondly, I enclose the signed contract. I can't wait to work for you.
  ~C
  X

TEN

Colette

"I'll be in my office, if you need anything. Find your own routine and make sure you rest." Michael placed the empty plate from the vegetable omelette, which Colette had cooked him, in the sink. She was eating the same meal but was only half way through. Like most men, well the four or five she knew, he inhaled his food rather than chewed it. "If there's a coffee going in about an hour, then I'll have one, please." He strode out of the room and left her alone in the cavernous kitchen. It had been a week since she was released from hospital. Michael had taken the week off to help her settle in and sort out the house in Surrey, but today was the first official day of her job. She got up at six am and tidied up their Chinese takeaway from the previous evening. She'd never had such delicious food in her life. Her brothers believed food should be a piece of meat, potatoes and vegetables. The closest she'd got to spice was a twist of pepper. In the Chinese, they'd had Kung Po chicken. The first mouthful had blown her head off, such was the ferocity of the chili. The more she ate, though, the more she couldn't get enough of it. After the meal, Michael had shown her how to go on the internet, and she'd looked up recipes for spicier food. She was determined to try everything. Michael had also told her about online grocery shopping. If she didn't want to go to the supermarket, then she could order everything instead. Online ordering was a bit much for her, so she decided a trip to the supermarket would be fine. How hard could it be? It was something she'd done often without any problems. There was a shop, a five-minute walk away. Armed with her shopping list and a couple of carrier bags, she found buried under the sink, she set off. The weather was warm for the time of year, so she just wore one of her long dresses. With her first wages, she was going to go clothes shopping. She looked around at what other people wore. It was mainly jeans and a fitted top or leggings and a tunic top. A few, because of the weather, had on shorts that barely covered their bum cheeks. She wasn't brave enough for that, yet or probably ever. Her brothers had told her she was born with childbearing hips. Skimpy clothing didn't really suit her no matter how much weight she'd lost recently with everything that had been going on. Mind you, with her new-found delight in exploring cookery, she'd probably end up putting loads of weight back on. At least she would be happy, though.

A group of teenagers caught her eye. They were up ahead in a bus shelter. They weren't doing anything wrong. Well, they were smoking, but they looked sixteen, so it wasn't illegal. What she did notice, however, was how loud they were being and the bad language they were using. One of the girls turned and looked at her.

"You a nun or something?" the girl sneered. She flicked the end of her cigarette, so it landed just by Colette's feet. She tried to walk around the bus shelter, not wanting any trouble, but two of the other girls stepped out in front of her.

"Hey bitch, our mate spoke to you. Ain't you got no manners?"

Colette kept her head low and timidly responded,

"Sorry, I was concentrating on where I was going, I didn't hear."

"Liar." The girl, who appeared to be the leader, knocked her shopping bags onto the ground. She knelt down to pick them up, but the girl stood on them.

"Answer me."

"I'm not a nun," she responded quickly.

"See, you did 'ear."

"I just want to go to the shop. I don't want any trouble."

The girls all cackled.

"I just want to go to the shop. I don't want any trouble," they repeated back, mocking her.

The girl lifted her foot off the shopping bags. Colette grabbed the bags, turned on her heels, and ran back to the house as fast as she could. The girls' roaring laughter echoed in her ears as she fled.

Why had they been like that? What had she done wrong? She just wanted to get some food. A silent tear tumbled down her cheek. She opened the front door quietly, not wanting to disturb Michael. She'd have another look at online shopping and cook something different tonight. She put all her things away and dried her tears. She'd only been out of the house for ten minutes. It wasn't time to take a coffee to Michael. She decided to do some cleaning, in the meantime. Her hands were still shaking, and she could still feel the tears burning behind her eyes. She picked up a duster and some polish. Getting rid of dirt would help. Tidying always made her feel better. She went into the lounge first. The previous housekeeper had worked until two days ago, so the place wasn't that messy. She started with a book case that contained ornaments. She removed them, placed them on a nearby chair, and cleaned the shelves individually. She could feel herself starting to relax. All of a sudden, there was a loud cackle of laughter from outside the window. The girls had followed her. She walked over to the window. Then, being careful to stay hidden behind a curtain, she peered out. She couldn't see anything. It must just have been someone walking past. She could do this. She didn't need to be so foolish, and she wasn't going to do online shopping next time. She was going to go to the shop and buy what she needed herself. She wouldn't allow those bullies, or anyone else like them, to destroy her. She returned to the book case and started to place the items back on the shelf. She picked up a delicate crystal ball. It was beautiful and didn't seem to be something Michael would own. She had learnt over the last few days he was very much a man's man. He enjoyed his sports and games. It didn't bother her. She liked to see him relaxed and happy. She wondered if this trinket had belonged to his wife. It looked like the sort of thing a woman would buy to decorate a home. It was feminine in nature.

The laughter came from outside again, and she dropped the ball on the wooden floor. It instantly smashed into hundreds of tiny little pieces.

"Colette." Michael opened the door. He looked at her hands and down to the shattered crystal.

"What have you done?" he shouted as anger flooded his entire body.

"I didn't mean it." She bent down quickly and tried to pick up the pieces. They dug into her fingers, though, and her fingers started to bleed.

"Get out of the way." He pushed her aside, and she fell onto the floor and cowered. "You're a stupid woman. That was the last thing she bought me."

"I'm sorry. I'm so sorry. There was a noise from outside," she gasped between sobs of distress.

"Noise?" His voice was still angry, as he carefully tried to pick up the pieces. "There'll always be noises, cars, people."

"They laughed at me."

"What?" She could tell she wasn't making any sense to him.

"I went out to try and buy the food for the recipe we looked up. They were in the bus stop. They laughed at me and stomped on my bags. I'm so sorry. I thought they came back, and I dropped the ball. I can never replace it. I'll go." She tried to scramble to her feet, but her legs would not work

Michael sat back and dropped all the crystal.

"What am I doing?" he sighed. "Three girls, all lippy and short skirts?"

She nodded.

"They attack anyone who walks down this street. They think they own it."

He pulled out his mobile phone from his pocket, hit the call button, and then the speaker button.

"Matthew Carter"

The familiar name came over the phone.

Colette scrambled further into the corner. Was he going to tell Matthew he no longer wanted her at the house?

"It's Michael. I need a favour."

"Name it? I owe you one for the Boss."

"There's a bus stop near my house. It's frequented by three female delinquents. I want them moved on, permanently."

"Permanently?"

"They've upset someone special to me."

"Colette?"

"Yes."

She followed the conversation, with more than a little bit of confusion. She knew Matthew had previously been MI5, and he probably still had enough sway with the police to get the girls moved.

"Will he get the police to arrest them?" she asked.

Matthew snorted on the other end of the line.

"No. Matthew will dispense his own justice."

"But that's illegal." Michael held up his hand to silence her.

"Do you need any further information?" he asked Matthew.

"No. I'll send you a message when I'm done."

"Thank you."

"Bye."

"Bye." Michael hung up.

"What's he going to do to them?"

"He won't hurt them, but he'll make sure they know not to harass people on this street anymore."

She looked down at the broken crystal.

"I'm sorry."

"It doesn't matter. It was only cheap. It was the memories attached to it more than anything. But they're in my heart and my head. I don't need a crystal ball to give me them. Come here?"

She tentatively scooted across the floor, and he wrapped his arms around her.

"I'm sorry for shouting at you."

"It's fine." She was trying to calm her voice, but it still sounded frightened and upset.

"Would you like me to take you to the supermarket?"

She shook her head.

"No. I'll try again tomorrow. I won't let it defeat me."

"Good girl."

She let out a loud wail.

"I'll never be normal, will I?"

"You will." He stroked his hand through her hair. "You're doing so well. There's so much to take in."

She looked up at him. Her eyes becoming captured by his comforting gaze. She moved her head up and pressed her mouth to his lips. He pushed her away.

"Colette."

"I'm sorry." She pushed out of his arms and jumped to her feet. He grabbed her hand before she could run away and stood beside her. He bent over, and this time, he kissed her. Her whole body tingled and warmed from the passion he conveyed to her. Michael pulled away again.

"Tell me to stop," he whispered.

"Show me how to be normal," she breathlessly replied. He scooped her up into his arms and headed towards his bedroom.

ELEVEN

Michael

"Are you sure this is what you want?" Michael placed Colette down in front of the bed. His room had been redecorated after his wife had died. It was masculine in the black and white clean lines. He sometimes lamented the loss of the feminine touch in this most secluded of places. His bed was made from black iron with a framework that would be perfect for using with cuffs. He'd never brought anyone here, though. His liaisons had always been at the club.

"I want you. I've known that since the day you first walked into the counselling room." Colette took a seat on the bed.

"Do you want me? Or is it that I can give you sex that's different?" he asked.

"Would you be upset if I said both?" It was involuntary, but she licked her lips with excitement when she spoke. He went from semi-erect to hard enough to hammer nails, within an instant. "I have known we'd be intimate together ever since James told me of you. Why else would he do so? He was matchmaking. I allowed myself to go along with it, but at some point, I realised I actually wanted to be with you, physically and emotionally."

"You have to be ready for what I will give, though. I don't know if you are."

"Trust me to trust you. Isn't that what a good Dom does?" She had him there. He switched the Dom on inside him and allowed his natural instincts to take over.

"Ok, We'll take it slowly this time. We'll sort a safe word at a later date but will use the traffic light system today. Green for okay, amber for nervous and we'll stop and discuss what's making you scared, red if you want to stop altogether. Do you understand?"

"Yes, Master."

The words were music to his ears, because they were given so freely.

"I want you to stand up and undress for me. I want to watch you unveil your body for your Master." A shudder went through Colette, with his demand. She timidly got to her feet and pulled the long dress over her head. Underneath, she had no bra on. She wasn't big breasted so didn't need one. Her nipples were erect, and he longed to wrap his tongue around them and taste. His heated gaze trailed lower to the plain white knickers she wore. They weren't overly sexy, but on her, they were perfect. They were who she was. She was still far too skinny for his liking, but she was starting to put weight on, and it suited her. She looked delicate, and he was worried he might break her. He reached out and ran his hand across her cheek, over her lips, down her neck, skimmed her breast, and trailed over her stomach until he came to the waist band of her knickers.

"I think I'll remove these." He brought his other hand up to the waistband and started to lower her panties. He looked up to Colette and saw fear flicker behind her eyes, just for a moment, before she whispered, "Amber."

He removed his hands and held them up.

"Talk to me."

"I don't want to stop," her voice quivered. "It's just, I told you about my brother's washing me after I'd been with James. They did it with steel pads, and they made me wash down there with one as well." Her eyes motioned down to her sex. I have little scars on my body from what happened. I don't know what damage it did to me there. It may not look normal or good."

"Hush." He brought her into his arms and held her tightly to his chest. If her brothers weren't already dead, he'd have taken a gun, found them, and shot them both, first in the crotch and then in the head. He wasn't normally a violent man, but what they had done to this beautiful girl, who he was falling for, could have driven him to it. He needed to not let her see his violent reaction, though. He wasn't going to let it spoil the moment. He gently tipped her back, so he could look straight into her eyes. "Listen to me. I find you incredibly sexy. I noticed the little scars on your body the first time I met you. They're a part of you. If they extend over your sex, then I'll love them there as well. They're who you are. I need you to do something for me. I need you to get out of your head. When you're in your head, you worry. Be in the moment, the here and now. Can you do that?"

"Yes, Master." She nodded.

"I'm going to remove these panties, now, because I want to see the whole of you. I want to worship every inch of your body."

"I'd like that." She bit her lip and stretched up to press a kiss of consent to his lips. He placed his hands on the waist band of her knickers again and pulled them down. He sank to his knees before her as he did. His face was level with her pussy. He let the knickers fall to the floor, placed his hands between her thighs, and separated them. Despite her nervousness, he could smell her arousal. He ran a finger between her lower lips. They were coated with a thin film of moisture. She wanted him and was relaxing. She let out a sensual groan.

"Good girl." He rewarded her by pushing her back onto the bed, parting her legs, and licking the length of her sex.

"Michael," she moaned and gripped the bed sheets.

He did the same thing again and dipped a finger inside her. She was tight. It had been a while for her, and he'd need to take it gently, because he was a large man.

"It feels good," she whimpered. "Again, please, again."

He was happy to oblige. She tasted like the sweetest honey. There were no scars, no damage. She was perfect.

"I'm going to make you come like this."

"But...you need to be inside me. You have to come with me." Her beautiful innocence shattered the barriers he'd built around his heart after his wife's death. This woman, laid bare before him, had captured his heart and was entwining herself around it.

"No. This is how a Dom treats his woman. The pleasure is all about you, and I will only take mine when you're completely satisfied."

He was still kneeling between her legs. She was looking down at him with flushed cheeks.

"I went back in my head for a minute, didn't I?" she asked.

"Yes, you did." Colette flopped back onto the bed.

"No more thinking. Master, please put your head back in between my thighs." He gave her a little tap on the clit, for her mischievousness. She let out a shocked but passionate cry. He knew when James had smacked her during sex she'd freaked out but not with him. She was writhing on his tongue as he licked her out faster and harder than he'd done with any woman before. She was a little, lascivious kitten emerging from behind the sofa to flex its claws. Those talons came down onto the bed covers and gripped hard when he felt her pussy start to pulsate around his tongue.

"I'm going to come," she called out and erupted on his face. She bathed him in her pleasure, and he lapped up every ounce of her essence. It was her first release from a man's mouth.

"That was...that was. Oh God! I can't breathe. So good. More!" Colette tried to sit up but collapsed back on the bed. He laughed.

"Hey, no sleeping yet, my little sex kitten. I've got a rather urgent problem in my pants, and I need you to free it."

"Sex kitten?" She sat up and looked at him with a raised eyebrow.

"I think I'm unleashing something, which neither of us were aware of, lingering deeply within you." He licked her pussy again. An aftershock must have rippled through her body, because she gasped.

"No more, just yet, please." She tried to catch her breath again. He stood up and undid the buckle of his belt. Even when he worked from home, he liked to wear smart trousers and a shirt. If he needed to run out for an urgent meeting, then he was ready to go. Colette's eyes darkened as she watched him. He undid the buttons of his shirt and shrugged it to the floor. She reached out to touch his chest.

"May I?"

He nodded.

She traced her hands over the carved lines of his torso and defined pecs. He had a tattoo of a thistle on his left side. He'd told her that he had one a week ago during a conversation about tattoos. It was in tribute to his wife, who'd been Scottish. Despite most people thinking the flower was a weed, it had been her favourite. It reminded her of the highlands where she'd grown up. She touched the purple flower, which topped the green stalk. It felt warm under her fingers.

"She'll always be a part of you, of us. We'll mourn and worship her together."

"Thank you."

Colette moved her hand to the zip of his trousers and lowered it. Then, after popping the button, she freed his cock from its confines.

"I've never tasted a penis before. May I taste yours?"

Most men would have come instantly, at that statement. It was used in role-play games when the female played a virgin, but in Colette's case, it was honesty at its purest.

"You may. Lick from the head down to my balls and back up."

Her tongue came out and did just that. He let his head fall back and his body relax into the pleasure it was receiving. Colette lightly squeezed his balls with her hands and took his length into her mouth. She took it a little too far, and she gagged and coughed and spat him out.

"Sorry."

He smiled down at her.

"Just take in as much as you can handle. The tip is the most sensitive part so focus on that. I'm a man. Any amount of my cock in your mouth is good enough for me."

"Yes, I read about deep throating, but I think I'll leave that for a while." She took him into her mouth again, this time, only taking in a manageable length and swirled her tongue around his shaft. His body heated with the need to fuck. He pulled out of her mouth.

"Did I do something wrong?"

She looked up at him with big eyes.

"No. I just want to be in you now. We can work on sucking my cock later. My other needs are a lot more pressing."

Colette squirmed her legs together.

"I'm not on any thing to stop babies. I didn't dare ask my brothers. While I was with James, the doctors put me on the pill because I had heavy periods. I stopped it a few years ago, and I was my periods had calmed so I didn't go back on it."

"We can explore contraception, at a later date." He went over to his bedside table and retrieved a condom. "Do you know how to put this on?"

She feverishly shook her head in the negative.

"I'll do it, but we can explore that as well." He ripped open the packet, held the tip, and rolled it down his cock. Colette watched his every move, with anticipation and interest.

"It looks funny in the condom."

"Not something you should say to a man."

"Sorry. My brothers didn't believe in contraception, so I haven't really seen a condom before. Sex was for making babies and all that sort of thing. I guess I'm lucky not to have hoards of nieces and nephews running around somewhere. Fortunately, they both believed in abstaining until marriage."

"You've disappeared back into you head," he teased. Her eyes shut and re-opened to focus on the cock he was now stroking. "I want you to put me inside you."

"Me?"

"Yes."

He lowered over her, so the tip of his cock nudged against her hole. She wrapped her fingers around him and slowly fed him into her entrance. Despite the fact she was guiding him, he set the pace. He didn't want to hurt her. She let go and gripped the sheets. A small cry left her lips.

"Take me, Colette."

"It hurts."

"Relax." He moved, so he could suck on her breast. He brought the nipple into his mouth and swirled it around before biting at the edges. Her pussy contracted tightly then loosened. He pushed all the way in to the hilt and stilled.

"Michael?"

"Yes."

"Is this what normal is?" A tear trickled down her cheek. He licked it up.

"Normal is whatever you choose it to be."

He pulled out and thrust back in.

"It feels very good," she whimpered again.

He did another couple of thrusts. He wasn't going to last long. He hadn't done anything sexually since his first visit to the hospital when he'd met with Colette. That first meeting, which on reflection, seemed to be the start of his second life. He'd used his hand, but it wasn't the same as being buried in a burning, hot pussy. It was then he realised they'd joined in the missionary position. He needed to keep taking Colette out of her comfort zone. She was doing exquisitely well. He withdrew from her, and she groaned at the loss.

"I want you on your hands and knees."

She didn't move her body, but her mouth made an attempt to answer.

"Colour?"

Still nothing.

"Colette, colour or I stop this now."

"Green." She got up and moved, so her ass was pressed against him.

"Good girl," he whispered into her ear and bit it.

She pushed back, and he slipped straight into the heat of her pussy.

"Fuck me, please, Master." To hear that phrase from her chaste lips had him buck into her like a wild animal. They moved together as one. She welcomed him, when he sank deeply, and when he pulled back, she chased him. His balls hung low and slapped against her clit with every thrust. He was going to come.

"Colette?"

"I'm coming."

She clamped down on him and wave after wave of erotic need pounded over his length. It set off his own climax, and he filled the condom with his release. They both stilled. The only noise that filled the room was the sound of their exhausted breaths. He grabbed the base of his cock and withdrew from her. She collapsed down on the bed. He joined her, brought her to him, and she nestled into the crook of his arm.

"Are you ok?" He pressed a tender kiss to her lips.

"I've never been better. I did as you said and stopped thinking. I became a bundle of pleasure. I can't feel my legs; it was so good." Her voice broke on the last word. "Thank you."

"You'll have good and bad days. We all do, but this can be your life, if you let me look after you." He was falling for the woman in his arms. He wouldn't let her go. He wanted to shower her with affection and care. She may not be a twenty-four seven submissive, as his wife had been, but she needed his care in different ways. His heart leapt for the first time in years. He was happy. He had a future, a future with Colette Fisher. "What do you say?"

"I don't ever want to leave."

TWELVE

Colette

Colette fiddled with the gold chain that adorned her neck. It had been a month since she'd left the hospital and moved in with Michael. They'd spent nearly every night together since. They'd learnt every inch of each other's bodies, and she was the happiest she'd ever been. She was in love, and she was *normal*. The day after they'd made love for the first time, she'd gone to the supermarket herself and bought loads of spicy ingredients. They'd made a wonderful Thai curry. She'd devoured every mouthful of it, and then, Michael had devoured her with tingling heat on his tongue from the chili. It'd been the most surreal moment of her life. She'd had multiple orgasms so many times she'd lost track of how many. She'd wanted to count at first, because she'd done a little calculation. It was said the average number of times an adult had sex a year was eighty-two. Well, if she had started having sex at seventeen, and she was now thirty, she would have been having sex for thirteen years. Eighty-two orgasms a year for thirteen years was one thousand and sixty-six orgasms. She had a lot of making up to do. Mind you, only twenty-nine percent of those woman reached climax every time they had sex, so there was no certainty as to the number of orgasms she had to catch up on. Michael, however, was trying his hardest to make up for the lost thirteen years in the least amount of time possible. She could still feel the ache between her legs from where he'd used an instrument he called a flogger between her thighs last night. She'd come hard, and then, he'd fucked her up against the wall. It had been exhilarating.

"Stop fidgeting." Michael wrapped his brawny fingers around her slender ones.

"I'm sorry."

"Colour?"

"Green. I'm okay, I promise."

They were standing outside the club Grayson Moore owned. She'd asked

Michael if they could go and see it. She wasn't promising him a scene or anything, but she just wanted to see what happened there. Now they were here, though, she felt sick in the pit of her stomach. She knew this was the place James had been beaten because of her. What if people inside knew who she was related to?

"We don't have to go in," Michael offered with his warming smile.

"I want to." She needed to be strong and put her big girl pants on. Well, that was definitely a figure of speech, because Michael, it seemed, had a thing for her not wearing any pants under the long dress she had on. Thankfully, this dress was sexy and not a sack like the ones she used to wear. The gold chain around her neck had been a present from him. It was to signify to everyone here that she was his and not to mess with her.

"If you feel uncomfortable, then we'll leave. I won't think anything of it." This was a special event at the club and everyone would be there. Michael needed to show his face. James wouldn't be there, though, as he'd become a father for the second time in the last few days and was on nappy duty while Amy rested.

"I know."

Michael took her hand, and they walked through the entrance. A guard scanned them through a barrier, and they entered a room, which was darkly lit. The sounds of joviality echoed around the large expanse. She had never been to an actual club before, let alone a BDSM one. She'd been to a pub once, but it was nowhere near as full as this. People were everywhere; some dressed in what she would term 'normal clothing' like hers, others were dressed in fetish clothing, and one even strode around after her master with nothing on.

"Breathe," Michael whispered into her ear, and she let out the breath she'd been holding.

"Michael." A masculine American accent called their attention to the left of the room. Seated there were a couple of faces she recognised: Matthew Carter and Sophie Moore, nee North, were looking at her. Matthew's face was impassive, but Sophie looked like she wanted to kill. Michael grabbed her hand and led them over to the table.

"Grayson." Michael greeted a tall gentleman who'd stood to offer his own welcome.

"Michael, we've missed you recently. I know some of the ladies are lamenting the loss of your skills with a violet wand." The man looked over to her. "I can see why, now. Is this Miss Fisher?"

"It is." Michael held his hand out for her to come to his side. "Colette, this is the actor and club owner Grayson Moore, and his wife Sophie, who you may know, Matthew Carter and his partner Sonia Anderson, and this is Callum Ashworth, and his very pregnant wife Marie. Sonia, you look amazing. It is incredible to think you gave birth a few months ago. How's Andrew?" All three of the women looked to Sophie for guidance on how they should react to this introduction.

James's sister stood, and Colette braced herself for violence. Instead, the young Mrs Moore wrapped her arms around her and brought her into a welcoming embrace.

"Sophie, let Colette breathe, or I'll put your padlock on. You didn't ask permission to touch her." Grayson rolled his eyes.

"She's doing well. I just wanted to say so, Master."

"Words. Use words." He shook his head this time.

"Yes, Master." Sophie resumed her seat, but when her husband wasn't looking, she stuck her tongue out at him. As if having a second sense at his wife's mischievous actions, Grayson reached out and took his wife's necklace in his hands.

"Stick that out again, and I won't let you use it on me later."

She didn't know why, but she found the entire interaction funny not distressing as she thought she might.

"Colour?" Michael whispered into her ear.

"Green," she replied.

The men all fell into an easy conversation. She looked around the room to see what else was happening. She saw a woman bent over a bench of some sort and a man smacking her backside. A young man was attached to what looked like a cross and was being whipped by a Dom. Her blood pressure started to rise. She repeated a little mantra in her head.

"This is normal. They consent to it."

A scream came from the corner of the room as a man pulled a woman by the hair and dragged her towards a hole in the wall. From her vantage point, she could see it was tiny and dark. No. Why would he do that? He pushed her in and shut the door.

"She likes to be made to feel enclosed. He'll go in there and fuck her, in a minute." Michael's voice permeated through the haziness in her brain. She repeated her mantra again.

"This is normal. They consent to it."

Everything around her started to fade into the distance. All except that door. It was all she could see. The woman's screams were all she could hear.

"Red." The words left her lips, before she had a chance to think clearly about what she was saying. Without saying goodbyes, Michael grabbed her hand, and they fled from the club. He brought her outside, and she gasped for air.

"Talk to me?" He placed his hands on her shoulders and looked deeply into her eyes. She tried to focus on him to regain her sensibilities.

"Cupboard. Cellar. I was locked in for a week."

"Your brothers locked you in a cellar for a week?"

She nodded.

"After they washed me. It's why I have scars in some of the cuts. They became infected, because I couldn't keep them clean down there."

"I'm sorry." He ground his teeth into his jaw, the veins in his temple pulsing in the moonlight. He was angry. He tried to hide it from her, when he was incensed at her treatment, but he didn't always manage.

"It's not your fault." She was coming back into her body now. "I'm calming down now. We can go back in."

"No. Enough for tonight. I'm taking you home."

"Michael." She dug her heels in.

Suddenly, he slumped to the floor in front of her. She stepped back and stared at him and up to the figures that replaced him. It was the couple who'd taken her and her brothers in.

"Colette, my child," her cult mother, Ruth, stepped forward. "He won't hurt you again, child. Come, let's take you away from this place."

Her cult father, Abraham, took her by the arm and started to lead her away from where Michael lay unconscious on the floor. She was in shock. What was going on? Why were they here? She allowed herself to be led. Her brain had switched off; she'd become the little girl who'd lived on the streets with her brothers. Michael disappeared into the distance, and they placed her in a car and sped off. A cloth was placed over her mouth. She regained her sense from the shock and tried to fight back, but it was too late. The chloroform claimed her, and she slipped into the darkness.

～

Thump, thump, thump.

The incessant noise woke her from the drug induced sleep. She sat bolt upright.

"Well, it's about time you woke up." Abraham was sitting on a kitchen chair. Ruth was busy at the stove, cooking. She recognised that stove. In fact, she knew the entire kitchen. It was her old one in the house in Surrey.

"What do you want?" she asked.

"Some answers." Abraham slapped the book down that he'd been holding. He must have been rapping it against the table to cause the thumping noise.

"Michael?"

"We'll get to that. The answers I want are more important than that piece of devilish trash. What I want to know is why your brothers are dead and how it seems to be your fault?" Abraham sneered at her. He was almost sixty and wore a dog collar as if he were some sort of priest. He wasn't. His education was limited mainly to tales of religious fantasies. He'd aged a great deal since the last time she'd seen him, over ten years ago. The skin hung loosely on his weather-beaten face, and his hair was grey save for a few flecks of the vibrant jet black it had once been.

"It isn't my fault. They messed with the wrong people."

"The same people whose club you went to tonight looking like a whore."

"Calm yourself, husband." Ruth turned around from the cooker and placed a bowl of what looked like fresh soup in front of Abraham. "You know the doctor says not to excite your heart. We can't finish your work, if you get ill again." Her cult mother hadn't changed much. She was still fresh faced, but then, in comparison to her father's almost sixty years, her mother was only forty. She'd been betrothed as a child. Colette wasn't certain, but given that Ruth's and Abraham's oldest child was twenty-six, she assumed Ruth was very much a child bride given to a man who would have been in his mid-thirties.

"How can I be calm when one of our own has strayed so far from the flock that she's become a murderess and nymphomaniac?" Abraham picked up the spoon and shovelled soup into his mouth.

"She's back with us, now. We can punish her for her indiscretions and bring her back to the true path." Ruth patted her husband's shoulder, and they both looked down at her.

"I haven't done anything wrong." She was still sitting where she'd woken on the floor in the corner of the room. She stood up using a nearby chair as her legs were still a little shaky. "This is my house, and I want you both to leave, or I'm going to call the police and have them arrest you for assaulting Michael."

Abraham slammed the spoon down.

"Ungrateful wench." He pushed the chair back. Ruth went to calm him again but gave up. "Ruth, remove my belt. I'll beat some sense into her."

"You won't touch me." She wasn't sure where this new found strength was coming from, but she was kind of wishing it would go back there, because it was only serving to make her cult father angrier.

"He's put the devil in her?" Abraham was going red in the face.

"Lock her away." Ruth had removed her husband's belt and handed it to him. "She'll curse us all."

"Get out!" She placed her hands on her hips and stared her parents down defiantly. It wasn't to work, though, as Abraham descended on her. He lashed out with the belt and caught her shoulder when she turned to avoid it. Pain shot through her body when he brought it down again with such ferocity she thought he'd split her skin in two. She cried out and edged away but hesitated when she saw where she was heading. The cellar. She couldn't. She couldn't go down there again.

"You were such a good girl," Ruth wailed behind her. "What did they do to you? Fight it, Colette."

"She's beyond help." Abraham brought the belt down again. This time it lashed across her back. The thin dress she was wearing offered no protection against the harsh leather. For once, she longed for her old attire. Another whack caused her to tumble forward and into the door. It opened, and she fell inside the cellar. She managed to grab the side rails, or she would have fallen down the stairs.

"You can stay in there, until we decide what to do with you. You aren't the child we took in. I don't know what you are anymore, but I won't welcome it. You'll repent or die."

Abraham slammed the door in her face, as she made a last-ditch effort to escape. The room went dark. Her body ached from the beating it had received. She sunk down until her knees were tight against her chest. Her face was wet where she'd been crying but hadn't registered it. She shut her eyes and started a new mantra.

"This isn't normal. This isn't my life. Michael will come."

THIRTEEN

Michael

Damn his head hurt. What they hell had they hit him with? Michael held a bag of ice against the lump that was no doubt forming on his temple.

"Have you found it yet?" He growled at Matthew Carter, the ex MI5 bodyguard. Sonia sat in front of a computer, searching for Colette's location. "When I had you put the chip in the necklace, I thought it was because she would freak out and run away, not because she would go and get herself kidnapped."

"Added benefit of my being an ex-spy. Everything important is chipped." Matthew tapped Sonia's own necklace. She rolled her eyes.

"It keeps you out of prison for breaking every privacy rule going. Especially when you put chips in your son's nappies!"

"You want to know where he is at all times."

"Yes, but even I draw the line somewhere."

"I drew the line at injecting it into him." Matthew raised his hand to silence his girlfriend's protest. "Back on subject, we've got arses to kick." He nodded his head to the computer screen, and Sonia turned her attention back to it.

"She's in Surrey. Not moved for the last hour, so it must be the base."

Sonia turned the screen round, so he could see it.

"That's her old home. Why would she be there?"

"She must know her kidnappers," Matthew surmised with a stroke of his stubbled chin.

"What?"

The bodyguard's phone rang.

"Hi Jasper, you've got the room."

He put the phone onto loud speaker.

"The people who took her are known as Abraham and Ruth Adamson. Fake names, they're really Bruce and Ruth Jenkins. Bruce is sixty-one. Ruth is forty.

They were married officially when Ruth was sixteen but had been living as man and wife since she was thirteen. They're part of the Order of Virtue, a cult set up in the sixties by Bruce's parents. His father was the leader. When he died in the nineties, Bruce took over and assumed the name Abraham. Ruth was born into the cult. Her father was the deputy, and she was betrothed to Bruce at birth. She was probably lucky they waited until she was thirteen to hand her over. From what I can see on the records, their known associates are Jacob and Joshua Fisher."

"Colette's brothers." Matthew slammed his fist into the table. "What the fuck, do they have to do with this? Can't they both just die and stay dead?"

"Wait." Michael went closer to the phone. "Colette told me about her upbringing. She was adopted into, what she called, a religious family because social services had failed her and her brothers. They'd ended up on the streets, when their real parents died."

"Jasper?" Matthew asked, and they heard tapping from the other end of the phone. It went silent for a few moments. He didn't have time for this. They knew where she was. They should be racing there. "We need full details." Matthew must have sensed his unease. "We go in blind, and she could get hurt."

He needed Matthew's knowledge and expertise. He needed Matthew. On his own, he wouldn't have a clue what to do.

"Right," Jasper came back. "Colette's mother died when she was five. There's no record of anything on social services for her, so it looks like what she told you is correct. The cult took them in. Looking at some of the things these people believe in, it completely explains why Jacob and Joshua were so messed up in the head. Do you want a hand in this? I wouldn't mind claiming a scalp of this magnitude, getting it off the streets of the UK. This guy's nothing more than a terrorist in my eyes."

"Are they likely to be heavily armed? Jacob was packing sawn-off shotguns, when we encountered him in America." Michael's stomach dropped at Matthew's words.

"No. They believe in old fashioned justice: stoning to death, hand removal for stealing, that sort of stuff. They could have knives, but guns aren't their style." He wasn't sure whether he was relieved or not. He tried to recall his history. Did they stone women for being promiscuous?

"We should be alright. I'll let Michael have his revenge and hand over what's left for you to bring to justice. I'm sure you can find a comfortable prison cell for Bruce next to someone who doesn't appreciate wives being taken at thirteen."

"I can think of a whole wing of people who don't appreciate that. Good luck. Message me after for clean up." Jasper hung up.

"You ready?" Matthew stood up and placed his phone in the pocket of his designer evening suit. They were still dressed for the club. He had blood from his head wound over his crisp shirt, but other than that, he was ready.

"Ready. Does Sonia need to change?" He hadn't actually asked if Miss Anderson was coming with them, because her reputation preceded her, and he knew she was just as feared as her lover.

"Nope, I'm good to go." She lifted the hem of her dress to reveal a knife taped to her leg one side and a gun on the other.

"Damn, that's so hot." Mathew groaned a wishful sigh. If it wasn't for the kidnapping, Michael knew what this couple would be getting up to right now. They both definitely had a masochistic streak.

"Later," Sonia promised and walked to the door. "Let's go get Colette before the freaks try to undo all Michael's hard work."

It didn't take them long to get to the house in Surrey. Sonia had some mad driving skills, and Jasper was apparently keeping the police off their backs, considering all the speed limits she'd broken. The house was a typical picture-postcard, in the middle of nowhere. That would be helpful in keeping them out of sight of nosey neighbours, because in communities like this, they were always around.

"Are we still playing it how we discussed?" he asked Matthew.

"They're not likely to be carrying guns," the bodyguard clarified the facts with Sonia.

"No. They're more likely to throw stones at us," she replied.

"Right. Well, that makes this a lot easier, then." Matthew cracked his knuckles. "These freaks have pissed me off. This was my first night out in months. My kid gets first dibs on Sonia's tits. now. I should be balls deep in her still tight little pussy."

"Matthew." Sonia punched her partner.

"Hush, woman. Instead, I'm having to rescue Colette, because they think sex is only for making babies. We go in the front door. No messing around." The big man lifted his leg up and kicked out at the door, smashing it to smithereens.

They all filed through the door. A tall gentleman with greying hair blocked their path. He was swinging a belt round.

"Ruth, protect our child. They've come for her. The demons of Beelzebub and his succubus." The man spat in Sonia's direction, at the last comment. "You won't take her."

"Oh, please. I'm very much awake when Sonia fucks me. Get your facts straight, before you start levelling names at people." Matthew stepped forward, but Michael placed his arm in front of him.

"I owe him. Let me," he demanded, and Matthew stepped back, with a 'be my guest' motion.

"You're the one who had your hands on my innocent girl." Bruce, well that was who Michael assumed he was, brought the belt down in a whipping motion in front of him.

"See, this is what I don't get about you. You're waving a belt around like a whip. We aren't that different. When I did it to Colette the other night, she really enjoyed it. I'm guessing the difference is I did it to give her the best orgasm I possibly could, but you would do it to hurt someone. I personally think you have it very wrong." Michael shook his head and took a step forward. The belt came down a little closer.

"Heathen, you disgust me. We're in no way similar. You're evil."

"Seriously, is that all you have?' He was getting bored with the pathetic insults this man had thrown at him. It was time to enact the plan he'd formulated. The belt fizzed through the air, again. Before it could find its mark, he grabbed it and used it to pull the stunned man, who was wielding it, towards him. He punched him hard in the face, and the insane preacher fell to the floor.

"If you've hurt her, then you'd better prepare to meet your maker, because I will destroy you." Matthew appeared at his side and restrained Bruce when he dizzily tried to get back up.

"Where the fuck did that come from?" the bodyguard questioned.

"You aren't the only one who should be balls deep right now."

Matthew snorted. "Go get Colette. Sonia will help you, while I deal with him."

He prowled off towards the kitchen. As he went, he heard another thump from behind him and these harshly spoken words,

"Prepare to find out what happens to men who take brides of thirteen years old."

"Michael!" Colette's voice called out. It was muffled but had him taking his steps a little quicker.

"Quiet child, father will deal with the man. We'll keep you safe." A woman spoke as he entered the kitchen. She was tiny and wearing similar clothing to those Colette used to wear. She protected a door to the cellar with a frying pan in her hand. Colette would be in there, and it was her feared place. She'd be so scared.

"If you're talking about your husband, Ruth, then you're mistaken. He's currently incapacitated. Now, get away from the door, so I can let Colette out." He stepped closer to the woman. Sonia was there at his side.

"No. We're on the side of the righteous. You can't win."

"Ruth, we don't want to hurt you, but if you don't open that door, I'll have no choice. You're as much of a victim here as Colette is." He put his hands down at his side and motioned for Sonia to step back.

"You were taken so young. It didn't have to be that way."

"I did my duty," she screamed back at him.

"You did. You took Colette in when she was at her lowest, after her biological mother's death. You gave her, and her brothers, a home... Let her out. Let her talk to you. If she tells you she wants to stay with you, then I won't take her. Let her make the decision." He was edging closer and closer, while he spoke. As much as he should hate this woman for her part in this, he couldn't. She'd also been a victim of abuse.

"You'll cloud her brain with impure thoughts."

"I promise you. I'll do nothing of the sort." He wasn't sure how he was supposed to prove that one, if she asked. Thankfully, she didn't but trusted him and moved to open the door.

"Colette, my child. I'm going to let you out, so you can tell this man to go away and leave us be."

"I understand." Colette's timid voice came from the other side of the door. It opened, and she stepped out from the darkness. He nearly lost his shit completely, when he saw the marks of the belt on her skin. Her dress was torn, red welts shone brightly against her pallid features. Sonia hissed beside him and made ready to spring into action, but he took a deep breath and calmed himself.

"This man seems to think you want to go with him to do lewd things." Ruth had tears in her eyes, when she spoke to Colette. He stepped closer to the pair.

"I do want to go with him."

"You don't child. He's wrong for you. Do you want to end up like your mother? That's what he'll do to you. Make you sleep with other men."

Colette shook her head.

"No, he won't. He loves me. My father never loved my mother. If he did, they'd still be alive, along with Jacob and Joshua, and we'd be a happy family."

"He's filled your head with so many fantasies."

"No, that's what Bruce and your parents did to you." Colette reached out, taking her cult mother's hands. "What I want isn't wrong. What happened to you, though, is. Let me help you? Let me take you away from Abraham."

"Away from him? He's my husband." Ruth pulled away from her. Michael was behind Colette, now, and she pushed her back into him, so he could feel her warmth. He couldn't reach and hold her yet. She needed to help the confused woman standing before her, first. Colette needed to find her strength to help another.

"He doesn't have to be."

"But I made a promise."

"You were too young to make that promise. Nobody will hold you to it. Not in this life or the afterlife."

"Don't listen to her." Bruce appeared at the door. He was still restrained by Matthew and had blood dripping from an obviously broken nose.

"Shut up," Colette bit out. "I'll not let you destroy any more lives. It's you and your stupid cult that are responsible for my brothers' deaths. I'll not allow you to take Ruth's life as well. You've taken enough of it over the last twenty-seven years. Matthew, get him out of here."

"No!" Ruth screamed and ran for her husband. Sonia caught her before anyone else could react. Colette collapsed back into his arms when Ruth fell to the floor in hysterical tears.

"My husband, my husband. You'll all rot in hell for this."

Sonia removed a syringe from her pocket, pulled the top off with her teeth, and plunged it straight into the woman's neck.

"My husband. I'll stop them. I will...." Ruth lay motionless. It was over. Matthew dragged Bruce out, when he started to struggle.

"Are you alright?" He turned Colette to face him.

"I thought she'd want saving." She sniffed mournfully.

"Not everybody does, I'm afraid. You're one of the lucky ones."

"What'll happen to them?"

"He'll go to prison for a very long time. He won't get out again, not unless it's in a wooden casket." He pressed a kiss to her forehead while checking out the marks the belt had made on her.

"And Ruth?"

"I'll talk to Dr Rahul and see what we can do. I fear she's too far gone, though. She'll spend the rest of her life in a different type of incarceration."

"The hospital?"

He nodded, and she went quiet.

Matthew came back into the room as Sonia was securing Ruth. He didn't have Bruce.

"Jasper's here." They both picked up Ruth's unconscious figure from the floor. "What do you want to do with her?"

"She doesn't know what normal is." Tears started to drip down Colette's cheeks. "How do you save someone who's never experienced hope. All she's known is virtue. She's going to be in so much pain and confusion."

"The doctors will manage it." This was the only answer he could give her.

"With drugs?"

"She won't feel anything, again. It's no disgrace."

"The pain stops, now. Please. No more. Take her to Dr Rahul; he helped me, and I want him to at least try." She turned and buried herself in his chest. He watched Matthew and Sonia leave the room.

Colette took a heaving breath.

"It's the right thing." She looked up into his eyes.

"Yes."

"Good."

He bent forward and kissed her lips.

"I was so worried about you."

"I was briefly scared, but then, I got pissed off. What gives people like him the right to tell me what to do?"

"A grand sense of self-righteousness."

"Well, fuck that!"

Whoa, his little lady had grown a set of balls.

"I want to go back to the club."

"It's getting late."

"I don't care. I want to go back there, and I want you to fuck me in the middle of the stage floor."

"That's probably a little extreme, isn't it? How about we go home, you can have a nice bath? I'll make love to you on the bed, and then, we can sleep in each other's arms for hours."

"Oh, that does sound nice. No. Oh, I don't know. Will you take me to the club, tomorrow tonight?" She bit her lip.

"If you ask me to, I'll take you."

"Good."

He wrapped his arms around her and led her from the room. In his head, he said a silent little prayer for his wife. He asked her to watch over Ruth, and he thanked her for sending him Colette, because only an angel was able to gift him something as wonderful as the woman in his arms.

FOURTEEN

Colette

"Ok, you know I said I wanted you to fuck me in the middle of the club? Maybe I was a little bit hasty there." Colette looked around at all the people who filled the club. They'd already seen Grayson and Sophie and Callum and Marie. Matthew and Sonia weren't there tonight as they were back looking after their baby. She felt a little guilty that by getting kidnapped, she'd ruined their first night out since the birth. They promised her it was alright, though, and they would have many more. That's what having lots of friends to babysit meant. She, then, promptly offered to babysit for them one night, which had Michael shaking at the thought of dirty nappies. It was nice that, despite her past, they were all accepting her into their lives. It couldn't be easy for any of them. Amy had sent her a message this morning wishing her well, offering assistance if she needed it. It was surreal, but her doomed relationship with James had brought her friends and a future. They'd gone the long way round to get there, but they'd finally succeeded. She had no feelings for James. He was her friend. She was in love with Michael and knew he was her Dom and always would be.

Michael wrapped his arms around her.

"I thought you may say that and booked a room just for the two of us. I'm not ready to share you, yet. I'm not sure I ever will be. You're mine and mine alone." He tapped her on the backside. "Now wiggle this into the room over there and strip. I want you in the slave position, ready for me, when I come in."

She wasn't waiting around. She'd been buzzing all day for her second attempt at the club. She went straight to the room and removed her dress. Michael had sent out for another one this morning. She was a bit concerned about the bruising she had on her shoulder from where the belt had hit her. She thought people would think he'd hurt her, so he had a dress with a cap sleeve delivered. The purple, silky material skimmed her body like a second skin. She didn't want to crease the dress, so she laid it neatly over a chair. She looked down at the high heeled sandals she wore. They made her legs look so trim and defined with muscles, when she walked. She didn't take them off. She wondered if Michael would agree to that. She hoped so. Her underwear was removed, and she knelt in her greeting position just as the door opened.

"Good Girl." She wiggled her bottom a little, like a dog being praised. "The shoes are a good inclusion. Well done on leaving them on. It makes me incredibly hard, just thinking about having your legs wrapped around my neck while I drill into you against the wall." She lifted her head slightly, to watch him re-arrange himself in his trousers. "Look at what you do to me." He shook his head. "I'll be coming in my pants like a school boy, soon." He bent down to her and grabbed her hair where she wore it in a fishtail braid.

"Safe word?"

"Disgrace." It was the word they'd decided on between them. It wasn't a word she needed to feel any longer. She was free.

"If you need to use it, do so. I'm trusting you with this, because I'm not going to go slowly today. I want you well and truly fucked, by the time I finish with you. Use Amber if you just want me to stop and talk about what we're doing. Do you understand?"

"Yes, Master."

"I want you on the bed. Arse in the air." She got to her feet, and with a seductive sway of her hips, climbed onto the bed and positioned herself. "Damn, that backside of yours is perfect." She squealed, when Michael leaned forward and bit into the soft flesh. "It looks even better with my mark on it. He smacked where he'd just bitten, and she squeaked out a moan. Her clit was throbbing already. "Tonight's going to be about decorating my precious toy."

She looked over her shoulder while he went to his bag and pulled out two clips she recognised from her research on the internet about BDSM. Damn, they really did have so many fun things to look up on the internet. She particularly enjoyed watching porn with Michael. When he talked about voyeurs, she thought maybe she was one. They could explore that at a later date, though.

"Face forward or I'll have to blindfold you."

She huffed.

He came back to the bed and slapped her arse again.

"Carry on and I doubt you'll be sitting down tomorrow, little brat." She wiggled her bottom. Embracing her inner minx was going to get her climaxing, if she played her cards right. He smacked it again.

"What do I have in my hands, since you were spying?"

"Nipple clips."

"Do you want to wear them?"

"Yes, please, Master."

Michael dipped underneath her and wrapped his lips around her breast. She gasped with the erotic pleasure that cascaded down towards her centre where she was starting to feel the need for stimulation. He removed his mouth and attached the clamp. She reared back and let out a cry.

"Fuck." It hurt.

He grabbed her other breast and pulled it into his mouth. The pain disappeared, in an instant, and was replaced with a dull throb. She shut her eyes and surrendered to the feeling. That was…until he placed the other clip on. The pain returned but was dulled again when he shifted and dipped his tongue into her open mouth. She captured his warmth, allowing it to focus her, once again, on the high of pleasure her body was preparing itself for.

"One more bit of jewellery, I think. We discussed anal the other week. Are you still consenting to it?"

They'd sat over dinner one night, and he'd asked her for her views on him sticking his cock up her arse. It was a pretty strange conversation to have over a homemade pad Thai, but she went with it, though she wasn't sure at first. He explained he wouldn't just go for it. He'd prepare her, so when he did eventually fuck her there, she'd be ready for it. She told him she was intrigued and would give it a go.

"I am, Master."

"Good. I'm going to start preparing you, tonight." He climbed off the bed and went to his bag, again. He pulled out another toy she recognised from her research. A butt plug. Her arse cheeks involuntarily clenched together.

"You'll need to relax, if I'm going to get this in."

"Easy for you to say. Shove it up your arse, and then, I'll relax." She wasn't sure where that came from; it was totally not her. She could act a brat on occasion, but that was a big brat. Michael dropped the plug on the bed and let out a bellowing laugh.

"I've created a brat bigger than Sophie Moore." He held his toned belly as he laughed. She turned around and pouted at him.

"It wasn't that funny. Now, are you going to stick that thing in me or what?"

Michael stopped laughing, and his eyes went dark as the black of night.

"It's going in." He picked up the plug and ran it over the folds of her sex. She knew she would be wet for him. She always was. The cold metal of the plug touched her clit, and she pushed back against it to feel the chill against her heated flesh. Michael brought his other hand down, in a smack of warning.

"Stay still."

He ran the plug over her highly sensitive flesh and took it back up to her puckered hole. He tested her willingness, and she instantly shut him out. It was a natural reaction. She couldn't help it. He brought the hand not holding the plug to her pussy, and a dexterous finger circled her clit. She mellowed as she felt the spark of electricity that instantly shuddered through her body. A pressure came to her puckered hole. It wasn't pain she felt. It was different. She couldn't explain it. She was just starting to feel full back there.

"It's in."

Michael came around to her front to stare into her eyes. She knew he was checking to see whether she was hiding anything from him. He did it often. She could never hide anything from this man.

"Colour?"

"Green."

"I'm going to take you doggy style again tonight, because that plug makes you look so good."

"It's my favourite position." It really was. From being the catalyst for a horrible series of events, it was now her favourite way of getting off."

Michael lowered his trousers. She licked her lips as he pumped his cock a few times. It was a work of art. The lines that went from the base to the tip seemed to frame its perfection. He disappeared behind her, and she felt him at her entrance. He pushed in, and she instantly lost herself to the pleasure. Her entire body started to shake with the intensity of what she was feeling. He pumped a few times, and she knew it wouldn't take long for her to climax. Michael pulled her up, so her back was against his chest. He wrapped a hand around her breasts which pulled down on the clips. Her bottom was pushed against his chest, and the plug was buried deep.

"So full," she gasped out.

Michael kissed at the back of her neck. He intermixed little bites with kisses. All the time, he kept a rhythmic pace with his cock driving into her welcoming body. She was going to lose her mind. Her vision became blurred, her head began to spin, and then, she was coming and coming. Her body was nothing more than a vessel for the pleasure her Master gave her. Michael screamed out her name and slammed deeply into her. She felt his shots of release coating her insides. She slumped in Michael's arms. Her body was like jelly, as he lowered her down onto the bed.

"I love you." She pressed a kiss to his lips, when he looked down at her.

"Forever," he replied.

She'd had the worst start possible to her life, but she found her place in this world, now. She was able to make her own decisions. She was able to feel pleasure. She was free, and all because the man wrapping himself around her took a chance on a girl in a hospital. A girl who couldn't even tie her own shoe laces, because the prescribed shoes didn't have them. She'd grown into a woman. A woman without disgrace.

FIFTEEN

Colette

Fifteen years later

Colette looked out, over the sun-drenched swimming pool. Jeremy, Jez for short, her eleven-year-old son, and Abigail, Abi for short, her twelve-year-old daughter, were chasing each other around. It was a beautiful summer day in the Florida Keys. They'd made their home here five years ago and hadn't looked back. Michael had decided, at the ripe old age of forty-five, he'd had enough of managing actors and wanted to retire. She hadn't fought him on the decision. In fact, she supported him from the minute he mentioned it. She'd formed a successful part-time career assisting victims of domestic violence, but her priorities always lay with her family. That was the way she was brought up, and that would never change. It was the one good thing to come out of her past. They'd decided on Florida after one idyllic summer holiday and had packed up life in the UK a few months later. Michael didn't last long being retired. He got bored and invested in Grayson Moore's Florida club. He was the manager there but only worked when he wanted to. Life was perfect.

She looked down at the photo album in front of her. Their friends had put it together when they'd left London. She flicked through the pages and landed on a picture of her with James North, taken a number of years earlier. He held his daughter, Isabelle, in his arms, and she held her new-born daughter. To hope for a friendship with him and his wife after everything that'd happened, would've been too much to ask, but it had happened. She was lucky.

"Thank you for allowing me to be so happy," she said to the picture as a tear dropped down her cheek

The door creaked, and she looked up to see Michael enter the room. Even at fifty, he still looked young. His hair was greying at the edges, but the Florida sun had dyed his blonde almost white, so it didn't show that much. He looked down at the album.

"Memories?"

"Yes," she replied. "So many."

He took the album from her and looked at the picture she'd had open.

"Regrets?"

"None." She kissed him. "It's been twelve years since that day. It seems a lifetime ago."

"James North made big sacrifices for everyone he cared for. The biggest he ever made was with Ryan. No one will ever forget that."

THE END

PART EIGHT

CONTROLLING THE PAST - PART ONE

FOREWORD

Important note from the author:

Please note this book is set in England. The age of consent for sexual activity of any orientation in the UK, regardless of whether male or female, is sixteen. Laws for other countries maybe different, but this book is set in England and adheres to the rules of that country.

Please enjoy.

ONE

Pete

1973 - Forty-five years ago

The melodic chime of the ice-cream van sang out, and seven-year-old Pete North placed his sand covered hand over his father's slightly pink bare chest. "Can I have an ice-cream please?"

They'd been at the beach near Broadstairs in Kent for a few hours, now, and the entire time his father had 'rested his eyes' under the burning intensity of the sunshine. It was an exceptionally hot day for England, and Pete knew his father would regret not covering himself in suntan lotion. Mind you, he wasn't sure there was much left in the bottle after his mother had smothered on the vile white, gloopy liquid. "Dad, please."

His father groaned and sat up.

"I thought you were building a sandcastle?"

"I finished it." He looked proudly over at the colossal structure, resting a bit further down the beach near the sea. It was his best work ever. Maybe, one day he could build a proper building.

Pete's mother poked her nose out from behind the book she was reading– something called, 'All things bright and beautiful by James Herriot'. "That's groovy son. Ken, I'll have a cream soda, please." Before his father could answer, Mrs North had settled her attention back to the book.

Pete's father got to his feet, and picking up his bell bottom trousers, which were lying on the sand, he searched in the pockets, and pulled out his wallet.

"What type of ice-cream do you want?" his father asked him as Pete also got to his feet and wiped his hands on his mum's kaftan.

"I want one of those with the chocolate in it. The '99' one."

His father rolled his eyes.

"I've no idea why they call them that. They've been called '99' since before I was born, and it has nothing to do with the price."

"It does seem a bit silly." He reached up with a pudgy hand and took his father's. "Mum, you're on sandcastle watch. Make sure the sea doesn't get it."

"Sure thing," his mum called from behind the book and fanned herself with it. Pete knew straightaway that if the sea came anywhere near his castle, it would be demolished. His mother loved her books and spent a great deal of time lost in them. He sometimes wondered what they contained but had decided long ago it was woman's business, and he was best to stay out of it. Girls were yucky things– they didn't like to play with worms or make mud pies. Where was the fun in that? He only needed one woman in his life, and she was his mother!

He trundled along, the sand kicking up as he struggled to keep pace with the bigger man's steps. His father bent down and scooped him up into his arms. The journey to the ice-cream van was much quicker this way, and they waited patiently until it was their turn.

"A '99', a cream soda, and I'll have…" His father paused in thought.

"Why don't you have a *Zoom*, Daddy? You like them."

"Yes, good thinking." His father tapped him on the nose. "I'll have a *Zoom*, please."

The ice-cream seller, whose sideburns joined up with his moustache, turned to prepare Pete's '99'. His father put him down on the ground and opened his wallet while Pete looked around. There were so many people at the beach today. He was sure most of the inner-city suburbs had ventured out to catch a few rays of sunshine. Varied musical tastes merged together: Elton John, Wings, Paul Simon, Roberta Flack and The Rolling Stones competed for the loudest sound of the summertime. He laughed at the awful noise all the different genres made.

"Here you are," his father said and handed him the vanilla ice-cream, which had a chocolate flake sticking out of it. Pete stuck his tongue out and gave it a long lick. Delicious, he thought to himself. He opened his mouth and was taking a bite of the flake when he noticed a little girl standing opposite them. She went to lick her own chocolate ice-cream, but it was already half melted and slid off onto the floor. Her face fell, and her bottom lip jutted out over the top one, trembling with her distress.

"Daddy." She tugged on the trousers of the man standing next to her. "I lost my ice-cream."

The man looked down and let out a long groan.

"Miranda, what did I tell you? You have to be more careful."

The little girl sniffed back the tears, forming in her eyes.

"I'm sorry. I was careful, but the ice-cream was melting, and it slipped."

"Probably, because you were staring into space and not eating the thing. Well, you can go without. I've had enough. It's too hot here and full of undesirables. We're going home…. Augusta," he called to a well-dressed and rather hot looking woman, standing nearby.

"Charles don't be so mean to the poor darling. It wasn't her fault!" the woman exclaimed. Pete found his tongue coming out and licking his ice-cream of its own accord while watching everything unfold

"Enough," the man spoke again, and the woman silenced. "I'll wait in the car.

You clean her up before she comes back. I don't want the leather getting sticky."

The man stomped off, and the little girl burst into tears.

"I'm sorry, Mummy. I didn't mean to drop it."

"I know, darling. You know what your father's like. He's not good around so many people like this. Come on, let's follow him."

The woman wiped away the girl's tears, but they kept falling.

"That was my first ever ice-cream. I really liked it."

Pete pulled his '99' away from his mouth and looked down at it.

"Wait," he called out as the girl and her mother started to walk off. They stopped and turned to look at him. "Here." He went over to them and offered the girl his ice-cream. At first, she hesitated to take it, looking up at her mother and then back at him. Her eyes were the brightest blue he'd ever seen, richer in colour than the sea he'd swam in earlier. "Please," he coaxed.

"Thank you." She reached out and took the ice-cream and had a lick of it before offering it back to him.

"No, you keep it." Her eyes went wide with surprise. "Just make sure you wash your hands before you get in your dad's car. Mine's just the same with his seats. They forget how messy we can be as kids, and once they have us, it's impossible to keep anything clean."

The little girl laughed, and Pete heard a chuckle from her mother as well.

"Say thank you to the young boy, Miranda," Augusta ordered.

"Thank you...um...I don't know your name."

"It's Peter, Pete North. That's my dad, Ken North." He pointed to where his father had finished paying and was watching them.

"Thank you, Pete. I'd better go." She took a long lick of the ice-cream, and he suddenly regretted his decision. But only a little bit because Miranda's tears had dried up, and she had a smile on her face as wide as the colossal moat he'd built for his castle.

Miranda took her mother's hand and skipped off happily with her. Pete rubbed his tummy when it gurgled. The ice-cream van put on its music and drove away. He frowned.

"Here." His dad handed him the *Zoom*. It wasn't a '99' with a chocolate flake, but he wasn't going to turn down the sugary treat. "You did a really good thing. I'm proud of you."

"It was nothing." Pete shoved the *Zoom* in his mouth and slobbered all over it, so his dad couldn't change his mind and ask for it back. "Her dad was mean, and I didn't like to see her crying."

"Get used to it, son. It happens with all women." Pete's father ruffled his hair as they headed back to the spot on the beach where his mother still lay, reading her book.

"I'll marry her, one day," Pete exclaimed as he sat on the edge of their picnic blanket.

"Marry who?" his mother asked.

"The girl I just helped." He smiled and licked the *Zoom* again.

"I thought you were getting ice-cream?" His mum looked at them both confused.

"So, did I." His father shrugged. "Although I think our little boy might have found an interest in women at the same time!"

TWO

Miranda

1984 – Thirty-four years ago

Miranda's head drooped forward, and she quickly righted it and stared out of the window again. It was her stop soon, and she needed to make sure she stayed awake. If she missed it, her father would be so angry. He was already upset with the fact she was coming home early from boarding school and spoiling his peace. It wasn't exactly her fault, though. She'd finished her O-level exams last week, and the teachers wanted to shut her dormitory down to allow them to re-decorate. She'd much rather have stayed at school and socialised with her friends. She was an only child. Being at home would be boring. She had at least twelve weeks before she could return to school to start studying for her A-levels. It would be the longest twelve weeks of her life.

The train pulled into the station, and she checked the sign to ensure it was her stop. She didn't want to have to call her father to let him know she'd got off the train at the wrong station. Picking up her handbag and rucksack, she walked past the few people still left in her coach and found her suitcase. She pulled the handle up and wheeled it to the carriage door. When someone opened it, she jumped down and bounced the case out of the train.

"Wait, Miss Braybrooke. I'll help you." She cocked her head to look up at the person calling her. It was her father's driver.

"Hello, Mr Pearson. It's alright.... I have it."

"Hush, child. It's my job. I wouldn't want you hurting yourself. Come on."

Miranda relinquished the handle of the suitcase over to Mr Pearson and stepped back.

"If you insist."

"I do. Put your rucksack over my shoulder as well."

She opened her mouth to argue but knew it would be useless. Mr Pearson had been her father's driver for several years, now—ever since her daddy had come into his title and money. Her father had become Lord Braybrooke when she was ten years old, and her grandfather, the previous Lord Braybrooke, had died suddenly of a heart attack. He'd suffered injuries to his chest during army combat service in World War One, and despite being very active for a further sixty years, it was always felt by Miranda and her mother he'd left them far too soon. The same was not the opinion of her father who, at the age of fifty-three, felt it was about time he inherited. She missed her grandfather every day. He was such a character, regaling her with stories from the years gone by, especially tales of what he got up to in the roaring twenties. He'd join her on long walks around the estate they lived on, and he helped her learn to ride horses at a young age. Her father had always been so strict with her. It was as if waiting to inherit had sucked the life out of him. She couldn't remember a time when she ever really saw him smile. Her grandfather, though, would have one permanently on his face.

The sound of the train's horn pulled her out of her reflections, and she followed behind Mr Pearson.

"Your father's waiting for you in the car, Miss."

"How is he?" she asked while skipping over a case left on the platform.

"The usual." Her chauffeur's response had her body deflate and the spring in her step disappear. They walked through the station and out the main entrance towards the shiny black 1984 Mercedes-Benz.

She was dressed casually in jeans, a fluorescent t-shirt, and jacket but wished she'd dressed smarter, maybe even in her pretentious school uniform. Her father was bound to criticise what she wore. Pulling the front of her jacket together, she zipped it up and hoped he wouldn't notice.

"Hop in, Miss. I'll put these in the car, and then we'll get you home. I suspect you want nothing more than a shower and something to eat." Mr Pearson popped the boot of the car and lifted her suitcase up with a puff of exertion. She knew it was heavy after carrying it across London and all the way from her exclusive girls-only school in Cambridgeshire. It was the one her grandmother had attended and was the best. She opened the door to see her father with his briefcase open on his lap and a folder of paper in his hand.

"Hello, Father." She climbed in the car and pressed a kiss to his cheek. He looked up at her, deep rooted lines of age seemed to have extended around his eyes. She tried to recall the last time she'd been home. It must have been for her sixteenth birthday in February. It was now June, so four months. Not long but he really looked to have aged. She frowned and immediately regretted it when he caught her concerned look.

"Don't look at me like that. If I'm looking tired, it's because I've had to work long hours this week managing the estate, so I can take this time off to come and get you. That school of yours is useless. I've paid them the same amount of money this term as I did for the same period last year and have got half the service."

She shrunk down into her seat.

"I'm sorry. I did ask if they would allow me to stay anywhere else, but they said it wasn't possible."

"Bloody typical. The state of education in this country! Mind you, the school was your mother's choice. It was good enough for her mother, and she was a 'Goldsmith', so it would be the best choice for you. I'll have you know the Goldsmith name isn't as big as it once was. Braybrooke is far superior, now, thanks to the associates I've made."

"You've done so well, Father. Our name is a great one."

"It is, and your useless mother hasn't given me a son to continue it. We need to consider your marriage and soon."

"Marriage?" she spat out.

"Yes, I need to start looking into the right people. We can't have you getting involved with the wrong person and making such a fool of the family name your uncle ends up claiming the title. No, we need you married as soon as possible and pushing out male heirs within a few years."

"A few years," she stuttered. "But father, I'm only sixteen. I've got my A-levels in a couple of years, and then I want to go to university. I've got so much more I want to do with my life, first."

She looked up at her father whose cheeks had patches of red spreading across them, a sure sign he was angry at her. Mr Pearson stopped him from exploding, however, when he opened the driver's door and sat down at the wheel of the car.

"Straight home, my Lord?" he addressed her father.

"Yes." The curt reply was given, and her father re-focused his attention back on her. "I mean it, Miranda. I won't let my good for nothing, anarchist brother have this title. You'll do as you are told, and you'll like it. I've given you the best life you could ever wish for. You've not wanted for anything, and you'll damn well do as you are told. No arguments." He threw the folder of papers back into his briefcase and slammed it shut before crossing his arms over his chest. "You're sixteen now, the time for childish follies is at an end. Now, you grow up." Her father turned his head to look out the car window and thereby ended the conversation. Miranda also looked away and stared out at the countryside of Surrey as it whizzed past the window. There'd always been so much competitiveness between her father and his brother, Henry. Uncle Henry wasn't interested in the title of Lord Braybrooke, far from it. He was happy exploring the world, and all things associated with the techno pop explosion, which was a sight to behold, considering he was nearly sixty. The title was more likely to go back a generation further to her grandfather's brother, if she didn't produce a male heir by the time her father died. Besides, even with the evidence of his ageing, she suspected her father wouldn't be checking out on life anytime soon.

The words that hit her the hardest, from her father's explosion, had been the ones spoken of her ungratefulness at everything he'd given her since childhood. It reminded her of an incident when she was five years old, which had shaped all future interactions with him. It may sound silly, but she'd never forgiven him for blaming her for dropping an ice-cream from her cone while at the seaside. Even worse, he'd not been a caring and understanding father who'd replaced it. No, he'd left her alone to mourn the loss of the treat until she experienced the kindness of a young stranger who gave her his. It was petty on her part to think this way, but it had been a defining moment in her relationship with her father, which had gone downhill ever since. This new assertion, on his part, that he would find her a husband and start her breeding had firmly killed any hope she had of reconciliation.

The car pulled up to their Tudor mansion, and she sighed heavily. The building was imposing, a fortress that destroyed hopes of any kind of joy. It was dark and gloomy, even the stonework gargoyles looked despondent rather than scary. Without saying another word, her father opened his door and stepped out of the car. She knew he'd disappear into his office until dinner time. Her mother appeared on the porch–if her father had looked slightly older, then her mother looked like she already had one foot in the grave. Her face was sunken, and she had dark circles around her eyes. Miranda jumped out of the car and went running up to her. Augusta Braybrooke, nee Naymouth, was nearly two decades younger than her husband. He was turning sixty in a few weeks, but she was in her forties. It was a marriage of convenience: a way for her father to obtain more money for his estates by accessing her mother's small fortune. She'd always wondered what benefits the marriage brought for her mother but never asked.

"My darling." Her mother held her closely. They were as tall as each other, now, and Miranda kissed her mother's cheek. "How did your exams go?"

"Good. I'm sure I'm going to get the grades I need to continue my education."

"I'm so happy for you. You've always been so clever. Come on, let's get you inside. I've brought afternoon tea up to your room, so after you've showered, you can tell me all about what's happened at school."

Miranda smiled. She worshipped and adored her mother. She was the one person who'd made her childhood tolerable. Sometimes, she imagined what it would be like if her father wasn't around anymore. A horrible thought that would likely get her struck down at some point and lead to her suffering an eternity in hell, but she could not help how she felt. Miranda wrapped her arm around her mother, and together, they headed off for an afternoon full of gossip. Maybe the summer wouldn't be so bad after all.

THREE

Pete

"Welcome, trainees. If you'd like to take a seat, our chairman will be with you shortly." The smartly dressed secretary broke out a tooth flashing smile and swayed her curvy hips as she walked out of the room. Like the two men sitting beside him who adjusted their cocks in their pants, Pete was sure he should be paying attention to the sexy little personal assistant, but he was too busy looking around the room they were in. It was an old-style building, probably from the early eighteen hundreds, and Georgian in period with large glass panelled sash windows. His body tingled with excitement at having been given this opportunity. Barrett's was one of the most prestigious banks in the UK, and thanks to his predicted excellent A-level grades, he'd been able to secure a trainee position within the firm as a banking clerk. He'd not always been financially minded. Building things was his great obsession, but he needed to make some money first before he could even begin to explore his real passion. "Hi, I'm Ian Henshaw." One of the other two men held his hand out to him. He shook it.

"Peter North."

"Albert Claridge." The other man, darker in appearance to them both, interrupted their introductions and held his hand out. Ian shook it first, and then Pete did.

"I hope all the women who work here are like that one." Ian chuckled. "It'll make looking at figures all day a lot easier."

"You'd never get anything done, if they all looked like her. You wouldn't be able to see straight!" Albert winked, grabbed his groin, and shook it.

"I think I'll just concentrate on trying to do a good job and forget the women for now." Pete looked up at the ceiling above them. It was ornately carved with a spectacular ceiling rose.

"It appears he's more interested in the décor than the women anyway." Ian laughed.

"Nerd," Albert added, but Pete ignored them.

A cough came from the doorway, and they all turned to face the older man who stood there in full morning suit, including a pocket watch.

"Mr North." The man's eyes narrowed. He spoke in clipped tones, and Pete gulped. "Would you come with me please?"

"Shit!" He heard Albert exclaim under his breath beside him. Albert and Ian both stepped back from him and reassumed their seats.

Reluctantly, placing one foot slowly in front of the other, Pete walked towards the man. He followed him out into the corridor, and down a long passageway. Pete's heart was beating fast. He'd worked so hard to get this job, and now he was wondering what had gone wrong? It had to be something serious because the face on the man as he'd told him to follow him had been thunderous. It left Pete suspecting he was about to be told his services were no longer required. He mentally ran his mind over the application form and the interview. He hadn't said anything false. He was certain of that, so what could it be?

"In here." The man pushed open a door. Pete's eyes went wide when he read the name on it – 'Ernest Barrett, Chairman' – shit, he was in big trouble. He entered the room and looked around to see it was empty. His hands were clasped in front of him, and he nervously twiddled his fingers together. The gentleman in the suit walked around him and towards a massive oak carved desk. It was lined with a faded green leather top. The piece of furniture looked almost as old as the building. "Sit down."

Pete scampered across the floor at the terse tone and sat as quickly as his legs would allow him.

"Mr Barrett?" he stuttered in enquiry, and the older gentleman burst out laughing. Pete sat further back in his chair, looking as if he was trying to get away from a mad man but didn't have the ability to run out of the room.

"You can relax." Mr Barrett said as he took his own seat and placed his hands on the desk. Pete noticed the expensive looking signet ring he wore. "I'm sorry for the pretence of being about to fire you. I have my own way of working out who'll be the best apprentice. Congratulations, you won."

"I don't understand." Pete scrunched his face up in confusion.

"Sorry. My secretary is purposely sent in as a distraction at the greeting. Your two colleagues fell for my trap and spent most of the initial introduction with their tongues hanging out like randy dogs. You, however, paid no attention to her, even if you were distracted by my building. It shows you'll be able to focus on the job rather than chasing the skirts we have to offer in the office."

"Oh. I do like women, though." Pete felt he needed to tell Mr Barratt. He didn't have anything against homosexuality–in fact, he'd explored that side of his sexuality a couple of times, as did so many of his peers, but he'd concluded he preferred women. He was certain of that.

"I'm sure you do. The difference is you won't allow them to become a distraction, and that's why you'll be working closely with me."

"Closely with you." His mouth fell open at the opportunity he was being presented with. Mr Barratt was one of the most famous bankers in the country. He was on the front page of many a newspaper due to his incredible financial planning. He was widely sought after by the rich and famous to not only take care of their money but also to double it with investments and interest. The current financial climate wasn't the best: the threat of strikes and changes in government looked set to lead the country into a period of austerity. If you wanted to survive, you needed Mr Barratt's advice and here he was being offered the chance to train directly under him. He was gobsmacked into silence.

"Yes, you'll work with me on some of the biggest clients the bank has. I'm going to get you started straight away by throwing you in the deep in with Lord Charles Braybrooke's account. I shall be meeting him in a few weeks, and I want you to study every inch of his monetary position and develop some recommendations. What do you say?"

"I...er...can I pinch myself to check I'm not dreaming?" he replied and squeezed a piece of skin on the back of his hand.

Mr Barrett let out his bellowing laugh again and got to his feet. He went over to a desk in the corner of his room and picked up a wad of papers and folders, a foot in height.

"I'm going to like you." Mr Barratt came back to the desk and placed the papers in front of him. This is what you need to read through. The Braybrookes have been clients of ours since the bank was started by my five times great-grandfather back in the seventeen hundreds. Lord Braybrooke is one of the biggest clients we have, and your interaction will be important in continuing that relationship. I cannot stress how vital it is you really read everything here because you must understand it all. You'll need to research current financial models and future risks. My assistant will be able to help you with that. You'll need to run any models you choose to adopt through the computers we have on the ground floor to ensure the probabilities of risk to the client are not too great. We aren't in the habit of making our clients bankrupt." Mr Barratt pushed the papers towards him. "You'll have a desk across the way with my assistant. Now, if you understand what I expect from you, then I suggest you start reading."

Pete got to his feet, picked up the massive pile of papers, and tucked them under his arm.

"I understand everything, Sir. Thank you for this opportunity. I won't let you down."

Mr Barratt sat back in his chair and lit up a cigar.

"I know you won't. I see a lot of myself in you. I think we'll work well together. Any questions just ask."

Pete nodded his head in gratitude, and stepping out of the office, he pulled the door closed and rested back against it. His heart was still beating so fast. He couldn't believe he was being given this chance. It would be the making of his career. His mum would be so proud when he told her.

Mr Barrett's secretary beckoned him into her office with a waggle of her finger. She was sexy, and he was a hot-blooded male, but she just didn't do it for him. He had it in his head he needed to succeed first with his career. He was certain the right woman was out there for him—one day, he'd meet her and know immediately she was his. From that moment, they'd never be apart again. He wouldn't let her get away. But for now, he had a lot of reading to do and wasn't going to let Mr Barrett down. He went into the room with the secretary and noticed there was a desk already set up for him. He took a seat at it and started reading. A few moments later, Albert entered the room carrying a pile of papers. Pete looked up and nodded at him in greeting.

"You got a client as well?" Pete asked.

"Client?" Albert strode moodily towards the photocopier and placed the papers down. Pete sucked in his lip when it dawned on him Albert had been given a different kind of task. The brown-haired man picked up the first piece of paper and fed it through the photocopier. He repeated the process with a sullen look on his face. Ian came into the room next carrying a tray of tea and coffee. Pete lowered his head into his paperwork and smiled. He was going to like this job –it would be the making of him!

FOUR

Miranda

"Miranda, will you hurry up?" her father shouted up the grand staircase to her. She pinned the last strands of her thick brown locks into place within her bun and pulled on the silk gloves her maid had laid out.

"Coming," she called down the stairs while reaching for her handbag and slipping her sparkling black court shoes on. In a flash, she ran out of her room, the door slamming shut behind her, and down the stairs to where her father paced impatiently.

"Women," he sighed with exasperation. "It takes you forever to get ready, and you still look a state when you say you're done."

Miranda looked down at her designer A-line dress in a teal colour. She thought it suited her colouring well, but obviously not.

"Should I change?" she asked.

"I don't have time for that. Get in the car. Why I agreed with your mother to take you today is beyond me. All you'll do is get in the way and send my blood pressure through the roof. And no doubt, she'll spend the day frittering more of my money away with beauty treatments that have little hope of working."

Miranda didn't respond to her father's diatribe. Instead, she hurried into the car and disappeared to the world inside her head for the journey to London. It was nicer in there where she had a father who respected and loved her.

The ride to London didn't take long with Mr Pearson weaving through the traffic. She was sure he should've been a racing driver instead of a chauffeur. He winked at her when he opened the door, and she smiled back before taking her father's arm. She looked up at the imposing building in front of them.

"Where are we?" she enquired.

"Barratt's Bank."

Her father's reply was curt, so she decided against asking him anything else. He took his briefcase from Mr Pearson, and Miranda followed him up the steps of the Georgian style building. The hubbub of the bustling streets of London disappeared when they entered through the door. A blast of icy air-conditioning hit them and washed away the heat of the British summer.

"Lord Braybrooke." A man dressed in a full morning suit stepped forward and dipped his head down in a show of courtesy. "Mr Barrett is expecting you. If you'd like to follow me this way, please."

Her father shook the man's hand firmly, to leave the poor fellow with no doubts as to who oversaw the situation.

"Miranda, keep up," her father ordered, and her court heels echoed across the wooden floors as she jogged to keep pace with the men's wide strides. They entered a lift, and it rose to the tenth floor. All the time, she watched her father's face. He was always stern, but this was something different. He was in complete business mode. Nothing or no one was going to distract him from whatever goals he had in his mind to achieve today. The lift pinged, and the men were off at a rapid pace again. She followed them as best she could, wishing she'd been allowed to wear her favourite jeans, trainers, and t-shirt instead. She didn't often get to wear casual clothes, but when she did, she had a fondness for slogans. The latest one she'd purchased told her to 'choose life'. There was so much irony in the statement she wasn't even sure where to begin to explain it, especially to her father after he'd rolled his eyes when she chose to wear it to dinner one evening. It wasn't quite the pearls and twinset he deemed appropriate.

"Miranda, for goodness sake will you stop dawdling? I don't have all day to wait around for you while you're off dreaming about fairies and god knows what else. Keep your mind focused on the task, which is putting one foot in front of the other and behaving like the lady you supposedly are."

She sighed heavily and looked down at the ground, wishing it would swallow her up. She was a constant disappointment, always had been and was likely to always be. Why couldn't she have been a boy? It would have made things so much easier.

The door to a massive boardroom was pushed open and there, sitting at the table, was the reason she was happy to be a girl. Her lady parts had suddenly awakened and were preparing themselves for the vision before her. Not the old man who greeted her father with affection but the slightly shy looking boy beside him who was regarding her. No, he wasn't a boy, definitely a man. His lip curled up into a smirk, which had her heart fluttering so fast it seemed like it would beat out of her chest. He stood and dominated the room. He must have been at least six feet plus a good couple of inches. His chest was broad in his suit, which was sculpted to his body and accentuated his narrow hips. She was salivating. He was fucking gorgeous. She'd never seen someone like him before.

"Mr Barratt." Her father's deep voice broke through her vision of the man's luscious lips, pressing against the sudden throb in her panties. "I'd like you to meet my daughter, Miranda. I'm showing her the ropes today. Giving her a bit of an insight into the running of the old business."

"Miss Braybrooke." The older man stepped forward and shook her hand. He was dressed formally with a pocket watch hanging from a chain, which was attached to his trousers. "It's a pleasure to meet you. I bet you're excited to learn more about your father's finances and what the future holds for you."

Miranda opened her mouth to answer but was cut off by the bellowing laugh of her father. "Good one, Charles. I see you still have a great sense of humour. All she'll be doing in the future is bringing her husband his tea and whisky while he works hard. Speaking of which….."–Miranda watched her father turn his attention to the hunk of a man standing next to Mr Barrett – "I'll have white, two sugars, please."

Mr Barrett coughed through the awkward silence that followed her father's instructions.

"Lord Braybrooke, there's been some confusion. Mr North here is my assistant. He's being studying your files for the last two weeks and has made some excellent suggestions on how we can improve your financial position.

The features on her father's face tightened, and his eyes darkened with anger.

"I don't pay you to have your assistants work on my files. I pay for your services and yours alone. Am I not the most important client you have? I would never have been treated this way when your father ran my account."

"Lord Braybrooke." Mr North stepped forward and inserted himself into the conversation. "I can assure you, Sir, Mr Barrett has worked closely with me at all times. He thought a fresh pair of eyes would be beneficial to your future prosperity."

"I don't give a fuck what he thinks or what work you've done together. I pay to work with Mr Barrett alone. and if he can't do that, then I shall leave right now and take my business to someone who'll treat me with the respect I deserve and not farm out my important financial future to a boy fresh out of nappies."

"Lord Braybrooke, Mr North is a trusted employee."

"I'm walking." Her father picked up the briefcase, which he'd placed on the table to shake hands, and made for the open doorway.

Miranda looked to where Mr Barrett and the young man, who still had her panties in a twist, stood. The older of the two looked stressed and sad at the same time. The younger picked up a folder, which looked to contain several hand-written notes, and gestured for the other to take it.

"Miss Braybrooke, should we leave Mr Barrett and your father to discuss business in peace? We'll only hinder them." Mr North urged the older man to take the folder one last time, and he reluctantly did. "Lord Braybrooke, I apologise for the confusion. I'll return with your tea shortly. I'll ensure Miss Braybrooke is taken care of while you work with my employer."

Miranda looked to where her father was watching what was unfolding. He had a supercilious look on his face, which she would love nothing more than to wipe clean away with a hard-thrown punch. Instead, she pulled her handbag a little higher up on her shoulder, stuck her nose into the air, and glided past her father and out the door. She did so without so much as a goodbye or acknowledgement that this course of action was either for or against his wishes. She was furious. He'd been rude and disrespectful. Foot-steps came up behind her, and a hand was placed into the small of her back. Warmth tingled through her body, and she let out an almost silent moan of satisfaction.

"I'll take you to Mr Barrett's office, Miss. You can wait in there for your father. I hope I read the signs right, and you'd also prefer to be out of the room."

She slammed to a halt and turned to face him directly.

"My father was just abominably rude to you, yet you were thinking more about getting me out of the room than smacking him in the face?"

A cheeky smirk crossed the man's face.

"I wouldn't say that. I've worked long hours on the project for the last two weeks. I'm probably running on adrenaline rather than sleep. If I didn't like my job so much, I'm afraid your father would likely have blood streaming from his nose, right now."

Miranda placed her hand against her mouth and giggled into it, trying to silence her amusement at the situation. Her blood still boiled deeply within, but she was glad she wasn't in the boardroom listening to the boring conversation the other two men were no doubt engaged in.

Another young man poked his head around a doorway and frowned at them,

"I thought you were in the Braybrooke meeting?" the newcomer asked.

"Change of plans. I'll be looking at Miss Braybrooke's finances as well. Her father wants her to start planning for her future." The other man looked her up and down, and she was certain she saw him lick his lips.

"Lucky bastard," he muttered.

"That I am," Mr North added and opened a door for her. "By the way, Albert, can you arrange for a white tea with two sugars for Lord Braybrooke? I'd keep your head down when you go in there to deliver it, though. He's a bit of a tyrant."

"Shit." Albert groaned and disappeared. She and Mr North entered a massive room decked out in the finest Chippendale furniture.

"Please, take a seat. Is there anything I can get you to drink? I'm Peter, Pete for short, by the way"

"Miranda." She shook her head. "No thank you, on the drink, I'm good. I want to apologise again for my father's behaviour. I wish I could say it was his age, but he's been like it ever since I can remember."

"That must make things hard for you?" He motioned for her to take a seat. She did, and he sat opposite her at the big oak desk in the middle of the room.

"I've not known any different. He's always been that way with me. One of my earliest memories is of him shouting at me on the beach because I dropped the ice-cream out of my cone." Pete leaned forward on the desk at her words, his brows furrowed together with intense interest. "If it wasn't for a kind boy giving me his ice-cream that day, I would have gone without. You don't do that to a five-year-old year girl."

"Broadstairs," Pete announced with a massive grin on his face.

"I'm sorry? She placed her handbag down on the floor and stared at him. Her own brows knitting together in confusion this time.

"You had, let me think…. it was a long time ago….." He bit his lip in deep thought, and it slowly started to dawn on her who he was. What were the odds? It must have been millions if not billions to one. "I had a '99', but you had a chocolate ice-cream. I've always remembered how happy you were when I offered you my half-licked cone with a bite out of the top of the flake. I'm not sure your mum was overly impressed. I think she probably saw the germs I was sharing." He laughed, and she joined in.

"I can't believe it was you. How is it possible?"

"The luck of the gods, I think."

"I like the gods. You've grown up a bit since then." Miranda blushed when the words came out of her mouth. She hadn't meant to be so blunt.

"I can say the same about you," he teased her.

"Thank you again for giving me your ice-cream."

"It wasn't a problem."

"And I really am sorry my father won't let you be in on the meeting. I'm sure you've worked extremely hard to impress him."

"A little." Pete shrugged his shoulders, and she got the feeling he was downplaying the task he'd undertaken and the disappointment he was experiencing. "Your father spoke of a future husband. Are you in a relationship?"

She shook her head in the negative.

"No, but I have a feeling he's going to be lining up the potential candidates for me….no scrap that, for him to choose from soon."

"This is the eighties not the Victorian era. You can choose your own husband. If you even want one."

She slumped down into the chair and started to fiddle with a button on her dress.

"Do I look like I'm living in the eighties? I'm sixteen, seventeen in a few months, and I'm dressed like someone from the fifties. I'd kill to wear a shell suit like other people of my age, but I can only do that when hidden in the privacy of my own home, so nobody can see."

"Your father's a tyrant."

"He wants what's best for me, I guess."

The man opposite her raised a quizzical eyebrow. "Ok, he's a bit of a bully," she finally conceded.

"I've got an idea." Pete jumped to his feet and went across the room to check the door was shut properly.

"What are you doing?" she asked, her skin suddenly feeling a little clammy at the prospect of being shut away alone with a man who wasn't a relative of hers. Her father wouldn't like it.

Pete came back to the desk and opened one of the drawers. He pulled out a mini radio and plugged it into a socket underneath the desk. He flipped a switch and static filled the room. She instantly covered her ears against the loud noise.

"Sorry. Mr Barratt always untunes it after he's finished playing it because he thinks nobody'll know he's listening to modern music. Pointless, since we can all hear it in the next room because he's going a little deaf and has it up so loud." Pete's laugh was so infectious that she got to her feet and came around to his side of the desk with a giggle on her lips. He flipped his finger across the switch to retune the radio, and she watched, wondering what that finger would feel like playing with her body. What was it about this man that put her mind straight into the gutter? He found a station and the latest rock music blasted out from the speaker. He quickly turned it down a bit and held his hand out to her.

"Dance?"

"Please." She took his hand, and he pulled her into the hard lines of his body. He must do plenty of exercise because underneath the suit, it seemed, he had the body to show for it. The song changed to, 'You Give Love a Bad Name' by Bon Jovi, and they held hands while rocking out and singing almost but not quite at the top of their voices. She head banged wildly at the chorus, unravelling the neat bun on her head.

They were both laughing so much as one upbeat song followed another, and her side hurt from a possible pulled muscle. She was unsure whether it related to the laughing or the rumbustious dancing they were doing. The instantly recognisable opening guitar riff of 'When Doves Cry' by Prince played, and Pete pulled her into him, and that's how they stayed for the whole of her favourite song. Just the two of them caught-up together in the emotion of the words and the freeing experience he was giving her.

"That day at the beach, I said something to my father after you left." Pete reached for a stray strand of her hair and tucked it behind her ear.

"What?" she asked looking up into his deep blue eyes.

"I told him one day I'll marry you." She gasped. "It was a childish comment at the time but seeing you here today"–he pulled her tighter into his arms– "I'm thinking maybe I knew what fate had in store for us, even then."

The door handle rattled, and they pulled quickly apart from each other as Mr Barratt and her father strode into the room. Pete reached for the radio and turned it off.

"Here you are," her father grumbled. "We've been looking for you."

She tried to form sensible words to explain what they'd been doing, but her body felt like jelly, and her mind was a pool full of nothingness.

"I thought it best to keep Miss Braybrooke away from the main floor, Mr Barratt." –Pete stepped forward– "I know both Ian and Albert are around and the issues you have with them."

Mr Barratt nodded at him approvingly.

"Good idea."

"I hope you don't mind, we put the radio on and were looking over some of your financial books. Miranda was particularly interested in this one." He grabbed a book from a nearby shelf and handed it to her. She read the title.

"The theory of investment value." She smiled up at the two older gentlemen in the room. "It seems a riveting read."

"That it is," –Her father stepped forward and ripped the book from her hand– "but too high brow for you. Household husbandry would better suit your future."

He discarded the book on the shelf like a poisoned chalice filled with hopes and dreams she could never have, because she was a woman.

"I have another meeting at midday. Come, we need to depart."

Her heart sped up. She was going to have to leave Pete, and she had no way of contacting him again. If Mr Barratt fired him because of her father, there'd be no way she could find him again. Her palms started to sweat with the realisation this could be the last time she ever saw him.

"I'm coming," she responded to her father and picked up her handbag. Pete stood off to the side, his face marked with lines of worry and fear. He felt exactly the same. Something was happening between them –it had started all those years ago, on the beach, and fate had brought them back together again.

Her father turned away and stomped out of the door, calling her name over his shoulder. Mr Barratt followed close behind. Miranda took the short time she had left to grab a piece of paper from the bank owner's desk and scribble down her home address on it. She thrust it into Pete's hand, and as she turned to run out of the room, she called back to the man now staring down at her address, "If you're going to marry me, you'll have to date me first. Find a way."

FIVE

Pete

It had seemed like an ingenious way of getting to meet with Miranda, at the time. But as Pete waited for the chauffeur, Mr Pearson, to deliver her to the rendezvous point, he was starting to worry. What if the driver had informed her father of what was happening? Miranda would no doubt get into big trouble. They'd managed to speak a few times over the last week, since meeting again for the first time in more than ten years. She had one of those massive great big mobile phones, which were becoming all the rage amongst the elite, so he'd called her, when he could, from a phone booth down the road from his house. The chats were limited mainly to sharing basic getting to know each other facts: favourite things, food, drink, colours, TV shows. Snippets about their lives growing up and what their hopes and aspirations for the future were. He still couldn't believe she was the same girl he'd given his ice-cream to on the beach. Either it was fate intervening and bringing them together, or he'd been so good in another life he was being granted the best of luck in this one.

He tapped his foot impatiently and looked down the road for any sign of a car approaching. Nothing. The suburban street he was waiting on was deathly quiet, which was a rarity in the ever-expanding metropolitan city that London had become. She wasn't coming. The damned driver had shafted them, and Miranda would be prevented from going out in future or shipped away from him never to be seen again. His shoulders slumped, and he fell back against the wall behind him. He really liked Miranda. When she'd walked into the office, she'd appeared like a vision of angelic beauty. She was a goddess in her teal dress with sensible shoes, and her hair neatly pulled back to show the perfect features of her face: full lips that were very kissable, and bright eyes that hinted at an air of mischief lying beneath them. He'd learned about her love of music during their dancing episode. It matched his own. He felt the despondency flooding through his body.

A car horn beeped, and he looked up. It was the car he'd seen Miranda climb into when leaving the bank. He pushed off the wall and waved it down. The driver swerved into the curb and came to a halt directly in front of him. The back door opened, and Miranda jumped out. She was dressed in a pair of distressed faded jeans and a T-shirt, which stated she was 'living the dream'. He chuckled.

"Hi. I'm so sorry I'm late. My father left behind schedule to go to the airport, and then Mr Pearson got stuck in traffic on the way back to get me. It's the only time in his life my father has ever been late. Do you forgive me?" Miranda looked up at him with puppy dog eyes. Just that look was enough to make him forgive her anything. His cock shifted in his jeans, and he willed it to stay down. The last thing he needed was a raging erection.

"Forgiven." He stepped forward and took her hand. A cough came from behind them. He'd forgotten her driver.

"I'll call you when I'm ready for you to come and get me, if that's ok?" Miranda turned to her driver and willed him not to show her up. The desperation was written all over her face.

"Where are you going?" Mr Pearson ignored her and focused his attention on Peter.

"A TV show recording." Pete pulled tickets from his pocket and showed them to the enquiring driver. Miranda squealed when she saw the name of the show. Mr Pearson flinched.

"Top of the Pops. Seriously! Oh My God, you got us tickets."

Pete nodded. "Mr Barratt felt guilty that I'd worked so hard on your father's account but wasn't actually allowed to attend the meeting. He gave me a little bonus, and I bought the tickets with it."

"I've wanted to go on that show for so long. I watch it religiously. I can't believe it." Miranda let go of his hand and wrapped her arms around his neck and pressed a kiss to his lips. She must have realised what she was doing too late for she pulled back and looked guiltily at the floor while biting her lip.

"Sorry," she whispered.

"It's ok," he reassured her.

Mr Pearson coughed again, and Miranda took a step further away from Pete. "What about after?"

"After?" He cocked his head towards the driver.

"Do I collect her here or somewhere else?"

Pete looked over to Miranda.

"Here," she murmured, and Pete saw the satisfied smile spread over Mr Pearson's face.

Pete stepped forward

"I can assure you Miranda's safe, sir. I simply want to get to know her better."

"There's a pie and mash shop down the road. I'll go and get something to eat. You have your phone?" Miranda nodded and tapped her handbag. "Call me if you need me."

"I will. Thank you, Mr Pearson."

"Go have fun, you two. A part of me is jealous. I enjoy Top of the Pops as well."

The chauffeur jumped back in the car and disappeared down the street before they could respond.

"I can't believe you did this?"

"I know how much you love music, and I'm told Frankie Goes to Hollywood is performing tonight."

"NO!" Miranda screamed again. "Paul Rutherford's so cute."

"Hey!" he teased. "I thought you were here on a date with me not to lust over a pop star."

"I am. It's just…. You know."

He jabbed her lightly in the ribs. "I know. Come on, the show starts soon."

He took Miranda's hand and led her through to the entrance of the studio where he showed their tickets. They then stored Miranda's lightweight jacket and handbag with the concierge before entering the studios. Pete watched Miranda. She looked a lot older than her almost seventeen years. Her jeans were skin tight and accentuated the luscious curves of her hips and arse. Her T-shirt was fluorescent pink and tight around her breasts. Damn, she's hot. She turned to face him, and he couldn't help but smile at how her appearance, now, differed from the way she'd looked at the office the other day. The prim and proper Lord's daughter was gone. Her twinset and pearls replaced by a black rubber necklace, and the tight bun hairstyle now a vivacious backcombed creation with crimped sections throughout and pink streaks, matching her t-shirt.

"What?" She interrupted his thoughts. "Am I dressed wrong?"

He shook his head.

"No, you're beautiful. Perfect."

She blushed a little.

"You're going to embarrass me."

He leaned forward and pressed his lips to hers and they kissed for a second time that evening.

"Thank you for agreeing to come on this date with me."

He wrapped his arm around her waist and pulled her against him.

"Thank you for finding a way to make it happen."

Music started up around them, and the opening melody of the show blasted out from the speakers. It was recognisable all over the UK now, and the fact he was actually here, sent shivers down his spine. He'd grown up, as Miranda had, watching the show every Thursday evening. Just like her, he'd made a mix tape every Sunday evening of the music from the 'Top Forty' charts on the radio. It was what people of his age did. He'd done it in his youth, and he wasn't planning on stopping now he was an adult. Music would always be a love of his, and he was glad he'd found someone to share it with.

The voice of Steve Wright, the presenter, rang out around the studio as he announced the first act, 'The Bluebells'. Miranda squealed with delight, and they rushed forward with the rest of the crowd to dance. He made sure to keep her close to him for the rest of the evening, especially when Frankie Goes to Hollywood came on. The studio was busy because the show was one of the most popular on television. When the final act finished, an exhausted Miranda collapsed against him.

"I need something to drink. I don't think I've ever danced so much," she said breathlessly.

"There's a café down the road. Shall we go there?"

"Please."

They collected her coat and bag, and he made her check everything was still in it and nothing had been stolen. When satisfied, he placed his arm around her shoulder and led them out of the building.

"Thank you for bringing me here. It's the most fun I've had in my life. Boy, that sounds really sad." Her face deflated, and he wanted nothing more than to take the hurt away from her.

"Well, we'll have plenty more years of fun to experience together."

"You meant what you said about having a future together?"

"Hell yes. Fate, Miranda, has brought us back together, and I'm not letting you get away again."

He pushed open the door to a café, and they took two seats by the window. A waitress immediately appeared, and they ordered two coffees and two slices of their cake of the day–black forest gateaux. Pete dove his fork into the chocolate devilment and watched Miranda. The sadness hadn't lifted from her. Her eyes had dulled from those that had been glistening with excitement during the recording of the TV show.

"Talk to me," he encouraged. She looked up from where she was pushing a piece of the cake around her plate.

"I don't want to hurt you."

"Why would you?"

He reached out with his free hand and wrapped his fingers around hers resting on the table.

"Because of my father. I don't think my life is my own to decide what I'll do. I'm destined to be a trophy wife to fulfil my father's desire to further his family name. He doesn't want my uncle getting the title, and a female can't inherit it, so he'll manipulate me into marrying his man of choice."

"His choice not being a banker's assistant who's not even worthy of looking at his financial papers."

"Exactly."

Miranda placed her fork down on the table and pushed the uneaten cake away before letting go of his hand and standing.

"I should go. You've given me an experience I'll never forget, and I don't want to lead you on as a result."

She made to flee from the restaurant, but he was quicker and was on his feet and grabbed her hand in an instant. The coffee cups rattled at the sudden movement.

"Don't go," he rasped.

"Pete, please." Miranda turned back to face him. Tears filled her eyes. He didn't let go of her wrist but with his free hand wiped away a tear as it tumbled down her cheek.

"I won't let you walk out of my life. There may be hurt down the road, but that's relationships. They're hard work. I've learned from watching my own parents, but as long as we don't give up, we'll beat the doubters and any opposition."

"I can't ever hope to beat my father. Don't you see that? I've never once gone against him in my life."

"But you have."

"What?" Miranda relaxed a little, and he loosened the firm grip he had on her wrist but still kept contact with her skin.

"You're defying him now. You're taking your life into your own hands and making decisions for yourself. If you'd asked him for permission to come on a date with me, what would he have said?"

"No."

"Exactly."

"That's different."

"It's not." He shook his head at her.

"I won't be able to continue telling lies to him. What if I fall in love with you? It's going to hurt so badly when I have to walk away, because I know he won't let me be with you?"

"Then don't let him win. Your father's just that, Miranda, simply your father. We don't live in the dark ages. This is the eighties, and we're free to make our own decisions. Don't let him dictate your future. If you want a career, go for it. You want to be a doctor, go to university because from what I know about you, you're intelligent enough to pass the exams. But, if you want to be a lady of leisure and live off your husband, I'll work as damn hard as I can to make sure I can provide you with that sort of life. You've just got to have the guts to say no to your father. If he's half the man he should be, then he'll support any decisions you make. If not, he'll chuck you out, but would it be such a loss? Are you so engrained into the life-style you were brought up in that you can't see beyond it and consider another?"

"That's not fair. I'm not in love with the privilege I have, but it's all I've ever known. I wouldn't know the first thing about surviving on my own."

"But that's it. You don't have to."

He led her back to the table and forced her to sit back down.

"Even if you didn't want a relationship with me, I think I've come into your life for a reason. It's the same principle as with the ice-cream. What your father has taken away from you, I can give back. I can help you find a life when now, as you say, you have none. Walk away from this opportunity, Miranda, if it's what you truly want to do, but if it isn't, then I suggest you eat your cake."

Pete watched his table partner intently while he resumed his own seat and started eating again. She looked between the door and the cake, back to the door and then the cake again. Eventually, she shut her eyes and letting out a long sigh, she opened her sapphire orbs, picked up the fork, and took a mouthful of cake.

"It's time to live, to love, to experience everything...together."

SIX

It had been a month since she'd met Pete for a second time after the ice-cream incident of their youth. Her summer would be over in a month and a half, and she'd be returning to her boarding school in a few weeks to continue her education. It had been a fight with her father to allow her to do so, but eventually, she'd bargained another two years for herself. Two years in which, hopefully, she could figure out some way of getting her father to allow her to live the life she wanted and not the one he would dictate. Her time with Pete was precious. They spent most of it sitting around in her bedroom talking, after he'd snuck in through the window, because she wasn't always able to get away. Mr Pearson was fantastic when they did manage to meet for dates. The chauffeur developed a fondness for Pete, and the two men often spent time talking together during the rendezvous. Pete arranged for them to go roller skating, and to see Ghostbusters at the cinema. He was even able to organise a trip back to Broadstairs when her father was away for a few days. He spent one evening holding her hair back as she emptied the contents of her stomach down a toilet while suffering from a bug. Miranda suspected her mother knew she was seeing someone but kept it to herself, which Miranda was grateful for. Her mother was a wonderful woman, but she didn't want her to have to lie to her father, because it would only cause trouble for her mother. Her parent's relationship had died years ago. Miranda's, however, was just starting. The physical side of her liaison with Pete was becoming rather hot and heavy. They'd started to fool around a lot, but it hadn't gone any further than him getting her off with his fingers. She'd felt guilty and offered to return the favour, but he'd refused because he didn't trust himself to be around her with his cock out. She'd felt it during their make out sessions and knew it was big and pretty much always hard. It must have been uncomfortable for him in that condition. She'd gone to bed the last time he'd left her, imagining him stroking himself off to thoughts of her. It was a glorious vision, and one that, before long, had her coming with her hand down her PJ bottoms. Her maid had spoken to her about sex a few years ago, but she'd already known what it was all about from the girls at her school. Several of them had long term boyfriends and were sexually active with them. She'd not really been interested in it because sex meant men, and men just caused trouble. Although Pete was nothing like that. She knew he worshipped her, and she was at the point in their relationship where she knew she no longer wanted a life that didn't have him in it. She saw herself married to him with a little boy and girl running around their feet. That was the future she wanted, not the one her father would force upon her. She needed to speak to Pete about it because she didn't want to hide their relationship any longer. She wanted it out in the open. It would be hard to arrange to meet up when she was back at school in Cambridge, so she wanted to do whatever she could to make sure it was possible to see him every weekend.

The recognisable tap to the window had her heartbeat fluttering, and she leapt from the bed and was across the room and unfastening the window in two seconds.

"Hi." Pete smirked back at her from the tree branch he was perched on. He had a bag in his hand, and she took it from him, so he could swing himself through the open window.

He pulled her instantly into his arms, and they locked lips in a passionate kiss.

"Damn, I've missed you." It had been only two days since they'd last met, but Pete's enthusiasm for her, had her panties instantly wet. "I was going out of my mind."

"You're such a dork, sometimes." She patted his chest and opened the bag to look at what was inside. "Pick and mix." She excitedly thrust her hand into the bag and pulled out a sugar-coated cola bottle. "My favourite."

"I thought we could watch a movie with some snacks."

"I like that idea." She padded over to the TV she had in her room and switched it over to the VHS player. "I've only really got romance films, though?"

"That's ok. I brought this." He pulled a video called Octopussy out of his pocket. "It's a spy film. Yes or No?" He waggled the video in front of him with a puppy dog look on his face.

"I'm guessing you are a James Bond fan."

"A little. I'd make a good spy, don't you think?"

She threw her head back and laughed so hard her sides started to hurt. When she finally calmed down and looked at Pete, he had a wounded look on his face.

"I'm sorry. I didn't mean…" She started to laugh again.

"Didn't mean what?" His eye's darkened, and the intense look on his face sent shivers down her spine. Her body was reacting in all sorts of strange ways again. She wanted him. She wanted him moving inside her and making love to her. She knew in that moment, watching his face glow with the affection he had for her, that she was ready.

"Make love to me," abruptly came from her lips before she registered what she was saying.

Pete's eyes went wide with shock.

"Ww…what?" he stuttered.

"I want you fully. Make me yours."

"Miranda."

"Please." She stepped up and placed her hands on his chest. The desperation in her voice was evident.

"I.. I..." Pete tried desperately to find words to say no to her. She brought her finger to his lips to silence him from saying something she didn't want to hear.

"Don't reject me, please. I've never wanted something more than I want you, right now. I know you're my everything. My life, my future, my love..."

Her last word hung thickly in the air between them.

"You love me?"

"Yes. I've loved you since you gave me your ice-cream. You were right, fate has decreed we're destined for each other, and I don't want to wait anymore. I want to shout from the rooftops you're mine. I want you as much as you want me but are too scared to admit."

Pete took a long shuddering breath and looked down at the ground. Had she read the situation wrong? Did he not want her? Was he just playing with her? She took a step backwards and held her hands over her heart. It felt like it was breaking.

"No." Her voice broke on the word, but she couldn't get any more words out because Pete was on her. His mouth attached to hers, and his tongue slid in-between her lips, tasting her and taking away all the negative thoughts from her mind. He pulled back but never let go of her.

"I love you. I've wanted you forever. I've been so scared of hurting you and of you not being ready. I've known all along that you're mine. Your body, mind, and soul are joined with mine, and we'll never be apart."

He scooped her into his arms and laid her down onto the bed. His mouth found hers again, kissing and tasting her delicate flesh as if it was one of the sweets in the pick and mix bag. His hands skimmed over her body, and all her nerve endings were ignited with sensations she'd never felt before.

This was it –this was her moment.

Pete opened the zipper of the jeans she was wearing, sliding his fingers inside to reach her pussy. She was soaked and ready for him. She always was when he was around. He pushed a finger inside her and a groan escaped her mouth, leaving the man touching her body in no doubt as to her acceptance of him. He pushed another finger inside. At the same time, his thumb found her clit and started to circle it. She was breathless for him already. Her orgasm was approaching so rapidly she wanted it to crash into her but at the same time she never wanted this feeling to be over.

"Harder," she groaned, and Pete lightly bit her lip. "Please...." Where the begging was coming from, she had no idea. She'd never begged for anything in her life. She'd just accepted she wouldn't be given anything and bemoaned her situation in silence, but this was different. With the man who would soon be her bedded lover, she wanted to beg and plead and cry and scream and worship him for the way he made her feel.

Her hands came to her jeans, and she tried desperately to push them down her thighs to give him better access to the treasure between her legs.

"No," he ordered, and she froze. "I'll undress you. It's my job." The masterful way in which he spoke had her writhing further on the bed with need.

Pete pulled her jeans down her legs and helped her sit up, so he could remove her t-shirt. He pulled his own t-shirt over his head and allowed her a few moments to take in his muscular stomach, broad shoulders, and tattoo. Holy Shit! He had a tattoo, and she didn't know. He brought his lips back to hers, but she pushed him away.

"What?" He looked confused and a little scared she was changing her mind.

"Tattoo," she reassured, and he looked down to his left side of his chest where the Polynesian tattoo covered it and spread up to his right shoulder. "Beautiful." She felt like she was a dribbling mess, but she was so in awe of the intricate design.

"You like?" he asked, and she nodded, having lost the ability to form comprehensible words. "I had it done for my eighteenth birthday. My mum cried, but my dad was impressed. I want to get it all over my shoulder and down my arm one day, but I need to be careful. Tattoos don't exactly go down too well in the banking industry. Best to make sure it's kept hidden at all times." He stroked his hand over the design.

"Did it hurt?"

"A little but nothing I couldn't handle."

"It's really beautiful."

"Thank you." His eyes sparkled with devilment while he looked at her like she was lunch. It was a menu she hoped he would enjoy. "Enough talking......more clothes removing."

Miranda looked down and realised she was having a conversation with Pete in just her bra and knickers. A sudden bout of self-consciousness hit her, and she tried to cover herself up, but Pete shook his head.

"No, you're mine to explore, now. Mine to devour."

She took his hand and led him towards the bed. Slowly, she placed her hands at the clasp of her bra but remembered at the last second he'd said her clothes were his to remove. She looked at him for permission to remove it, and he nodded his approval, so she undid the bra and lowered it to the cradle of her arms. Summoning up as much of her inner sex goddess as she could, she let go of the gossamer fabric and allowed it to fall to the floor. Her perky tits, not too big and not too small she thought, were bared to the man standing in front of her, and judging by the lascivious look on his face, he liked what he saw.

"Panties." He ordered her to remove them with a flick of his head. She placed her hand in the elastic banding, which held them up, and lowered them down her svelte legs before standing up and displaying her naked body to him. She was natural down below. Some people, in a decade that was starting to see medical enhancements and beauty procedures explode, liked to have all the hair removed, but she wasn't keen on having that area so exposed. Pete reached for his own jeans and started to palm his cock through the rigid fabric.

"I knew this would be how you looked. Innocent and pure with a body built for sin."

He backed her up further, so she fell onto the bed with her legs parted and inner most parts on display for him.

"Mine." The word escaped from his mouth and seemed to come as shock to both of them.

"Yours," she repeated, stroking her finger down the length of her slit to demonstrate just how much she was his.

Pete undid the buckle of his jeans and slid them down his muscled thighs. She already knew he liked to go to the gym a couple of nights a week. He'd told her he was teased for being a wimpy kid at one stage, but then he'd found the gym and hadn't looked back. The muscle certainly looked good on him. His boxer briefs followed suit, and she gasped when his erect cock sprung free from its confines. She'd not seen one this close before. Ok, the girls at her school had shared pictures from porn magazines, but she'd never had a real-life one in front of her. It was strange but stunning at the same time. Its rigidity caused it to reach up to his belly button. In fact, his length and width was more impressive than some of the photos she'd seen. She suddenly felt a little self-conscious. This would be her first time, and something that size would have to hurt.

Pete came over to the bed, settling between her thighs with his mouth close to the cleft between her legs, his tongue came out and licked up her slit. Her head fell back as her nerve ends danced with delight. His tongue swirled around her clit, applying pressure and alternating between fast and slow. It drove her to the edge of climax, and then he slowed it all down again. He pushed a finger inside of her, following it with another. Both stretched out to ready her for his cock. Her head started to swim with all the sensations flooding her body –surreal and sensual, crazy and vibrant, all at the same time. She was swimming and drowning in happiness.

Pete pulled away from her and turned back to his trousers.

"What is it?"

"Condom."

"I'm on the pill. Bad periods when I was younger."

"I've never been so happy to hear that."

Pete came back over to her and settled his cock at her entrance. Miranda took in a deep breath and waited for him to push inside her. Instead of wondering what it was going to feel like for her, she imagined what he would be aware of in the intimacy of the coupling. But then a thought popped into her head –this was her first time but was it his?

"Wait." She stopped him as his hips drew back. He groaned but halted.

"What? Are you ok?" His eyebrows furrowed together, and he searched her face for signs of distress. She composed her features, though, to make sure none of her concerns showed at the thought she was given him her greatest gift, and this might not be his first time.

"Are you a virgin?" she blurted out.

"What?" he questioned with dumbfounded shock.

"Have you done this before?"

"I'm clean," he told her, and she recollected a disease her teachers had taught her about in sex education, which you caught during intercourse.

"That's not what I meant. You know, this is my first time. We've discussed it before, but I've never asked –will this be yours?"

Pete shut his eyes.

"As much as I want to play the big man and say I'm a pro at this sex thing, it's my first time also. I'm currently praying and pleading in my head that the second I put my cock inside you I'm able to make you feel something. I'm reciting banking terms in my head just to stop from coming too soon."

She leaned forward and brought his lips against hers.

"Account holder...compound interest...debt-to-income ratio," she teased.

"Fuck! When you say it, it's the sexiest thing I've ever heard."

Pete looked down at his cock sitting just outside her entrance and then back at her. He was asking for permission.

"Yes," she whispered, and he thrust slowly in until he was fully seated to his hilt.

She felt the barrier to her virginity break and, despite the momentary pain, rejoiced at the fact they were finally as one. He gave her a moment to settle to the feeling of him, and she needed it for the overwhelming sense of fullness was threatening to engulf her in a powerful climax. Pete pulled his hips back and speared back into her. The sounds of their slick bodies moving together filled the room. Her soft moans of delight and his grunts of need echoed in her mind. It was a sound that would stay with her forever. Her first time and it was beautiful because it was with the man she would devote the rest of her life to loving.

Pete moved faster and faster, and the sensations inside her coiled tighter than a spring. Every part of her tingled with the awareness of her pleasure. A fire surged through her body and straight to the bunch of nerves between her thighs.

"Come," he ordered, and she complied. Her body convulsed against the powerful climax. Pete stilled, and his cock pulsed his own release deep into her body. The warm spurts mixing with her own essence to create a unity from the pleasures they'd taken.

When the stars stopped flying around her head, she registered Pete had collapsed onto the bed beside her. He'd withdrawn from her, and her tender flesh ached pleasantly.

"Wait here." He kissed the tip of her nose and rolled off the bed. She watched his pert backside as he strode confidently, but with a hint of exhaustion, into her ensuite bathroom. There was a rustling, and then she heard the turning on of taps followed by the sound of running water. That ceased, and he reappeared with a damp towel. He pressed it to her pussy, while she lay collapsed like a beached whale on the bed. Her legs were still there, but she was incapable of feeling them just yet. He cleaned her up and pulled the covers down, so she could nestle into her bed. He looked towards the door. She'd had a lock on it since she turned fifteen. It was something her mother had insisted on for her although she wasn't sure why. She should have thought about it before they'd had sex, but she'd been so caught in the moment she'd forgotten. She nodded at him to lock it. He obliged and came back into the bed next to her.

"You may need to take some paracetamol tomorrow because you'll probably feel sore. As much as I want to do that again and again tonight, we have a lifetime ahead, and I'm not going to damage you on the first night." A naughty grin spread across his face, and he pulled her into his arms.

"Stay," she begged.

"Until you fall asleep."

"I wish you could be here when I wake up." Her eyelids fluttered shut as exhaustion took over her body.

"I know. It won't always be this way." Pete kissed the top of her head, and she snuggled further into the warmth of his skin.

"I want to tell my father about us," she murmured half awake and half asleep. Before the darkness claimed her, she was sure she heard him reply.

"Not yet. I don't think I'll survive losing you."

SEVEN

Miranda

Miranda was dreading returning to Cambridge for her studies. She'd wanted to look at advancing further in English Literature and Art, but her father had insisted she do Economics and Mathematics, instead. She was good at those subjects, but they weren't her favourites. She would have no choice, though, if she hoped to avoid talk of her being married off to further her father's future ambitions. He'd mentioned it a few more times over the summer holidays and had even taken her to a social function where she's been introduced to several different men. She'd hated being there the entire time. None of the men spoke to her the way Pete did. She knew she'd lost her heart to the man she'd given her virginity to. With his commitments to his new job, and her father's ability to watch her like a hawk even though he had little interest in her, they had spent as much time as possible together over the summer.

One of the most exhilarating times they'd spent together was when Pete had showed her the new Ford Cortina he'd bought with his savings. It would enable him to drive up to meet her in Cambridge for weekends when she was away studying. They'd driven out to Broadstairs and had christened the back seat of the car numerous times before they returned home. She loved the car and had named it 'Cindy'. Pete hadn't been overly impressed with the name. He felt his car was more masculine than feminine and should have a boy's name, but she was adamant the car was a girl. She asserted it was the only other female that he would be allowed to ride, ever.

Miranda looked down at her watch. Pete was late. It was a Saturday morning, and the last before she had to return to college tomorrow. They were going to spend the day together. She'd not been feeling at all well the last few days. A stomach bug had twisted her stomach and left her feeling exhausted and dizzy, but she wanted to enjoy the carefree time she had left. Her father had been away for the last week but was due to return later in the evening, so he could spend 'time' with her before she left. She wasn't sure why he bothered. He hadn't spent any time with her in the last sixteen years, so one night wouldn't make any difference. She'd rather spend the night with Pete buried deeply inside her. She giggled and covered her amusement with a hand over her mouth. She was turning into a bit of a sex fiend. She couldn't get enough.

A rap came from the window, and she jumped off her bed and sped across her room to open it.

"Hey, beautiful." Pete smirked with a playful raise of his eyebrow.

"Hey yourself." She licked her lips in anticipation of him finally climbing through the window and ravaging her. She'd been fantasying about it since she woke up this morning.

"How are you feeling?" Pete asked and gently brought her into his arms, kissing her slowly. His tongue darted out and ran across the seam of her lips before delving in, tangling with hers in a passionate greeting.

"A lot better. I haven't been sick so far today, but breakfast was a boring affair of a slice of plain toast because I couldn't really stomach anything else."

"Are you sure you shouldn't see a doctor?" Pete frowned, and she pressed her lips against his, again, to reassure him she was fine and all that afflicted her was a stomach bug.

"I'm fine. I promise. It's probably nerves at having to go back to school. I don't want to leave you, I'm having so much fun." She pouted and pulled him to sit with her on the bed.

"If it continues, you have to promise me you'll go to the doctor straight away."

"I promise." She leaned in to kiss him and then pulled back with a smile. "So, what are we doing today? Are we going out in Cindy?"

Pete groaned.

"I'm never going to be able to think of my car as anything but Cindy, now. You've damaged me." He ran his hand through his hair. The top part was getting a little long since he chose to spend all his free time with her rather than at a barber.

"Cindy is beautiful. It's a perfect name for your car."

He shook his head.

"Come on." Pete stood and held his hand out to her. She took it, and he led her back to the window and down the tree that he'd climbed up to reach her bedroom. Mr Pearson appeared from his workshop, overlooking her room and nodded at them. Pete waved back.

The chauffeur came over to them.

"I'm collecting your father at five pm. Make sure you're back and ready for dinner. He'll want it straight away as he has another meeting at eight pm."

She huffed. So much for spending the last evening with her father. Three hours was all she got. Most of that would be spent sitting in silence, eating a meal that no doubt would be his favourite and not hers, regardless of what her mother had promised. Lady Braybrooke was overridden at every stage of her endeavours to make her daughter's life better.

"I'll make sure she's back well before five." Pete pulled her hand up to his chest and held it by his heart. Mr Pearson nodded his acceptance.

"Drive carefully," the chauffeur warned.

"It's ok. We aren't going far. I've got some roller skates in the car, and we're going to go to the local park and have some fun."

"Now, I'm more worried"–Mr Pearson shuddered– "those things are death traps. Humans weren't intended to have wheels attached to their feet. No. Solid ground is best for me. If I want to do some spinning, I'll grab myself a dolly bird and head to the ballroom for a spot of foxtrotting." Miranda tried not to laugh when Mr Pearson held his arms up in a perfect hold position and wiggled off back to his workshop in a series of foxtrot promenade steps, mixed in with a couple of quickstep chassés

"He's insane." Pete chuckled quietly while leading her to his car, which he'd hidden off her father's land in the forest area surrounding the grounds.

"He is, but I wouldn't change him for anything. I miss him when I'm away from Braybrooke Hall. It's boring not having anyone to make me laugh." She went quiet and shuffled her feet on the summer sun-dried earth."

"Are you really nervous about going back?"

Pete leaned her against the car and stroked his hand down her cheek.

"I'm going to miss you. There's a big part of me that doesn't want to go. I want to stay locked here in this moment, but I know if I stay here, my father will forge ahead with his plans for my future. I will lose all control over what I want. I need to go back to school and get some qualifications, which will hold me in good stead when I walk away from here."

"It will be tight, but I can support you, if you want to walk away now."

She shook her head.

"No. I need to do this for myself as well. I don't want to be the stay at home woman. I want to do something with my life."

"You're doing something just by taking a chance. There are so many people out there who don't even do that." He brought himself closer to her and pinned her tenderly against the car.

"I want to be able to turn around and tell him I don't need him. That I've found my own way in life, and he needs to accept it. I've dreamt so many times of how I would do it, but I know the reality won't be anything like the fantasy."

She inhaled deeply and wiped away the tears that were forming in her eyes. She was so emotional lately. It was the thought of all the change.

"You'll try, won't you?" she uttered almost silently.

"Try?" Pete questioned.

"Us. Try to continue what we have. Try to come and see me?"

Pete pulled her closer into his arms and nestled her head against his heart.

"Miranda. I'll be with you whenever I can. I would walk away from everything here in London and find a job in Cambridge tomorrow if you gave me the word. I've told you. This is fate. You're mine. We may be kept apart for a little while longer, but we've found each other twice now, we can't be separated. I'll wait for you. I'll fight for you. I'll be yours, forever. This…" –he moved her back and placed his hand over his heart– "beats only for you. I want you. I love you. Never doubt what's in here."

"I love you." she whimpered back at him. "Damn." She looked up at the sky and silently cursed the fact she was all over the place today. "I'm a wreck. I'm sorry."

"Never apologise. I'll call you on that brick of a phone everyday if I can't get to

Cambridge to see you. I'll be there every weekend without fail. Say the word, and I'll drop everything. I was going to do this later, but….."

Pete let go of her and dropped to his knee. He reached inside his jacket pocket and pulled out a small box. He opened it to reveal an engagement ring. She gasped and started to shake all over. Was this a dream? Was it really happening?

"It's not a proper diamond, yet, but it will be in the future. The car kind of wiped me out, but I needed it to get to see you. Miranda Braybrooke, I first set eyes on you eleven years ago, and I've not wanted anyone else since. Will you marry me?"

Tears now streamed down her cheeks. Words tried to form in her mouth to answer him, but the emotions overwhelming her prevented anything that would sound remotely intelligent from coming out. Instead, she nodded her head, and then as common-sense came flooding back to her she cried,

"Yes, yes, yes." Pete pushed the ring onto her finger, and then standing back up, he brought her into his arms and twirled her around while kissing her.

"I love you!" he shouted.

"I love you, too," she repeated after him, and he sat her down on the ground. Bile suddenly flooded into her mouth, and her head started to spin violently. Before she knew what was happening, the ground was coming up to meet her, and her world turned black.

EIGHT

Miranda

"Miranda?" The familiar gentle feminine voice pulled her back from the blackness. "Miranda, can you hear me?"

"Miranda?" That was Pete's voice, and it was laced with fear and trepidation. "We need to call a doctor?"

Her eyes sprang open. If they did, her father would be told she was unwell and that would lead to so many questions and the possible discovery of her relationship with the man currently holding her hand.

"Mum?" The form of the other voice in the room stood over her, holding a cold compress to her forehead.

"It's alright, my darling. You fainted, and Mr North brought you back." She looked around and realised she was lying on her own bed in her bedroom. "He said you hadn't been well. Why didn't you tell me? I knew you weren't eating as much as normal and seemed so tired." Her mother pulled the compress away from her forehead and held the back of her hand to Miranda's cheeks. You aren't hot, but you still look a little flushed. When was the last time you were sick?"

"Yesterday," she answered, and Pete squeezed her hand tighter.

"Have you eaten today?" Her mother continued her questioning.

"I had a slice of toast a few hours ago."

"It could be the lack of food from previous days." Her mother's complexion turned paler. "I need to ask you some questions before we decide whether we need to call the doctor or not." Miranda watched as her mother stood away from the bed. It was then she noticed Mr Pearson stood in the room as well. Lines of worry etched onto his face.

"Mr North, it might be better if you let me have a few moments with my daughter."

Miranda shook her head fervently and held tighter to Pete's hand. She didn't want him going anywhere.

"It would seem she wishes me to stay with her if that is alright, Lady Braybrooke?"

Her mother lowered her head in acceptance and went over to Mr Pearson and whispered something into his ear. His eyes went wide, and he scurried from the room.

"Mother?" Miranda exclaimed. Her own feeling of trepidation rising with each passing moment.

"Sorry, darling." Her mother came back to the bed and took her other hand. "How long has your relationship with Mr North been going on? I see the ring on your finger." Her mother's head flicked to where the engagement ring was glistening on her left hand.

"Since June."

"Not long."

"We're soulmates, Lady Braybrooke," Pete interjected.

"I see it in the worry showing on your face, Mr North. Please don't fear my reaction on that score. I'm not my husband. I suspected my daughter was seeing someone. You should have told me, darling."

"I'm sorry, Mother. I didn't want to put you in a position where you would need to lie to father."

"I can handle him myself." Her mother stumbled over the words and ran a finger over the back of Miranda's hand. "Is your relationship physical? Erm...intimate."

"Sexual?" Pete offered, and Miranda felt her cheeks flush bright red.

"Yes." Her mother turned a pinker shade herself. Miranda had never learned about relationships from her parents. It wasn't the done thing amongst the upper classes. Not when school could provide the full details and not just the brief outline an embarrassed person would.

"Yes. Our relationship is sexual and has been for a few months, now."

Miranda's stomach lurched again. She let go of both hands holding hers and brought her hands up to her mouth as the knowledge of what could be wrong with her dawned. She frantically tried to remember when her last period had been but kept coming back to the same answer: when she'd finished school for the summer. She hadn't had one since then.

"Do you need the sick bowl?" Pete held up a bucket. She could tell by the look on his face he was more concerned about her vomiting again than contemplating the reason behind her current bout of sickness.

Mr Pearson chose that moment to rush back into the room with a box under his arm. He handed it to her mother, and Miranda knew instantly what it was. Her mother twisted the box around in her hand and checked a date on it.

"Still in date."

"No," Miranda lamented.

"Miranda?" Pete pulled her closely. "What is it?"

"You need to take it, my darling. We need to be certain before we tell him."

"No. He can't know. He can't know, ever."

"What?" Pete grabbed the box out of her mother's hand in frustration. His face went white as a sheet as he realised he held a pregnancy test in his hand. "You're on the pill, though? We didn't use a condom."

"You had the stomach bug just after you returned from school. If you'd vomited the pill, then you could have lost protection."

Miranda felt her head starting to spin again with everything she was trying to take in.

Pete dropped the test on the bed and pulled her closer.

"It's ok. We just got engaged. I wasn't expecting a baby straight away, but if the test is positive, then we'll just be a family sooner rather than later."

"I'm not seventeen, yet," she mumbled almost incoherently.

"Doesn't matter," Pete reassured her.

"You need to take the test, my darling," her mother urged, again.

Miranda looked to where Mr Pearson stood on the balls of his feet. His hands were clasped together in front of him. He looked older than she thought he'd ever looked before. She'd done that to him. He adored her more than her father ever would, and her situation was causing him worry.

She picked the test up and slid from the bed. Pete helped her walk on wobbly legs to the bathroom. He made to enter with her, but she pushed him away.

"We do this together. I'm staying with you."

"But I've got to...." she whispered and looked towards her mother.

"Pee into a bottle. I know. Still going nowhere. When we're living together, finally, we'll have no shut doors between us."

"Ok."

They both entered the bathroom, and Pete shut the door behind them. He took the box from her hand, opened it up, and handed her the container.

"It says you need to wee into this." He pointed to the contraption in her hand. "Then, we have to wait."

"Will you at least turn around while I do the first bit? It feels strange."

He nodded and turned his back to her. Miranda placed the container on the sink and pulled down her jeans and panties. She retrieved the container and placed it under her while hovering over the toilet. She did her business and placed the container back on the sink while she flushed the toilet. She followed the instructions on the test packaging and then washed her hands.

Pete turned around when he heard the toilet go and brought her into his arms. Her mind was reeling. She wasn't sure how long she'd been unconsciousness, so time was a bit fluffy, but no more than half an hour ago they had been discussing a future that was nothing like this. If she were pregnant, she wouldn't be able to go back to school. It wouldn't change her plans to marry Pete, however, it would mean it'd probably happen a bit earlier than they'd expected. She and Pete could have created a small human, and it may be growing inside her. The thought warmed her, and she slid a hand across her belly to rest it there. Pete brought his to rest on hers.

"I'm not going anywhere, no matter what that says."

"I know." She leaned back into him, and he kissed her neck. "We should go back outside. My mother will want to know straight away. She will need to prepare for what we'll tell my father."

"She won't have to tell him anything. I will." Pete picked up the test from the sink, and she winced a little. He was touching the test containing her pee, but it didn't seem to bother him in the slightest.

When enough time had passed, he held the test up and looked at it and then to the instructions. He exhaled deeply and handed it to her. She didn't need the instructions, though, to tell from the result staring back at her: she was pregnant.

NINE

Pete

Pete slipped out of the room and left Miranda sobbing into her mother's lap from the shock and fear of what would happen next. Her father's impending reaction weighed heavily on them all. He needed a few minutes to collect his thoughts. He was going to be a father and a lot sooner than he thought it would happen. Strangely, though, he wasn't scared. He knew Miranda would make a perfect mother. He'd try his hardest to be a great father, and if he followed his own father's example, then he'd do alright. The door closed behind him, and Mr Pearson filled the corridor.

"Is this where you hit me for getting her into trouble?" he asked.

"It takes two to tango. I can see you love that girl and won't be going anywhere."

"I'm not. Even on my death bed, she'll be my first, last, and only thought."

"You know her father's going to try and implement the death bit." Mr Pearson raised a telling eyebrow at him.

"I don't doubt it at all. I just have to hope I made so little of an impression on him at the bank that he forgets I'm just a trainee."

"That, or you discover in the next few hours you're some rich and titled gentleman. That would probably be the best thing you could do."

"Yes. But I don't think it's going to happen. Ken and Elise North aren't really the gentry type. Not when my father was born in the East End."

"I was hoping it would be at least Kensington way."

"Sorry."

Pete shrugged his shoulders.

"I wish I could give you some indication on how Lord Braybrooke is going to take the news, but I've got no idea. He likes to play games and to win them, having only a daughter is the biggest loss to him. She's a pawn in his aspirations. He won't take this lying down. You need to be ready to fight for her and the child. It'll get hard, but you'll have my support as much as I can give."

"Thank you. Your vote of confidence means a lot. I won't let her down."

Mr Pearson held his hand out. Pete took it and shook it. The older man then ran his hand over his brow. "It's time for me to go and get him. Prepare what you're going to say. I'll be back in half an hour."

"Good luck with that. Try and keep him in a good mood."

Mr Pearson let out a belly laugh.

"I don't think good mood and Lord Braybrooke have ever been used in the same sentence before. You are a great joker."

Pete gulped.

Mr Pearson reached into his large pocket and pulled out a mobile phone.

"I was going to give this to you when she went back to school, but I think you need it now." He handed him the phone. "It's a spare. He never looks at the bills anyway, so you've got it if you need to call her and can't be with her. Her father never lets her leave her phone behind."

Pete took the phone and looked down at it in shock and confusion.

"You don't have to."

"Take it. I really need to go." The chauffeur hurried down the corridor. Pete looked at the phone in his hand. The urgency he felt in his bones to speak to one particular person overruled his need to return to Miranda. He punched the numbers he'd memorised into the device and pressed call. The phone crackled into life, and the digital ringtones echoed into his ear.

"Hello?" His mother's voice came on the other end, and he sighed in relief. It worked.

"Hi, Mum."

"Pete. Are you ok? I thought you were doing extra work all day?" He heard the clatter of dishes in the background, and he knew his mother was cooking up a feast again for their dinner. Saturday night was always fish and chips night, followed by one of her cakes covered in glazed fruits.

"Is Dad there?"

"Of course. I think he's checking the football scores. Hang on." The phone went muffled, and he heard his mother shouting out 'Ken'. There was more rustling, and after a few minutes, his father's voice came on the other end of the line.

"Hey, kiddo. You ok?" Despite the fact he was eighteen, his father still called him kiddo. It was a nickname that'd always stuck.

"Hi, Dad. Do you remember the summer we went to Broadstairs and I gave that little girl my ice-cream after she lost hers?"

"Your first love. How can I forget?" His father laughed.

"I've asked her to marry me."

"What?" His father sounded confused, but given he probably wasn't making much sense, Pete wasn't surprised. He'd told his parents he'd met someone but nothing else.

"I found her again. She's the girl I've been dating. Dad, we had an accident. She's pregnant."

He heard his mother gasp and surmised she must have been listening into the conversation as well.

"Well it's too late for me to tell you to be careful." There was a hint of anger in his father's voice, but Pete knew he was trying to mask it because of the love and support he always got from his parents. "How is she?"

"Feeling sick. She fainted. Dad, we may need somewhere to stay. Her father, he's not a good man. He's nobility and treats her like dirt. We're going to tell him later, but I think he may abandon her. I love her, Dad, and I want to be with her forever."

The line went silent for a few moments. His father was thinking.

"Dad?"

"Elsie, go change the sheets on Pete's bed. I'll start tidying up his room. We'll make some space in the wardrobe for her to put her stuff in. It'll be alright son. You love her. That's all you'll need."

"Thank you." He felt the lump forming in his throat. "I better get back to her."

"We'll be here when you come home."

Pete finished the call and put the phone away. He took a few more moments to compose himself and re-entered Miranda's bedroom. She was standing in front of a full-length mirror looking at her sideways reflection.

"I think I can see a little bump already." Miranda stroked her completely flat belly. Her mother smirked at him and mouthed,

"Is everything alright?"

He nodded at her and went over to Miranda.

"Mr Pearson has gone to get your father. I think you should pack a little bag of essentials just in case."

Miranda's eye's widened, and she looked over at her mother who nodded in agreement.

"Nobody knows what his reaction will be. All we can do is wait."

It was the longest half an hour of Pete's life. Numerous different outcomes had run through his head by the time the wheels of the returning car kicked up the gravel on the driveway. Lord Braybrooke's stern voice came up the stairs in a bellow for his wife and child to join him for dinner. Augusta got to her feet and straightened the long dress she was wearing. The matching pearl earrings looked far too big for her ears, but Pete knew it was the fashion. Miranda had gone so white she looked like a ghost.

"I think I might be sick." She held her hands over her mouth, and Pete rushed to her side with the bucket again. She dry heaved over it a few times before deciding she'd be alright

Lord Braybrooke's voice came up the stairs again, this time with more anger in it.

"We need to go now before he gets too angry." Miranda grabbed his hand and dragged him towards the door. She stopped at the threshold and kissed him. "I love you."

"I love you, too," he replied without hesitation and opened the door for her to go through. They were instantly met with the imposing figure of her father and a pale Mr Pearson standing behind him.

"What the hell is going on?" Time seemed to stand still as her father spoke. Venom laced each of his words with a stinging bite.

"Daddy, I'd like to introduce you to Peter North." Miranda held herself up tall and didn't seem to allow the big man to intimidate her. Pete knew differently, though, from the shaking of her hand.

"Why was he in your bedroom?"

Miranda's mother appeared behind them, and her father's eyes almost stood out on stalks with the shock.

"Augusta?"

"Please listen to them, Charles. What they have to say is important."

Pete cleared his throat and stepped forward.

"Lord Braybrooke, it's a pleasure to finally meet you." Pete held his hand out, but Miranda's father only looked at it like it was covered in dog shit. "Miranda and I have something we wish to tell you. I asked her to marry me earlier, and she said yes."

Her father burst out into a fit of laughter. It wasn't exactly the response Pete was expecting. In fact it hadn't figured in any of the scenarios he'd imagined over the last thirty minutes.

"Mr Pearson, would you escort this vagabond out of my house? If he thinks he can come here and make stupid promises to my daughter, then he has another think coming. I'm not a fool. Give him some money to make him go away... permanently. I'm sure that is all he wants."

"I'm pregnant," Miranda blurted out. "He's the father, and he's not going anywhere.

Flames of fury licked up the sides of Lord Braybrooke's cheeks, and Pete was certain that if it were possible he would be seeing steam coming out of the ears of the man in front of him, right now.

"Pregnant?" her father repeated.

"Yes."

Without another response, her father turned on his heels and stomped off down the stairs. Miranda looked to her mother.

"Is that it?"

She shook her head.

"You need to follow him."

Solemnly, they followed down the stairs towards the sound of Miranda's father. He was on the phone. "I need you here, now."

Silence.

They walked into the lounge to find him pouring himself a brandy from an ornate decanter perched upon a dark mahogany dresser.

"Do you realise what you've done?" He spoke into the amber nectar and not directly at them.

"Daddy, please." Miranda stepped forward, and Pete let her go. He was on hand should he be needed to protect her, but this wasn't a battle he could fight for her. It was one she needed to win herself. "I fell in love. Please, this is a happy accident."

"You're sixteen." Her father spun around to face Miranda. His eyes were black as the night with the anger coursing through his veins.

"Age is nothing but a number when it comes to what I feel. Pete is a good man. He's intelligent and... and... I know you're worried about the future of our family name, but he'll be a good asset for it."

"You actually think I'll allow him to inherit after me. A kid who has fooled around with my daughter and got her in the family way." Lord Braybrooke turned his malevolent focus back to Pete. "Who are you? What is your pedigree? Your parents? Your finances. Tell me?"

Pete had been right. Their meeting in the bank was so insignificant to Miranda's father he'd forgotten him.

"My name is Peter North; my parents are Ken and Elsie. I have some money and a good job. My prospects for a superior position are good. I can get references should you wish. I can and will look after your daughter." He dared to take a step closer. "I'm not stupid, Lord Braybrooke. I know the situation we find ourselves in is not ideal at our age, but I want to care for you daughter and marry her. I'll do it with or without your blessing, but we really would prefer with."

There was the bark of laughter again.

"You think I'll allow this marriage to happen?" The doors behind them flew open and two heavy set men thundered in with fists clenched.

"Daddy, no." Miranda reached out to grab her father, but he pushed her away.

"You disgust me. You've always been a selfish little brat. I thought for once you might think of someone other than yourself and accept the man I chose to be your husband, But I can see you've opened your legs for the first person who's shown any interest in you."

"That's not true," Miranda countered. "I love him."

"You love the idea of affection."

"Well, is it any wonder given I've been starved of it most of my life?" Miranda slapped her hands over her mouth, realising at the last minute that what she was saying would antagonise her father further.

The two men bore down on Pete with fists smacking against open palms. This was about to get painful, very painful, judging by the men's expressions. Miranda's mother and Mr Pearson entered the room.

"Charles, please listen to them. This isn't some sordid encounter. This is emotional."

"You knew?" her father bellowed, and it felt like the whole room shook.

"I only found out today, but I've seen the affection Mr North has for our daughter. He truly loves her. I'm sure we can sort something out. You could educate Mr North on what you need for a successor. He could be a powerful future holder of the name with your guidance. I'm sure he'd even consent to taking the name Braybrooke for Miranda's sake if you asked?" Pete knew Augusta Braybrooke was trying to play to her husband's weaknesses to make him see sense, but the look of disgust on his face told him it wasn't working.

Determination spread across Lord Braybrooke's face, and it sent shivers down Pete's spine. The devil himself was in front of them and about to wreak havoc.

"You two"–he pointed to the burly men who now stood either side of him–"deal with him." One of the men grabbed him, and the other sent a stomach crunching punch into his torso. He gasped out in agony.

"Daddy." Miranda ran to get in the way, but she wasn't quick enough. Her father grabbed her by the hair and pulled her in closely to him. She screamed, and it scared Pete enough to try and break free of the men. He wasn't strong enough, though, and another blow came, this time breaking his nose and shooting blood all over the floor.

"No!" Miranda screamed again.

"You slut," her father screeched. "You've destroyed everything. How can I ever sell you for a virgin, now, when you have this insignificant's spawn inside you? I should beat you black and blue until you lose the foetus, but I won't be responsible for taking the life of your mistake. No, you'll have to live with what you've done forever."

Pete tried his hardest to keep focused on what was being said to Miranda. Was he casting her out of the family? The beating would be worth it if Miranda would be free to live her life.

"Mr Pearson?"

The chauffeur stepped forward.

"Take Miranda and put her in the car."

"Sir?" He stepped forward tentatively. "What then, Sir?"

"We'll take her somewhere this lowlife can never find her. She'll have her brat, and then I'll give it away, so she can never see it again. Afterwards she'll be married off and bedded as the whore she is, but this time at my whim."

"Sir." Mr Pearson hesitated.

"Charles." Augusta Braybrooke came up to her husband and got down on her knees in front of him to beg. "Please, don't do this."

The Lord's large hand came out, and he slapped it hard across his wife's face. She tumbled onto the floor, her head hitting the side of a table. Her body lay limp.

"Mummy." Miranda, who was still being held by her father, was hysterical by this point.

"Shut up." Her father shook her. "Get her in the car," Lord Braybrooke ordered the chauffeur again just as another punch sent Pete down onto his knees. His world was starting to blur at the edges, but he needed to remain focused.

"No." Mr Pearson stepped forward and used as much of his dwindling from old age bulk to intimidate his employer.

"You've been helping them." Realisation dawned on the Lord's face.

"They're in love."

"Get out," Lord Braybrooke ordered.

"Not without Miranda, Pete, and Lady Augusta. I won't watch you destroy their lives, any longer, with your greed and envy." From his slumped position on the floor, Pete was proud of the way the chauffeur was standing up for them. Miranda had pulled her mother towards her. The Lady appeared to be dizzy and disoriented but was moving, albeit slowly. A shadow walked in front of him, and before Pete could open his mouth to warn Mr Pearson, one of the two brutes who had been attacking him sent a vase smashing over the driver's head. He collapsed to more screaming from Miranda.

Lord Braybrooke gritted his teeth and snarled at the same time, grabbing Miranda and pulling her to her feet.

"Finish them. Leave my wife for me to deal with."

Pete tried his hardest to stand up, to fight back, but he was too weakened. All he could do was look on as Miranda was dragged from the room by her father.

"Miranda!" he shouted after her and received nothing back but her frantic cries for help. He went down on his hands and knees, crawling towards the door. He knew he wouldn't make it through when he felt the debilitating pain of something shattering the bones in his leg. The darkness claimed him, and Miranda was gone.

TEN

Miranda

Days of loneliness and captivity turned into months, and the entire time Miranda's abdomen swelled with the child growing inside. Occasionally, a midwife would come and check on her but apart from that, she saw no one. Her food was delivered by the same mute servant who never even raised her eyes from the floor to look at her. She had no idea where she was or how long she'd been there, but the fact the baby within her blocked all view of her feet and its head was engaged, according to the last midwife visit, indicated she was near to full term. The baby would be born and taken from her. She'd no idea if Pete was even alive. If he were, had he given up on her? The tears fell as she tried to get comfortable on the rundown bed, which was the only piece of furniture in the primitive dungeon she lived in.

Her father had visited a few times, and the contempt and disgust she felt for him had grown each time. The way he'd spoken down to her had extinguished any hope she'd held for him having any goodness in him. He was an evil man and cared for only himself. He hid behind the pretence of making decisions for the future good of the title, but he couldn't really care less about that. It was purely selfish, and she knew when this was over she would be sold to the highest bidder as a trophy wife. Money –everything was about that. Her father wanted as much as he could get for himself. He wanted prestige and to own the greatest name in the country. At least by marrying, Miranda would lose the name Braybrooke and never have to use it again. She couldn't wait.

It was impossible to get comfortable. Her back had been aching all afternoon, and all she wanted to do was curl up into a little ball and sleep through the rest of her life.

She looked up when the door opened. Her father stomped in with the midwife behind him.

"Get up," he ordered her. There was still an edge of defiance in her, which grew every day, so she ignored him. "I said get up," he repeated louder and with more venom.

She rolled over, so she didn't have to face them. Next thing she knew, she was being pulled from the bed and flung across the room.

"Lord Braybrooke, please, the child." The midwife came to her side to check on her, but Miranda slapped her away and protectively cradled her arm around her stomach.

"I couldn't give a fuck about that thing inside her. I want it out, now. So, get it out!"

"I really don't think this is a good idea." The midwife tried to comfort her again, but Miranda just stared daggers at her.

"You said she was thirty-eight weeks, meaning the baby will live if it's born. Now, do what I pay you to do."

"Don't touch me!" she screamed.

"Oh, for crying out loud." Her father came over and pulled her to her feet. She was helpless with her size and lack of strength, compared to him. He dragged her out of the room and along a dark corridor she vaguely remembered from when she was brought here. She tried to quickly do the maths in her head. She'd have been roughly six weeks pregnant when she arrived. That would've been thirty-two weeks ago. She choked out a garbled cry for Pete. It'd been so long. It would be March now. She'd missed the autumn and winter while hidden away. Her father stopped and slammed her against the wall. She whimpered with pain.

"He's gone. You'll never see him again. Get used to it, you little whore. We're going to get this bastard out of you, and then I'll deal with you, just as you deserve. You'll spend the rest of your life flat on your back. I've got just the husband for you, and he isn't bothered by the fact you're not a virgin. It tells him just what sort of woman you are. You think I'm the devil? Well, I've got nothing on him. His relatives are notorious in society, especially his cousin the Duke of Oakfield." Her father pulled her away from the wall and resumed hauling her towards another room. He kicked the door open as he approached, and several of the people inside, who were dressed in medical scrubs, jumped back. The room was white and clinical. There was a bed in the middle of it.

"Your patient," her father snarled and thrust her towards them. She tried to turn and run before she was caught, but being heavily pregnant left her incapable of fast movement. One of the men caught her and sneered. She noticed beneath the face mask it was one of the men who'd been in the room that fateful day when she'd told her father what was happening. She raised her hand to slap him for what he'd done to Pete. For all she knew this man was her lover's murderer. He caught her tiny wrist, though, and flipped her around to bend over the table and pulled up her top.

"Doctor," he ordered, and a timid man stepped forward. "The epidural."

Miranda knew in an instant what was happening. The knives on the table in front of her gleamed brightly in the clinical light. They were going to cut her baby from her.

"No." She tried her hardest to struggle, but the weight of the man behind her prevented any movement. The doctor disappeared from her vision, and she cried out when a sharp pain shot through her lower back. A cold liquid flooded into her body, and she was pulled up onto the table and held down.

"How long?" her father asked.

"The drugs should work in about ten to twenty minutes and up to another forty minutes for the baby to be born," the doctor replied.

"I'll be back in forty-five. You better have it out by then," her father responded and went for the door.

"Daddy, please," Miranda called out.

Her father turned.

"Please, don't do this. Please. Let me go. I'll disappear. You can choose whoever you want to give the title to. My uncle can't dispute it if I lie. Say that the person is your son. I'm sure if you can do all of this, then you can hire someone to falsify a DNA test. Please. Let me go. I'm your daughter."

Her father threw back his head and laughed. Miranda blinked back the tears in her eyes.

"Finally, you show there's a bit of me in you and not just the soppy neediness of your mother. She'll be so pleased to know that." Confirmation her mother was still alive slammed into her with the realisation that possibly the same could be said for Pete. Maybe he was out there looking for her. She just needed to hang on. "Too little too late, though." Her father turned heel and walked back out, slamming the door behind him.

"No!" she screamed and tried to pull away from the man holding her down. She scratched at him and bit down on his arm. He had no choice other than to let her go, but as she slid from the bed, the drugs coursing through her body started to work and her legs went from under her. The feeling in them gone. "No!" she cried as she was un-ceremoniously picked up and dropped back on the bed. The man she'd bitten, seething at having a chunk taken out of his arm, took great delight in removing the clothing from the lower half of her body.

"Do it now!"

he ordered, and the doctor went white.

"I can't. The drugs haven't fully spread through her system."

"I don't care." Her father's hired thug picked up one of the surgical knives and handed it to the doctor. "Now, or I'll be using that on you."

Another man came to her feet and held them down while the man who'd ordered her torture placed both his hands on her shoulders and stared down into her eyes from his vantage point at her head.

"We need to cover her lower half from view." The midwife stepped up with a cloth and stammered out her nervous words. Miranda didn't doubt they were being paid handsomely for what they were about to do, but professional ethics still weighed heavily on their minds. She looked up to the man looming over her. His facial expression told her no covering up would be done, and she would witness every sick and twisted element of what was about to happen to her.

The doctor stepped up and with a gulp pressed his hand on to her abdomen. Thankfully, the drugs had worked quickly, and the sensations around her midsection and legs were gone. She felt nothing. A tear dropped from her eye when the doctor looked at her and whispered, "Sorry.".

He pulled his hand back and made the first cut with the knife. Fortunately, the swell of her abdomen hid her view of everything. Seeing her insides would probably have caused her to be violently sick. She lay as still as she could. There was no point in struggling, now. She needed to help those who were about to rip her child from her belly. To deliver her baby safely, she needed to remain calm and quiet and allow them to do their work. Her impending motherhood washed over her with this new found eerie compose.

Before long, she heard the cry of a baby. Her breath caught in her throat as the new-born was delivered onto her chest. The man holding her let go of her arms, and she instantly brought the baby to her and held it tightly. It was perfect, beautiful, and a miracle all wrapped up in one tiny bundle. She looked down and saw it was a boy. Pete would have been so proud to have a son. She silenced the distraught cries of the infant with a 'coo' and kissed the top of his forehead.

The room around them had fallen silent except for the noises she and the baby made. His tiny lips moved, and his tongue darted out looking for food. She didn't care who was around and removed her breast from the bra she still wore. The baby knew instantly where to find food and with a little bit of trouble latched on to her breast. It felt natural. Tears streamed down her face. She was vaguely aware of work continuing around her, the afterbirth being removed, the umbilical cord being clamped and cut, and stitches being put in place, but all her focus was on the baby.

"She shouldn't be feeding it." The man who she'd bitten spoke up, but the midwife pulled him away.

"The first milk is important."

"It's not an it." She spoke without diverting her attention from her son, "His name is Ryan. Ryan Peter North."

Miranda pulled her gaze away from the baby for a moment when the door opened, and her father walked in. He looked from her to the baby.

"Is it ready?" he asked with zero emotion in his voice. This baby was his grandchild, but it could have been a dirty rag on the floor for all he cared. That sent shivers of fear through Miranda.

"Yes," the midwife spoke up.

"Bring it." Her father turned and left the room, again.

The midwife came up to Miranda with tears forming in her own eyes. "I'm sorry." Before Miranda could register what was going on, Ryan was removed from her chest, wrapped in a blanket, and taken towards the door. He started to scream for her, for her milk, for his mother. She tried to move, but the men were back and holding her down.

"No!" she screamed repeatedly. She was thrashing around on the bed trying her hardest to go after her child as he was carried from the room. "Ryan!!"

"She's going to do herself damage," the doctor shouted. "give me a sedative, now."

"No." She tried even harder to move, but the people around her were too quick, and the needle flooded the tranquillising fluid into her arm. As it took her body into oblivion, she knew she would never see her son again.

ELEVEN

Pete

Another dead end.

Another false hope.

Another time when he would return home without Miranda and their child.

He looked up once more at the run-down castle in the Highlands of Scotland before getting in his car and heading back towards the cheapest bed and breakfast he'd been able to find.

Pete had done the calculations so often now. He knew Miranda was due any day or had probably already had their child, depending on how far along she was when they'd discovered her pregnancy. Eight months had gone by so quickly. Although given he'd spent half of it unconscious in a hospital bed, it wasn't surprising. His mother had sobbed by his bedside as his father explained he'd been found in the gutter outside Barratt's bank with a shattered leg, a broken jaw, and internal injuries so numerous his parents were told if they were religious, to call a priest for last rites. It was another three months before they'd allowed him out of the hospital because it had taken him that long to be able to walk again. His leg would cause trouble for the rest of life, but he hadn't lost it, which had been the initial fear.

As soon as he was strong enough, well maybe sooner than he should have, he quit his job and was out looking for Miranda. His first port of call had been to find Mr Pearson. The elderly chauffeur had been in the same hospital as him. Neither of them had spoken about their injuries to the police. As far as the authorities were concerned, they'd both been attacked by an unconnected mystery assailant for their wallets. He had, however, tried to report Miranda to the police as missing. But, it seemed money talked when it came to a person being recorded as unac-counted for, and his plea for help had fallen on deaf ears. It was up to him to find

Miranda. Hopefully, before her father damaged her irrevocably if it were even possible at this late stage.

"I'm back," Pete called as he entered the accommodation in which they were both staying. Mr Pearson, or *Jim* as Pete had come to know the chauffeur, had taken longer to heal from his wounds. In fact, his arm was still in a sling from the fracture he'd received, and Jim's memory was poor at best, now, because of the impact of the vase against his skull.

"Did you find her?" Jim was out of his chair and expectant.

"No. It was another dead end."

"Damn it." The old man hit the side of the chair with his good hand. "We're running out of time."

"I know." Pete went over to the fridge in the corner of their room and pulled out a beer. He'd found himself drinking a lot more recently. It numbed the pain and help him sleep. March in Scotland was damp, and it did little to help the fragile bones in his leg. Then there were the thoughts constantly running through his mind concerning Miranda and what was happening to her. He flipped back the pull ring and took a long drink.

"We have that other lead. I'll try that tomorrow."

"It'll come to nothing." Jim sat back down in an armchair, his body hunched over in defeat. The old man thought of Miranda as his daughter. He cared for her in a way Miranda's own father never had.

Pete ambled over to Jim and put his hand on his shoulder.

"I promise you we'll find her. I won't stop until I do. I've found her twice now in my life. The third time will be forever."

A quiet knock at the door drew both their attentions.

"Were you followed?" Jim asked.

"No, I checked repeatedly."

"If he knows we're looking for her…"

Pete held his finger up to his mouth to silence Jim.

"Who is it?" he called out.

Silence.

He and Jim looked at each other, a bead of sweat developed on his brow.

Jim picked up a bat they'd brought with them, just in case. It had been resting in the corner of the room. He motioned for Pete to open the door. Reluctantly, Pete stepped forward. His mouth fell open when he saw who was on the other side.

"Lady Augusta."

Miranda's mother stood in front of him. A fur coat wrapped around her to guard against the chill in the air. She pushed past him and into the room.

"I'm sorry for my rudeness, but I don't have much time. I'd hoped and prayed you'd pull through, but your injuries….They were so severe. I know if I hadn't forced them to take me from the property by causing such a scene, they would have killed you both."

"Miranda?" Pete stepped up to her. His fists were clenched with the need for information. "Where is she?"

"That's what I'm here to tell you. She's been kept from me as well." Augusta burst into tears. "The baby, she's had it. They…they did a caesarean as soon as they could."

"I'm a Father?" Pete's ears started to ring with the blood whooshing around his head. "Where is it...er...he? She?"

"He, Ryan, she named him Ryan." Miranda's mother stumbled, and Jim was up and helping her into his chair.

"The beer." He waved towards the can he'd left on the desk.

Pete retrieved it and offered it to Augusta.

She took a sip and screwed her nose up in repulsion.

"Thank you. I'm sorry."

"Lady Augusta, where is my son?" He knelt in front of her.

"I don't know. My husband, he's always been insane, but the last few months even I don't recognise him. It's like he has become so consumed by everything he's lost all his humanity."

"What did he do to you?" Jim asked and placed his hands around Augusta's.

"Miranda. We need to focus on her."

"Augusta." Jim squeezed, and it was the first time Pete saw the fatherly care for Miranda also extended to her mother.

"He took his rights from me as my husband....violently. I'll heal just as you will. Miranda is the one I'm worried about. Pete."– Lady Augusta turned her attention from his roommate to stare directly at him– "she's to be married to a man who'll treat her even worse than her father. She's not strong, now, with the loss of her baby. I've tried to search my husband's records to find out what has happened to him, but there's nothing. He's disappeared off the face of the Earth, and although I know my husband won't kill him, you won't be able to find him. He'll have made certain of that."

"If he's alive, there's always hope, but I agree with you we need to get to Miranda. Where is she?"

"She's at a house outside Dumfries. It's a remote location. I saw her yesterday for the first time. She's very weak but capable of running should it be needed." She reached into the pocket of her coat and pulled out the address and another piece of paper.

"What's this?"

"It's notice of your intended marriage. You can marry in Gretna Green without parental consent. I placed the notice a week back when I was told this other marriage was to take place. Go to the address tonight and rescue her. Take her to Gretna and hide for the next few days, and then, you'll be able to marry. Find the Blacksmith."

"What?" Pete shook his head as confusion clouded his mind.

"Marrying her is the only way to stop this. Bind her to you and make her yours forever. It's the only way her father will give up. I've been looking through all his family history and the governing documents of his properties and titles. Only Miranda's first husband will be able to inherit. Should she divorce, then it's null and void, and the estate goes to my brother-in-law. She'd be completely useless to him and his aspirations. She'll be free."

"I'm not sure I can get my head around all of this." Pete rubbed his forehead. "Free. To live. The one thing she's wanted to do forever. To be herself and make decisions based on her own learning and hopes for the future."

"Yes. Free."

The room fell silent.

"What about you?" Jim knelt also. His old bones creaking.

Augusta reached out and stroked her hand down his face. This was a gesture that would've been intimate in so many situations, but in this instance, it was one of respect. "I lost my freedom the day I married Lord Braybrooke. My decisions have been made for me, and I'll live by them because it's all I know. This has been who I am for so long, now, I don't know any different. What's on the other side would destroy me. I wouldn't survive it." Her voice broke on the last word, despite her desperately trying to stop it from doing so. "Go save my little girl."

With those final words, Pete got to his feet, stepped back, and allowed Augusta to rise gracefully out of the chair. She adjusted her coat again, so it wrapped around her tiny frame as a barrier to the cold and the world. Within the protection of the fabric, she could be whoever she wanted to be and not just the downtrodden wife of a tyrant. Augusta bowed her head to them both and left them alone in the silent room.

The ticking of a clock reminded Pete time was passing. He had the address of where the woman he loved was, and he was standing here lamenting the fate of her mother.

Jim, who'd risen to his feet as a show of respect to Augusta when she left, bent and retrieved a briefcase from under his bed. He clicked the locks to open it and pulled out a gun. Pete's eyes went wide.

"Let's go." Jim pushed the pistol into the back of his trousers. "Don't fail me now, boy. When you've lived through a World War, handling one of these is nothing. Try facing down a grenade."

"I think it's just dawning on me what we're going to have to do to save her."

"Whatever we need to." Jim responded.

"Whatever we need to."

TWELVE

Miranda

It felt like a cold wind had swept over her body as Miranda looked into the mirror in front of her. The last time she looked at her reflection, she was imagining how she'd look with the child she'd conceived with Pete, heavy in her belly. The girl staring back at her this time had lost all of the excitement and spirit of that previous one. This one was broken beyond all repair. The baby was no longer there, cut out of her stomach and taken away after barely drawing his first breath. The hope for a future filled with love and devotion torn away by a man who was supposed to love her.

Her hand moved to the chain and locket around her neck. As much as she hated the midwife for what she'd helped do, she also respected her for her actions afterwards. She'd returned later that evening to check on Miranda and had brought a locket, containing hair from her son. She'd apologised and told her about her own children she never got to see. They'd been taken away from her because she couldn't afford to look after them. The job the midwife had just undertaken would allow her to get them back. A child for a child. Miranda hadn't thanked her. She'd simply taken the locket and placed it around her neck. That had been six weeks ago. Today, she'd been given the all clear after her caesarean and was to be married.

She'd met the man once when her father had brought him to where ever it was in the world she was staying. She wished she could say he was handsome or even a nice man, but he was neither. He was at least fifteen years older than her, and his physique was nothing in comparison to Pete's lean and toned muscular body. His eyes were beady, and they bore into her as though he was having lustful thoughts. She'd ignored him at first, but that had only seemed to increase his feelings of inadequacy at having to buy a wife rather than have one fall in love with him. In front of her father, he'd punched her in the face for showing him disrespect. Her father hadn't cared, though, and sanctioned the action as necessary because of her insolence. The bright purple bruise surrounding her eye stood out against the paleness of her reflection. The white wedding gown she was forced to wear doing little to give her colour.

She turned away from her image. It was tormenting her even further, causing more problems in her already jumbled mind. With a long exhalation, she trudged over to the window and looked out. The world outside was blossoming with the signs of spring. Daffodils bloomed in yellow, flowers of hope for the coming year. She had none. She was more like the snowdrops that had withered and died, having blanketed the grass only a few short weeks ago with their splendour.

Pete must have died or given up on her. She'd still had no word from him. He'd not come when their baby had been taken, and he wouldn't come today. She was alone, broken, ashamed. No one truly loved her.

She wiped a tear away from her eye, which had been clouding her view of the field in front of her. Oh, the irony, now she was seeing things. Pete stood on the other side of the grassy expanse. She was going insane. Actually, maybe that was the best thing that could happen. If she saw him everywhere, at least she would remember him. However, when Mr Pearson appeared at his side, she rubbed her eyes and took a second look. Her old chauffeur had his arm in a sling but was moving with determination.

"Pete?" she questioned to no one in particular because there was no one who could hear her. "Pete." She tried to open the window to call to him, but it was locked. She ran across the room to another one, facing the same way. It too was locked. She rattled it furiously in frustration before banging to get his attention.

He finally looked her way, and the smile that spread across his face when he saw her, warmed her heart. He was here for her, and she had to get to him. She knew her father was somewhere on the property with his thugs and her soon to be husband. In an instant, she was across the room and trying the door. She'd been locked in the room when she'd first come here, but her father had been leaving it open, recently, because he knew she was too broken to even contemplate escaping. Not anymore, though. She flung the door open and sped into the corridor and down the stairs. She tried to focus her brain. From the way they were heading, he'd come in at the left side of the house. She silently cursed her melancholy nature for not allowing her to explore this place better. It was near the kitchen, though, she knew from the smells wafting her way. There'd be a door. Her heart leapt at the thought of freedom.

"Miranda." Her father's demonic voice froze her to the spot. "Where do you think you're going?"

She turned slowly to face him, the hatred she had for him bubbling beneath the surface of her body. Her mother hung off his arm like the trophy she was. On the other side was the man she was to marry. Something snapped –years of oppression and hatred surged through her with a strength she didn't think she'd ever have. This man took her baby. He had her cut open. He'd treated her like dirt all her life. No more.

"I'm leaving." Her head went high, and her shoulders squared when she spoke.

Her father raised a seemingly knowing eyebrow. "You are, are you? And where will you go?"

"With me." Pete's voice came from behind her, and his arms snaked around her waist. He rested his hand gently on her stomach as if knowing she was still tender in that area, despite healing well from the operation.

"You again. I'd hoped you'd succumb to your injuries. I see my men didn't beat you hard enough. I'll have to get them to double their assault this time."

"I don't think so." Mr Pearson appeared next to Miranda with a gun pointed directly towards her father. She looked up at him with shock, and when she looked back at her father, she noticed the expression on his face was similar. The look on her mother's face surprised her more, though, for it was a look of awe at the turn of events.

"What is going on?" the man she was to marry asked. "I said I would take her on but not if I'm to have this hassle before I even get her into bed."

Pete's hold on her strengthened, and Mr Pearson fired a warning shot into the wall behind her intended.

"Fuck this!" the man exclaimed and made for the front door.

"We have an agreement!" her father shouted after him.

"Not if I'm going to get shot at. I don't need the hassle when I can buy another woman with a lot less trouble."

Mr Pearson shot again, and the man she was to marry left at a more rapid pace.

"You'll regret that." Her father pushed her mother aside and bore down on them. Mr Pearson shot at his feet, missing by millimetres.

The two hired thugs ran into the hallway with their own weapons drawn.

"Go." Her former chauffeur turned his head towards where she and Pete stood.

"Jim?" Pete questioned.

"Go. Run. Make her free. Love her forever and give her everything she deserves."

"No." She tried to protest as Pete dropped his arm from her waist and took her hand instead. He pulled her towards the door just as gunfire filled the room, again. "No!" she screamed and looked back just in time to see her mother jump in front of a bullet, intended for her father. She fell to the floor unmoving. "Mum." She tried to pull back, but Pete held her too tightly.

"Go," Mr Pearson ordered again, and Pete tugged on her arm. She knew if she stayed, she'd die just like her mother was now probably doing.

"Miranda, please," Pete whispered into her ear. She turned to him with tears streaming down her face and nodded. In mere seconds, they were running through the corridor and into the kitchen and safety.

"Kill him." Her father's voice bellowed behind her and shivers went through her body when a hail of gunfire followed.

She had no time to process what was happening. She weaved through the kitchen with Pete, knowing her father's men would be on their trail soon. They emerged into the fresh air, and even though she wanted nothing more than to stop and vomit, she knew she had to push on. He led her into the forest with a call of 'over there' behind them. Before long, they arrived at the Cortina he'd spent his money on all that time ago.

She let out a loud cry of relief at seeing the car.

"Get in," he ordered and jumped into his own side. The instant she closed her door, he pulled away, spinning the wheels and kicking up the forest floor.

Her father's men appeared, and one of them went flying over the windshield when Pete floored the accelerator and roared out of the grounds of her father's property. She was at the point of hyperventilating, but it didn't seem they were being followed.

"It's ok. Stay calm. It's not over, yet. We need to get to Gretna Green."

"Gretna Green?" she asked.

"Yes. Once we're married we're free."

The journey should have taken half an hour, but at the speed Pete was driving, it seemed to take no time at all. She was tired, and her incision hurt from all the exertion, but she was on the verge of freedom. When the car pulled up outside a blacksmiths, she looked over to Pete.

"Are you ok?"

He placed his hand over her stomach again.

"I had a boy."

"I know. Ryan. Beautiful name."

"How?" she asked and leaned closer into him.

"Your mother. She's the one who told me where you were."

"What? Why?" The news her mother had saved her gripped her heart in spasms of pain. "I don't understand."

"We tried to save her. To make her stay behind, but she said she couldn't. I think that's why…"

"…She jumped in front of the bullet: to die. Death was preferable to life."

"She's been through so much."

"But if my father had died?"

"She wouldn't have been able to survive without the only life she knew."

"I can't believe it had got so bad. I knew he was a monster but…"

"I believe she hid a lot of what he did to her from you. Your mother was too far gone to live. I know that sounds horrible, but with her last breath, she made sure you were free. Mr Pearson also. They're the true parents you need to remember, not the man you called father." Pete pulled her into his arms and kissed the top of her head.

"We're parents."

"We are. Our little boy is out there somewhere, and I'm not going to rest until we find him. It may take a few months or a few years, but before either of us die, we'll know our son again. We'll tell him we love him and none of this was our choice."

"I'm scared."

She brought her hand to the locket around her neck.

"Marry me, Miranda."

She gripped the locket tightly in her hand.

"Yes."

THE END

PART NINE
CONTROLLING THE PAST - PART TWO

ONE

Miranda

Present Day

"Should I ask why my daughter is sitting there silent and with a face like thunder, or is it best that I don't know?" Miranda enquired from the leather front seat of the SVAutobiography Range Rover they were travelling. She turned around to where her daughter, Sophie, glared daggers at Grayson who was both the driver of the vehicle and Sophie's husband.

"Because my husband's an arse..." Sophie started to speak but her husband interrupted

"Fifteen."

"Motherfuc...." her daughter countered, but Miranda found herself inter-rupting this time.

"Sophie. Not in front of Ash."

Eight-year-old Askhii, Grayson's son from a previous relationship with the now deceased Sally Bridgewater, looked up from the film he was watching on his iPad.

"It's alright, Grandma. Mum is just upset with Dad because he wouldn't let her wear a dress she liked for the flight." Miranda's heart warmed to hear the little boy call her Grandma.

"It was a one of a kind. He seems to forget that as the wife of a world-famous movie star I need to look good at all times." Sophie's pout deepened, and Miranda couldn't help but be reminded of the 'diva-strops' her little girl had been well known for as a child.

"It showed too much leg. Argue again, and it'll be twenty." Grayson did not take his eyes off the road, but the twist of his lip showed that he was enjoying the playful interaction with his wife.

"It showed the right amount of leg!" Sophie kicked the back of the chair like a petulant child.

"Twenty."

"Mum, tell him."

Miranda knew exactly what the count of twenty meant, and she really didn't need to think that her daughter would find it hard to sit down after her spanking later. She was just grateful that Ash had gone back to his iPad. The boy had developed so much since he'd moved in with Sophie and Grayson. The first few years of his life had been spent in foster care after his mother sold him to the highest bidder when born. The evil bitch was dead, now, and no one needed to ever worry about her again. If Ashkii asked about her one day, Miranda knew that Sophie and Grayson would only talk favourably about the woman, even if they both hated her. The fact that he called her Grandma, and Sophie Mum, was all she focused on because it meant so much to them all.

"I'm not going to get involved in your arguments. Your father would tan my backside for interfering in a Dom's rules."

"Mum! Yuck!" Sophie cringed, and Miranda turned back to face forward in the front passenger seat. She couldn't help but notice the wide smirk on Grayson's face at her comment, though.

"Grandma, is Grandad already at Uncle James' castle?" Ash placed the iPad down on the seat beside him and leaned forward into the space between the two front seats.

"He is. He went ahead with Uncle James to make sure everything was prepared." They were on the way to her son James' castle in the Yorkshire Dales. A few weeks ago, Pete had asked her, following a romantic dinner at an eighties revival evening, to renew their vows. The relationship between them hadn't always been easy. For a short time, they'd split up, and the relationship between them had been incredibly strained. James had been brutally assaulted by his ex-girlfriend's brothers because his sexual preferences were slightly wilder than the norm. Her son was a Dominant, hell it ran in the family. Her husband had demonstrated tendencies at the start of their relationship, but over the years it had developed, and they enjoyed a healthy sexual relationship, despite her reaching the age of fifty a few months previously. Age was nothing but a number to her, now. She felt as young as the couple sitting in the car with her. After the assault, her husband had made a mistake that threatened to tear them apart. He'd slept with a consort. It was a bitter and difficult time, but she and Pete had been through so much at the start of their relationship that no matter what, they were destined to be together forever. She forgave him, after a lot of grovelling on his part, because he was her heart, and she was his. With the addition of James and Sophie, that love had grown to become a family. They never forgot the missing piece though. She brought her hand up to the locket she still wore around her neck. She never took it off unless an emergency arose and it was necessary. Pete had been true to his word, and they'd searched high and low for their son Ryan but always came up with dead ends. She'd not seen her father since the day she fled Dumfries and married Pete. A few days after the wedding, Pete sent her father a copy of their marriage certificate along with a signed declaration that the marriage had been consummated and received word back that she was no longer to have anything to do with her father. If he saw her again, he would have her forcibly removed from his property. She knew that day she was finally free of the man who'd tormented her for most of her life. Her father died a few years back, an apparent suicide by gunshot to the head. She knew better, though, by the way Pete had returned home to her the night of her father's death. He was defeated. She'd asked no questions, not even of Matthew Carter, her son's bodyguard and best friend, who'd spent the day with her husband. James and Sophie didn't know of the existence of their brother who was out there somewhere, hopefully alive. She and Pete had made the decision to keep it from them, due to the traumatic nature of the events surrounding Ryan's birth. James and Sophie had grown up knowing Elsie and Ken, Pete's parents, as their grandparents. They'd never asked questions about her parents, accepting that they'd *died* before they were born. James may have searched further when he came into his billions. In Matthew, he certainly had the ability to do so, but he never mentioned anything, and she never asked. Ryan was her and Pete's secret, and one they rarely spoke about together because while missing him so much, it was the only way they could function, at times. He would be thirty-three now –so many missed years.

"Mum, you ok?" Sophie tapped her on the shoulder, and she came out of her memories with a start. "I'm sorry –have we upset you?"

"What? Sorry? No. Not at all. I see every day how in love you are. I'm missing your father. I've got so used to being with him all the time, again."

"We'll be at the castle soon. I'm sure he's waiting for you. I spoke to James earlier, and he said that Dad had a mopey face on him most of the time."

"I think it's probably more your brother is the mopey one from the lack of sleep associated with another new-born."

"Oh, but Isabella wouldn't annoy her daddy while she's a crying baby. She'll wait until she's eighteen and dating."

The entire car burst out laughing as they all knew that James was in for one hell of a ride when Isabella reached the age at which she discovered boys. Despite being only a month old, she was already the most stunning baby. She had the same big blue eyes as Amy, her mother. James had once told Miranda that Amy's eyes were one of the things that had first attracted him to her, now, daughter-in-law.

"At least I don't have to worry about that with my boy." Sophie placed her arm around Ash and pulled him into her. "He's going to be a mummy's boy for life."

Grayson snorted a laugh.

"Hey." Sophie lightly kicked his seat again.

"Thirty," Grayson mischievously proclaimed.

"You're kidding me. I didn't do anything."

"That's a matter of opinion."

Miranda rolled her eyes.

"How do you live with these two, Ash?"

"Headphones and an iPad, Grandma."

Grayson flipped on the indicator to come off the motorway and drive down into the Dales. The automatic car revved as it pushed up into the mountain passes but the noise coming from the engine sounded strange. Grayson looked back into the wing mirror, undoubtedly checking on the car behind them, containing his security detail. He had just returned his focus to the front of the car again when a loud crunch echoed through the vehicle. Miranda watched as he slammed his foot onto the brake pedal, but the car didn't slow.

"Shit!" he shouted out and flicked a switch on the car to turn it from automatic to manual to use the gears to slow down. It didn't work, and at considerable speed, Grayson fought to keep the car on the road. At that moment, Miranda had never been so grateful for the stunt training the young actor had received.

The car behind them sped up, presumably the driver had realised something was wrong and was attempting to overtake on the narrow roads so that he could keep oncoming cars out of the way. Grayson looked around, trying to find some other way of slowing the car. Miranda was watching him, but when she looked up, she realised they were heading straight for a sharp bend that veered off to a shallow drop below.

"Grayson," she screamed, and he looked up.

"Brace," he shouted.

Out of the corner of her eye, Miranda saw Sophie bring the still seat-belted Ash over her lap to shield him, so he couldn't see what was happening. Miranda protected her own head within her arms as the car slammed into the bend, travelling at twice the speed it should have been going. Time seemed to stand still as she peered out from between her fingers. Grayson was fighting with the wheel, and Sophie screamed as the car ricocheted off the side of the road and spun around. The tires screeched on the ground. Grayson was punching the brakes with his feet in the hopes they'd work again, but it was to no avail. She felt the car continue to move forward with the force of inertia. If it went over the side of the mountain, it would fall onto the side that Grayson and Sophie were sitting. She felt herself lurch forward, and the seatbelt tightened against her shoulder and stomach, holding her as safely in place as it could, under the circumstances. The car was sliding along the ground, now, and the air bags deployed preventing their heads from smashing against the seats.

The car continued to slide along the ground for what seemed like forever. She could hear screams coming from her mouth, but everything was surreal as if she was in a dream and all this wasn't really happening. The car hit the edge of the drop, and she felt it slide over and down. They were going to die! Thoughts of Pete, James, Amy, Thomas, Isabella, and finally Ryan flew through her mind. The car jolted and with a horrendous sickening crunching noise, ground to a halt. Her body juddered with the motion of the crash, but she was alive. Her breaths came out ragged, and she tried to clear her thoughts.

"Sophie." Grayson's deep timbre was filled with fear.

"Ok. Bleeding, but ok."

"Ash?"

"I'm alright, Dad. My arm hurts."

"Miranda?"

She looked at her son-in-law, the shock of what had just happened starting to kick in.

"Alright," she stammered.

"We need to get out. The car is full of fuel, and the lines could be cut. Miranda can you open your door?" Grayson released his seatbelt and reached back to assist Sophie and Ash to undo theirs. She didn't move.

"Miranda?" Grayson spoke again.

"Mum?" Sophie sobbed.

"She's in shock." Grayson's voice sounded muffled as Miranda tried to focus. What had he said to her before? The door….. that was it. She twisted in the seat, her side was hurting, in fact pretty much everything hurt now. She pushed at the door, but it wouldn't budge. The angle they were at meant she needed more strength to open it because it was going upward not outward. She could feel it giving, though.

"I'm not strong enough," she told Grayson as everything flooded back into clarity.

"Good to have you back, Mum," he reassured.

"Grayson?" A call from outside the car.

"Mike?"

"Yes, Boss." It was one of his bodyguards.

"We're all ok. Can't get the door open, though."

The next thing she knew, the door was being thrown open, and the familiar face of one of the bodyguard's she'd seen at the airport appeared. Sirens started to wail in the background.

"Mrs North," the bodyguard addressed her and reached over her. "Put your arms around me. I'll pull you out."

She instantly did as instructed and felt her seatbelt loosen. Grayson had undone it. The bodyguard pulled her up and out through the window as if she were light as a feather. He passed her over to another bodyguard, who was behind him, and he helped her clamber down.

"Can you walk, Mrs North?"

She nodded –her legs felt like jelly, but she knew she'd be able to stand on them.

"There's a clearing over there. Make for that."

The sound of the sirens grew louder and then stopped, presumably turned off when they arrived at the spot from where they'd just fallen. Shouts sounded from above.

"Down here," Mike called out.

"Sophie."

"Mum's coming out behind me, Grandma."

Ash slammed into her side. He had tears in his eyes, but she could tell he was trying to be really brave and not cry. She took his hand and led him towards the clearing where she'd been directed. Sophie followed. She was limping and being supported by one of the bodyguards.

Grayson was the final person to be pulled free from the car. His face was marked with cuts from the shattered glass that had smashed in from his driver's side window. His bodyguard helped him down from the car, and they all walked at a quick pace away from the vehicle as the police and ambulance crews appeared in the clearing.

Miranda looked down at Ash who was still cuddling into her leg.

"It's ok. You're safe."

Bang.

A loud explosion ripped through the air, and they all ducked. The car had exploded. Grayson and his two bodyguards, who were still close to the vehicle, were propelled through the air and landed with great force on the ground. They weren't moving.

"Gray!" Sophie screamed and despite the fact she had been limping moments earlier, raced back through the clearing to her husband, closely followed by Ash. On seeing Ash run after his mother, Miranda's own legs began to carry her towards them.

"Ash, stop."

"Daddy," the little boy called out, completely ignoring her.

One of the policemen raced past her and grabbed Ash before he could go any further. The spirited child was desperate to check on his father, so he kicked and screamed, but the officer was stronger.

"Grayson." Sophie slid to the floor next to her husband, and Miranda, who was now assisting with keeping Ash away from what could be a horrendous sight, watched on with bated breath.

Eventually, after what seemed like forever, Grayson groggily started to sit up. Miranda let out the breath she didn't realise she'd been holding as Sophie wrapped her arms around her husband and smothered him in kisses. The policeman let Ash go so he could join his parents. Gradually, the other men shifted, and Mike, Grayson's bodyguard, got to his feet and came to her side.

"You alright, Mrs North?"

She looked up at him. He had a massive bruise forming on his head, and his clothes were scorched from the explosion, yet he was asking how she was.

"I'm fine," she answered before collapsing on the floor with shock.

TWO

Pete

Pete was quicker racing through the hospital than his son who trailed behind him.

"Miranda North." He pushed aside a lady who stood waiting at the reception and used his intimidating height to elicit answers about his wife.

"Sir, please. I'm dealing with this lady first." The receptionist looked at him over her thick rimmed glasses. She was one of those ladies who would normally terrify you, but he was already scared enough.

"Yeah. Wait your turn." The other lady pushed him back and glared at him, a stare that had him wanting the ground to open and swallow him.

"I'm so very sorry." James stepped up beside them and flashed the welcoming North smile. "We've just received some very distressing news about my mother and sister. My father is slightly aggravated to see them."

"No excuse for rudeness." The woman with the evil stare responded and pushed them both out of the way to resume her conversation.

"Boss," Matthew, his son's bodyguard, called, flicking his head for them to follow him. "I got hold of Grayson's man. They're this way."

Pete shoved his son in the direction that Matthew had indicated.

"Move quicker," he urged his son as they made their way through another white-walled corridor in a hospital that seemed like a never-ending maze.

"Dad, calm down. If you go in there like this, then it'll upset Mum."

"I just need to see for myself they're ok."

"I know." James stopped, bringing him to a halt also. "Dad, the bodyguard who called said they're all fine. Shaken but alright."

"I know. It's just…" He felt the emotion within him welling up. When the call had come in to say that his wife, daughter, son-in-law, and grandson had been in an accident, they'd been decorating the banquet hall for the vow renewal. He'd wanted to do as much as possible for her so that she could just enjoy the experience. Their first wedding, though beautiful, had been associated with so many mixed emotions, leaving them unable to rejoice in the occasion.

"I know, Dad. I've been there with Amy. Mum's ok."

James brought him into an embrace. He and his son may have had their issues over the past few years, but these had been resolved and the affection between them and their close relationship as father and son was now stronger than ever.

"You've got to be kidding me. Grayson! We've just been in an accident?" Sophie's indignant voice echoed through the corridor.

"I'll make it thirty-three if you carry on. Now sit down and let the doctor look at your ankle. I'm fine. They're just superficial burns."

"No." Pete winced as his daughter's elevated reply had people looking towards the room he guessed the couple were in. "Look at his burns first."

"Enough, Sophie."

Pete pushed the door open to find his daughter being forcibly examined by a doctor while her husband stood over her. His clothes were tattered and burned away in places, the skin underneath red and raw. Ash sat on a chair in the corner of the room, wrapped within the arms of Miranda. She looked up when they entered the room and let out a small sob.

Sophie stopped struggling when she saw them and allowed the doctor to look at the wounds she appeared to have on her head and ankle.

"Grandad." Ash leapt from Miranda's arms and came running to him. Pete picked him up and cuddled him closely. Ash wasn't blood, but damn, he felt like it.

"Are you looking after Grandma for me?" Pete asked him.

"The doctor said she's got something called shock. They gave her a cup of tea, and she seems a lot better now. Matthew?" Ash addressed the bodyguard, who was standing next to him and assessing the little boy for injuries.

"Yes, little man?"

"Can you get Grandma another cup of tea? I think two cups is better than one. They wouldn't let me go and get her one."

"Of course. You want anything?"

"Lollypop? Just to overcome my shock."

"Of course." Matthew winked at him and walked out the door.

Pete placed Ash back down on the ground and led him back to where Miranda was seated. He stroked his hand down her cheek and leaned in to kiss her on the lips.

"You ok?"

She nodded, and her eyes filled with unshed tears.

"Calming down. I was so scared." Her voice broke on the last words.

"You're safe now."

He kissed her again.

"I love you," she whispered to him.

"I love you, too," he responded without hesitation.

"Sophie, listen to the doctor." James' voice boomed out.

"Grayson was the one sent flying through the air by a great big fireball. They should be looking at him and not me." His daughter sobbed.

"Back in a minute," he reassured Miranda before getting up.

"Pumpkin," Pete addressed his daughter. Grayson and James, who'd been standing around her hospital bed, parted to allow him through.

"Daddy, tell them to check Grayson out first, please," Sophie cried. "He's being a stubborn Dom."

"No, he's looking after you. You've got a head wound. The doctor needs to look at that first."

"But Grayson could have one. He flew so very high." She let out a big whimper, and her husband brought her into an embrace.

"The doctors checked me thoroughly before bringing me here. They need to check your head now, and then they can patch me up."

Sophie sniffed back her tears.

"When I saw you go through the air, I thought I'd lost you."

"I know." Grayson kissed the top of Sophie's head.

"Come on, little sis." James jostled her shoulder. "You know that Gray is made of harder stuff than that. He regularly does stunts like that on film sets. Now, let the doctor take you for scans. They need to check you've got a brain in there."

"Hey." Sophie whacked her brother, and Pete knew in that instant that his daughter was calming down.

The accident had been a shock for them all, but apart from a few cuts and bruises, they all looked to be in one piece. It could've been a lot worse, but he wasn't going to think about that.

Matthew returned with the tea and a lolly for Ash. He'd also brought a coffee for Sophie. He made another trip and returned with coffee for the rest of them. Pete drank his, sat next to Miranda with his arm wrapped around her shoulder. Sophie was wheeled out of the room to undergo a head scan, and when the results came back negative for any issues, steri-strips were placed over the cut to close it. Her ankle had swollen terribly, but a scan also confirmed that it wasn't broken. It was placed in a brace, and she was told to keep off it for a few days. That led to even more tears from his fashion-conscious daughter because it meant she wouldn't be able to wear the new Jimmy Choo shoes she'd bought for the vow renewal. Grayson had his wounds cleaned. He had a rather large burn on his back, which he was told may require surgery if it didn't heal properly. He was given strong painkillers and ordered to rest. He assured the doctor both he and Sophie would do so. Ash was checked over and given a clean bill of health. He was a little upset that he didn't get to have a cool bandage like his mother and father, but when the nurse found a sticker, proclaiming him the best patient ever, he wore it with pride. Miranda was the last to be examined. She'd whacked her hand against the dashboard when the car tumbled, and it was swollen with a sprain. She was bandaged up and also told to rest.

Grayson's security team arrived with a fleet of cars to transport them back to the castle for the night. Pete travelled with Miranda in one vehicle. His wife leaned into him and allowed the exhaustion of the day to send her to sleep. Grayson had asked Sophie to travel with James because when Ash had seen they were to go in a car again, the young boy had turned as white as a sheet. Grayson travelled with him in a car driven by Matthew because, according to Ash, the bodyguard was the best driver. Sophie had slept most of the journey, it seemed, but Ash had held on firmly to his father, clutching him more tightly whenever the car made any unusual movements. Pete had seen the worry on Grayson's face when they'd arrived at the castle an hour later.

"He'll be alright. It's a lot to take in plus he's tired. We'll get some of Mrs Aimes' food into him then bed, and he'll be right as rein tomorrow. You'll see, children recover a lot quicker than we do."

"Thanks, Dad." Grayson acknowledged his advice with a weary smile.

Later in the evening when the women had retired to bed, Pete sat with his son and Grayson by the fire in the library. Grayson was nursing a brandy in his hand and staring deeply into the fire, lost in thought.

"How's Mum?" his son asked him as he brought over the bottle of brandy to refill Pete's glass.

Pete took a long gulp and allowed the amber nectar to soothe the tension threatening to erupt into a migraine.

"She's fine. Just tired. You know your mum. Tea solves everything."

"It's the first thing I told Amy about her." James chuckled and resumed his seat.

"We'll get them all involved in the vow renewal preparations tomorrow. It will distract them from the fact they'll no doubt be sore in the morning."

"Just don't mention shoes," Grayson added with a smirk.

"Sophie still distraught?" James questioned.

"I may be phoning Jimmy Choo personally tomorrow and asking him to bring out a line of ankle braces just for Sophie to wear at the wedding."

They all laughed. Sophie being concerned more about her footwear than her injury was a sign she wasn't allowing the situation to distract her from looking good.

Matthew entered the room with his brows furrowed. James got back to his feet and poured his friend a drink.

"Andrew still not going down?"

"He's cutting his first tooth. Sonia's going to sit with him for a while. I needed to talk to you." Matthew took the glass and sat down on one of the armchairs by the fire.

"What is it?" James leaned forward and placed his elbows on his knees. His features narrowed with concern.

"I spoke to the officer investigating the crash."

Pete also leaned forward at those words, and Grayson came out of his reflective state.

"It would seem the brakes were tampered with," Matthew continued.

"What?" Pete exclaimed. James hissed in a sharp intake of breath. Grayson just looked down into the now empty glass he held.

"I suspected that," the Native American said solemnly. "I've done enough advanced driving courses for my stunt driving. I know when something isn't right. What about my inability to slow the car down with the gears?"

"Manual override was also impacted. You didn't stand a chance. If it had been a bit further up in the dales, with some of the drops there…"

"Don't," Pete interrupted, the brandy churned in his stomach, making him nauseous. "I can't think about that."

"Any ideas why? Who?" James was the practical one amongst them. He'd been through so much in his life it still left him devoid of emotion, at times, but never when his wife was concerned.

Matthew shook his head.

"Anyone had any issues they haven't told me about?"

They all shook their heads. The only problem Pete had ever had in his life was to do with Lord Braybrooke, and he was dead now.

"Do you think it's to do with Sophie?" Grayson asked.

"Sally Bridgewater?" James added.

"What?" Pete knew nothing of what they were talking about.

"No. I don't think so," Matthew replied, appearing deep in thought.

"What's going on?" Pete enquired.

Grayson nodded his head towards James to speak.

"There was an incident, recently. It was Sophie who killed Sally Bridgewater," James explained, and Pete gasped.

"What?"

"It was an accident and couldn't have happened to a more deserving woman if you asked me, but it did happen." James shrugged.

"I don't...is she ok?"

"She has nightmares, sometimes, but we're dealing with it," Grayson reassured him.

"Ok." Pete tried to quieten the dumbfounded way he was feeling about this revelation.

"What do you suggest?" James asked Matthew.

"I want to put you all on lockdown until I can investigate more. Nobody comes or goes without my say-so. It's not going to be difficult while you're here. I'm going to double security around the castle. Grayson, can I get some more of your men over here?"

"Of course." Pete was aware that Grayson had a large security retinue in America but only travelled with a few guards when he came to England because he knew James had a crew of his own to protect his family. Even Miranda and Pete had people who followed them around. James took no chances when it came to the safety of his family since the incidents involving him and Amy. Sometimes it was restricting, but Pete and Miranda went with it because they knew it allowed their son to relax and be happy with his life.

"You do whatever you need to do. I'll transfer an additional amount over to your account to cover the cost." James told Matthew.

"Are we still continuing with the renewal ceremony?" Pete asked.

"Yes," Matthew replied instantly. "That doesn't change. We need to tell the women about the extra security details because, let's face it, the second I tell Sonia what's happening, then Amy will know." Sonia was Matthew's partner, but she'd been Amy's bodyguard, at one time. Now, she was Amy's friend and confidant. The two of them discussed everything together, which Pete knew was sometimes a bone of contention with their men.

All three of the men nodded to show agreement with Matthew's response.

"If it's ok with you, James, I'd like to call in a friend of mine from MI5. He's helped us out a few times, and I know he's taking a break from government security, at the moment. He could be beneficial in finding out what's going on."

"Jasper?" James asked.

"Yes. I know this may sound strange, but too much has happened over the last few years to us all. It's beginning to not feel like coincidence anymore." Matthew got to his feet and placed his empty glass on the sideboard.

"What are you saying?" Pete asked.

"James' attackers coming back. The issues with Sally. Marie and Callum's problems with those thugs. Even my wife coming back from the dead. Something just feels wrong." Matthew stated, his face marked with tension and confusion.

"You think they're all linked?"

"As much as I hate to say it, I'm beginning to think so, yes."

The room fell silent. All four men lost in their own thoughts and worries for their families. Each had something to lose, and the fact that there was someone after them tore them all apart. Pete just had to hope they were all strong enough to face what was coming for them.

THREE

Miranda

Miranda shifted in the bed when she felt it dip with the weight of Pete getting in. She opened her bleary eyes and peered across the bed to where he lay. She still couldn't believe after all these years he was still beside her. In those moments of desperation when she was pregnant with Ryan, she had thought she'd never see him again.

He turned and saw she was awake.

"I'm sorry. I didn't mean to wake you," he apologised and pressed a kiss to her forehead.

"It's alright. I've only been sleeping lightly anyway. Whenever I fall asleep, I feel the motion of the car rolling again."

"It'll take a few days to recover. I remember when I had that crash in Cindy. I felt like I was spinning for days afterwards."

She smirked at the mention of his old Ford Cortina. The car had become a lifeline to them, and they were both devastated when she'd met an untimely demise, as the result of a patch of ice on a road outside Cambridge, fifteen years after they'd got her.

"Are Sophie, Ash, and Grayson alright?" she asked.

"All sleeping. Grayson put Ash's mattress in the room with him and Sophie, so they could keep an eye on him. He was a little reluctant to go to sleep as he feared he'd have nightmares. He's only eight, and it's frightened him. Give him a few days, and he'll bounce back."

"I think it scared us all." Miranda brought her hand to the locket around her neck. She could've died, today, and never had the chance to find Ryan.

"I'm still looking."

"I know." He brought her closely to him. He smelled freshly showered, something he always liked to do before bed no matter what. A hint of brandy was still

on his breath, though. The men she surrounded herself with were all alpha domi-
nants. She could picture them all downstairs, brandy in hand, discussing how they
would protect their women. She allowed herself to be calmed by this vision and
laughed.

"What?"

"Nothing."

He raised an eyebrow at her. Not a knowing one, but the type that said she was
going to be in trouble if she didn't tell him the thoughts running through her head.
Lies earned a spanking. It was an adage she knew both her children lived by, especially Sophie who, it seemed, had a constant problem with sitting down
comfortably.

"Okay," she huffed. "I was thinking about you and all the boys"–because let's
face it they were boys compared to Pete– "downstairs with brandy in hand and
putting the world to rights."

Her husband chuckled, and she felt it vibrate through her body –such was their
closeness as she lay cradled in his arms.

"It was a bit like that. James, Grayson, and Matthew are definitely alpha males,
and through them, I've learned a lot about how to look after the woman I love."

"Oh yeah?" Miranda pushed up on his chest to allow herself to come to a sitting
position. He moved his arms, placing them behind his head. "What have you
learned exactly?"

"That's for me to know and you to experience."

Miranda rolled her eyes when her husband finished his sentence with a waggle
of his eyebrows.

"Well then, give me that experience."

Pete's face turned serious.

"You need sleep to rest and recover."

"I need you inside me and moving at a rapid pace. That's what I need. A damn
good fucking to take away the spinning feeling. Leaving my head totally spaced
out from coming instead of stressing."

"Wow!" Pete exclaimed. "It still never fails to get me from semi-hard to hard
enough to bang nails in, in a few seconds, when you stop being prim and proper
and demand what you need in such a dirty way." Miranda could feel her cheeks
start to blush. Despite the intervening years, Pete still made her feel like the young
girl he'd fallen in love with before they'd experienced the scars of losing their baby.
She suppressed the thought. Her mind was awash with different emotions since
the accident, and she knew she needed Pete to fuck her into oblivion, so she could
sleep like a log.

"Fuck me...." She paused and thought carefully about the next word she was
about to say before expelling it from her lungs with breathless lust, "Sir."

It was a clear night with the full moon shining in through the windows. She'd
always liked to sleep with the curtains open since her time in the dungeon.
Initially, it had been difficult to get used to the light nights during the summer, but
the sun setting at ten pm and rising at four am no longer bothered her. Although
the light in the room was dim, now, she saw Pete's eyes darken at her words.

Before she had a chance to register what was happening, she was flipped over
onto all fours.

"If it gets too much for your wrist, just say," Pete whispered into her ear.

"What are you going to do?" she moaned back at him when she felt his hand slide between her thighs and the folds of her sex. She'd slept in one of Pete's t-shirts for so long, now, she never wore anything else. Even during the brief period they were apart, she still used an old one he'd left behind. It was so faded and tatty by the time they'd reunited that Pete incinerated it and gave her a new one with great pride. Neither of them had the perfect bodies. Her hips had birthed children and had never quite gone back to the slimline version of her youth. Pete was going gray on top and a few too many cakes were starting to leave a little extra weight behind despite the fact he worked out regularly. They were normal people their age, not the fantasy created by plastic surgery, and she wouldn't have it any other way.

Suddenly, she felt Pete's hand smack her bare bottom.

"Ouch." She shifted, but he pulled her hips back closer to him.

"That's for thinking I'm no match for those thirty-year olds down the hallway."

"I never said that," she protested, and he smacked her again. "What was that for?"

"Nothing other than the fact my handprint looks sexy on your backside." He pulled her hips into his groin, and she felt his hardness ready for her. "Do you trust me?"

"Yes." Miranda didn't need to hesitate on her answer. She trusted him implicitly.

"Red?" he questioned.

"Stop all activity, no resumption," she replied.

"Amber?"

"Stop and discuss."

"Green."

"Go for it." She allowed the edges of her lips to curl up into a playful smirk.

"Let's play, then." Pete jumped from behind her on the bed, and she shifted back around so she could watch him.

"What are you going to do?" She saw him retrieve one of her scarfs from the wardrobe and a box from a drawer.

"Matthew and I had a bit of a discussion on the way up here. He gave me some ideas. As well as a lecture on making sure I treat you right. I think he's got a soft spot for you." Pete collected a glass of water and came back to the bed.

"He misses his mother. It's been a little while since he's got over to France to visit her, and ever since she lost her arm, he's been really concerned with how she copes with the disability." When Matthew's long thought deceased wife had reappeared a while back, his parents had been caught in the cross-fire. His mother had lost her arm due to gunshot wounds, and his father had lost his ability to think properly after he was shot in the head. The two of them lived with relatives close to Bordeaux, so he knew they were well cared for. He went to visit as often as he could, but it wasn't always possible with his job and now Andrew.

"Maybe we can get James to bring his parents over to stay for a little while?"

"I'll talk to him. Anyway, stop distracting me."

She raised the fabric of her t-shirt to display herself to her husband. Her folds shimmered with her arousal.

"Fuck me!" Pete exclaimed and dropped everything he was holding onto the bed.

"I was rather hoping you would fuck me?" She laughed, and her husband pounced on her, pinning her to the bed. His hands roamed over her body while their lips joined and savoured the taste of lust that they both had for each other.

"Damn, I love you." Pete pulled away and brought the scarf into his hands. "I'm going to blindfold you."

"Green," she replied and allowed Pete to first remove her t-shirt and then put the blindfold over her eyes.

"I want you to lie back and part your legs," Pete ordered with an authoritative tone, sending shivers straight to the throbbing bundles of nerves between her thighs. "Relax."

She shut her eyes, despite having the blindfold on, and listened to his movements. She felt his breath on her body when he leaned in closer to trail a path of kisses from her breasts to her pussy. He stopped where she knew the small scar from her caesarean was and pressed extra kisses to it. The blemish wasn't big but could be seen. Thankfully neither James nor Sophie had ever asked questions about it when they were younger.

Pete lowered the path of his mouth, now alternating between kisses and small bites, setting her skin on fire. Her body tingled with the anticipation that being deprived of her sight provided.

When Pete trailed his tongue up the length of her sex, she groaned in pleasurable desire. He wrapped his mouth around her pussy, and she felt him eating her out like she was a final supper laid bare for his decadence. She could feel the orgasm building within her. It wouldn't be too long before she'd be quaking underneath his mouth from a powerful climax. He pulled away, though, and the disappointed groan, which left her lips, earned her a smack to the side of her hip.

"Pete," she squirmed, the response from her husband doing nothing to calm her need for satisfaction.

"No coming until I say, and it's not time yet."

The whimper that left her mouth was strained with frustration.

She listened closely to Pete fumbling around with something on the bed, and she remembered the small box he'd retrieved from a drawer. Wrapping was removed, and then whatever he had was swirled around in the glass of water. She could hear it hit the sides of the glass. When the cold droplets of water fell onto her pussy, instinctively, she went to shut her legs, but Pete rested between them creating a barrier that prevented her from hiding away. A pressure pushed against the entrance to her sex. It wasn't Pete because it felt different –no, it was a toy. She opened her legs wider to allow him to nudge the device inside her. It felt large, and she stretched to accommodate it. When seated, he allowed her time to adjust to the intrusion before taking her wetness and sliding it down to her puckered entrance. They'd done anal several times before, but not recently, and it surprised her.

"Relax," his gravelly voice warned, and she complied with several deep breaths. Next thing she knew, there was pressure at her other hole and a device slipping inside.

Her entire body felt like it was on the knife's edge of an orgasm when a click sounded, and the devices were switched on. The gentle movements stimulated her and left her feeling incredibly full. Pete shifted on the bed, and she felt the head of his cock nudge at her lips.

"Colour?" he questioned.

"Green," she breathlessly replied with the force of an orgasm already building rapidly down below. She opened her mouth and welcomed his cock inside her warmth.

"You're going to take all I give you. I'm going to feed you my cock until you swallow it deeply and choke." She felt him push inside her, to the back of her throat. Sucking Pete's dick was one of her favourite pastimes, and he often commented that she was worthy of the title 'better than a porn star' when it came to fellatio.

"So full," she murmured around his length, her tongue licking up and down the ridges that framed his penis. Pete grabbed her hair and took control of her movement. He fucked her mouth with wild abandonment, all the time increasing the speed on the vibrators buried in her pussy and arsehole. She was glad he'd taken charge because she damn near lost her mind when the orgasm she needed tumbled into her with a dramatic climax. She screamed around his dick as he buried himself deeper and came in her mouth. His essence coating the back of her tongue and running down her throat. She swallowed as much as she could, but his love for her was too much, and her mind was flying too high with the pleasure cascading through her body. His cum flooded out of her mouth and dropped down her chin and onto her breasts. Pete pulled back, allowing her to gasp for breath and fill her oxygen-starved lungs.

"Are you ok?"

"Yes."

He leaned forward and checked before turning the devices off and removing them from inside her. She whimpered at the tender feeling of her body. He pulled the blindfold away from her eyes and helped her to lie back.

"Time for you to sleep." He jumped off the bed and went to the bathroom to retrieve a wet towel, which he used to clean her. He dropped it onto the floor and climbed in next to her before bringing her into his arms and settling in for sleep.

"Thank you," she murmured, her body exhausted and her mind finally starting to switch off. "If you let me sleep for a few hours, then we can go for round two."

Pete chuckled and kissed the top of her forehead. "Not sure about that, my love. I think you're mistaking me for the thirty-year olds down the hallway."

She tried to raise her arm to pat his chest in a playful gesture of annoyance, but her body was already well on its way to the world of slumber.

FOUR

Miranda

"Mum have you seen my Tiffany bracelet?" Sophie delved deeper into the bag in front of her and started to throw the contents over her shoulder. "I know I brought it with me. What the hell have I done with it?"

Miranda couldn't keep the laugh in any longer. It erupted from her at the same time as Amy's and Sonia's. This exact scenario was reminiscent of her daughter's wedding day when she panicked and lost her garter. Amy placed down the brush she'd been using to style her long blonde hair into a fishtail plait and got to her feet. She wandered over to the dresser behind Sophie and picked up a box.

"Is this it?"

Sophie nodded enthusiastically.

"Thank you. For a PA, I'm a such a forgetful clutz at times. Amy, I love you." Sophie hugged her sister-in-law.

"I hope in a different way to your brother." Amy screwed her nose up, and the laughter bellowed out again.

Thomas, who was approaching eighteen months and had been walking with that cute toddler amble for a few months, now, teetered over to her. He started a conversation that probably made so much sense to him but was still nothing but babble to her. Amy had fallen pregnant with her second child very quickly after her first but was coping well with two children under two. She'd given up the day to day management of her dancing school to her friend Elena but remained an executive partner for when she was needed. Often that need involved her leaving the children with Miranda and just catching a moment's breath by dancing for an hour. Her writing was something she continued with but without the pressure of having to identify when her next release would be. For all intents and purposes, Amy North was a full-time wife and mother and couldn't be happier. Miranda brought Thomas onto her lap, and he showed her the new car that he'd been given by James.

"Brmmm." Or what sounded like that came out of his mouth.

"Yes, cars go broom."

"Careful Miranda, he's just eaten a rusk. He could have dirty hands." Amy came to her side, grabbing a towel on the way.

"It's alright. When you're a grandma, you have to expect a few grubby hand prints, even on your wedding vow renewal day."

Sophie let out a laugh and slammed her hands over her mouth.

"What?" Miranda asked.

"Nothing."

"Sophie? Do I need to tell Grayson to add five to his current count?" Miranda raised a playful eyebrow, and Thomas, sensing the mischievous nature of the moment, clapped his hands and bounced up and down on her lap.

"You wouldn't!"

"Then spill."

"I hate being the baby in this family. You're all supposed to tease Amy, now. She's younger than me." Sophie moaned.

"I think you'll find they tried when I first married James. I'm not as easy to do it to as you."

Sophie stuck her tongue out.

"Fine, all I thought was that it isn't just when you are a grandma you get grubby hands on you on your wedding day. I'm pretty certain by the time Grayson had finished with me on our wedding day my dress was filthy."

"Oh my god, I don't need to hear that!" Miranda exclaimed.

"Well you shouldn't have asked." Sophie placed her hand on her hip and wiggled her eyebrows.

"Glad I did, though, as it reminds me of just what your father and I got up to last night and will definitely be repeating during the next few days. I'm not leaving the bedroom."

All the other women in the room placed their hands over their ears and started to sing,

"La, la, la."

"Just because I'm a few years older doesn't mean we've stopped doing it."

"Mum, please."

Sonia coughed to clear her throat, and they all looked at her.

"Is it still as intense?" she asked.

"Is what still as intense?" Miranda wanted to clarify. From what she'd heard, Sonia and Matthew were more into a masochist style of BDSM.

"All of it, the feelings, the dominant nature of the partner, the orgasms." Sonia blushed a little red on the last word.

"Yes. Does it stay that way?" Amy asked this time and lifted Thomas from her lap when he held his arms up to his mummy.

Miranda went quiet for a moment. She needed to think about her answer. So much had happened between her and Pete, but the love they shared for each other still grew if that was even possible. Once she collected her thoughts, she knew her answer.

"It gets better. More intense, more dominant, more orgasms."

"Ewwww." Sophie shuddered, and they all started to laugh again.

Miranda felt a tear come to her eye. Before she could rein it in, the pearl slid down her cheek.

"Mum." Sophie came running to kneel in front of her. "What's wrong?"

"Nothing." More tears fell –so many thoughts started to run through her head but the main one to emerge was the memory of the night long ago when Pete had returned from visiting her father with Matthew. He'd given her no details of the visit other than her father was dead, and he didn't know where Ryan was. She'd not asked at the time because she wasn't ready to face more talk of her father and what had happened to him. She was ready now, though. She needed to know and before the renewal. There was a door in her life that had to be closed before she could embrace the future. "Go get your father."

"What?" Sophie spluttered. "Mum talk to me, please. What's wrong?"

"I promise you it's nothing bad. I just need to ask him something before the ceremony."

Sophie's voice was almost a whisper, "Is it about when James made him leave?"

"No. That door is closed. I just want to ask him about something from our youth."

"About the ice-cream?"

They'd told James and Sophie the story of the first time they'd met as children when they'd been at Broadstairs with their families on holiday.

"Yes." She nodded.

"I'll go," Amy offered. "I think James can look after this little monkey, so we can get dressed properly."

Sonia got to her feet.

"I think Matthew can take Andrew for a while, as well. He seems to think he needs to run the security despite the fact Jasper and all of Grayson's men are here. He can relax and take the day off for once."

Sonia and Amy left the room with their sons while Isabella remained sleeping silently in her crib in the corner.

"Mum. You promise me you're ok."

"I'm not calling the vow renewal off. I promise."

There was a knock on the door.

"That was quick. Come in!" Miranda shouted out.

But instead of Pete entering, Jasper, Matthew's ex MI5 colleague, appeared.

"Can we help?" Sophie asked.

"I'm sorry to disturb you. I was asked to give you this." Jasper pulled a package from behind his back. "I think it's a present, which has arrived for you. Security have apparently cleared it."

"Thank you." Miranda took the box and placed it down on the dressing table. "I'm sorry if the trouble we're having is upsetting your original plans for your time off. I must say we're so grateful to have you here, though. Matthew assures us you're a fantastic officer, so we feel incredibly safe in your hands."

"You've not impacted on anything, Mrs North. I'm honoured to help. Matthew and I worked closely together in the past. He had my back every time, and I've got his, now."

"You're a wonderful man." She reached out to squeeze Jasper's hand in a show of gratitude but was a little shocked when he pulled back quickly.

"Sorry. I have issues with touch," he explained, and she nodded.

"Jasper," Sophie interjected. "You've got strong muscles. Do you think you could help me move Isabella and her crib down to the main reception room? Might as well get her settled down there for the wedding."

"Good idea." Jasper smiled at Miranda's daughter and effortlessly picked up the crib and cooed at Isabella when she momentarily stirred. They tiptoed silently out the door.

She was finally left alone to catch all her thoughts. The castle had been a hive of activity since first thing this morning, and she was still feeling a little sore after the car accident. There was a knock at the door, and Pete popped his head in.

"You alright?" His eyes were filled with worry.

She nodded and motioned to the bed.

"Aren't we supposed to do that bit after the ceremony?" He wiggled his eyebrows suggestively.

"That's not what I asked you here for."

"Damn"–he rearranged himself within his pants– "what is it?"

She took a seat on the bed, and Pete came to sit next to her.

"I want to know what happened the day my father died."

Pete's face fell.

"Honey, why drag up the past, now? It's long since buried."

"I need the closure. I have to hear how he died before I can move on properly."

She watched him shut his eyes and let out a long breath as he made his decision on what to say.

"Everything, Pete. You have to tell me everything."

"Ok." He stood, but rather than begin his story, he went over to a dresser in their room, which she knew held hidden glasses and brandy. He poured one large glass and placed the bottle on her dressing table next to the box Jasper had brought in, reminding her she needed to open it. However, the present was quickly forgotten again when Pete walked back to her, gave her the brandy, and started his story.

"We went to see him on the premise of a business deal. You know the sort that would make him lots of money. He was more than happy to meet us. I knew the instant I walked in the room, though, he'd recognised me. Slightly ironic given he'd never remembered my face before. Obviously stealing his daughter away from him left a lasting impression, finally."

"He was just arrogant. He didn't want to know a person if they couldn't make him money. In his warped mind, you weren't on his level and therefore inconsequential and not worth remembering. The only reason he probably remembered he had a daughter was because he could sell me to the highest bidder."

"I wish I could say that wasn't true, but alas we both know differently. Anyway"–Pete shifted so he was more comfortable– "it had been twenty-five years since I'd last seen him. He'd aged so much in that time and not in a good way. For an eighty-five-year-old, I remember thinking he looked a lot older if that were even possible. He could barely walk and used a wheelchair, I suspected, as there was one in the room. His eyesight appeared to be failing, given he squinted a lot, but his mental capacity was there. He was still sharp as a tack. When he saw me, he called for security? However, Matthew was able to easily incapacitate them. I'm not proud of myself for this next bit, but the anger within me re-surfaced for what he'd done. I couldn't tamper it down. The words I used to let him know what I thought of him were ones I don't think have ever left my mouth before. They washed straight over him, though, and he laughed at me. I saw red and raised my fist ready to lash out. Thankfully, Matthew prevented me from laying a finger on him. It was what he wanted. It was at that point I calmed down and allowed my brain, not my heart, to take over. I started to tell him about our life. I showed him pictures of James and Sophie, let him know how successful I'd become in my career, and how James was well on his way to his first billion. I told him how in love we all were with life. I may have exaggerated a bit, given what James was going through with the assault at the time, but I wanted him to know everything he'd missed out on. Family, love, and devotion. But, still nothing –do you know what he asked me?"

"No."

"Did James know who he was because he needed money to repair Braybrooke Hall? I hadn't thought about it before then, but the building was in disrepair. In fact, Matthew investigated his finances after we left, and he was heavily in debt. All his scheming had failed."

Miranda ran her hand over her head in frustration.

"Money, it was always about money."

"Title and dominance but not in the way that we know it. Matthew warned him that should he ever try and contact James, it would be the last thing he did."

"I'm so glad Matthew came into our lives. I'd be lost without him."

"Yes." Pete shifted again, the tension of the conversation weighing heavily upon him. She leaned over and stroked at the back of his hand in comfort.

"It was then I asked him about Ryan. I told him if he needed money to repair Braybrooke Hall, I wanted to know where our son was. He refused the offer. Told me the whereabouts of our son would go to the grave with him. Matthew started to tear his office apart looking for information. We took copies of his hard-drive, details of his financial transactions, and when we searched back through it all, there was nothing, not one lead. It was as if our son had vanished into thin air. That was the first time I truly questioned what had happened to him. The first time I believed he might have died."

"No." She felt her heart breaking. "No, I would know. I would know if he was gone. He can't be."

"Sssh"–Pete reassured her with a kiss to the lips– "he's alive. I know it because of something your father mentioned. He told me our son had the life he deserved being the illegitimate child of a nobody. That was it….to him I was a nobody without the background or wealth that he valued so highly. It was the reason for everything he did. Pure hatred and the fear he would have nothing if he allowed us to be in a relationship."

"I don't understand?"

"We were better than him. He saw it when we were together. Your mother was the same. She was better than him, not just because of her ancestry but also in character. He was lacking and compensated in the wrong way. He was a sad man. So, I gave him a choice, thinking of him as nothing but mercenary."

"Choice?" Miranda leaned forward.

"I laid the offer back out on the table: our son for the money he wanted. I knew if he asked for a bit more than we had, then James would be able to help, so I offered him ten million. Enough to make the repairs and live out his life in peace and prosperity. He had assurances the transaction would be done without reference to where the money came from. As far as people were concerned Miranda Braybrooke had died around the same time as her mother. We reassured him she wouldn't return to society and shame him, and his good name would remain intact. I told him he could either accept the offer or choose to end his days with a pistol, but with no guarantees I wouldn't destroy his reputation. Both Matthew and I expected him to take the money."

"He chose the pistol," she blurted out, knowing that once her father had chosen a path, he'd never waver from it. That was who he was. Spite had filled him, leaving him twisted and bitter. He was a man devoid of compassion even in her childhood, but by then he would've been virtually unrecognisable.

"Yes, having kept his secret from us for all those years, to preserve his title, reputation, and property, he then chose in his final moments to increase his vindictiveness by taking it with him to the grave."

"You shot him?" She could barely get the words out.

"No. I held the gun to his temple while the room filled with his maniacal laughter. It still haunts me to this day. But, no, I couldn't do it. Matthew took over, and your father died just as he lived, full of insanity. I just hope that by taking his life Augusta and Jim can find peace in their eternal rest."

Pete looked down at the floor. His eyes filling with tears at the thought of the man he'd become such good friends with. A few years after his death, they'd discovered that her father had, at least, had him buried in consecrated ground, albeit in an unmarked grave. To cover up what had really happened the night she'd escaped from the house in Dumfries, Jim, or Mr Pearson as she still thought of him, had been blamed for the murder of her mother. It was believed that, subsequently, he'd been killed by her father's guards while they were defending their employer. Alright, it was partly the truth but there was no mention of her and Pete's role in the story. She sensed more lay behind the unshed tears in her husband's eyes.

"I'm sorry. There is something I never told you."

"What?" Her hand entwined with his.

"I had your father's coffin removed. I didn't want him to remain buried next to your mother. It would haunt her. I had it swapped with Jim's. Matthew is a master at these things. I asked, and a few weeks later he told me it was done."

She placed her hand to her face again, the knuckle of her index finger resting under her nose to help stifle the sobs.

"Thank you. Thank you. She found peace, finally. They both found it together. As for my father, it's one of the biggest insults he could ever be given. A grave of a nobody."

"You're not angry?"

"No. Not at all."

"I know Braybrooke Hall went to my Uncle, but he didn't want it and sold it to the public. It's run by a trust, which uses it as a tourist attraction. A part of me has always wanted to visit, but I didn't want to go, knowing my father was there, even though dead. Now I can. I can go and say goodbye to my mother."

"You can. I'll take you in a few days if you want?"

"I'd like that."

Pete leaned forward and pressed a kiss to her lips.

"Are you alright now?"

Miranda looked over to the antique clock on her bedside table.

"Goodness, it's almost twelve. We're to marry in an hour. Out"–she jumped up from the bed and started to shoo her husband– "Come on, out. I need to get ready."

"Jesus, woman. You're crazy." He laughed.

"Sooner we marry,"–she licked her lips- "sooner you can get me back in this bed."

"Bye." Pete turned on his heel and sped out of the door. She let out a laugh. The tension of the conversation having dissipated with the knowledge that her father had died a coward and resided now in hell. Her son was alive, and she'd talk to Matthew, again, about finding him. Perhaps, see if they could try and find some new avenues to explore. Maybe Jasper could help.

Jasper, she suddenly remembered the box. In her hurry to get to it, she tripped on a car left on the floor by Thomas. She fell forward onto her dressing table, sending the brandy and the box flying off it. They both landed with a thud on the floor, the brandy glass shattering and spilling everywhere. The lid of the box fell off, and a flash of white light blinded her. It took a few seconds to gather her senses, and when she did, the room was filling with flames. The small box must have contained something explosive, and it had mixed with the flammable brandy. The fire spread rapidly with the curtains nearby catching alight in seconds. She ran towards the doorway to her room to raise the alarm, but when she turned the door handle, she found it was locked.

"What?" she exclaimed and tried again. Nothing. She turned back to the fire, which was spreading, and thick smoke now clouded the room causing her to choke on the acrid air.

She bunched up her fist and thumped loudly on the door. She had to get out of here, or she'd be burned alive.

"Help!" she screamed. An alarm sounded outside. The fire alarms had been activated and rapid footsteps clattered along the hallway.

"Get everyone out and call 999." She heard Matthew order.

"Help!" she screamed again.

"Who was that?" a feminine voice asked in panic.

"Sonia, get everyone out," Matthew ordered.

"Ok."

"Help!"–Miranda screamed even louder– "I can't get out. The fire's in here."

"Miranda." Matthew's voice came from the other side of the door.

"Help me, please." She coughed as the thick smoke twisted around her.

The door rattled.

"No key."

"Mum." She heard James' voice.

"Get out," Matthew ordered.

"Not fucking happening," came James' swift response.

"Stubborn arse," Matthew cursed. "We're going to have to kick the door down. Miranda, can you get to the side of the room?"

"Yes." She looked to her left and saw a space where she could take cower while they rescued her.

"Stand back,"–Matthew called seconds before what she assumed was his foot thudded against the door– "damn English oak. You couldn't have furnished the house from Ikea like any normal person."

Another thud came as she heard James say, "It's authentic."

"It's damn near impossible to kick in."

"We could use the sideboard as a battering ram."

"Not just a pretty face."

"Fuck you and help me lift this thing," James demanded.

The next thing she knew, the hammering grew louder and more regular. Her head was starting to spin from all the smoke she was inhaling, the breathable air in the room was being replaced with carbon monoxide. Finally, after what seemed like forever, the door splintered onto the floor, and Matthew's broad form filled the space. Before she could draw another breath, he had her in his arms, and they were speeding out of the castle and onto the front lawn where he laid her down on the cool grass. Sophie rushed at her with water, and Grayson who appeared to have been holding Pete back with several of his bodyguards let go of him, and her husband came to her side.

"Is she ok?"

"Is there an ambulance on the way?" She heard Matthew ask, in between her attempts at breathing fresh air into her smoke-filled lungs.

"Box," she spluttered.

"What?" Matthew bent down at her side.

"Box. Exploded. The gift."

"What's she on about?" Matthew questioned, and she grew frustrated that she couldn't manage to speak properly.

"The gift. Jasper." She tried again.

"You mean the box Jasper brought in exploded?" Sophie questioned.

She nodded.

"What's this?" Jasper bent down beside them.

"You brought a gift to Miranda."

"Yeah, a little black box addressed to her and Pete for their wedding vow renewal. Security told me it had been cleared. A man named Mike?"

"It exploded." Matthew scowled.

"What the fuck? Sorry." Jasper blushed at his language in front of them all.

"Is everyone out?" Matthew asked.

"Yes. All accounted for, including the staff."

Miranda looked at Pete –his face was white as snow. She then turned to face Matthew.

"Whatever is happening here, I think it just escalated." Matthew stood up and nodded towards James who was cradling a crying Thomas in his arms.

The sound of sirens flooded the courtyard of the castle as several fire engines and an ambulance arrived. People started to run everywhere, and she felt someone trying to examine her, but all she wanted to do was escape and hide. Why did she have the feeling that whatever was behind the attack on them, related back to her father? Even dead, he was haunting her from the grave.

FIVE

Pete

The stale air was filled with the stench of smoke. A large section of the east wing of his son's castle lay in a mass of scorched wood and tattered timbers. Thankfully, most of the property was undamaged and still habitable. All that had been lost was a few priceless antiques. Only things, and not people. He'd nearly lost Miranda. She'd been in the room where the fire had started. His stomach turned at the thought.

The damping down took most of the day. Miranda was taken to the hospital while they assisted in salvaging what they could. The quick work of the fire brigade saved so much. He was tired and dirty, and hunger was something that had long since passed. All around him, he saw weary faces. When Miranda returned a few hours later with a clean bill of health, she was sent to rest in one of the rooms in the west wing. It was an area that was mostly used for paying guests. James rented out the castle when they weren't in residence.

He'd come back to their replacement room, earlier, to shower but had just stood staring out of the window ever since. He'd seen the fear in her eyes. It was the same look she had when her father took her away from him. Was it too much of a coincidence to believe that he could, in some way, be behind this. He was dead for fuck's sake. How could he be? Their minds were playing tricks on them –such was the exhaustion and the pressure of the last few days.

Miranda shifted on the bed. "Pete," she called out.

"I'm here." He went straight to her side and cradled her within his arms.

"Is the damage bad?"

"It's not good, but nothing James can't have his men come in and fix within a few months."

"I'm such an idiot" Miranda placed her head in her hands.

"It's not your fault." When she'd finally been able to get her breath back, his wife had told them how she'd tripped and sent the box and the brandy flying onto the floor, causing the fire. She'd been so apologetic to their son, but James had told her categorically it was in no way, shape, or form her fault. Whoever planted the explosive device was to blame. In fact, her tripping possibly saved her from more serious harm when the device could have blown up in her face. Jasper had it sent back to MI5 to see if there was anything that could be determined from it. Matthew was rather impatiently awaiting the results. The man hadn't stopped since the first sound of the fire alarm.

"But if I hadn't knocked the brandy over...."

"We'd be sitting by your hospital bed hoping you survived after an explosion in your face. Property can be replaced. People can't."

"Why is this happening? I don't understand."

"I wish I knew because I'd be putting a stop to it. None of us have done anything wrong. Not really. We're good people. It's so frustrating."

"It is." Miranda shifted on the bed. He watched her slide her legs from under the covers. She was naked, except for a t-shirt she'd borrowed from Matthew. Most of their clothes had been destroyed, and what little could be saved, smelled atrocious. They'd go shopping tomorrow, or rather they'd have a highly vetted person bring clothes to them because Matthew wouldn't allow them out of the house. Slowly, his wife padded along the wooden and rug covered floor to the new dressing table she was using. She took a long look in the mirror.

"Go get me the girls?"

"What?"

"The girls. Get them for me?"

"Why?" he questioned and joined her by the dressing table.

"Because I need them to find me something to wear, do my hair and make-up, and make me look like a bride. And if you say why again, Peter Kenneth North, then I'm going to bash you on the head to knock some sense into you."

She still wanted to get married, again. He tried to hold in the smile at her resilience. It was a beauty only he ever really saw.

"People are tired. Let's do it tomorrow."

"No." She turned to face him and placed her hands on her hips. "Whoever caused this, I'll not let them win. All we need for this wedding is the people in this Castle. They are the guests. We don't even need a priest –we're already married. All we're doing is re-affirming our vows to each other. We can look up the service on the internet, and one of the others can read it: James, Matthew, or Grayson. The girls are my bridesmaids, but if one of them wanted to do it, then they could. Pete, please. I want to do this. Now. Here. I won't let him win."

Him. The word confirmed Pete's thoughts.

"Your father?"

"Don't tell me that the thought hasn't crossed your mind. That somehow this is linked to him. The escalation just at the time of our vow renewal. We were directly targeted today. Either one of us could have opened that present."

"If it is"–Pete tried to damper down the anger rising in him– "I won't rest until I put his ghost to rest."

"That's why we have to show him we're stronger."

"I'll go get the girls."

The house was a flurry of feverish activity for the next hour. He was thrown in a shower and then squeezed into a suit borrowed from James because his was burnt in the fire. They were similar in size although his son just had a slightly narrower waistline, which needed fixing with a safety pin to extend the waist and to hold his trousers up. He was told that Miranda had a dress but from where, nobody would tell him.

Before long, they were all gathered and were ready to celebrate. Miranda took his breath away when she walked down the aisle. She was wearing the same wedding dress that, just under two years ago, Sophie had worn. He'd forgotten it had been stored here after dry cleaning. It was a princess style dress, which was full-on theatrical and gave her the appearance of being the queen and matriarch of the family that she was.

"You look amazing," he uttered breathlessly when she came to his side, and he kissed the top of her forehead.

"I can't believe I fit in it. With a couple of safety pins." She laughed.

"Believe me, you're not the only one held together with them." He winked, and she laughed back.

Their family and close friends assembled around them, forming a circle. Matthew stood off to the side, his finger to a microphone in his ear. Sonia nodded towards James who gave his best friend and bodyguard a glare, leaving the big man with no uncertainty that he was to join the circle. Matthew reluctantly handed his earpiece over to Jasper and pushed his way in between Sonia and Amy.

James started the ceremony traditionally,

"Dear Beloved, we are gathered here today…"

Pete drifted off as his son spoke. He only had eyes for Miranda, and when he looked down at her, he saw she only had the same for him. James finished his speech, and Amy took over. Miranda whipped her head around at this, and their daughter-in-law leaned in to explain,

"We're all marrying you. Your friends and family."

"Oh, how beautiful"–Miranda turned back to him– "was this your idea?"

"I wish it had been, but Sonia is the genius at work here, not me."

Miranda smiled gratefully at their friend.

Amy continued and everyone else took a turn in saying a passage from the speech they'd printed off the internet. When it came to the vows, everyone went silent to listen to them. It was his turn first.

"I, Peter Kenneth North, take you, Miranda North, to be my wife, again. I've made mistakes, so many of them, but I've never stopped loving you. My heart is yours. It's been entwined with yours since we were children. So many times, we've been forced apart, but we always find our way back together. Destiny has defined us. You've given me the gift of beautiful children"–he purposely left out the number of them, but he knew that his wife would understand he meant three and not two. They were symbiont to each other's thoughts in many ways– "a part of me and you combined."

"No sex talk," James interrupted with a heckle.

"Hush, you, or I'll make Thomas do the same to you and Amy one day."–Pete winked at his son and continued his speech– "When I first met you, you were stunning, but each day you've grown more beautiful. Until death do us part, and even then, for evermore."

Miranda wiped a tear away from her cheek.

"I, Miranda North, take you, Peter Kenneth North, to be my husband, again. I love you. I had so many words planned that I wanted to say to you at this moment, but I'm struggling not to break down. You and me. Always and forever."

He pulled his wife further into his arms and nestled her face against his chest as she sobbed.

"Oh god, we're going to need to re-do everyone's makeup." Sophie cried out her own whimper. Pete watched as each of the couples in the circle moved closer to their significant others. Hands touching, eyes looking longingly. Here, in this place and time, he was home. A heavy weight sat in his heart from the missing piece of their equation, though. His eldest son.

James stepped forward,

"We now pronounce you man and wife. You may kiss the bride."

Pete leaned over and pressed a chaste kiss to his wife's lips. He whispered, "I'll save the heavy stuff for when the children aren't around."

Out of the corner of his eye, he saw Jasper start to shuffle away. It looked as though the emotion of the ceremony had even got to the heavyset MI5 man.

"Jasper,"–he called out and was acknowledged with a dip of the head– "would you mind taking a picture of us all? I'm not sure when we'll all be together, again, with Sophie and Grayson being so far away in California most of the time. It'll be good to have one."

"Of course." Jasper pulled out his camera phone and held it up while they all assembled. Matthew and Sonia stepped aside.

"No,"–Miranda beckoned them over– "you have to join us."

"It's better just family." The bodyguard smiled back.

"If you don't think you're a part of this family after as many years of service you've put in with James, then you need your head examined, Matthew Carter."– Miranda continued– "You and Sonia are like another son and daughter to us. Please, we want you in the photo."

They both stepped forward, and everyone formed a line.

Jasper held his camera up and snapped a few pictures of them all.

"I'll send them over in a few minutes."

"Can we have cake now?" Ashkii stepped up. All the children and babies had been so quiet during the ceremony he'd almost forgotten they were there.

"Of course, we can"–Pete held his arms up– "Mrs Aimes, cake please."

The housekeeper and her family, who'd also been watching the ceremony, stepped aside to reveal a massive three-tiered cake.

"Goodness me. We'll be eating it for ages." Miranda looked worried at the size.

"I thought it might be nice to hand it out in the village, afterwards," James informed them.

"Good idea." Miranda patted her son on the hand and stood on tip toes to kiss him on the cheek.

"Cake, cake," Ashkii and Sophie started to chant.

Grayson raised an eyebrow at them and joined in.

"Ok." Pete picked up the knife and Miranda wrapped her hand around his. Together, they pushed the knife into the cake and cut a piece, which they pulled out. When he handed the slice to Miranda, Pete noticed a piece of paper in the gap he'd left. He stuck his hand in and retrieved it. Sadly, what was written on it would turn him off ever eating the delicious dessert again.

"Mr North." Matthew stepped forward and took the paper from him.

"Fuck."

"Pete, what is it?"

Miranda was touching his cheek.

"It *was* him."

"I don't understand?"

"The message, it read, 'A touching family reunion but isn't someone missing?'."

SIX

The Past – Ryan twelve years old

"You good for nothing, lazy, disgusting brat. Why I keep you around, I don't know? It's not as though the money they give me for you is even worth it." Ryan's foster mother, Chantelle, whacked him hard around the ear, and he was sure he could feel his brain rattling around in his head. He cursed his birth parents for leaving him here. It was a daily ritual he performed in his head. His arm was still in a cast from where his foster father, Dwayne, had broken it a few weeks back. He'd been trying to help them out by cleaning the house because he knew it would make them happy. It wasn't his fault that he'd knocked into the table and sent the plates crashing to the floor, breaking them. "I'll be asking for more money to replace all of my stuff you've broken. Do you even know how much plates are?"

He thought to himself the ones he was given to eat off were probably no more than a pound from one of the cheap shops on the high street, but he knew better than to argue with Chantelle when she was in this sort of mood,

"I don't. I'm sorry." He held his good arm across himself to ward off another attack.

"You're a good for nothing freak. No wonder they gave you to me. Wish I'd said no. Get the fuck out of my sight. You can go without dinner tonight. I've got better things to do than cook for you."

He scampered out of the room as quickly as his lanky legs could take him. Dwayne was on the sofa in the lounge with the TV playing, but he wasn't watching it. The needle sticking out of Dwayne's arm told Ryan that the lights were on, but nobody was home in his foster father's head. The man was lost to his latest heroin fix. That was the true reason they kept him –it meant they could afford to stick rubbish into their veins.

He opened the front door and stepped outside onto the walkway of the run-down east London council house he lived in. There was a chill in the air. Winter was on the way, but there was no point in asking for a coat; the only think he'd be given was a beating. He wasn't enrolled in school or any clubs, and he didn't have regular meals because the people who were supposed to be looking after him weren't prepared to spend any money on him.

His stomach rumbled and reminded him he hadn't eaten since he'd had a slice of stale toast that morning. He was tall for his age, but there wasn't an ounce of fat on him. When he'd been, reluctantly, taken to hospital for his broken arm, the doctors had told Chantelle and Dwayne that he needed to have more milk, cheese, and spinach because his bone density was weak for someone his age. He had to ask his parents what spinach was because he'd never heard of it before. He was shocked there were such things as vegetables. He couldn't recall a time he'd ever had any. Most of his meals consisted of takeaways or baked beans on toast. His little belly groaned again, and he put his good hand over it to relieve the pain that spasmed through it. If Chantelle wasn't going to feed him, then he'd have to find his own dinner. He knew just the place. His long and lanky legs sped up, and he reached the back of the pizza shop, in no time at all. The delicious smells made the knot of agony in his stomach twist even more. But when he opened the lid to the first bin, a rancid smell met his nostrils.

"Nope, too old." He put the lid back on and dry heaved a few times to rid himself of the nausea induced by the rotting food.

He opened the next one.

"Bingo." The remnants of lunchtime food rested at the top of the bin. He grabbed a few pieces and was lucky enough to find some full slices that contained his favourite topping: pepperoni. It was a good day.

He brought the first slice to his lips.

"Don't eat that." A deep voice came from behind him. He spun around to see an old man watching him. His hair was white at the edges, but he was dressed well. On either side of him stood two stocky men. They were scary.

"Who are you?" Ryan asked but backed away from them at the same time.

"I'm a concerned party," the man offered and stepped closer.

"A what?"

"A friend."

"You aren't my friend. I don't know who you are. If Chantelle and Dwayne owe you money from that stuff they put in themselves, then you need to go threaten them. I don't have any money, or I'd be in the shop buying the pizza not getting it out of the dustbin." He'd learned at the age of five that there were people who would try and use him to get money from his foster parents. They'd taken him one day and kept him locked in this house with a woman who seemed to have lots of men visiting her. He'd been there for a week before Chantelle and Dwayne had shown up with a fistful of cash, and he'd been allowed to go home. He'd kind of liked it at the other house, though. They gave him food and let him watch what he wanted to on the TV. They all just laughed at him when he'd asked if he could stay there. The second time it happened hadn't been such a pleasurable experience. He'd been beaten with a stick, and it'd left a big scar on his back.

"Would you like a pizza from inside the shop?" the man asked.

"What?"

"Would you like a pizza from inside the shop? A hot one." The old man tapped one of the men beside him. "Get Ryan a pizza of his choice. We'll be in the car."

"Pepperoni!" he shouted at the man who turned to go around to the front of the shop. It occurred to him that he should be worried the man knew his name, but he was so damn hungry he was beyond caring.

"Shall we?" The man motioned for him to follow.

"You going to hit me?" Ryan didn't move.

"Pardon."

"You going to hit me?"

"Certainly not."

"Kill me?"

"Hadn't even crossed my mind."

"Do that thing I saw Dwayne doing to Chantelle once. With his dick and pushing it in her arse."

"I can assure you that's something I'll never do." The old man's cheeks reddened with fury.

"Ok. What car you got?"

"I have a BMW."

"Cool. You've got some money."

"I have." the man agreed, and Ryan started to follow him.

"Yeah, that's a posh car. I've seen it on the programmes Dwayne watches. I like the car programmes he has on a lot better than some of the other ones. I really don't like the ones with all the women together. It looks yucky."

"Your foster father has an interesting choice of television viewing."

"Yeah. I'm not sure why I can't watch my programmes. Half the time he doesn't even know what's on."

They approached a black BMW, and Ryan let out a wolf whistle.

"This is such a cool car."

"Thank you." The old man chuckled.

The man who had gone off to get pizza reappeared. The smell distracted Ryan from the car, and he grabbed the pizza box and pulled the first slice out and shoved it in his mouth before anyone could take it away from him. It was probably the most delicious thing he'd ever tasted. He moaned with delight around the cheese and tomato goodness. Its sustenance sliding down and filling his tummy.

"Is that good?" The old man raised an eyebrow towards him.

"The best," he mumbled back with a mouth full of food.

"Good. Ryan, do you know who I might be?"

He stopped mid-bite.

"What do you mean?"

"Do you know who I am?" the man asked, again.

Ryan studied him while finishing his mouthful. He wasn't certain, but he had a few ideas. Maybe, another mouthful would help him determine the truth. He brought the pizza up to his mouth and bit down. Slowly, he chewed and swallowed.

"Are you a relative of the person who gave birth to me? The 'bitch' as Chantelle often calls her."

The old man laughed.

"I am. I'm her father."

"So that makes you my grandfather?"

The old man nodded.

"How do I know you aren't lying."

"You don't. You must trust me. I no longer speak to my daughter. She and the person who is your father are no longer allowed in my house after they abandoned you. I knew that she didn't want you, but I had no idea the lengths she'd go to get rid of you. If I'd known, I'd have never let her out of my sight as her due date approached."

"You know my father as well?"

His grandfather nodded.

"I'm sorry to say, yes. He destroyed my family and poisoned your mother against me, not that she took much persuading. It's my understanding that it was her decision to get rid of you. The heartbreak killed my wife. She died shortly after you were born."

"My grandma?"

"Yes. She would've been, I suppose."

Ryan didn't feel like anymore of the pizza. The portions that he'd eaten sat heavily in his stomach.

"Do you know where my parents are?"

"No. They left my life, and I haven't tried to contact them since. I've spent all the time I could looking for you. I came here as soon as I found you and learned about the way they've been forcing you to live.

"Are you going to take me with you?" Hope suddenly sprung in Ryan's heart for a different life. Something away from the drudgery of the one he was suffering, currently.

"Would you like to come? I'm old but can help look after you. We must be careful, though. Your parents can't find out I have you with me. They'd be so angry that I'd fear for my life and yours."

Ryan bit his lip to temper down the anger he felt at his grandfather's revelation.

"I'll be quiet. They won't know."

"Good. We can get you clean clothes and lots of food. I know you've not had much schooling. I'll hire a tutor to help you learn everything you want to know."

"Can I learn how to be a spy?" Ryan leaned forward, his eyes widening with excitement and his heart beating faster. "I saw this show the other day on the television. It was so good. The spies were so skilled, and they had cool weapons."

"If that's what you want to do, then I'll do everything in my power to help."

"Thank you." He handed the pizza box to the burly man standing next to him and flung himself at his grandfather. His thin arms wrapped around the old man's torso, and he buried his head in the man's chest. "I love you, Grandfather."

The old man stiffened, and Ryan put it down to the stress of having searched for him for so long.

"Before we go, we have to do something. Your foster parents –they can't tell anyone where you've gone."

"Ok, I'm sure I can just get in the car and go with you. They probably won't even miss me."

"No. We have to do this properly." His grandfather's face darkened. It was a look that scared him a little, but this man was promising a better life. His current one was shitty, so at this point, he was willing to try anything. "Let's go."

Ryan jumped into the car and played with all the cool buttons that allowed him to phone someone, produce ice, and even play music loudly through the entire journey. The car pulled up outside his rundown estate, and Ryan showed them to his house. When he opened the door, both Chantelle and Dwayne were in drug induced highs on the sofa.

"Drugged up, waste of spaces." He heard his grandfather mutter under his breath.

"They're like this whenever they inject the contents of that bag into their arms. It gives me peace."

"No child should see this." His grandfather frowned and slammed his fist on the door. "Prepare two more syringes," he ordered his guards. "Be careful what you touch."

The men set to work heating up the white powder until it bubbled. They pulled the needles from Chantelle's and Dwayne's arms and re-filled them before shoving them back in.

"Done." One of the men stepped towards them. "You want us to inject."

"No."

"Ryan, do you know what'll happen to them if they take too much of this drug."

He did. He'd seen it once before when he was eight. Chantelle had taken more than she should, and she got sick. An ambulance had come for her, and he'd been hidden away. It wasn't until Chantelle had come back that Dwayne had beaten her black and blue for being so stupid and nearly dying. That is what happens when you take too much of the stuff.

"You can die."

"They haven't been very nice people to you, have they?" His grandfather pointed towards his arm. "Did he do that?"

Ryan nodded.

"She doesn't feed you. They won't let you watch what you want. They beat you. They call you names. Do they deserve to live?"

He gasped.

"I can't."

"Why not? Have they ever shown you one kind moment? One kind word?"

He tried to think hard, but every memory he had of the two people who'd raised him since birth involved violence, drugs, and hatred.

"No."

"Do it. Get revenge for all the years of suffering. Nobody'll know. My men have made it look like an accident. Send them to hell." His grandfather's words stirred something inside him. An insane need to destroy the people who'd treated him like dirt. He needed to extinguish the memories that plagued his brain. His little feet carried him forward towards Dwayne, first, and his fingers surrounded the plunger of the needle. He inhaled a deep breath, and he pushed. Dwayne sat up. Ryan jumped back. His foster father's eyes widened, and his mouth moved but nothing came out. Then, he slid back down into the chair.

Ryan looked up to his grandfather who was smiling happily. "Well done. Now, her."

He went over to his foster mother and did the same. She didn't sit up, though.

She just slumped further down into the chair. The men with his grandfather went to the two comatose bodies and checked their necks.

"Gone," one said.

"Same," the other added.

"Do you have anything that you want to bring with you?" his grandfather asked. Ryan looked around at the filthy squalor, surrounding them.

"No," he replied and followed his grandfather out to the car. They climbed in, and as the the car set off, nobody spoke. He wasn't stupid –he knew he'd just killed his foster parents. Surely, he should feel sadness or guilt, but none of those emotions were inside him. No. Happiness flooded his body, and a feeling of being free.

He picked up the box containing the remaining pizza before looking back, one final time, at what was to be his past. He pitied the poor people pulling up in the Ford Cortina, a man and a woman. They were just about to discover the sort of man he was to become.

Present

From where he was stood, Ryan knew that nobody could see him. They were oblivious to him in their state of panic. The final parts of his plan where falling into place, and he couldn't be happier. His mother and father would pay for abandoning him. His siblings would bow down at his feet, and Matthew Carter would suffer for killing his grandfather before he'd had the chance to name Ryan as his heir. They would pay, every last one of them and anyone who associated with them.

They had no idea who he was or what he was capable of. He was the best of the best, a top operative in MI5, even better than Matthew himself. The idiot had just brought him right into their midst, a mistake that would cost him. He didn't use his birth name anymore. No, he lost that years ago when he took the name, Jasper Braybrooke. The heir to his grandfather's fortune until Matthew killed him before the will could be changed. He'd seen the close relationship between the bodyguard and James, and it disgusted him. Now was the time –the time to put the final parts of his plan in place. Take them out one by one, starting with James. He pulled his phone out of his pocket, pressed to dial the number he'd saved in it, and left the room. The call connected.

"Hello. I have some information for you, which I think you might find of great interest."

SEVEN

Miranda

"Mum, you and dad need to start talking. What's going on?" James stepped up to her and folded his arms directly across his chest in a show of defiance. She knew enough about her son to recognise that he wouldn't stop until he had answers.

"James"– Amy tapped her husband on the shoulder– "let them sit down. It's a big shock. I'm sure we're all thinking things, following the message."

"But we weren't the ones targeted this morning, resulting in half my castle being destroyed."

Amy raised an eyebrow at him. "Think before you speak."

Miranda shuddered when her son growled at his wife.

"Stay out of business that doesn't concern you. Go put the children to bed."

The air sucked out of the room when Amy's expression turned to one full of thunder and fury.

"Because of the situation we're facing, I'll let that one pass, but if you ever speak to me that way again, I'll serve your balls up to you on a plate."

James shook his head and placed it in his hands.

"I'm sorry. I shouldn't have said that. I'm worried."

"We all are. Doesn't help if we start losing it amongst ourselves. I agree with you. That note meant something to your mum and dad, but they have just shared a loving event. The wind has been knocked out of them. Let them sit and work through their thoughts. They'll let us know what they're thinking when they've recovered."

James pulled his wife into his arms and kissed the top of her head. "I'm sorry." He turned to Miranda and reached out a hand to hers.

"Mum, let's sit you down. Sis, bring a drink."

Miranda went with her son to seek comfort on the sofa, but she noticed Pete remained glued to the spot. Amy went to him and nudged him tenderly towards them. Her husband wasn't fully there, though. He was reliving things in his head. When he sat, Miranda took his hand, and he looked over at her. He appeared to have aged, in a matter of moments, and his eyes were bloodshot and weary. He'd been strong for so long the pressure was finally getting to him.

"It's time." She looked directly at her husband when she spoke. "We can't protect them any longer."

"Mum?" Sophie queried, handing her a shot of whisky.

Matthew came to stand in front of her.

"We can't be certain it relates to what you are thinking."

Nothing had been directly spoken, but Miranda knew the bodyguard had read her mind regarding the reasons for what was happening.

"I know, but even if it isn't, it's time. Pete and I may not have long left. I want to go to my grave knowing that someone is still looking."

Matthew bowed his head and stepped back. James took his place and knelt down onto the floor.

"There are things that your father and I have tried to protect you from. Whether it was right or wrong to hide the truth from you, it was done out of love."

"Mum, you're scaring me." Sophie worried her lip and nervously stroked at Miranda's hand.

"Hush. It'll be ok. Just listen. I've never given you many details on my mother and father. We told you that they died before you were born, and I wasn't on good terms with them, anyway. That's only true in the case of my father. My mother, she died the day your father and I were married."

Sophie gasped.

"I was only seventeen at the time but had already been through so much. After our brief encounter as children, your father and I met again when I was sixteen. I fell pregnant shortly afterwards."

She looked at James who she could tell was doing the mental arithmetic in his head.

"Unless you've lied about your age that wouldn't be me."

"No, it wasn't. We had...have another son."

Pete jumped to his feet, and she longed to go after him, but she needed to finish her tale. He poured another glass of whisky and stood in the corner of the room. James turned to look at him and back to her.

"You gave the baby up?"

"No, not by choice. My father, he was a horrible man." She felt her throat start to tighten and a lump form at the back. "My father was Lord Charles Braybrooke. I'm of aristocratic blood. He didn't approve of the man I love, your father. He didn't approve of much that I did." She stopped to try and compose herself, memories so horrid filling her mind: the knife slicing through her stomach, the first cries of her baby, and the silence when he'd been taken from her. "He had your father beaten and hospitalised and me stolen away and hidden for the term of my pregnancy although he didn't allow me to go to nine months. When the baby was deemed viable enough to survive without intervention, he had him cut from my stomach."

This time, it was Sophie's turn to get to her feet. She had tears streaming down her face. In an instant, Grayson had her pressed to his body, providing her with the comfort she needed in that moment. Amy ensured Thomas was happy playing with Ash and came to sit on the floor with her husband. He wrapped his arm around her and pulled her in closer to him. Pete remained in the corner of the room, but she noticed that Sonia had handed Andrew to Matthew and held her hand out to Pete, allowing him to draw strength from her.

"What happened to the baby?" James' question could barely be heard even in the silence of the room.

"He was taken from me while still on the operating table. I've not seen him since"–she broke on the last word– "we've searched endlessly, but never found him. I know in my heart he's alive. He has to be."

James turned to Matthew, "You've been helping them look."

He nodded back.

"Thank you."

"What happened after that?"

"I was kept hidden away until I healed. My father came to me and told me I would be married to a man he'd chosen for me. Thankfully, my mother had found Pete and a friend who'd, previously, helped us be together. Pete rescued me, but my mother and our friend were killed. I married Pete the same day and became worthless to my father. He never sought us out again and died a very lonely man."

James let go of Amy, got to his feet, and walking over to Miranda, pressed a kiss to her head. He then went to his father and pulled him into a big bear hug.

"Thank you for not giving up on her."

Sophie sat back down and placed her arm around Miranda's shoulder.

"We'll find him. Not sure how I'm going to feel about having another brother to boss me around, but we'll find him."

"I'm sorry we never told you."

"I won't lie that I'm not a little angry, but it's in the past. We need to think to the future."

"We do." James led his father back over to them, and the four of them embraced. Miranda found so much strength in just that little display of affection.

"What I don't understand is, if your father's dead, then why is someone coming after you?" Grayson had his hand to his chin in thought.

"He didn't die naturally." Matthew stepped forward.

"You killed him?"

"Yes, and I think that's one of the reasons I'm being targeted as well. Sally Bridgewater knew too much about me. Stuff that's not in the public domain."

Miranda watched Sophie wince at the mention of Miss Bridgewater.

"I think the reporter had been used as a pawn to further the needs of whoever is coming after us. Sophie, I can't prove it yet, but regardless of what happened in that room between you and her, I'm not sure she was dead when you left it."

"What?" Sophie wobbled on her feet, and Grayson reached out to support her.

"Someone's targeting us, trying to destroy anyone who's remotely related to anything we do. I think whoever did this may have started as soon as Lord Braybrooke was killed."

"But who?" Miranda tried to think of who her father would have left to do such things. The men he worked with when she was younger would be old men now and incapable of such feats.

"There's only one person I think it could possibly be." Matthew stepped forward, and Miranda held her breath. But before Matthew could answer, Pete replied for him.

"Our son."

The room suddenly exploded with men in black balaclavas and guns.

"Armed police. Nobody move." Miranda had no time to think about what her husband had just said. She held her hands in the air, immediately, as instructed. Everyone else did the same and looked around the room, stunned by what was going on.

One of the men stepped up to James and pushed him forward onto the floor. Her son knew better than to react or do anything out of the ordinary. He looked up at her from where he was lying on the floor. His eyes were wide. Another officer came over and pointed a gun at her son's head.

"James North, I am arresting you…"

"Wait," Matthew called out. "I'm ex-MI5, Matthew Carter, there's a current MI5 operative in the building, Jasper…fuck he doesn't use a surname. Let me stand down, and you can tell me what's going on."

The man pointing the gun didn't take his eyes off James but replied to Matthew,

"You have no jurisdiction. We have information and are acting accordingly. I would suggest as you are holding your son that you hold your tongue also and let us do our job." The officer then leaned forward and pressed his gun directly against the back of James' head

Miranda saw Matthew's face drop when he realised he was helpless to prevent what was happening to her son.

"James North"–the officer started again– "I'm arresting you on suspicion of money laundering. You do not have to say anything, but it may harm your defence if you do not mention when questioned something, which you later rely on in court. Anything you do say may be given in evidence. Do you understand?"

"Yes," James replied loudly and clearly. Miranda could feel her heart beating so fast, and she was sure the air was trapped in her lungs because none was coming out of her mouth.

"Cuff him and search him."

Amy let out a loud scream when they tried to put the cuffs on. Thankfully, Isabella was in her cot, and Ash, despite his young age, had taken Thomas and was distracting him with a car. "No." She tried to race forward but was instantly restrained by a couple of other police officers.

"Amy, stay calm. We know it's a mistake. I'll explain everything and be home in a few hours. Look after Mum." James tried to keep his voice deep and command-ing, but Miranda could hear the waver in it. She'd seen it in his eyes when the gun was pointed at his head.

"James," Amy sobbed, and Thomas looked up from Ash's lap.

"Dada."

Miranda knew as well as anyone in the room it was the young boy's first proper word.

"Dada ok," James reassured him, and Amy was released and pushed in the direction of her son.

They all stood in numb silence as James was searched and, eventually, pulled from the room. Money laundering was a very serious charge. Her son was in deep trouble.

The police officer who'd arrested James went over to Matthew next.

"Better get your boss a good lawyer. This one isn't going away." The cop laughed, and they all filed out of the room. Pete and Matthew followed without a word, leaving Miranda alone with her shell-shocked family and tumultuous thoughts.

Her son. The little boy she'd cradled in her arms was doing this. It was the only explanation.

EIGHT

Pete

"I want some information on my son, and I want it now." Pete banged his fist against the front desk of the police reception. James had been brought straight to Scotland Yard, and they'd travelled back down through the night to be with him. Amy, Miranda, Sophie, Grayson, Sonia, and all the children had returned to his son's house in Knightsbridge to get some rest while he and Matthew had gone straight from the airport to the world-famous police headquarters.

"Sir, if you don't sit down and wait, I'll be forced to have you arrested for breach of the peace," the snotty-nosed receptionist ordered.

"You've had him for ten hours, now, and we haven't been told anything. These charges are ridiculous. My son's well known for his charitable donations to the victims of terrorists, not for providing funds to those doing the harm. I want to see a supervisor, immediately."

"Sir, everyone is busy. If you let us do our job and confirm you son's innocence, then he'll be free in no time, and you'll have the answers you seek. Now, I'll ask you one final time to sit down and wait, or I'll have you arrested."

Pete growled low in his throat. He was going to get nowhere with this job's worth.

"Be interesting to see how you can get me arrested when everyone's so busy." He turned heel and stomped back to his seat where Matthew was on the phone.

"How did they get access to his personal account? It's locked tighter than the fucking Bank of England safe?" the bodyguard shouted down the phone, and the receptionist shouted out for them to be quiet. Pete very nearly gave her the finger but thought better of it.

"This is ridiculous, Jasper. See what you can do with your boss and call me back. You know as well as I do that he hasn't done this"–Matthew continued– "ok, bye."

James' bodyguard, and best friend, hung up his phone and put it back in his pocket before turning to face Pete. "Any news?"

"The usual crap. Everyone's busy, and the receptionist's trained to not deviate from the manual they gave her when she started the job. What did Jasper say?"

"It looks like someone hacked into James' personal account and transferred money to unknown bank accounts. It only happened yesterday. I've got Jasper doing a trace to locate where the transfer was done. His boss is a little reluctant to help, though. More concerned with finding out where the money has gone and how to get it back before it goes to people it shouldn't."

"How much?"

Matthew shook his head.

"Fifty million."

"Shit."

"Yep."

The door was flung open as Callum and Marie Ashworth rushed in. Pete stood to greet them. Matthew had called James' accountant from the plane to let him know what was happening.

"Any news?" Callum asked, and Pete shook his head. "Damn. All the accounts and assets are frozen. Both the business and personal. I've had to send everyone home. We can't do anything with the business. There are police everywhere at the office, tearing everything apart."

"They won't find anything." Matthew stood up and started pacing the room. "James is as clean as they come. This is a waste of public funds." The last part was said rather loudly to make a statement.

"But it's putting doubt in people's minds. That's the whole point of this." Pete resumed his seat, and the others sat as well. "If it gets in the press. It ruins his name."

"Matthew told us what's been happening in Yorkshire, and who you suspect is behind it all." Marie spoke for the first time. Pete could tell she'd been crying. Her eyes were puffy and red.

"Yes. My first born. He's either trying to kill us or destroy us. He must think we abandoned him. If I could only find out who he is and tell him that it wasn't us."

"We'll find him. You have my word." Matthew stood. "Callum, can you stay with Pete? Just try and find out what is happening with James. He's got a lawyer in there with him, but if they're still interviewing, he won't be able to get out to talk to us."

"Where are you going?" Pete asked.

"I'm wasting time sitting around. We need to find your son, and even if it's the death of me, I'll find him by sundown."

Pete went to stop Matthew, but before he could, the big man had left the building.

"There's a Starbucks down the road. Why don't I go and get us some decent coffee? No offence, but you look like you need one." Maria stood and placed her handbag over her shoulder. "I just want to check on Owen and Olivia, as well." Pete knew that Marie and Callum were adoptive parents to Marie's four-year-old nephew Owen and parents to six-month-old Olivia. Owen's mother had been killed in a drive-by shooting when she was pregnant with him. Fortunately, the doctors were able to save the baby. Marie had lived in squalor, for a long time, when she was forced to pay back drug debts her sister had accumulated and look after her sick mother. Thankfully, she'd found Callum, and they lived happily together in Kensington, now. Both worked at James' firm: Callum as the Finance Director of North Enterprises and Marie as James' PA. Although she was currently on maternity leave, Pete knew she still spent most of her time in the office because the replacement PA providing maternity cover just wasn't up to her exacting standards, or his son's. He doubted anyone ever would be. The two of them worked so well together. James had even had the office next to his turned into a creche complete with a trained child caregiver. Often when Pete visited his son, he would find Thomas, Andrew, Owen, and Olivia in there together. He knew it wouldn't be long before Isabella joined them…but, if the worst happened, then she wouldn't. If this charge stands, then James would lose everything he'd worked for. That was a distinct possibility, anyway, if the press got wind of what was happening.

"At this point in time, I think I'm in need of a quadruple espresso. The last time I slept must have been close to thirty hours ago."

Marie touched his hand reassuringly.

"I'll get them to make it extra strong."

Marie left him alone with Callum.

"The banking world has changed so much since I took early retirement. How bad is this financially for James?" he asked Callum. The accountant's face fell.

"It's not good. The bank will have submitted a form to the national crime agency when they saw the money being moved. Even for James, fifty million is a lot to transfer, but I suspect the country it went to is the real reason for the concern."

Pete cocked his head.

"Afghanistan."

"Shit."

"Yeah."

"I've been looking through all his accounts, this morning, just checking there's nothing else that looks wrong. I think it's all ok, though. Just this one transaction."

"That's something."

"In the grand scheme of things, yes. The bank freezes the account until the crime agency has investigated. That's why I find it so strange he's been arrested. They must have had a tip off about the transaction."

"From the person who made it?"

"Would be my suggestion. I just hope they sort it quickly because, in a few days, it's global payday. The shit really will hit the fan, then, if wages aren't sent over."

"I think the biggest problem will be keeping the media away. The stocks will have been suspended as well. I'm sure people are starting to dig."

Callum looked across at the receptionist.

"You're really getting nowhere with her?"

"Nothing."

Callum stood and motioned for Pete to follow him outside. He did so.

"What is it?" he asked when they were away from the busy reception area.

"I want to make a phone call but in there is not the right place."

"To whom?"

"The big guns."

Pete furrowed his brows together in confusion. His exhausted brain wasn't allowing him to think straight.

Callum retrieved his phone, placed it on speaker, and dialled a number. It took a while before it was connected.

"Callum?" a deep masculine voice enquired.

"Dad." Suddenly, it hit Pete who Callum had called. His father was the Prime Minister of the country.

"I've been expecting you to call," the voice on the other end of the phone informed them. "Where are you?"

"I think you already know the answer to that because I'm guessing I just interrupted a cobra meeting." Pete knew from watching news reports that this was the government's name for meetings that involved terrorist activities.

"Scotland Yard. Have they said anything?"

"We can't get past reception. Although I haven't pulled the I'm the Prime Minister's son card, yet. That's my next step if you can't give us some news."

"Us?" Callum's father halted. "Who are you with?"

"I'm with James' father. That's it. We're not by anyone else, and this call is on the private phone you gave me."

"Ok. Hello, Mr North."

"Hello, Prime Minister," Pete nervously stammered. Despite the fact the man on the other end of the phone was Callum's father, he was nervous knowing the powerful position he held.

"Dave, please."

"Dave."

"Look, you know I can't tell you everything, but what I can say is we do know this is a set up. The police need to investigate the crime and where the money has gone, but everyone here knows James in some way. He's a good man, and we don't believe the story. He is being thoroughly grilled by the police. I'm receiving regular transcripts, but between his calm nature and the solicitor he has, they've found nothing to incriminate him except for the transfer of money to a holding account in Afghanistan. That's not enough to charge him. They only have a few more hours left to interview him. I've been asked to extend his detention but declined the request. I could face issues as a result, but I'm prepared to explain my actions if I do. I know there's a man on your team with links to MI5. He needs to work together with them to find out where the money was transferred from, including finding the computer so it can be proven James has no link to it. That's the only way to prove his accounts were hacked. Once that happens, he's in the clear."

"Matthew's already working on it. He's with an agent friend of his right now."

"Good. I'll talk to the head of MI5 and ensure he has all the clearance he needs."

"No. You need to start distancing yourself from this. If people find out, questions could be asked. I'm going to get pulled into this, Dad. I'm the finance director of the company. People will go from me to you, and if they find out you've made demands like that, it could be problematic."

"You think I care about that, son? I've been Prime Minister for long enough, now. I'm done. I was going to resign on your mother's birthday this year, anyway. I've been putting everything into place. I'm tired, and we want to live the rest of our lives away from the spotlight."

Pete looked up from the phone to Callum and saw the man exhale deeply with relief. He knew that he'd grown up under the spotlight of being the Prime Minister's son, and it was a burden that weighed heavily on him.

"You don't know how happy Mum will be to hear that."

"Very. Look, my advice to you both is to go back inside Scotland Yard and wait. James will be released in a couple of hours. It won't be the end of it. He'll lose his passport and be under surveillance around the clock, but he won't have a charge against his name. Call his employees back into work tomorrow and continue as normal. The press is already asking for statements. I'm going to give them something to keep them quiet. Get James' team to do the same."

"I'll get on this straight away." Callum agreed with his father's advice.

"Just stay calm. We'll sort this out," Dave reassured. But after the last few days, Pete couldn't be certain because unless they found the person behind the plot, more troubles would surely come their way. Eventually, something would happen, and they wouldn't be able to solve it or rescue the person involved. He needed to remain positive, though.

"Thank you for your help," Pete replied.

"I have to go," the Prime Minister said, before hanging up.

"You ok?" Callum asked Pete.

"Just about." The sound of heels clicking on the pavement behind them, alerted them to someone coming. Marie appeared with caffeinated goodness in her hands.

"Why are you out here?" she asked her husband.

"Fresh air," he replied and winked at her. Whether that was a secret code between them or not, he didn't know, but Marie didn't ask any other questions. Pete followed them back inside to drink his coffee and wait. His whole body was sagging with exhaustion and worry. Marie and Callum eventually left him alone to sort out the running of North Enterprises in the absence of his son. Pete spent the next few hours pacing the floor of the reception area. Eventually, more than twenty-four hours after being arrested, James appeared out of a side door, looking exhausted and pale. His solicitor didn't look much better. The lawyer said his goodbye, and Pete thanked him for his work.

"What happened?" he questioned his son as he led him to where a car waited for them. A bodyguard from Grayson's team had been stationed there by Matthew.

"They found no evidence to charge me. I'm not in the clear, and my assets are still frozen, for the time being. But, at least, I can go home to my wife and children. Is Amy ok?"

"Hysterical when they took you away. Sonia called a doctor to give her something to calm her down. Sophie and Sonia have been looking after Isabella and Thomas ever since."

"I need to get home to her. She's always been so scared of losing everyone after her parents' death. This would have stirred up old memories."

"In you get." Pete opened the door for James who, near enough, stumbled into the car with fatigue.

"Dad, what was his name?"

"Who?"

"My brother?"

Pete took his seat and fixed his seatbelt in place. It had been such a long time since the name of his son had left his lips, and it felt strange. He and Miranda always referred to him as their son, or firstborn, so to call him by his name seemed to hurt even more.

"Ryan. Ryan Peter North."

He inhaled deeply to centre himself from the emotion clouding his own exhausted mind.

James slumped down in the seat. "You were right."

"What?" He didn't understand.

"It's my brother doing this. The account the money went to was in the name of Ryan North."

NINE

Miranda

Miranda didn't think she'd ever fussed over James as much as she had since he'd walked through the door this evening. He looked exhausted, and she made sure he was seated with a cup of tea in his hand before Pete pulled her away, so Amy could get near her husband.

"Sorry,"– she apologised– "over anxious mother here."

"Never apologise, Miranda. I know how hard it was for you, seeing him go through that. We know it isn't over yet, but we have him home, now. That's all that matters." Amy circled her arms around her husband. He leaned forward and placed the cup of tea on the table, having taken a sip. That pleased Miranda no end. Tea was the cure for everything.

"Do you mind if we digest everything tomorrow, please?" James stood and pulled Amy under his arm. "I'm beyond tired. I want a shower, and then I want my woman in my bed."

"James!" Miranda exclaimed, blushing.

"I don't have the energy even for that, Mum." James shook his head and led his wife down the corridor. His children were already asleep, and Miranda knew that her son would check in on them before he eventually collapsed. He was a fantastic father. Just like his father had been to him, despite the odd blip.

She turned to her husband who she was sure, by the looks of him, was asleep standing up.

"Bed." She nodded. Her own body, having barely rested in over twenty-four hours, was struggling. Pete took her hand and led her down to the quarters of the house that had once been her own private accommodation, during the time she and Pete had spent apart. However, that was a distant memory, now, and she wasn't going to dwell on it. Her husband's phone rang, and he quickly shut the door to their rooms so as not to wake anyone.

"Matthew?" Pete answered and put the phone on speaker, so she could hear as well.

"How is James?"

"Tired. Amy's taken him off to bed."

"Sonia's going to watch Isabella for them tonight. Amy's expressed some milk so that they can both get some sleep," Miranda added.

"That's my girl"–Matthew sounded tired himself– "It's only nine, so I'm going to do a few more hours work and then come back for some sleep."

"Don't exhaust yourself," Miranda told him.

"Oh, before I forget, does your family have any links to Cambridge?"

"Yes. My grandmother's family were from there, and I went to boarding school in the city. Why?"

"I was looking further into your father's accounts. I found payments to a school in Cambridge, but from the dates, they wouldn't have been related to you. I looked at security footage from around the area. It's not the best quality. Technology has advanced a lot since then, but your father is seen taking a child into the school. I can't see the kid's face properly as it's covered with a baseball cap and glasses."

"What dates?"

The other end went silent for a moment, and then she heard Matthew flipping over sheets of paper.

"1997."

"How old does the child look?"

"It's difficult to tell. Twelve, thirteen. Looks like a boy from the clothes, and he's pretty tall."

"The dates fit. It could be Ryan." Miranda had hope. Although the thought that her son was with her father started to gnaw at her gut.

"What month?" Pete asked.

Silence again.

"September."

Pete rubbed his brow as though he was willing his brain to try to think.

"That's a month after we found his supposed foster parents dead from the overdose."

"No,"–Miranda felt her legs starting to give way– "please no."

"Your father had him all along." Matthew sucked in a sharp breath.

"He must hate us. The things my father has probably told him." Tears filled her eyes.

"Matthew, please find him. We have to put him straight about everything." Pete pulled the phone closer to his ear and turned it off speaker. He walked away from her, and she stopped listening to them. Her brain couldn't take in anymore. Her father had been a demon to her when he was alive. But, even now, he was destroying her. She wasn't sure how much more she could take from him. The man had been dead for eight years and was haunting her every move, including through her son. It was the only explanation. He'd taken her little boy and twisted him into a reflection of himself: an individual full of bitter thoughts. How was she supposed to save him? Finally, she allowed the emotions of the last few days to hit her. For so long, she'd been strong, but she wasn't sure she could be any longer. The floodgates opened, and her tears fell. The sobs wracked her body, and with heaving breaths she tried to bring air into her pained lungs. Her heart hurt. Her

whole body ached as she wailed for the past, present, and future in one giant
outpouring of emotion. Pete ran back into the room, picked her up, and sat
cradling her to his chest.

"It'll be ok. We'll find him." He tried to reassure her, but she needed this. It was
her moment of weakness in so many more moments of strength. Her husband
stroked her hair and rocked her closely in his arms. She felt a drop of water run
into her hair, and when she looked up, Pete was crying as well.

"I failed you both."

"No, you didn't."

"I should've got to you sooner. Protected you better."

"No. Nobody knew what levels my father would go to," she pleaded with him.

"I'm not the man you needed."

"You are. You're everything I've needed. You're James and Sophie's world. They
are who they are because of you. This is nobody's fault but my father's. We'll beat
him, though. We will win. We'll save our son and live a life that he never had." The
strength within her was flooding back with the determination to beat the man
who for fifty years, now, had haunted her every move. "We'll find our son and
bring him home, no matter what we discover. Our strength and love will beat the
malignancy that my father has planted within his mind."

She sat up and kissed her husband. He wiped away her tears and his own.

"I need to be inside you," he whispered.

"Take me," she consented and moved so that she was straddling him. She was
wearing a skirt, allowing him easy access to where she felt her body heating. He
undid his trousers and pulled his already hardening cock out. No matter how
often she saw it, her breath always hitched at its beauty. He pulled her panties to
the side and slid her down on his length. This wasn't about taking it slow and
playing with each other's bodies. This wasn't even about the art of dominance and
submission. This was purely a raw need to be one on one with the man who
completed her. Fate decreed they were soulmates as the only people who truly
understood each other. When they were together as one, they were bonded in
unity and strength. The world around them could crumble and fall, but they'd
survive.

She gasped out a long breath of pleasure from the intrusion and gripped down
tightly around his dick. They didn't move. Just sat staring into each other's eyes.
She could feel him lengthening and hardening even further inside her.

"Always this." Pete kissed her on the nose.

"Always. Us against the world."

"Protecting what is ours."

"Ryan is ours. Us combined. We'll bring him back into our fold."

Pete slid his hands down her legs and lifted her skirt to bunch at her waist. He
placed his hands under her backside and pushed her up his length.

She let her head fall back and her body become lost in the shifting of her pussy
over her husband's cock. She sheathed him within her warmth as he pulled out to
the tip. The movement was slow –a deliberate coupling designed to ignite their
shredded nerves into fiery passion. She took over the movement herself, quick-
ening the pace. Her head came back upright to see Pete watching her every undulation. He took his hands off her backside and pulled her top over her head. He
removed her lace bra in a swift movement, freeing her breasts, which he took into

his mouth. His tongue swirled over her peaking nipples, his teeth nibbling at the sensitive flesh and heightening the sensations of need coursing through her body. Her pace increased so that she was riding him like a cowgirl, taming a wild beast between her legs. Every time she slid down, her clit rubbed against him. Her breath quickened, and Pete's urgency increased. They were going to come together, their bodies entwined in need and comfort.

Pete stood and flipped them around so that her back hit the mattress. He pistoned into her harder and harder. She no longer knew where he finished and she began. He was her, and she was him.

"Come," he demanded, and her body obeyed. He was her master, lover, husband, and her forever after. She shattered in a flurry of calls of his name. Her pussy contracted around his dick as the spasms of her orgasm took over her body, obliterating the tension that had manifested itself within her. Pete thrust hard into her and stilled. His cock jerked, and he was coming, flooding her insides with his essence –warm and comforting. There was no longer any risk of further children, resulting from the coupling, so this moment had become just about them. Breathe, live, love, and hope.

Her husband collapsed down next to her and pulled her into his arms.

"I need to shower."

"I need to clean up and undress."

He kissed the top of her head, and she saw his eyes flutter shut. He opened them only for the heavy lids to close again. He was exhausted both physically and mentally. They still had most of their clothes on, but she didn't have the energy to move or to really care. Her own eyelids started to close. Tomorrow would be a new day. Matthew would find her son, they'd save him, and their family would be complete. She should make her scones. She was sure Ryan would like them. She snuggled deeper into Pete's embrace as he started to softly snore. The sound comforted her. She'd sleep for a few hours and then start baking. She might need a few ingredients, but that wouldn't be an issue.

TEN

Ryan

It was late, gone midnight, and he'd had enough of being in the company of his grandfather's murderer. Ryan wanted nothing more than to put a bullet in Matthew Carter's head like the bodyguard had done to the only person who'd ever loved him. He still remembered the day he got the news about his grandfather's death. He'd been due to go down to the Braybrooke estates to sign papers, giving him the heirship of the name and lands. Instead, he was told that he needed to leave the home he'd been living in for the last few years because it was no longer his to reside in. He'd had so much promised, and it was stolen by the man in front of him. It was a miracle he'd not killed him sooner.

"Can you check on the school manifest, again, please. It must be ready by now." Matthew swung around in the chair of the investigation room they were in and pulled up footage from the night Sally Bridgewater was killed.

"What are you doing?" Ryan nodded towards the video.

"I just have a feeling about the night the reporter died. Something doesn't add up."

"What do you mean?"

"I don't think Sophie killed Sally, but I can't explain how she died."

Matthew wasn't as stupid as he looked. Ryan had been there that night. He'd killed the intrepid reporter. She was a victim of her own selfishness, and Sophie was a casualty of her own stupidity. His sister had left the room without even checking Sally for a pulse. If she had, she would've found her alive. The reporter had regained consciousness and thought that he was there to help her. He'd been fucking the woman. She had a tight cunt despite how many times she must have opened her legs for a story. It was the only decent thing about her. She was a nasty individual as demonstrated by the fact that she gave her own son up shortly after he was born. Any woman who did that deserved to have his hands around their throat and the life squeezed out of them. He'd rejoiced as he'd watched her die. She'd made life miserable for so many people. He did the world a favour. Just like he would when his own mother dies. Some people weren't cut out for being parents. They were too selfish. Oh, Miranda and Pete made a good act of being the perfect mother and father to James and Sophie, but he knew the truth. They picked and chose the children they wanted. He didn't make the grade for whatever reason, but he was better than them and, eventually, it would show. They'd cower at his feet before he took everything from them. Death no longer affected him. How can it when at twelve years old you steal the life of the scum who was looking after you? The drugged-up wastes of space that your biological parents sold you to.

"You ok?" Matthew cocked his head at him. "You look stressed?"

"Tired," he replied and pulled up his emails to check on the manifest again. He knew his name would be on it. Not that Matthew knew his second name. He didn't use it here. To all at MI5 he was Jasper. That was it. Alright, payroll had his full details but nobody else. He didn't give a second name. He didn't have to, and nobody asked. Matthew shoved his surname in everyone's faces. 'Carter' was like a badge of honour to him, but he'd die a traitor's death. Ryan had details of every kill the bodyguard had made outside of the law, every crime he'd committed in the name of the North family, and when the man lay rotting, he'd piss on his good name by releasing it. Sonia made her bed by choosing to lie in it with Matthew. She'd have nothing when all this was over. No, he wouldn't do that to her. He had a soft spot for her because she'd suffered from parents who'd abandoned her, too. He'd see her right, but not to the same luxury she was used to. He could always do with a housemaid when he took over North Enterprises and its assets.

"It's more than that." Matthew interrupted his thoughts, again, and he tried hard not to imagine the man with his brains splattered all over the desk. If he let his mind wander, it would happen. He was that close to pulling the trigger.

"Some of what's happening is bringing up memories of my own past. I probably just need a few hours' sleep. You're right. We'll get this manifest and then rest for a bit. We'll start making mistakes if we work too hard. The first thing you learn at spy school." He laughed.

"Training seems like such a long time ago." Matthew set up a scroll on the video, and Ryan watched.

"It was. A lifetime ago."

"Why did you join?" Matthew asked, not taking his eyes of the screen. This was the way they'd worked when they'd been friends, before his grandfather died. He'd respected Matthew and vice versa. They were similar in experience and age. But the second he recognised the ammo that shot his grandfather, the respect died.

"It's a long story."

"I think we've got time. The school must have the biggest archives going, judging by how long it's taking them." Matthew laughed.

"Did you have a happy childhood?" Ryan asked and pulled up his own video to make himself look busy. He knew he wouldn't find anything on it, though. He wasn't anywhere near the property during this incident, but Matthew had insisted that it could be linked. Clutching at straws much?

"It was good. I've a large family in France, and we spent summers there. Happy memories. What about you?"

"No. I was glad to reach adulthood. The people who called themselves my parents should never have been allowed children. I was their only child, and they treated me like a slave. Beatings, and no food, that sort of thing. I was blessed the day I got out of there. They are the reason I became a spy. It allowed me to get rid of people who shouldn't be allowed to breathe the same air as us. The people out there who are sick, twisted, and far beyond being recognisable as human."

"There's a few of them out there. My dead wife for starters." Matthew huffed but still didn't move from the screen of the computer. Ryan's emotional state was becoming volatile, again. Talking about his past always made him feel that way. It was like there was a part inside him that was defective and replaced his reason when it was triggered. He'd always wondered if that was why his parents hadn't wanted him. They knew there was something wrong with him when he was born. James and Sophie seemed so sensible. Yes, James had killed but not as much as he had. His brother could step back from the voices in his head and not allow them to rule him. Ryan, however, hadn't found the way to shut them off, yet. All he heard was – 'Kill, kill, kill. Get revenge for those who have shunned you. You may not be worthy of their love, but it's them who will suffer.'. He rubbed at his temple as the permanent stress headache he'd had the last few weeks, came back with a vengeance.

"What happened to you parents?" Matthew finally took his eyes off the screen and swung round to face him.

"They're dead." His reply was cold.

Matthew lowered his head. Ryan didn't need to confirm how, when, or who had taken their lives. Matthew knew.

"Vengeance. Don't let it rule you. It's over. Put the memories behind you and move on."

Matthew swung his chair back to face the screen just as a figure dressed in black walked across it. It was quick, and in the shadows, but Ryan knew instantly that it'd be him. The computer in front of Ryan brought up a new email as Matthew frantically rewound his screen and used the swipe keyboard to zoom in.

Ryan opened the email. There it was, the entries to the school on that day. At the top of the list as if in neon lights was his name.

Matthew gasped and swung around, his chair flying backwards. James North's bodyguard knew because on the screen was Ryan's face.

"You."

He allowed his lip to curl up into a snide grin.

"Finally,"–Ryan teased– "thought you were a great detective and everything. You never had a clue."

"You killed Sally Bridgewater," Matthew spat out in disgust.

"Don't say it like you think it was the wrong thing to do. You were on the verge of doing it yourself."

"But to blame Sophie?"

"I didn't blame her. You didn't check the body properly. You've grown sloppy." He pulled his gun from his pocket and held it directly in line with Matthew Carter's chest. The bodyguard was no longer a serving member of MI5 so was frisked when he entered the building. He had no weapons, no phone, and no means of protection on him. He was a lamb to the slaughter. "Shame you had to do it after you killed my grandfather."

"Jasper"–Matthew held his hands up– "you have to listen to me. All is not what it seems. You need to talk to Miranda and Pete."

"What, for more lies? I think I've had enough of them in my life, don't you?"

"She didn't want to give you away. It was her father." Matthew was backing across the room. There was a panic button located on the wall, and he was heading for it.

"Don't lie"–Ryan snarled– "he was the only one to save me."

"No. He was playing you."

"You're sick." He tried to tamper down the voices in his head, telling him to fire. To shoot, and to end the menace to society in front of him.

"You were a good agent. One of the best. Why? Why get involved in something like this? Taking justice into your own hands. I lost everything!"

"Jasper. Please. You need to put the gun down. I can prove everything I'm saying. You must listen to me. Put the gun down, and we can go and talk to Miranda and Pete. There's no major harm done, yet. You're right, Sally deserved to die. She was a disgusting piece of work. What's happened with James can be corrected in an instant. Please put the gun down."

"Did he beg for his life?"

"What?" Matthew inched closer to the panic button.

"My grandfather?"

"No, he told us that he'd take your location to the grave so that Miranda and Pete would never know where their little boy, they'd spent years searching for, had gone. He was a bitter old man who'd been responsible for alienating himself from any family he'd ever had. You need to listen to me. Don't do this, Jasper. It won't end well. Please. Miranda needs her son."

"She has her son, the precious James North, the boy she chose. The only one who was good enough for her. Well, I guess she picked the right one, given he made billions and has kept her in a life of luxury. I would've just put her down in a blood bath." He spat at Matthew and cocked the trigger on the gun.

"No, she's a good person. You wouldn't have killed her."

He laughed so loudly that the sound echoed around the small room like an eerie cackle of a madman. Maybe that was where he was descending, into insanity. It certainly felt like it, now. Why could nobody see his grandfather for the man he was. The kind old gentleman who'd saved him from eating out of a dustbin.

"Jasper, Lord Braybrooke was a bad man. You must listen to me. What he did to Miranda, he had you…."

Bang.

The gun went off without him even realising he'd fired it. He looked from the pistol to where Matthew was standing. Red started to seep through the front of the white shirt the bodyguard was wearing. The world slowed down –he'd done it. He'd shot the man who'd killed his grandfather. His plan was coming together. Matthew made a last-ditch attempt for the panic button but failed when he fell to the floor. He didn't move. It took Jasper's breath away. He'd killed him. He'd done it, so why wasn't he elated. It felt wrong inside his chest.

No, he couldn't think that way. He had to continue with his plan for revenge. The time was nearing when he'd end it all.

Calmly, he picked up his phone and tucked the gun into the back of his jeans. His jacket was slung over the chair in the room. He picked it up and pulled it on. The leather material felt luxurious and warm in contrast to the cold feeling, spreading throughout his body. He looked down at Matthew who still hadn't moved.

"One down. Mother and father, I'm coming for you."

ELEVEN

Pete

Pete rolled over in the bed to find it empty. He bet his wife was up at first light and baking. It was the way she coped during times of stress. He pulled the covers back and swung his legs out of the bed – he was still in last night's clothes. Damn he must have been exhausted. He pulled them off and threw them at the linen bin. He headed into the bathroom, did his business, and brushed his teeth. He'd shower later. If Miranda was baking, then he wanted what she was offering, first. Rummaging through his wardrobe, he found a pair of jogging bottoms and a Bon Jovi t-shirt from the eighties. Perfect. He dressed quickly and made his way into the kitchen.

There were no smells of baking, though.

Only Amy and Sonia talking. The latter sounded worried.

"He didn't come home, and I've been calling him, but he's not answering." Sonia nibbled on the tip of her finger in anguish.

"Who?" He stepped forward and poured himself a cup of coffee.

"Matthew." Amy opened the fridge and passed him the milk. He thanked her with a nod of appreciation.

"I'm sure he's just working hard on trying to find Ryan." James strode into the kitchen. He was dressed in only a pair of jogging bottoms. Amy licked her lips at the sight.

"Yeah. I'm sure he is, but it's unlike him not to check in every few hours or so."

"He may have thought you were still asleep." Pete looked over at the clock on the oven. It read 8:30am. Damn, he'd slept late.

"I think I'll try him again. It can't hurt." She picked up her phone from the counter and dialled.

Sophie and Grayson entered the room, next.

"Morning," they both greeted.

Sophie took a seat at the table while Grayson poured two coffees and handed one to his wife.

They looked at the empty table, and it was then he realised that Miranda wasn't in the kitchen.

"Where's your mum?" he asked.

They all looked around.

"Isn't she still in bed?"

He shook his head. "She mentioned something last night about baking." Grayson pulled the phone out of his jeans pocket and dialled a number. Sonia was still trying Matthew.

"Mike. Mrs North…any idea where she is?"

"Yeah. She wanted to go to the supermarket. I sent her with Mark and Kenny."

"Thanks." Grayson hung up and put the phone away. He sat down and motioned for Sophie to sit on his lap. She obeyed, instantly.

"Your mother and baking." He shook his head.

"You love it, Dad." James came up and lightly tapped Pete's stomach. It wasn't as flat as it had once been. One too many cakes and hot dinners.

"I'm sure if Amy keeps cooking, you'll have exactly the same in a few years."

"Doubt it. Amy keeps me well exercised in other ways." James sidled up to his wife and wrapped his arms around her.

Sonia put the phone down.

"Still no answer?" Pete asked.

"No. He gave me a number for MI5, once. I'm going to try that and see if someone can check on him for me."

"Wasn't he with Jasper? Have you tried him?" he questioned. Sonia slapped her forehead, indicating she was stupid.

"Of course. I think I'm exhausted."

She picked her phone up and dialled a different number.

"Jasper?"

Sonia's brows knitted together. Pete wasn't sure why, but a cold shiver spread down his spine.

"Jasper?"

Sonia stumbled backwards and went as white as a sheet. James leaped, from where he was holding Amy, to grab her just before she fell to the floor. He took the phone out of her hand and while supporting her put it on speaker.

Demonic laughter came from the other end of the phone. They all looked at one another, but when a feminine scream sounded, the bottom of Pete's world fell out. He knew that voice anywhere.

"Miranda." He jumped forward and grabbed the phone from his son. "Miranda."

"Hi, Dad."

Jasper's voice came over the phone.

"Jasper?" he questioned.

"I think it's Ryan, isn't that what you named me? I forget. It's been such a long time since I went by that name. Ever since my grandfather rescued me. Such a shame he was murdered. I've taken care of the perpetrator of that crime, though."

Sonia's legs completely gave way this time, and James struggled to hold her up as she registered what Jasper meant. James himself looked sick to the stomach.

"What do you want?" Pete tried to keep his voice calm.

"It's time to end this. I want you, Sophie, and James to come to the roof of North Enterprises. Just you three. Nobody else or my mother gets a bullet in her. I think it's about time we had a little family discussion. Deviate at all, Dad, and I mean it, I'll make the bitch a pin cushion of bullet holes."

"You have my word."

The phone line went dead.

Sonia's cries broke the silence in the room.

"I have to go and find him."

Grayson pulled his phone out of his pocket again.

"Mike?"

"Boss."

"I think you'll find that Mark and Kenny are dead or severely incapacitated. I need two men to accompany Miss Anderson to MI5 headquarters. We believe Matthew Carter could be"–Sonia whimpered– "injured."

"I'll have them bring a car round immediately."

"I'll need another one as well."

"Boss, what's going on?" Mike's voice was hesitant.

"We know who's doing this."

"Who?"

"Questions later. When we get to our destination, you're to stand down. Nobody is to enter North Enterprises unless they have my permission."

"Understood, Boss." The line went dead.

Pete tried to catch his breath –Jasper was his son. Why hadn't he seen it. The man had similar physique and build to James. He thought back to all the photos his mother had of relatives on the sideboard of his childhood home. He could see it now. Why couldn't he then? Jasper had a look of his uncle about him. James was different, more squared featured like Miranda's father. It was something that haunted his wife.

"I have to go. Amy, will you watch Andrew?" Sonia was already on her feet and running out of the door.

His daughter-in-law nodded.

"Wait." But it was too late. Sonia had left.

"James, you can't go there. Not alone, please," Amy pleaded.

"Sophie's not going," Grayson added.

"What? I am. That's my mum."

"And I'm your husband, and I'm not allowing you up there without me."

"Enough!" Pete shouted. He was struggling to take in all that was happening. His first born was holding his wife hostage, and Matthew Carter was probably dead. "Enough. Please. Let me think."

"Dad?" James came up to him and placed his hand on his shoulder. "She's been through worse and survived."

"Not with her own son. She held him, James. He fed from her before he was torn away. She's lived with that memory for thirty-three years."

"And she'll have more. Good ones."

James turned to Grayson.

"Amy, call Marie and Callum, get them here to look after all the children. We're all going to the building. Grayson, I know you're trying to protect Sophie, and I'd say the same if it were Amy."

"But…" Grayson interrupted as Amy left the room to make her call.

James continued, "I'll protect her with my dying breath, if I have to."

"No!" Sophie sobbed.

"And I'll protect you both. Family, we're all coming out of this alive"–Pete stepped forward– "All of my children and my wife.

Grayson's phone dinged.

"Car's here."

TWELVE

Miranda

"It's beautiful up here. The view's amazing. I can see why he chose this building for his office." Ryan, the man in front of her, would never be Jasper again. Not now she knew who he was. How had she not known all along? There was so much of Pete in him when she looked at him properly. His eyes were the same shape. But thirty-three years had passed. She'd spent a life time away from him. Her baby. She couldn't help but remember his little face as it looked up at her from the operating table. She saw vulnerability both then and now when he turned to face her.

"They're here. They seem to have disobeyed me and brought Amy and Grayson. No wait. Wow, those two have just got back in the car."

"Ryan, please."

"I'm not Ryan… I'm Jasper. The name your father gave me."

"Please. Don't do this."

"Why, Mum? The guilt for leaving me starting to break into that frozen heart of yours."

"I never left you," she partly shouted despite trying to remain calm. She'd realised the moment her son had taken her and shot both her bodyguards that he was not mentally stable. His mind was twisted so badly he couldn't see truth from lie. That was how her father worked.

"Liar."

"You've listened to my father's side of the story. Will you not listen to mine?" she pleaded. He hadn't tied her up, but she was sat on the roof top. The air was cold, and the sky had darkened. It would rain soon.

"Because I'm sick of hearing your lies."

"You've never heard one lie from my mouth."

"What? You expect me to believe after all these years that you are the perfect mother? My god, you've raised a girl who can't even tie her own shoelaces without a man doing it for her. Sophie's a child. And don't get me started on James. He's a murderer. I know all about him and Colette Fisher's brothers. I saw what was left of Jacob's genitals. What kind of sick man does that to another human being. That's what you raised. A sick freak."

"No. Sophie's not a child. She's loved by Grayson. You've heard what she's said about their relationship. It's been well published. It may be different from the norm, but it's what they both want. She knows Grayson has her best interests at heart and trusts him to do what is right for her. That's the love they share. Conventional isn't always right. Sometimes, it doesn't suit people." Ryan started to pace up and down the side of the roof. She knew his gun was tucked into the back of his trousers. "James isn't a freak either. He's loving and protective. Colette's brothers were freaks. They were forcing woman into lives that were against their wishes. They beat him because he touched Colette in a way that's natural. Sex isn't something to be ashamed of. It's something that happens because we love each other."

"Is that what happened with you and Dad?" He stopped pacing.

"The sex?"

"I'm not going to discuss my sex life with my son." She looked down at the ground.

"What, you embarrassed? Too late for that, Mum. You opened your legs wide, so my dad could stick his dick in your filthy cunt. You didn't like what resulted, so you gave it to people who spent the money you paid them on heroin. Do you know by the time I was five years old I could have injected myself? I'd seen them do it so often. You had your five minutes of fun. I got the lifetime of crap as a result."

"I never wanted to give you away."

"But you did."

"I didn't." Ryan jumped down from his vantage point on the roof and bore down on her. He pulled the gun from his trousers and held it out in front of him.

"You wanted me to rot in hell because I was an inconvenience."

"I wanted to love you."

"You hated me."

"I loved you."

"Lying bitch." He pushed the gun against her temple as the door to the roof opened and the rest of her family stepped out.

"Finally." Ryan pressed the gun harder. "Mum and I were just discussing how wonderful our dysfunctional family is."

"Take the gun away from her head, and we can discuss it further." Pete walked to the forefront with James behind him and Sophie tucked away from the bullets, should they start flying. Damn alpha men.

"You don't get to tell me what to do, Dad. You're a few years too late for that."

"Maybe some discipline from a parent is what you need," Pete snarled, and Miranda felt the gun dig deeper into her temple.

"You're too much like him." Pete came over, so he was standing directly in front of them.

"Who?" Ryan asked.

"You're grandfather. Stubborn, bitter, and refusing to listen. I was there when he died. Couldn't have happened to a better man, if you ask me. He was disgusting."

"Shut up." Ryan inhaled deeply, his nostrils flaring.

"You've listened to his made-up stories. Now, you're going to listen to our truths."

"Pete, no," she whimpered. She knew exactly what her husband was doing. He was antagonising their son so that he would remove the weapon from her and aim it towards him.

"Your mother lived a life of hell under that man. He spoke down to her at every opportunity. She was nothing but a money-making venture to him. His own wife chose to die because of the damage he'd done to her."

"Pete," she pleaded, the tears streaming down her cheeks. Out of the corner of her eye, she saw that Sophie had been placed behind a pillar by James, and her son crept around the edge of the building towards Ryan's other side. What were they planning?

"She wasn't even allowed to listen to music because it spoiled his serenity and peace. Yes, we were young and made a mistake. Your mother was sixteen when she fell pregnant with you. I was going to stand by her and marry her, though. I loved her. We wanted you the second we knew you existed."

"Lies!" Ryan shouted, and a flock of pigeons scattered from a nearby roof.

"Never. We went to your grandfather and told him Miranda was pregnant. He had his thugs beat me up so badly I spent months in a coma. He took Miranda from me that day. The next time I saw her, you'd been born. That was how long he kept us apart."

"He wouldn't. He saved me from those people you left me with."

"We never left you with anyone. He's the one who did that. We searched everywhere. Every day, we followed leads. One time, we thought we were close to finding you when we went to your foster parents' house and found them dead."

"Cortina." Ryan pulled the gun back a little.

"What?" Pete froze, his hands slightly extended into the air.

"I remember. As we were leaving, a Cortina and two people got out."

Miranda's stomach lurched, and she couldn't help but retch on the small croissant she'd eaten for breakfast that morning. Ryan pulled the gun back when she vomited.

"That was us."–she heaved– "We missed you by moments. We were too late."

"I don't understand."

Pete took a step closer to him.

"Charles Braybrooke took you back to his house that day, didn't he? Braybrooke Hall?"

Ryan shook his head.

"He said I wasn't allowed at Braybrooke Hall in case you had people watching the house and took me away, again." For a thirty-three-year-old man, his voice sounded so small and young. Her son had been taken by her father from one minefield to another. "He took me to a place in Dumfries. Later, he sent me to school in Cambridge. He changed my name to Jasper Braybrooke, so you wouldn't find me."

"Dumfries is where you were born." Miranda wiped her mouth with the back of her hand. Ryan no longer had the gun pointed at her head, but it was still close enough to shoot her if anyone made a move that spooked him.

"The house?"

She nodded.

"I thought I didn't like that place. He said that you'd discovered I was gone from the foster parents, and I needed to hide down in the dungeon room. I spent five days down there before I was transferred to Cambridge."

Why couldn't he see it? That his grandfather hadn't been looking after him. He'd been hiding him so they, she and Pete, couldn't find him. Was he so starved of love for the first few years of his life that he'd clung to the first person who'd paid him attention? Her father had known what he was doing all along. He was paving the way for this to happen. The ultimate revenge on his part. The son kills the family.

"I spent nine months in the dungeon." She'd been gentle with him up until now. But to be kind, she needed to be cruel. She had to break the fantasy he had of his grandfather being a knight in shining armour. She needed to show him the truth.

"Nine months?"

"Well, not exactly. I was probably six weeks when I found out I was pregnant, and you were born three weeks early because that's when they told him you were viable and able to breathe on your own."

Sophie poked her head out from behind the pillar. She looked devastated. James was still working himself into a position, presumably, so he could try to wrestle the gun away. She and Pete were still in prime position, though, directly in front and to the side of their son. She wanted to reach out and bring him to her chest.

"Viable. Breathe on my own."

She slowly got to her feet. It startled Ryan a bit, and he pointed the gun back towards her. She lifted her t-shirt and lowered her jeans a little to reveal the scar on her abdomen.

"They cut you out of me."

"Cut? You had a caesarean."

"Not by choice. The pain medication was not even fully working when they made the first incision."

"Lies. That could be from James and Sophie."

"You're not a fool, Ryan. You would've researched us. You know I had them naturally."

"My father pulled me out of the dungeon one day and had me strapped to a bed. He ordered a small medical team to cut you out of me."

"No."

"Yes."

Her hand went to her necklace, and his eyes followed. They zoomed in on the locket.

"You were delivered onto my chest. I held you. Your little face was all crinkly but still the most beautiful thing I'd ever seen. You were hungry, so I latched you onto my breast, and you suckled while people worked around us. I didn't even hear them or see them. People were stitching up my abdomen, and I didn't feel a thing because I had you in my arms. My son, my little boy. But, then, they took you from me. My father came into the room and had you ripped from my arms."

She looked up from where her hand was at her chest and into her son's eyes. They were filled with tears.

"No," he stammered.

"Yes."

"I got this necklace that day, and I've not taken it off since. Do you want to know what's inside it?"

"No, you have to be lying. He wouldn't; he was going to name me his heir. I was going to be his future. He saved me from the people you left me with."

"He would never have made you heir. He was setting you up for a fall." Her breathing was so fast, now, the sound pounded in her head, but she needed to keep her focus on the man falling apart in front of her.

"Stop lying," Ryan cried. Before she'd spoken, his voice was filled with anger and fury, but now it was laced with only despondency and failure. She opened the locket in her hand and showed it to him. Behind the glass plate was a lock of his hair.

"Your first curl."

"No."

His entire body deflated, and in an instant, both James and Pete pounced. The gun was wrestled from Ryan's hand and thrown across the floor of the roof towards Sophie. She grabbed it.

Ryan lashed out and punched Pete directly in the face. He stumbled backwards and into a wall, his head banging loudly against it before he slumped to the floor.

"Pete." Miranda ran towards him.

James and Ryan stilled.

"Dad." Sophie was at her father's side.

"Dad,"–Ryan stammered- "I've been so wrong."–Her son looked behind him to the edge of the roof– "I'm sorry."

He took off towards the edge.

"No!" Miranda shouted just as he went over. James was there, though, his arm extending out and grabbing his brother.

"Fuck! I can't hold on," her youngest son shouted in agony and a loud popping sound filled the air. Miranda realised that the arm James had used was the one with the damaged shoulder, caused when he was shot by Amy's evil uncle.

Sophie scrambled across the floor, and grabbing hold of her younger brother's feet, she pulled with all her might. A shadow fell over them. Grayson, Amy, Sonia, and Matthew appeared. The latter looking pale and still covered in blood. They were all there in an instant and pulling both the men from the edge. Pete stirred from his momentary loss of consciousness and was helping before she had time to register what was happening. James came back first and then Ryan.

Amy smothered her husband in kisses, despite the fact he was still cursing and screaming. His arm was out of the socket, and he couldn't move it. Sophie went to Grayson, and he brought her into his arms, holding her so tightly it looked like he'd break her. Matthew collapsed onto the ground, breathless, and Sonia checked under his suit jacket to see what injuries he'd sustained.

Pete sat next to Ryan. Both were dazed and confused. Miranda scrambled to her feet and wrapped her arms around them. In time, it changed to both her and Pete holding Ryan tightly.

"Mum, Dad." His words were those of someone seeing clearly for the first time. A broken man but with hope of repair.

"Ssh." she cooed. "It's ok. Everything's going to be ok. We've got you. Your family has you. You're home."

EPILOGUE

Amy

Amy opened the lid of her laptop and entered the password to switch it on. She'd promised James she wouldn't write while she was here, but there was something on her mind that really needed putting down on paper. She opened the word document and started to type,

Dear Reader,

Here we are. We've come full circle; our story is at an end. So much has happened: heartache, love, betrayal, and life. A tale that started when a girl of twenty-one boarded a plane to Lanzarote has given way to a series full of emotion. I know that you want conclusions. Loose ends tied up with neat bows so that your hearts and minds can rejoice. Well here they are:

Michael and Colette

You pretty much already know their happy ending. Our friends, yes, a word which at one time seemed alien whenever Collette was mentioned, live happily in Florida with their two children. We see them often, though. Colette is like a different person from the one I was first introduced to. She has banished the scars of her past and thrives under the love of her husband. She's finally free, and it's a glorious thing to see.

Alexia and Marco

Mistress Alexia still appears on occasion, but the Dominant within her is very much submissive to Marco. They run Grayson's Vegas club as their own, now. The branding is

the same, but the club is theirs. A gift from the actor. They overcame the expectations placed upon them by their fathers and live happily with their third child on the way.

Callum and Marie

I hated Marie when I first met her, but I guess that was the protective instincts within me for 'my man'. Now, she's one of my closest friends, and we talk each day. James promoted her after the incident with Ryan. She knew North Enterprises just as well as he did, so he made her chief executive when his previous one took early retirement. From her humble beginnings in the tenements of London's slums to one of the most powerful businesswomen in the country. Although she still bows down like any good submissive to her husband, Callum. He continues as Finance Director of North Enterprises, and his skill and knowledge combined with those of his wife have seen the company flourish. More and more, they take on the day to day running while my husband steps back to be with his family. That doesn't mean Marie and Callum's own family suffers –far from it. Olivia is now five and ruling the roost. She reminds me a lot of Sophie, and I'm sure my own son, Thomas, has a soft spot for her. Owen is nine and becoming just like his father –the adoptive one, not the biological one, I must add. I wouldn't want to confuse anyone. I think of Callum as his only father, biological or not. Owen has already stated he's going to be Prime Minster like his grandad Dave once was. David Ashworth's name is now legendary as one of the best politicians our country has ever had. He's been asked to come out of retirement several times, but he's happy just being a husband and getting under his wife's feet.

We see so much of Callum and Marie. They're trusted by my husband as members of our small inner circle. We both learned the art of submission together, taught by our skilled husbands. Our scenes together have become widely discussed within Grayson's London club. When together, Marie and I both like to be punished for topping from the bottom.

Sophie and Grayson

My sister-in-law and crush-worthy husband relocated from America back to London after everything that had happened. Grayson placed his career on hold for a while, but they didn't suffer financially, for he'd made enough from the Renegade films to last a lifetime. Certainly, enough to keep Sophie in designer dresses. She still acts the diva she is, but we all know it's her soft heart that shines through. It took her a long time to come to terms with the fact she hadn't killed Sally Bridgewater. She had blamed herself for so long and resigned herself to eternal suffering, believing her actions had taken a life. It was difficult for her to accept the alternative reality. Eventually, she worked through her issues, and the birth of her and Grayson's daughter three years ago helped. Rayen, Native American for Blossom, gave strength to both Grayson and Sophie and a little sister to a teenage Ash. The boy has flourished under the love of a family. His start in life could have damaged him in ways we've all seen the effects of, but he's probably the strongest out of that branch of my family. He's getting so big. He has the makings of his father's physique, and the girls will very soon be paying far too much attention to him.

Both Sophie and Grayson have continued to embrace their heritage, and they work hard to build better lives for people on both sides of their nationalities. Now, the couple are focused on philanthropic work, and both are actively involved in helping children from the slums and the more impoverished native reserves. Grayson still does the occasional acting job, though. He could never leave it behind, and we were all shocked, recently, when he made a guest appearance in a well-known British soap opera. He looked so funny with a pint in hand and arm resting on a bust of Queen Victoria.

In the end, though, with Grayson and Sophie, it comes down to the relationship they have between the two of them. Sophie needs guidance and submission twenty-four hours a day. She needs a master who'll be there for her, and never once has Grayson let her down. They'll be the same even in old age. He'll be putting her over his knee and smacking her backside for cheekiness, I'm sure.

Matthew and Sonia

I'd never been so glad to see Matthew as I was up on the roof top. To look at your husband dangling precariously over the side of a building, screaming out in agony because his arm is ripping from the socket.... it's the stuff of nightmares. Sonia told me she'd found Matthew lying in a pool of blood and thought him dead. She'd barely been able to breathe let alone check on him because she didn't want confirmation of the news that would destroy her. She'd lost so much in her life already, to lose the man she loved would've finished her off. She found strength, though. She felt it came to her from the heavens –from her mother and father, reunited, and forgiveness passed between them. A gunshot wound was not enough to keep a man like Matthew Carter down. He'd been knocked unconscious when he'd fallen, but somehow the bullet had avoided all his major organs. He allowed the injury to be temporarily stitched and swung into action to save his best friend, my husband. I owe Matthew more than I can ever repay. He and Sonia still live with us. It might seem strange, but we are a foursome without the sex. We scene together of course, but both men are too possessive to ever let the other one touch. Sonia and I touching, however... they seem to enjoy that. Matthew no longer bodyguards for James. He runs the security at North Enterprises and Sonia assists.

After everything that happened, Matthew went down on one knee and proposed to Sonia. She accepted, and just a few weeks later in a low-key ceremony, they became man and wife. I don't think I've ever cried so much. They celebrated in private together, and nine months later, Ben was born. Two years later, they had Chloe. Heaven help her when she's dating. Her father already gives Owen and Thomas the death stare when they so much as look at her.

My husband once said he and Matthew didn't have a normal boss/employee relationship. He was right –they are male soulmates and their bromance, if you know what I mean, was never like that. You don't get one without the other, and I wouldn't have it any other way.

Miranda and Pete

I am blessed with my parents-in-law. I don't think you could have two better people supporting you. They're the head of our little gang of friends and relatives. We feed off them for our strength.

They'd buried so much and suffered for so long. To have a child physically cut from your womb must leave unfathomable scars, but they survived and nurtured not only the man I love but also everyone else who encounters them.

Miranda still feeds copious amounts of tea to anyone who comes to her with a problem. Somehow it works, though, because when you leave her, you feel like you could take on the world.

Pete made mistakes in the past, and he suffered for them, but when he was beaten and left for dead by Miranda's father, he could have walked away. But, he didn't. He spurred a generation on by fighting for the woman he loved. Over the years, I've developed just as close a relationship with him as Miranda. I lost my true parents at far too young an age, but in Miranda and Pete, I've found new ones, and I love them with all my heart – just don't tell James I've given them the keys to the playroom on a few occasions. According to him, his parents don't have sex. I know differently. They're like rabbits and always at it.

Ryan

I should hate him. He's the reason for most of the suffering in the stories you've read. But I can't. He broke after the incident on the roof, and it took him a long time to recover. But he finally had a family, and we brought him through the darkest days, together with Elena, my friend, who is now the head of my dance school. But that's a story yet to be written.

James and I

And so, to the final couple, we started all this so long ago in Lanzarote. A chance encounter that spawned a series. My god, it seems like a lifetime has passed. James saved his brother on the rooftop that day, but he made a sacrifice to do so. One which has never left him the same. When he rescued me from my uncle, he was shot in the shoulder. The wound healed, but the strain of holding onto Ryan tore the muscle apart again and ripped his arm from the socket. They put everything back together, but he lost the use of his arm. It's only recently he's begun to get some feeling and movement back into it. I'll never forget the day in the hospital when he looked at the doctor, who'd just given him the diagnosis of his injury, and asked if he'd ever be able to hold his children with it again. I cried, and then I cried some more, and then I found the strength to help him get through what was happening to him. It wasn't easy at first. My husband, as you've seen, is a proud man and likes his independence, but he battled with so much at first. Just dressing was a chore and seemed to be an endless struggle. I'd stand and watch him trying until finally the defeat would show on his face, and he'd allow me to help. One day, though, Isabella fell over, and he was there for her. He used his good arm to bring the other around her and wrap her in a cocoon of comfort. It gave him the hope he needed, and we've been trying different therapies ever since. I know despite having limited movement, now, he'll fully recover, eventually.

James and Ryan, along with Sophie, have developed a close relationship. The sibling love I saw between Sophie and James has been transferred to include Ryan as well. They had issues they needed to work through. Ryan suffered a lot of guilt over James' injury, and Sophie's distress while coming to terms with the death of Sally, but his youngest sibling forgave him easily. I love to watch them together. It brings me great joy, especially when Sophie's being teased by both her brothers.

James took a step back from North Enterprises. As I've said previously, he allowed Callum and Marie to take on a lot of the responsibility. He'd worked hard all his life to build up his business and when he was cleared of all suspicion against him and his fifty million was returned, he made the decision to semi-retire and spend more time with us. I gave my dance school over to Elena as a present. She refused it at first, but you can't hand back what's already signed over to you. I'd proven my point that I could be independent. I wasn't the little girl who had relied on her parents, and then on her uncle for everything. I'd become strong. I'd become a North. Together, we've raised our family and enjoyed our ability to just live life to the full. Thomas and Isabella were joined by two more siblings, Henry and Charlotte. After that, Matthew dragged James to see his doctor, demanding they gave him a vasectomy because contraception had this strange habit of not working with us. For a bodyguard, we were becoming too big a family to protect.

Well, dear reader, that's it. That's what has happened to all of us. We have all lived happily ever after. Giving you the ending you need, and the conclusion you love.
    Thank you.

Amy started to type, 'The End', but James appeared at the door.
    "I thought you weren't going to write while we were away?"
    She bit her lip and looked down.
    "It was only a few words."
    "Come here," he beckoned, and his eyes darkened with lust. She shut the lid of the laptop and got to her feet.
    With her hips swaying, she went to him and knelt down to present herself to him in slave position. "You know what happens to naughty girls?"
    "They get punished."
    "They do." He wrapped his good hand around her hair and pulled her to her feet. The next thing she knew, she was against the wall behind her.
    "Take off your clothes."
    She obeyed without question, and her white summer dress and matching panties fell to the floor. The heat of the Lanzarote sun warmed her body, or was it the stare coming from James? This was the first time they'd returned to the island since they'd met.
    "Full circle," she said to him. He nodded.
    "Place your hands above your head and don't move them." Once, the authoritative tone had scared her, but now it sent shivers down her body and prepared her for what would happen next.
    He pressed a hot kiss against her lips, and then trailed his mouth further over her neck, and down to her breast.
    "Good girl's get rewarded."
    "And bad girls."
    "Get nothing," he teased and lowered his hands to her thighs. He parted them and slid his finger through her wet folds.
    "How long have you been like this?" he asked.
    "Since you walked into my life."
    He circled her clit with his thumb, and her body sagged against the wall with a jelly-like feeling in her legs.
    "You don't come until I say."
    "Yes, Master."
    James pulled his hand away and went to the zipper of his shorts, which he undid, deftly, having become an expert at using only one hand. Sliding his shorts and pants down his toned thighs, he revealed his hard cock. Memories of the first

time she'd seen it flooded back. It had been beautiful then, and it was even more so, now, because she knew how it could make her feel. He stepped out of the garments and returned to her. He lifted her left leg, and wrapping it around his waist, he positioned himself at her entrance.

"Mine," he growled.

"Forever," she replied, and he slammed deeply into her in one hard thrust.

"May I touch you?" she asked

"Always."

Amy slid her hands down her husband's back and over the skin marked with scars. Last time they had been in this position, she wouldn't have been able to do this, for he didn't allow her to touch him. He'd held her hands above her head as he'd taken her —ashamed of the scars, marring his back. That was the past, though. If he was a deviant, then she was one with him. James pulled back and found a steady rhythm as he took her against the wall. The coupling possessive and a sign of his dominance over her. She found his lips and kissed them hard. His swivelling hips brought them both quickly to orgasm. She flew high and free, her body quaking and milking his. Eventually, they both came down, withdrawing from her, James lowered her leg gently.

"Did I hurt you?" he asked, a hint of worry in his voice.

"Never."

He leaned his forehead against hers.

"We're going to be ok, aren't we?" he questioned, and she cocked her head in confusion. "For the rest of our lives, we're going to live happily."

"Nobody knows the future," she replied and led him out of the study they'd been in and towards the bedroom.

"No, I supposed they don't. We have to make it work ourselves."

"No, we have to control it."

He laughed.

"Well, Mrs North, let's control the future...together."

THE END

Thank you for reading the Control Series

AFTERWORD

Dear reader, thank you for choosing my book to entertain yourself with. I'm more grateful than you know.

Anna
x

ABOUT ANNA EDWARDS

Anna Edwards is a British author from the depths of the rural countryside near London. When she has some spare time, she can also be found writing poetry, baking cakes (and eating them), or behind a camera snapping like a mad paparazzo. She's an avid reader who turned to writing to combat her depression and anxiety. She has a love of traveling and likes to bring this to her stories to give them the air of reality. She likes her heroes hot and hunky with a dirty mouth, her heroines demure but with spunk, and her books full of dramatic suspense.

CONNECT WITH ANNA EDWARDS
www.AuthorAnnaEdwards.com
Newsletter: http://bit.ly/NewsletterAnnaEdwards
Facebook, Friend: TheAuthorAnnaEdwards
Email: anna1000edwards@gmail.com

THE CONTROL SERIES

The Control Series: A complete, dramatic, witty, and sensual suspense romance set predominantly in London.

Surrendered Control

Divided Control

Misguided Control

Controlling Darkness

Controlling Heritage

Controlling Disgrace

Controlling Expectations

Controlling the Past

Also available:

The Control Series Boxset

Surrendered Control audio

THE GLACIAL BLOOD SERIES

A world of shifters and witches, magic and mayhem, unforgivable lies and unbreakable love. A world where family is born not only through blood, but bond. With plenty of the threats to come—and a secret that remains untold.

The Touch of Snow

Fighting the Lies

Fallen for Shame

Shattered Fears

Hidden Pain

Stolen Choices

A Deadly Affair

Power of a Myth

Banishing Regrets - Coming 2021

DARK SOVEREIGNTY SERIES

A complete dark and suspenseful series set amongst the elite of a London society intent on finding power in the wrong place.

Legacy of Succession

Tainted Reasoning

A Father's Insistence

Legacy of Succession audio

SING WITH ME

SAVING TATE COLLECTION

Sing with Me by Anna Edwards,

A With me In Seattle Universe Novel from Lady Boss Press.

Pre-order now

Amazon US: https://amzn.to/2X37NAy

Amazon UK: https://amzn.to/3bAvGog

Amazon CA: https://amzn.to/2WA4vWM

Amazon AU: https://amzn.to/3cDqQs2

Blurb:

Tate Gordon is the lead singer of Saving Tate, the hottest new rock band in Seattle. Having been mentored by music legends, Nash, for several years, the group are about to head out on their first world tour. Tate's excited, but he's struggling at the same time with the secrets he's been keeping. His friends don't know the truth about his youth or the confusion running through his head. Will Tate's past destroy everything the group have been working for when his past returns in a chance encounter?

Zoey Danson is a hot commodity in the record industry, and her boss wants her to travel with one of his top clients, Saving Tate, as they embark on their world tour. She's not entirely sure about being stuck on a tour bus with four famously horny men but mounting debts, thanks to her deadbeat mother, mean she doesn't have a choice.

When Zoey ascends the steps of the tour bus, looking hot and carrying a clip board with a full itinerary, sparks instantly fly between her and Tate. Can these two keep it professional, or will their instant attraction lead to an explosive disaster no one could have foreseen?

Sing with me is part of Kristen Proby's 'With me in Seattle' world and the start of a brand new rockstar romance series from the author, Anna Edwards.

Also in the Lady Boss Press World from Anna Edwards:

Easy Rumba

Playing Again

Drawn by You

ALSO BY ANNA EDWARDS

Beauty's War - Gods Reborn with Claire Marta
Apollo's Protection - Gods Reborn with Claire Marta

Oliver - Part of Blaire's World

Redemption - Book Ten of the Cavalieri Della Morte

Overexposed - A Skeleton Kings Prequel

Cruel Angels with Dani René

Happily Ever Crowned with Lexi C. Foss
Happily Ever Bitten with Lexi C. Foss

Frozen Sector

Printed in Great Britain
by Amazon